America

Christin

American Goddess

By James Aiello

American Goddess
©2020 by James Aiello

.

Dedicated to America with Love from your friend James Aiello

American Goddess

CHAPTER 1

It's 8:22 pm November 4th Election night in the United States of America and here I sit all alone in the dark, with only the light of a single white candle glistening in the mirror. The light is the only thing which shows, it is truly my own reflection gazing back at me. I cannot believe that I, Christina Powers, on this election night am poised on the verge of an historic journey as the first woman President of the United States of America. And after living through the most vicious campaign in American political history, as well as the most horrendous day of my entire life, all the polls show me way ahead of both my opponents. It appears as though I cannot lose. As I sit here pondering my future, I can faintly hear the chanting from the crowds in the streets outside my window here at Rockefeller Center, "Christina! Christina! They chant.   The sound is maddening.

As I gaze into this mirror with my hands clenched tightly and tears running down my face, I begin screaming in my mind, "Oh, God! Oh, God! How did it get to this point? Why have I taken this course with my life?"   So many questions are going through my mind.

I once thought I knew who I was, where I was going, and how I was going to get there; but it seems fate has a mind of her own. Events are out of my control now and I know I must follow this path wherever it leads. Or has this always been my destiny? I have no answers to these questions. In a moment of silence, it comes to me like a vision in the mirror, "Oh, God!" I plead once more. "Oh, yes." I think to myself, "It's all coming back to me now."

For you see, it was 1973, and I was an eighteen-year-old pop star poised on the brink of super stardom, with two Platinum albums, two Grammy awards and a sure bet to be nominated for my first Academy Award. I felt as though I was on top of the world. As if I had it all. All at the tender, naive, age of eighteen. 'Or so I thought.'

I was also the apple of my uncle's eye, who just happened to be 'Frank Salerno' the legendary performer whose entertainment career spanned over twenty-five-years. He was Italian, forty-five-years old, six-feet-two-inches tall, with brown hair, brown eyes, and he weighed about two-hundred-pounds. He had two children Anthony and Debbie. Frank was also the alleged godfather for the entire West Coast of the United States.

Frank was the one person in my life I could always count on. This man was my rock! At that time, I was fast becoming one of the biggest stars to be signed on the Salerno Record Label. It was a glorious time for me, for I had always stayed to myself in the past and no matter how hard I tried, I never seemed to fit in. 'Oh, yes! There was Barbara Goldstein,' I can't forget her. We met in 1970 at the Grammy awards just after I won my first Grammy for best new artist of the year. We became close friends, and she became my mentor. She was the kind of woman I wanted to be, strong and Independent with the

2

voice of an angel. She also happened to be one of the only friends I chose for myself who my uncle approved of.

My mother was Frank's sister and shortly after my birth both my parents died after being in a car crash, 'or so I was led to believe.' I attended exclusive Catholic schools straight through my high school graduation. I never bothered continuing my education after high school because I had a dream; and that was to become a great performer like my beloved Uncle Frank. As for the affection of my cousins, Frank's children, there was none. They made it noticeably clear that I was in their way. I hardly knew any love or even friendship to speak of at all as a child, except for that which came from my uncle himself. Frank always showered me with his love and affection. He took care of my every need, from every song I sang, to every part I played. From my schooling right into my career and every date I ever went on, Uncle Frank had it all planned out. I wanted to be a star, and Uncle Frank was going to take me there. Until the day 'Johnny' came into my life!

It was a beautiful spring afternoon, and I was having lunch with Kathy Brown. She was twenty-two, beautiful and her prime-time TV show was number one in the Nielsen Ratings. We were paired together to be best friends' courtesy of my Uncle Frank. He felt it would be good for both our careers, to be seen together in public.

So, there we were, two of the most desirable and eligible young women in America, having lunch together at Tavern on the Green in Central Park. We were just finishing our meal, when the Maître d' came to our table, "Pardon me, Miss Valona and Miss Brown, the two gentlemen at table eleven would like to give this bottle of champagne to you ladies to have with your meal." Oh, by the way, my name was Christy Valona at that time.

"Thank you." I replied, "please tell the gentlemen it is not our custom to drink champagne with our lunch, but we will accept the gift if they will join us for some fresh vegetable juice."

"Why did you do that?" Kathy asked with a look of distress. "Now we have to have lunch with two perfect strangers. What are we going to say to them?"

"Sometimes you have to go with your feelings, Kathy." I winked, "Something tells me this is one of those times."

"Well I have a feeling too, Christy, and it's telling me to get the hell out of here."

"Don't you dare leave me here alone with them, I'll slap you, girl." I said with a giggle, half meaning it.

Then it happened. There were two men approaching our table, but I could only focus on one. He was a splendid six-foot-tall, blond haired, blue eyed god! His muscles rippled through his tight-fitting baby blue designer sport shirt, which enhanced those blue eyes of his. Peeking through the 'V' of his open collar, the curls of his thick blond chest hairs cascaded across his well-defined physique. He was incredible to look at!

As he reached our table, he stretched out his hand to mine and with a slight southern twang in his voice, "Hi Miss Valona, my name is John Everett. It's my pleasure to meet you." As he touched my hand, I felt it, in that instant I knew I had to know more about this man, this beautiful, seemingly gentle giant who was holding my hand.

He reached over to Kathy, "Miss Brown, it's also a pleasure to meet you." He then gestured toward his dark-haired companion, "This is my friend and colleague, Steve Grady."

After we exchanged greetings, I invited them to sit with us. In an effort to break the ice, I struggled with my thoughts for a moment. Trying to be witty, I smiled, "I hope you like vegetable juice, guys!"

"I take mine straight," John said with a boyish smile. Looking straight into my eyes with those baby blues, he added, "I think you're an incredible performer, Christy. May I call you, Christy?"

"If I may call you Johnny?"

"But my name is John."

"I know that, Johnny," I answered with a slightly seductive smile.

With that he gallantly replied, "Whatever my lady would like!"

Our meeting over vegetable juice was going quite well. Kathy and Steve seemed to hit it off nicely, but you could never really tell what Kathy was genuinely thinking about when it came to deal with men. As for Johnny and me, it was magic. He told me he was a pitcher for the New York Mets and that Steve was his catcher. He also assured me with great enthusiasm and confidence, the Mets will win the World Series this year.

He seemed to have a real zeal for life. This was something I had felt in myself but had not seen in anyone else until then. He told me he was twenty-four-years old and he grew up in Virginia. Although he loved the excitement and vitality of life in New York and playing with a major league team, his ultimate passion was to one day return home to work the soil with his own hands. That is where he truly felt as though he was one with God and nature.

As we finished our conversation, the four of us made a dinner date for that evening. Johnny was going to pick me up at eight o'clock and Steve was picking up Kathy. We were to meet at La Shazonz' Restaurant in downtown Manhattan.

I felt a childish anticipation throughout that exceptionally long afternoon, as I primped for that evening's rendezvous. I brushed my long wavy dark black hair and made up my eyes with just a touch of blue liner to enhance the blue of my eyes. I slipped into a tight black evening dress, which deliberately had a very low-cut neckline. I tied up my hair with a white silk scarf and donned a pair of black leather heels. I was dressed to kill.

"What is this I'm feeling?" I thought. I have met many men in the past three years of being a performer and none of them ever made me feel like this. I felt as if I were glowing inside! "Was he feeling the same," I wondered?

American Goddess

Finally, the hour came. Johnny picked me up at my Park Avenue penthouse which I purchased with the earnings from my first record album. When I opened the door, he was holding two dozen red roses with one pure white rose sitting in the middle of the bouquet.

His eyes opened wide when he saw me, "Good evening, Christy." Handing me the beautiful bouquet, "You look awesome, tonight."

"Thank you, Johnny." I eyed him up and down, "You don't look too shabby yourself and thank you for the lovely flowers. Red roses are my favorite flowers and the white one makes them a little more special." I smiled, "Would you like to come in for a minute while I place these in a vase?"

He entered the living room as I headed for the kitchen. When I returned, he was standing by the fireplace where I kept all my awards. He looked at me through adoring eyes, "I was just admiring your collection, very impressive. You should be proud."

"Thank you," I answered, gracefully. "I am proud of my achievements. I've worked very hard for them."

"Your home, it's beautiful," he turned to gaze at the rest of the room.

"Thank you again. Would you like to see the rest of it? I decorated it myself."

"Yes, I would," he replied enthusiastically.

As I took him on a tour of my home, he really seemed impressed with what I had done with it. When we reached the master bedroom Johnny stood in amazement as he looked around the room. My heart started pounding in my chest as I felt my blood pressure rising. I was becoming nervous by my overwhelming feelings of desire for this man I had only met a few hours earlier.

Johnny's first gaze fell on the black marble fireplace which was majestic in size. As he took in the rest of the decor, he noticed the paintings and sculptures of angels throughout the room. "Wow! Someone's into angels, aren't they?" He exclaimed.

"Yes, I am. I've been intrigued by angels since I was a child. They have comforted me and filled an empty void in my life in many ways, and that's why I've decorated this room with them. This is my sanctuary."

He looked over to the canopy bed and stood in awe of the splendid white marble roman column like pillars, which held up each corner of the canopy. The canopy was made of sheer white chiffon drapes, which cascaded down from the ceiling and flowed gently between the columns to meet the pearly white marble floor, inlaid with twenty-four-karat gold. "Your bedroom is out of this world! You have an incredible imagination to have decorated it this way."

"Why thank you, Johnny," I replied with modesty. "But it's getting late, we'd better go. I'm sure Kathy and Steve are wondering what's taking us so long."

He looked at his watch, "Holy cow, 'little angel,' it's 8:15 already! I'd guess we'd better get going." He escorted me to his car, and our evening was on.

American Goddess

Kathy and Steve were already waiting at the bar when we arrived. The Maître d' escorted us to the best table in the restaurant. It had a fabulous skyline view of Central Park West. Dinner was splendid and the four of us got along as if we had known each other for years. Johnny and Steve were so witty together. It was obvious they were best friends. I could not remember the last time I had laughed so much. Johnny made me feel so free that by the time dinner ended, I knew he was special.

We all decided the night was young, and we should go to Furn's for a drink. Furn's was the most exclusive club in town and only the elite were allowed in. As the four of us approached the entrance, the cameras from the tabloids were snapping all around us. The night seemed enchanted. We were led to a table, which was reserved for patrons such as ourselves. To my surprise the diva herself, Barbara Goldstein, was also out on the town that evening with one of America's top black female singers and performer, Eartha Kit. She was seated two tables away from ours with Eartha who was preforming at the Copacabana nightclub the following evening. They were there with two extremely attractive gentlemen. I was about to ask to be excused for a moment, to go say hi, when Barbara noticed us and came to our table.

"Christy!" With a big smile she embraced me.

"Barbara!" Enthusiastically, I returned her hug, "I didn't know you were back in town. I thought you were still shooting out on the West Coast."

"Not anymore, the film is finally finished and it's time to start promoting it. The premiere is next Friday. It would make me incredibly happy if you would come as my guest."

"I'd love to Barbara, but I can't. I will be out on the West Coast myself next Friday. Uncle Frank has a script he wants me to audition for at Paramount."

With wide eyes she asked, "Is it the script for the film, 'Samantha's Father'?"

"Yes," I answered, with a devilish look in my eye.

Her grin became as bright has mine as she said, "You know, whoever nails the part of 'Samantha' is going to skyrocket in popularity."

I smiled mischievously, "I know girlfriend, and I want it."

Just then Eartha hugged me from behind, "Christy, sweety, it's so good to see you. Are you still coming to my show tomorrow night at the Copa?

I kissed her cheek, "Keep those front row seats opened for Kathy and I, we are both planning to be there."

She hugged me again as she continued, "Oh, by the way, congratulations, I hear you're a shoe in to be nominated for an Oscar. That is wonderful girlfriend, and I'm so happy for you. I just know you are going to get it. Your performance in 'Blue Lady' was breathtaking."

As Eartha was speaking to me, Barbara turned to Kathy, "Hello, Kathy, it's so nice to meet you, and oh my, my, John Everett and Steve Grady, I just love you guys. You're both such great ball players."

The four of them exchanged greetings, after which Barbara put her arm around Eartha's shoulder, "Why don't you guys come join us at our table?"

"Maybe another time." I kissed her cheek and whispered in her ear, "It's our first night out together and I'd like to keep Johnny all to myself for a while."

"He's a living doll," she whispered back, "We'll do dinner, and you can let me know how it went."

I laughed, "With our notorious appetites? Don't you remember the last time we did dinner? I am still doing two hours on the stair master every day. I'll call you next week; it's safer for both our figures."

We both laughed as we said our goodbyes.

Then I turned to Eartha, gave her another kiss on the cheek and said, "I love you Eartha, but I'm keeping Johnny all to myself tonight.   Kathy and I will see you at tomorrow night's concert."

We all said are good buys and I turned my full attention back to Johnny. The magic between Johnny and I continued. We were in a fantastic dream together as we held each other on the dance floor. We danced till midnight. Finally, we said goodbye to Kathy and Steve, and Johnny drove me home.

When we reached my front door, Johnny took me in his arms and kissed me passionately. "Well, I guess I'd better get going, I have practice in the morning and a game in the afternoon." We embraced again as he softly continued, "May I see you tomorrow, Christy?"

We relinquished our embrace, "I'd love to see you tomorrow, Johnny."

He kissed me once more with such passion I thought I'd melt. He released my lips, "Good night little Angel." As he turned to leave, he stopped, turned back, hugged me softly, "Christy I can't leave you, please let me stay the night."

Trembling in his arms, "Johnny, I can't, I've never."

He looked heartbroken as he whispered, "Please forgive me. I have never been this forward in my life. I'll leave; may I still see you tomorrow?"

"Of course, you may."

This time as he slowly turned to leave, I felt a fire explode within me burning with a passion I had never felt before. I reached for his hand, "Johnny, please don't leave me tonight. I don't know what this is I'm feeling, but I have never felt this way before. I want you to stay with me, please." As these words flowed from my mouth I thought, "How could you be saying these things?" You have never been intimate with a man before and now I was longing for this man I had only met for the first time this afternoon.

Johnny looked intently into my eyes, "I was praying you felt it too, Christy." He kissed me deeply, "I won't leave you angel. I'll stay as long as you want me to."

He swept me off my feet and carried me into the bedroom. The room was dimly lit with only the light of a splendid full moon filtering in through the bay glass doors, which led out onto the open balcony. He gradually stood me up alongside the bed and we embraced. Slowly and oh so softly he kissed my cheeks as his large hands slid so gently through my hair. My silk scarf floated to the floor as one hand tenderly held the back of my neck, the other hand began to caress my breasts. His lips met mine again and this time I became frightened, so I softly pushed him away, "Johnny, please slow down, I'm scared. I've never made love before."

He gazed so shyly into my eyes and with complete sincerity in his voice, "I've never made love before either, Christy."

Hearing him say that seemed to take all the fear away, as I pulled him to me and kissed him tenderly. I felt so weak in the arms of this man whom I knew at that moment I loved. My body began to softly shiver with a feeling of extreme ecstasy. He began to slowly undo the buttons on my dress and let it slide down to my ankles. As he was undressing me, I found myself undressing him. I had to see him, touch him, taste him and make love to him. The passion swelled between us, "Johnny, oh, Johnny," I whispered in his ear as he laid me on the bed. The heat of our bodies was scorching as his flesh met mine. The fire grew hotter as we touched one another, kissed one another, and loved one another. We caressed each other from head to toe. It was incredible. There was lightning flashing through our souls and then in our hearts. When we were wild with passion and thought we could take no more, he slid back on top of me and held me passionately in his arms.

With a gentle quiver in his voice, "Christy, I love you. I do not understand how I know this. I just do. I love you; I need you. I'll love you now and always."

I held him so close to my pounding heart and cried in a soft voice, "I love you too, Johnny, I love you too." I drew him to my melting body. My soul screamed in ecstasy and pain, as he gently took the gift of my virginity. Gentle soft tears slowly began to drip from his deep blue eyes as he accepted my gift of love. My tears began to flow with his. The love we felt together at that moment was eternal. We sealed our love that night with the fire of our souls. We were one and we knew it. The night was filled with passion and pleasure. So much so I felt as if I had never lived until that moment. We embraced and shared our love throughout that glorious night. Our bodies and souls were one when the rays of the morning sun found us.

"I love you, Johnny." I lifted myself out of his embrace and looked in amazement at this magnificent man as I softly stroked his body.

"You're beautiful, angel," rising up to kiss me, "and I love you with all my heart."

We embraced again and the fire flared. We had an insatiable thirst we could not quench. 'Oh, how I loved him so.' As much as we wanted that night's love making to never end, it did, and we knew we had to come back to earth.

"We'd better get up, it's seven o'clock." I kissed his cheek, "Why don't you shower while I fix us some breakfast?"

"Okay, angel," embracing me, "I love you, Christy."

He rose from the bed and headed for the shower. I slipped on my robe and headed for the kitchen, quickly put on the coffee pot and popped some bread into the toaster. I went to the bathroom to freshen up and when I entered the room, I could see his silhouette through the shower doors. He was sliding a washcloth all over his body.

"This man is perfect." I thought as I slipped off my robe and entered the shower with him. As soon as I did, he took me in his arms, and kissed me passionately, "I am so in love with you my angel and I'll always want you."   His hands slowly began to caress my breast. Then he began to gently make love to my entire body as the warm shower water dripped from our naked bodies. I surrendered everything I was to him in that shower that morning. The love we made was so pure and innocent that we both knew it was a love to last a lifetime'. We knew it was real love and It was wonderful.

Afterword's we got dressed and headed out to the kitchen to find burnt toast and muddy coffee. We looked at each other and laughed.

"That's okay, angel, I have to go anyway. I have practice at nine o'clock." He grabbed me, kissed me, "Can you make it to the game this afternoon? I'm pitching."

"I wouldn't miss it for the world, what time does the game begin?"

"Four o'clock. If you come to the players' entrance at 3:30, I'll be waiting for you."

"I'll be there, my love," We kissed, and I walked him to the door. One last embrace and he left my arms. I closed the door when he was out of sight, leaned back on the door and began to cry.

"These emotions are so strong," I thought, "I could never express them in words." I walked over to the couch, picked up a pen and paper and began trying to compose my thoughts. This was at 8:30 in the morning. By 1:30 that afternoon, I was at the recording studio putting music to the lyrics. Writing was what kept me sane that day as I prayed for afternoon to come. All I could think about was Johnny and I just knew I was all he could think about.

Finally, it was 3:30. I ran to him the instant I saw him, and I leaped into his arms. He embraced me and we were whole again; and the flashing of the tabloid cameras caught it all. He led me through the dugout to a seat he had saved for me. It was so close to the pitcher's mound we could see each other's eyes. As the game began, my heart grew with excitement. My eyes were focused on every move he made; they were so strong, smooth, and fast; that I was mesmerized. As I watched, I could hardly believe this beautiful gladiator was the man I loved. My heart began to fantasize deeper and deeper with every pitch. In my mind, I could see myself wipe the sweat from his brow with the tips of my breasts. There we were, the two of us, making love with our eyes in front of the world. He was magnificent that day and to the cheers of fifty-thousand screaming fans he bowed for a no hitter. Steve ran something out to Johnny. It was a bouquet of two dozen red roses with one white one in the middle. Johnny walked over to where I was seated, bowed, and handed them to me. The crowd went wild.

As we tried to leave the stadium, the press with their cameras, were all around us. It was 7:30, by the time we left the ballpark and by nine o'clock that evening, the whole country knew we were in love. We were so high on love, we thought we would live forever, yet so tired and hungry, we thought we would die at any moment. But it was off to a celebration party at the Hilton, to celebrate his tenth no hitter of the season, and Johnny was the main attraction. As Johnny finished receiving all those slaps on the butt from the biggest names in baseball, I slipped away and went over to speak with Patrick Victor. He was the orchestra leader and a friend, "Hi, Pat." We embraced, "Do you think you could do me a small favor?"

"Anything for you, Christy," he answered with a smile. "What is it?"

"I have this copy of sheet music with me. Would you please have someone copy it for your musicians and have them try to play it for me? Pretty, please."

"I'll do my best and let you know."

Thank God they were finally serving hors d'oeuvres when I rejoined Johnny at our table. To my surprise Kathy was also seated at our table with Steve. I greeted them both with a warm smile and embrace. Steve popped the cork from an expensive bottle of French champagne, "Will you ladies have some champagne with us now?"

Kathy and I looked at each other with a devilish look in our eyes, grabbed for the bottle at the same time and acted as if we were going to splash it all over them. Astonished looks came over their face's and we laughed so hard I thought we'd burst. After our outburst we all started to drink, maybe just a little too much, especially Kathy.

From the stage Patrick Victor announced, "Excuse me, ladies and gentlemen, tonight we have a dear friend of mine here with us. Right now, I would like to invite her up on stage to do a number for you. Please give a hardy welcome to Christy Valona."

The room began to applaud as I walked to the stage. I was a little nervous as I took the microphone in my hand, but I wanted to do this, so I said, "Good evening, ladies and gentlemen. I would like to give a special gift to an incredibly special friend of mine, John Everett. This is a new song I wrote, just for him."

With that the music started and I began to sing. I sang from the core of my heart to the man I loved. I found strength and passion whirling up within my soul as I sang to Johnny. The words burst out of me like fire. I sang like I had never sung before.

"Where, my Johnny is, that's were, I long to be. He is so tall and oh so strong and

he's, in love with me-e-e. He said, he loves me, with all his heart, and soul. That is why, I know, that I'm, Johnny's girl-oh-oh. And when he leaves me, my heart, waits, impatiently, because I know, he loves me so, tenderly-e-e. And when, he comes home, I run, to his open arms, because I know, he loves me so, and that is why I'm, Johnny's girl-oh-oh. And when he holds me, oh so close, my soul screams in ecstasy. Because I know, he loves me so, I'm, Johnny's girl-oh-oh. And when he kisses me, gentle tears, fall, from his deep blue eyes. And that is why, I'll shout it from on high, that I'm, Johnny's girl-oh-oh. Yes-s-s, we seal our love, with the fire, of our souls. Filled, with love, passion, and pleasure, we hold each other, oh so tenderly-e-e. And that is why, I'll shout it from on high, that I'm, Johnny's girl-oh-oh. Where, my Johnny is, that's where, I've got to be. Because I know, how much he loves me so, I'm, Johnny's girl-oh-oh. I'm, Johnny's girl-oh-oh, Oh yes, I'm, Johnny's girl-oh-oh. And Johnny, he, is my man-yes-Johnny, he is my-man.   My.... Man...."

I was incredible and the crowd knew it. I got a standing ovation and Johnny met me at the stage when the song was finished. We embraced to the applause of our friends and colleagues. After the celebration it was off to the Copa for Eartha's show. The night was enchanting. We were living a fairy tale and we loved it. It was 2:00am by the time we arrived at Johnny's condo in Tarry-town, just north of the city. We spent the rest of that night with our bodies mingled in pure ecstasy.

In the morning we showered together, AGAIN! Then I made him a real breakfast. Johnny dropped me off at my penthouse at 8:30, kissed me and left for practice. We made plans to meet at 6:00 that evening at my place.

I entered my home to a barrage of phone messages from Uncle Frank. I picked up the phone and called him on his private line at his corporate headquarters in Las Vegas.

"Hello."

"Hi! Uncle Frank," I said with excitement in my voice.

"Where the hell have you been, Christy?" He interrupted my thoughts, "And what the hell is going on out there? My phone has been ringing all night because of your reckless behavior. Have you seen the headlines in today's papers? Photos of the two of you embracing are splattered all over the country. Dammit girl, I thought you were more mature then that! When you asked me on your birthday to let you buy that place and live in the city alone, I said yes, because I trusted your loyalty to me. I told you I did not want you dating anyone unless I approved! Why have you disobeyed me?"

"Please calm down, Uncle Frank," I exclaimed. "It's not what you're thinking. I'm in love, Uncle Frank, I'm truly in love."

"Well, if you're truly in love baby," his voice began to calm, "then how come I'm the last one to find out?"

"It all happened so fast, we only met two days ago."

American Goddess

"Two days ago! Are you serious? What the hell are you thinking? How can you be in love in two days?"

"I don't know how; I only know I am." With enthusiasm, "Wait till you meet him Uncle Frank. He is wonderful! He's everything I ever dreamed he'd be and if you're not happy for me, I'm just going to cry."

"Don't cry baby," he said with a reassuring tone. "Let me just compose my thoughts for a while. I have a hectic schedule today, so there is nothing I can do about this now. I will be flying out tonight. If all goes well, I'll see you around 11:00pm your time."

"That's wonderful, Uncle Frank, I can't wait to see you. I cannot wait for you to meet him. You are just going to love him. I know it!"

"All right Christy, just do me a favor and don't do anything foolish!" he said harshly.

"I won't do anything foolish, Uncle Frank, I promise. I love you so much and thank you for coming. It means so much to me."

His reply was noticeably short, "Okay, okay, I have to go. I will see you tonight. Goodbye for now."

"Goodbye, Uncle Frank."

As I hung up the phone, I got an extremely uncomfortable feeling from our conversation. Uncle Frank had never used that tone of voice with me before and it concerned me because I did not understand it. I decided to dismiss these feelings. I was so happy at that moment and I was not going to let anything take those feelings from me.

I quickly changed my clothes and headed for the recording studio around 9:00am. The crew and I worked furiously that day and by 3:00pm we had recorded a masterpiece; a masterpiece which I wrote in only three hours for my beloved Johnny. I titled it, 'Johnny's Love.' I rushed home with my heart pounding at just the thought of seeing him. I quickly began to prepare for a romantic dinner, accompanied by candlelight, champagne, and soft music. By 5:58pm I was out of the shower and dressed to impress. Just then the doorbell rang, and I ran to answer it. I felt like a puppy anticipating the entrance of his master. I opened the door and he swept me up into his arms and carried me to the sofa, kissing me wildly all the way. "I love you! I love you!" He kept repeating as he placed me on the sofa. Our bodies immediately exploded with passion. He was back in my arms and I was alive again.

I finally served dinner shortly after 10:00pm that night. Needless to say, it was not very appetizing, but we ate it anyway. The meal really did not matter because we were living on love. Over dinner, I told Johnny about the conversation with Uncle Frank. I shared my concerns with him over the way Frank spoke to me. I told him he should be arriving any minute. Johnny stood up from his seat at the table, walked over, knelt down, wrapped his arms around me, "Don't worry angel, you're right, he will love me. I'll make sure of that, I promise."

American Goddess

I was so reassured by his words as he held me tightly that I felt encouraged by his strength. I kissed him, "I have something for you."

"You do?" He smiled as he gently tickled my waist.

"Yes, I do." I playfully slapped his hand, "Now let me go get it."

I walked to the living room, opened my purse and pulled out a key. I took it over to him, "Please take this Johnny. It is the key to my home, and I want you to have it. I want you to be able to come here anytime you want."

He smiled and took the key, "I guess great minds really do think alike."

He slipped a small, sealed envelope out of his pocket and handed it to me. I opened it and inside was a key to his condo. We looked at each other and laughed. Nothing more had to be said. We were giving ourselves to each other with those keys and we both knew it.

Then the doorbell rang, and we knew it was Uncle Frank. For some reason, my heart began to race as Johnny walked me to the door.

"Relax, Christy, he's your uncle. He loves you and we're going to get along great."

I squeezed his arm, "You're right." But in the back of my mind, I could not help but feel concerned, for I was raised by this man. He was always wonderful to me, but I could also remember how frightening he could be, when I was disobedient. So, I hardly ever stepped out of line.

As I opened the door, I will never forget the look of shock on Uncle Frank's face when he saw Johnny standing there with me. He burst into the room, pushed Johnny up against the wall and screamed, "You bastard! You fucked my niece! I should have you killed for this!"

Johnny was in shock! As he held my uncle back, all Johnny could say was, "I'm sorry sir. I'm sorry! Now please try to calm down and listen to us."

I screamed, "Please, Uncle Frank, please stop this!"

He flung his arms free from Johnny's grasp, stood back, straightened his suit and with anger, "Christy, how could you do this to me? And to yourself! Dammit, girl!" He raised his fist to me then dropped it in disgust, "I thought I raised you better than this!" He lowered his voice, "You've brought shame to me."

All I could do was cry. I was devastated. I could not stop crying. Johnny grabbed me and held me up as he forcefully said, "Mr. Salerno, I am very sorry you feel this way, but I love your niece and she has done nothing to bring shame upon herself or upon you. I will marry your niece tonight if she'd have me!" I looked up at Johnny and my heart leaped.

"Okay, Okay, I've heard enough," Frank shouted. "I think you should leave now, so I may speak with my niece alone."

"I'm deeply sorry Mr. Salerno, but I can't do that. We are in love and I'm staying with Christy tonight."

American Goddess

"You're what! Like hell you are! Can't you see you've done enough harm?" He swung his hand toward the door and shouted, "Get the hell out before I throw you out!"

Johnny stepped in front of me, "I'm not leaving!"

Uncle Frank looked straight into my eyes and shouted, "Christy, tell him to leave, **now**!"

My heart froze and as if my mouth was in slow motion, "A! Ahhh!"

Commanding he shouted, "**Christina!** Don't you dare disobey me, or I will walk out that door and you will regret it!"

The tears just flowed down my cheeks as I looked at him and pleaded, "Please, Uncle Frank, don't do this. Please don't force me to make that choice."

He screamed, "Damn you, **Christy**!" Then he turned, walked to the door and slammed it on his way out.

I buried my face in Johnny's chest and cried. Johnny picked me up and carried me to the bedroom. I clung to Johnny as we lay in bed. He held me so tenderly and stroked my head, as the tears softly fell from my eyes. The wind slowly began to pick up that night. We could hear the rain start to fall out on the patio. The thunder rumbled and the lightning flashed. The storm grew until the wind roared. It sounded so cold that my body felt frozen, as I listened to it right outside my window. I did not know until that moment that the heart could hurt so badly, and yet feel so full of life all at the same time. As I drifted off to sleep, I felt safety in Johnny's arms, but I also felt fear. For if there was one thing I knew about Uncle Frank, it was no one crossed him and got away with it.

In the morning we woke up still embraced in each other's arms. Johnny slowly lifted himself up, gazed down at me and in the most loving tender voice, "Will you marry me, Christy?"

Looking up into his deep blue eyes, my tears began to flow again, as I grabbed him and cried, "Yes! Johnny, yes! I will marry you."

The rest of that day, I was on cloud nine. I was so happy with the thought of being Mrs. Johnny Everett that I did not think of Uncle Frank at all. Neither one of us went to work. We got in Johnny's Porsche and drove endlessly. We talked about our love as we drove; our marriage and how many children we would have.

Johnny drove me to his dream house that day. It was a five-thousand-acre farm in Wells, Virginia, just south of Norfolk. There was a beautiful big old white colonial house, with three large barns seated behind it. Johnny told me he played here as a child and how he had saved through the years to buy this place. He told me how he dreamed of one day bringing his bride here. Then we dreamed together of how we would live here. He would run the farm, and I would be right beside him. We dreamed of having our children and raising our family here. Johnny's dream became mine that day. All I wanted was to be his bride and bear his children. 'Oh, how I loved him!'

American Goddess

The time came to leave the dream, but we took it with us in our hearts. After we left that beautiful farmhouse, Johnny took me to meet his parents. Their home was only five miles down the road. When we got there Johnny introduced me to his parents as his fiancée. His parents hugged us both with excitement, then his mother ran to the phone. After she hung up the phone, she ran to the kitchen and started to immediately put out a big spread. His father stayed and entertained us as his mom ran back and forth in the kitchen. I tried to offer her some help, but she lovingly threw me out.

Within thirty minutes Johnny's whole family came through the front door, his brothers Billy and Mark with their families, then his sister Joanne with her family. By the time dinner was placed on the table, I had met Johnny's whole family.

After dinner, right in front of everyone, Johnny came over to where I was sitting, knelt in front of me, "Christy, this ring was my grandmother's." He placed it on the ring finger of my left hand, "I love you, angel, and it will honor me if you will accept this for your engagement ring."

I hugged him, "Thank you, Johnny, I love it!" It was just an old thin gold band, but I loved it!

As we were leaving, Johnny's mom was handing all the ladies' handbags back to them, which had been thrown in the bedroom on the bed when we arrived. It was quite amusing to watch her fumbling as she gave us the wrong bags.

She looked at me with an expression of pure love, threw her hands in the air and said, **"Oh well, I'll figure it out tomorrow!"**

We had a great time that afternoon. Meeting Johnny's family was wonderful. I fell in love with them and they fell in love with me.

When we arrived back at the penthouse there was one message from Uncle Frank, "Christy, honey, I'm sorry. I do love you baby, so please call me back at the Hampton Estate."

With a great sigh of relief, "Oh, thank God! I want to call him now. All right, Johnny?" I looked into Johnny's eyes for his approval, "You don't think it's too, late do you?"

Looking at the time with a smile, "2:00am, nah, it's not too late." He kissed me, "Go call him, you little screwball."

I called Uncle Frank and got him out of bed. We both, very emotionally apologized to each other. After talking for an hour, he seemed to accept the things I was telling him about Johnny and me. I told him of our intent to wed and he was finally happy for us. He invited us to dinner that evening to celebrate. He would have his car pick us up at 7:00pm. I hung up the phone and turned my full attention back to Johnny.

We climbed into bed together and our passion rose instantly. We could not keep our hands off one another. The fire of our imaginations eclipsed our souls as we made love, and that night became filled with endless pleasure.

American Goddess

The next morning, we started our day the same way we ended our night, making love. Then Johnny was off to the ballpark and me to the studio. I was so inspired by our love I stopped recording, sat down and wrote 'Johnny's Love" in twenty minutes. The crew and I spent the rest of that day putting music to the lyrics. I insisted 'Johnny's Love', and 'I'm Johnny's Girl' be placed on my new album. I also had the title of the album changed to 'Johnny's love.'

Johnny met me at the penthouse at 6:00pm with a fresh change of clothing in his hands. He dropped his bundle on the floor as soon as he saw me. We embraced and just held one another on the sofa for the first ten minutes. It was such a warm tender feeling to have him back in my arms. Then we got ready for dinner.

Uncle Frank's car was there at seven o'clock sharp, and the next thing we knew we were on our way to his estate in the Hamptons. I could see Johnny was impressed as the guards let us in through the steel gates. We traveled down the two-mile driveway, past the well-lit guest homes, then up the hill to Frank's oceanfront, four story mansion.

Uncle Frank greeted us warmly at the front-door and immediately apologized to Johnny for his outburst of anger the night before. He continued to express his joy and concern over our engagement. We were served dinner in the informal dining room. The meal was exquisite and as we ate Uncle Frank said, "John, I want to be very candid with you, I have had your entire background researched and it appears as though you are a very talented and respected young man. Forgive me for prying into your life, but this is my niece you're planning to marry. I promised her mother on her deathbed, I would give my life to keep her beautiful little angel safe."

My heart was moved by Uncle Frank's compassion as he spoke of his love for my mother and me. At last, I thought I finally understood my uncle's obsession with my life, and it made me love him even more.

Johnny spoke up, "I understand completely, Mr. Salerno, and I would expect no less from myself, if I were in your position."

Uncle Frank interrupted, "Let's stop being so formal, John, please call me Frank."

"Thank you, Frank, and let me assure you, my intention for Christy is honorable. I love her with all my heart."

As I sat there listening to the two men, I loved most in the world talk about my future, I felt so safe and secure. I knew nothing in the world could hurt me as long as Johnny and Uncle Frank were by my side. 'Oh boy, how naive I was!'

Uncle Frank said, "All I ask of the two of you is that you hold off on the wedding until after you finish your summer tour, Christy. And by that time John, you will have completed this year's baseball season. I also request that the both of you, please, allow me to take care of all the wedding plans as my wedding gift to you and I hope to have the honor of giving the beautiful bride away."

American Goddess

Johnny smiled, "That sounds agreeable to me, Frank." Turning toward me, "As long as it's okay with you, angel?"

"That sounds wonderful to me too, Uncle Frank, all I ask is my tour schedule be planned to correspond with Johnny's baseball schedule."

"I think I can manage that, baby."

We finished dinner, then talked some more over coffee in Uncle Frank's study. As we were getting ready to leave, Uncle Frank warmly embraced me, "I love you, Christy, and my only concern is your happiness." He took Johnny's hand in his and embraced him with the other arm, "You be good to my little girl son, and welcome to the family." He hugged me again, "By the way, good luck tomorrow with the audition."

"Oh my God," I replied with surprise. "I totally forgot about the audition for 'Samantha's Father.'"

"Well, I hope you're ready for it."

"I'm ready for it, Uncle Frank, but I'm not going to try out for the part."

"You're not going to the audition?" Uncle Frank asked, with a look of surprise.

"Uncle Frank, I really don't want to take the part anymore. All I want to do is get through the summer and then marry Johnny."

Uncle Frank looked at me strangely, "Well, if that is what will make you happy, then you have my blessings." He hugged us again and we walked out the door.

Johnny and I were so happy when we left Frank's that evening. We had our whole lives ahead of us and fate was smiling on us.

That summer was incredible. We traveled the country together. Johnny played ball like a god and I sang my heart out to him. Johnny did not lose a single game he pitched that summer, and I was there cheering him on every step of the way. The magic of our love seemed to touch the whole nation. We were America's golden couple. We were in every newspaper and on the cover of every magazine in every corner store. Wherever we went, cheering crowds mobbed us and fan letters poured in from all over the country. America loved us, and we loved America. We could do no wrong. We were living a fantasy.

By the time the Mets won their way to the pennant that year, Johnny was the crowning star of the games. At the same time, my career was soaring with 'Johnny's Love' at the top of the record charts the whole summer. My concerts were bringing in record crowds and the money kept rolling in. The amount of money I made that summer was staggering! I could not believe one person could make that much money in four months. But that was not my concern. I left that part to my business manager, 'Uncle Frank.' I was in love!

The summer finally led us to the pennant playoffs. It was September 24th, 1973. The fifth inning of the seventh game of the pennant series was being played. The Mets were playing the Cardinals. The game was being played in New York and my Johnny was pitching. The score was one to nothing, the Met's favor. Johnny was pitching a perfect game up to that point. The tension was high between the players. It had been a hard-fought playoff, and this was the game that would lead one of these extraordinary teams to the World Series. Joe Rosa was at bat for the Cardinals. There was, what seemed to be, a personal battle being played out on the field between Johnny and Joe throughout the playoffs. Joe was a powerhouse home-run hitter and every time he came up against Johnny, he kept him from hitting even one ball. When Johnny pitched the third ball, it was a wild one. The ball hurdled through the air and hit Joe in the leg. The battle turned physical. Joe ran out on the field with the bat in his hand and swung it at Johnny with all his might. Johnny ducked the bat and jumped on Joe. Both teams ran out onto the field and leaped on them both. I jumped to my feet and screamed in horror, "Johnny! Johnny! Oh My God! Johnny!"

The battle seemed endless. I stood there helpless, frantically looking just to catch a glimpse of Johnny in the midst of these thundering gladiators. Finally, the dust cleared, and Johnny emerged unscathed. My heart leaped when I saw him, and the crowd went wild. Johnny brushed himself off, picked up his cap, placed it on his head and blew me a kiss with two fingers. I melted!

He composed himself and continued the game. Joe Rosa was unbelievably barred from the game for only two innings. In the eighth inning, they were up against one another again. Only this time Joe got what he was after, a home run. The crowd booed as Joe ran the bases. The score was now one to one in the eighth inning, and Steve Grady was at the plate for the Mets. Ralph Lowe was pitching for the Cardinals and doing a hell of a job. Johnny and Ralph had been pitching the whole game. Then Steve slammed the ball over center field for a home run. The crowd went wild again. It was now two to one, our favor. The Cardinals were up at bat. It finally came down to two outs, when the Cardinal's manager called time out. To our surprise, a lineup change was announced, and Joe Rosa was up at bat. You could hear a pin drop with the first pitch. "Strike one," shouted the umpire and the crowd screamed. "Strike two," shouted the ump and the crowd screamed again.

The stadium was breathless as Johnny wound up for the third pitch.

"Strike three! You're out!" screamed the ump and the whole place exploded.

The entire team ran out to Johnny, grabbed him and flung him in the air. They carried him around the field screaming and poured champagne all over him. As we screamed, the crowd began to jump onto the field and chase after them. All at once there was a mass of humanity right in front of me. I could see the team go into the dugout and Johnny was out of sight. I sat there for a few moments just crying. I was so proud of him that day and I loved him so much.

I finally made my way to the lockers and waited there with the press for our hero to emerge. Then, there he was, my Johnny coming down the hall toward the waiting room. We ran to one another and I leaped into his open arms. He embraced me, swung me around in the air and shouted for all to hear, "I love you angel!"

I held his arm as the press swarmed us. He was the man of the hour. The entire team came running out from the lockers. When they reached us, they screamed and showered us with champagne. We were soaked. We finally left the press behind and headed for our limo. We were escorted out of the stadium by four police cars with sirens wailing. The car arrived at the penthouse at 5:20pm. We needed a quick respite before heading to the Plaza Hotel for dinner and the celebration party, which was to begin at 8:00pm. As we entered the penthouse Johnny picked me up and carried me to the bathroom kissing me all the way. He placed me down laughing, "You're a little sticky, angel."

I looked at us and began to laugh. We hugged and kissed then took our sticky clothing off and jumped into the shower together. I took the washcloth from his hand and began to wash his body. He leaned his back against the side of the shower wall and as I washed him, I watched his large, limp, muscle slowly become enormous. My body shivered with passion. I kissed his lips and slowly slid my tongue from his neck down to his hard nipples. I began to softly massage them with my tongue and the tips of my teeth. As the warm water ran off our bodies, I moved from one nipple to the other. Johnny was moaning and his body began to softly twitch with excitement. I found myself being drawn to his throbbing manhood. My lips began to quiver with anticipation, as I slowly took him into my mouth. Our bodies went wild together in perfect rhythm, until Johnny screamed in ecstasy. As he exploded, I drank from him as if I were drinking from the fountains of the gods. I felt his lightning shoot through the essence of my being, and the heat of my passion exploded within me. The feelings of pleasure and lust were magnificent. We embraced again, "I love you; I love you," was all either one of us could say. Slowly we began to finish washing one another.

After we rinsed off, he picked me back up still dripping wet and carried me to the bed.

He was so incredibly hot. He was like a wild beast that just killed its opponent for the prize, '**and I was that prize**.' He devoured my flesh over and over again. It was exquisite.

As we dressed, I began to feel lightheaded, like I was going to faint. I reached for the bedpost to hold myself up. Johnny grabbed me just as I was beginning to fall, and as he laid me on the bed, I could faintly hear him say, "Christy, baby! Christy, wake up!" I slowly came back as Johnny held me, "Are you all right, baby?"

"I think so, Johnny." I answered slightly dazed.

"What happened, angel?"

American Goddess

"I don't know I just felt weak. It must be from all the excitement of the day."

"Do you feel all right now?"

"Yes, I'm feeling much better. Let's get going. We can't keep your public waiting, you know."

"We don't have to go any place if you're not feeling well."

"I'm fine now, baby." I answered reassuringly as I gently squeezed his shoulder. 'And I was.'

Then it was off to the Plaza. As the limo drove us through town that night, there were people all over the streets. The city was alive with excitement. There were celebrations everywhere. The limo pulled up to the Plaza and we climbed out. We entered the ballroom to a standing ovation. It was Johnny's ovation. I turned to him and curtsied then he bowed to me and escorted me to our table. The cameras were lighting up the room. Steve and Kathy were seated at our table that night and we were glad to see them. We had at least ten different toasts to Johnny and the team before dinner even arrived. By the time dinner was over and the band began to play, we all had plenty to drink, and once again, **especially** Kathy.

Johnny and I danced and danced. The night was divine, and our love seemed to outshine the brightest star. Then Steve and Kathy danced between us and we changed partners. I was dancing in Steve's arms, but I could not keep my mind or eyes off Johnny.

As Steve and I danced, I began to feel slightly weak again, so I excused myself and headed for the ladies' room. I washed my face, took a few deep breaths and began to feel better. After a moment, I put my face back on and headed back to Johnny. As I entered the room, I could see Johnny across the well-lit, crowded dance floor. He was uncomfortably attempting to hold back Kathy's drunken advances and Steve seemed embarrassed by her behavior. As I watched her hang her arms around Johnny's neck and begin to whisper into his ear, I also noticed everyone else in the room witnessing this behavior and trying to act as if none of it was taking place. Steve turned and walked out of the room. I on the other hand had fire in my eyes as I walked over to them, grabbed Kathy and pulled her off Johnny. I held her tightly by the wrist, looked her straight in the face and with a sharp tone which echoed throughout the ballroom, "If I ever catch you putting the moves on Johnny again, I'll beat the crap out of you!"

She gave me an evil look, "I'm sorry if you got the wrong impression, Christy." as she pulled her hand from mine, "Don't flatter yourself, I'm not after your man." With that she turned and walked out the door.

Johnny immediately took me by the hand and with a silly smile, "I think you better just dance, 'little lady,' and cool down."

As we danced, "Was she coming onto you? Or was I just acting like a jealous fool?"

"She sure as hell was coming onto me, angel, believe me," Johnny answered with a

American Goddess

slight snicker. "But you have nothing to worry about with me, I'm all yours." Then he held me tightly as we danced one more dance.

It was 1:00am when we arrived back home. We were physically exhausted and emotionally charged. Johnny took me in his arms and held me ever so close. Looking lovingly into my eyes, "We're almost there, Christy. Just think, in two weeks you and I will have won the World Series and we will be wed. We will have the most romantic honeymoon you could imagine. Oh baby, I cannot wait to carry you off to our dream. Then we will begin our lives angel, our lives together."

"I love you so much, Johnny."

We slowly walked out arm in arm onto the balcony, "Look at it, angel. Isn't this the most beautiful city you've ever seen?"

The city lights were filling the sky, "Oh, Johnny, it is beautiful."

Johnny kissed me, "And tonight it's all ours."

As we stood there in each other's arms gazing out over this beautiful city, on this glorious night, we knew our love was eternal. We embraced passionately and Johnny slowly began to unhook the back of my gown and it fell to the floor. He slid my bra off my shoulders to expose my breast to the warm night air. As he began to lick my neck, I felt a chill run up my spine. He squeezed my breasts together with both his masculine hands and softly buried his face in my flesh so closely he could hear the throbbing of my heart. He slid his head back and forth licking and kissing both my nipples with such warmth and tenderness I thought I would explode. I felt so much like a woman as he grabbed me up in his arms, laid me down on the cool carpeting, and gently finished undressing me. His tongue was hot as he moved down to my navel. Sliding my legs apart he brought his smooth warm lips to my quivering essence, slowly moving his tongue round and round until passionately and wildly he drove it deep within me.

I moaned, "Oh God, Johnny. Johnny, oh Johnny," I pulled him up and began to rip his clothing off. I kissed him madly, "Make love to me, Johnny. Please make love to me." I wanted him so badly.

Slowly he placed the head of his massive manhood gently into the opening of my surrendering body. As he slid deeper, harder and faster into my fiery soul, I cried out in pure ecstasy, "Oh God, Johnny, I love you."

He screamed, "Oh, baby!" as we both simultaneously exploded in a whirlwind of passion and pleasure.

The weight of his body collapsed on mine and we held each other tightly with the sweat of our passion dripping from our bodies. After a while, I slipped out of his embrace. I returned to his arms with a damp washcloth and towel. I washed the sweat from his body that night, and it felt so right. I felt I could never love him more than I did at that very moment. I laid my head on his shoulder and we drifted off to sleep surrounded by the city

American Goddess

lights.

We woke up at 7:00am that morning to the persistent messages from Uncle Frank. He wanted me to call him right away. It was very important. I finally got up, brushed the hair from my face and answered the phone, "Hello, Uncle Frank," I said with a half yawn. "What's wrong?"

"I have to meet with you as soon as you can fly out here."

"Where are you? What's going on, Uncle Frank?" I asked again with concern.

"I'm at the Vegas house and I can't speak about it over the phone. That's why it's imperative I see you tonight. I can't leave here now I'm not feeling well enough, otherwise I'd come to you."

"All right, Uncle Frank, I'll catch the first flight out."

"What's going on, baby?" Johnny asked as I hung up the phone.

"I don't know. That was Uncle Frank. He sounded as if there was something wrong and he needs to see me as soon as possible. He can't leave Vegas, so he wants me to fly there today." I hugged him, "I'm sorry baby, but I have to go."

Reassuringly, "I know angel," playfully he lifted me up, "What would you say if I said I'd like to come with you?"

"Could you?" I asked as he placed my feet back on the floor.

"Sure, I could. I have the next two days off and I'm all yours."

I booked a 10:00am flight to Vegas for that morning. I called Uncle Frank, told him what time to expect us, and he said he'd have a car waiting.

I was so glad Johnny was with me because my mind went wild with crazy thoughts wondering what the problem could be. During the flight Johnny could see I was concerned. He tenderly took my hand, "Don't worry, Christy. Whatever it is, we'll handle it together."

"I love you, Johnny, but what if it's his health, what do I do? He had a severe heart attack only two years ago. I almost lost him then."

"Try to stop worrying honey. I'll give you some of my mom's famous advice for a good case of the worries. Oh, let me see," putting his hand to his cheek, "She would say something like, 'try not to fix something before you know it's broken.' My mom is filled with little ditties like that."

I smiled as I gazed up into his eyes, "Oh well, I'll figure it out tomorrow. She's wonderful, your mother." We laughed then I placed my head on his shoulder and we stayed that way until the plane landed.

It was 5:00pm when the limo pulled up to the main door of the thirty-three-story building which was the headquarters to Frank's empire. When we entered Frank's office, he walked over to me, put his hands on both my shoulders and exclaimed, "Thank God you're here baby, it's almost too late." Turning to Johnny, "Hello, John. I'm sorry but I'm going to have to ask you to wait in the outer office while I speak with Christy."

Johnny looked at me, "Do you want me to stay with you?"

"Yes, I do." I looked at Uncle Frank, "Johnny's my fiancé and I don't want to keep anything from him."

"All right then. Come sit down." He headed toward his desk.

We took the two seats in front of his mammoth desk. He opened the top drawer, took out a large thick envelope and with a wide smile on his face, tossed it to me, "You got it, baby!"

I opened the envelope and inside was the script to 'Samantha's Father'. For a second the blood raced through my veins with excitement. Then I looked at Johnny and remembered our dream. I looked back at Uncle Frank, "You called us out here for this? I thought it was your health! How could you do that to me Uncle Frank? You couldn't tell me this over the phone?"

Johnny glanced down at the package, saw what it was and said nothing.

"I'm sorry I didn't tell you, honey, but I had to get you here. You must start studying this script right away. Filming begins in four days in LA." He tossed me another envelope, "I also wanted to give this to you myself, baby. You have officially been nominated for an Academy Award."

I didn't even open the envelope. I was so taken aback over getting the part of Samantha, all I could say was, "How is this possible? I didn't even try out for the part."

Frank looked straight into my eyes, "I did it, baby. I did it for you. I called in a lot of favors for this one and we got it!"

I reached over and grabbed Johnny's hand for strength, "Uncle Frank, I don't want the part."

Frank got up from his chair, walked over to the window, then turned back to face us again, "What do you mean, you don't want this part? Do you know what this part will mean for your career? Do you know or even appreciate what I went through to get you this part?"

"Yes, Uncle Frank. I do know what this part means. I also appreciate what you had to do to get me this part and I love you for it. But after Johnny and I are married, I'm not going back to work. We are going to start our lives together and that doesn't include performing."

Frank walked up to where I was seated, slammed his fist down on the desk right in front of my face, "That's what you think! You have two years left on your contract with me young lady, and you're going to take this part!"

Johnny stood up, "I've heard enough of this. If Christy says she's not taking the part, she's not!" taking my hand, "Let's get the hell out of here Christy."

Uncle Frank yelled, "Don't you dare walk out on me, Christy! You signed a contract and I am holding you to it."

Johnny becoming visibly angered, "You can take your contract and shove it, Frank!" And we walked out the door.

We headed for the airport and caught the first flight back to New York. After the frenzy of trying to get a flight back home eased, Johnny lovingly put his arms around me, "Christy, my angel, I love you. You made me so happy and proud today, when I heard you defend yourself to your uncle. And when I see what it is you are willing to give up for me, it brings tears to my eyes." He kissed me gently, "Baby, are you sure you can leave all this behind to raise a family with me?"

Oh God, my heart melted. I cuddled close and with tears in my eyes, "Johnny, my sweet, wonderful, Johnny. I love you more than life." We finished the flight in each other's arms.

It was 2:00am when we finally climbed into bed. We were physically exhausted, emotionally disgusted and totally in love. I took the phone off the hook and for the first time since the day we met, we fell asleep without making love.

We were awakened at 10:00am by the continual ringing of the doorbell. I threw on my robe and ran to the door. When I opened it, there stood a uniformed officer who thrust an envelope into my partially opened hand and departed without uttering a single word. Not even good morning. I stood there a moment, thinking, "What the hell was that?"

Johnny came out of the bedroom, "Who was that?"

"A police officer, I guess. He stuck this envelope in my hand and left."

"Well, it's addressed to you, maybe you should open it," he chuckled.

I kissed Johnny's cheek as I started to open it, "Good morning, baby. Come on in the kitchen, I'll put on some coffee."

As we entered the kitchen, I was reading the letter, "It's a summons! It basically says, **'I have to appear in court at the City Hall building, room 717 at 2:00pm this afternoon for an informal hearing in front of Judge Christopher.'** It's regarding a suit brought against me by dear Uncle Frank, for breach of contract!" I took a breath, "I can't believe this, it goes on to say, **'if you fail to appear, there will be a bench warrant issued for your arrest.'"** I threw the paper on the floor, "I still can't believe this!"

Johnny held me, "Calm down, Christy. It's going to be okay."

"I hope so, Johnny, I hope so." I answered slightly giggling.

He led me to the table, "Here, you sit down, and I'll make the coffee." As Johnny put the coffee on, "How in the world did he get a summons in one day?"

"He can get almost anything he wants in this city. He has that kind of clout."

"Why don't we get cleaned up and go for something to eat. Then I'll come to court with you."

"That sounds great to me, Johnny," with a sigh of relief.

American Goddess

We headed for the shower and as I passed the phone, I placed it back on the receiver. By the time we got out of the shower there were five phone calls for Johnny; two from Steve, two from his coach and one from Stephan Brown the owner of the New York Mets. All saying call now!

I looked at Johnny and I was scared, "He's getting to you now."

He hugged me wearing a smile, "Let's not fix something we don't know is broken," throwing his hands up in the air, "Or something like that," and we both started to laugh.

I couldn't believe he was able to bring some light to such a horrendously dark moment. I just started to kiss him all over his face and we laughed again. In the midst of our fears, we chose to cling to the innocence of our love. After we composed ourselves, Johnny picked up the phone and called Stephan Brown, 'who guess what,' had to meet with Johnny in his office at 2pm promptly 'which by the way,' was across town from City Hall. Johnny hung up the phone, turned to me, "I guess we're on our own, angel," hugging me confidently, "We can do this, Christy. I know we can."

As he said these words, I knew I could be strong without him by my side. Johnny and I were one, whether we were together or not and I was not going to let my uncle intimidate me any longer.

We finished dressing and went for lunch. After lunch we kissed and made plans to meet back at my place immediately after our meetings. We kissed again and went our separate ways.

When we parted that day, we took with us the utmost confidence we would return victoriously. Unfortunately, I was totally dazed when I returned home at 8:00 that evening and to my dismay, Johnny had not yet arrived. I took my clothes off, threw them on the bedroom floor, and headed for the shower. I felt like I had to wash the stench of the afternoon's meeting off my body. After showering I dried off, threw on my robe and headed for the sofa to wait for Johnny.

When Johnny opened the door, he looked like a little boy who just received an old-fashioned southern thrashing. I stretched my arms out to him, "Come over here, sweetie."

For the longest time we just held each other like two wounded pups. After a while, Johnny said to me with an exhausted tone, "How are you, angel?"

"I could be better."

"Okay, you tell me what happened, and then I'll tell you."

"I don't know if you're ready for this, but here it is," I began with a disgusted tone, "It seems I have no choice but to be on a plane to LA tomorrow morning."

"And if you're not, then what?"

I took a deep breath, "Johnny, my love, first I'll be sued for thirty-million dollars for breach of contract. Second, I will be totally penny-less because Uncle Frank managed to trick me into signing power of attorney for all of my finances over to him." I started to cry,

American Goddess

"Third, he would have you pulled out of the World Series games." I held him tightly and with tears still falling from my eyes, "Fourth, if I marry you, all of your financial assets will be frozen to pay off my debts. Including in my uncle's own words, our little dream house."

"That fucker!" Johnny exclaimed angrily, "I got the same thing. We can't let them get away with this baby, we just can't."

"What are you saying, Johnny?"

"Exactly, what I'm saying. What if we just say to hell with them? I'll drop out of the game and we'll take off together."

"Oh God, Johnny, try to be realistic here. We'll be letting him steal all of our dreams if we do that."

Looking slightly puzzled, "What do you mean?"

"Johnny, the World Series, it's your dream; our, dream. Our family on our farm; it's our dream. If we leave, we lose it all. Baby, for a lousy two years it's not worth it. He can only hold me to the contract for two more years and I'm willing to play his game that long, so I can have you and we can have our dreams come true."

"I guess you're right, angel." Johnny put his sleepy head on my shoulder, "So what time are you leaving in the morning?"

I kissed his cheek, "four o'clock honey."

This was the second night we both just fell asleep. It was 3:00am when I got off the sofa with Johnny. I covered him with a quilt and went to clean up. It was 3:45am when I kissed a very sleepy Johnny goodbye. I left a note on my pillow saying, "**I love you, Johnny, with all my heart and I will be thinking of you every moment of the day. Baby, I will call you every free second, I have. All my love to you, honey. Love You, Christy.**"

Then I was on my way to LA and the shooting of 'Samantha's Father.' The schedule for the next couple of weeks was unbelievable. Johnny was with the team almost 24 hours a day. They were playing the LA Dodgers, so at least I knew Johnny would be coming out to the West Coast. As for me, my shooting schedule was intense. They seemed to be deliberately keeping me hopping. I had ten complete costume changes in one day. The only time I got to see Johnny was at a game. The only place I got to touch Johnny was in the dugout for a few minutes before the team was rushed out to a locked hotel room. The team was forbidden to have any social life at all until after the series was over. In the dugout before the opening game, Johnny gave me a present. I opened it and saw a pendant so beautiful it took my breath away. It was a square, aquamarine stone with baguette diamonds all around it.

"Johnny, it's beautiful!" I exclaimed.

"I chose it because the stone matches the color of your eyes," he replied with an adoring look.

American Goddess

I kissed him passionately, "I love it, Johnny."

Just then, the manager called Johnny back into the dugout and he was out of my reach once more. Johnny pitched the opening game in L.A. that day and I screamed and cheered as he dominantly won the game. The Dodgers won the next two games. The next game the Mets won, making the score two to two. The fifth game was to be held in New York and Johnny was pitching. I was not able to make it to that game and much to my dismay Johnny lost the first game he had pitched since the day we met. This made the score three to two, Dodgers favor, and the next game was crucial.

Johnny finally called me at 2:00am and he sounded so sad, "Christy, I need you. I can't make it without you anymore," starting to cry, "I lost the game today, angel, and you weren't there."

My heart hurt deeply as I heard him crying, "Johnny, please don't be sad. I love you so much and it's killing me not to be with you."

"Oh, baby," he replied as we cried together, "I love you, Christina. I love you."

That was the first time Johnny called me by my full name. I felt as if he was crying to me as his equal, because we were both in need of strength, and we gave it to each other over the phone that long dark night.

"Honey, we have to be strong. Remember what you said to me? We can make it through anything together."

"I know, angel! I know. Christy, baby, if we win Wednesday's game, I'll be pitching Thursday at 9:00pm. Christy, will you please, please, be here with me? I need you to be here! Baby, this time, I'm the one who's scared."

"Oh yes, my Johnny! I'll be there, baby, I'll be there, I promise."

We fell asleep on the phone that night to the sounds of each other's breathing. It was 6:00am when I woke up. I told Johnny I would call the airport as soon as I hung up. I called and reserved a 1:00pm flight for that Wednesday. I called Johnny back to let him know, and then it was off to the studio. It was Wednesday morning and I was in the middle of shooting a scene when Johnny had an emergency page sent for me. I ran to the phone, "Johnny, what's wrong?"

With panic in his voice, "Christy, they've changed the line-up and I'm pitching! The game is tonight at 9:00pm!"

I looked at my watch, "Honey, don't worry I'll be there! I love you, Johnny." I hung up the phone and called the airport. I told them who I was, gave them a credit card number and hired a private jet to New York. I ran out of the studio, jumped in the rental car and sped to the airport. Just as I got there, I heard my name being paged again. I ran to the phone thinking it was Johnny. My heart was pounding as I answered it, but the voice on the other end was unrecognizable.

I heard, "Christy, it's me, your cousin Anthony. It's Dad, he's had a massive heart attack and he's dying."

My head began to whirl, "Are you sure, Anthony?" I asked with a disbelieving tone.

"Christy," Anthony said with a tone of urgency. "If you want to see him once more before he dies, you'd better come now!"

I looked down at my watch, "Where is he?"

"He's at the Vegas home."

I was torn. What do I do? I looked at my watch again and figured if I spent ten minutes with Uncle Frank, I would still have an hour to spare. So, I went for it. I had the jet go to Vegas first. I had a town-car waiting and I was off to see Uncle Frank. When I arrived at the mansion, I ran to the door and flung it open. I looked around and could not find anyone. I ran up the towering spiral staircase straight to Frank's room and found him standing there. I walked up to him and with all my might slapped him across the face and angrily shouted, "What kind of sick joke is this?"

He began to laugh at me, "You'll never make it to the game now, he'll lose, and he'll hate you for not being there, because you will have let that sap down."

"You monster," I shouted! "Why are you doing this to us?"

He screamed at me, "I love you, Christy, and if I can't have you, no one will."

I stepped back throwing my hands in the air while screaming, "I'm your niece, what the hell are you talking about?!"

He slapped me with all his strength knocking me to the floor and shouted, "You're not my niece. I own you!"

I scrambled off the floor, "What are you saying? Am I your daughter?"

"No," he answered wickedly."

"If I'm not your niece or your daughter, who the hell am I?"

"No, Christy, you're not my niece or my daughter. You're mine," Frank said emphatically!

I screamed, "Why do you keep saying that?! Who am I?! Who are my parents?!"

A look of complete insanity radiated from him, "I was in love with your mother. I loved her with all my heart. But she was like you, she didn't love me back."

I stood there trembling, "Who was my mother?"

He gave me an evil look, "You don't need to know that."

I ran over to him, grabbed his arm and with hatred in my voice screamed, **"I DO NEED TO KNOW! I DO!"**

He began to cry like a baby, "I loved your mother. She was a rising star with golden possibilities, and we were in love. Until she met **him!**"

"Who were they? Frank, tell me!" I screamed again.

"They had an affair when she was just becoming well known. He was a young state senator from New England. He got her pregnant, but they could not be together. She could not find it in her heart to kill the child, so she had it. You're that child."

"Is my mother alive," I asked with pain in my voice?

"No, she took her life with an overdose of sleeping pills."

"Is my father alive?" I asked as tears began to flow.

he replied ruthlessly, "No, he was assassinated."

I screamed again, "Who were they? Tell me Frank! Tell me!"

With an enraged expression his jaw clinched, "Your mother was the 'queen of Hollywood' Marilyn Monroe and your father was once the President of the United States, John F. Kenny. And I am the only person in the world still alive who knows that.

I backed away from him screaming, "Do you know what you're saying? Are you mad?" He grabbed me and tried to kiss me, and I screamed, "Stop it, let me go! Let me go!"

As I struggled to break free from his arms he screamed in my face, "You're a **FORBIDDEN CHILD** Christina, and you're mine!"

I screamed and wildly fought my way out of his powerful grasp. I ran down the steps crying all the way, and as I ran, he screamed at me, "You can't leave, your mine! Come back here now!   Come back here or you will never perform again!"

I opened the door and ran down to the car. I jumped in and sped away in hysterics. I tried desperately to calm down and compose myself before reaching the airport.

It was 4:00pm when I boarded the jet and was on my way to Johnny. During that exceptionally long flight to New York my mind was racing with thoughts of what Frank had said. "Could it be true? Am I truly the daughter of President John F. Kenny and Marilyn Monroe?"

I finally stopped thinking of myself and my thoughts turned to Johnny. My heart almost stopped when it was 9:00pm and we still had half an hour to go before reaching New York. When the plane landed, I had a car waiting and I sped to the game. I turned on the radio and heard the announcer screaming, "The LA Dodgers have just won the World Series!" I cried out, "Oh God, no!"

By the time I arrived at the stadium it had started to rain heavily. The parking lot was nearly empty. I sped through it madly looking for Johnny's car. When I spotted it, I sped up to it, slammed my foot on the brakes and screeched to a stop. I jumped out of the car into the pouring rain and ran with all my might through the parking lot to the player's entrance. I opened the door and ran down the cold dark hall. I stopped dead in my tracks when I saw him walking toward me. I grabbed him and cried, "Johnny, I'm so, so sorry, baby!" He became weak in my arms and we both fell to our knees.

He cried out, "I lost the game. I failed you. I lost the dream."

I held him so tightly on that cold floor and with desperation, "I'm here now, Johnny, I'm here."

All at once he pushed himself away from me and with disgust in his voice shouted,

American Goddess

"Where were you, Christy? I looked for you! I needed you and you weren't there!"

"Johnny! I'm sorry I didn't make it, baby, but Frank . . ."

He cut me off in mid-sentence and as he stood up, he flung his arms in the air and shouted, "Frank! Frank! Frank! I can't take any more of Frank!" Then he turned and walked away from me.

I pleaded, "Johnny, please, I'm begging you." But he just kept walking away. As he moved out of sight, I fainted. I woke up two hours later in the hospital with my doctor standing over me. He smiled, "Good morning, Miss Valona."

I sat up, "What am I doing here?"

Still smiling, "You passed out last night, young lady. I think a woman in your condition should be a little less active."

I looked at him and started to laugh and laugh until finally I could say, "Are you telling me I'm pregnant?"

Still with that stupid smile, "Yes, you are."

I shook my head in disbelief, "Oh God! When you're screwed, you're screwed."

He thought I was nuts and wanted to have me psychologically evaluated, so I said, "Live through a day like I just had and then tell me that."

I signed out against the doctor's advice and left the hospital. As I headed home, I began to think about Johnny. In my heart I realized he loved me. I knew he was probably looking for me that very moment.

I stopped quickly at a florist shop and bought two dozen red roses with one white one in the middle. On the card I wrote, "**Johnny, my beloved, we're going to have a baby!**"

With anticipation, I ran into my penthouse looking for Johnny, but he was not there. I drove to his condo in Tarry-town and my heart leaped when I saw his car. I grabbed the flowers and ran up to the door. I opened it and ran in yelling, "Johnny! Johnny my love!"

My heart crumbled when I burst into the bedroom and found him lying in bed with Kathy beneath him. I screamed, "You bastard!" as I drew my hands to my face, "How could you, Johnny? How could you?"

I threw the flowers right in his shocked face and ran out crying. **It was horrible. I was devastated**. I cried frantically as I sped wildly through the streets. I rounded a corner, lost control and plunged down a six-foot embankment to an abrupt stop. I sat there crying in the dark for six hours. As the sun rose, a police car spotted me and back to the hospital I went.

While I was there, everything went through my mind. Johnny, Frank, my mother, my father, my career. They were all gone now. I did not know what was out there for me, or for a child. Then I thought of the possibility of my child being raised by someone as sick as Frank. That thought, at that moment, caused me to harden my heart so much, that without a second thought, I had one of the first legal abortions performed in our nation.

American Goddess

I came home from the hospital the next day and lay in bed for two days crying. I was surprised on that second day when Johnny walked into the room. He came over, knelt down beside me, took my hands in his and with tears of love in his eyes, "Christy, please forgive me. I am so sorry. Please tell me you still love me?"

I grabbed him tightly and cried, "I forgive you, Johnny! I love you!" We were back in each other's arms and we felt the love run so deep again.

His eyes began to glow and with an excited tone, "I can't believe we're going to have a baby!"

Instantly, tremendous pain shot through my heart as I began to cry even harder. Only now they were tears of sadness and with my voice cracking, "Johnny, I had an abortion."

He looked at me and screamed in horror, "You killed my baby? Christina, how could you kill my baby?"

I had no answer, for there was none. I looked at him and saw so much hatred and anger in his eyes that I knew he could never forgive me. I couldn't stand to see him look at me like that, so I screamed at the top of my voice, "Get out! Get out!"

With tears flowing down his cheeks, he turned, walked to the door, opened it and gazed back at me. Then he turned again, slammed the door and walked out of my life. **My heart and soul died in that split second. And there was no innocence to be found.**

CHAPTER 2

It was December 10th, 1973, my nineteenth birthday, when finally, it all crumbled. At 8:00am I received a call from my attorney informing me the IRS had decided today at 10:00am would be the day they were to arrive to seize my penthouse with all its contents, for back taxes. He said, "They want your car and the title at that time as well."

I tried to tell him this car was my baby, "They can take my home, my jewelry, my clothes, and my money, but not my car!"

It was a 1972 Pontiac Grand Prix and beautiful. It was emerald green with a black vinyl roof. I loved it and Frank hated it, which made me love it even more.

I told him, "This is the first car I bought on my own and I picked it out by myself. Frank picked out everything I ever owned, except for this car and he has taken it all back, but I'll be damned if he'll get my car!"

I hung up the phone and took the only cash I had from under my mattress, which was sixty-six- thousand -dollars. I packed whatever I could fit into two suitcases, grabbed one bottle of champagne, carried them to **my car** and took off. **I HAD, HAD ENOUGH!**

You see, my life was pure hell after Johnny, and I broke up. I stayed in my room for seventeen days; I only ate a few bites I could manage to keep down. I could hear the messages on the answering machine, but I could not utter a word. In the midst of the madness of those seventeen days, I felt such shame, I wanted to die! "What had I done?" I asked myself over and over, "How could I have taken the life of our child?"

In the depths of my anguish, I took a blade to my throat and began to slice it. The blood from the first puncture began to drip down the edge of the cold steel blade and touched my hand. I began to shake, I threw the knife across the room and cried, "Oh God I can't do it!" I thought, "You coward! You can kill your own baby without a second thought, but you can't take the life of the murderess." I flew across the bedroom, grabbed the knife and put it to my throat. This time I meant it! I began to slice my throat once again, then I screamed out, "I can't!" as I threw the blade as hard as I could. It struck the mirror, shattering it into a million pieces all over the room. I looked at it, and then I looked at the wall where the mirror had been, and I could not see myself. There was nothing there, and I just began to laugh hysterically as I said to myself, "You decide to stay, then you give yourself seven more years of this shit, by breaking the freaken mirror." With that I laughed some more. When I finally stopped laughing, I left that bedroom and decided to make it my life's goal to get Frank!

When I finally listened to my messages, I found out I was in deep **shit.** It seemed I had checks bouncing all over town. **BIG ONES!** I had a seventy-thousand-dollar American Express bill for chartering a jet. All my credit cards were worthless and from out of the blue came the IRS. They were after me for the three-hundred-thousand-dollars in back taxes for 1972 and I hadn't even thought about 1973, yet. Paramount Studios was suing me to the tune of three-million-dollars for walking off the set of 'Samantha's Father' and to top it all off, my checking and savings account balances were **ZERO**, thanks to Frank.

It also appeared that while I was incognito, the papers and the tabloids had a field day at my expense. They read, **"Christy, the Dragon Women who slew the white knight's heart, at his defeat!"** or **"The Temptress, who brought down the New York Mets!"**

All this wonderful press did wonders for my public affairs. I was shunned from the hearts of most New Yorkers, and every time I appeared in court for a summons, it was more than apparent.

When I tried to get work in the field of my dreams, it appeared that had been taken from me too, for I could work nowhere in the entertainment industry. And, on one of my exceptional days, I received a very apologetic note from the chairperson for the Institute of the Academy Awards stating, **"We regret to inform you of a miscount in the votes for the 1973 awards nominations. It appears that your nomination for 'Blue Lady' was one of those that were miscounted. When recounting the votes for your performance, it was not considered to be of Academy Award standards."**

After I read it, I crumpled the letter, threw it over my shoulders with a shrug, snapped my fingers and said, "Oh well! I'll figure it out tomorrow."

Then there was my visit from Barbara. She came over sometime around Thanksgiving. I was lying in bed, half a-wake at 1:00pm when the doorbell rang and rang. I finally got up and staggered over to the door. I peeked through the peephole expecting to see a uniformed bearer of 'good news', when there she was.

I opened the door and she said, "What the hell is the matter with you? You don't know how to work your answering machine?" She hugged me, "I'm sorry I haven't been here sooner, Christy, but it's a 'fucking' man's world, and even I couldn't sneak a way to see you before this."

With half a yawn, "Come on in Barbara."

She gave me a strange look and followed me into the very messy living room, "So tell me, Christy, what's going on?"

I leaned over, tiredly kissed her cheek, and bewilderingly shook my head, "It's good to see ya, Barb."

I proceeded to tell her everything. I needed to talk, I needed a friend, I needed to be able to try to trust someone and thank God, it was Barbara! She told me how Frank brought all his muscle to bear on the entertainment industry in order to keep me out and her hands were tied as well. If she, or anyone else in the business tried to give me work, there would be retaliations.

I understood all too well what Barbara was saying that day. At that moment, I decided 'no man' will ever hold my life in his hands again, and I would live **MY LIFE by MY RULES!**

After Barbara left that day, I found a white envelope in my bathroom. I opened it and there was one-hundred-thousand dollars cash in it, with a note which read," **Use it with good judgment, Christy, Love Barbara. P.S. don't forget we have a dinner date."**

The first thing I did was pay off all my bounced checks. Then I stuck sixty-six-thousand dollars under my mattress.

So, when I pulled away from my Park Avenue penthouse on my nineteenth birthday at 8:30am I was saying goodbye to the past and hello to the future. I drove endlessly that day. It wasn't until 11:00pm that I decided I had to stop and feed my hunger. I pulled into a truck stop off Route 95 south of Thompsonville, South Carolina. I filled the tank with gas for the second time that day, then headed for the restaurant.

American Goddess

When I walked in, I felt a little uncomfortable to say the least. The place was filled with southern truck drivers, all looking at me. I ordered a hot pot roast dinner with all the trimmings, I was hungry! While I waited for the feast, I noticed a little jukebox on the wall, right at my booth. As I flipped the nob with my thumb to examine the choices, a title caught my attention. It read, "The Love I lost." I popped a quarter in the slot and punched B8. I could hear through the crackling of the speakers, a male voice singing a country western ballad. He was singing a story of how he had lost the love of his life. It told of his heartbreak and pain, and how years from now he'd still be wondering why. As I listened to his pain, I could feel mine, and I knew I would always feel that void.

She was a cute little waitress in a grease spotted pink uniform who rescued me from my memories with a meal fit for a king. As I began to devour my pi'ece de re'sistance, I could not help but overhear the conversation going on at the booth next to mine.

It sounded something like this, "Boy she's hot!" One of them said, with mustard hanging off his six-inch beard, which lay on his three-hundred-pound belly.

Then the dirty skinny one, with the two black teeth, "Shit man, she looks a little like that Hollywood slut everybody is talking about; "You know?" "Christy something, she's the bitch who destroyed that ball player's career. You know? What's his name?"

I wanted to crawl under the table and die. I thought, "Oh my God, even people like that, feel like this about me." I suddenly lost my appetite. I got up and as inconspicuously as possible, walked over to the waitress, stuck a fifty-dollar bill in her hand and walked out.

As I walked through the dimly lit parking lot toward the car an actual flying saucer appeared over my head. I looked up in wonder and as I looked a bright ray of lite burst from it and covered me. All of a sudden, my skin began to tingle. I looked at my arms and they were starting to glow. I put my hands to my cheeks and my whole body began to burn. In fear I fell to my knees, covered my face in my hands and I could still see the light. Horrified I screamed at the top of my lungs, "Ahhhhh!" and it was gone.

I looked to see the same two truck drivers looking down at me and the fat one said, "Are you alright lady!?"

I stood up still shaking. I looked at those guys then took off running to the car, started it, though it in drive and hit the gas. As I hopped back on route 95, I said out loud, "What the fuck was that!!?" Then I looked at my hands and they were normal. I shook my head and said, "You better pull it together girl, or they are going to lock you up in a loony bin!"

I found myself gazing out the window of my room at Motel 6, off route 95 at 2:00am. Boy was I depressed. I thought, "How the hell in the world am I going to be able to start a new life, when I'm have out of my mind?"

The room was dark behind me as I looked over the pool, in the center court of the motel, filled with these thoughts. Out of the corner of my eye, I saw a flash of gold light glistening behind me. I felt a chill as I turned around quickly into a dark room. I saw nothing. I moved over to the light sitting on the desk and flicked it on. I looked down and there on the desk was a Bible with a brilliant gold cross carved into the center of it. With curiosity, I flipped the cover open to see an atlas of the world. I could see where someone had taken a red pen and circled the city of Rome. Underneath was written in quotes; "YOURS." I closed the cover, knelt down on my knees, made the sign of the cross, "Lord I don't know how to go on from here so please help me. And thanks for the Bible; I'm taking it with me." Then I climbed into the bed and passed out.

The next morning, I was out of the Motel by 9:00am. I drove to the town, stopped at a bookstore, bought a pen and paper, and wrote Johnny the following letter.

"Johnny, you will always be, the love I lost. My heart and soul died with the slamming of the door. Reflections through broken mirror pieces, our shattered lives appeared before me and in your eyes the pain was too hard to bear. In anguish, I know we could never forgive, and I have to be strong to survive, the love I lost. I must take my future into my hands and live life by my rules, in order to survive, the love I lost. I will live my life with passion and have lovers as I desire, and I will survive, the love I lost. Our love was destroyed with such viciousness I know it could never be repaired. My love for you will burn deep within me, but I must banish this pain and ban you from my thoughts, in order to survive. I will never want you back, but I will always ask myself why? Why, did I lose, the love I lost? How, did I lose, the love I lost? No matter how many lovers I may hold, or how many roads I must travel, you will always be, the love I lost. No one will ever fill your place in my heart, and you will always be, the love I lost. I will look back after all the years and lovers and ask myself why? Why I lost, the love I lost."

Then I drove to the airport. As I pulled into the entrance of the parking lot there was an attendant giving out parking tickets. I took one from him, parked my car, and placed one half of the stub on the dashboard and the other half in my purse. With that I kissed the steering wheel, "I'll remember you, baby." Then I grabbed my belongings and headed into the terminal.

As I waited for the plane to depart, I went to the airport gift shop, purchased an envelope and addressed it to Johnny. I slipped the letter I wrote to Johnny and I titled it, 'The Love I Lost'. Then I placed the ring which Johnny had given me into the envelope, sealed it and placed it in the mailbox.

Then I heard over the loudspeaker.

"All passengers for flight 221 to Rome will be boarding gate 17 in five minutes" **And I was off to Rome.**

American Goddess

CHAPTER 3

It was December 15th, 1973, when I started my new life in Rome.

First, I changed my name to 'Christina Powers' then cut my long black hair to just above my shoulders. I wasted no time in getting myself established. I rented a cute one bedroom fully furnished, basement apartment just north of the Coliseum that fit my budget perfectly. The next step was to find employment. Since I did not have much experience at anything I could think of, I took the first position offered to me, which was a waitress at the cafe only two blocks down the road. I was working the evening shift from 4 to 11pm and it was convenient because I could walk to work. The first week, I broke enough coffee cups to last a lifetime. By the end of my second week, I was waitressing like a pro.

By the time I was finally established and self-supporting at a level I had to grow accustomed to, it was January 28th, 1974. But I still had sixty thousand dollars under my mattress.

For the first few months, I didn't make many new friends. My mastery of the Italian language, at the time did not help my social life at all. When I tried to be sociable, unless we were talking about menu items, I didn't have much to say.

It was sometime in early June when I met Jimmy, my sweet Jimmy. He was so cute and funny I couldn't help but fall in love with him. He was a twenty-two-year-old, five-foot eight-inch, one-hundred and twenty-pound, ball of energy. He had dark brown curly hair and deep brown eyes. Boy was he sexy!

It was a beautiful warm spring night, so after work I decided to go for a walk. The streets in downtown Rome were alive with people. It felt good to feel all the life and energy in the air. It brought back memories of a time past. As I strolled down the avenue around 1:00am, I began to hear music coming from the building on the corner. As I reached it, I could hear the rhythm more clearly. It was a rhythm I was not familiar with, but I found it very catchy. I gazed up at the neon sign, **"Rome One Discotheque."**

I decided to check it out. I entered the packed nightclub and headed straight for the bar. I couldn't help but notice there were no other women in the place. I thought, "This is strange," but I still took a seat at the bar. The style of the music was just too enticing for me to leave.

The bartender came over to me and shouted in English over the sounds of the music, "Hi, honey! Did you know this is a gay club?"

He screamed it with such dramatics, I felt like an idiot for not knowing. I shout back, "No, I didn't know. May I stay anyway?"

"Sure honey, what can I get you?"

"A White Russian please."

American Goddess

With that he flicked his right hand, just from his wrist at me and shouted, "A White Russian! La, de, da.! You see this crowd, how about a Bud?"

I gave him a slightly puzzled look, as I chuckled to myself, "Sure, a Bud would be fine."

When he returned with my Bud, he introduced himself to me, "Hi, honey, here's your Bud." He leaned over to me and shouted in my ear, "By the way, my name is Jimmy Severino and I'm the queen bee around here. So, if you're going to hang out with me, looking that good, we better get that out of the way right now!"

That morning at 4:30am Jimmy took me for breakfast where our bond of friendship, mutual respect and love began.

After that night Jimmy and I became inseparable. Every minute we had free; we were together. And every night Jimmy worked at the Roma, I was there. If they didn't know any better, all the boys at the Roma, would have thought we were lovers. It turned out Jimmy was an American and most of the men who patronized the Roma One Discotheque were American too. And if they weren't, at least they spoke the English language. This fact helped make hanging out at the Roma, a delight. I didn't mind shouting, as long as it was in English. Jimmy was never a good bartender, but the owner kept him on because most of the guys who came in were attracted to him. They all loved him, and I swear, I think he slept with them all at least once! Besides Jimmy's jovial disposition, he had many talents. He was a damn good piano player and seamstress. Boy, could he sew. But the talent I loved most of all, came out when he was on the dance floor. He was an incredible dancer. The way he could move his body to this new music style, which was spreading like a wildfire throughout all the gay clubs in Europe was phenomenal. Whenever he would let loose his magic on the dance floor, everyone would give way to his moves. He was so good I just had to have him teach me his moves. And boy did he! We played and danced that whole summer. It seemed time and living life like a silly schoolgirl was healing the wounds of the past. Or at least I thought so.

It was September 22nd, 1974, at 10:00am when Jimmy entered the front door of my apartment. We had planned a day trip to the Coliseum and when he walked into the kitchen, I was sipping my first cup of coffee of the day. He was carrying an American tabloid in his hands when he sat beside me, "Christina, you're not ready yet, girl?"

I gazed up over my coffee cup, "Oh don't be such a spaz', pour yourself a cup of coffee and sit down with me for a few minutes. It won't take me long to get ready."

As we sipped our coffee, Jimmy began to read the tabloid. I got up, put my cup in the sink, and walked over behind him to kiss his cheek before heading for the shower. As I kissed his cheek, I could see at the bottom of the page he was reading an article which caught my attention. It read, "**The New York Mets' star pitcher, John Everett, was wed on September 1st, 1974, to his high school sweetheart, Mary Wilson.**"

American Goddess

I lost it! The pain shot through me like a thunderbolt. I ripped the paper out of his hands and crumpled it. Jimmy watched in disbelief as I fell to my knees and began to cry. Jimmy jumped from his seat, flew to my side and screamed, "Christina, what's the matter, girl? What is it?"

After I finally got a hold of myself, I told Jimmy who I was and then I proceeded to tell him the whole story. He was a big help! He sat there on the floor with me and began to cry. There we were the two of us, sitting on the kitchen floor bawling and I thought, "Well, at least I'm not crying alone."

Looking seriously into my eyes, "You know what you need girl-friend."

"No, Jimmy, I don't know. You tell me."

"To get happy girl!" He pulled a joint out of his pocket and lit it up.

I gave him a nasty look, "Get out of here with that stuff, you know I don't smoke pot."

He kissed my cheek, "Well, today you do." Then he handed me the joint. I took one puff, then another. By the time we made it to the Coliseum that day, I was high! We laughed all that day and into the night. I couldn't believe that with only one joint, I was able to push Johnny and the article right out of my thoughts. It seemed like a magical cure for heartache. By the time I hit the bed that night, I considered myself to be a full-fledged advocate for marijuana usage.

During that Fall our partying became more intense and I became the new queen of Roma's. The guys loved me, and I hit it off with all of them. It was easy to fit in with all these gay men because I didn't have the concern of someone coming onto me. That was the last thing I wanted. These men, in this bar, gave me a sense of belonging. They helped me feel beautiful again, which was what my ego needed.

It was December 31st, 1974 and the Roma was throwing a New Year's Eve Ball, with a drag show to boot. I was sitting by myself at a table in the corner of this packed, frenzied night club, at 11:58pm. Jimmy was off with his latest love, somewhere on the dance floor, when the clock struck midnight. Suddenly, the place became an explosion of noise and it hit me, **"MY CONTRACT IS UP!"** The thoughts and feelings of entertaining again flared up within my heart and I became overwhelmed with anticipation, "But how?" I asked myself, "Frank would still be able to keep me from working and the people of my own nation have disowned me." My thoughts raced so fast I didn't even notice Jimmy when he grabbed me back into space, time, and the party, with a quick tug on my arm. As I was dragged out to the dance floor, I thought, "Oh well! I'll figure it out tomorrow."

It was 4:00am when Jimmy walked me home. We were, to say the least, stoned out of our minds! When we entered my apartment, Jimmy closed the door, "Do you mind if I stay tonight, Christina?"

"No baby, I don't mind," as I kissed his forehead and headed into the bedroom. I took my clothes off, put on my night gown and I climbed under the covers. Two minutes later,

American Goddess

Jimmy climbed into bed with me with nothing on. I looked at him strangely, "What are you doing in my bed with nothing on?"

He answered meekly, "It's too hot in here."

"Go turn the heat down and put something on."

He whined, "I don't want to sleep alone tonight, Christina. Please, let me stay in here with you?"

I thought, "I guess so, it can't hurt, after- all he's gay." So, I said, "Okay."

Suddenly I found him clumsily trying to climb on top of me, with an erection no less. Holding back my laughter, "Jimmy, what are you doing?"

With a very shaky voice, he stuck his nose in my face, "If there was ever any woman in this world I would sleep with, it would be you."

Chuckling, "Oh that's sweet Jimmy thank you very much. Now get off me!"

At that he laid his head on my chest and began to pout, "Oh! Come on, Christina, please just once."

I looked into his big brown, puppy dog eyes and shrugged my shoulders, "Oh well, why not."

The moment his erection touched my leg, I had a flashback of making love with Johnny; and instantly a thought hit me like a ton of bricks! I flew up in the air knocking Jimmy off the bed and onto the floor, where the back of his head hit the dresser and I screamed out, **"I'm a fucking genius!"**

Jimmy looked up at me totally bewildered, and with one hand holding the back of his head shouted, "You're a fucking nut! That's what you are!"

I ran to the kitchen, grabbed a pen and paper and started to write something like this, '**Aa, baby, baby, Ou, baby, baby. Yes, yes, aa, aa, oh God, baby, baby, touch me, touch me, just like that, baby, baby.**' Jimmy put his shorts on and followed me into the kitchen. When he reached the table, he looked down at this secret code I was scribbling, "You're a fucking genius, all right." Then he scratched his head, turned and went to bed.

Later that morning over coffee, I handed Jimmy a sheet of paper," Let's put the hottest disco beat we can create to this."

Jimmy read it, looked up at me standing beside him, "What is it?"

I slapped the back of the head and as he yelled, "Ouch!" I said, "It's our new hit single, you dope."

Then it was off to work. The first thing I did was to take the sixty-thousand dollars I had remaining in cash, out from under my mattress. Jimmy and I put music to the lyrics, and we knew it was hot! As we were putting together a band to perform our music, I was registering and certifying myself, with the Italian government as Powers Records Incorporated. I now owned my own record label, and I was going to make it work!

Within two months, we were ready to go to the Italian public with one-hundred-thousand copies of our first release, 'Oh Baby! Touch Me Like That!' It was the most sensuous recording ever to be placed on vinyl. The only problem was it was so hot no radio station in Italy would play it!

With my financial neck on the chopping block again and with no one hearing our new recording, it was time for self-promotion. Jimmy and I planned every detail of my first performance. From my metallic blue eyeliner, bright red lips, flaming red nails, sliver sparkles in my long black wavy hair, black silk chiffon skintight gown which gently dropped off the upper curves of my breast and down to my ankles with a slit that came up the center to just below my upper thigh, to reveal my black silk-lace stockings and black heels. I was looking hot! Every move was choreographed to enhance the sensuality of the rhythm.

It was finally opening night. Our first performance was at the Roma, itself. It was March 18th, at 12:15am when I was going back on stage for the first time in more than two years. The D.J. was still spinning the last record before calling me to the stage.

I turned to Jimmy with the jitters, "I don't think I can do this Jimmy." and I started to walk away.

Jimmy ran up behind me, grabbed my arm and yelled, "You got us into this, so you get us out!"

"But I can't, Jimmy! I just can't do it!"

He gave me a hug, "If you could perform as Christy Valona, you can certainly perform as Christina Powers, can't you?" I looked up at him sheepishly and nodded my head in agreement, "Well then you shouldn't be afraid to perform tonight."

"I'm not afraid to perform, Jimmy."

"Well then what is it?"

I looked dead in his eyes, "I don't think I can carry this off. It's one thing to pretend I'm making love in a recording studio, but it's another in front of all those men."

Jimmy shook his head, hugged me again, "Is that all it is, Christina? Everyone out there is a friend and besides, they're all gay. So if you can't do the act in front of them when you have the act down perfectly, you'll never do it in front of a straight audience."

I looked at him, "My mind tells me you're right, but my heart tells me I can't be that provocative in front of all these men."

He looked at me and with a flick of that wrist, "Oh, just tell your heart to shut-up and get your sexy little buns out on that stage, girl!" We looked at one another and started to crack up.

He lit a joint, passed it to me, "Take a hit off this, then you go get'um girl!"

All of a sudden the dance music stopped, and I heard the D.J. begin to say, "Let me have your attention, guys! Tonight, we have a special treat. Our very own Christina Powers is going to perform her new recording, 'Oh, baby! Touch Me Like That' for the first time

American Goddess

right here at the Roma. Now let's give a big round of applause, to our girl, Christina!"

I swallowed my fears, took one more toke for luck, flicked the joint on the floor and slowly sashayed out onto the stage. When I reached the microphone, I was stoned and feeling no pain. I picked up the mike with my left hand and said in the sexiest way I could, "Hi, guys! Are we all hot tonight?"

They all screamed back, "Yes!"

"Great! Now hold on to your seats because I'm going to make you even **hotter!**"

I waved to the D.J. to start spinning the rhythm as the guys cheered. The stage and dance floor were lit with only strobe lights and the spotlight was on me. Swaying my hips as the smooth sensually tantalizing rhythm began to emerge, I moaned loud enough for all to hear, **"Oh, baby, touch me like that; Oh yes, yes, touch me like that; It's ecstasy, ecstasy, when you touch me like that."** as I simultaneously and sensually moved my right hand over my head. I let it drift down to my right breast as I gently moved the top of my gown, just enough to expose my right nipple through the black, silk chiffon and moaned, **"Oh, baby, touch me like that, I need you, need you, to touch me like that, it's ecstasy, ecstasy, when you touch me like that. I love, love, when you touch me like that."** as my fingernails gently stroked my breast. Then I moved my entire body slowly and smoothly, from side to side slithering down to the floor into a catlike position. Arching my back, I swayed my hips and cried out with the voice of an angel, **"Oh, baby, baby touch me like that! Touch me like that! Oh yes, yes, touch me like that! It's heavenly, heavenly, when you touch me like that."** I slowly began to rise from my feline position as I purred. Now standing I slid my hands slowly between my legs, parting the slit in my gown and seductively revealed my sensual black silk stockings up to my thigh. When my hands reached the crease of my swaying hips, I let the slit of my gown gently drift back into place and cried out again, **"Oh, baby, baby touch me like that. Oh yes, yes touch me like that."** Sliding my right hand slowly up my thigh, between my breasts, over my shoulder I reached for the stars, as I lifted my left hand holding the mike close to my lips, tilting my head back so I was looking straight up and sang out, **"Oh, baby, baby touch me like that, touch me like that."** Then the music stopped, and I took a bow.

The boys went nuts! Jimmy came running out to me, jumped into the air with his right arm rising up over his head, then pulled it down to his side like a prize fighter, shouting, "Yes! Girl! Yes!" He leaped into my arms and we both almost fell off the stage!

When we arrived home that night, we were on adrenalin high! I hugged Jimmy and said with excitement, "We have to setup a whole European tour now. Oh yes! We need some more songs too." I threw my hands in the air and said, "Oh well, I'll figure it out tomorrow." With that, I turned and headed for the bedroom.

As I walked away Jimmy said, "New songs? How in the world are you going to top 'Oh, baby, touch me like that?"

41

American Goddess

I turned to him, gave him my, 'it's no problem look' with a sexy wink and a girlish tone, "I'll sing." At that point, I went to bed.

By the time we had our tour setup; beginning with all the gay night clubs in Italy, we had a seven cut soundtrack to bring with us. And let me tell you, they were seven of the hottest, sexiest songs Jimmy and I could imagine.

The date was June 1st, 1975. I was so hot on stage; I knocked them dead at every club I played. I became the queen of the gay night life, with groupies to boot!

Our touring schedule was intense, and the album began to sell like hot cakes. So much so, that finally in September, it began to filter into the straight clubs. After that it was on the airwaves!

By November 1st, we had the number one selling record in all Western Europe and the money was starting to roll in. Jimmy, the band members and I were on the road every day and in the clubs every night. When we were not trying to get some sleep, Jimmy and I were writing and writing. The fame and the music of Europe's new disco queen Christina Powers hit the American shores without me even being there to promote it. The demand to purchase the recording in the United States began to grow in record numbers!

On December 1st, Powers Records Incorporated received a call from Mr. James Smith, the Executive Vice President of Columbia Records Incorporated. He offered to swing a deal which would open the American markets to Powers Records Incorporated and for their star performer, Christina Powers, with only a 60% take on the gross. I informed Mr. Smith I would have to speak with my associates on this matter and I would return his call with a counteroffer, as soon as possible. As I hung up the phone, my head was spinning with the thought of heading back home. 'But how?' was still the question. For as soon as Frank discovered I was Christina Powers, he would be able to stop me again.

It was 8:00pm December 10th, my twenty-first birthday when Jimmy and I were just getting off the plane at Rome International Airport. We were coming back from a three-night engagement at the 'La Vie en Rose, which was the hottest night club in Paris, when Jimmy said, "I have a little surprise for you Christina."

"You do?" I replied as we walked toward the exit doors of the airport.

As the doors opened, he replied, "Yes, I do!" As soon as we hit the fresh air, Jimmy raised his hand over his head and summoned a limo for us.

I gave him a puzzled look, "What's this?"

He took me by the hand and ushered me into the limo, "This is just the first phase of your birthday gift!"

I looked at my sweet Jimmy as the driver swept us away, "Oh thank you, Jimmy. This is a great surprise." I thought knowing Jimmy as I did, "I hope so!"

He handed me a small, wrapped gift, "Happy birthday, Christina!" I opened it and inside was a little heart locket hanging from a delicately woven, gold chain. I opened the heart and inside was a carved inscription which read, "You're a fucking genius! Love Jimmy." I looked at him and we laughed so hard, I thought I'd never stop. I finally had Jimmy snap it on for me.

The driver drove us to the new, much larger apartment, Jimmy and I rented together, back in September. It also happened to be in a much better part of town.

When we entered, Jimmy swiftly led me to the bathroom, pushed me in and with the flick of that wrist and a girlish wiggle, "Dress to impress, girl! We're gonna have a hot time on the old town tonight!"

Laughing I pushed him out of the bathroom, "Okay, sister! Now get your dramatic little ass out of here."

After we changed, it was back to the waiting limo at 9:30pm destination unknown, and I was dressed to 'the nines.

As the driver drove us deep within the heart of the city of Rome, I couldn't help but notice the style of the architecture on the buildings around us. They were exquisite! There were angels, gargoyles, lions, naked bodies and heads of gladiators, carved in all of them. It just went on, building after building, until the car stopped at a large, gold plated gate, which just fit between two large buildings. As the gates opened, the driver pulled in and proceeded down a mile-long driveway. The walls of these two enormous buildings ran along either side of the driveway.

Instantly I became nervous, turned to Jimmy, "Where the hell are we going? It looks like a **claustrophobic's nightmare!"**

Jimmy Smiled, "Relax!" as the car entered a clearing to expose a thirty-acre flower garden, spread out in front of the most beautiful Italian villa I had ever seen.

At that moment, I became a little suspicious. I grabbed Jimmy by his arm, "What is this? You don't know people like this!"

He interrupted my spasm, "I said, relax! Some of Rome's elite dignitaries are throwing you a surprise birthday party."

I let go of Jimmy, looked around at all the limos and thought, "This might not be half bad after all."

I kissed Jimmy as the car reached the door, "Let's go get'um!"

The second the doorman led us into the main foyer of the villa, I turned on Christina Powers as if I were turning on a light switch. With that, I became Christina Powers, the sultriest, sexiest, songstress in all of Europe. I played the part to the hilt. Every move, every glance had a sexual connotation attached to it. I felt myself feeding on it and I wanted to become it. This was my ace in the hole.

The foyer was awesome! It had to be a hundred square feet in diameter. The ceiling hovered three stories above the floor. The room was filled with the most well-dressed

American Goddess

people that I had seen in one place, in a long time, and they were all dancing to my music under a ceiling filled with golden chandeliers. The walls had a white background with golden chariots. They appeared to be racing around the room. Directly across the room from where I was standing stood a towering staircase of Italian, white marble. It was breathtaking! At the top of the staircase, I could see the figure of a man beginning to descend. He was expensively dressed in a black silk tux and the rock on his left ring finger, was blinding. He appeared to be in his late fifties. I'd say six-feet-tall, two-hundred and twenty-five-pounds, with slightly graying hair filtering back from his temples, into his raven black hair.

As he entered the room, I could see he commanded respect from all who greeted him. As I watched from across the room I thought, "Now here's someone with clout! This is our host?" I wondered, "Who is he?"

Turning to Jimmy, "Jimmy, who is he?"

Jimmy answered with a smile, "You're not going to believe it, but we were invited here by Dominick Giovannetti, himself."

"You're kidding!" I said, turning back to Jimmy. "But why?" I wondered if he knew who I really was and if Frank had something to do with this. You see, everyone in Italy, including myself, had heard of Dominick Giovannetti, The Italian Godfather.

"Because he loves your music and he wanted to meet the woman behind the voice. That's all I know."

"If that's true, this could prove to be a very interesting evening."

As Dominick reached me, I placed my fingers into the palm of his hand and curtsied. The second he looked into my eyes; I knew he had no idea I was Frank's niece. As we were introducing ourselves to each other, my mind was racing, and it hit me. "This man could be my ticket back to America," and I was going to be nice to him.

After our greeting, he swept me away from Jimmy and into the heart of the room. I felt a little guilty leaving Jimmy standing by himself in a room full of strangers. Then I thought, "Oh well, he's a big boy." as I charged right into the center of attention with every move I made.

Dominick personally introduced me to everyone in the room. We joked, laughed and flirted our way through the crowd as we sipped champagne from Dominick's private collection. It was turning out to be a fabulous evening after all. Dominick and I were hitting it off superbly as the evening progressed.

It was around midnight when my large beautifully decorated, three-tiered birthday cake arrived. The waiters served us tiny little pieces of cake and I thought, "I knew I should have grabbed a bite to eat." When we finished our feast, Dominick led me onto the dance floor. The song that was playing was an incredibly soft Italian love song. We began to dance as the lights dimmed. As we danced so awfully close, he told me he was a very

44

happily married man with grandchildren and how highly he was viewed by the people of his Italy!

So sincerely, he whispered in my ear, "But what wouldn't I do, for a woman like yourself." Smiling, "Would you like to see the balcony?"

Very seductively, "I would love to, Dominick." He escorted me to the balcony which looked out over the well-lit ancient Roman Coliseum. He handed me a small golden wrapped gift box as he kissed my cheek, "Happy birthday, Christina."

I opened the gift gently to heighten the suspense. Within this precious wrapping was the most brilliant ten karat diamond necklace I had ever seen. I was stunned! I looked up into his eyes and seductively winked, "It's beautiful, Dominick, and I'm more than flattered, but the only reason I can accept such a fabulous gift is because it's my birthday. I would never insult such a thoughtful giver by not accepting it."

He kissed my cheek, "I see a woman like yourself does not come frivolously."

I smiled softly, looked up into his eyes sweetly, "You're right, Dominick. You're absolutely right. I don't come frivolously!" I kissed him very gently, "Thank you for the lovely gift."

In that sultry Italian voice of his, he whispered as he bent his head down to kiss me, "I'm pleased you like it."

Before he tried to take advantage of me, "It's getting late and I really must leave now, Dominick. It's been an exceptionally long day."

With lust in his eyes, "But the night is young, Christina. I was hoping you would like to spend the evening here with me."

Just to tantalize him, I kissed him tenderly, "Not tonight, Dominick. I'm exhausted and my heart wouldn't be in it."

He kissed me back, "Would you please have dinner with me tomorrow evening?"

I graciously slipped out of his embrace, "I'd love to have dinner with you, Dominick." We made plans for his car to pick me up at 7:00pm the next evening.

As our limo drove Jimmy and me home, I thought, "I've got him right where I want him. Now to bait the trap just right."

The next evening promptly at 7:00pm Dominick's limo arrived. I started setting the trap by looking the hottest I've ever looked. When I climbed into the limo, the driver almost fell off the curb as he closed the door behind me. I was sizzling! Within thirty minutes, we were pulling up to Dominick's two-hundred-foot yacht, and I was impressed!

He greeted me at the door with champagne in hand and with a distinguished nod of his head, "You look ravishing, Christina."

I handed him my black cape, "Thank you, Dominick. You look quite debonair yourself."

With wide eyes he exclaimed, "Debonair! I was hoping for something more like attractive."

American Goddess

I smiled as he led me to the bar, "You misunderstand me, Dominick. I find the debonair look more than attractive."

He moved close to me, putting his hands on my shoulders, "I'm happy you're pleased, Christina."

I looked up into his eyes, "You have pleased me, Dominick. Just your presence is pleasing to me."

His face lit up with that one, "I have a very special evening planned for us, beginning with dinner in the glass enclosed sky room. Our meal will be more appetizing under the city lights."

"That sounds lovely." I delicately rose from the bar stool and out from under his grasp.

He proceeded to escort me to dinner. I looked around the room, "This is a fabulous yacht. Would you mind taking me on a tour?"

He walked over to me, put those massive hands of his back on my shoulders, "let me lead the way."

As we toured the yacht on our way to the sky room, I had to use the utmost restraint not to knee him in the groin for having his roaming hands all over me. But because I needed him, I was good, and I held my temper.

As we shared a lovely filet minion with all the trimmings, he said, "What is it that entices a woman of your caliber?"

I smiled at him devilishly, "Power."

"Power, that's interesting, why would a lovely lady like yourself be enticed by power?"

I leaned toward him, "Because I need someone, with power."

"Now that's a dramatic statement. You need someone with power. Why, may I ask, do you need someone with power?"

I reached over with one hand and stroked his temple seductively, "Not just someone with power, Dominick. I need you and your power."

He took my hand, kissed it, "Do tell, Christina. How can I, with my power, assist **you**?"

I very carefully told him who I was and what I needed from him.

With a look of shock on his face, he exclaimed, "So you're Frank's niece! I heard he had crushed you for trying to break your contract." He stood up, "What's in it for me, if I decide to help you?"

"If you will help me get back to America and keep Frank at bay, I. . ." with the most seductive voice I could muster, "will let you feel what it's like to sleep with the most extraordinary woman on earth."

His eyes opened wide, "That's a powerful offer, Christina. May I hold my decision until the morning?"

American Goddess

Gazing at him with confidence radiating from my seductive eyes, knowing I had him by the balls, "Yes, you may, Dominick. But I promise nothing more than my passion for one night."

With a look of amazement, "That's an offer I can't refuse."

I took him by the hand and led him to the bedroom. As I began to perform for Dominick, I found my thoughts of destroying Frank, feeding my passion. I devoured Dominick with every kiss. With every sensual touch he became mine. I totally violated my innermost being on this dog in heat, as I forced the flames of lust to incinerate my fears and magnify my profound hatred for Frank.

By the time the morning sun shone in through the portholes, I had Dominick wrapped around my finger. That morning, after one more interlude just to ensure my triumph, he held me and assured me he could, and would, put a stop to Frank's influence over my career.

As I was leaving, Dominick kissed me passionately then handed me a card, "This is my private number, use it and I'll be there." As he placed it in my hand, "I only give this number to the special people in my life." Kissing me again, "You are an amazing woman, Christina Powers, and I know you will get whatever it is you want in this life."

I kissed him gingerly, slipped out of his grasp, "Thank you, Dominick I will." With that, I turned and walked away. As I sashayed toward the limo, I knew Christy was gone and I was now, truly, Christina Powers, the woman behind the music.

Later that afternoon, I was making arrangements to meet with a representative from Columbia Records, Incorporated, to sign a deal that would open the American markets to Powers Records Incorporated, with only a 10% take on the gross. All of this was possible, thanks to one phone call from my extremely grateful friend, Dominick Giovannetti. With a little more assistance from Dominick's American attorneys, I quietly paid back all the debts I left behind. After that, it was back to work.

On January 2nd, 1976, Jimmy and I released our second album. It was hotter than the first. This time we kept the same sensuality in the lyrics, but we spiced up the rhythm to make them more melodic. By April, the album, 'I'm The Love Master' was number one on the European charts. At the same time, my first album, 'Oh, Baby! Touch Me Like That' was finally soaring across America. In May, my touring of the nightclubs was over, and I had advanced to the stadiums. The Europeans loved me. The demand for personal appearances throughout Europe grew and grew. The spotlights, press and cameras were all back. I loved it, but it was not America yet.

It was June 1st, when I received a call from Mr. James Smith informing me, "I'm The Love Master" had become number one in just two weeks. He also said the demand from the American public was increasing. They wanted Christina Powers. I hung up the phone and just sat there at my desk thinking, "It's time for my return home." Then a feeling of anxiousness shot through me as I thought, "I know they want Christina Powers, but will they still want me when they know who I really am?" I shrugged my shoulders and said out loud, "Oh well! I'll figure it out tomorrow."

It was July 23rd when Jimmy and I were getting ready to leave Rome, for NEW YORK CITY! As I packed, I reflected on how my life here in Rome had taken me full circle, heading back to where I started. I remembered the drawing of a circle around Rome and thought, "How ironic. Ha! Ha! Ha!" Then I grabbed my suitcases, one bottle of champagne and ran out the door for the airport. **DESTINATION, AMERICA!**

CHAPTER 4

It was July 24th, 1976, at 10:00am when our plane touched down at LaGuardia International Airport, in the United States of America. **MY HOME!** I was so excited I had butterflies in my stomach just knowing that I would soon be back in my beloved city, Manhattan. I was told to expect some reporters, so I dressed for the occasion. As Jimmy and I were exiting the plane, I looked out over the metal detectors and I never expected to see what I saw! The airport was swarming with reporters and the place went wild with screaming fans as soon as I stuck my head out the door. I was stunned. I could not move.

Suddenly, Jimmy shoved me out onto the ramp, "Come on, Christina, you're holding everybody up!"

When Jimmy finally witnessed what it was that caused me to freeze, he screeched, **"Holy shit!"** as he proceeded to cut off the blood supply to my right hand.

Somehow, I got a hold of myself, "Just follow my lead, Jimmy, and please stop breaking my hand."

As we both began to slowly move toward this screaming crowd, we were freaking! I immediately turned Christina Powers on. As we proceeded to head toward the flashing lights, I posed for the cameras like only the QUEEN of Hollywood herself could, and it hit me like a ton of bricks. I knew in that moment I was her **daughter.** As I smiled for the cameras and tried to answer a hundred questions for the reporters, my mind raced with thoughts like, "I am her daughter! It's true! Somehow, it's true! What does this mean? Are Frank and I truly the only ones in the world who know this? How will this affect my life?

American Goddess

What do I do with this knowledge?"

It was starting to drive me mad, right there in front of the whole country! So, I stopped my mind from racing and thought, "Oh well! I'll figure it out tomorrow." With that I was able to give my full attention to the reporters.

Finally, we were through the crowd, in the limo and on our way to meet with Mr. James Smith from Columbia Records. We still had to finalize our contract and iron out any last-minute glitches with my upcoming American tour.

By the time we reached Manhattan it was already 2:00pm. As the limo drove through the city, I thought of how this city I loved so much, once loved me. Then I thought of Frank. I knew I was within arm's length of him now, but how do I arrange for his demise? I didn't know the answer at that moment, but I knew if I thought about it long enough, it would come to me. It had to be just right.

After an evening of dinner and hobnobbing with the top brass of Columbia Records, Jimmy and I finally arrived at our Fifth Avenue penthouse, which was so graciously provided by Columbia records. It was only 11:00pm when we walked in the door, but we were exhausted. We both went straight to our respective rooms, to wash up for the night. When I finished showering, I put on my robe and headed out to the enticing scent that was drifting in from the other room.

When my nostrils finally found the origins of this aroma, I saw Jimmy sitting on the sofa. He had his legs stretched out and his feet lying on top of the coffee table, with a big bowl of buttered popcorn sitting on his lap. He was watching TV as he stuffed his face with fists full of popcorn.

I gave him a dirty look, "You shit-head! You're having buttered popcorn without me."

I jumped over the back of the couch, which sat in the middle of the floor, and landed on the sofa just next to Jimmy. He fumbled a little as I landed, but he saved the prized buttered popcorn. I lay down across the sofa and placed my head on Jimmy's lap. He placed the bowl of buttered popcorn on my stomach and as I began to eat exactly like Jimmy I asked, "Whatcha' watching?"

"A Star is born."

I lifted from Jimmy's lap just enough to take a sip from his soda, turned to the TV and looked dead at the star singing on the stage and it hit me. I jumped up off the sofa, knocking the soda and buttered popcorn all over both of us and shouted, "**I'm a fucking genius!**" At that I swiftly ran for a pen and paper; and as I ran, I heard Jimmy scream as he tried to frantically wipe the ice-cold soda off his chest, "That fucking girl is nuts!"

After I had the items I so desperately needed, I sat down at the big oak desk in the den and began to write. I was writing my thoughts for a screenplay about a young girl who would become a disco diva. It was 3:00am when I could not see any longer, so I dropped the pen and staggered to my room. It was dark, except for the light which shone through the sides of the curtains. As I flicked the light switch, I was thinking, "Where in this country would be the best place to build my soon-to-be empire, Powers Incorporated?" But the light didn't come on. So, I walked over to the curtains to expose more light. As I reached the curtain, I caught a flash of light glistening in the corner of my eye, and I got a chill. I quickly opened the curtain so I could see the lamp on the night table. I calmly walked over to the table, reached down and flicked on the light. There on the nightstand laid a Poughkeepsie Journal newspaper. I pulled back the covers, climbed into bed, shut off the light and passed out.

I was dressed and on my second cup of coffee, when the phone rang. I could hear Jimmy stumbling out of bed to answer it. I continued to glance through the road map sitting on the table in front of me. As I sipped my coffee Jimmy yelled out, "Christina, where are you?"

I yelled back, "In the kitchen, Jimmy."

He came in carrying the cordless phone, "It's, Joseph Cole, for you."

"Oh yes," I said, as Jimmy brought me the phone. "He's our new orchestra leader, we met him last night, remember?"

Jimmy handed me the phone, "Good morning, Joe. I was just about to call you. What's up?"

"Good morning, Christina. I just wanted to touch base with you before today's rehearsal and tonight's performance."

"Joe, do me a favor and rehearse the melody with the orchestra today. I have some place I have to go, but I'll be back around 7:00pm for the final rehearsal."

"Are you sure about that?" he asked with concern.

"Trust me on this one, Joe; I'll be there by seven."

He answered with an unconvinced tone, "You're the boss, Christina, so I guess I'll see you tonight."

I clicked off the phone as Jimmy flopped down beside me with a cup of coffee, "What are you doing up and dressed already?"

I took my last sip of coffee, "I'm going to a town called Poughkeepsie. It's about an hour and a half north of here."

Jimmy perked up, "Poughkeepsie, why are you going to Poughkeepsie?"

"Just a feeling," I answered, as I rinsed out my cup.

With a suspicious tone, "A feeling! You know you really are a screwball. Do you realize you have to perform, 'I Am the Love Master,' live on national TV tonight?"

"Yes, Jimmy, I know," I calmly replied.

"Do you want me to come with you?"

I looked him straight in the eyes, "You should know what I want you to do. The stage and lighting for tonight's performance has got to be exactly as we have planned it. When

American Goddess

I come back Jimmy, all I want to do is sing."

He gave me a stunned look, flick of that wrist, "Yes sir!"

I kissed his forehead, grabbed the brochure of the real estate brokers in the Poughkeepsie area, which I had sent up to me at 6:00am that morning. Then I walked out to the rental car I had waiting for me, all before 8:00am.

As I buckled myself into the driver's seat, I tossed my briefcase on the seat beside me. It contained four pocket recorders, which I used to record my thoughts. Two for my screenplay and two for new releases. As I drove to Poughkeepsie on that beautiful bright, sunny day, I was wasting no time! You see, I had decided how I would **get Frank** and that would be where it would hurt him the most. **His pocket**!

It was 10:30am when I found the location of the first real estate agent on my list. I parked the car and headed in. As I entered the door, I could see a secretary seated at a mid-sized desk in front of four small cubicles. It appeared as though they were struggling to survive the slump in the local real estate market, which I had only discovered two minutes before turning off the car, from a local radio talk show. I walked over to the secretary and asked to speak with the first available Realtor.

The Realtor seemed pleasant as she approached me with a smile. She reached out her hand, "Good morning, my name is, Terry Baggatta. How can I help you?"

I introduced myself, "I'm looking for a very special piece of property. It has to be at least eight hundred acres of prime real estate. I don't want it to be too close to the city, but I don't want it in the boonies, either. Oh yes, it also has to be in close proximity to your largest airport.

She looked at me as if she were going to faint, "I don't believe this. I just received a listing this morning that fits your needs perfectly."

I smiled, anxiously rubbed my hands together, "When can I see it?"

Terry said enthusiastically, "Right now if you wish."

Still smiling, "I do wish."

Then we hopped into her car and off we went. It turned out to be a thousand acres of pure heaven, with a thirty-thousand-foot riverfront view. It was right on the majestic Hudson. It had running streams flowing over the creek beds, which led the waters splashing through the towering pines, on its way down to the river. This place was beautiful. The property was right off Route 9W in the town of Milton, N.Y. It was only twenty minutes from Stewart Airport, which Terry assured me would be a thriving airport in the near future. As we drove back to Terry's office, I knew this was the place for my new empire.

Terry and I worked up a thirty-million-dollar offer, on this seventy-million-dollar piece of property. And I didn't even have the money yet! But I was still compelled to leave her a deposit check for one-million-dollars, which was every penny Powers Records had earned to date. As I signed on the dotted line I thought, "Oh well, I'll figure it out tomorrow!"

By 4:30pm I was on my way back to New York, and my first American performance as, Christina Powers! I was appearing on a national TV show called The Nancy and Danette Comedy Hour. The show was being broadcast live from Radio City Music Hall, to honor their one hundredth taping. It was America's number one variety show. I knew all of America would be watching, so it was crucial I be extremely hot tonight!

I arrived for the rehearsal at 6:50pm. As soon as Jimmy and Joe saw me, they dropped what they were doing and headed right for me. They immediately began to inform me everything was set to go. The three of us began to make a quick spot check on everything. The lighting, stage and props were all in place and timed perfectly to the choreographed rhythm of the music and my performance. It was a job well done. Joe assured me the orchestra was tuned to a tee. All that was missing was me. I turned to both of them, "Great job, guys! I'll go change and we can get started." With that, I quickly walked toward the dressing room.

Jimmy came charging after me, hung his arms around my neck and with a girlish excitement to his mannerisms and voice, "Christina! I'm in love! His name is Bobby."

I kissed his cheek as we walked toward the dressing room and with a loving smile, "Again, Jimmy."

He was glowing, "This time it's for real. We met here this morning. He's the lighting director here at Radio City. He's gorgeous! We spent the entire day working together." As we reached the dressing room, he hung onto the door while I began to take off my clothes, "We know we really have a special kind of bond together. I can't explain it, but it's there."

I walked back over to him, "I'm happy for you Jimmy." As I pulled him off the door and began to usher him out, "And I can't wait to meet him. Now get out of here and let me get ready for the rehearsal."

With the flick of that wrist, he backed out of the room, "That's great, because I'm bringing him home tonight." With that, he turned and wiggled his chunky little buns down the hall. I shook my head and thought, "Oh well!" as I closed the door to finish getting ready.

When I walked out onto the stage, I was ready for my first and only rehearsal, prior to my live national performance! As Joe cued the orchestra, I began to sweat. The music started and I began to rehearse, 'I Am the Love Master!' The lyrics to the Love Master were one of my most sensual recordings. The rhythm was the fastest and hottest disco beat to date and number one on the billboard charts. My one and only rehearsal was awful! I was tripping over the stage props; my voice was cracking, and I couldn't keep up with the orchestra. When we finished, Jimmy, Joe and everyone who had anything to do with the show that night, looked at me in horror! I looked around and saw them all glaring at me as if they had just witnessed a five-car collision.

I dropped the mike on the stage floor and ran off to my dressing room, with my hands shaking as if I were holding a jack hammer. Jimmy came running after me and as we reached the dressing room, I slammed the door and started to cry. Jimmy grabbed hold of me, "Christina, what's the matter with you?"

Uncontrollably I shouted, "Jimmy, I'm so nervous I'm freaking out here. Do you know what's riding on this?"

Jimmy gave me a hardy shake and very calmly, "You can do this, Christina! You know it by heart. We created it."

Still crying, "Jimmy, I know I can. I'm just so nervous."

With a steady reassuring tone, "Just relax, Christina, and tell me what's making you so nervous. Then we can deal with it calmly and logically."

Wiping the tears from my face, "Thanks, Jimmy, I'm starting to feel a little better already."

"Good, now let's talk, girlfriend," he replied with a sigh of relief.

I looked into his comforting eyes, "We have everything riding on this performance tonight." Then, with a giggle as if I were a little insane, "I just gave every dime we've made, one million dollars as a deposit on a thirty-million-dollar piece of property."

Jimmy's face appeared as if he had just run face first into a plate glass door, as he screamed, "You what! Are you fucking nuts? How could you?"

With a blank expression, "I don't know! I just took the pen and signed my name."

With that he shouted, "Why in the world would you put all of our money on the line like this, Christina?"

I shrugged my shoulders, "It was just a feeling I had."

All at once he shook me by my shoulders and screamed like someone who had just been driven mad, "Just a feeling! Just a feeling! I can't fucking believe you! You are fucking nuts!"

Just in the nick of time, I was rescued from this man who was about to rip my hair out by its roots, by someone banging on my dressing room door and a bewildered voice screaming, "Are you guys all right in there?"

Jimmy, recognizing the voice dashed to the door, flung it open with full cinematic dramatics, leaped into this man's arms and began to sob, "She's nuts! She's nuts!" This man came bursting into the room and somehow calmed us both down.

After we composed ourselves, I discovered this man was Bobby, Jimmy's newest love.

Jimmy, clinging to Bobby's arm, "Christina, I don't care how you do it, but you had better pull this one-off tonight, girlfriend."

"Jimmy, I know that. I just need to relax."

American Goddess

Jimmy looked at his watch and pulled a joint out of his pocket, "You only have 45 minutes to relax. You better smoke this."

I looked at him as if he were nuts, "Jimmy, we're not in the back of a nightclub. Don't you think someone might smell that?"

Jimmy put the joint back in his pocket, shook his head, "Well, I don't know what to tell you then. Just try to relax, I guess. We'll get out of here and let you get ready."

Feeling totally drained, I rubbed my forehead with my left hand, "Okay, Jimmy, just let me rest and call me when it's time."

Bobby walked over to me, pulled out a little brown bottle, opened it and took out a tiny little spoon. He scooped some white powder onto the spoon, stretched his hand toward my nose, "I could lose my job for this, but snort some of this and it'll help you relax."

I looked at him then I looked at Jimmy, who was looking at me, "That's cocaine isn't it?"

Jimmy snapped, "Oh, shit! Don't get moral on us, just snort the crap and let's get through this nightmare. Okay?"

I looked at them both one more time and snorted it. Finally, they left me alone. I just sat there on the floor trying to calm myself. When I got up, I showered, changed, made up my face and I still had ten minutes to spare.

When the knock sounded on the door, I took a deep breath and swallowed my heart. Then, '**she**' took over and Christina Powers walked out onto the stage. As I stood there on stage, waiting for the curtains to rise, I drew a deep feeling of strength up from the depths of my soul and held it captive. Then, I heard it as if it were in the echoes of my dreams, screaming at me, "Ladies and gentlemen, here she is! The Queen of Disco, Christina Powers!"

All at once the lights, sounds, curtains and cheers of the audience, went up simultaneously. I gazed out at this sight while holding my seductive stance in my glistening gold gown, painted up like a queen. Oh, what a rush I felt! Then my performance began. The rhythm and I became one as we began to swirl together with sensual movements, which slowly intensified. The concert hall went black. All the bright intense, flashing lights were on my every move. As I moved, I swayed and slithered every muscle in my body. And when I sang out, I sounded like an angel." "**I'm, I'm, I'm the love master, yes, baby, oh yes baby, I'm the love master. You heard me right. I'm the love master, that's right, the love master. That's what I said, I'm the love master. As I spin my web, I've got you; I've got all of you.   The lover of your dreams, that's who I am, and I've got you; I've got all of you.   Now take me and fill me completely, with your love power. Now fall to your knees and taste the power of my love, cause I'm the love master. My love drips like nectar of pure ecstasy, passion, and the pleasure of love. With every look, every glance,** and touch, I become your love Master. No man, no, no, no man can resist the Love Master." Then I ripped my angelic, golden gown off my body, to reveal a black leather, gold-spotted leopard, full length skintight body suit. I danced like a fiery demon from hell and sang out with a voice that was hypnotizing. I hit all the props right on cue. With each prop I hit, the stage flared up with flames and silver sparks showered my most seductive moves. The crowd was going wild with cheers. They loved it!

When I ended my performance belting out, "Yes, Yes, I'm The Love Master. Ecstasy, ecstasy, taste my ecstasy. Yes, Yes, I'm the Love Master", and vanishing into an aqua-blue smoke cloud, while clutching my breasts, the place went mad with passion and deafening screams for me!

As I stood there above this roaring crowd, I was flying with emotions of incredible power. I left my nation a disgrace and returned a queen! I took bow after bow. That night the world watched the creation of what was to become a true, 20th century sex goddess, with all the trappings. It was as if I had spun a spell of love and lust on everyone watching. From that night on, I made cocaine a part of every performance."

After the show that night, there was a party being held at the Plaza Suite in the heart of the city. It was to celebrate, Nancy and Danette 100th show. As I slipped my right leg out of the limo door in front of the Plaza entrance, I was looking my usual hot self! I performed every step of the way into the Plaza, through the flashing lights and the crowds of beautiful people, all wanting to meet me. Jimmy, Bobby and Joe, followed my lead. As I stepped into the ballroom, the applause went up and I was finally home.

The party was fabulous and without even trying, I took center stage from my gracious hostess', Nancy and Danette. It was like old times. Then, I thought of Johnny and the pain of that flashback made my eyes begin to water, so I quickly changed gears and gave my full attention to the party.

While I was being the life of the party, Mr. James Smith of Columbia Records, came up from behind, touched my shoulder, "Excuse me, Christina, but I'd like to introduce you to a friend of mine."

I turned to acknowledge this introduction, "This is Senator Tom Kenny, from Massachusetts."

I extended my hand to greet this man and thought, as we casually spoke to one another, "Oh my God, could this man really be my uncle? Am I a Kenny?" As our chat continued, I found myself dodging some very sophisticated advances and I thought, "Oh shit! I am a Kenny."

The next morning the whole country knew, Christina Powers was once Christy Valona. It was plastered in every newspaper across the country. Beginning at 9:00am that morning, the flowers, cards, letters and phone calls came flooding in. All of them, welcoming Christina Powers home, With Love.

But the only call I accepted that morning came from Barbara, my one true friend from my past. It was wonderful to finally speak with her again. She grilled me on everything I did over the last two and a half years and I did the same with her. She was out on the West Coast, so we made plans to spend time together when my tour reached Los Angeles. The rest of that day was spent at the recording studio with all the gang. We had two weeks to finish the third album, before beginning our U.S. Tour.

Needless to say, we worked our asses off night and day to finish it. The title was, 'Love in The Heavens.' It had nine incredible cuts, one hotter than the next, and it was coming with me on tour.

On August 9th, we were getting ready to go on a six-month tour. So, I grabbed my suitcases, one bottle of champagne and ran out the door to the waiting caravan of buses. **I was off to see America!**

CHAPTER 5

As we toured the nation, my fame grew. I was bringing in the largest crowds ever seen in concert history. The sales of 'Love in the Heavens' my third album, soared to the number one spot its first week. My shows and public appearances also helped to bring new life to my career and increased the sales of my first two albums. The European market was finally being surpassed by the American market and by Christmas 1976, between the concerts and record sales, I was bringing in more than three-million-dollars a week, which was the gross take for Powers Records.

The schedule I kept was intense. While being on the road four nights a week performing, I managed with Jimmy's help to finish my first screenplay, 'Life, Passion and Fame'. We also had an entire soundtrack to accompany our planned future motion picture. When I wasn't working, I was raking up every high-ranking male politician and dignitary across the country and sticking them in my back pocket for future use. Everything you heard about me in those days was true. I had to seduce them all, especially the ones that were just out of reach. It became an obsession. In my spare time, I purchased the property of my dreams with the assistance of Dominick's American attorneys, for the mere sum of thirty-six million dollars. There was no grass growing under my feet, as I jockeyed into position to get Frank!

While I was whoring, Jimmy settled down to a one-on-one relationship with Bobby. Bobby joined our team as head of stage, lighting and props, as well as my personal cocaine connection. My daily life had become consumed with wicked thoughts, passions, and behaviors. All fueled by hatred! Hatred for Frank! I made sure every step I took brought me closer to destroying him. Somehow, I hid my inner fire from all those who knew me, including Jimmy.

Thanks to Dominick, and my own popularity with the American public, Frank stayed out of my way. But I knew he was out there lurking somewhere. So, I monitored every aspect of my life like a compulsive paranoid dictator. From every penny that came into my hands, to every person I had around me, I had it all under control. I became **THE BOSS**.

My last performance of the tour was February 2nd, 1977, in Hawaii. After the last show, I started a week vacation with Barbara. I needed some time off before I began casting and shooting on the new Powers Motion Pictures and Records Incorporation's first, full length motion picture. Starring, 'yours truly'. But this week was for Barbara and me. We stayed incognito at the Hyatt on the beach. The weather that entire week was perfect, sunny and beautiful with warm breezes. The temperatures ran at a steady ninety degrees during the day and the eighties at night. It was like paradise and this had been the first time I took notice of the weather in six months. It felt rejuvenating to be part of nature again. The heavenly days were filled with blue skies and incredibly starry nights and my soul drank from its pureness.

Barbara and I were having a wonderful time. We were at the beach by 8:00am every day, just soaking in the sun and each other's company. Our nights were started by an early dinner, then out on the balcony to soak in the balmy breezes. We stayed incognito right up to the last night we were on the island, which was a Saturday evening. It was around 8:00pm and we were going to the Governor's Mansion for a formal dinner party. There were about three hundred guests in attendance, and you know me, I was **looking hot**.

Barbara and I were mingling with the guests when I noticed an extremely attractive man on the other side of the room. His presence seemed to be attracting the attention of most of the woman in the place.

I turned to Barbara, nonchalantly pointed him out, "Do you know who that is?"

She glanced toward him, "That's, Tony Demetrees, don't you know him?"

"No, should I?"

She looked at me kind of funny, "He's only America's hottest new leading man in Hollywood. I thought you would have heard he got the leading role in 'Samantha's Father' after you walked off the set. The movie made him an overnight sex symbol!"

American Goddess

I looked at her and with a slight giggle, "You're kidding. That hunk would have been my leading man? Maybe it's a good thing I left the film after all."

He was a looker. He was 6 feet tall, deep black hair, dark blue eyes and from what I could see, he had a body that would not quit!

As we sipped on our champagne, I turned back to Barbara, "I wonder if I should try to get him for my leading man?"

Barbara smiled, "It wouldn't hurt the movie to have him in it, but I hear he's under contract with Frank."

"On second thought, the last thing I need is to have something that good looking hanging around." With a wink I added, "I'd never get the film done." As she laughed, I was thinking, "I'm not ready to come against Frank for anything. Not yet anyway."

Then Barbara asked, "Did you see the finished movie 'Samantha's Father?'

"No, I didn't, why?"

She took a sip of her champagne, "Kathy Brown was given the lead role after you left. The film won her an Oscar. Rumor has it she fucked you out of that part, literally." Her words struck a chord and they cracked the wall around my heart, just a little bit.

Trying to hide my embarrassment, "You mean to tell me everyone heard about her and Johnny?"

Her answer was blunt to say the least, "Christina, if you're coming back to Hollywood, I have to tell you this. Everyone in Hollywood also knows about your abortion."

"You're kidding!" I said with alarm. "Barbara, you're a good friend. I know that wasn't easy, but I love you more for being honest with me."

"I love you too," she kissed my cheek, "Christina, there's one more thing you need to know. Tony Demetrees is engaged to Kathy Brown, and I'm sure, if Tony is here, then Kathy is somewhere close by." Barbara put her arm around my shoulder, "I'm ready to leave now if you are?"

I turned to her firmly, "No, Barbara, I'm not going anywhere. As matter of fact, I just changed my mind. I do want Tony Demetrees for my leading man after all, and I'm going to go get him. Right now!" I grabbed Barbara by the hand, "Come with me, you know it could be bloody if I see her and I'm alone. Besides, you have to introduce me to Tony."

With that, I turned Christina on full power, as I seductively charged through this elite crowd toward my prey!

Barbara with an encouraging spark to her tone, "You're so bad Christina I love it!"

I thought, "There is no way Kathy is getting away from me tonight without some damage being done."

American Goddess

As Barbara just happened to bump into Tony she said, "Tony! What a surprise." She grabbed his hand, kissed his cheek, "I didn't know you were on the island, are you vacationing?"

Returning her kiss, "We just finished shooting on Maui, I thought you knew that?"

With a slight chuckle, "I don't catch all the gossip, Tony, just most of it."

Still not noticing me, this sex goddess standing right next to him he said, "It's so good to see you Barbara, you look wonderful."

Smart-ass Barbara continued her conversation with Tony, as I just stood there. I was ready to kick her when she finally said, with a surprised expression, "Oh, Tony! Please let me introduce you to a dear friend of mine." As she said, "Christina Powers," he turned toward me. When his eyes met mine, I smiled softly, winked sensually at this great lady killer and I knew in that moment I'd conquered my prey. Somehow, I could see in his eyes a future beyond the one night stand I had planned for Kathy's fiancée. Catch my drift?

As the three of us continued the conversation, I was so seductive I radiated sensuality with my slightest move. My performance was so subtle no one in the entire room noticed, except him. It felt as if my soul left my body and mingled with his. As we talked, I was hypnotizing him with my eyes. The power I felt over him was incredible, I fed on it and somehow, I knew it was real, like witchcraft of some sort, fueled by raging fires of revenge.

Then it happened. Kathy came in the door on Frank's arm. I broke my spell weaving and froze in fear.

Barbara quickly jumped in, "I'll go run interference and **YOU,** please go out the side door! This isn't the place or time for a confrontation."

I turned slightly shaking, "I'll meet you back at the hotel." Barbara dashed off to greet Frank as I looked at Tony, "I'm very sorry, but I must leave now."

He took my hand and led me to the side entrance, "I can't let you just leave like this, please let me take you back to your hotel." I graciously accepted his offer. Tony and I slipped around the outside of the Governor's Mansion and sent for his car. Neither Frank, nor Kathy, saw us leave. But I knew it wouldn't be long before they found out. That gave me one shot and one shot only to nail Tony.

We climbed into Tony's car. It turned out to be a vintage 1959, black Cadillac convertible with black leather seats. The car was cool. We drove out of the main gates of the mansion, down the road toward town with the top down.

As we drove, Tony remarked, "Christina, you look absolutely radiant with the wind softly blowing through your hair."

American Goddess

"Thank you very much. I love your car and it feels good to have the top down. I feel like the night sky is right at my fingertips." I ran my fingers through my long black hair, stretched my hands out past the windshield, and straight up to the stars.

Tony smiled, "Thank you, it was my father's car and I have it shipped everywhere I go." With curiosity he added, "That must have been a very awkward moment for you, almost running into both of them like that."

I turned to him, "Well, since my life seems to be an open book, yes I was very uncomfortable." I smiled, "Thank you for rescuing me."

"Christina, I think you're an excellent performer, and I was extremely disappointed when I learned you were not going to be my co-star in 'Samantha's Father.' I was looking forward to working with you."

"Thank you again, Tony, I truly appreciate the compliment. I hear you're an incredibly talented entertainer, yourself."

We were entering the heart of the city as he said, "Thank you, Christina, I'm not too shabby if I must say so, myself." We laughed, then he asked, "Do you really need to go right back to the hotel now?"

"No, not at all, why, what do you have in mind?"

He gave me a gorgeous smile, "I would never forgive myself if I had the disco diva herself, in my car on a beautiful Saturday night and didn't ask her for just one dance." Then he looked me straight in the eye, "What do you say?"

I looked at him, smiled, ran my fingers through his wavy soft black hair, which was also blowing in the breeze, "I'd love to go dancing with you, Tony."

Just then he pulled, as if it were planned, into the valets' driveway at Platinum's. One of the hottest discos in town. As we climbed out of the car Tony said, "I hear you're the best hustler around."

I laughed, "I'm not too bad." As I said these words I was thinking, "In more ways than you could imagine, Tony."

I kept my innocent smile as he opened the door for me, "I'm not too bad, myself."

When we walked in Tony handed the top bouncer a hundred-dollar bill. We were escorted to a very secluded section of the establishment. We sat at a private bird cage style booth, where we both ordered White Russians. We could hear the music just fine and we could also hear ourselves as we talked. The entire place was decorated in black mirrors with red and gold carpeting. The room where our booth was, was attached to the main bar and dance floor, and separated by a beautiful indoor rainforest with little flowing streams. The only lighting in the rainforest and where we were seated was provided by dim little lights in the ceiling.

As we sat there in this interesting setting sipping our drinks Tony asked, "Do you know your name is the buzz word in the entire entertainment industry right now?"

60

American Goddess

I smiled, "To tell you the truth, I didn't even think about it until tonight."

With an interested tone, "I hear you're starting casting on your new script and that you just branched out your record label to include films."

I looked at him," Well if I intend to survive in this business for the long haul, I need a solid base to grow on."

He looked at me in awe, "Not only are you beautiful, but intelligent as well. That's very intriguing in a woman."

I smiled again, "I take that as a high compliment." I stroked his hand gently for just a moment, "Since you know so much about me, please tell me a little about yourself."

He reached for my hand, "How about after a dance?" Without hesitation I agreed.

He led me out onto the dance floor, which was lit by brilliantly flashing lights. It felt like magic. It was incredible how well we danced together. We started to dance the Latin hustle on that packed dance floor and people couldn't help but notice. When they realized who we were, they gave us the floor. Let me tell you, we used the entire thing. He spun me one way, then the other. He lifted me up in the air as we spun, and I landed on the floor in the split position. Then he lifted me up to my feet. It was as if we had danced together for years. I followed his every lead. We moved together in a perfect sensual rhythm across the dance floor one way then danced as if we were floating on air back the other way. As we danced, we devoured each other's inhibitions, stimulating each other's imagination.

When we finished our dance, everyone began to applaud. I hugged Tony right on the spot, "I want you to play the lead role in my new film. I already know just by one dance, what kind of chemistry we'd have on film."

On the way back to our booth, I held my arm around his waist, as he held his around my shoulders. We walked through the rainforest, over a little wooden bridge which crossed over a small babbling brook. I gazed down at the running water; out of the corner of my eye I saw the shadow of a large man right behind me. I turned quickly to gaze at the figure and there was no one there. I felt a cold chill shoot down my spine, "Tony, do you mind if we leave now?"

I could tell Tony sensed my urgency, "Sure, let's get your cape and get out of here." So, we did.

As we climbed into the car I asked, "Do you have to go right home?"

He looked at me, smiled, "No, what do you have in mind?"

I glanced over at him as we drove away, "A nice walk on a secluded part of the beach would be pleasing."

He reached over to me, gently squeezed my hand, "That sounds like a fine idea to me."

American Goddess

He headed out of town along the coastal highway until he found a secluded beach. We strolled hand in hand on the beach that night, with the crystal-clear light of a full moon illuminating our path.

As we walked, "Tony, I'm very serious. I would love to work with you on this film. I already have Eartha Kit signed onto the project and I know she would agree."

"Well I might be able to work it into my schedule, if the price and timing are right."

I smiled, "The price I'm sure we can deal with, but what is your time frame?"

"I have six months off before starting the last film, of a five-film contract with, Salerno Pictures. I also have something in the works with Paramount for the next six months."

Intently I asked, "Is your Paramount deal finalized?"

"Not yet."

"That's good, now we can talk figures, because I plan to be releasing the film in only three months."

Wide-eyed he looked at me, "Three months! Boy, when you know what you want you don't waste any time going for it, do you?"

I smiled, "When we were dancing, I knew I had to have you." I paused for a second as his eyes lit up, then emphasized, "For my leading man."

His eyes lost their glow, "You've given me a lot to think about tonight."

I gently squeezed his hand, "Let's stop talking shop now and just take in this fabulous night." With that, we walked and walked for the longest time down the white sandy beach, listening to the crash of the waves on the shoreline.

As we walked Tony turned to me, took me in his arms, kissed me gently and said, "You are the most incredible woman I've ever met." He kissed me again, only this time with passion. We stood there in each other's embrace, with a gentle warm breeze blowing through our hair. I let my full-length blue silk cape, drift to the sand, as our gentle encounter, slowly turned passionate.

He began to gently nibble on my ear and whisper, "Christina, I want you, right here right now." He kissed my lips deeply and as we came up for air, "I've never wanted anything more in my life, than I want you at this very moment."

As I slowly surrendered to his passion fueled by mine, I whispered softly and seductively, "Tony, take me. Take my love from me and fill me with yours." We resumed our kissing as we undressed each other slowly and passionately under the canopy of the heavens, until our flesh became one in the soft warm sand. I could hear the wave's crash as we made love and I could not resist the urge any longer. I gently pushed him up by his shoulders, to release our lips and held him there, "Come follow me."

I kissed him again, rolled out from under his body and rose to my feet. In my purest of fleshly apparel, I looked down at him, smiled, blew him a kiss and ran across the sand toward the crashing waves. As I reached the edge of the white foaming shore, Tony was right by my side. He grabbed my hand as we both ran into the sensually stimulating, tingling sensation of the cool ocean water.

As we swam, splashed and laughed, we were drinking in the beauty of our bodies until we could no longer resist one another. We embraced in the midst of the waves. We were so enthralled with one another, neither of us saw the wave that lifted us off our feet and splashed us down into the water on the edge of the beach. As the water rushed over our bodies, he plunged his powerful loins deep into my lusting essence. Our sex was wicked, and our surroundings were divine. We consumed one another, over and over, until finally we collapsed on my cape, dripping wet with salt water. As we held each other under the starless sky of dawn's first light I thought, "This is real love, it wasn't just lust." Then my emotions turned dark, "It's not enough to steal him from Kathy for only one night."

As we laid there in a loving and tender embrace, I pulled the wild card out. I looked deep into his spellbound eyes and with a tone of deepest love, "Tony, marry me! Marry me tonight! We could fly to Vegas and be married by 10:00 this evening. Then we can always be together like this."

I held my breath as he lovingly looked back at me, "Christina, I would marry you this second if I could." With that, we melted into a passionate embrace.

It was 6:30am when we left the beach and headed for my room at the Hyatt. We were totally in love, or so Tony thought. As we drove, we made our plans for the day. Tony was to drop me off so I could pack and make our flight arrangements to Vegas, as he headed to his hotel to pack. Then he would pick me up and off to the airport we would go.

As we pulled up to the Hyatt, Tony leaned over, kissed me lovingly, "I love you, Christina, and I'll be right back for you."

I kissed him back, "Tony, I love you too and I can't wait to be your wife." I climbed out of the car and watched him drive away. I thought as I walked to my room, "I got him! Now to get him off this island pronto, so I can keep him."

It was 6:48 in the morning when I entered the room I shared with Barbara. When she heard me enter, she came out to find me looking like a drowned rat. She put her hands to her face and in horror, "Oh, my God! What in the world did they do to you?"

I looked at her like she was crazy, "What are you talking about? Nobody did anything to me. I went swimming."

"Didn't they find you?"

"Didn't who find me?"

"Oh, thank God! I thought they found you and tried to drown you." She started to crack up with laughter.

American Goddess

I was still looking at her in bewilderment, "Would you please try to make a little more sense so I can at least figure out what you're saying."

She stopped laughing, "You're right, it's not funny." She looked back at me and started to laugh again.

Shaking my head, "Barbara, we don't have time for this."

She contained herself long enough to say, "Last night about two hours after you and Tony left, one of Frank's men told him you and Tony were seen together at the Platinum's Disco. Frank and his goon left Kathy behind and took off together to go after Tony. I tried to stall them, but Kathy ran interference and rushed them out the door!"

As she was saying these words, I got a cold chill. I remembered the shadow and I thought, "How strange, could that shadow have been a warning of some kind? Ooh! This is too spooky even for me. I think I'll figure this one out some other day." Then I shook my head, "Don't worry about it. We have to pack now. I want you to be my maid-of-honor at my wedding in Vegas tonight. I'm marrying, Tony Demetrees."

Her mouth fell open, "You're not kidding me, are you?"

I walked over to her, put my hands on her shoulders, kissed her cheek, "Nope! I'm not." Then I headed for the phone.

As I called the airport, Barbara turned toward me looking dumbfounded, "Isn't this carrying the payback a little to the extreme?"

After I booked the three of us on a 11:00am nonstop flight to Vegas I said, "It's not like that at all, Barbara we love each other."

She burst into hysterics, "Christina, you can sweeten it up with any feelings you want. But believe me girl, we are one in the same and I know you better than you realize." Looking at me with the sincerest expression, "Christina, the stench of revenge cannot be sugarcoated. Take it from someone who's been there."

I smiled at her, "I hear what you are saying, now please hear me." I stopped, looked her in the eyes, "Just be happy for me in the moment, 'cause that's the way I am choosing to live my life. For the moment!"

She embraced me, "I love you, girlfriend, and I am so pleased you've found some happiness, no matter who gets trampled on, because you deserve it." With that, we both slightly laughed a little sadistically. Then we went to prepare for our journey.

As I showered, I thought, "If Frank can manipulate people to get what he wants, then so can I. And right now, Frank, I want Tony!"

It was 9:30am when Tony came to the door to pick us up. I had just finished speaking with Jimmy. I told him to have his ass in Vegas and meet me at the Golden Nugget by 7:00pm for my wedding. Then, I just hung up.

When I opened the door, I kissed Tony, "I love you, Tony." I turned to Barbara, "My man is here, now let's go." She came out from her room with two bags and handed them to Tony as she happily greeted him. I grabbed my suitcase; one bottle of champagne and it was **off to Vegas**.

CHAPTER 6

February 17th, 1977, we had a double wedding in Vegas. That night Tony and I were wed, Jimmy and Bobby took their vows of marriage at the same time we said ours. It was the first double wedding where one of the couples wed was a same sex marriage in the state of Nevada. It was not legal, but we did it anyway. Barbara stood up for the four of us. After the flashy ceremony, it was back to the airport. But this time we were flying to LA in Barbara's private jet. We partied all the way back to Los Angeles. By the time we arrived, it was 3:00am, the next morning and we were toasted. The limo took us to Barbara's Malibu beach house, where we all finally collapsed.

The next day we spent recuperating by the warmth of the fireplace, in the glass enclosed family room, which overlooked the stormy waves of the Pacific Ocean, on that cold February day. Tony and I clung to one another all that day. It was wonderful to have a strong man's arms around me again. We didn't let the headlines in the LA Times disturb us at all. It read, **"Christina Powers' Love Power, Sweeps Tony Demetrees, from the arms of his betrothed Kathy Brown, right to the altar."** The headlines also told the whole free world about our double wedding. As we read these headlines Tony appeared a little sad when he realized what we had done to Kathy, so I kissed his cheek, "We're in love Tony and we mustn't let ourselves feel too bad for her." As I comforted Tony, the only thing I was really concerned about was whether this publicity was going to hurt or help my new film. But I shared my concerns with no one.

When we left Barbara's home the next morning, I left an envelope in her bathroom on the back of the toilet tank. It had one hundred-thousand dollars cash in it and a three hundred-thousand-dollar gold diamond stick, butterfly pin with a note which read, **"I used it with good judgment, Love Christina."**

Needless to say, Tony and I did not have much of a honeymoon. The next day, we were off to Columbia Pictures to begin auditioning and casting for 'Life Passion and Fame', starring **Christina Powers** and **Tony Demetrees**. We worked out the figures to

American Goddess

Tony's liking. I gave him a four-million-dollar contract for one picture. We worked our asses off! Tony, Jimmy, Bobby and I worked almost eighteen hours a day. We would shoot from 5:00am to 9:00pm then, we were off to the recording studio until 2:00am. It was intense, but we knew we were creating a masterpiece, so we were driven. Jimmy and I finally stopped living together when I moved in with Tony at his oceanfront penthouse in Malibu. But that did not mean I saw any less of Jimmy, for he and Bobby rented an apartment together only two blocks from us.

Somehow, amidst this mad pace, Tony and I flew to New York and hired the top architects in the city and put them to work on the design for the future headquarters of Powers Incorporated. Tony and I worked together like fire. Not only on the screen, but with every aspect of the building of my empire. We also had fun together as we worked, which made all the hard work go faster. The four of us went full steam ahead. It was as if they caught my fire and began to burn with me. We set up a makeshift operation in downtown LA, not far from the studio Columbia Pictures, lent us for the filming of 'Life Passion and Fame'. With the help of an employment agency, along with Jimmy and Bobby, we hired office staff for our new location. Then, they went to work recruiting new talents of all kinds for my final inspection. From writers to singers, we concentrated on our recording label first. It was our moneymaker thus far, but I had full intentions to begin to play with the big boys, right after we made our millions on 'Life Passion and Fame.' I knew this film was a work of genius on paper, but it was up to us to bring it to life on the screen.

Tony and I had extraordinary passion between us, and we brought that passion to life on the film with every take. It was magical how we performed together, in more ways than one. Tony and I were becoming one! It was as if my dream became Tony's dream. I slowly began to really fall in love with him and I slowly began to let him, truly let him, into my life. When we did find the time to make love, it was honest love! It was beautiful, sensual and passionate. I didn't realize how much I missed this kind of passion in my life. **It was the passion of love.** We lived our lives like this and so did Jimmy and Bobby, from February 20th to the day we finished the last edit on 'Life Passion and Fame' on June 7th, and it was just in time, because my record sales had begun to slip. Before plunging into the promotion for the release of our film on June 21st, the four of us decided to take a few days off for a much-needed rest. So, we were off to our perspective honeymoons' in Lake Tahoe, Nevada leaving all of our cares behind.

The four of us took a cabin together to begin our four days of marital bliss, on a very secluded part of the lake. Our view of this lake, surrounded by majestic mountains, was fabulous. The cabin's forty-foot deck jetted out over the crystal-clear waters of Lake Tahoe. When you walked in the front door, you entered a large open knotty pine room with living room furniture laid out beautifully around a large fireplace. Off to the left of

American Goddess

this room was a completely updated kitchen, on the right was a formal dining room. The entire first floor was open in the back to the deck, which held a captivating view. On either side of the beautiful living room and just before you entered the kitchen, or the formal dining room stood two spiral staircases one on each side. The staircases led up to an open wraparound balcony. The balcony looked over the first floor in the front and out over the lake in the back. On either side of this balcony were our rooms with private baths. The whole place was done in knotty pine. We had just enough provisions to last the four days. When we sat down at the kitchen table for coffee that first morning the weather was 'bright' and 'sunny' and already eighty degrees.

As we sat around the table sipping our coffee, Jimmy was reading a brochure on the area's attractions. Tony got up from his chair, walked over behind me and began to massage my shoulders, while looking at all of us, "So what would you guys like to do today?"

Smiling, "What can you do out here in the wilderness except to just take in the beauty of it all?"

Tony kissed my cheek, "There are lots of things to do out here, baby, like fishing."

"Can't we just sit out there on the deck?"

Jimmy spoke up, "No, Christina, I'm not going to let you get us out here just to sit for four days. I want to do something."

With that Bobby said, "I'm with, Christina, I can handle just staying here."

"Oh, come on you two," Tony added. "We have to do something fun."

So, I replied, "I guess they're right, Bobby. We should do something, after all, who knows when we'll have free time again."

"Okay, whatever you guys want to do. Count me in." Bobby agreed.

Tony asked, "Jimmy, what's in the brochure?"

"Oh, lots of fun things, like boat trips, fishing trips, mountain climbing and sky diving." Then acting a little like a monkey as he jumped up and down in his seat, "Ooh, ooh, ooh, here's one, listen to this. **Come run the white-water rapids on your own inner tube down the winding, rolling, Snowy Hill River, until you emerge into the waiting arms of beautiful, majestic Lake Tahoe.**"

"That sounds great," Tony said as he slapped his hands together!

Then I said, "Okay, I'm game." Once I did, Jimmy dashed to the phone to make the arrangements.

It was 1:00pm when we grabbed our tubes and headed to the river to begin our ten-mile trip down the white-water rapids to the lake.

As I sat down in the middle of my tube wearing my cut off blue denim jeans, I jumped up quickly and shouted, "Oh shit! This water is cold!"

American Goddess

That's when Jimmy spoke up, as he bravely sat in the cold water, "Oh, don't be a pussy! Just get in the water."

"Okay, okay, don't rush me." Then I flopped my ass into the cold water and off we floated down the river.

The four of us started out in a chain, all holding someone else's hand. I held Tony's, Tony held Jimmy's; and of course, Jimmy held Bobby's. It turned out to be fun! I could not believe floating down a river would be so much fun. The first few sets of rapids we went down were great. They were nice and gentle, with just a touch of the cold water splashing on us.

We were laughing and having a great time, so I yelled out, "Hey, Jimmy, this was a great choice! I know my ass is turning blue, but I love it!"

Then, we started down our second set of rapids. This one was a little faster than the first set and it forced us to break our chain. There was a little more splashing, but nothing I, **jungle woman** Christina couldn't handle! Very quickly we began to be rushed into the next set of rapids. As we hit the first set of rolling water, I noticed Tony, Jimmy and Bobby were drifting off to the left side of the river, while I was drifting off to the right side of the river. By chance, I caught sight of a woman up on a hill just off the river's bank. She was jumping up and down while waving her arms. It appeared she was yelling something, but I could not hear her over the sound of the water, until the current brought me closer to her. At which time I could finally understand what this crazed woman was screaming, "Don't go that way! Turn back, it's not part of the **courseeeee**," as I sped by!

I looked and noticed the river forked just ahead of me, and I thought, "Oh, my God! Thanks for telling me lady, but how in the hell do I not go that way!" I was being swept away so I screamed out, "Tony! Help me," as I went flying over the rocks, heading the wrong way. I saw Tony as he jumped off his tube, grabbed it and came flying through the rushing water. Then he jumped back on it and headed down after me. I went flying over four-foot drops, screaming all the way. I smashed into twenty or more rocks, all head on, clinging to this black inner tube for dear life, and I could not believe what I saw next! I was heading straight for a tree which lay across the entire river. I screamed and held on as I collided with this unmovable beast **and when I did**, I flew head over heels while still holding my ass in the tube, landing in the middle of a five-foot deep whirlpool, which began to swirl me as if I had just been put on the spin cycle of my washing machine. Just as fast, it flung me headfirst into the ice-cold rush of white water. As I struggled to rise from the bottom of this whirlpool, I caught sight of something gold flashing out of the corner of my eye. So, when I stood up out of the water, I took a deep breath and when I did, I could see Tony about twenty feet away coming toward me. Then, I dove back into the ice-cold depths of the water and found the origin of the gold flash. I reached for a medallion of some sort on the bottom of the riverbed and just as I grabbed it, I found myself flying out of the water with such a force it nearly broke my neck, as Tony swept me up into his arms and carried me to the shore.

When we reached the shore, I was banged up and freezing. I just grabbed Tony and held on. As Tony rubbed his hands on my body to warm me up, he excitedly asked, "Are you all right, baby?"

I took a moment to examine my bruises, "I've been better, but I'll survive."

Shaking his head, "What the hell were you doing?"

"What was I doing? I didn't do it. The water did!"

With a bewildered expression, "I don't mean that I mean jumping back in the water like you did. You scared the shit out of me."

"Look at what I found down on the bottom of the river," I opened my hand to show him the gold piece I had grabbed.

Tony took it from my hand, "This is different, I've never seen a medallion quite like this before." Just then, we heard the panicked screaming of Jimmy and Bobby. I put the gold piece in my pocket, and we stood up to see where Jimmy and Bobby were calling. We looked down to the end of the river and there they were. It seemed we only had another one hundred yards to go on this little detour we took, before running back into the main river. So, I climbed on top of Tony in his tube. We floated the rest of the way back down the river, to where Jimmy and Bobby were frantically waiting.

They rushed to our aid, helped us out of the tube and kept repeating, "Are you guys all right?"

When I was finally on my feet with the help of these two bumbling idiots, I slapped Jimmy across the back of his head and shouted, "You and your stupid ideas! We could have been killed."

Jimmy started to cry and sobbed, "I'm sorry, Christina."

I held him, "I'm sorry Jimmy, it's not your fault."

He slowly stopped sobbing, "Well, we can't stop now. We still have five more miles of this."

With that, we all laughed as we climbed back in our tubes. Except for one difference, I was floating on my right side with my body lying next to Tony, as he laid face up. I placed my head on his left shoulder, slid my right leg over his knees, placed my right hand on top of his wet crotch and we floated on his tube just like that. To be honest, I loved the little detour.

As we floated, I could feel the slight throbbing of a growing mass in the palm of my right hand. I immediately felt a warm flash shoot through my body, even though I was still in that very cold water. I quickly raised the temperature of our bodies when I slid on top of Tony and began to sensually shower him with kisses, as I was rhythmically grinding my thighs into his groin. It was becoming quite the hot little ride when it was abruptly stopped by the riverbed. We looked up to see Jimmy and Bobby standing over us.

Tony looked at them, "Don't you guys have something better to do?"

Bobby threw his hands in the air, "You guys should take a look at this, before you get too carried away."

When we stood up, it appeared as if most of the water just vanished. There was only a small steady flow going over the rocks, but not enough to float on. I looked over to the right side of the riverbank and there was my tube floating away. We picked up our tubes and started to walk. As we walked, we found ourselves slowly waving our hands in the air at a few annoying horseflies. Then, from out of the depths of hell, came this swarm of demon horseflies. It was un-fucking real! They dive bombed us like kamikaze pilots. They were eating us alive! It got so bad I started screaming. I thought I was going mad. Then Tony grabbed me, took his big black tube, and started swinging it in the air in a desperate attempt to get them off me.

I screamed, "Jimmy, if I didn't love you, I'd shoot you right now!"

Jimmy shouted as he frantically flung his shorts through the air, beating back the attack, "They're eating me too, you know!"

Once I stopped laughing at the sight of Jimmy, in his wet underpants I shouted back, "That's no consolation Jimmy." Just as I did, I caught my left foot under a rock and went crashing onto the stones again. Tony helped me up and I now had a limp, too!

I turned to Jimmy, "Strike the love part, Jimmy. When I can walk again, I'm going to kill you."

Finally, the water rose, and we were quickly swept away from our impending doom.

It was 6:00pm when I hobbled into the cabin. I looked like I had fought the Vietnam War by myself and lost. I was black and blue from head to toe and with all the red spots; I looked like I had jungle fever. If I weren't hurting so much, it would have been laughable.

Then I crept over to the spiral staircase, "I'm going for a hot bath, would someone else please think about dinner tonight."

Tony kissed my cheek, "How about Chinese? I could run into town and pick some up."

I kissed him back, "That sounds good to me, baby." Then I slowly proceeded up the steps and right into a hot tub!

After dinner that evening, the four of us sat out on the deck with our Chablis wine. The night was beautifully warm, and it felt liberating just to be sitting there absorbing this awesome display of nature. As we sat there, we were able to look back at the day's events and finally laugh about it. Boy did we laugh!

Then I remembered my find, so I took it off. I had put it on my neck chain shortly after my bath. As I showed it to them, I proceeded to tell Jimmy and Bobby how I came to have it in my possession. We all agreed the piece seemed incredibly old and was solid gold. It was about the size and shape of a man's pocket watch. **In the center was a carving of a naked goddess standing on top of a flaming ball of fire, and she appeared to be breaking the chains which bound her to this inferno.**

As we remarked on its beauty, jokingly Jimmy said, "Well, if you had drowned, we would have never known of its existence."

With a laugh I said, "Maybe I was meant to find it, it's probably a good luck charm." We all laughed at my words, as I placed it back around my neck.

As Tony and I lay on the soft bed together that night, he looked deep into my eyes, "Christina, honey, I love you. You are the best thing that's ever come my way. Baby, every time I look at you, I gaze in wonder at your beauty, your intelligence and your strength." He kissed me softly and in a gentle loving tone, "You're so full of life Christina and I thank God you are my wife."

I kissed him, "Tony, I love you more every day. I never thought I could feel like this." I kissed him again as I pulled him over to me. Our love soared that night, as we came together in hot passion. He was incredible as he softly caressed my beaten body. I felt no pain! All I could feel was intense love for this man, this magnificent man who was now truly my husband. I surrendered all my emotions as I cried for the first time while making love, since Johnny.

"Oh, God Tony, I love you, I love you. Take me, baby, take me." I cried, and I meant every word. I begged him for more and more and he gave it to me. He satisfied me in ways I thought I would never feel again. It was lovemaking in its purest form. We were both in heaven together.

I woke up to the chirping of the birds outside our open windows. I looked at the alarm clock and it read eight o'clock. Tony was still sound asleep, so I tip-toed into the bathroom. When I returned, I put on my robe while Tony was stirring in the bed. So, I kissed his cheek, "Don't get up, baby, I'll go put on some coffee and bring you a cup."

Returning my kiss, "Sounds good to me, I'll go to the bathroom and meet you right back here." With that, he walked one way and I limped the other.

When I walked out onto the balcony, I could not help but notice Jimmy kneeling on the floor on his hands and knees. He was down in the large living room, facing an open door. I could see he had the screen door propped open with a coffee cup. On closer inspection, I could see he was holding a camera in his hands and there were peanuts on the floor, just outside the front door. And to top this whole scene off, Jimmy was only in his underpants, socks and a tee shirt.

Finally, I could resist no longer, "Jimmy, what are you doing down there like that?"

He turned his head almost 160 degrees and in a soft whisper, as he put one finger over his lips, "Look, out there on the porch."

American Goddess

I bent over the rail, "Jimmy, I don't see anything."

With a boyish snicker, "It's a squirrel and it's eating the nuts I'm putting out for it. I'm trying to get a close-up shot."

I whispered back, "Put the nuts a little closer to the doorway so I can see him too."

Jimmy slowly placed a nut just at the doorway and I could see this sweet little squirrel just nibbling on it. It was adorable and we were amazed as Jimmy got his shots.

Then all at once, the wind blew the screen door closed with a **crash!** This sweet little squirrel made a horrifying screech, leaped three feet into the air, at the same time Jimmy let out with a scream and jumped four feet into the air. They both started to slide across the slippery oak floor like cartoon caricatures as they tried to run away from each other.

I cried out hysterically, "Run Jimmy, it could be rabid!" At which time, the squirrel turned and charged right toward Jimmy. Screaming, Jimmy slid across the floor as if he had just gotten hit by a lightning bolt. I screamed in horror as I watched helplessly, "Run Jimmy! He's coming right for you!"

Bobby ran in with the broom and started swatting at it. It jumped, made a turn in midair, landed right on the staircase, and charged up the steps. It stopped at the top, looked straight into my eyes and started running toward me screeching all the way. I shrieked as if a herd of elephants were heading right for me. Turning to run, I saw Tony coming out of the bedroom then he dashed back in. Being left to fend for myself, I flung myself down the spiral staircase in a desperate attempt to escape. As I struggled to my feet, I looked up and there he was still coming after me. I screamed and ran to the sofa Jimmy was standing on, leaped at him and we both went crashing into the coffee table. I looked up quickly to see if the monster was still on my trail, and saw Tony throw a blanket over this flesh-eating beast and let it out the front door.

I stood up in total shock, took a deep breath and shouted, "Jimmy, are you trying to kill me? Or is this your idea of fun?"

He stood there as chicken as I was, "Oh my God, girlfriend! I thought we were goners!" The four of us immediately lost it. We must have laughed a good twenty minutes as we tried to have our coffee and toast.

After we finally stopped laughing, I reached over toward Jimmy from my chair, put my arms around his neck, kissed him and said, "Jimmy, I love you. You're the best friend anyone could want, but I think if I stay here with you in this wilderness much longer, I'll be going home in a casket."

I kissed him again as we chuckled. Then, I turned to Tony as I released my hold on Jimmy. I stretched my hand out, took Tony's hand in mine, "Baby, would you be too upset if I asked you to take me to one of the hotels in town."

American Goddess

Tony looked at me and smiled, "Actually, Christina, I do mind. You see, baby, I have a little wedding gift for you, but I forgot it at home, and I can't wait to give it to you. So, would you be too upset if I took you home."

I squeezed his hand, "Oh, Tony, that's sweet and no I don't mind going home." Then Tony called the airport and booked us on the 1:00pm flight back to LA. We grabbed our suitcases, I grabbed one bottle of champagne and **it was off to LA.**

CHAPTER 7

It was 5:00pm when we loaded the trunk of Tony's black Cadillac with our suitcases at LA International Airport. As we drove toward our home in Malibu, Tony seemed a little excited and he had a childish smile on his face. As I watched him, I thought, "What is he up to?" I could take the suspense no longer, "All right, why do you have that smirk on your face?"

His face lit up like a Christmas tree, "What smirk? I don't have a smirk on my face."

I chuckled, "Oh, then that must be a neon sign I see flashing on your face."

As I was saying these things Tony drove past our building, "Where are we going?" Knowing there was not much out past our building, except scenic views.

"I just thought a little ride might be nice."

I slid across the seat, kissed his cheek, "Hmm! That sounds romantic." Then I laid my head on his shoulder as we drove up the scenic Malibu Coast.

Shortly after we passed the gates to Barbara's mansion, Tony began to slow down as if he were looking for something. Then, he pulled into an open gate and proceeded up a winding, wooded driveway, "Where are you going?"

He patted my thigh, "To Barbara's, house."

"If you're going to Barbara's, then you're at the wrong place," Looking at him strangely I added, inquisitively, "What's up? Why are we going to, Barbara's?"

The driveway led up to a brilliantly light tinged, bright yellow, brick mansion with all white trim. Tony parked the car right at the front entrance, "You'll see when we go in." With that, he got out of the car came around to my door opened it, "Come on, she's waiting."

American Goddess

I gave him another strange look, "Tony, this is not, Barbara's house."

He reached for my hand, grabbed it and gently pulling me out, "This is her new place. She said she'd leave the driveway gate open for us."

"Oh," I said with surprise, "I didn't know she was moving."

Then, I looked at this magnificent three-story, brick mansion as we walked up the six steps of a twenty-foot wide staircase, which was attached to a one hundred foot long, eighteen foot deep, Italian marble front porch and I exclaimed, "Holy, shit! Would you look at this place? It's gorgeous!"

There were six, thirty-foot-tall, three feet in diameter circular marble Roman style columns holding up, this blast from the past, Greco-Roman architectural styled, front porch. When, we reached the large eight-foot double hung doors, Tony slipped a key into the lock. All at once, he flung the big doors open, swept me off my feet and shouted, "Welcome home baby!"

Then, he proceeded to carry a completely shocked woman over the threshold. As he placed my feet back on the floor, he kissed me, "I love you, Christina! I bought it for you. I mean us. Oh, you know what I mean."

I hugged him so-lovingly as I giggled my reply, "Yes, I know what you mean." Kissing him, "Oh, Tony, it's just beautiful and I love you for it! Thank you, thank you my love."

He took my hand tugged my arm with excitement, "Come on Christina, let me show it to you, baby."

As we toured the interior of our new home, I said with a surprised tone, "Tony, this is our furniture. When did you find the time to do this?"

He smiled proudly, "I had it all moved here yesterday. I thought it would do fine for now, at least until we can find the time to decorate it ourselves."

I was so excited; I began kissing him childishly all over his face, "I love you, Mr. Demetrees."

He returned my kisses, "I love you too, Mrs. Demetrees."

The mansion towered majestically on top of a cliff, which overlooked the glistening Pacific Ocean on that early evening sunset. There were lovely flower gardens everywhere and on either side of the mansion, stood two, large water fountains. As you passed through the front doors, you entered a large marble foyer with a six-foot round, crystal, chandelier hanging from the ceiling. Across from the front doors, were two marble staircases which curved up both walls on either side of the foyer to a beautiful landing on the second floor. The inside was Italian marble, slate, wood and stone throughout the entire place. It had fourteen bedrooms, sixteen bathrooms, three kitchens, three formal living and dining rooms, two libraries and three towering balconies which overlooked the ocean. On the grounds were two guest homes, a ten-car garage, a house for the staff and two barns with riding stables, all on two hundred acres.

American Goddess

The place was incredible! I had not lived in a place like this since I moved out of Frank's mansion.

After our tour, Tony pushed a button on the wall intercom in the small kitchen and said, "James, would you and Carman, please come up?"

A male voice responded, "We'll be right up, sir."

I looked at Tony, "Who are, James and Carman?"

Before Tony could answer, two people in their late fifties came into the room. At which time Tony said, "James, Carman, I would like you to meet, Mrs. Demetrees." Turning toward me, he added, "Christina, let me introduce you to, Mr. and Mrs. James and Carman Pavone. Carman is our cook and housekeeper. James is our chauffeur and gardener. They live in the staff quarters."

We exchanged greetings then Carman said, "It is very nice to meet you, Mrs. Demetrees. Now please excuse me, I have to get back to the main kitchen or we'll be having burnt lasagna for dinner."

With that, she took off down the hall with James still saying, "It's nice to meet you, ma'am," as he ran off after her.

She was walking determinedly toward the kitchen, then she abruptly stopped dead in her tracks, turned and hollered up the hall, "Oh Yes, dinner will be served in the blue dining room at seven o'clock," and just as quickly she ran out of sight.

I turned to Tony, "They seem nice enough, but live-in help. Do we really need them?"

Tony kissed my cheek, "The way you work me, you don't think I'm going to cook and clean up after you too. Do you?"

I laughed, "We'd better bring our suitcases in; we only have twenty minutes till dinner you know."

Tony laughed, "James, has already brought them up and put them in our room."

"Wow!" I replied with a surprise, "Maybe we do need help after all."

Tony chuckled, "Come on; let's go sit on the deck while we wait for dinner."

Tony sat down on a big white rocker, which was part of a twenty-piece wicker set on the first-floor deck. I sat on Tony's lap and said to him, as we looked out over the ocean, "Baby, this place is beautiful! But what did you pay for it?"

He gently patted my thigh, "Don't worry about the price. We can afford it."

I kissed his forehead, laughed then replied, "Tony, I'm not worrying about the money, I'd just like to know how much you dished out for me, that's all."

He smiled, "Eight-million and you're worth every penny!"

Wide eyed, "Eight-million-dollars for one house, I'm glad you think I'm worth it!" I flung my legs over the armrest of the rocker and slipped further down into his lap. I gazed up into his eyes and I sweetly kissed him, "Tony, my love, thank you for my wedding gift. I love it!" I kissed him again, only this time much deeper. When we finally came up for air, "Baby, I have a wedding gift for you too." Gazing lovingly up into his eyes, I softly continued, "Tony, we are going to have a baby."

His face appeared as if he were in shock, "Are you serious?"

I shook my head to indicate yes, smiled, "Yup, I'm pregnant baby."

He held me closely and with enthusiasm, "Oh God, Christina! We are going to have a baby! You have made me the happiest man on earth, and I love you with all of my heart." Then, we just laid there holding each other until Carman called us for dinner.

After a scrumptious lasagna dinner, we took a walk arm-in-arm around the grounds and down to the stables. When we got there, Tony said, "I hope you can ride?"

I smiled devilishly, "Nobody rides better than I do. Why don't we go to our new bedroom and I'll show you just how well I can ride?"

He kissed me passionately, "Let's go!" Then we began to walk back to the mansion. As we passed the beautifully fragrant gardens on that warm starry evening, Tony asked me, "So when is our little one coming into the world?"

"I'm not sure, I only found out yesterday when the Doctor called with the results of my test."

Tony turned toward me quickly, "We'd better get you to the doctor then, 'Little Woman.'"

I laughed at Tony's, John Wayne imitation, as he said, 'Little Woman'. Then I said, "I'll call Doctor Hedderman tomorrow morning."

"That's good baby. We have to stay on top of these things you know."

As we climbed the steps of the front porch, Tony put his arm around my shoulders, "We're here, Christina." He rubbed my belly, "Our new baby, new home and new life together. May it be filled with lots of love, lots of happiness and lots of babies."

As he said these words, I felt joy, which quickly turned into a dim, faint pain in my heart as I thought of Johnny, and what might have been for one brief second. Then, I dismissed the thought and gave my full attention to Tony.

When we reached our third-floor master bedroom I said, 'imitating Mae West', as I pulled Tony by his hands, "Come with me little man, I've got something to show you."

He followed willingly as I led him into the bathroom. I turned the bath water on warm and began to undress him. As I unzipped his pants, he immediately became aroused, so I knelt down, slipped his pants to the floor and kissed the tip of his beautiful manhood and as I gazed up into his eyes, "Don't get too hot yet, baby. We have a lot to celebrate and all night long to celebrate it."

I finished undressing him and led him to the tub which was nice and steamy by this point. As he climbed into the large four-person bathtub, I was gently stroking his beautiful body. I proceeded to continue my seduction of Tony as I climbed in and began to kiss his entire body. I lathered him with a huge sponge; then, he began to wash me and as he did, I felt our passion growing even hotter. That's when I slowed our pace by rinsing and drying us both off. I led him to our bed, pulled back the covers and opened the curtains to a bright starry night. As we fell onto the bed, I began to devour his body with my love. Our bodies soared together in the heat of passion on that brilliant night! It was all so wonderful. As we made love, we were celebrating our new life together as one.

As we laid in each other's arms just before sleep crept over us, I began to think, "That was the closest I came to perfect ecstasy since Johnny." I snuggled a little closer to Tony and thought, "Oh God. I truly do love Tony, so why can't I get Johnny out of my heart?" With that thought I screamed out in my mind, "Stop haunting me Johnny! I don't love you anymore and I want you out of my heart so I can love Tony completely." I felt a tear running down my cheek and I stopped my mind dead and thought, "Oh well! I'll figure it out tomorrow."

The next day, doctor Hedderman informed me to expect a little bundle of joy on October 10th, which just happened to be the same as my true mother's birthdate. After I told Tony, I called Jimmy and Bobby, and told them to come right over as soon as they got back into town. Then I called my office manager and had her send out a memo inviting everyone who was anyone in Hollywood to a celebration party to announce our expected gift. It was to be held at our home that coming Saturday night, June 13th, at 8:00pm which was only two days away. I also invited the press and tabloids. The timing was perfect. One thing I learned from Frank was to never look a gift horse in the mouth. However, I did leave two names off my guest list, Frank and Kathy.

It was Thursday night, June 11th, around 8:00pm when Jimmy and Bobby came to the door just in time for dessert. As soon as Jimmy opened the door he said, "It's no surprise Christina, I saw the house before you did."

I kicked him in his ass as he walked by me, "You did, did you? Why you shithead! How in the world did you keep your mouth shut?"

We laughed as we walked into the living room. While we talked about the house, Carman brought in some coffee and pineapple whipped cream cake.

We were having our dessert and I turned to Jimmy, "Jimmy, I have a confession to make, I lied to you about something."

He looked at me as if he went into shock, "I can't believe you lied to me! I would never lie to you."

"Don't get so melodramatic, Jimmy. Remember I said the test was negative? Well that is what I lied about. I am going to have a baby."

All at once, he jumped up in the air, spilled his coffee all over Bobby and started screaming, "Oh my God! That's wonderful!" As Bobby jumped up and shouted, "Oh my God! That's hot!"

American Goddess

That Saturday night we had the most glamorous party in town. Barbara, Eartha, Jimmy, Bobby, Joe Cole and the rest of the crew, as well as most of our Hollywood friends were there. They all came to our home to celebrate with us along with the press. Tony and I were dressed to the hilt. He was so handsome in his black tux and I was ravishing in my dark maroon, satin, full length gown. As we welcomed our guests, we opened our new home and our new life, to our friends and our country. We were so proud of ourselves and our achievements that day and the party was a smashing success.

The next day, the whole country knew I was having Tony's baby. Our photos were plastered all over the free world and we planned to keep it that way for the next two months. It was time to get back to work. We promoted the upcoming release of our new film and double record soundtrack, day and night around the entire country. We did TV and radio talk shows, all day and night, in thirty-six cities, in seven straight days. While Tony, Eartha and I were traveling, Jimmy and Bobby were signing new acts onto the Powers Record Label. It appeared the whole record industry was jumping on the disco bandwagon. So, Powers Records started pumping out one disco hit after another. Yes, there were other disco divas in those days, but none like me, for I was the Goddess of Disco and the whole world knew it.

Saturday, June 20th, at 7:00pm we held the premier of, 'Life Passion and Fame' at the Palladium, in downtown Los Angeles. We spared no expense to assure we had a lavish opening, with all the Hollywood hoopla! Tony and Eartha were standing on either side of me. Tony and I looked like a king and queen as we greeted Hollywood's elite at the front door of the Palladium. As the limos pulled up, through the crowds and the flashing of the press with their cameras, we could see from where we were standing, each guest as they climbed out of their limos and walked up the red carpet toward us. I was smiling, happy and proud, as we greeted our friends. Then, I felt the expression on my face turn evil as soon as I saw Frank and Kathy climb out of one of the limos and start walking toward us. Tony quickly grabbed my arm, "Just relax Christina, we can deal with him."

I turned to him and forcefully, "I've heard those same words before. Believe me Tony, he's a prick and she's his slut, and if they're here, something is up.

Eartha squeezed my hand and leaned up to my ear, "Stay calm girl.""

Tony under his breath said, "Isn't that a little strong? I still happen to have a contract with Frank, remember? So please don't put me in the middle of this war you and Frank have going."

I looked at him angrily and sharply said, "When you married me you put yourself in the middle of it. So don't try to sugarcoat it with him now, because it won't work."

When they reached us, Frank said, "You look well, Christina and I see."

I just cut him right off, "What are you doing here?"

American Goddess

He smiled, "I've come to see your work."

I snapped back, "You're both not welcome here."

Frank turned to Tony, "Is this true, Tony?"

Tony quickly answered, "Of course not Frank, please come in."

I stood there trying not to **rip his face off**, as he was inviting Frank in. Then, he continued with, "Kathy, it's good to see you. You look wonderful tonight." I almost bit my tongue off as I smiled for the cameras. Then finally, the show started.

The premier was a smashing success, but that was not what I wanted to talk about when Tony and I climbed into bed that night. He rolled over to me, kissed my neck, and with anger in my voice, "Don't even think about it! How could you humiliate me like that? In front of all those people no less."

"Me! I was trying to save the moment. Do you realize what you said to Frank Salerno in front of all those people? He's your uncle. You should know better than anyone, what kind of man he is. Nobody talks to Frank like that and gets away with it."

My reply was sharp, "Well I do! He's a no-good bastard, and I don't want him in my life, in anyway, at all."

Tony knelt up in the bed and gently grabbed my shoulders, "Christina, I love you and I thought it took a lot of balls for you to stand up to Frank like that. I'm proud of you. You fought the boss-man and won. But baby, I still have to do one more film with that man, so please, for my sake, please don't let him come between us. After the film, I don't care if you stand on the top of the World Trade Center and shout obscenities at him, just please wait until the film is done."

With that, he gave me his little boy look and I slowly melted into his arms. As I did, I said, "Tony, I'm sorry, I should have thought of you, instead of just myself."

I proceeded to gently kiss his shoulders and as I laid my head on his chest, he said, "Baby, I love you! We really pulled it off tonight you know. This film was pure genius and it's going to be a hit for us."

I kissed him passionately, "I love you too Tony, and yes we were like magic on the screen." Then we came together in the tenderness of pure, loving passion.

That weekend, 'Life Passion and Fame', brought in a record breaking sixty-eight million dollars and Tony and I became the most popular couple in America. The demand for the two of us to make personal appearances shot through the roof and we did our best to fill them all. Over the next two months, the movie and record sales were bringing in hundreds of millions of dollars worldwide. At the same time, the soundtrack to the movie which was titled, 'Come Lay with Me' was number one on all the record charts. I was singing the number one cut on the album, 'Come Lay with Me' at every appearance. Between traveling and personal appearances Tony and I would write. We started writing the lyrics for my next album and screenplay, as well as the lyrics we sent to Jimmy and

American Goddess

Bobby, to be recorded by our new head liners. We also broke ground on the future site of what was now called Powers Incorporated, in Milton, N.Y. The building design we chose for our future home, was the most complete environmentally friendly design of its time.

By August 30th, we were back in the recording studio, working all day on my fifth album entitled, 'Everlasting Love.' All night we wrote our next screenplay entitled, 'Listen to the Wind'. It was a story of two strangers who fell in love in one night, as they talked on the beach. We also found out that day that Tony would have to start filming his next movie with Salerno films, on January 2nd, 1978, in London, England. I was not too pleased to receive this information. I tried to convince Tony to try to break his contract through the courts, but he refused. So, I thought, "Oh well! I'll figure it out tomorrow. And if I don't, at least I would have Tony all to myself until then."

We released our fifth soundtrack, 'Everlasting Love' on October 5th, 1977 and I was as big as a house. By now, I was done with being pregnant, but the baby wasn't! I felt like a twenty-two-year-old sex symbol in hiding. I was so fat; I thought I was having a cow instead of a baby. As October 10th, my due date came and went, I hated being pregnant. I thought I would go out of my mind if this kid didn't come out soon." Then I started to get scared. All this talk of breathing the pain away, I knew was all bullshit and it was going to hurt. October 12th, I was really bitchy. Everybody just stayed away as I paced through the entire mansion like a waddling duck with three little spying Indians, following in the distance. The place became an insane asylum. Especially when Jimmy and Bobby insisted on moving in with us until the baby came.

It was October 14th, at 2:00am when my water finally broke and I wet the bed. I turned to Tony, "Tony, I think it's time."

With groggy eyes he looked at me, "Baby, did you say something?"

As I started to climb out of our wet bed I shouted, "Baby, my water broke. I think it's time to go to the hospital!"

His face immediately turned white when he discovered the bed was wet. He flew up out of the bed and shouted, "Oh God, Christina! What the hell is all over this bed?"

He ran into the bathroom and jumped into the shower mumbling, "Oh shit! What is this stuff?"

I looked at him like he was nuts and shouted, "Tony, its only water! So, get the hell out of that shower and take me to the hospital!"

I ran out into the hall and yelled, "Jimmy, Bobby, get up it's time!"

I heard this loud screech from Jimmy, and he kept it up as he shouted, "Oh shit, Bobby wake up! Christina, hold on! Don't have that baby yet! I'll be right there!"

I shouted as I threw my hands in the air, "What the hell kind of morons are you guys?"

American Goddess

I had finished dressing by the time Jimmy and Bobby dashed into the bedroom. Jimmy grabbed me by both my upper arms, shook me and screamed in my face, "Are you all right?" His head popped around the room like a jack-in-the-box and he shouted again, "Where's, Tony?"

I looked at him, broke out of his crane like grip, "First of all I'm not deaf, second stop trying to shake the baby out of me it's doing a good enough job on its own." Taking a deep breath, I calmly replied, "Would you and Bobby, please get Tony, out of the shower while I call the hospital."

He stepped back, put his hands on his hips, "What the hell is he doing in the shower?"

"I don't know!" I answered, as I headed for the phone, "Would you please just get him out!"

I sat by the front door with my bag in hand, ready to go for ten minutes before the three of them came down the steps. Tony got some color back in his face, when he saw I was just fine. When they reached me, Jimmy and Bobby both grabbed me by either arm to help me up, "I'm fine guys, you don't have to hold me let's just go to the hospital and get this over with."

Tony, still not saying much, went for the car. When he pulled the car up to the front of the house, he jumped out, ran to me and gently helped me into the front seat. As I climbed into the car, I got one! And I screamed, "Oh shit! That hurts!"

Tony flew into the driver's door, stuck his nervous face in mine and shouted, "Are you okay, baby?"

I kissed his cheek, "I've been better, so let's just go."

As Tony drove us the twenty-mile trip to the hospital, I began to get some bad ones. So bad I thought I was going to give birth any minute and I finally screamed out, "Oh, God! I think it's coming!"

Bobby immediately passed out in the back seat. Tony stepped on the accelerator and we all almost broke our necks from the force of the jerk. Jimmy grabbed my shoulder and screamed, "Put your hands down there and hold it in until we get to the hospital."

Then, Tony hit a bump and we all hit are heads on the roof. First, I cried out in pain; then, I screamed, "Tony! Slow down! You're going to make this baby fall out right here on the car seat."

He came to a screeching stop and I almost went through the windshield. As Tony sped up to ten miles an hour, Jimmy was chanting in the back seat, "God don't let it come now! God don't let it come now!"

Tony went over a set of railroad tracks at five miles an hour, to the honking of twenty or so cars behind us, as I cried out in pain again. That's when Tony finally said something, "I can't go any slower."

American Goddess

I screamed at him, "Would you please give this car some gas, and get me to the freaking hospital now!"

With that, he almost broke our necks again as he floored the car. Finally, we were at the hospital! Jimmy flew out of the car and ran into the ER as Tony helped me out of the front seat. I noticed Bobby was still out cold on the floor of the back seat. Jimmy ran back with a hospital nurse, who put me in a wheelchair, wheeled me into the hospital and straight up to the elevators. When we reached the door to the OB/GYN unit, Tony stopped us all dead, knelt in front of me and pouted, "Christina, I can't come in there with you."

"What do you mean you can't come in?" I shouted as I looked him straight in the eye. Then I got another one and I screamed, "I don't give a shit what you do! Just someone get this kid out of me!" My driver pushed me through the doors, and we left Tony and Jimmy out in the hall.

By the time the doctor came in the room, I was in agony! He smiled at me and with a cheerful tone, "How are you, Christina?"

I looked at him like, **duh**, "I'm having a baby, Doctor Hedderman. How the hell do you think I am?"

He smiled again, looked at his assistant, covered his face with a blue mask, "Now Christina, don't be a testy one."

I got another labor pain and during my pain, I could see panic-stricken eyes popping out through a blue cap and mask. Realizing they were Tony's eyes, I looked at him and screamed, "You idiot! I thought you were staying out!" I screamed out with tears of pain rolling down my cheeks, "Do you see what you did to me?" Tony just stood there like he was frozen solid. I cried out in pain again, "Oh shit! Tony, I'm hurting! I need you!"

He instantly ran to my side, held my shaking hands tightly, and as the sweat poured off our foreheads he said, "I'm here, baby! I'm here."

We heard the first cry of our new baby girl as we buried ourselves in each other's eyes, which were filled with pain and joy. We named our little baby girl, Joy. This little Joy of ours was so precious. She had beautiful curly black hair and a little chubby round face. Her eyes were crystal blue and she was a six-pound, ten-ounce, little ball of energy. She captured our hearts and we loved her from the instant we heard her first cry.

The next day we were in every headline across the country. The flowers, letters and cards, from well-wishers filled the hospital mail room. America's new golden couple now had a little bundle of Joy, and we instantly became known as America's golden family. That evening we discovered my latest album, 'Ever Lasting Love' shot to the number one spot. When we left the hospital the following day, we ran right into the center of a fanfare, with press and cameras. After a short interview Tony, Joy and I were off to begin our new life together as a family. Oh yes, Jimmy and Bobby came too! They were great. They catered to Joy's and my every need.

The next two months were wonderful. Tony and I stayed home with Joy almost every day. By December 10th, my twenty third birthday I was back on top of the world! We had the best of both worlds. I was in love with Tony and our life as a family, was a dream come true. My career was skyrocketing, and it seemed no one could dethrone my music from the top of the record charts. Even though we were home it did not mean we were not busy. We had six more household staff members and one full-time nanny, which had nothing to do so far. We had two private secretaries, one for each of us. We managed the helm of Powers Motion Pictures and Records, from home. Our wealth and fame kept growing. Powers Motion Pictures was releasing three new films by the first of the year. Powers Records had twenty-three-top names signed to our label. We had it all!

After my birthday dinner that evening, Tony received a call from an "old friend," Frank Salerno. It went like this. We had a small gathering of a few friends over to celebrate my birthday with us. We were all gathered in the golden formal dining room chatting over cake and coffee, when Carman excused herself, walked over to Tony and said, "Sir, you have a phone call in your study."

"Please just take a message for me and tell them I will call them later."

"I tried that sir, but the gentleman caller said to tell you he was Mr. Salerno and that it was urgent he speak with you now."

"Thank you, Carman."

Tony excused himself then headed for the study to take the call.

I tried to act nonchalantly over the call amongst our friends, but as the first half hour approached and Tony had not returned, my concern was beginning to show. I finally could take the suspense no longer, so I excused myself and went to find Tony. As I approached the study, I could faintly hear through the slightly ajar door, what seemed to be the end of Tony's conversation with Frank, "I don't like this at all Frank." I opened the door, "Don't worry Frank, I will honor my contract. Now I really must get back to my wife's birthday party. Goodbye."

When he hung up the phone, I looked at him and I knew something was wrong, "What did he say to you?"

Tony kissed my cheek, "I'll tell you later, let's get back to our guests."

Later that evening as Tony and I climbed into bed, I turned to him, "So tell me what he said? But first, start with what you disliked so much."

Shaking his head in disgust, "Well baby, you're not going to like it either, but Kathy Brown is my leading lady. Shooting starts January 12th. I need to be in London just as we planned, January 2nd, and the script for 'Billy Boy' will be arriving shortly."

American Goddess

I looked very seriously, "I smell a rat, Tony. This is a setup if ever I saw one and you're right, I don't like it."

Tony took my hand, "Christina, I have no choice, I have to do the film no matter who they co-star me with, I have a contract."

Squeezing his hand, "Why don't you just break the damn contract? So, what if we get sued. I'd rather lose everything then to lose you."

Tony pulled me close to his chest, "You're not going to lose me, baby."

With concern, "Tony, you don't seem to understand. She is going to try to get you back. There I said it, I just love you Tony, and I'll go out of my mind knowing she's with you. I've seen her in action before and **she's a bitch**. Please, Tony, I know she wants you back, baby. I have to be honest with you, there has been a sort of rivalry between the two of us for a long time now and there's nothing that would please her more, then to steal your love from me."

Tony looked straight into my eyes, "You mean like you did to her?"

I was taken aback. I could say nothing in reply. He kissed my cheek, "You really don't think I didn't know about your feud with Kathy when I met you? I knew, Christina! I knew right down to how Kathy only went after John, because Frank put her up to it." As he said those words, I felt a pain shoot through my heart, which flared up more anger and hatred for them both. "I also knew the real reason you proposed me. The one thing you did not know was that I loved you long before I met you that night. I was in love with you when you and John Everett were engaged. You thought I just fell in love with you on the beach that night, but the truth is I loved you so much my heart broke when you walked off the set of 'Samantha's Father' before I could even meet you." He squeezed me tightly, "Baby, what I'm saying is, yes, I did have feelings for Kathy, but when you asked me to marry you, you made my dreams come true and you've filled my life with magic every day since then." He pushed me from his chest, looked down into my eyes, "Baby, if there is anyone who should worry about losing anyone it's me, not you. You will never lose my love Christina, never."

Tears of love began to fall, "Tony, I do love you and you never have to doubt that."

He bent down and gently kissed the tears from my cheeks. The love we made that night felt so honest and peaceful that we decided we were going to trust in our love and get through this film together.

January 2nd, 1978 came and Tony left. I slowly began to go mad. There was no chance of Joy and me going with him because that would have made it worse. So, on January 3rd, I went straight to the gym and started a rigorous training program. I had just a little too much baby fat left for me to be seen out in public. On January 5th, I was back in the recording studio working on my next release. Tony called every evening to say hi to Joy before I put her down for the night. I would call him back and we would talk for hours. I sent Tony a new photo of Joy and me, once a week. But it was hard, we deeply missed one another.

On February 14th, I released my sixth album entitled, 'Love Affair, Long Distance' It was a very special album with four cuts which were each sixteen minutes long. It had a new rock and roll kind of twist, to a very upbeat disco rhythm. It was a ballad of a fairytale love story. But the best thing about the recording was I sang my love to Tony on every cut and he, as well as the whole world knew it.

March 2nd, I heard the news my sixth album topped the number one spot. I also received a letter from the Academy Awards Institute, informing me 'Life, Passion and Fame' had won eight academy award nominations. The ceremony was to be held in Hollywood on March 29th, at 5:00pm. I was also asked to perform the hit single from the film, 'Come Lay with Me.'

Even with all this news I was still going mad. I got a sick feeling every time I thought of Kathy being with Tony. Oh, God! I cringed at the thought of her touching him! In order to cope with the thought of Tony and Kathy performing love scenes together on screen, I buried myself in work and my little Joy. Then, I had a brainstorm and decided to go on a four-month, twenty city world-wide tour. It was scheduled to begin on April 1st, at the London Coliseum because I needed to see Tony, and this was the way to do it. I ended at Shay Stadium in New York, on July 4th, with a planned blow-out concert.

March 29th, the night of the Academy Awards, I was back in shape and dressed to kill. As I walked up the red carpet with Jimmy and Bobby, on either arm, through the flashing of the cameras, I wished Tony was by my side. He was nominated for best actor, but his current shooting schedule would not allow him to be present. I also felt a little bad we would miss our nightly call, for the first time since he left. I dismissed my sad feelings and jumped right back into the mood. As soon as we entered the doors I thought, "Screw you, Frank! I made it here without you. Then I got nervous. I turned to Jimmy and in a low voice, "Jimmy! What if I don't win? God forbid! I'll look like a fool!"

As we were escorted to our seats Jimmy squeezed my hand, "Did you bring some cocaine?"

I looked at him as we took our seats, "Yes, I have some."

"Good, now go to the lady's room, snort some and just relax. You'd be doing us both a favor."

I looked at him, Bobby and then at my shaking hands, "You're right! I'll be right back."

Now mind you, I was not a drug addict. I was a municipal user only, but that night was my first exception.

It was 7:00pm when a runner came to me with a note. I was being asked to come backstage, to prepare for my performance. I kissed Jimmy and Bobby for luck, and then followed the runner backstage.

American Goddess

I was looking like a queen in my full length golden laced, soft midnight black satin gown, with my trademark slit up the center seam. I knocked them dead as I sang 'Come Lay with Me!' I ended the song to a five-minute standing ovation; then, the announcements came. I won for best song of the year, best screenplay and best leading lady. I was flying so high! I was on top of the world that night! I walked out of there with three Academy Awards for myself and one for Tony. I was so excited and the only person I wanted to see was Tony; so, I decided to skip the celebration party and go home to call him. Believe it or not, Tony was anxiously waiting for my call and we talked one hour past our normal time.

The next morning I was working in my study on my next screenplay with my right hand and playing with Joy with my left hand when I received a call. To my surprise, it was Dominick Giovanetti on the other end of the line. I stopped what I was doing, "Dominick, it's so nice to hear from you."

"Christina, it's good to hear your voice. I want to congratulate you on your great success and your new family."

Happily, "Thank you Dominick that means so much to me to hear you say that. You're a very special friend."

Dominick chuckled, "My beautiful Christina, I'm so pleased you feel that way because I'm in town right now as we speak. I am here to do some business with your uncle, tomorrow night as a matter of fact. That is why I would be very pleased if you would join me for dinner tonight."

I was stunned and all I could say was, "Tonight, Dominick? I have the baby, and I'm trying to get ready for a trip abroad tomorrow. I don't think I can make it."

"Christina, I think tonight would be a good time to renegotiate our contract."

"Would it make any difference if I said, I was happily married?"

He chuckled again, "My dear Christina, could you be turning me down?"

I quickly replied, "No Dominick, you're my guardian angel and I would never turn you down." I swallowed my heart, "Would it be acceptable to you, if I asked you to have your driver pick me up here at 9:00pm after my little girl is asleep?"

With an authoritative tone, "That would be pleasing to me, until 9:00 then. Good day, Christina,"

When I hung up the phone, I grabbed Joy and began to cry. I knew I had no choice but to meet with Dominick and it was killing me.

That night after Tony said goodnight to Joy, I said, "Tony, I have some last-minute things I have to straighten out with the orchestra tonight. So, don't wait up for me honey. I'll just call you tomorrow before we leave."

"No Christina, I want you to call me no matter what time you get in. You are my wife. I'll miss saying goodnight."

American Goddess

Trying to be reassuring, "Oh Tony, I truly love you with all my heart baby."

His reply was blunt, "You just remember that! I don't like other men being around you without me being there. That's why I wish you would cancel the tour and just come spend some time with me."

"Tony, we need the money. You know the business is not stable enough to support itself yet. So once again, the mighty buck is still the bottom line."

"You're right and I have to agree with you. I guess that's why I love you so much."

"I love you too Tony. Now, I have to get going if I'm going to get back."

We ended the call and I put Joy to bed. I told Jimmy the same thing I told Tony when I left the house that night.

I felt like dirt when I climbed into the back seat of Dominick's Limo. I looked back at our home as the driver drove down the driveway away from the house and my heart screamed out in fear, "Don't leave your home! Stay here safe with Joy in your arms!" But I knew I could not heed the cry of my heart. I felt myself wanting to scream out, "Tony, help me! God, help me!" But there was no help for me that night as I willingly allowed myself to be raped by this man, over and over.

As I casually glanced at the clock on the nightstand, I thought of Tony waiting for my call. It was 4:00am when Dominick had finally had enough, and it was 5:00am when the limo dropped me off at my front door. I stood there by the door for a short time with my soul wounded, naked and ashamed. It took great courage for me to walk up those steps and open that door.

When I did open the door, Jimmy was waiting in his underwear and ran to me, "Where have you been? Tony has had me calling all over for you."

As he talked, I leaned up against the wall, slid down to my knees and just lost it. I started crying and it seemed like I could not stop. Jimmy stopped talking and grabbed my arm, "Christina, what is it, baby? What happened to you?" Starting to cry, "Stop crying and tell me what's wrong?"

I stopped crying, thought very quickly, "I witnessed a car accident last night and the parents of these two little twin baby boys were killed. So, I stayed at the hospital with them until they were picked up by child welfare." I thought, "A little over dramatic, but not bad considering all the stress I'm under."

Sympathetically, "You poor thing, why didn't you call?"

"I was so shook-up Jimmy, it didn't cross my mind. Would you please call Tony and tell him what happened, while I try to compose myself in the bathroom."

When I left for the bathroom, I was praying Tony would buy the story coming from Jimmy first. I knew Jimmy would elaborate on my state of mind before I had to talk to Tony. Oh God! I hated lying to Tony, but I knew if I told him the truth, I would be pushing him right into Kathy's open arms. And no way was I letting that happen! So, I lied through my teeth when I spoke with Tony. He seemed to believe my story and was overly concerned for my well-being. But he was still upset for my inconsiderate behavior by not calling; so, I apologized, and we made plans to meet at his suite in London at six o'clock the following night. We said I love you and goodbye. I hung up the phone and went to the shower to scrub the filth from my body. Then I went to the bedroom, climbed in bed at 5:57am and cried my heart out.

At 9:00am I grabbed Joy, four suitcases, one bottle of champagne and headed for the airport.

I slept during the whole flight to London that day as Jimmy and Nanny Sue, took care of Joy. I was still tired when we got there. It was 11:00am April 1st, when Joy, Nanny Sue, Jimmy, and I, settled down in Tony's suite at the Regency in downtown London. I searched for telltale signs of Kathy being there and found none. Then I thought, as I waited for Tony to come in, "Oh, God, how do I face him? Will he be able to tell that I have broken the sanctity of our marriage? Will he see it in me, feel it in me?" I stopped my mind dead and thought, "I'll play this one by ear."

Tony did not come in until 2:00am the following morning. When he did come in, I had been sitting up waiting at the door and biting off all my nails, "Hi Tony, I'm sitting here in the living room in the dark."

He walked into the living room, "What are you doing sitting up in the dark?"

"Waiting for you to come in."

"I'm sorry I'm so late. Kathy and I got hung up on a couple of scenes,"

"Until 2:00am?" A phone call would have been nice."

"I just didn't think of it. I was so busy," he replied sarcastically.

"Oh, it's like that, is it? You're just playing some kind of a game because of the other night. Well, I think that sucks and I'm going to bed! Goodnight." Then, I stormed off to the bedroom and Tony never came in.

By 5:00am I was crying again. I wanted him to come to me so badly, but he didn't.

Later on that morning, he was playing with Joy when I came into the living room. I kissed Joy and Tony on the forehead, "Good morning Tony. I'm sorry I stormed off like I did last night. It was childish of me."

He picked up his jacket, "I won't be able to see you until after your performance for the Royal Family tonight. So, I'll meet you backstage just before we are to be presented to the Queen and Prince."

He turned and walked out the door and I thought, "Oh, God, he must know. Somehow, he knows. Could I have been set up by Frank and Dominick? Oh well, I'll figure it out tomorrow. Right now, I have to prepare to perform for the British Royal Family."

That evening, my performance was remarkable. Tony showed up right on cue, just as he said he would. We met the Queen, went to Buckingham Palace for a Queen's Ball in my honor and we acted like nothing was wrong. We arrived home at 1:00am, and Tony said, "Christina, I can't stay here with you tonight." The tears started to roll down his eyes, "You're lying to me and I can't stand it. I love you, why did you lie to me?"

I grabbed his hand, "Tony, I love you too and I can't let you walk out on me like this. If we talk, I know we can work it out."

Biting his lip, "I know you were out in a limo and at the Regency the night of your car accident."

My response was quick, "Tony, if you will listen to me, I can clear this all up."

"I'm listening."

"Yes, you're right I lied to you and I'm deeply sorry I did. But it was not for what you're thinking. Do you remember asking me once, how I got away with talking to Frank, like I did?"

"Yes, but what does that have to do with the other night?"

"I'm getting to that. You see when I was in Italy, my Uncle Dominick took care of me. He almost went to war with Frank because of what he did to me. Well, Uncle Dominick was in town that night and since it was the only chance, I might get to see him, I went. I just didn't want you to know I had two uncles in the mob."

Tony pulled me to him, "Please don't hide anything from me again."

I kissed him, "I won't Tony, I promise I won't. Now please come to bed with me."

After that, we had an incredible night of love making and we were back together again. We had four more days of heaven together that April. Every time the three of us could be together, we were. The passion and desire of being together again was stronger than ever before. We took courage in the knowledge Tony's film would be finished in eight months and he would be done with Frank's contract for good. That is when we could be a family again.

Then, the time came for the tour to go on the road. As we said our tearful goodbyes, I thought, "If I could get us through that one, I could get us through anything."

We sent Joy back to Malibu with Nanny Sue, and it was back on the road for me and back on the phone for us.

It was 7:00am July 4th, 1978, when Jimmy and I entered NBC studios, in downtown Manhattan. I was appearing on the Good Day Show, with Jane Smalley. Jane was interviewing me, and her questions were to stay on the topics of my July 4 blowout concert at Shay Stadium, and the unveiling of a sixty-foot billboard of me, in a very sensual pose with mike in hand. The billboard was part of the concert promotion, being held at 1:00pm that afternoon in Times Square. She was also to ask me about hosting this year's special summer International Music Awards Ceremony in LA on July 20th, and how I felt about my twelve nominations.

American Goddess

During the interview, I explained to Jane my concert performance was the hottest thing going all summer and I was incredible. I also told her how I arranged and signed a twenty-million-dollar deal, the first contract of its kind with HBO. The deal included the live broadcast of my performances exclusively on their cable channel and the recording of the concert live for my next soundtrack. It would have all my prior number one hits, and two new cuts.

Jane and I were having a particularly good interview as I gave her all this information. It had been fun, right up until her last question, "Christina, may I ask you one more question I know the whole nation would like to hear you answer?"

Feeling uncomfortable yet, still smiling, "Sure, Jane."

"How do you cope with the fact; your husband is off in another country filming a very racy movie with his ex-fiancée?"

I smiled confidently, "It's not hard to cope with it at all, Jane. I'm Christina Powers! Once a man has been with me, he could never go elsewhere."

"But..."

I stood up before she could ask another embarrassing question, "Thank you Jane, but I must run, I have a lot to do today." I looked into the cameras and winked, "Good Day America."

Once the cameras were off us, I glared at Jane, "That was the most pressing question you could come up with?" Then I turned and walked out.

Jimmy and I left NBC studios, hopped in the limo, and headed for Shay Stadium. It was a beautiful warm, sunny morning around 8:00am, when we went to check on the setup for my performance, before the unveiling of my sixty-foot poster in time square at 1:00pm. I was staying on top of everything. Tonight's performance had to be hotter than anything I'd done yet and I was going to see to it that it was.

The moment the limo left us off at the stadium, I noticed we were standing right in front of the players' entrance and I froze as I was hit with a rush of a thousand flashbacks of the night, I ran through the cold New York October rain, across the parking lot to these doors right in front of me to find Johnny in the hall devastated. Jimmy grabbed my hand, looked at me strangely, "Are you all right?"

I took a deep breath, "Yes, I'm fine," as I slapped Jimmy on his ass, "Come on, let's go to work." With that I put it out of my mind, and we headed for the players' entrance.

When we reached the doors, we were talking, and Jimmy opened one door wide for me to enter. As I began to step in the doorway, I froze again. Only this time as if I saw a ghost! I turned as white as a ghost, when I realized Johnny was standing right in front of me. When our eyes met, we were both stunned. Instantly all the banished forgotten feelings came flooding into my consciousness and I became weak. I reached for Jimmy's hand and stepped back so Johnny could pass. When he came out into the sun light, I noticed he was carrying a small child in his arms. As he passed, he calmly looked at me, "Christy, it's nice to see you, you're looking great."

Somehow, I managed to say, "John, it's good to see you too."

Then a woman came out of the doorway behind him, reached her hand for mine, "Hi! Ms. Powers, it's nice to meet you." Smiling ear to ear, "I'm Mary Everett, John's wife."

Somehow, I snapped myself out of a state of shock, reached out, took her hand and hugged her warmly, "It's very nice to meet you also, Mary." I kissed her cheek, released my friendly embrace, reached for Johnny's free hand, shook it, "Oh my God, John! This must be your son."

Johnny looked at me with the smile of a proud father, "Yes! This is my son, John Jr."

As he spoke, I looked down at Mary's left hand, to see her wedding ring and it wasn't there. My ring! Johnny's grandmother's ring, the one he gave to me, was not on her finger! I quickly glanced up into Johnny's eyes and he acknowledged my discovery with a wink. The moment he did my heart cried out for him. I wanted to hold him and scream out, "Johnny! I love you! I miss you! Please forgive me! I need you!" But I stopped myself because, I could see the same thing in his eyes and our emotions were now forbidden by our new lives.

I reached into my purse, "I would love it if you guys would be my guests at my performance tonight." I pulled out six front row tickets and a card with my personal phone number on it. I gave them all to Mary, "Mary, please take these tickets. There are six of them so please bring some friends." I kissed her cheek again, "And Mary, my personal card is in with those tickets, so if you guys are ever in Malibu or if you ever need anything, please call me."

Mary took my gift, "Christina, thank you. You're just as nice as John's mom says you are, and we'd love to come to your show tonight."

We said our goodbyes, and I watched Johnny walk away. As I stood there in a daze, Jimmy slapped me out of it with the palm of his hand on the back of my head, "You didn't even introduce me. You just left me standing there, holding the fucking door like some idiot, as you start having a conversation with your ex-lover and his wife."

"I'm sorry Jimmy. I was completely caught off guard. I never even thought I might run into Johnny, while we were here."

We started to walk through the dark hallways, toward the player's dugout, when Jimmy said, "Are you sure you didn't come here in the middle of baseball season, just so you might run into him?"

I replied a mischievous, "Hmm, I never thought of that. Sometimes your mind is more devious then mine, Jimmy."

Jimmy laughed, "You're right, he is a stud! But I still think Tony is hotter looking."

American Goddess

I gave him no reply as we kept walking. We were just heading out onto the center of the ballfield where the stage was being worked on, when it hit me like a lightning bolt shooting through my body. I could see, feel and hear the whole thing in my mind. It was like vision or quick dream, in a three-dimensional image, with lights and sound. I turned to Jimmy, grabbed his shoulders and shouted, **"I'm a fucking genius**!" Then I kissed his cheek and shouted, "Quick, come with me!"

As I started to run toward the stage, I could hear Jimmy saying, as he ran to catch up to me, "Here we go again!"

When I reached the stage, I found Ann Markel my stage manager, and started shouting orders at her, like, "Ann! I want you to cut a twelve-foot hole in the center of the stage and have it mounted on a forty-foot, hydraulic lift. Then run a cable one hundred feet above the stage and mount six super spotlights on it so that they will shine straight down on me as the stage lifts me up. I also want six sets of super spotlights to hit me from every corner of the stadium." Turning to her I added, "And I want it by tonight's show! You got that."

She gave me an overwhelmed look, "You got it, boss."

I found Bobby and told him just how and where I wanted the lights, cameras and stage props to be set up and placed. After that, I ran over to Joe Cole, "Joe, how well do your people have the two new numbers down?"

Joe smiled, "We're right on key with them, Christina."

"Good, because I'm going to have a new number for you guys in one hour and I want it down pat by our 5:00pm rehearsals! You got it?"

He looked at me as if I were nuts, then smiled, "Yes ma'am!"

Then Jimmy and I sat down with pen and paper and went to work. As I started to write on the paper, I first wrote the words down. Then I started to write the music and melody, right over the top of the words. As I did, Jimmy looked at me with amazement, "Oh my, God! You are a fucking genius! How in the world do you do that?"

I looked at him and smiled, "It's not that hard Jimmy, I know the song by heart."

Shaking his head, "You are nuts, you know that? What the hell are we doing this now for anyway? We're supposed to be in the city at 1:00pm, remember?"

I finished writing, "Were not going. Now let's spice these lyrics and melody up and we'll have a hit record by tonight."

Jimmy read the lyrics, "Christina, are you sure you know what you're doing?"

"Yes! I am writing my third and last encore for tonight's performance. Now shut up, sit down and help me."

He snatched the paper from me, "Where did you get this song from?"

American Goddess

I grabbed it back, "It's the letter I wrote to Johnny. Do you remember me telling you about how I mailed my ring back to Johnny, and in the envelope, I also placed a goodbye letter? Well this is that letter."

With concern, "Do you realize what these words are saying?"

I looked into his eyes, "It's a song, so I don't want to hear one more word about it, okay."

Jimmy sat down with a puss on his face, "Christina, I can't let you do this without trying to tell you to please, think about what singing a song like this, might feel like to Tony?"

I grabbed his hand, looked deep into his eyes, "Jimmy, this is the last time I am going to say this. It's just a song." And on that note, we went to work.

It was as if I were possessed. I had to have it done, and perfected, for that night's show. Johnny was going to be there and that was my driving force. By 5:00pm that afternoon, we were rehearsing 'The Love I Lost' and we were rehearsing it the way only Christina Powers could. I had everything set to go, from my wardrobe to every step I made on the stage. It was all choreographed, timed and setup by everyone working that night and it was done down to my every detail. We had the rest of the show down pat, so I had us all working on and perfecting just this one song for that night's show. We worked on that project from 10:00am, that morning and by eight o'clock that night we had a masterpiece ready to go.

The show started at 9:00pm on the dot and it was turning out to be exactly the way I planned it. The **hottest** show I had ever performed. I kept one-hundred-thousand fans, all screaming for more. And I gave it to them! One hot set after another. I could see Johnny and Mary sitting with Steve Grady, his date and another couple. I could hardly keep my eyes off Johnny as he watched my performance with amazement.

Then it was time for my third and last encore of the night and the stage curtains opened for me one more time. I stood there looking like a goddess, in my emerald blue skintight, full length gown, with a slit up the center seam. My long wavy black hair was draped over my shoulders and I wore tear shaped diamond earrings. My makeup was divine, and I had on blue high heels to match my gown, with clear silk stockings.

Then the orchestra started to play and as the whole country and most of Europe, watched on HBO, I began to sing my heart out just to Johnny.

The rhythm started very slowly with the string section of the orchestra. I began to sing very slowly and softly. The lyrics recalled a fiery and gentle love, of a time passed.

"With the slamming of the door, gone was, the love I lost. Our love was so strong, so pure and meant to last a lifetime, but now in reflections of broken mirror pieces, shattered lives appear before me. And in the eyes of the love I lost, the pain was too hard to bear. We destroyed our love with such viciousness that there was no innocents to be

found. And I knew we could never love again. The love I lost. The love I lost. In anguish my heart told me I had to be strong to survive, the love I lost. Oh, the love I lost."

As I sang, I gently floated around the stage with all the stage lights flashing on me. "I must take the future into my hands and live life by my rules, in order to survive, the love I lost. I will live my life with passion and have lovers as I desire, and I will survive, yes, I will survive, the love I lost. I know the memory of this love, and the pain it has caused, will always be within me, but I must banish you from my thoughts, in order to survive, the love I lost. The Love I Lost.

As the tempo of the rhythm increased, so did mine, until I was belting it out with every ounce of my strength, "I will never look back, but I will always ask myself why? Why, did I lose, the love I lost? How, did I lose, the love I lost? No matter how many lovers I may hold, or how many roads I must travel, you will always be, the love I lost. The Love I Lost. No one will ever take your place in my heart, and you will always be, the love I lost. The Love I Lost."

Then, the thunder of the orchestra's tempo increased again, and I looked deeper inside myself to find the strength to match its rumble with that of my angelic voice. All at once the center of the stage began to rise with me on it. As it reached its full span of forty feet, the edges of the circle began to spin with thousands of red and white sparkles, which showered down upon the stage below.   I reached the height of my range with my last angelic note and held it, "I will look back after all the lovers and years of my life, and ask myself why? Why I lost, the love I lost. The love I lost." While I sang the super spotlights, all hit me at once and my emerald blue gown began to glisten, as it lit up the night. With the help of mirrors an image of me still singing rose off the platform as the lights appeared to be lifting me. Then my image just disintegrated as if I were being beamed up by angels into heaven. With that the skies above the stadium became filled with grand finale fireworks, which lasted for twenty minutes. The whole place went wild. People were screaming and passing out all over the place. The crowd grew so excited the guards had to block the stage to keep them from coming after me. I had to be helicoptered out of the place before they could quiet the crowd down and manage a safe evacuation. It was an incredible performance.

Johnny knew I was singing to him and so did anyone who knew anything about my life. And that was the whole free world. Later that night back at my hotel room, I received a bouquet of two dozen red roses, with one white one in the middle and a note, which read, "Ditto!" I held those flowers in my hands and cried. When I finally got around to calling Tony, it was 3:00am. There was no answer, so I drifted off to sleep. The next day the fame of my performance made me a first class, worldwide, bonafide sex symbol. And every radio station in the nation wanted 'The Love I Lost' as soon as possible.

American Goddess

I flew back to the West Coast, to my little Joy and to prepare for hosting the 1978, International Music Awards, on July 20th. I tried to reach Tony all week, but he was never in and he never called me back. Then on July 17th, it was spattered all over the front page of every tabloid in the country. The headlines read, **"Tony Demetrees and Kathy Brown appear to be having a very explicit public affair, as they hit the nightspots all over London."**

When I read them, it felt like a knife piercing my soul. Then I called the London studio and told them who I was, then said, "I want Tony on the phone, 'Now!' It's an emergency." After having to wait ten minutes, I was steaming even hotter, when someone came to the phone and said that he was not in, but I could reach him at Miss. Brown's personal number. I asked for it and the bastard wouldn't give it out. If I could have reached through the phone, I would have strangled the asshole. I hung up and called my attorney, Lesley Stine, "Lesley, I want you to serve Tony with divorce papers, 'Now!'" I was humiliated for the entire world to see and I was not taking it lying down, if you get my drift.

July 19th, at 1:00am, the phone rang. I picked it up, "Hello."

It was finally Tony, "Christina, what the hell are you serving me with divorce papers for?"

"Now you call. You son of a bitch! After I've served you with divorce papers! Well, now I don't want to speak to you."

With a desperate tone, "Christina, wait! Please don't hang up on me. We have to talk."

Angrily, "There is nothing left to talk about. You made your bed with that bitch, now sleep in it. Do you know I have to host the I.M.A.'s tomorrow night and because of your behavior I somehow have to be able to hold my head up high, in the midst of my disgrace? So why don't you just talk to my lawyer?"

He cried out, "Christina, I love you, baby. Please talk to me!"

I shouted back, "You should have thought of that before you climbed into bed with that slut." Then I hung up the phone, took it off the hook, laid down on the bed and cried my heart out. I was so hurt by the fact Tony slept with Kathy that I was blinded to anything I might have done to cause it.

It was July 20th, at 9:00pm when I walked out onto the stage of the Crystal Palace, in the heart of LA to host the 1978, special summer International Music Awards. I was dressed to kill! I wore a milky white, silver trimmed Stargenzy Original, full flowing, calf length gown, with a diamond tiara in my hair and matching diamond earrings with silver high heels.

I caught sight of the audience and my heart became filled with surprise and warmth, as the audience rose to a cheering standing ovation. All my friends and colleagues in the entertainment industry as well as the whole country were applauding and supporting me. The lights of the cameras flashed wildly every time I came on stage. I also swept the awards that night with an unprecedented twelve International Music Awards. It was a fantasy lived.

As I walked through the mob of screaming fans and hundreds of press, with their flashing cameras I had Jimmy, Bobby and Joe, all around to buffer me from the onslaught of press and their questions. From out of this mass of confusion, came Tony. He grabbed my arm with forceful power. Then right there in front of all these people he shouted loud enough for most to hear, "Christina, you have got to listen to me."

I calmly replied, "Tony, this is not the place or the time, for this. Can't we discuss this later?"

"Only if I'm coming home with you tonight, Christina, baby, I walked off the set. I'm home for you and Joy now."

With that statement I really got pissed off, "Tony, you're not coming home with me tonight and now is not the time to walk off the set. I'm not going to be here to pick up the pieces for you."

With a disbelieving tone, "Why did you do this to us? I loved you! I trusted you."

Anger radiated from my eyes, "You got it wrong, Tony. You did it when you slept with that tramp."

"No, Christina, I'm not the one who slept with their ex-lover first."

I snapped back in anger, "I never slept with anyone but you since the day we were married."

His voice began to break up, "What about the song you sang to him?"

"It was just a song Tony. I didn't sleep with him."

Tony cried out, "Just a song! Just a song! You cried your heart out to him for the whole world to hear. You told the world I would always be second best in your heart! Your second choice! How did you think I'd feel? Happy, because maybe you will sell a million copies? No Christina, you humiliated me! You broke my fucking heart and then you ask me why I slept with her. You put me in her bed and I'm just as fucking human as you are! I'm begging you baby, forgive me and I'll forgive you!" Tears fell from his eyes, "I love you Christina, and I don't want to live without you. Don't do this to us, don't destroy our family."

I looked so lovingly into his eyes and I thought, "Tony, I never wanted to think about how you might feel over the song. I'm sorry too baby and I will take you back." Then I looked at the mob of reporters all around us and thought, "Not in front of all these people, I have to be the Queen." I felt as though I was still being humiliated, so I ripped my arm out of his hand, "Just get away from me right now, Tony." Then I turned and began to push my way through the crowd.

American Goddess

As I did, I heard a blood curdling cry, "Christina, I love you!"

I slowly began to turn, as if in slow motion and I heard someone yell, "He's got a gun!"

My eyes caught Tony's and he had a gun in his hand. I screamed, "Tony, no!" At that moment he pulled the trigger, **bang**! The blood from his head splattered everywhere. I screamed! **"Tonyyyy! Noooll!"**

I ran to his side with my heart exploding in pain and I cried out, **"Tony! My love! No! No! Tony! What have I done to you my love? Tony!"**

I was in **hysterics** as I tried to stop the blood with my white gown. My Tony was lying in a pool of blood and he was dead. I was screaming and shaking wildly until someone tried to take me from his side. With that I lost it and started to fight everyone who came near us. Then, four strong men tackled me, and I felt a sharp pain. After a few more minutes of fighting these men, I began to feel dizzy. **Then there was nothing**.

CHAPTER 8

I woke up three weeks later in the hospital. It seemed I had gone temporarily mad, and they had to keep me sedated. Every time I did come out of my sedation, I became physically and verbally combative, so they would shoot me back up with the tranquilizers. I guess it was the only way my mind could cope with what I saw, felt and experienced. There are no words for it. It was simply horrendous. How I lived through Tony's death and the state of shock I went into was a miracle in itself. When I did finally regain my senses and realized I was in a hospital bed, I also realized at that same moment, somehow, I had to face what I had done. I quickly looked around that hospital room and thought, "If I had only said what I truly felt, I'd still have my Tony here with me now. If I had only!"

But the millions of what ifs I had done this or said that which ran through my mind didn't make a damn bit of difference. They could not change what happened. Nothing could bring Tony back to me. He was dead and I was alone with Joy. This was my reality, and I knew it. I thought, "Oh, God! How do I face my own daughter? I killed her father. How do

American Goddess

I hold her in my arms and tell her that her mother is the murderess who caused the death of her father? How do I go on? Why should I go on? How do I get anywhere from here when all I want to do is die?" As I lay in that bed, I knew I had no answers, to these questions.

I was discharged on August 20ᵗʰ, 1978, from the hospital, one month to the day of Tony's death. My discharge came only after one week of convincing my new psychiatrist, I was able to handle going home. He put me under constant surveillance for that week, but he was sweet about it. He truly cared about me as a patient and I know he felt what I was going through. He tried so desperately to help me in that week, and I appreciated that, but at the same time he wasn't letting me go home until he was sure I could handle it, and that, I didn't appreciate. By the end of the week, I had him semi-fooled. I told him all the things I knew he wanted to hear in order for me to be discharged; only I was never truly candid with him. I just wanted out. So finally, He felt it would be beneficial for my recovery to send me home, but only under the close supervision of my dear Jimmy. I was also put on a regiment of anti-depressants and three office visits with the Doctor per week.

When Jimmy picked me up in the limo that day at 10:00am from the hospital, he came alone. This was at my request. I had to speak with Jimmy alone. After my chair was wheeled through the hospital, even though there was nothing wrong with my legs, I was swamped by what seemed to be every camera and reporter in the nation, all shouting at me! I buried my face under Jimmy's arms as we pushed our way to the waiting limo, where we flung ourselves into the back seat. As our limo drove away from the mob, I was shaking! When we were out of sight, I reached over and grabbed Jimmy's hand. I looked deeply and sincerely into his eyes as my tears slowly rolled down my cheeks, "Jimmy, you have got to help me. You're the only person in this world I can count on now." My tears began to fall faster, "Because Jimmy, I can't handle this. I'm out of the hospital, but I still can't handle this. I don't know how I'm dealing with it and I don't know how I'm going to. So please, Jimmy, please be with me!"

Jimmy's tears began to fall with mine and as he looked back at me through his tears, "Christina, I love you. This is me, your Jimmy! I will always be here for you, you're my girl. I'd never let you down."

We embraced, "Thank you Jimmy, but you have to do me another big favor."

"Anything Christina, what is it?" He cried.

I pulled back from him, turned away feeling just a little bit ashamed of myself, "You have to keep taking care of Joy for me."

He pulled my cheek back toward him to once again make eye contact, "Of course I'll keep taking care of Joy, Christina. Bobby and I have already moved in lock, stock and barrel. We are also on top of everything at Powers Incorporated, so don't you worry about anything but getting better. Okay?"

I kissed his cheek, "Jimmy, it's not just that. I need you too." I stopped. I could hardly say the words, but I knew I had to, "Jimmy, you have to keep Joy away from me. I can't see her."

He looked at me strangely, "What do you mean you can't see Joy?"

I grabbed his hand desperately, "I can't explain it to you because I don't understand it myself. I just can't look at her. I can't touch her. I can't smile at her." Then, I lost it and really started to cry.

Jimmy hugged me sobbing, "All right Christina, all right."

As we held each other tightly I said, "Thank you Jimmy, I love you." I stayed in Jimmy's strong comforting embrace the rest of the way home.

The limo entered the opening gates and proceeded through the wooded, winding, driveway up to my wedding gift. Once James brought the limo to a stop in front of the mansion, I had Jimmy go right in to make sure Nanny Sue and Bobby were not downstairs waiting for me with Joy. When the coast was clear, I opened the limo door and slowly climbed out. When I looked up at the mansion, I realized I was standing at the same angle as the day Tony lovingly pulled me out of his `59 Caddie, to see Barbara's so-called new home. That's when I began to feel a little shaky.

Jimmy ran over to me and helped steady me on my feet. Then, Oh God! I began walking up those steps and over the threshold which Tony carried me over. Then it was into the house Tony led me so happily through by my hand. The same furniture was still there. My heart began to **break** when I remembered how we had planned to decorate it together. I could not hold back my tears any longer; they just streamed down my face as I walked through every room. I had no expression, no sound, just tears. Every room I went into I saw Tony's face, I felt Tony's touch and I smelt Tony's scent. I walked straight into our room to the bed where Tony and I slept, played, talked, made love and first fell in love. I took all my clothing off, laid down on Tony's side of our bed, squeezed his pillow tightly and cried, "Oh God, Tony! Forgive me!"

Jimmy came in every few minutes to check on me and see if I needed anything. But I would just wave him out. Then, I cried even harder. The pain was so unbearable! I missed Tony so much. I finally cried myself to sleep sometime around 11:00pm that night.

The next morning, I felt a gentle shake on my shoulder as I heard Jimmy say, "Christina, come on its 10:00am, time to get up. I have a nice breakfast here for you, eggs, bacon, toast and hot coffee."

I woke up from my tear induced sleep, stretched, yawned and wiped my eyes, "Oh Jimmy, why did you wake me?"

American Goddess

Jimmy kissed my forehead, "I didn't want to wake you, but you have a doctor's appointment at 1:00pm so you really do have to get up."

I sat up in bed, "Oh shit, I don't want to go see the Doctor, I don't want to do anything."

Jimmy encouraged me, "Come on, get up and eat something. Then go get cleaned up and you will start to feel a lot better. You know you have to see the doctor, or you might have to go back in the hospital."

Shaking my head, "I'll try Jimmy, but I can't make any promises."

Sadly, he said, "The hospital sent over your mail. There is a bedroom full of cards and letters all wishing you well. Would you like me to bring some in for you to read?"

Sarcastically I replied, "Wishing me well! I don't need anyone to wish me anything."

Jimmy wore a nervous expression, "Christina, I have some bad news for you."

"Bad news! Ha! Like that's new. What is it?" I asked with disgust.

He walked over by the windows and opened the curtains. I could see it was a cloudy dark dreary morning and that made me want to stay in bed all the more. Jimmy walked back over to me, sat on the bed and very sadly said, "The whole horrible scene was caught by Hollywood Tonight's news team on video. It has been replayed all over the country, maybe even the world."

I instantly got a sick feeling, "Thanks Jimmy, I really didn't need to know that right now did I? Now get out of here and let me get ready."

Jimmy shook his head sadly, "I had to tell you. They played the film again last night along with some footage of us leaving the hospital yesterday. I just don't want you to see it by chance, without knowing the film is out there."

Realizing how hard that had to be for Jimmy to tell me, "Thank you Jimmy, I don't mean to snap at you."

Jimmy kissed me sympathetically then left me alone. When he closed the door I got out of bed, threw on some old blue jeans, a gray sweat top, an old pair of black sneakers, ran a brush through my scraggly hair and I was ready to go.

It was 2:30pm when I climbed into the limo after my useless appointment with The Doctor. As James began to drive us home, I pushed the button to bring down the partition glass so I could speak directly to him, "James, did you go to Tony's funeral?"

James glanced at me through the rear-view mirror, "Yes ma'am, I did."

"James, would you take me there now?" I nervously asked.

Politely he answered, "Are you sure you want to go there by yourself mam?"

"Yes James, I'm very sure."

"Whatever you wish, ma'am."

His reply was as dignified as always, but for some reason I felt uncomfortable with it now, "Two things I would like to request from you James. First, please call me Christina from now on. Second, please tell me what Tony's funeral was like?"

American Goddess

His eyelids lifted nervously, "Thank you, I'd be honored to call you Christina." Then as if he felt totally comfortable calling me Christina, he gave me a fatherly wink as he glanced back at me through the mirror and calmly added, "Christina, it was a beautiful funeral. Thousands of his friends and fans came to show their love and respect. When they all left, a small group of close friends and family stayed behind to pay a special private homage to his memory. We all prayed for your speedy recovery as well."

"Thank you, James, I needed to know that."

James pulled into the cemetery, drove to some burial sites, and stopped, "We're here, Christina. It's the third row in on the left and the ground is still loose. The missus and I stopped by yesterday."

"Thank you, I will be back shortly," I climbed out of the limo and headed for Tony's burial site.

As I walked past the headstones looking for Tony's, a soft rain began to fall. When I reached the third row in; I turned to my left and there it was, Tony's gravesite. The stone read, "**Here lies Tony Demetrees, who was all heart. This man was loved by millions!**"

I knelt in front of that stone, "Tony, I'm so sorry." As soon as I said these words my tears began to fall. Then I took off the medallion I had found in Lake Tahoe, scooped up some dirt and began to bury it with my Tony. As I patted the last of the dirt down over the medallion, I cried out, "Tony, can you hear me? I'm sorry baby! Oh God, help me! I want my Tony back!" At that moment I became a grieving widow. I threw myself on the loose wet soil and shouted at the dirt, "Tony! Please come back! Please Tony, I can't live like this without you! Tony, Tony, pleaseee forgive me MY BELOVED!"

As I screamed and cried these words, the drizzle turned into a torrential downpour. I laid there in the mud wailing my crushed heart out, until James grabbed me, pulled me up out of the mud, "Let's go home, Christina."

He led me back through the pouring rain, to the limo. When James opened the limo door for me, I tried to head back to Tony, but he grabbed my arm, "He's not there, Christina. He's in a better place now."

I looked at him through my muddy tears and somehow, I knew he was right. Tony was not in that grave. Then I climbed into the car and I didn't say another word as we drove away from the cemetery.

For the next two weeks, except for my six visits with the psychiatrist, I did nothing but stay in my bedroom. I did not want to talk to or see anyone. Jimmy was great he made sure everyone just gave me my space.

It was about 6:00pm on a Friday, when I just couldn't take the silence and those freaking anti-depressant pills anymore. Just taking the damn pills was depressing me. So, I threw them in the toilet and flushed it. I opened the medicine chest, reached up to the top shelf to a prescription bottle, opened it and took out my little brown bottle of cocaine. Then, for the first time since I started to use cocaine, I used it for more than just my shows. This time I was using it for me, and I took two snorts, one in each nostril. I climbed into the shower, cleaned up, put on some jeans, one of Tony's red flannel shirts, grabbed my purse, the keys to Tony's `59 Caddie, and I was going out.

I tried to sneak out through the mansion to the garage, but as I reached the garage door, Jimmy caught me, "Christina, you're up! Where are you going?"

"Hi Jimmy, I'm just going out for a ride. I have to get out of here for a while; I'm starting to go stir-crazy."

Jimmy smiled, "That's great, Christina. You need to get out. So where are you going?"

"It looks so nice out this evening I thought I'd go shopping for some new clothes."

Jimmy's smile grew wider, "That sounds like fun. How about I come with you?"

I kissed his cheek, "Jimmy, I really want to go alone. You don't mind, do you?"

His smile disappeared, "That's Okay, I don't have to come with you. Just be careful, all right?"

I kissed his cheek, "I love you Jimmy, and I'll be fine." Then I opened the door and headed for the Caddie.

When I pulled out of the driveway, I was heading for Rodeo Drive, and all the best shopping in Hollywood. As I turned onto Rodeo Drive, I noticed a blood red Mercedes Convertible sitting on top of a six-foot-high platform. I quickly turned into the car lot of a Mercedes dealership and drove over to it. I climbed out of the Caddie and walked over to the car on the platform. I walked around it then I went up the ramp to see the inside of this gorgeous car. It had two bucket seats and they were black leather. By the time I walked down the ramp, a tall, fairly attractive, blond haired man, in his late twenties, was standing there waiting for me. He shook my hand, "Hi! My name is Eddie Smith. Here is my card. I am the sales manager here at, Smith's Mercedes. Can I help you with anything?"

"This car," pointing to the convertible, "I'll take it."

Eddie cleared his throat as he looked at me in my old blue jeans, "Miss, this is an eighty-thousand-dollar automobile. Are you sure this is the car you want?"

I gave him a dirty look, "Mr. Smith, don't patronize me, just sell me the car. I'll pay you for it now and I'll have it picked up in the morning."

Eddie immediately apologized, "Please forgive me, Miss? I'm sorry I offended you."

My smile returned, "You're forgiven, Eddie. Now sell me the car."

He waved his arms graciously toward me, "Well follow me this way Miss, and I will draw up the paperwork."

When we reached Eddie's office, he invited me to sit down, "Okay, the first thing I need is for you to fill out this paperwork."

American Goddess

I put my hand on my hip impatiently, "Eddie, I really don't have time for this. May I please just sign my name and pay for the car. Maybe you could fill them out for me?"

"It depends on how you want to pay for the car."

"Well I can give you a check now or give you a credit card."

He smiled his reply, "If you put it on a credit card, then I can take care of it all for you." He looked at me 'kinda' funny, "You look awfully familiar Miss. Do I know you?"

I put down my Master Card as I winked, "Have you ever heard of Christina Powers?"

With a look of surprise, "I sure have, and I can't believe I didn't recognize you." Then he ran my card through his little machine, "Miss Powers, I hope you will forgive me for my bluntness, but I must say something." Looking a little nervous, "I am sorry for your recent loss and I know you're still grieving, but I would like to ask you if maybe when you're feeling a little better, I might be able to take you out for dinner some evening?"

I looked at him strangely, "Eddie, that was a number one move, and it took a lot of balls to make it." I took my credit card out of his hand and turned away leaving him speechless. When I reached his office door I turned back, took a card out of my purse and flicked it on his desk right down in front of him, "Eddie, call my personal secretary for the information you need. Then, take my address off the card and pick me up tomorrow at 7:00pm for dinner, and bring my car with you." Then I turned and left.

The evening was still young, so it was off to the biggest designer clothing center of the West Coast. By 11:00pm that night I had treated myself to a three-pound lobster feast, at Captain Ed's Seafood Palace. I also happened to spend thirty-thousand-dollars, on a whole new designer wardrobe, of the most outrageous styles of the day. I arranged for it all to be delivered the next morning. It was around midnight when I arrived home, so I left a note for Carman to deal with the morning's delivery. I told her to place the stuff in the guest room closet closest to my room for now. I went straight up to my bedroom and began to go through Tony's belongings. I thought it was time to give some of his things away. As I went through Tony's things, I came across some photos of us rafting at Lake Tahoe. I looked at the photos and my eyes began to water. But I just could not put the photos down. I just kept staring at them. I held them along with a pair of his pants to my breast, laid down on the bed and said as the tears fell, "Tony, I'll be with you soon my love." Then I cried myself to sleep again.

The next morning and most of that day I spent going through the rest of Tony's things. I packed up most of it and had it put away in storage up in the attic. Those I wanted to keep, I left in the closet. Like the suit Tony wore the night I met him and his bikini briefs. I just could not find it in my heart to pack these things away. As I was doing these things, sometime around 4:00pm Jimmy tapped on my bedroom door, "Christina, it's me, can I come in?"

I hollered out, "Come on in Jimmy, the door is unlocked."

American Goddess

He opened the door, stuck his head in, "Christina, I have Joy in my arms, and she's been looking for you."

I felt my heart begin to race and with fear in my voice, "Jimmy, please don't bring her in here. I can't see her yet."

"Christina, I am bringing your daughter in to be loved by her mother."

I got off the bed and ran into the bathroom, "Jimmy, get her away from me right now or I'll walk out of this house and never come back."

I heard Jimmy say to Bobby, "Here, take Joy back to Nanny Sue." After that he came over to the bathroom door and tried to open it. I opened the door for him, and he said, "What the hell kind of mother are you? Joy is your and Tony's daughter. Now straighten up your act and go see Joy before I do something I will regret."

I started to cry, "Jimmy, get out of here and stop trying to help me. I can't see her now. Why can't you understand that?"

"Because it makes no sense to me at all," he shouted. "Christina, she's your child and she needs her mother."

I screamed at him, "Jimmy, don't push me! Can't you see I killed Tony? I killed her father! How can I look at her and tell her that? I can't see her now! I just can't! So, don't ever do that to me again! I just need some time and I'm begging you to give me that time." I closed the bathroom door and said, as I cried, "Just go away Jimmy, please."

I heard him say, "Okay Christina, I'll give you your time," as the bedroom door shut.

I cried in that bathroom for the next hour. Then I reached for my cocaine, took four snorts, climbed in the shower and was ready for my dinner date by 6:45. Let me tell you, I was looking wild! I had my hair all flared out like I stuck my finger in a light socket, and I wore a blood red designer outfit. It was an all-leather pants, vest and jacket, skintight suit with chains connecting the slits on the sides of my pant legs and vest, along with my new red high heeled patent leather biker boots and I still looked hot. I snuck through the mansion and down to the front door. I snuck out because I was trying not to run into Jimmy.

As I walked around the front yard waiting for Eddie to come with my new car, I took two more snorts of cocaine. By the time Eddie pulled up the driveway to where I was standing, I was feeling no pain. He looked at me, smiled and said, "You look fantastic!" He climbed out of the driver's seat, "Here is your new 1979, Mercedes LX 750 Convertible."

"Tony, oh I'm sorry. Eddie, would you please drive?"

He escorted me to the passenger's door, opened it and held it for me. Then he closed it behind me and went back to the driver's seat. It was a beautiful, warm, evening, and Eddie had the top down. As he drove away, I asked, "So Eddie, where are you taking us?"

"I hope you like seafood," he enthusiastically answered. "I made an 8:00pm dinner reservation at Captain Ed's Seafood Palace, on Rodeo Drive,"

American Goddess

I smiled, "Well, you picked the right place, because I sure do like a good seafood dinner."

"You sure bought yourself a nice car here. It handles great." Eddie said as he looked over at me with adoring eyes.

"Thank you, Eddie." I looked up at the sky with its shades of red sunset rippling through the clouds, "It is such a beautiful evening, I could just lose myself in those clouds."

He glanced over at me, "Don't do that, I don't want you to miss any part of our date."

"I'll try to stick around for the good parts, Okay?"

Wide-eyed he replied, "Whoa! You are good." Then he laughed and proceeded to tell me all about himself, all the way to the restaurant.

Over dinner Eddie remarked on how well I could eat a three-pound lobster without getting messy. I told him it was only because we were in public and I started to laugh a little. I stopped because he didn't even crack a smile, and I thought, "He didn't get it! Oh boy!"

At that, he proceeded to tell me about his two cats, three dogs, four horses, five pigs and six chickens, that he had grown up with on his parents' farm in Ohio. By the time we finished dinner I didn't know if I was out with a down home country boy like Old MacDonald, or a sophisticated lady killer like James Bond. The one thing I did know was, **he could talk**.

As we waited for the valet parking attendant to bring the car, I took the parking receipt out of Eddie's hand, "This time I'll pick the place if you don't mind?"

He looked at me like I just stepped on his manly right to control the date, "I guess so, it's your car."

It was 10:00pm when I pulled out of the restaurant driveway and onto Rodeo Drive. I was looking for the first disco I could find. All I wanted to do was move my body on a dance floor. I was so filled with penned up emotions I couldn't release, and I hoped that dancing would be my relief. Besides that, I was still full of spunk and ready to go from the cocaine. I also did not want to hear this guy talk about himself anymore.

Finally, around 10:30pm I spotted the Pink Flamingo Disco. I pulled into the parking spot, "Well Eddie, we're here." We climbed out of the car and went in. It wasn't too busy yet, so I found a table right by the dance floor, and close enough to the speakers so I didn't have to listen to him ramble on and on. Then I sent Eddie for a White Russian and I went to the lady's room. While I was in the lady's room, I decided to take two more snorts of cocaine.

When I returned to our table Eddie was not there. All of a sudden, he came up from behind me and grabbed my arm. I jumped, ripped my arm from his grasp and turned quickly. Then he yelled, "Sorry! But come with me." So, I followed him to another table less noisy and he said, "I thought I'd sit us over here, so we can hear ourselves talk."

I took a mouth full of my White Russian, "Good thinking." I took another gulp of my drink and Eddie's eyes opened wide as I drank it down, placed the glass down in front of him, "Eddie, would you please give me a refill?"

He took the glass, and looked up at me strangely, "I hope you don't drink as much as you eat." Then he went for my drink and I thought, "Screw you asshole," realizing what I was out with!

Eddie returned with my drink, put it down on the table in front of me, "Here you go, this time try to come up for some air before you down this one. There is a line at the bar."

I took a gulp, "Thanks," grabbed his hand, pulled him up, "Come dance with me." Then, I dragged him out on the dance floor. Oh boy! Did I dance! I went wild on that dance floor. I danced rings around him and everyone else on the floor. I felt like I became part of the music and lights, I lost myself in the rhythm of each song. The only reason we stopped was because Eddie was about to pass out. When we got back to our table, I needed another drink, so I caught my breath as I waited for Eddie to bring it to me. When he did, I took it, drank it down like water and very sweetly, as I gave him a peck on the cheek, "Eddie, would you please get me another?"

He picked up my glass with frustration and headed right back to the bar. I knew that would keep him busy for another ten minutes at least. When he returned with my drink, I drank it down, took his hand and led him back to the dance floor. At first, he was reluctant to come, so I grabbed his balls, looked dead in his eyes, "Eddie, if you don't want to lose **these things**, then you better come with me." After that he was right on my tail if you catch my drift.

I was so high when we walked back onto that dance floor that I went into overdrive. I was dancing so hot; I was becoming a spectacle on the dance floor. Then, I got hot on Eddie. I was all over him. I was dancing so seductively around him, underneath him, backing into the side of him and rubbing up against him, that I had him throbbing on the dance floor. He took me in his arms as we danced and began to kiss me as he rubbed his hard groin against my thigh. I was beginning to lose myself. I kissed him deeper and rubbed my thigh harder up against his. We were almost at the point of having sex on the dance floor. It was hot! And I was getting hotter! Then the music changed again. This time they played 'The Love I Lost' by Christina Powers. I heard the rhythm and then I heard my own voice begin to sing the song which caused the whole awful thing. I broke away from Eddie's hot embrace and screamed when I realized what I was doing. I ran out the door and down to the car. I opened the door, climbed in, put the key in the ignition and started it. I just started to cry my heart out. I genuinely thought I was in Tony's arms and he was kissing me and telling me how much he loved me. I saw Eddie come running toward the car, so I put it in gear and pulled away.

I hopped on the interstate and headed toward home as fast as I could go, which was about 100 mph. As I remembered it, I think it was around 2:00am when the flashing red lights appeared. When I pulled over, I was shaking, and my face was full of tears. Then a female California Highway Patrol Officer came up to the driver's side, flashed a light in my face and said as she saw my condition, "Miss, are you alright?"

I looked up at her with tears falling from my eyes, my hands shaking, "Officer, I don't think so I just have to get home."

"Do you know how fast you were going, miss?"

"Fast."

"I need to see your driver's license, registration and insurance card," she flashed the light all around the car, "Have you had anything to drink tonight miss?"

I took my driver's license from my purse, handed it to her along with the registration and insurance card, "Yes, Officer. I have had a few drinks tonight."

She opened the door, "Can you please step out of the car, miss?"

I pleaded, "Please, don't make me get out of the car." Then I looked straight into her eyes and with all sincerity, "Miss, I'm a woman who is going through a very emotional time in my life. Please just call me a cab, so I can go home."

I heard a male voice coming from the other side of the car, "Miss, get out of the car now and put your hands up."

I turned quickly and raised my hands at the sight of a gun pointing at me then I dropped my hands, "Go ahead and shoot!"

"Hold on Sam." The female officer said. Then she looked at me, "Miss, please wait here." She walked around to the back of the car and I heard her, "Sam, do you know who this is?"

"No, who is she?"

"Look at her license. It's Christina Powers."

"Holy shit, the movie star!"

"Yes, the movie star. But not just that, she's also a human being who just tragically lost her husband."

"Your right," Sam replied sympathetically.

"I'll tell you what Sam; let's not radio this one in. You follow me and I'll drive her home."

"You got it partner."

Those two wonderful officers drove me home and saw me safely inside.

The next morning, I woke up around 9:00am to a beautiful, sunny, Sunday morning. I showered, threw on a pair of cut-off-jeans, a tank top and a pair of sneakers. I grabbed

American Goddess

a pen and paper and headed for my Mercedes. The top was still down when I climbed in. I started it up, opened the garage door and took off for unknown places. I stopped about one hour down the coast to gas up the car and myself, with a Big Mac, fries and a large coke. Then it was back on the road, still heading south on Route 5. I decided to stop at a place called Imperial Beach, just before Tijuana and found a place to park. Then I took my pen and paper and went to sit on the beach. As I sat there on the beach that day watching all the people having fun, I started to write. From 1:00pm till 5:00pm I unconsciously wrote the lyrics for eight of the most sexually, tasteless, lyrics I had ever written. It was almost as if I had made a conscious decision right there on that beach to become, America's bad girl! But I made no decisions at all.

Monday morning September 1st, at 7:00am I went into my office at Powers Incorporated and called all my top people into the number seven recording studio. For the next two weeks, we all worked on my eighth album entitled, '**American Goddess**.' All my music had always been very sexy, sensual, and hot. After all, I was the Goddess of disco. But those were nothing like the eight new singles I was about to release on my new album. The first track on the recording was titled the same as the album, '**American Goddess**.' The second track, '**The Queen Of 42nd Street!**' The third title, '**Ladies' of Fire in the Night!**' The fourth, '**Ecstasy in my arms.**' The fifth, "**Love on the run.**' The sixth, '**Dark hearted queen**', and '**Trapped in a nightmare**'." Each one destined to tear up the dance floor. This album was called hardcore disco by most of its critics. But when I released the finished cut on the airways on September 22nd, it only took one week for it to make the number 3 spot on the billboard charts. It was poised to take the number one spot away from 'The Love I Lost', which had kept the number one spot from July 21st, and stayed there until October 21st, thanks to my tragedy. After releasing the album, I went right to work on shooting our already casted screenplay. It was the one Tony and I wrote together for each other to play. It was titled, 'Listen to the Wind'.

We started shooting 'Listen to the Wind' on September 24th, and I had everyone working sixteen-hour days. As I threw myself into work all day, I also threw myself into the hottest discos in LA, all night. The press began to call me the 'Queen of the Night' and I lived up to my reputation. During this time in my life, I also kept my new cocaine supplier well fed. I released my second film, along with my ninth album, both entitled, 'Listen to the Wind' on December 10th, my twenty-third birthday. As soon as the film hit the theaters, I began a three-month concert tour on December 15th, to push the film and album. It turned out to be my hottest tour ever. The last encore of my performance, I stripped right down to a 'g' string and two feathers, which I held over the tips of my breasts. I left them all screaming for more. The hotter my music and performances became, the more my public begged for them to be even hotter. So, I gave them what they wanted, one song hotter than the other and one performance sexier than another. It became an obsession to top myself with each creation. My ultimate goal was to have each project earn more money than its predecessor and for the last nine albums and two films **I had been doing it**. There was one thing different with my approach, in the way I had been achieving this goal since my day on the beach, and that was I had become a total bitch at work. I was smiling for the cameras and my fans, but everyone who worked around me began to hate me. I became a true Hollywood **ice queen**. I shouted orders out like Hitler. I told them what I wanted, how I wanted it done and when I wanted it done, which was usually immediately, and it had better be done right the first time! Not only that, but during the eight months between July 20th, 1978, the date of Tony's death, and March 18th, 1979, when I returned home from my concert tour, I did not see Joy once.

The limo pulled into the driveway of my Malibu mansion, at 6:00pm. I had called Jimmy ahead of time to let him know I was returning home and to have Joy out of sight. Joy was now eighteen months old and I had not even acknowledged her first birthday which was October 14th, 1978.

As I approached the steps to the house, I was greeted by Jimmy who was standing at the foot of the front porch, "Welcome home Christina."

We hugged, "Hi Jimmy, it's good to see you."

"We have to talk about Joy, Christina."

I shook my head 'no', "Not now Jimmy, I'm tired."

Then I headed for the front door as Jimmy, raising his voice in anger, "We need to talk right now Christina. This can't wait anymore."

I stopped on the sixth step, turned, "All right Jimmy! What the hell is so urgent?"

"What!" He replied sharply, "I tell you I want to talk to you about your daughter, and you ask me what the hell is so urgent. The real question Christina is what the hell is wrong with you? Bobby and I have been taking care of everything here, including Joy and Powers Incorporated, while you've been whoring all over the country. Every time I'd look in a newspaper, there was something written about you and your nightly escapades."

I turned back toward him and sarcastically snapped, "What I do Jimmy, is none of your business and just for the record, I have not slept with anyone since Tony. So I don't care what the papers say, I didn't go to bed with any of those men."

He shook his head in disbelief, "Christina, whether you've been fucked is not the issue. Joy is the issue, and how many times you have seen her in the last year. Christina, Bobby and I have decided to leave you here alone with Joy. Bobby is upstairs with her now and no one else is here."

I dropped my suitcase on the steps and headed for the garage, "Jimmy, I'm leaving! I can't see her now and if you try to force me to be with her, I will put her up for adoption."

I reached the garage door with Jimmy right behind me, "Go ahead Christina, run and keep running. That will solve everything."

American Goddess

As I reached the garage door, "Jimmy, I am sorry, but I can't see her!"

I opened the door and headed for the Mercedes. As I climbed in the car Jimmy grabbed my arm, "You know what Christina, I don't care what you fucking do. I don't even like you anymore."

I pulled my hand away, turned the car on, opened the garage door and took off.

As I drove away from my own daughter that evening, I felt like I was dead inside. I did not feel anything at all for Joy and I couldn't even cry about it anymore. I headed for the Hyatt Regency Hotel in the heart of downtown LA and took a room for the night. I had nothing to change into, to wear out dancing that night, and I was definitely going dancing. I went to the dress shop in the lobby and bought myself a new outfit. Then I went up to my room, showered, got dressed in my new three hundred-dollar, baby blue three-piece sequined blouse and jacket suit, with clear stockings and black heels. Once I was looking hot, it was back downstairs to the Park Place Restaurant in the lobby by 8:30pm.

As I ate my dinner, I noticed five men at the table next to mine, all dressed in business suits. They seemed to be talking about how important personal computers were going to become to the growth of our nation's economy in the years ahead. I found the conversation to be extremely interesting and I also found the man doing most of the talking, very interesting as well. Not because of his looks, for he happened to be the least attractive man at his table. He appeared to be in his early forties, about five feet, eleven inches, maybe 190 pounds, brown hair and eyes with wire-framed glasses. He also had a mustache and he was slightly balding on top. What I found so interesting about him was the things he was saying and how he was saying them.

As I nonchalantly listened to their conversation, every guy at that table looked over to check me out at least three times, except for the one doing the talking. He didn't look my way once and I thought, "Maybe he's gay. Shit! Even gay men check me out at least twice. Hmm, maybe I should meet this guy?"

Just then I realized these men had finished their meal and were getting ready to leave. So I thought quickly and as he passed my seat I deliberately knocked my White Russian on the floor and all over his shoes. I quickly stood up with my napkin in hand, "Oh no! I'm dreadfully sorry I messed up your shoes. How clumsy of me. Please let me help?" I just pushed him down into my seat, knelt down in front of him and started to wipe off his shoes with my napkin.

I knew he was taken aback by my heroic behavior when he said, "That's not necessary miss, I can clean them myself."

I quickly rose to my feet and acted as if I didn't realize I was on my knees wiping a stranger's shoes, "Oh, how embarrassing," I said coyly. "Please forgive me again. It was just a natural reaction to help, I guess."

He smiled, "I appreciate that very much, but I'm fine."

American Goddess

I looked at him apologetically, "At least let me pay you for your shoes."

He stood up, "You don't have to do that, I have another pair in my room. Well, I better catch up with my colleagues."

I reached my hand out to him, "Please, at least let me introduce myself. I'm Christina Powers."

Without the slightest change in his expression, "It was very nice meeting you, Christina Powers, and my name is Lee Bradford. Now I really must go."

Then I thought, "Can this guy really not know who I am?" So, I said, "Well at least let me buy you a drink in the lounge."

He looked at me strangely, "Well, I guess so. I will meet you in the lounge in about an hour. Say 10:30."

Smiling, "That sounds great, I'll be there."

I finished my meal, went back up to my room for a few lines of cocaine, and it was back down to the lounge.

It was 10:40pm when I arrived at the Starlight Lounge in the hotel lobby. As I entered the door, I saw Lee sitting at the bar with the same four guys from dinner. The Starlight Lounge happened to be where most of LA's elite business crowd gathered. The lounge was quite large and spread out with a stage and dance floor. The atmosphere was still warm and cozy even though the lounge was large. The lighting was dim, but all the mirrors and fresh flowers made it seem brighter than it really was. I noticed there was a nice sized crowd which appeared to be 90% men. When Lee noticed me entering the lounge, he came over to meet me and said as he began to escort me to the bar, "Ms. Powers, I'm so glad you came. After I realized who you were, I didn't think you would show up."

"Thanks a lot! What kind of person do you think I am?"

He looked apologetic, "I didn't mean to be derogatory. I guess what I'm trying to say is, you're Christina Powers, and I'm–well nobody special. Why would you want to have a drink with me, instead of one of my colleagues?"

I looked at him strangely, "Lee, let's get something straight right now. First, I didn't spill a drink on any of their shoes. Second, I didn't come down here for anything but to show you a kindness, for your graciousness, over my clumsiness. Now I would still like to buy you a drink, if you would allow me."

His face turned slightly red, "Yes of course, and please forgive me, Ms. Powers. I'd enjoy a drink with you, and the guys are dying to meet you."

I gently grabbed his hand, "Lee, would you mind if we sat at a quiet booth. I just came off an intense tour, and I'm really not up to a group conversation tonight."

He stopped walking, "I don't mind at all Ms. Powers, but the guys sure will."

American Goddess

I looked at him sweetly, "Please call me Christina, and how about if I take a seat at that booth over there," I pointed to a booth way in the back, next to the restrooms, "while you make my apologies to your friends for me. Please tell them I'd be more than happy to meet them all another time. I'll just be waiting at that table for you."

"That sounds fine to me, and I'll be right back." Then I went off to the booth, while Lee went to the bar.

Within two minutes Lee was taking a seat on the bench across from me, "I'm back and once again Christina, please forgive me. It's just that I never had a beautiful woman like yourself ask to have a drink with me."

I chuckled, "Well thank you for the compliment, that's very nice of you to say. But you should really think more of yourself than you do. I think you're an extremely attractive man."

He smiled, "Well thank you Christina, but maybe you should use my glasses."

I laughed, "That was cute Lee, you're so witty, and I can't tell you the last time I laughed." I reached over, patted his hand, as I noticed a barmaid coming, "Well what would you like to drink?"

"Scotch and water."

The barmaid reached our booth, "What can I get for you folks?"

"We would like a Scotch and Water and a White Russian," I answered.

She replied with a smile, "Thank you and I'll be right back with your drinks."

I turned back toward Lee, "So Lee, tell me when you realized who I was?"

Appearing somewhat embarrassed, "Well to be honest with you Christina, I didn't know who you were until my colleagues told me you were a big star."

I looked at him strangely, "You really didn't know who I was, even after I told you my name?"

"Please don't be offended I just don't have much time to go to the movies and I only listen to classical music."

I chuckled again, "I'm not offended Lee, just surprised. I thought everyone knew me. So you really never heard any of my music?"

"I wish I could say yes, but I can't, because I don't believe I have."

"What is it you do that keeps you so busy," I asked inquisitively?

"I work with and design new computer programs."

"That sounds extremely interesting Lee. Please tell me more about what kind of programs you design."

He smiled, "I can tell you I am working on a new prototype of a home-based personal computer and that's all I can say. There happens to be a lot of people who would like to know exactly what I'm working on in my lab, but that has to remain top secret."

"Top secret, now I'm really intrigued. Do you work for the government?"

American Goddess

With that the barmaid came over to us and placed our drinks down on the table. I handed her a twenty, "Thank you and keep the change."

In answer to my question Lee said, "Well, yes and no. I work for myself, but the government has purchased many of my inventions for national defense purposes, as well as the space program."

"Your work sounds extremely exciting Lee, and I am somewhat familiar with computers. In my line of work, we are beginning to use computers for more and more things every day. But why would a home-based personal computer be considered top secret?"

He leaned close to me and in a low tone, "Because the first company to come up with a small inexpensive, home based personal computer, which will have versatile applications and be user friendly, will change the way we live and work forever, not to mention the monetary gains for such a revolutionary invention."

As I listened to Lee speak about his work, he began to become more technical as he went on, until he finally lost me completely. I found myself in awe at this man's intelligence and I slowly became a little more interested in the man as well as in his words.

We had been so involved in our conversation that neither one of us noticed the lounge slowly filling up with people. Then we heard someone over the loudspeaker say, "Ladies and gentlemen it is 11:30 and we are about to begin our comedy show, which will be hosted by a special surprise guest tonight. So, without further ado, please give a hardy welcome to the incomparable, Kathy Brown."

As soon as I heard her name my blood began to boil. Then I saw Kathy walk out on the stage. I totally lost complete interest in everything Lee was saying and went into a dead stare at Kathy, until Lee said, "Christina, are you, all right?"

He shook my hand, which snapped me out of my trance, "I'm sorry Lee, what did you say?"

"I said are you, all right?"

"Actually Lee, I'm not. Do you know anything about my life?"

"I'm sorry I didn't mean to monopolize our conversation. And once again, I don't know anything about you."

I smiled, "Lee, you have nothing to be sorry for, I was genuinely enjoying our conversation. As a matter of fact, I could listen to you talk all night. I find you to have a very dynamic personality. But, since you don't know anything about me and my life, you could not realize who that woman on the stage is."

He looked for the first time at the stage, "No, I don't know who she is, should I?"

American Goddess

With that I really laughed out loud, "I'm sorry for laughing, but that woman and I have had bad blood between us for years. If you've ever read a Hollywood tabloid you would know that."

"If her presence is making you uncomfortable, we can leave. I'm sure there must be someplace else we can go close by."

I patted his hand, "Lee, please forgive me, but I'm not going anyplace. I have a score to settle with that women and I have just decided tonight is going to be the night I'm finally going to settle it. So, if you would like to leave now, I'd understand."

His face appeared nervous, "I'm not sure what you mean when you say you have to settle a score with her, but there is no place I'd rather be than here with you right now. So maybe I can help you somehow?"

As Kathy was giving a small monologue I said, "Lee, there is nothing you can do to help me, because I don't need any help. But I can at least tell you a little about what happened."

With that I told him the whole story of how she slept with my husband and helped to cause his death. Afterward he said, "I'm sorry to hear that Christina, it sounds like it was a very intense situation."

"To, say the least!" Kathy finished her monologue and introduced the first comic.

Lee patted my hand assuredly, "I don't know what you have in mind for your revenge, but I do feel that if we stay here this could become another newsworthy story." Taking my hand, "Please Christina let me take you out of here. I don't believe you're thinking very clearly right at this moment and you might be compelled to do something I'm sure you will regret later."

I shook my head, "Oh shit! You're right, let's get out of here."

As we were getting ready to leave, Kathy walked right by us on her way to the lady's room without even noticing me and I thought, "Are you kidding me! This is too good to be true."

I immediately excused myself and went into the lady's room behind her. There were two women seated at the make-up table and I could see Kathy's shoes from under the stall. The two women stood up and started to walk out so I followed them to the door. As they exited the lady's room, another woman was trying to enter. I put my hand on her chest to stop her from entering and she said, "Hey! What do you think you're doing?" as I closed the door and locked it.

I walked over to the front of Kathy's stall to wait for her, as this woman kept knocking on the door.

When Kathy opened the door, her mouth dropped to the floor the moment she saw me standing there and I felt fire in my eyes as soon as I saw her face. I grabbed her and flung her into the sinks behind us and shouted, "Hi, Kathy! You bitch! I'm going to give you what I promised a long time ago and beat the living shit out of you."

She tried to run so I grabbed her and punched her right in the face. She punched me in the stomach with all her might and at that moment, I realized I had a formidable opponent, but I knew she could not overcome my tomboy childhood, as I belted her left jaw knocking her into the sinks. She bounced off the sinks and pushed me back into the stall door as she screamed, "Fuck you, Christina! You're the fucking bitch! If you had just left Tony and me alone, he'd still be alive today."

That was all I had to hear! I leaped at her, grabbed her by the hair, put her in a headlock and began to belt her in the face. She was screaming like I was killing her and believe me I think I was! She kneed me in the crotch and knocked me into the sinks. She grabbed a can of hair spray and began to hit me over the head with it. I grabbed her hand and twisted it around her back and put my other arm around her neck. I held her with my body and pushed her forward smashing her face right into the paper dispenser on the wall, and I heard '**Snap**' as her nose broke. Blood began to run all over us as she screamed and tried to break free. She slipped out of my hold and bit down on my hand like a Doberman Pincer. I swung her around and punched her with all my might right smack in the nose. She reached out and dug her nails right in the back of my neck and pulled. "You bitch!" I screamed, then I walloped her again.

As we fought like two wild animals, we could hear people were trying to break down the door. She grabbed my right breast through my blouse, dug her nails in again and ripped my blouse off, taking my skin with it. I grabbed the can of hair spray and backhanded her right across the head, and she fell to the ground screaming. I leaped on top of her and proceeded to smash her face into the floor, as she screamed, "Help! Help! Somebody Help!" and that's when the door finally gave way to the constant pressure. Someone then grabbed and pulled me off her. I turned and it was Lee, holding me back from killing her.

Someone else helped Kathy up off the floor and she yelled, "Someone call the police, this fucking bitch tried to kill me!"

I yelled, "Kathy, don't you think you've been humiliated enough. Call the police in on this and you'll never live it down. But on the other hand, I will become the heroine. So go ahead, call!"

She looked at me with tears and blood running down her face, "Don't call the police, I only fell." Still looking dead into my eyes, "Christina, if you want to kill someone, it should be Frank, not me. He put me up to sleeping with John. I never wanted to try to break you two up, but you know how convincing Frank can be at getting his way."

I looked at her with disgust in my expression and said nothing. I just turned and held my blood-stained head up high as I walked out past the crowd of on-lookers.

American Goddess

As I reached the front door, Lee was right behind me with my jacket and purse, which I totally forgot about. He opened the door for me, "Christina, please let me take you home."

I turned to him, "I'm staying here tonight, so you can walk me to my room if you'd like?"

"I wouldn't dream of letting you walk through here alone, especially after that fight! So yes, I would be happy to walk you to your room."

We proceeded to my room and as we entered the elevator Lee said, "Are you all right, Christina? You look like hell."

First, I looked at myself, then I looked at the three men in the elevator with us who were staring at me, I looked back at Lee and started to laugh. I didn't stop laughing until we reached my room on the 16th floor. I turned the key, "Lee, won't you please come in for a few minutes? I could sure use someone to talk to right now."

"I have no place to go and I'd rather stay with you until I know you're all right."

He came in behind me and as I closed the door I said, "Lee, would you please excuse me for a few minutes while I clean up and change."

He eyed me again, "Sure, you go clean up. I'll entertain myself until you return."

As I showered, I thought about everything Kathy said, and I realized for the first time since Tony's death, I did not kill Tony. He pulled the trigger not me. I had been blaming myself for months now for Tony's death and that realization made me decide right there in that shower, I did not have to blame myself anymore. I thought about the last thing Kathy said and it made me hate Frank even more. I did not think I could ever hold as much hate in my heart as I held there for Frank, but I did. I was now more than ever driven by my hatred to crush Frank and I knew my day for revenge would come. I turned off the shower and began to dry off. As I was drying, I began to realize what I had just done to Kathy. I was so angry I think I could have killed her with my bare hands if Lee hadn't pulled me off of her. I began to shake at the thought I could actually get angry enough to kill someone. As I trembled, I threw on a robe and went out to speak with Lee with a towel in my hand, still drying my hair.

When I came out of the bathroom, Lee was sitting on the sofa with two cups of coffee and some Danish. As I sat down on the other side of the sofa Lee said, "I took the liberty of having room service bring us a snack; just in case you were anything like me when you're upset. I usually head for the first thing I can eat."

I wrapped my hair up in the towel, "That sounds great Lee, thank you. Please excuse the towel; I didn't want to leave you while I took the time needed to dry my hair."

"Don't excuse yourself to me, the towel looks like a queen's turban on you."

"Thank you, Lee that was a very nice thing to say, especially since I have a black eye to go along with it. Maybe you need your eyeglasses checked," we both laughed.

American Goddess

When I reached for the coffee cup my hand started to shake from the weight of it and I almost dropped it. Lee steadied my hand, "You're not all right at all are you? Christina, are you sure you don't need to go to a hospital?"

I laughed, "Oh, God! That's all I'd have to do. Tomorrow the whole free world would know, even you." We laughed a little more, "Lee, I'm really not hurt too badly, I'm just a little shaky. After all that was a hell of an adrenaline rush, let me tell you."

"I guess so, from what I could hear I thought you were killing each other."

"Lee, we were trying to kill one another. The bad blood runs deep between us. That's why I thank God you broke in when you did. I might have actually killed her and she's not worth it. In the scheme of things, she's small change." Then I reached over, touched his hand, "Thank you for being here for me, you could not imagine how alone I feel in this world. I have isolated myself from my own daughter, as well as all the people in my life who mean anything to me. Lee, I have been hurting for so long now, I can't remember what it feels like not to hurt." My tears began to run again, and I could feel them stinging my eyes, "Please forgive me again Lee, I don't mean to be crying on you."

"Would you please stop apologizing to me and just let it all out. Christina, if there is one thing I know it's this. If you keep everything locked up inside yourself, you will never be able to start the healing process." He moved closer to me and gave me a gentle hug, "I have a big shoulder and it's free for you anytime you need it."

I looked up into his kind eyes, "Come to think about it, I could use a big shoulder right now." He placed his left arm around me, and I laid my head on his chest.

We sat on that sofa for the longest time just like that. It felt so good to finally feel the warmth of a man's arms around me again. I started to feel alive again and I found myself slowly nuzzling closer to him. I gently moved until my lips found the flesh of his neck and I began to softly kiss him. I felt my passion begin to grow as I slowly began to unbutton his shirt. In a soft voice Lee said, "Christina, I know you're not in your normal frame of mind right now, so before we go any further I have to ask you if you're sure this is what you want?"

I looked up at him and with a tender loving voice said, "Lee, if for only one night, will you make love to me?"

He leaned down and began to softly kiss me. I let myself melt into his kisses and the passion slowly began to flow between our lips. Our fire was beginning to crackle when I broke from his embrace. I stood up in front of him and with only the dim light of the lamp on the end table I took the towel off my head and threw it on the arm of the sofa. I gently untied my robe and let it fall to the floor. I could see his heart in his throat and a bulge in his pants as soon as my robe fell. I stood him up and began to undress him, starting from his suit jacket to his socks and I saved the pants for last. As I unbuckled his pants and began to bring down his zipper, I could hear his heart pounding through his chest. I led him over to the bed, held him and began to kiss him deeply. Slowly I let his pants fall to his ankles, reached down and slipped his underwear over his nicely curved cheeks and then over his throbbing erection. I sat him down on the bed, knelt down in front of his loins, slipped his feet out of his clothing, brought them up and laid him down flat on the bed. I climbed up on top of him and proceeded to make love to every inch of his body. I needed to feel him, I needed to feel the passion, I needed to feel alive. I needed the fire for life back again and I needed the sex! I was incredible! I nearly killed the man, but he kept up with me, if you get my drift. That night of love making was rejuvenating and it definitely was love making. I felt a connection to this man as we made love and all I wanted was to make him feel my love and passion. After we climaxed, we held each other and I said, "Lee, I want you to know we were truly making love and you were wonderful. I also want you to know no matter what you may say about your looks, I think you are extremely attractive. Thank you for making me feel so loved and wanted. I will never forget this night." Then I kissed his lips and we fell asleep.

I woke up at 5:00am that morning and Lee was still asleep. I looked at him sleeping there and thought, "He's not a great looker, but he's sure a sweetheart and not too shabby in the sack either."

I quickly dressed, took a pen and paper and left Lee this note. **"Lee, you are the nicest man I've met in a long time and I had an incredible time with you. So much so, that I know I could get to like having you around. But, for your own safety I am not going to leave you my number. Have a good life Lee, Love Christina."**

I decided not to pursue Lee because I knew deep down inside myself it would only be because I wanted to get in on the ground floor of the up-and-coming computer age. So, for the first time in a long time, I put the personal feelings of another before my own desire for power and revenge." **Then I headed for home.**

American Goddess

CHAPTER 9

I walked into Joy's room at 5:45am on Sunday March 19ᵗʰ, 1979. Joy was now, one-year-five-months and five-days-old. It had been one day short of eight-months since the last day I saw my sweet loving Joy. I looked down at her sleeping in her crib like an angel and I felt a warm feeling come over me. I quietly moved the reading chair closer to Joy's crib and sat beside her. As I watched her sleep, tears began to roll down my cheeks. I guess I fell asleep myself because I did not hear Nanny Sue come in the room. I was surprised when she touched my shoulder and said in a low tone, "Mrs. Demetrees, its 8:00am, I usually wake Joy up now. Would you like to get her up instead?"

I looked at her and answered in a soft low voice, "Thank you, Nanny Sue. I would like that very much." I stood up, reached into the crib, picked Joy up, "Joy, honey, Mommy's home."

She looked at me, started to smile, "Mommy!"

I held her close, "Your Mommy loves you Joy, with all her heart and I will never desert you again." We played and laughed as I washed and dressed her.

I was down in the family kitchen feeding Joy her breakfast when Jimmy and Bobby walked in. They both almost fell over when they saw me, and Jimmy joyfully yelled, "Oh my, God! Christina, you're back! And look Bobby, she's feeding Joy. It's so good to see you with her."

I gazed up at them both, "Hi guys, what would you think about the four of us going to Disneyland today?"

Jimmy jumped into Bobby's arms and shouted, "Thank, God! Our girl's back, Bobby." They both came over to me, and the four of us had a warm group hug.

As we hugged, Bobby looked at me with curiosity, "Christina, do you have a black eye?" I looked at them both staring at my eye and I started to laugh.

As I laughed Jimmy asked, "So what's so funny about a black eye?"

I stopped laughing long enough to explain, "I kicked the hell out of Kathy Brown, last night." Then we all started to laugh. When we finally stopped laughing, I told them both about my accidental run-in with Kathy. After that we all had our breakfast and it was off to Disneyland for the day.

It was a beautiful, warm, bright, sunny day when James drove all of us including Carman and Nanny Sue, to Disneyland in the limo and the seven of us went in together.

I was dressed very inconspicuously with blue jeans, black tee shirt, sneakers, baseball cap and wide sunglasses. I also carried Joy most of the day as we walked through the park.

American Goddess

About halfway through the day, we came across the haunted castle and of course, everyone wanted to go in. But I decided to wait outside with Joy who was too little to enter, while everyone else went in.

When I said I wasn't going in Jimmy said, "Christina, you have to come in with me." Then he turned to Bobby, "Honey, would you please stay out here with Joy, so Christina and I can go in together?"

Bobby knelt on the ground and said like, 'Dan Acroyd' might, "Oh gee Dad, do I have to?"

We all started to laugh, "No Bobby, you don't have to, I'd rather stay here with Joy anyway."

"No Christina, I'm only kidding. You go ahead with Jimmy; I happen to like my arms without black and blue marks anyway. You know how he is with those hands of his when he gets nervous".

I laughed, "I know what you mean."

Jimmy came over to me with his puppy dog eyes, "Please! Please! You have to come with me. We haven't done anything crazy together in months."

I looked at him with his hands up like a begging poodle, "All right, you talked me into it."

I handed Joy over to Bobby, and Jimmy and I got in line with James, Carman and Nanny Sue. When we finally reached the end of the line, the chairs for the ride would only fit two adults comfortably, so Jimmy and I took a seat by ourselves. As the ride began to take us into the screaming, pitch black darkness, Jimmy and I were both starting to get scared. Things were popping out at us from every angle and we were screaming and having a great time. Jimmy and I were holding each other tightly to help intensify our fear, when a figure of Frankenstein's bride came running toward us with her three-inch long fingernails coming right for our faces, and we both screamed at the top of our lungs. Then it hit me like a charge of dynamite, and I flew up out of the seat almost knocking Jimmy out of the chair and yelled, "Ahhh! **I'm a fucking genius!**" as Jimmy screamed out in horror, "Ahhh! What is it?" and grabbed at his chest.

When Jimmy could breathe again, he shouted, "I told you girl! You're a fucking nut! And you'll always be a fucking nut!"

He hugged me and shouted, "Hey world, she's really back!"

Joking around I slapped his hand, "Shut up, you asshole!" Then I kissed him, "Jimmy, you are truly my best friend and I love you."

It turned out to be a wonderful day and I was finally back to myself and my family. We had arrived at the park at 10:00am and we went on all the rides and saw all the shows. Finally, we left at closing time which was 9:00pm right after the fireworks. When we got

American Goddess

back to the limo, Joy was sound asleep in my arms. It felt so good to have my baby back in my arms again and I knew I no longer had to hide from her.

The next morning, I decided to take two months off from work. I spent every minute of Joy's waking hours with her during those two months and when she slept, I was writing. First, I wrote the lyrics and melody to an entire album of ballads which came from my deepest innermost feelings of love for Tony and Joy. There were nine cuts on the album. Each one told the world just what I went through after Tony's death, and how the love of Joy saved me from myself. This was my tenth album, and I titled it **'For the Love Of Joy.'** After I finished it, I sent it into the studios with Jimmy. I wanted everything set up and ready to start recording as soon as I returned to work. At the same time, I started writing my third and most brilliant screen play with movie soundtrack, to date. The idea came to me while I was on the ride with Jimmy in the haunted castle at Disneyland. They were both to be titled, **'Halloween In Hell!'**

During that time Joy and I had the chance to come to know one another all over again. We had so much fun and I took her everywhere with me. We laughed, played, and I found out I could truly be a good mother.

One day during my vacation, I received a call from Tom Davis, who was one of the attorneys I had hired in New York, to oversee my building project in Milton. He informed me the project was going well and the builders had reached the point of building the first stage of my planned construction. This was the completion of six of the main studio buildings, which was the point I had requested to be informed, so I could make a personal inspection.

The plans were to have the project built in three stages. There was to be three main developments on the property which would be considered individual industrial parks. Each of these three parks would have six large campuses like buildings, spread out amongst the woods. Each park would have its own master control center, to monitor the activities throughout the three parks. There would also be offices, recording studios and movie lots. In addition, each park would have buildings set aside, as well as its own twenty-acre area for future ventures and endeavors of Powers Incorporated.

So, on April 16th, 1979, it was off to New York to inspect the progress of the future home of Powers Incorporated. When Joy, Nanny Sue and I left L.A. it was hotter than hell. The summer had come early to California and we already had two weeks of 90+ degree temperatures. But when we got off the plane in New York at 6:00pm we walked straight into the beginnings of a freak spring **blizzard**. It took the limo nearly four hours to get us from LaGuardia airport to the Plaza Hotel in downtown Manhattan. Then we spent the next two days snow bound in our suite.

Finally, on April 19th, Tom Davis who was a very attractive six-foot tall black man, and I took the ride upstate by ourselves, because it was still too cold to take Joy. When

American Goddess

we finally reached Milton, we drove through the town until we found the sign that read, **"The future home of Powers Incorporated."** We turned down a sloppy, muddy road and headed to see the completion of stage one of my dream. Tom drove us from one building to the next in his four-wheel drive Ford Bronco. After a six-hour detailed inspection of the interior and exterior of six very large buildings, I found myself feeling extremely pleased with the work that had been completed.

Just before we left, I stood in one spot and looked all around me at this dirty, muddy, winter wonderland and thought, "You must be freaking nuts, Christina. What the hell are you spending six-hundred-million-dollars, out here in the freaking wilderness for? You asshole, everything you need is in Hollywood and that's where you live." I looked at Tom who was standing beside me patiently waiting to leave and I shrugged my shoulders and said, "Oh well! I'll figure it out tomorrow."

Tom gave me a strange look, "Whatever you say, Ms. Powers."

I looked at him and started to laugh, "It's an inside joke Tom." Then I gave him the okay to continue work and it was back to the city.

The rest of my time with Joy went too quickly. Before I knew it, it was May 15th, time to go back to work. When I arrived at my office in the temporary headquarters of Powers Incorporated in southern LA, I immediately called all my personal staff off the other projects we had them on. Then, with only working nine-hour days, we still released a completed album on June 1, entitled 'For the Love of Joy.'

On June 5th, it was full steam ahead for all of us, on my third film and eleventh album as Christina Powers. As I said, I entitled it, 'Halloween in Hell!' I knew 'Halloween in Hell' was going to be an ambitious and expensive sixty-million-dollar gamble. I also knew if we could pull it off before this coming Halloween, we'd make at least a half a billion. Be assured we worked day and night for the next four months, so that we'd be able to release our film to the world on October 5, and we did it!

The film was about a young nursing student who finds herself caught up in a macabre situation on Halloween Night, in the year 2000. It turns out that she must do battle with the demons from hell to keep them from releasing Satan himself on mankind at the stroke of midnight. If she failed, Satan would enslave the whole human race. The film was full of nonstop action and horror, with high-speed auto chases, plane crashes and the murders of all the heroine's family and friends by horrifying demons.

The pace of the film was intense right up to the unpredictable terrifying ending, where myself, playing the heroin, is finally defeated and possessed by all the demons of hell at 11:45pm Halloween Night. At which time I started to dance the dance of the demons, to open the gates of hell and summon forth Satan himself, at the stroke of midnight. I danced and sang for the last ten minutes of the film, just like I was truly possessed. Miraculously, at 11:59 the heavens opened above me, and angels flew down and released me from the demons, just as Satan rose up from out of his fiery, smoky hole in the ground, at which time I grabbed a sword one of the angels lost in their battle with the demons, and I plunged it into this hideous creature's heart. He explodes and I saved the human race from everlasting torment, with a little help from my angelic friends.

On September 14th, we finished the last day of shooting on 'Halloween In Hell' and it was time to start promoting our ahead of schedule release date of October 1st, for the new 'Christina Powers' film. I knew it would be a winner because the film and my performance were phenomenal. I also knew the accompanying soundtrack would be the only other album released that year by any performer, to knock 'For the Love of Joy' out of the number one spot on all the record billboard charts. After 'For the Love of Joy' was released my fan club membership went from ten million worldwide to forty-six million. This number turned out to be the largest fan club ever, for any performer in entertainment history. My fans and I seemed to create a personal and loving relationship through the years. The whole world knew I was telling them all I would survive my heartbreak through the lyrics on that album. Even though 'For the Love of Joy' had none of my typical dance songs on it, it still became my best-selling album to date. I also had to increase my fan club staff from ten employees to thirty employees, just to keep up with the mail that came in every day.

Finally, it was October 1st, at 8:00pm and I was hosting my premiere night at the Palace Theater in downtown LA. I was dressed in a black full-length gown, which ran all the way to the floor. It had a three-foot-long train, which slid along behind me as I walked. It was similar to the gowns 'Elmira' might wear today, on her 'Horror Night' TV shows. I planned it to be a formal invitation bash. I had all the top brass of Hollywood on my invitation list. All but Frank of course.

Jimmy, Bobby, Barbara and Eartha were with me at the front entrance of the theater greeting all our guests as they came in, when to my astonishment I saw Frank walking up the red carpet toward us. He had Kathy Brown on one arm and another bimbo on the other. He also had two of his well-dressed goon's right behind him.

The lobby of the theater was nearly full with most of my influential guests when they reached us, and Frank said, "Christina, you look lovely tonight, and your attire suits you. I didn't receive my formal invitation, which I assume was an oversight by your staff, so here we are."

I looked him straight in the eye, "There was no oversight, and you know it! So, please just turn around and leave right now."

He looked at Barbara, "She must be mistaken, don't you think so, Barbara?"

Before Barbara could say anything, I interjected, "Frank, Tony is not here tonight, so if you don't leave now and quietly, then I will be forced to call your bluff and make a scene neither one of us will live down for a longtime. So make your choice and make it quick, because I'm becoming more and more nauseous the longer I have to look at you."

.I could see the veins in his neck begin to bulge as his anger grew, "Frank, take your looks of admiration and get out, now! Because this is my last warning and I know you want to cause a scene with me a lot less than I do with you."

"Christina, I'm very sorry to disappoint you, but I don't think I want to sit through another one of your over hyped movies after all." Then, he turned and walked away with his entourage bringing up the rear.

Barbara turned to me, "You have some set of balls, girl." And the five of us immediately started to laugh.

The premiere was a complete success, and everyone loved the film. Jimmy, Bobby, all the crew members and I, were flying higher than a kite that night at the celebration party. It was held in the ballroom at the Regency Hotel which was adjacent to the theater. It was about 11:00pm as I stood there with my crystal glass of champagne in hand. I was talking with Barbara and Eartha as well as a group of five or six other people. All of a sudden, I heard Tony's voice echoing in my mind like a crash of thunder shouting, **"Christina!"** I turned quickly to look behind me and for a split second, I actually saw Tony standing there. I looked into his tear-filled eyes and I saw he was holding the limp body of Joy in his arms. Then he was gone.

Instantly I dropped my glass and screamed in horror, "Ahhh!" As I started to shake, everyone came running to me. I screamed out again, "Jimmy! Jimmy! Where are you?"

Jimmy and Bobby both came running through the crowd yelling, "What is it?"

I looked at Jimmy with panic in my eyes and screamed, "We have to get home now! Something's wrong with Joy!"

I grabbed their arms and the three of us ran through the crowd and down to the parking lot, to where James would hopefully be waiting with the limo. When we reached the parking lot, Bobby shouted and pointed across the line of limos, "There he is over there!" We ran across the parking lot to where James was waiting.

James almost went into shock when he saw us running toward him shouting, "James, hurry we have to get home now!" He ran around the limo and jumped into the driver's seat. I jumped into the front seat with him, as Jimmy and Bobby jumped into the back.

I caught my dress and tore it at my knees on the door as I slammed it shut and shouted, "James, step on it and get us home NOW!" Then I tore the rest of my dress off from my thighs down, as Jimmy was opening the partition between the front and back seats. When it was completely down Jimmy, yelled frantically "What's going on, Christina? I'm having a fucking heart attack here!"

American Goddess

I looked at them all, "I don't know how I know it, but something is terribly wrong at home."

We raced through Los Angeles toward Malibu on Route 1. When we reached Topanga Beach, James said, "Oh my God! Christina, look at the sky ahead."

We all looked up and to our horror the sky was bright red. Then James really gunned it. We were doing 90 miles an hour down Route 1, toward what was becoming the biggest brush fire we had ever seen. When we reached Rambla Pacifica Road, we were stopped by a state police roadblock and the officer said, "The Santa Anna Winds have flared up a whopper of a forest fire for the next ten miles in, and no one is allowed past this point."

I stuck my head out the window over James' lap and shouted, "I'm Christina Powers, and my daughter is up that road, we have to pass."

He shook his head 'no', "If she's up there the rescue squad will surely get her out, so please just turn around. We have to keep the road open for emergency vehicles."

Panicking and not caring about any emergency vehicles, I pushed my foot down on the accelerator and shouted, "James, drive! Drive!" and we flew right past them.

As we got closer to the mansion, we found ourselves in the middle of a raging fire on both sides of the road. James had to drive over downed burning tree limbs in order to reach our driveway. He sped up the driveway until we were stopped by burning trees about three-hundred yards from the mansion. We jumped out of the limo and ran up to the house. We could hear the sounds of sirens but there were no fire trucks to be seen. As we rounded the bend of the driveway, I could see the entire right side of the mansion was engulfed in flames, and I screamed, "Oh, God, no!"

As we reached the front porch, Carman and two other employees came running out of the half burning front door. They were coughing so bad they could hardly speak as they ran down to us in the front yard. When they reached us, I screamed in horror, "Where's Joy, Carman? Where is she?"

Carman cried out, "I tried to get to her and Nanny Sue in the nursery, but the fire and smoke is everywhere."

"Oh my God!" I screamed, "Joy is still in there!"

I started to run and James grabbed me, "No Christina, you can't help her now."

I ripped myself from him and shouted, "The fire is on the right side of the mansion and the nursery is on the left." I took off and ran up the steps of the porch right through the partially burning front door and straight into an inferno in the foyer. The entire right side of the staircase was engulfed in fire, but I could still make it up through the flames which were burning on the left side. I charged up the staircase and headed through the thick smoke until I reached the nursery. When I entered Joy's room the smoke was so thick, I could hardly breathe. I was coughing and shouting, "Joy! Joy! Where are you? Nanny Sue, where are you?"

American Goddess

I fell to the floor and crawled over to where her youth bed would be. When I found it, I felt the bed for Joy, but she was not there. I frantically searched the floor on my hands and knees praying to find her, until I finally felt her little hand under-mine. My blood raced through my body with all the force of Niagara Falls as I picked up her limp, lifeless, body.

I pulled her close to me and screamed, "Joy! Joy! Wake up!" But there was no response. I tried to give her mouth-to-mouth resuscitation, but the smoke was too thick. I turned to try and crawl my way back out the same way I came in, but I could see the flames were now at the bedroom door. I stood up in the center of that mass of smoke and started searching wildly with my right arm flinging through the air, looking for anything that would help me find my bearings. I found the iron reading chair, and holding Joy in my left hand, I flung the chair with my right hand with all my might toward the direction of where I hoped the window would be. The chair went crashing out of the bedroom window and as soon as it did, the flames came bursting into the room as the smoke poured out of the window.

I stuck my head out of the second story window and screamed out, "Jimmy! Somebody! Help us!" But no one was on that side of the mansion to hear me over the roar of the fire. I looked behind me at the approaching flames and I had no choice. I held Joy as close to me as I could, and I jumped out the window.

When my feet hit the ground, I lost hold of Joy and we both went flying into the broken glass, just missing the iron chair I had thrown out the window. Then I ran to Joy, picked her back up and started giving her mouth-to-mouth resuscitation again. I started to run toward the front of this burning inferno to where I prayed help would be. When I reached the front of the mansion, I could see Bobby and James, struggling to hold a fighting and screaming Jimmy back, from running into a fiery death.

I screamed out as I ran toward them, "Jimmy! Help us!" When they finally heard us, they all turned to see our smoke stained, bloody and partially singed bodies, running toward them. They all started to run toward us. The minute they reached us, there was a series of large explosions which knocked us all off our feet and the heat, smoke and sound of the fire grew so quickly we almost didn't get away from the mansion fast enough. We all stopped running when we reached the driveway which was about one hundred yards from the house.

Jimmy grabbed me and yelled, "Christina, let me take her!"

As Jimmy took Joy from my arms, he looked at Bobby and yelled, "Bobby, help Christina, I'll continue C.P.R. on Joy!"

Bobby grabbed my left side which I was limping on and shouted, "Come on everybody, we have to keep running, the fire is beginning to encircle us."

I looked at him frantically and shouted, "Let's help Jimmy, Bobby. I'm all right."

American Goddess

At that we all made a mad, one-mile dash through the burning woods, away from the crumbling mansion and toward the main road. We could not run up the driveway because it was in flames and so was the limo.

That one mile run through the woods burning all around us, was the longest and scariest run any of us had ever made in our entire lives. I clung to one side of Jimmy, as Bobby clung to the other side of him. While Jimmy continued to give Joy C.P.R., Bobby and I were dragging Jimmy in one direction then the other, as we ran whatever way we could to get through the flames. Right behind us was James and Carman, but we were not able to see the other two household employees.

When we finally reached the main road, we found ourselves right in the middle of more flames and it was closing in on us from all directions.

I desperately looked around at this hopeless situation and screamed out, **"Oh, God! Please help us!!"** Then from over the roar of the fire, we could hear the whirling of a helicopter's blades as it approached us. We all started to jump and scream as the 'chopper' began to descend toward us.

When it landed, two medics jumped out and ran over to us and I shouted, "My daughter! Please help her!" Then one medic took Joy from Jimmy's exhausted arms and began to work on her, as the other one helped us into the 'chopper' and it was off to LA Memorial Hospital.

I pleaded with God in my mind to save my baby, as the medics began to artificially breathe for Joy with a black breathing bag. Then they proceeded to evaluate her condition and radioed their findings to the hospital. We were all in a state of shock by the time the 'chopper' landed on the roof of the hospital. As soon as we landed, the emergency crew came running to us. They grabbed Joy and disappeared with her before I could even get out of the 'chopper'. We were taken to the emergency room, and the E.R. staff began to evaluate us for injuries.

Panicking again I shouted, "Where is my daughter?"

A doctor came over to me, "Are you the mother of the child just brought in on the 'chopper'?"

"Yes!" I answered desperately, "Where is she?"

"She's in the triage burn center, which is the best burn center in the world. What I need from you is to sign a release form so we can legally treat your daughter. Also, if you are up to it, I need to ask you some questions about your daughter's health."

I signed the form he had and answered all of his questions. Afterward he said, "Now please let us treat your wounds and we will inform you of your little girl's condition."

"I want to be with her now!" I demanded.

"I'm sorry, but I can't let you do that. It is a very sterile area, and it would be impossible to let you go in there in the shape you're in now."

American Goddess

After we were treated, they sat us in a waiting room and Bobby looked at me and in a somber tone, "Did you see Nanny Sue, Christina?"

I looked at him sadly, "No."

The five of us sat in the waiting room for what seemed to be an eternity for some word on Joy's condition. Finally, at 3:15am a doctor walked into the waiting room and said, "Is Mrs. Demetrees here?"

Jimmy and I stood up, ran to him and I said, "How is my baby, Doctor?"

He had a desperate look on his face, "She is still hanging onto life and we have done all we can do at this point. She is now on a respirator, but her lungs are severely damaged. The next few hours will be crucial for her if she's going to survive."

My tears immediately started to fall, "May I please see her now?"

He answered sympathetically, "Yes, you may, come with me and I will take you to her."

Anxiously Jimmy said, "I'm her father and I need to see her too."

The doctor looked at him strangely, "You may come also Mr. Demetrees, but only one person at a time and for only **five minutes each**."

We followed him to the intensive care unit of the burn center. When I reached Joy's room, I walked up to her. Her precious little body was hooked up to a respirator, I.V.'s, and life support monitors. She was enclosed in a large see-through plastic container. They had her suspended in the air, by what looked like wires in the center of this enclosure. I put my hands on the outside of the container and cried because I couldn't even touch my baby.

My five minutes with Joy passed too quickly, when a nurse came in, "Mrs. Demetrees, I must ask you to leave so Mr. Demetrees may come in."

I kissed the plastic container, "Joy, it's Mommy honey, I love you my little angel, and I will be right here when you wake up." I turned to leave. When I came to Jimmy, I hugged him tightly, "Jimmy, I'm going to the chapel for a few minutes, if anything happens come get me."

Then I left to find the hospital chapel. When I opened the door to the chapel, it was dimly lit with only two lights. One semi-bright light was over the door as you entered and one small light on the other side of the room was glowing over the top of a statue of the figure of Christ. I walked the twenty feet or so to where the statue was, and I knelt down in front of it. I began to pray out loud, "Dear God! I don't ask you for much and I know I don't go to church anymore, but please save my daughter's life. She is so little and helpless; she needs me, and I need her!"

I felt a sense of urgency and I started to cry and scream out, "Please, God! I am begging you to help her. Tony, Tony, I know you can hear me! Please save our daughter!" Just then the door opened. I turned quickly to see the tall figure of something or someone standing there. With the tears flowing from my eyes, it looked as if I was seeing a glistening angel from the light shining over the door behind this dark figure. I wiped the tears from my eyes and begged, "Can you save my daughter?"

This figure began to come toward me and in a strong, stern voice, "Christina Powers, you're a sinful woman and you must repent for your sinful ways before God will answer your prayers and save your child." I reached out to touch this heavenly image, but it was just a man.

I stood up and shouted, "What are you talking about? If God will only save my daughter after I've repented for sins, I don't believe I've committed, then I don't want anything to do with your God."

"You dare to blaspheme God, while you plead with him to save the life of your daughter? What kind of an abomination from hell are you?"

I slapped him in the face with all my might and this six-foot man went flying into the pews. I ran out of the chapel and continued to run back to Joy's room. When I turned through the opened doors of the burn unit, I saw Jimmy walking toward me with tears pouring down his face.

I stopped and shouted, "**Jimmy is Joy all right**?" All he could do was shake his head 'no'.

I screamed, "Oh God, no!" Then I fell to my knees in the middle of that hall and cried my heart out, **as another piece of my soul died**.

CHAPTER 10

As I was sitting on that cold floor in the hallway of the hospital crying my heart out, I felt a warm soft breeze flow over my body and immediately a sense of peace came over me. Somehow, I knew Joy was out of pain and safe with Tony. I felt someone touch my shoulder as they knelt down beside me, "Jesus is speaking to you, Christina, please listen to what he is saying."

I turned toward the voice and it was the same man who was in the chapel. I felt so weak I just leaned my head on his shoulder as my tears began to subside, "Would you please help me up? I need to go to my daughter."

As this stranger was helping me off the floor Jimmy and Bobby came over to us and Bobby said, "Thank you sir we'll help her from here."

Then with Jimmy and Bobby on either side of me, we walked toward Joy's room. As we headed slowly down the hall this same man came up to us, placed a card in my hand, "Christina, this is my card. Please call me anytime you want to know what Jesus is trying to say to you."

He then turned around and left without saying another word. I slipped his card in my partially torn and burnt bra and continued walking toward Joy's room with Jimmy and Bobby.

When we reached Joy's room and opened the door, there were two nurses in the room with Joy. They were washing her, and one of them was holding Joy's little arm way up in the air, so high that it lifted her little body just enough to reach her hand under Joy's back. When she saw us open the door, she stopped washing Joy, came over to us and said in a very rude tone, "I'm sorry, but you're not allowed in this room until we have prepared the body."

I looked at her sternly and sharply replied, "Miss, you're washing my baby and I don't like how you're doing it. So I will take over from here."

She looked back at me angrily, "I can't let..."

I interrupted her immediately, "You can stop talking right now, or I will have your license in the morning."

I walked over to Joy, took the washcloth from the other nurse's hand and began to wash my baby's bruised and singed little body.

As the two nurses left the room, Jimmy came over to me reached his hand down into the wash basin grabbed the other washcloth and began to help me wash her. We looked into each other's tear-filled eyes, as we washed our little girl, "Mr. Demetrees, I truly do love you."

When we finished washing Joy, we put her little hospital gown on her. I turned to Jimmy and Bobby, stretched my arms out to them both and they came over to me and we just held one another. There was a tap on the door and as it opened, a young nurse was standing there and she politely said, "Please excuse me. I am Sue Sereikis and I'm the nursing supervisor for the burn unit. I just wanted to see if there was anything, I could get for you folks?"

The three of us broke our embrace as I said in a very low sad voice, "Sue, can you please tell me where my baby's body will go from here?"

She answered me very sincerely, "Mrs. Demetrees your daughter will be held here at the hospital in a safe, clean cooler, until your funeral director comes to pick her up."

"Thank you, Sue." Then I bent down, kissed Joy on her forehead, "Its Mommy honey and I love you baby with all my heart. You will be with me in my heart every day of my life, until I can hold you again." I kissed her again, "Joy, honey, you go with Daddy now." I could no longer hold back my tears, "Daddy will be taking care of you now my baby." **Oh God! How my heart broke as I said goodbye to my baby. It was the hardest thing I ever had to do.**

Then the three of us slowly turned and walked out of her room together. We held each other up as we walked in a dazed state down the hall, where we met James and Carman in the waiting room. We all just looked at each other with no one knowing what to say and everyone trying to hold back their tears. I said in a totally defeated voice, "Since the five of us have no place to go, I suggest we take a taxi to the Regency Hotel. I think we should try to get some rest."

James spoke up, "Why don't you four sit here and I'll get us a ride. Then I'll come back and get you guys." So that's what we did.

I rented a three-bedroom suite for one week at the Regency. James and Carman took one room, Jimmy and Bobby took the other, and I went for the last bedroom. It was 6:00am when my head hit the pillow. As exhausted as I was, I still could not fall asleep. So I got up at 8:00am on the dot and called Hess funeral home which was the same funeral establishment Jimmy hired to do Tony's funeral. I made an appointment with the owner, Mr. Hess, for 10:00am to make the arrangements for Joy's funeral. After I set the appointment time, I had Mr. Hess promise me he would go immediately to the hospital and pick Joy's body up. I could not handle the thought of Joy being left in the hospital morgue any longer.

I called my Senior Personal Secretary, Judy, at her home and had her send clothing to the hotel for all of us, along with a new limo. I also put her to work on finding us all temporary housing at one of the more elite apartment buildings in town, at least until I could try to think about permanent living arrangements. As soon as I hung up the phone, I went to the shower to clean up and get ready for my appointment with Mr. Hess.

About ten minutes after I finished my shower, the clothing which Judy had sent to the hotel for us arrived. I placed all the clothing out on the sofa with a note telling the others to go through the clothes and find what fits. I also told them where I was going and that I would be back as soon as possible. I dressed and walked down to my limo, which I had waiting to take me to my appointment with Mr. Hess. As the limo driver left L.A. and headed toward Malibu, we could still see the smoke in the sky from the fire.

When we reached Hess Funeral Home on Route 1, I climbed out of the limo, took a deep breath and slowly headed into the funeral home. I knew this was going to be a hard thing to do, but I didn't realize how hard until Mr. Hess took me in the back room and began to show me some tiny coffins. When I saw them, the realization I was actually going to have to place my child in one of those coffins made me begin to feel faint. I grabbed onto Mr. Hess' arm to steady myself, "Mr. Hess, I can't do this right now. Would you please pick out the best one you have for Joy?"

He helped me back out of the room, "Mrs. Demetrees, if you would please send me something for Joy to wear, then I can take care of everything else for you."

I looked at him sincerely, "Thank you Mr. Hess, I would truly appreciate that, and I'll have a dress sent to you this afternoon. And please call me Christina."

He nodded his head, "Thank you Christina. I need to know one more thing. When would you like to have the showing? We can hold it tomorrow afternoon and evening and have the funeral the day after, or we could wait another day."

"Let's have it tomorrow, I don't think I can handle waiting another day." Then I gave him a hug, thanked him one more time and left.

It was October 4th, 1979, at 11:00am when the funeral procession pulled into the cemetery. The weather was cold and rainy that day. This was the first rain we'd had in months and I was burying my little Joy ten days before her second birthday, in that cold rain. This was also the second time I was at this cemetery in the past year, and as I recall, it was raining then too.

As the men started to lower Joy's golden coffin into the ground right over her Father's, I realized I would never attend my own daughter's birthday party, for some reason it hit me right there as she began to disappear from my sight. **I had missed her first birthday party**. I had been fairly strong through all of it up to the point when Joy completely disappeared out of my sight. That's when I lost it. I began to scream and cry, "No! No! Joy! God, why did you take my daughter from me?" With all my closest friends around me, I turned to them and shouted, as the rain poured down, "What the **fuck** is life all about? Why would God take my child from me?"

Jimmy put his arm around me and softly said, "Christina, none of us truly know the answers. All I know is we are still alive, and we must go on living. Maybe there is something we need to learn from death, or maybe not. Christina, if we are to learn something from Joy's death, then we will. For right now let's just let some time pass before we start looking for the answers." Then he hugged me, lifted his eyebrows just a bit, "Okay?"

I wiped my eyes and calmly sighed, "Okay."

I bent down, grabbed some dirt to toss on the casket and in my hand was the Medallion I buried with Tony and I thought, "Well I guess you want me to have this." Then I brushed it off and stuck it in my pocket as Jimmy placed his arms around me and said, "Come on baby, let's go back to the hotel," and with that we turned and walked away, leaving Joy and Tony behind.

The next morning, I received a visit from a Detective Fred Ulrich of the California State Fire Investigation Bureau. I learned from Detective Ulrich that three other people lost their lives in the fire that night. He said Nanny Sue's body was found where the nursery once was. He also told me the bodies of the other two employees, Flow and Mark Sentamore, who came running out of the burning mansion with Carman that night, were found in the woods about two miles from the mansion. Detective Ulrich also needed some information on all of my household employees. I answered what I could of his questions, I gave him my Secretary's number and told him if he needed anything more to call her. I was a little curious, so I asked, "Detective Ulrich, why do you need information on all of my household employees?"

He answered very officially, "It's all routine Ms. Powers, nothing to be alarmed about." Then he added, "I'd like to thank you for your help, and if I might say, it has been a pleasure meeting you." I thanked him and walked him to the door.

Shortly after Detective Ulrich left, I decided to take a ride out to the mansion. I could not believe what I saw when I rounded the bend of the driveway. There was nothing left to that once magnificent building but rubble and ashes. I stepped out of the car and slowly walked up the sidewalk toward what once was my home. When I reached the porch steps, I decided I had to look through the rubble for anything that belonged to Tony and Joy. I slowly and carefully climbed down into the ashes and began to look through the debris. I spent the next three hours rummaging through the burnt ashes and all I could find was a slightly singed bottle of champagne. I picked up the bottle, wiped it off and thought, "Oh my God! That's all that's left... 'one bottle of champagne,' nothing left to the life Tony and I made together. **NOTHING AT ALL!"**

All of our personal photo albums, every stitch of clothing I saved of Tony's, along with all of Joy's things were gone. It was as if there was nothing to confirm I ever lived that life with Tony and Joy. Just then a breeze picked up and the ashes started to blow away in the wind. As I watched the wind blow, I realized everything I loved was gone and that I was alone in the world. Sure, I had Jimmy, but he was not Tony. When I could no longer take the pain of my hopeless search, I climbed out of the ashes and decided somehow, I would rebuild my life.

American Goddess

When I got back to the hotel that evening, Jimmy and Bobby had just returned with two boxes of great smelling pizza. They had gone into the office that day and also went to look at the six-bedroom penthouse Judy had found for us as a possible rental. James and Carman went to stay with their daughter. This was only a temporary living situation for them because I gave them both some needed time off. James and Carman were going to leave my employment because Carman felt responsible for Joy's death. I convinced her there was no one to blame and that I truly felt like they were a part of my family; so, they decided to stay on with me. Boy was I glad, because I really would have missed them as family members first, then as trusted, irreplaceable employees. They were going to move back in with Jimmy, Bobby, and me as soon as we were reestablished in semi-permanent living quarters. After I washed the champagne bottle, I went into the living room to where Jimmy and Bobby were. When I entered the room, I noticed they already had opened one of the pizza boxes. I walked past them, placed the bottle on the mantel, then I walked over, poured myself a glass of Coca Cola, grabbed a piece of sausage and mushroom pizza and said, "This was a great idea guys, mmm, it's good too!"

Jimmy was downing a piece of pie as I sat beside him and when he swallowed, he said, "Christina, the penthouse was great, so we went ahead and rented it. It's on the 16th floor of the Elsmere building, which happens to be the most elite building in LA for the city's gay population."

I laughed, "That sounds great guys. Maybe it will be like our old days in Roma, Jimmy."

He laughed, "Not exactly like those days I hope."

Over our pizza Jimmy and Bobby gave me the rundown on the ten motion pictures and twenty albums we had in the works at the studio. Afterward, Jimmy said, "Everything is running smoothly right now Christina, so if you need more time off go ahead and take it."

"No Jimmy, I think it will be better for me, if I just go right back to work. So I'm going to try to get some sleep tonight, and go in with you guys in the morning."

The next day when I went into my office I discovered, 'Halloween in Hell' had grossed a phenomenal two hundred million dollars in its first weekend. It seemed the news of how I somehow knew something was wrong with Joy, and how I ran out of the premier to try to save my daughter's life catapulted 'Halloween In Hell' to be the most financially successful motion picture of all time.

The album which accompanied the film had shot to the number one spot the very next afternoon. The six days since Joy's death, the gross earnings for the film and soundtrack were five hundred ninety-six million dollars worldwide. In those six days the stock of Powers Incorporated soared to a whopping fifty-two-dollars a share.

American Goddess

The newspapers, tabloids and television, all told story after story of how people lined up for blocks and waited hours to see the film. Then there were the stories of how people were fainting in the theaters and there were about six deaths by heart attack, blamed on the film. They also told how the Christian community had condemned the film, my performance in it, and how they had organized a protest to ban the film. However, I think it only helped feed the film's fire. It appeared that the whole world was talking about 'Halloween in Hell' and the horrendous death of my daughter, which just happened to take place on the premier night of this extremely horrifying and emotionally charged film.

Around 10:00am I went into one of the empty soundtrack mixing rooms, put on a set of headphones and began to really listen to my soundtrack of 'Halloween in Hell.' As I listened to one song after the other, I began to feel a chill. The titles to the individual cuts were, 'Halloween In Hell', 'Dance Of The Demons', 'Dark Demon Lady', 'Bride Of Satan', 'Demon Temptress', 'Death On Route 666' and the one with the scariest lyrics of all, 'The Fiery Queen Of Hell Has Come.'

As I listened, I thought, "How in the world could I have written all of these lyrics? Each song I sang glorified Satan. What if that man in the hospital was right? No, it can't be. All I did was create another money maker." I shrugged my shoulders to accompany my thoughts, "Shit, if Mickey Mouse can scare the hell out of people, so can I. That guy was just an asshole. Now the true question is, how in the world do I top this one?"

When I finished in the mixing room, I went back into my office. I walked over and sat down at my desk where I started to try and come up with my next money maker.

That night I climbed into bed and tried to fall to sleep, but I could not stop my mind from replaying over and over again the things I discovered that day. I thought about the film and the way I performed in it. I thought about the lyrics I sang on each cut on the soundtrack. I thought about how my fans have reacted to the film, versus the way the so-called Christian community had. Then, I thought about what the man in the hospital said to me. I didn't think I was ever going to fall asleep that night, but finally, I drifted off.

All of a sudden, I heard a horrible scream! I flew up out of the bed to find myself once again running at night through a burning forest, only this time without a stitch of clothing on. My feet were blistering, as I ran over the hot burning cinders. It seemed like the fire was screaming at me. It was wailing horrifically as the flames reached out for me from the burning tree limbs. As I ran, the fire was trying to grab hold of me by my bare skin with its flaming hot claws. Then, the fire all around me began to take on the forms of hideous burning men. These horrifying burning beasts began to leap off the trees and started to run toward me from all directions. I screamed in horror as they began to encircle me, chanting in a horrible screeching tone, "Christina! Christina!" With every step I took, the sound became louder and more horrifying.

American Goddess

The fire raged into an inferno as they made a complete circle around me. I had about twenty feet left before I'd be consumed by their flames. Then all at once, a bright light began to shine from over my head. I looked up to see Tony and Joy coming toward me and I screamed out, "Tony! Help me!"

He reached out his hand to me and started to yell, "Christina, grab my hand!"

I stretched out my hand to him, but I could not reach him. Then I heard Joy yell, "Mommy, take Daddy's hand."

I jumped up as high as I could, but I still could not reach Tony's hand. Just as these fiery beasts were about to grab me, I screamed out with all my might, "God, please help me!"

With that there was a great thunder, and the fire was gone. The light began to grow so strong that I covered my eyes with the palms of my hands, but I could still see it. I heard the rumble of a voice so strong that I fell to my knees in fear. The voice shouted, "Christina, you have blasphemed my name and sinned against me! Yet you dare plead to me for your life!" As the voice of God spoke to me, I became so terrified I dug my fingernails right into my legs, causing them to bleed profusely. The voice echoed through my body, "Christina, the punishment for your sins have been decided. You shall never be allowed to see Tony, or Joy again for all of eternity and you are to be banished into the fiery flames of hell until the time I remember you!"

Then the light began to fade, and I could once again see the flames of the fiery beasts approaching me. I screamed out from the depths of my soul, "God no!" With that I felt the fiery hands grab me and I began to fight wildly as I screamed, "No! No!" Then I heard more yelling,

"Christina, wake up! You're having a nightmare! Wake up!"

My eyes flew open and I saw Jimmy and Bobby trying to wake me up. I screamed out, "Oh God, Jimmy. It was horrible!"

I, along with the entire bed was soaked from sweat. I grabbed hold of Jimmy and just held him as I sobbed. After about ten minutes, I was finally able to calm myself and tell Jimmy and Bobby all about the dream.

Jimmy kissed me, "It was a horrible dream, that's for sure. But it was only a dream Christina, so why don't you try to put it out of your mind and go take a shower while Bobby and I change the bed." When I emerged from the shower my bed was ready, and I finally fell back to sleep around 3:00am that morning.

I woke up at 6:00am to the annoying sound of my alarm clock. I turned the alarm off, stretched and climbed out of bed. After I dressed, I walked over to the nightstand drawer, opened it and took out the card that was placed in my hand by the stranger at the hospital. It read, **"Evangelist Reverend Timmy Swinebert, Spiritual Leader of the Swinebert Full Gospel Church and President of Swinebert University of God, in Greater**

Dallas, Texas." Included on the card were two phone numbers, a business number and a handwritten personal number.

At 6:45am I placed a call to Mr. Swinebert at his personal number and he agreed to set an appointment to meet with me at 1:00pm that afternoon, in Dallas. I thanked him and hung up the phone. I placed his card in my purse and headed out for breakfast. Over breakfast I told Jimmy and Bobby I decided not to go into the office with them. After Jimmy and Bobby left for work, I headed for Dallas. I did not tell them where I was going, because I knew Jimmy would have something to say about it, and **I did not want to hear it.**

CHAPTER 11

I caught the 9:00am flight on October 15th, at LA International, and I was on my way to Texas. The day was bright, warm, and beautiful when I got off the plane in Dallas. I headed straight for my waiting limo and it was off to my meeting.

The time was 12:40pm when I arrived at Mr. Swinebert's University. I was becoming fairly impressed as we drove past a dozen or so buildings on the campus. It appeared as if Mr. Swinebert's ministry was doing quite well. When we reached the three-story administration building, I climbed out and headed for my meeting.

As soon as I opened the office door I was immediately and graciously received by Mr. Swinebert's secretary. She rose from her desk and came to greet me with a bright smile and outstretched arms. I was taken aback a little as she hugged me and said, "God bless you, Sister Christina! It's so nice to meet you."

I stepped back and replied, quite officially, "It's Ms. Powers, and I'm here to see Mr. Swinebert. I have a 1:00pm appointment with him."

She laughed like a little scatterbrain, "Silly, I already know that Sister Christina, I've been expecting you. Come with me and I'll take you in to see Brother Swinebert."

When we reached the massive, solid oak double doors of Mr. Swinebert's office, my jovial guide tapped twice on the door. Then, she opened it just enough to poke her head through and said with a slight giggle, "Brother Swinebert, Sister Christina is here."

American Goddess

I heard him reply with an excited tone, "Show her in, Sister Nancy." As Sister Nancy opened the door, I could see Mr. Swinebert coming toward me. He was well dressed in a black three-piece suit. He was about six feet tall, two hundred and ten pounds and fairly muscular. I'd say he was forty-five years old and he had the beginnings of gray mixed in with his well-trimmed, soft, brown hair. His captivating, sparkling brown eyes helped to enhance his distinguished look, which I found to be slightly appealing. As he reached me, he took my hands in his, smiled and with a southern twang to his manly voice, "Miss Powers I'm so glad you've come."

I pulled my hands away, and replied very politely, but formally, "Mr. Swinebert thank you for seeing me on such short notice, and please call me Ms. Powers, not miss."

Still smiling, "Of-course, please come on in Ms. Powers."

He led me into his large office which I noticed immediately had eight stuffed and mounted trophies of wild animals, two on each of the four walls around his office. Scattered between these were numerous photos of Mr. Swinebert, with hundreds of other people. We walked the thirty-foot span toward a group of bearskin style covered office chairs. A petite woman in her thirties with curly shoulder length, dyed blonde hair and brown eyes, wearing a Donna Reid style Polka dot dress, stood up from one of the chairs, hugged me and sweetly said, "Hi, Sister Christina, I'm Sister Tammy Swinebert, Timmy's wife! It's so nice to meet you."

I smiled cordially, "Hello, it's nice to meet you as well."

She gasped, put her little hands to her mouth, "Oh my! Sister Christina, proper 'Christians' never greet someone in that manner. Saying hello to someone is like telling them to go to hell, you know, hell is low?"

I looked at her strangely, "What are you talking about?"

Mr. Swinebert quickly interrupted, "Sweety, Ms. Powers, is not a Christian yet."

Her face immediately took on an incredibly sad expression, "I'm sorry, I thought you became a Christian the night of your daughter's death."

Feeling quite offended and without my smile, "Mrs. Swinebert, I am a Christian. I was baptized a Catholic as an infant."

She clutched her hands to her chest and gasped, "Gee, I'm messing everything up here. I'm so sorry."

I smiled, "Thank you for the apology. I think the problem is we are both on two different channels." Then I laughed, as she looked at me with a blank stare and I thought, "She didn't get it, oh boy!"

Mr. Swinebert hugged his wife, "Tammy, sweetie, I'm sure Ms. Powers is a terribly busy woman. So why don't you say goodbye now and leave us be."

This time she only shook my hand, as she said, "Well, I hope we meet again, Ms. Powers."

American Goddess

When she finished shaking my hand I answered very sweetly, "It's nice to have met you, Mrs. Swinebert."

As she left the room Mr. Swinebert said, "Please take a seat, Ms. Powers."

"Thank you," and I sat down in one of the furry chairs. Mr. Swinebert took the seat next to mine, "Please Ms. Powers call me Tim."

"Of course, I'll call you Tim, and please call me Christina."

After taking a sip from his glass he inquired, "Now tell me Christina, how I can serve you today?"

Looking seriously at him, "Tim, you told me Jesus was trying to speak to me. I've come all this way today, because I would like to know what you mean by that."

He took my hand in one of his, squeezed it, then he put his other hand in the air, closed his eyes and quite loudly, "I praise you Jesus! God of all power and might; for you have called another child out of the fires of hell and into your salvation."

Astonished at what he was saying, I pulled my hand out of his, "Would you please stop this, you people are freaking me out here. I came to ask a question, not to be mauled and insulted."

I got up to leave and Tim begged me, "Please Christina, forgive my outburst. It's just that when I see the Power of God's Hand at work in another child's life, I become filled with the Holy Spirit and I must proclaim the glory of Christ. So please stay and allow me to answer your question."

I sat back down, "I guess I can understand that."

"Christina, Jesus is telling you He loves you. He wants you to look at your life and judge it for yourself. Then give your life to him and let him help you change your evil earthly ways."

Feeling offended again, "Are you saying God would take my daughter's life, to make me change my ways?"

He grabbed his Bible, opened it, "Do you believe in the Bible?"

"I'm not sure; I have never really read it."

He looked at me with concern, "Please allow me to read some scripture to you I feel God wants you to hear. In James, 2:11, God has said, '**Do not commit adultery and do not kill. Now if you commit adultery and kill, haven't you become a transgressor of the law? Then by denying your transgressions, you blaspheme my name. Now you shall have judgment without mercy, for you have shown no mercy. And mercy rejoiceth against judgment**.' He closed the Bible with force, "Do you understand what Jesus is saying?"

He looked as if he were looking right through me, "Yes, I think I do know what He is saying, but what does God want from me?"

He smiled, "In Acts 8:22 God says, '**Repent therefore of this thy wickedness and pray God, if perhaps the thought of thine heart may be forgiven.**' Turn your life over to Jesus so you may have all eternity with your loved ones in the presence of the Lord. If not, then you choose Satan, and eternity in the flames of hell."

As he said these things I thought of the dream and I knew I wanted to be with Tony and Joy. I also knew I didn't want to be burning in hell for one second, no-less an eternity. I took a deep breath, "So what does it mean to give your life over to Jesus?"

With authority, "It means you become born again. Jesus said in John 3:3, '**Except a man be born again, he cannot see the kingdom of God.**' He also said, '**Except a man be born of water and spirit, he cannot see the kingdom of God.**'

Curiosity made me ask, "I have heard the term born again, but what does that mean?"

His eyes lit up, "You must first repent for your sins then be baptized in the name of Jesus Christ and change your life. God wants to use you, Christina, to reach the world with his message of salvation."

I looked at him as if he were nuts, "Whoa! You said a mouthful and I don't know if I can swallow it all, especially since I don't even know what you're talking about."

"Christina, have you ever seen my television crusades?"

"No Tim, I can't quite say that I have."

This time he looked at me like I was nuts, "You haven't? Well I just happen, 'Praise God' to be holding a crusade tonight in Houston. Why don't you come and see what I'm talking about for yourself?"

I shrugged my shoulders, "Why not! All right I will take you up on your offer."

He grinned from ear to ear, "Good, because we have to leave right now if I'm going to be ready for tonight."

"May I first use your phone? I need to call my office."

"Of course, why don't you use the phone in the back room for privacy?" He pointed to a door on the other side of the room. I got up, walked over to the door, opened it and headed for the phone to dial the number, "Hi Jimmy, I just want to let you know I don't think I'll be home tonight. I'm also checking up on you. How are things?"

With concern he said, "Where are you?"

I answered evasively, "I'm in Dallas checking something out, and I'm not sure what it is yet. Right now, it's just a feeling."

With a nervous tone, "Just a feeling! Well, whatever it is, please don't throw every dime we have into it like the last time you had a feeling."

I laughed, "It's nothing like that."

With a sigh of relief, "Thank God! So how can I reach you?"

"You can't right now, I'll have to call you back."

American Goddess

"Okay. Well just in case I don't see you tomorrow, I'll leave your penthouse key with the building security officer. We are moving in tonight you know, now, with no help from you, thank you very much."

I chuckled, "I'll give you a kiss when I come home darling. Will that do?"

We laughed a little like old times, "It will do for now. Do you know where the Elsmere building is?"

"Yes, and I'll see you there. So don't worry about me, I'm doing fine."

"I love you girlfriend, so you keep in touch."

I replied in kind, "Same here." I hung up the phone and headed for Houston, Texas with Tim Swinebert.

As we flew on Tim's private jet to Houston, Tim talked more about the Bible and his personal relationship with Jesus Christ. He read scriptures which told what it meant to be a born-again child of God. He articulated his message with such warmth and gentleness, I truly felt touched.

When we arrived at the Houston Coliseum, I witnessed a transformation take place with Tim, from this soft-spoken teddy bear, to suddenly becoming more like myself, a strong demanding perfectionist. He took charge of the entire set up, which happened to be quite impressive.

The minute we entered the work area, he started giving orders. There was a thirty-piece orchestra to back up a sixty-member choir, stage lighting, sound, and television crew setups. Everything had to be perfect for that evening's crusade. I could see by the way Tim was handling things, he knew exactly what he wanted for every minute of his sermon.

As the evening approached, the coliseum was becoming a-buzz with life. There were Christian radio and newspaper reporters all interviewing Tim. Then when one of the reporters realized who I was, this nice, peaceful, well-mannered interview, suddenly turned into the frantic ones I'm used to. With the blink of an eye, they all charged towards me and started shouting questions at me simultaneously. But Tim swiftly managed to reestablish control over the interview.

Afterwards, we met with dozens of local church leaders. I just quietly followed Tim as he introduced me to them all. When we reached one of the gentlemen there, Tim introduced him to me as his father, The Reverend Timmy Swinebert Senior. I discovered this sixty-year-old, tall, heavy set man, was the founding father of Tim Junior's Christian empire. He was a very pleasant man upon our meeting, but there was something about him which put me on my guard. After we finished speaking, Tim Senior called us all into a twenty-minute prayer, which I thought would never end, asking for the service to be blessed. Finally, it was time for Tim Junior to take center stage.

American Goddess

Tim opened his sermon with a prayer, followed by thirty minutes of everyone in the Coliseum singing of their love with praises to Jesus Christ. I didn't know what to make of these thousands of people all around me, all doing something different. Some were singing and dancing, while others were jumping up and down crying and screaming.

Finally, Tim calmed them down and began his sermon. He started by talking about how our sins affect everything in our lives. He said, "In order to see the power of sin in our lives, all we have to do is look at the first sin, which was the sin of Adam and Eve. Because of that first sin, now all mankind must suffer the penalty of that sin which is death. This is why we all must die. So, when you sin and think it does not matter, think again; because it influences everything that takes place in your life." He went on to say, that Jesus died on the cross, paid the penalty for that first sin, for all of us. He said, "This was done because Jesus was a perfect sacrifice. So, when Jesus died, he gave us all the opportunity to come to him and be born again. When you die, you are assured eternal life in the presence of Christ and with all your loved ones."

Then he jumped around the stage praising God and working the crowd up into a frenzy of crying and praising God. After that he said, "You must all come to the altar, for now is the time to accept Christ as your Savior. Then, He will forgive your sins and accept you as his child. This is how Christ will open the doors to Heaven for you." Suddenly music started playing and Tim began to cry with real tears as he begged people to come to the altar. He shouted, "Give your lives to Christ now, before it's too late!"

I found Tim's performance to be quite hypnotic. So much so, I almost walked to the altar myself. Suddenly Tammy Swinebert came over to me with a big smile, grabbed my hand and shouted over the crowd of wailing people, "Come Christina, Jesus is calling you! Please let me walk up with you."

A little leery of her aggressiveness, "Thank you Tammy, but I'm not ready to take such a long walk."

Her eyes grew wide as she lowered her voice, "If not for yourself, then give your life to Jesus for your daughter's sake."

At that point I had had enough, and I shouted at her, "Please, Tammy, I don't like someone trying to convince me to do something I already said no to once." I pulled my hand from hers, "I need some fresh air I feel like I'm being suffocated in here. I'll meet you out by the limo." With that I turned and walked away from her as fast as I could and thought, "This one could get on my nerves fast!" After that I waited for Tim and **Tammy** to come out.

It was 11:00pm when Tim finally walked toward the limo driver and me as we were chatting about Jesus. When he reached us, he said, "Christina, I must stay here tonight at the Hilton. Shall I reserve a room for you?"

"No, thank you." I answered quickly. "I must catch the first flight back to L.A. so if you would provide me with a ride to the airport, I would be very grateful."

He sighed sadly, "I wish you could stay, but I understand." He looked at the chauffeur and added, "Billy-Joe, take us to the airport please."

"Where's Tammy, Tim?"

"She is going to the hotel, and I'm taking you to the airport. I'll have my jet take you back to LA right away."

"Thank you, that is very generous."

As the limo pulled away Tim said, "Please tell me Christina, did you feel the power of God this evening?"

I looked into his big brown eyes, "I felt something this evening Tim, but I can't say it was God. What I can say is, I will start to read my Bible because of it."

He grabbed my hand, moved close to me and said, as I thought I was going to be kissed, "Praise God! Christina, God has just told me to be your spiritual teacher."

With that we pulled into the airport, where the private jets are kept and I replied, "Thank you Tim, please let me think about your offer. I'll call you in a few days."

When we climbed out of the limo, Tim took me in his arms and hugged me very nicely, "God speed to you Christina, and I will be waiting for your call."

Graciously, I thanked him, and it was off to LA on Tim's private jet. As the plane took off, I thought, "You know, he was not that bad and a lot of what he said made sense." I also felt a sense of peace from within my heart as he talked. I could have listened to him for hours.

It was 3:15am when I opened the door to our new home in the Elsmere building. The lights in the foyer were on, so I closed the door behind me and walked right into the living room. When I flicked on the light, I could hear some noises from the back room. As I headed toward the dark hall, I looked for a switch to turn on the light, but I could not find one. The noise became louder. It sounded like someone screaming while being choked. Instantly I became alarmed and thought, "What the hell is going on?"

I saw a light coming from under the doorway and I jumped in the air when I heard another really loud scream, making me run toward the sound. As soon as I reached the door, it flew open and I screamed, "Ahhh!" as this green faced monster screamed, "Ahhh!" at the same time it reached out for me. I kicked it right where it hurts, knocking it back into the light of the room and I heard a loud squeal. I ran into the room ready to do battle, only to find Jimmy bouncing around on the floor holding his balls, with a green facial mud mask on screaming, "Oh fuck! Oh shit! Oh, fuck that hurts!"

I wanted to laugh but Jimmy was hurting so much, "Oh my God! Jimmy, are you all right?" I reached down to help him, "I didn't know it was you, all I heard was screaming and choking and I thought someone was being killed."

American Goddess

When I heard the choking again, I turned to see Bobby coughing so hard, his face was turning red. I helped Jimmy up, then I walked over to Bobby, "Bobby, let me look at you."

He replied with a rough voice, "Hi, Christina, I'm not feeling too good."

Bobby started to cough again as Jimmy said, "I was just going to get him a drink and some more cough medicine, when you attacked me."

As we talked, I felt his forehead and exclaimed, "Shit Bobby, you're burning up." I turned to Jimmy, "What's his temperature?"

"I don't know, I didn't take it yet."

I gave him my 'Duh' look, "I'll look for a thermometer while you get him the medicine and for God sake please get that shit off you face."

I went into the main bathroom, opened the medicine closet and as I suspected, there was a first-aid kit there. I knew Judy would think of everything, so I took the kit back to the bedroom where Jimmy was giving Bobby his medicine. I opened the first-aid kit, took out the thermometer, and shook it down, "Open your mouth Bobby, and place this under your tongue."

As we waited, Bobby was struggling not to cough as he held the thermometer in his mouth. When I pulled it out, it read, **"104.6 degrees**."

Thinking, "Shit, that's high!" I said, "Maybe we should call the doctor."

As soon as I said that Bobby began to cough again. This time he was coughing up blood. I grabbed a handful of tissues and helped Bobby catch the blood and said, "Jimmy, come here with Bobby, I'm calling an ambulance."

Jimmy ran over to me and took the bloody tissues from my hand. I turned and went to call for help.

I washed the blood off my hands and waited for the ambulance. When the medics came to the door, there were two of them. One tall and skinny, the other short and fat. I greeted them, then led them to the bedroom where Bobby and Jimmy were. As we walked, I told them his temperature and that he started to cough up blood. When they entered the room behind me and saw Jimmy holding Bobby up, so that he didn't choke on his own blood, their faces went white. They stopped walking and the tall thin one asked, "Miss I know this is a gay building, but is he gay?"

I replied with annoyance, "What are you talking about? 'Is he gay?' He's sick."

With a tone of fear, the short fat one, "I'm sorry, but you're going to have to take him to the hospital yourself."

In shock I replied, "You guys must be joking, my friend is sick, now do your job and help him."

Again the fat one spoke out, "Look lady, your friend probably has that new 'gay plague', that's killing gay men all over the country. And I'm not going near him."

American Goddess

They started to walk out, "Listen guys, I'm Christina Powers and I don't know anything about a plague. But I promise you both, if you don't help my friend, I will have your heads in the morning."

They looked at each other, turned around, walked back into the bedroom and helped Bobby. Then they took us to the hospital without saying another word.

When we arrived at the hospital, Bobby was asked if he was homosexual. When he said, "Yes", to my horror we began getting more of the same treatment from the hospital staff. Even so, I thank God it was not on such a dramatic scale as our two paramedic friends. Just the same, there was fear in most of the faces of the staff members we came in contact with that morning. When the ER doctor finally came in, he hardly touched Bobby at all as he tried to examine him. I could see he was not doing anything for Bobby, and Jimmy was beginning to get upset, so I quickly spoke up before Jimmy lost it and asked this doctor to call Doctor Heddermen for me. He stopped what he was doing, "Is he your family doctor?"

"Yes, he is," I answered. "And I would like to see him as soon as possible."

With a tone of relief, "Great, I'll go call him right now." With that he quickly left the room.

It took him fifteen minutes to come back to our room and when he did, he only stuck his head in the door, "Doctor Heddermen will be in soon." Then he closed the door and left without saying another word.

As we waited in our little room for Doctor Heddermen to come, I could not believe the treatment we were getting. I finally turned to Jimmy, "Jimmy, did you hear anything about a new gay plague?"

He looked at me with a worried expression, "Just last week. I read something about it in the 'Gay and Lesbian Herald.' It said there were an alarming number of gay men who were coming down with some rare disease and dying. The paper also said it was a 'conspiracy' which was being covered up by the government to wipe out the gay population. So, when I read that part of the story, I didn't think it was real."

I lowered my voice, "Well, Bobby is finally sleeping so let's wait and see what Doctor Hedderman says before we get crazy."

When Doctor Heddermen arrived, he examined Bobby then said, "Bobby, you have pneumonia and from what I can see, your coughing is what caused the bleeding. You ruptured a blood vessel in the back of your throat."

Jimmy asked, "Doctor Heddermen, does Bobby's pneumonia have anything to do with this new disease, everyone is calling the 'gay plague'?"

Doctor Heddermen laughed, "No Jimmy, and there is no new disease killing gay men either."

I spoke up, "Then someone better tell your co-workers."

American Goddess

With that I told him everything that happened, and he said, "From what I know, there has been some unexplained illness and deaths popping up around the country. But it's not an epidemic. The reason the staff is so jumpy is because we have had two cases in the last week."

I shook my head with concern, "Well, I think you should have a meeting with your people then and tell them there is no epidemic. Even if there was, they need to treat their patients a lot better than they treated us."

"I think I'll do just that." Then he turned back to Bobby, "Now Bobby, I'm going to keep you here for a couple of days. I'll send a nurse in with something to help stop the cough. I'm also going to order an IV. I want you on an antibiotic drip for a few days and we'll see how you respond to that."

Bobby nodded trustingly, "Whatever you say doc."

Doctor Heddermen turned to Jimmy and me, "It's going to take about an hour before Bobby gets a room; so, why don't the two of you go home and get some sleep."

"Jimmy, he's right. Why don't we go home?"

Jimmy looked at me through faithful loving eyes, "You go ahead Christina, I'll stay here with Bobby."

"Okay, why don't you take the day off? I'll go into the office today." Then I kissed them both and headed back to the apartment.

Bobby stayed in the hospital on I V antibiotic therapy for two weeks before he was able to come home. When he did, I gave him and Jimmy the next two weeks off from work.

As for me, well, I went back to work. Over the next few weeks, I checked up on every project we had in the works and reviewed all of our future plans. I read fourteen scripts for movies, and the lyrics for sixty-two albums. I ended up rejecting most of them. However, I did put my stamp of approval on six films and twenty-six albums. I put a stop to the ones I rejected, and had the writers start from scratch with new ideas. I also found the time to double check all the books. I wanted to make sure my hand-picked staff in the accounting offices were doing their jobs. Thanks to a huge shot in the financial arm by 'Halloween in Hell', the net cash worth of Powers Incorporated had soared to a whopping two-billion-dollars and still climbing.

On December 1st, after my verification of this great financial news, I had my New York and LA attorney offices prepare to send their best representatives to my office to meet with myself and my top management. The meeting was set for December 7th, at 10:00am. This would also be the first day Jimmy and Bobby would be returning to work. I wanted to be on top of every aspect of my business before I left. You see, I had made arrangements to go away for the first two months after Jimmy and Bobby returned to work.

American Goddess

Between doing all this, I still made time for studying the Bible. I needed to know for myself what God was saying to mankind through the Bible. If I thought of Tony, Joy and the dream once a day; then, I thought about them a thousand times a day.

On December 3, at 9:00am, I received a call from detective Fred Ulrich. He asked if I could meet with him sometime that day. I looked at my schedule and set up an appointment with him for that afternoon at 5:00pm, here at my office.

It was 2:00pm when Judy paged me and told me Barbara Goldstein was on the line for me. I had her patch the call into Studio 9 where I was working, then I picked up the phone and said, "Hi hot stuff, how are you?"

She replied with a sincere tone, "I'm fine, but how are you doing?"

I chuckled a little, "I'm getting through it Barbara, it's not easy, but I'm doing it."

"That's good news and I'm glad to hear it because Christina, this is not just a social call. I wanted to ask if you had seen Detective Ulrich recently."

I replied with curiosity, "No, but I received a call from him this morning. He said he needed to speak with me, so, I set up an appointment with him for this afternoon at 5:00pm. Now tell me why you're asking?"

"Good," Her voice intensified, "I'm glad I got to you first."

"What's up?" I asked with concern.

"I think we need to talk before you meet with him, but not on the phone," she said mysteriously.

"Well you've roused my curiosity. So, where and when do we meet before 5:00pm?"

"Can you meet me out in front of your office in ten minutes?"

"I don't think I have a choice here, so I'll be right out."

As soon as I walked out of the front door, Barbara pulled up in a limo, opened the back door from the inside, and said, "Climb in." I did, and off we went down Hollywood Boulevard. I looked at Barbara, who had an overly concerned expression on her face, and I said, "The intrigue has got me Barbara, and that look on your face is starting to spook me. Start talking."

She took my hand in hers, "Okay, there are two things Christina, but you never heard them from me, you got it?"

"I got it baby; this conversation isn't happening."

"All right then, first, I just heard from a good friend, who happens to be an inside source. This person has informed me you have some kind of insurance policy which allows you certain freedoms Frank would like to take from you."

With wide eyes, "I guess you do have an inside contact."

"It seems that Frank is trying to work around that policy, and it has something to do with the laws which govern the stock market. Frank is pumping millions of dollars into trying to influence certain congressman to help pass a new set of laws to govern the stock exchange. My sources say once these laws are enacted, Frank intends to instantly maneuver a corporate takeover of Powers Incorporated, just so he can throw you out of the entertainment industry once again. He wants to make an example of you for anyone who dares to challenge him."

Alarmed, "But how? Powers Incorporated is not listed on the public stock exchange. I have never sold any of the stock."

"I don't know much about it myself Christina, but I do know if Frank wants you, he is going to try anything to get you."

"Holy shit," I exclaimed! "I thought I was covering all the angles and the bastard can still out-fox me."

"Christina, there's more." Her look of concern intensified, "Now promise me you will hold on to your rage, because you're not going to like this one."

She stopped talking for a moment and I said, "I'm already freaking out now Barbara, so you might as well get it over with!"

"You have to promise me you'll stay calm!" She begged, "Or I'm not talking."

"I promise I will not lose it." I reassured her.

She proceeded cautiously, "Christina, listen to me very closely and please heed what I am about to say, before you do anything." Shaking her head, "Okay kiddo, here it comes." She slapped her hand down on her knee with frustration, "Shit Christina, this is going to hurt you, and I don't know how to tell you, so it doesn't."

She started to cry, so I squeezed her hand, "Stop it now Barbara and just tell me for God sakes. I'll handle it, whatever it is!"

She took a deep breath, "Detective Ulrich is going to inform you of the fact that the fire was the work of a well-planned arson. The way the fires were started they were assured to incinerate both of our properties." I 'gasped' as Barbara continued, "I have already spoken to Detective Ulrich and he asked me about the disagreement you had with Frank at the theater the night of the fire." At that I grabbed the edge of the leather seat and began to squeeze it with all my might.

Barbara let go of my other hand, reached out and put her arm on my shoulder, "Then he asked if I knew how come you went running out of the party like you did. I also heard from Eartha this morning and he questioned her about it as well. After her call I made some calls of my own and there is more. I heard Frank put the word out to torch our homes as soon as he walked out of the theater that night. But there is no way to prove it."

Horrified, "Are you telling me Frank had the fire set that killed my daughter and there's nothing I can do about it?" I shook my head, "I'll tell the detective what I suspect. There must be something he can do."

American Goddess

Desperately she pleaded, "Christina, listen to me. I believe in my heart what I was told is true, but I also know no one can prove it. That is why I am telling you this now, before the detective does. I want you to think about the best way to get Frank without trying to kill him yourself. Because Christina, I know you and I know you could lose it and actually kill Frank. I just don't want to see you in prison. Before you act baby, please think about it first."

"So what am I supposed to do, nothing?" I asked in desperation.

"Right now, Christina, I don't know what you can do, I only know what you should not do. Christina, you're a bright woman and I love you, so just don't throw it all away. Now, I'm going to slip away as fast as I came."

That's when the limo stopped, and we hugged. I kissed her cheek and said, "I love you Barbara, and thank you. I'll never forget the things you have done for me."

She smiled with love in her eyes, "When you need me, just call."

I climbed out of the limo and she drove away. I took a deep breath and headed back to my office. As I walked through the halls, I thought about everything Barbara had said, then I thought, "If no one can prove Frank gave the order for the fire, what can I do?" As I entered my office I didn't know how to react to Barbara's news. All I felt was weak, confused and overwhelmed. Not just by what Barbara told me, but by everything that had happened to me. I sat down at my desk and thought, "Oh well! I'll figure it out tomorrow!" With that in mind, I opened my safe and took out the bottle of cocaine I had stashed in it and for the first time since I went home to Joy, I took two lines of cocaine and I instantly felt a sense of relief.

Once I was feeling a little more relaxed, I remembered the feelings of safety and peace I felt when I was with Tim Swinebert that night in Houston as we talked about God. So I picked up the phone and called him.

When Detective Fred Ulrich did show up, I answered his questions to the best of my ability. After my questioning I invited Fred to join me for dinner, which he graciously accepted. After dinner, I asked him to drive me home, so he did, at which time I invited him in for a night cap. As we sipped our champagne out on my balcony, I decided it was my turn to question him. So with a tone of sincerity I said, "Fred, I need to talk to you. I need to ask you for your help."

With a slight look of disappointment, he replied, "What is it, Christina?"

I looked deeply into his eyes, "Fred, I think Frank Salerno may have caused the fire that killed my daughter. The only problem is I don't know how to prove it."

His look turned suspicious, "So what is it you're asking, Christina? I'm not sure what you mean."

I replied innocently, "I want to know if you have any clues as to who started the fire?"

American Goddess

"I have a few leads."

"Can you please tell me if any of them include Frank Salerno as a suspect?"

He looked at me guardedly, "Yes, I have thought of that myself. I have researched both of your pasts and I think you may be right."

"Oh boy! I'm glad to hear that. All I'm asking Fred is that you please find out the truth for me, and if it was Frank then please see that justice is served."

He leaned over gently kissed my check, "Christina, I promise you I will solve this case."

"Thank-you Fred," I answered sincerely. After that we continued to spend the rest of the evening together just chatting on the balcony. Fred actually turned out to be a nice guy and I felt I could really trust him.

On December 7th, 1979, at 10:00am in the main conference room, I called attention to our meeting by saying, "The first thing I wanted to say is congratulations and thank you. This year Powers Incorporated has seen such a phenomenal increase in our financial success that it means we have graduated to a full-fledged player in the Hollywood game." I received a round of applause after which I said, "Although we are doing quite well it doesn't insure, we will be here tomorrow, especially if we can't surpass 'the competition.' That's why I would like to vote on and hopefully pass a few amendments. First, I make a motion to pass a 20% pay increase across the board to all our employees, at a cost of ten-million-dollars a year. Second, even though we will eventually base our corporate headquarters in New York, I move we purchase this building outright to keep for our California headquarters, at a cost of thirty-million-dollars, a one-shot deal. Third, I move we purchase two corporate jets. One for my personal use as President of Powers Incorporated the other to be used by the Top Brass, meaning all of you, at a onetime cost of forty-million-dollars, per purchase. Then with an estimated two-million-dollar annual operations cost; the total cost for my proposed expenditures for the year is one-hundred and twenty-two-million-dollars; leaving cash on hand of seventy-eight-million-dollars. The best part is this will only increase our annual expenditure by twelve-million-dollars a year, and 'gang' I think we need these things for the company's future growth."

Upon completion of my report, we took a vote and my proposals passed unanimously. As I passed out copies of our financial report for the year I added, "This year belongs to us all. Most of you here came on board with Jimmy and I back in the beginning, that's why Powers Incorporated belongs to us all, not just Jimmy and me. Yes, it's true that I hold 70% and Jimmy holds 20% of all the stock, leaving 10% held by the rest of you. But I want you all to know you still have a voice and we want to keep hearing from you because Powers Incorporated belongs to everyone in this room, and we all hold the only stock to our dream. Now, I must tell you we are facing a big challenge to the survival of Powers Incorporated. I can't tell you exactly what it is right now, but I would like to inform you of what I intend to do to meet that challenge." I took a deep breath, big gulp of water, looked at Judy who was taking notes, "Ready, Judy?"

"Go for it, boss."

I smiled confidently, "We need to learn everything there is to know about the stock market. So, I move we hire the best 'broker' on Wall Street, to keep us on top of the game. I want a few insiders in Washington because we need to know what bills might be in the works to change the laws concerning the market. I also want to know who might be sponsoring these bills, and who or what committee is writing them. I want a personal Press Secretary for all of our headliners. I want as much control of the news going out of this place as possible." I stood up and added, "Listen closely 'gang', I don't want any of our business dealings slipping out of this room by anyone." I then handed out different assignments to each of them in groups of three, because I had decided earlier who I wanted doing what. When I regained their attention I added, "I really need to make sure you all follow these instructions to the letter. I know everything I have on some of your lists may not make sense now, but it will in the future. Now that we are done, I am leaving Jimmy and Bobby at the helm. I will be out of the office for a few weeks doing some research. If you need me, Jimmy will be able to get in touch with me. Thank you again ladies and gentlemen and hopefully you'll have completed your assignments, which I expect to find done and ready for me when I return two weeks from now." I said my goodbyes to them all, grabbed my re-stocked stash of cocaine, and it was off to Texas.

I had decided to accept Tim's offer to tutor me on the scriptures, so I rented a suite at the Dallas Hilton and began my personal Bible lessons with the 'master' himself, the great Reverend Timmy Swinebert.

For the next two weeks, I spent almost fourteen hours a day with Tim. Tim put his whole agenda and family on hold for me during those two weeks and he taught me as much about Jesus Christ and the Bible, as one person could possibly comprehend in a two-week span. Tim not only made learning the Bible easy, he also made it fun. We studied in the car as we drove all over the state of Texas during my entire stay. We studied from the beaches to the mountain tops. We studied the Bible on horse- back, on bicycles and on a five-mile hiking trip. To the ultimate Bible study of them all, a thousand feet up in a hot air balloon! For the first time since Joy's death, I was alive, and I didn't feel the pain. I felt free and I began to feel a oneness with Jesus Christ as I learned of his will.

Before we knew it, our last day had come, and we were on our last outing together. We were having a lovely picnic basket lunch on South Padre Island Beach, on the southern tip of Texas. The day was sunny and warm, and the sky was a bright turquoise blue, with beautiful, big, white, fluffy, clouds which were scattered about like giant marshmallows suspended in the air. It was my kind of day. We had our swimsuits on and we were sitting on a big beach blanket. As we ate our lunch, the warm breeze blowing over my body, along with the sounds of the water crashing on the beach, and the four lines of cocaine I did in the restroom, all had an erotic effect on me. As I watched and listened to Tim talk, I started to notice in a swimsuit the preacher looked pretty good. I caught my thoughts, "Christina, stop it! This man is a man of God! How could you start to look at him in that way?" Then I thought, "God, forgive me! Here I am trying to learn about your word Lord, on how to stop sinning and what am I doing? I start thinking of seducing the man who is teaching me. What am I? Am I an evil person? God, I hope not! Please help me stop thinking like this, God. I don't want to have these thoughts." I took a deep breath as I thought, "Okay, stop it right now Christina, and pay attention to what Tim is saying." So that's what I did.

When I came back down to earth, Tim was saying, "Christina, Jesus loves everyone, even the worst of sinners. The reason why He died on the cross for us was because he knew we were all sinners. But once we come to know Jesus and are born again He takes the power of sin from us. This is why we know we are saved and will go to heaven with our loved ones."

Curiously, I said, "Tim, when you speak to me of God's will for my life, I can truly feel the love Jesus has for me. It makes me love Jesus more every day for what he did for us all, by dying on the cross."

Tim grabbed my hand and moved closer to me with a look of romance in his eyes. I looked deep into his eyes and I felt my willpower instantly fading, so I found myself sliding over to meet him anticipating a warm kiss, but none came, "Christina, God is calling you! Can't you hear him? He's calling you to act now and be born again. Jesus wants you to lead the world to his saving grace and to turn the people from the sins of the world; the sins which you have helped to create by your once immoral lifestyle. Now, you can make up for your sins by saving others with the 'Word of God' and bring them to Jesus Christ." All of a sudden he hugged me, "Christina, you have that power because of who you are. God can use you to reach millions of lost souls. Please, Christina, realize the truth and become born again; then, come with me and leave your world of sin behind. Just think you and me, teaching the 'Word of God'. We can tour the world together and bring the lost sheep back to Jesus." He released our embrace and looked deeply into my eyes, "Christina, I'm serious. Don't go back to Hollywood, come with me. I am beginning a six-month, nationwide crusade next month. Come with me and tell the world what Jesus Christ has done for you. How his love and power has changed your life for the better. You can be an example of the mercy of God for the entire world to see." At that he kissed me and with enthusiasm added, "If you do this, then I will call you Sister Christina, and you can call me Brother Tim."

American Goddess

I hugged him joyfully, "Tim, I do want to be baptized. Right now as a matter of fact, in the ocean."

He threw his hands in the air and exclaimed, "Praise the Lord!" Afterward he kissed me again, took hold of my arm, "I will baptize you, but not here. It must be special." Then he grabbed my hand and pulled me up off the blanket, "Let's get going. We can be back in Dallas by 5:00pm if we leave now. We will hold a special baptismal ceremony this very evening. We don't want to keep Jesus waiting any longer." So off we went back to Dallas and my baptismal ceremony.

On December 21st, at 8:00pm at the Timmy Swinebert, Full Gospel Church of Christ, in Dallas, Texas, I prepared to be baptized by Timmy Swinebert himself. Tim had his whole congregation show up to encourage me as I took my baptismal plunge. 'Oh, by the way, a photo showed up on the front page of every newspaper in the 'Country' the very next day.' Still, it was wonderfully spiritual, and I was giving my life to Jesus Christ, and that's what really mattered.

Tim led me to a pool which was set up on the stage and said the words that would change my life forever! "Christina, I baptize you in the name of Jesus Christ. Receive the power of the Holy Spirit." He then submerged me into the water, and I came out of the water to the cheers of everyone. When I took my first deep breath, I felt something shoot right through my body. At that very moment, I knew I was touched by the Holy Spirit and it was real. Or else it was the shock of hitting that ice-cold water. Well, it was one of the two.

When I could breathe and see again, I saw and heard all the Elders of the church who were standing all around me. They were all talking at the same time and I couldn't understand one thing they were saying. Then Tim said to me in front of the entire congregation, "Sister Christina, did the Holy Spirit speak to you as you were baptized?"

I shouted with astonishment for all to hear, "Yes! I think so! I think he wants me to learn all the languages of the world!" And they all looked at me like I was nuts.

After that, everyone began to sing and dance. It was incredible. I decided that night I was going to begin to learn every language I could for Jesus Christ. I would take them one at a time, until I mastered them all. No matter what they thought.

I returned to my suite at 11:00pm and I walked straight over to the dresser and took out my stash of cocaine. I thought, "You don't need this anymore, you're born again. Jesus has freed you from this."

With that in mind, I went to the bathroom and began to dump it in the toilet. As I started to see it falling out of the jar I stopped, I could not dump it. I went back into the bedroom and put it back in the dresser drawer. After, I knelt down beside my bed and began to pray, "Lord Jesus, I'm tired! I'm only twenty-four years old and I can't deal with my life anymore." I felt my tears begin to fall, "Lord, please help me! I can't take the pain of Joy's death any longer. And I can't keep this hatred I have for Frank in my heart anymore, it's destroying me. Jesus, I can't fight any more battles, I give up and I give my burdens to you. Lord, I chose to give you my life when I was baptized, and my life is out of control. I look all right on the outside, but I'm slowly dying on the inside. Please give me the strength to do your will Lord, because I have no strength of my own left. Amen."

I got up, opened the dresser drawer and cut four lines of cocaine. As I looked in the mirror at myself snorting the cocaine, I said out loud, "Lord Jesus, please forgive me, I don't know why I'm doing this, but I am."

After snorting, I sat down with pen and paper and proceeded to write six of the most beautiful songs of praise and love to God, 'I could imagine'.

The next morning, I flew back to LA and it was back to work. For the next two weeks, we worked like dogs to release my twelfth album entitled, 'The Power of His Love' before I was to leave again. But I had not, as of yet, informed anyone of my plans to take a leave-of-absence. So as soon as we finished the soundtrack, I called Jimmy into my office, "Jimmy, I am going away for a while and I'm leaving you in charge."

"Again! Where are you going now?" He exclaimed with irritation.

"Well Jimmy, I have decided to join Timmy Swinebert, on his nationwide crusade for the next six months."

Jimmy's mouth dropped to the floor as he shouted, "What? You can't do that! What's wrong with you, Christina? You need to be here now. What about the things you have us all working on? You have us all preparing for a war with a corporate giant, and you're going on a fucking holiday."

I calmly replied, "Jimmy, none of that, matters anymore. What matters is that we are able to stand before Jesus Christ on Judgment Day and be declared worthy to enter heaven. Jimmy, I have to do what God is calling me to do and right now that has nothing to do with this place at all. I have a Higher Calling and I have to answer it Jimmy." I reached my hand out, touched his and added, "Jimmy, you will be able to reach me at any time and when you need me, I'll come back. But I must do this first."

Jimmy pulled his hand away from mine, and with a sharp tone responded, "Oh God, Christina! Here we go again. You go ahead and do what you have to do. I'll take care of everything, just like I usually do." Then he got up, walked to the door and slammed it on his way out. After he left, I grabbed my things, and on February 1, 1980, I was off to the airport, where I climbed onto my new private jet, and flew to Texas.

On February 3rd, I began my nationwide crusade with Timmy Swinebert in Las Vegas, Nevada. At the onset, Tim talked about conquering sin in our lives with the power of the Holy Spirit.

American Goddess

After his sermon he said, "Now I would like to introduce to you a newborn again child of God! She is a true witness of the power of Jesus Christ. Brothers and Sisters, please welcome, Christina Powers."

I walked out on the stage and received a standing ovation. When they calmed down, I proceeded to proclaim to the fifty-thousand people in front of me, as well as the whole country on TV, how the power of God's unconditional love had changed my life. I told them how Jesus Christ had saved me from the depths of hell and had freed me from a life of sin and now he has called me into a life of service; where-in, I will serve my Lord and Savior for the rest of my life.

After that I said, "Brothers and Sisters, I tell you now Christ can save you too. So come to the altar and give your life to Christ." With that, I watched in amazement as everyone in the whole place came to the altar that night.

The next morning the papers read, "**Christina Powers, Hollywood's Bad Girl, gives up her glamorous life in Hollywood, to serve Jesus Christ as a 'Born Again Christian!'**"

After the story hit the headlines, Tim's usual crowd of fifty-thousand people a night, turned into an amazing, one-hundred-thousand people every night. The crowds swarmed the crusades just to hear me witness. So, I gave them what they wanted, HOPE! Every night I got up and sang my songs of love and praise to Jesus, and then I'd proclaim the miraculous power of Jesus. What I didn't proclaim was the fact that in order for me to get out on the stage and give them what they wanted, I had to get stoned on cocaine first.

As I toured the country with Timmy Swinebert, I kept in touch with Jimmy back at the office once a day. I helped guide Jimmy's every decision over the phone. Then I would preach to him for the last ten minutes of how happy I was now that I found Jesus.

During our April 16th, phone conversation, Jimmy said, "I have some bad news for you. First, I haven't said anything to you Christina, but Bobby has been sick all month. Finally, Doctor Heddermen admitted him back into the hospital last night. Christina, I'm really concerned about Bobby. Now he has some kind of mouth fungus. It's so bad he hasn't been able to eat any solid foods for the last two weeks."

He stopped speaking and I could hear him start to cry. Realizing he was upset, "Jimmy, relax! Bobby is going to be fine and I will try to come home next week. So just take some time off to be with Bobby, and I will handle everything over the phone with Judy. When I get home, we will take care of Bobby together."

His voice broke up, "Christina, can't you please come home now? I really need you."

With a tone of certainty, I replied, "Jimmy, I will pray for Bobby and he will be fine. You just have to believe God answers the prayers of the faithful. That's why I can't come home now, and I must remain a faithful servant."

His voice became sharp with anger, "Fine, Christina, you keep praying and while you're at it, pray for your new album, because 'The Power of His Love' is losing money. I had to stop production on the album last week. We're already over stocked by three-million copies."

I was taken aback by his statement, "How can that be Jimmy? When we released it, the sales were climbing fast"?

"Well two weeks after you told the world you were a Christian, the mainstream radio stations stopped giving it air play. They branded it a Christian album and tossed it off the air."

I became angry, "That album is fantastic! How could they do this to me? I never thought I would be kept off the air again. I'm Christina Powers; they can't just toss one of my works out the window."

"Christina, face it. If the album was what your fans wanted, the stations would be playing it."

"No Jimmy," I insisted. "Even though the album is not my normal style, if people were hearing the music, I know it would still be selling."

Sarcastically, he admonished me, "Of course, you're right again! Well, I have to go, remember Bobby? He's not here today, he's sick again."

"Well give him a kiss for me, tell him I'm praying for him; so goodbye for now Jimmy." And on that note, we hung up.

On April 29th, I received a call from one of my New York attorneys, Tom Davies. When I answered the phone he said, "Hi, Christina, I have some information for you. As of yet there are no new proposals being sent to congress which have anything to do with the stock market. The only thing I could find out was that Mr. Salerno has been and continues to be, working very closely with Senator Davage, from Nevada, Wesly, from Texas and Relm from South Carolina, all Republicans! What they're working on, I don't know yet. Even with all that, I still don't see how he can touch you. You have no open stock on the public market."

"I don't know either Tom, but thanks, you've done well. Just make sure you keep your feelers out. I don't want to be surprised."

"They won't sneeze without you knowing about it."

After we hung up, I sat there for a minute and realized I still had to figure out what that snake Frank was up to. Then I thought, "Oh well, I'll figure it out tomorrow."

On May 1, one hour before the start of our New York crusade, I took Tim to the side, "Tim, I can't do this anymore."

With a surprised expression, "What do you mean, Sister Christina?"

"I can't go out there any longer and profess to these people Christ has saved me from sin, especially when I am still addicted to cocaine and I have not been able to stop using it." I hugged him, "Tim, please help me! The more I pray to God to stop, the more I find myself needing it. So, until I truly feel God working in my life and I stop using cocaine, I can no longer lie to the world."

"Christina, my sister, I love you!" He exclaimed, "And I will not let Satan defeat you anymore."

Immediately, he called all the Elders who were traveling with us and had them meet us in a back room behind the stage. They all laid their hands on me and began to pray. As they prayed for me, I could feel my body begin to shake. Probably, because I had not received my high for the day yet, and as I trembled, Timmy Senior said, "Jesus, we ask you to deliver our sister from the bondage of the demon of cocaine. We rebuke you, demon of cocaine and exorcize you from the depths of our sister's soul, in the name of Jesus Christ."

As I knelt on the floor with all these men encircling me, Timmy Senior poured oil all over my head and shouted, "Through the power of the Holy Spirit, I cast you out in the name of the King of Kings, Jesus Christ."

All at once like a miracle, the desire for cocaine, as well as my shaking left me and I jumped up and shouted, "Praise God! I'm free from the demon of cocaine! I felt it leave my body." After that announcement we all held one another and praised God some more.

When I walked out to witness to the crowd that night, I was flying high, but on Jesus Christ this time. I proceeded to glorify Jesus Christ for his gift of mercy and love, after which I confessed to the crowd, as I witnessed to them by saying, "Brothers and sisters, I need to speak candidly to you. I am ashamed to say this to all of you, but I must. You see, I have been less than honest with you all. As I have been witnessing with Brother Timmy Swinebert, of the power of Christ in my life, I was still addicted to and using cocaine." The crowd gasped, "But I praise God; because Jesus Christ has just freed me from my cocaine addiction and I can truly say, I no longer have the desire, or the need, to use cocaine any longer. Jesus has truly set me free!"

The crowd went wild praising God and once again they all answered the altar call that night. As they came up to the altar by the thousands, I knew I was truly serving God now.

As time passed on our tour, I began to notice things which started to bother me. Tim would get on the stage every night and preach hell fire for all those who didn't know Christ, as well as those who did know Christ and still chose to live in sin. He preached against alcoholism, but at the same time, I had seen him under the influence of alcohol more than once after a crusade. He condemned womanizing and looking with an eye of lust, but I had suspected that the looks I was getting from Tim were more than just spiritual for a long time now. One night after he had a little too much to drink, he made advances towards me. Since I knew he was under the influence of alcohol, I chose to dismiss it. I had also caught him more than once checking out other women with eyes of lust. After that, he condemned lying and yet I had caught him in two or more lies. As I thought of these things, I began to become concerned and I thought, "What's going on here?" Then rationalizing it, I thought, "Christina, he's only human. So stop looking at the negative things and look at how he is getting the word of Christ out to the world. Besides, if God can forgive my sins, then I guess I can overlook Tim's little indiscretions.

We were in Albany, New York, on July 1, when I received a call from Jimmy in my hotel room at 9:00am. He immediately started screaming into the phone, "You know what, Christina? You are a self-consumed lying bitch. You dared to call me your only family when Joy died, but I know now that was just because you needed me, and I like a fool was there for you. But when I needed you, you never came. I've been waiting for you to come home since April, when you said you would be home the following week." Starting to cry, he yelled, "You lied! You said you would pray for Bobby. Well Christina, Bobby is dying. He has a rare skin cancer and the only people who have been getting this cancer are the ones who are dying from the 'gay plague'."

Now crying myself, "Oh God, no! Jimmy, I'm so sorry. I will be home today Jimmy, I promise. I will leave right now! Please don't hate me Jimmy, I do love you both." I hung up the phone, immediately called Tim and said, "Tim, I must leave now. A family member of mine is ill and may be dying; so, I am leaving right now."

"Christina, you can't leave now," he demanded. "We have a crusade tonight. Why don't we just call in the Elders and we will pray for your family member. Then you can leave after you do God's work tonight."

Bluntly, "Tim, I said I have to leave, so goodbye." Then, I hung up the phone and headed for home. When I arrived, Jimmy was taking care of Bobby at home, because the hospital would not readmit him. Jimmy told me before we went in to see Bobby that the fungus in his mouth came back and once again, he was not eating any solid food at all. He also said Doctor Hedderman had him on a diet of something called 'Ensure' and that every time he gave Bobby some, he started to throw it up.

When we walked into his room, I was shocked. It had only been five months since I saw Bobby last and he looked **horrible**. He had dark red and black skin blotches all over his face and body and he had lost fifty pounds. He could hardly sit up in the bed. I could tell he was in a lot of pain, just by the look on his face. I could hardly believe what was happening to him. I hid my feelings of shock as I sat on the bed next to Bobby, kissed his forehead and said, "Bobby, listen to me. I believe I know how to help you."

Jimmy asked, "How, Christina? No one else seems to know anything about this disease."

I looked at them both with the deepest sincerity, "Come with me and I will have the Elders anoint you with oil Bobby, as we pray for Christ to heal you. Jesus can take this disease from you; I know he can."

American Goddess

Jimmy was angered by my statement, "Please Christina, I've seen what your prayers can do, and we don't want them!"

Bobby patted Jimmy's hand and softly whispered, "Stop it Jimmy!" Then he grabbed my hand, looked me straight in the eye, "Christina, for as long as I have known you, you have always had a special gift for knowing things. So, if you honestly believe this will help me, then I believe it too." He reached his other hand toward Jimmy and guided him to sit down beside me on the bed. As the three of us held hands he continued, "Jimmy, I trust Christina, and I want to do whatever she says."

Jimmy had tears in his eyes as he kissed Bobby, "You're right Bobby, our girl is back and the three of us will be fine now."

We all hugged, and it was back to the crusade, which was now in Hartford, Connecticut. When we arrived in Hartford, we took a three-bedroom suite at the Radisson. The weather was so perfect it was almost impossible to believe that three people could be so depressed on such a glorious day. As soon as we checked into our room, I called Tim, "I'm here with my step-brother. He is dying, so would you please call the Elders together for him so we can anoint him with oil and lay hands for God's healing on my brother."

"Is he able to come to the Coliseum, Christina?"

"Yes, Tim, he can make it."

Assuredly, "Good, I will call together the Elders and meet you in the sound room at the Coliseum. Let's see, its 10:00 now, so say around 1:00pm."

I sighed, "God bless you Brother Tim. I love you so much for doing this." I hung up the phone and proceeded to joyfully tell Bobby and Jimmy, we were going to pray that very afternoon.

When we walked into the prayer group of Elders, I held the door so Jimmy could push Bobby in his wheelchair. I introduced the two of them to the Elders and Tim asked Bobby what his illness was.

Bobby replied, "I have something called 'Kaposi's Sarcoma'."

Instantly, one of the elders rudely interrupted, "Excuse me, but isn't that the skin cancer which is caused by the 'gay plague'?"

Bobby answered innocently, "Yes, it is."

All of a sudden Tim's face turned as white as a ghost as he looked down at Bobby. Then he looked up at me, and at all the other 'Brothers,' who were looking down at Bobby, and he asked abruptly, "Are you a homosexual?"

Once again Bobby answered innocently, "Yes I am."

Sternly, Tim shouted, "Do you denounce your homosexuality, repent for your sins and accept Jesus Christ as your personal savior?"

American Goddess

Instantly Jimmy piped up with, "We accept Jesus Christ as our personal savior, and we repent for our sins." With that flick of his wrist, "But we cannot denounce our homosexuality, because that's part of who we are."

Tim went into shock and adamantly cried out, "Then may God help your brother, because I can't." Outraged he slapped his hand down on his knee and shouted at Bobby again, "Damn you boy! Are you stupid? You can't accept Jesus Christ as your personal savior, repent for your sins, and still be a homosexual!"

I was horrified and about to slug him when Bobby said, "I'm sorry! But I can't change who I am."

Outraged at Bobby's honesty Tim yelled, "Well then I cannot pray for you."

That's when I couldn't take it anymore, "Now just wait a minute, Tim! This is Bobby's life; we are talking about here! Isn't it God's will that we pray for and love every one! Don't the Ten Commandments tell us to love thy neighbor as thyself?"

With a stunned expression on his face Tim replied, "Christina, I would do anything for you, but this is asking me to go against God. This would be a sin to pray for someone who openly admits to being a homosexual and refuses to repent for it. If we were in the ancient times of the Bible, I would have no choice but to order your brother stoned to death, right now."

I was shocked and my face showed it, but before I could say anything, Jimmy shouted, "Christina, this is who you call, **loving Christians**? This is what you think is **Godly**? Well I think you're all sick." Then he grabbed the handles on Bobby's wheelchair and said, as he turned away, "You can keep your prayers, because none of you pray to the Jesus Christ I know. Now if you will excuse us, we're getting out of this 'hellhole' of 'hypocrisy' right now."

With that he headed out the door like a bolt of lightning. I looked at Tim and all the Elders, then I looked back to see Jimmy leaving the room and I didn't know what to say. So I charged out of the room after Jimmy and Bobby. When I reached them, Jimmy was helping Bobby into the rented town-car and they were both crying. I grabbed Jimmy by the shoulders and pleaded, "I'm so sorry! I had no idea they would act like this." After I finally calmed them down, I continued, "Please wait here, I have to give Mr. Timmy Swinebert a piece of my mind, right now."

I stormed back into the Coliseum and I was '**Pissed**'! When I reached the door to the room where I left Tim and all of the Elders, it was partially opened. I stopped at the door before going in because I could hear them talking about us. Timmy Swinebert Senior was saying, "Brothers, listen to me. I think my son may have over-reacted."

I heard Tim Junior say, "Dad, I won't pray for a fagot. He deserves to die."

Tim Sr. replied, "Son, don't you realize how valuable that girl is to our ministry. If she walks out on us, we lose millions of dollars. So I say you go after that pot of gold and apologize to them all. Tim, I don't care what it takes for you to bring her back here, but you bring her back. Then we say a prayer for that boy. Shit son, I don't give a damn if he lives or dies either. The prayers don't work anyway. Just as long as she thinks the prayers work, and she thinks we're doing it for her, that's all that matters. So if it keeps her under our control, then, who the hell cares if we pray for a fagot."

I felt fire in my eyes, and I was about to burst in, when I stopped myself. I turned and quietly walked away, without being seen by anyone. As I walked through the parking lot toward the car, I thought, "God this can't be happening! How in the world could I be deceived like this without realizing it? Christina, this is a travesty! You can't allow this to continue. They are deceiving millions." When I reached the car, I told Jimmy and Bobby what I'd just heard, and on the ride back to the hotel I said, "Jimmy, I need your help to stop this wickedness."

With a malicious tone he replied, "Start talking girlfriend! I'm listening."

Deviously I told Jimmy exactly what I wanted him to do.

As soon as we entered the room, I picked up the phone and called Tim. When I got him on the line, he was so apologetic, it was **sickening**. Before I could say anything he immediately said, "Sister Christina, Praise God! You called. I have heard from Jesus and he convicted my heart. Jesus has told me I was wrong, and if we pray for your brother, Jesus will be faithful to our prayers and heal him!"

With enthusiasm, "Praise God, Tim! I thank you from the depths of my heart."

With a tone of authority, he continued, "If you bring your brother to the service tonight, we will heal him."

Sounding desperate and needy I begged, "Please Tim, can you come over here now. I need to speak with you before tonight's crusade. I'm in the penthouse suite on the top floor of the Radisson Hotel. Can you please come now? I need you."

"Yes Sister Christina, I'll be right over."

The suite we had was on the top floor and it had a direct access to the roof of the building where there were a number of well-maintained flower gardens, which were scattered throughout a Kentucky blue grass lawn. When Tim arrived, it was 4:00pm and I had Jimmy hiding out on the roof. When I opened the door, I had two glasses of scotch in my hands, which happened to be Tim's preferred drink. As soon as he entered the room, I handed him one of the drinks, hugged him and said, "I need a drink and I don't want to drink alone."

He took the drink, "Are you all right Sister Christina?"

"Do you mind if we talk out on the roof, it's such a beautiful afternoon?"

"No, I don't mind, that sounds nice."

I led him out onto the roof, and as we gazed out over downtown Hartford I said in a sensual tone, "Tim, look at it. We are on top of the world you and I, and God is giving it to us." I moved close to him, "Tim, just think of it, you and I reaching the whole world together for Jesus Christ." I placed my glass down, hugged him, looked passionately into his eyes and seductively said, "Tim I think I'm beginning to have sexual feelings for you." Then I put my lips next to his ear and softly whispered, "Tim, I think I'm falling in love with you and I don't know what to do about it."

As soon as I said these words, he became a mad man full of passion and he was all over me. His lips were everywhere. I began to push him off as I said, "Tim slow down. I think we should talk about this," but there was no slowing him down! As he began to rip my clothing off my body, I knew there was no way I was stopping him now. I saw Jimmy coming out of hiding, so to stop him from blowing his cover I waved him away with a hand motion. Then I began to rip Tim's clothing off as I gestured to Jimmy to stay hidden. Swallowing my heart, I began to rape Tim as viciously as he was me. The lust between the two of us was unbelievable. As we laid our naked bodies down on the soft blue, green grass, the demons of lust exploded within us both. Our bodies burnt as we quenched the fires of our fleshly lusts. It was the most degrading and demoralizing thing I had ever done, but I had to do it, if only to expose Tim and his organization for the **hypocritical monsters** they were!

At that evening's crusade, Tim had the audacity to preach on the sin of homosexuality. He said, "People, the penalty of the sin of homosexuality is death. I warn all those who are homosexual, God will not be mocked. That is why he has sent the 'angel of death' to visit all those who are homosexual with the new 'gay plague.' This is why the plague is only killing homosexuals. God has told me he will slay all those who dare to sin in such a vulgar manner."

His words incited a chant of hatred toward all of those who are gay and praises to God for bringing his hand of justice to them in this so-called divine plague. It was so frightening I thought I was in Germany during Hitler's reign.

Then, it was my turn to minister to the enraged crowd of one-hundred-thousand spectators. As I picked up the mike to sing, the crowd was giving me a standing ovation and I said, "Brothers and sisters, I have something different to say tonight. I want to tell you what I discovered this very day. That is, that Mr. Timmy Swinebert is a filthy swine. His ministry is full of lying thieves. He preaches against one thing then he goes out and does it. The next thing he'll probably do is go have sex with some guy in the back of a bookstore."

Stunned, Tim screamed out, "I rebuke you, you lying beast from hell! Depart from Sister Christina's, body."

The crowd thinking I was possessed, started to scream out in unison, "Depart from her you demon! Depart from her you demon!"

I shouted, "I don't need to be exorcized Tim, **you do!**"

American Goddess

He started to walk from the other side of the stage toward me, as I pointed to him, "Ask your 'god' here, how come he committed adultery with me, just this very afternoon!"

That's when the crowd gasped as Tim screamed, "Blasphemer! You are a demon from hell and a liar!"

I shouted, "Tim, I'm way ahead of you. I knew you would say that. That's why I have photos of the two of us to prove it. So take me to court for defamation of character why don't you?"

I turned to the crowd as Tim stopped dead in his tracks, "People, this is nothing but a tax free, money making, lying, scheming, brain washing organization and I can no longer be a part of it!"

Tim turned to the crowd and began to cry with tears pouring down his face. Then he screamed with all his might, "She is a harlot from hell and she seduced me with her witchcraft. Brothers and sisters please forgive me for falling into the web of demons, with Satan herself."

After that display of alligator tears, I shouted, "Tim, you should be asking God to forgive you, not your bank roll. People, he squanders your money on private jets, mansions, fancy meals, and young woman. This whole ministry is a farce, and I only allowed him to seduce me to prove it to you. I hope for your sakes, you will be able to see the truth for yourselves. Brothers and sisters please listen to me, what we as Christians do not truly understand is that the blood Jesus shed for us is priceless. It covers all of us, even if we happen to be gay, lesbian, or transgender. God loves us all and all he wants is for us to have a personal relationship with him. To come and discover why he paid such a high price for us to have eternal life with him. We as the body of Christ have to start letting God be the judge not the church. God does not take pleasure in religious leaders standing on pulpits condemning anyone. When all that really matters is what it says in John 3-16 and 17, "For God so loved the world, that he gave his only begotten Son, that whosoever believeth in him should not perish, but have everlasting life. For God sent not his Son into the world to **condemn** the world; but that the world through him might be saved."

Then I put down the mike and walked out through a shocked mob, as Tim cried in hysterics in front of the whole world. After the release of the photos, in a worldwide scandal, it seemed I had brought the fifty-year Swinebert Empire, crashing down into a pile of rubble, **and all in only one day.**

American Goddess

CHAPTER 12

Around 3:00am the morning after I slew the Swinebert ministry, the three of us found ourselves still quite shook up. Jimmy, Bobby and I, were in the air on our personal jet, which we paid for from honest money, somewhere between Hartford and LA. We were sitting together in the living room compartment all on one big sofa with me in the middle, when I reached out, took one of each of their hands, "Guys, I love you both and I'm really sorry for having put the two of you through this."

Bobby glanced at me lovingly, "Christina, don't apologize. The way they reacted to this disease and my sexuality had nothing to do with you. What you did was out of your love for us and we know that."

We all hugged, and I said with sensitivity, "Listen to me guys, even though Timmy Swinebert and his ministry is a farce, that doesn't mean there is no God. Bobby, I believe in Jesus Christ, and I believe if it's his will God can heal you. So why don't the three of us pray?"

Jimmy quickly grabbed two pencils which were on the coffee table, stuck one up each nostril and said, "Ha! Like, God has time for the likes of the three of us." We lost it and started laughing like crazy.

After our outburst I said, "Come on guys, let's get down on our knees and pray it can't hurt." So, that's what we did.

After two days of rest and reflection on what we had just lived through, it was time to get back to work. There were four things which needed my immediate attention. My first priority was Bobby and the so-called 'gay plague' which was killing him, and hundreds of others like him. Second, to somehow absolutely find out if Frank had anything to do with Joy's death; if it turned out he did, then justice would be **MINE**! Third, was to figure out how to out fox, the fox on the Wall Street scene, before he could pounce down and devour Powers Incorporated. Fourth, I had to start writing my next manuscript. It would tell the world the story of a young female performer, who gets caught up with fraudulent religious leaders and how she exposed their inner den of iniquity.

Oh, by the way, two weeks after my incident with Timmy Swinebert, the album, 'The Power of His Love', did the impossible and beat the unbeatable. The sales of 'The Power of His Love' soared past the top selling album of all time, 'Halloween in Hell'. And once again the money was pouring in, our stock were going up, and my popularity was soaring. There were thousands of letters pouring in every day, with 98% of them telling me how much they loved me and how sorry they were to hear what happened to me. There were letters from little old ladies who told me they were sending Tim money from their SSI checks every month. They actually thanked me for exposing the Swinebert Ministry for what it truly was.

164

American Goddess

It was overwhelming to me. There were millions of people from all over the world, all telling me they loved and cared about me. As I realized these letters came from the hearts of real people, it finally meant something to me, which was more than just the money I was making off of them. It was more than my desire for revenge, which was the driving force behind everything I thought and did. It was as if blinders were taken off my eyes and for the first time in my life, I truly began to look at others first, instead of just myself. I could see there was a great need in the world around me. I realized there were other things happening around me, outside of my world. I had always lived as though my life was the whole universe and everything revolved around me. I finally realized it didn't and that in the scheme of things I meant nothing. I was just a speck in time and what truly mattered was the world around me. This awakening of mine changed my focus and I knew I had to use my popularity to truly make this life here on earth a little better for as many people as I could.

There was that 2% of the mail which told me I would burn in hell for what I had done. There were also a few death threats, which I decided to take seriously. So, I hired a private security firm to supply eight full time bodyguards to be around me on a twenty-four-hour basis. Something told me not to take any chances. After all, look at my true family's history. I wanted the security, but I still needed my privacy. So, I requested they work two per shift and they had to stay where I would not have to be aware of their presence.

All of a sudden, on the morning of August 26th, Bobby began to go downhill. He was having horrible coughing bouts and I knew he had once again come down with pneumonia. I called Doctor Heddermen who told me to meet him at the hospital emergency room with Bobby as soon as possible. Bobby was admitted into a private room in the intensive care unit. He was incubated with a feeding tube and given mega doses of IV antibiotics. He was also put on a morphine drip to help lessen the pain. It was horrible to see him dying like this and we were helpless. Jimmy and I took turns staying with him because we could not find one private duty nurse willing to take the case. It was so frustrating, no one really knew anything about the disease and if they did, they shunned it because it was a 'gay' thing. I truly wish I did not have to say this, but in August of 1980, the hospital staff was incredible in their attempts to steal whatever dignity Bobby had left. No one wanted to go near him. Everyone was afraid.

I tried to understand what everyone was feeling, so I never complained. As for Jimmy, he was feeling so belittled by the stares he received every time he entered the hospital that he wouldn't complain for fear of some sort of retaliation against Bobby. All that changed when one-night Jimmy came down with a fever and I stayed home to look after him. I called the hospital to inform the nurses in the intensive care unit no one would be in that evening to care for Bobby. I asked, "So please look after him for us and I'll be in to stay with him in the morning."

The weather was rainy, cold, and damp on that fateful morning of August 31st, as I drove to the hospital. When I went into Bobby's room, I found Bobby lying in his own feces and the bed was sopping wet with cold urine. I went ballistic as I stormed to the administration office ranting and raving all the way. When I reached the office, I demanded to see the hospital administrator at once!

When I entered Mr. Mallard's office, I told him the condition I found Bobby in, the treatment he had been receiving since we arrived at the hospital, and I was disgusted with the reaction of the hospital staff members. Mr. Mallard said, "Ms. Powers, please try to calm down. I do understand your feelings, but I also want you to understand something too. The only reason Mr. Shaw was admitted into this hospital in the first place, was as a courtesy to you. So if you're not satisfied, I suggest you take him to County General where all the other patients with his disease reside."

I was shocked when I heard his words and my expression showed it as I swiftly replied, "You mean to tell me, you're not accepting patients into this hospital because of a certain type of illness?"

Very sarcastically he replied, "It has become our policy for the time being, not to accept these patients until we know more about this disease. We are in a very delicate situation here, because, if we accept these patients, we risk losing our regular patients, who have informed us they will not come here if we have patients with the 'gay plague' admitted into this hospital. The problem is the other patients, and the staff are afraid. Due to our financial situation and our main contributors, our hands here in the administration office are tied. So, you see Ms. Powers, we are actually being forced to send these patients to County General and like I said, if you're dissatisfied, I'll be more than happy to transfer Mr. Shaw to County General.

I felt fire in my eyes as I replied with indignation, "Well thank you ever so much Mr. Mallard, but we're not going to County General. Los Angeles Memorial is going to take care of Bobby and you are going to have your staff take care of him with dignity and respect, or I will be on the local news this evening telling the public how your hospital is discriminating against certain patients. Now the choice is yours. Speak with your staff and take care of Mr. Shaw, or do I create a public scandal for the hospital? So what's it gonna be, Mr. Mallard? The ball is in your court!"

He was shocked by my response and his face showed it, "Ms. Powers that is not going to accomplish anything except to cause hard feelings between the hospital and yourself."

I sarcastically snickered, "Ha, ha, ha. You know what? I think it will accomplish something more, like destroy the reputation of your hospital."

American Goddess

He grew angry and I knew he was biting his tongue, "Ms. Powers, we don't have to carry this incident to such an extreme. I will talk to my staff, and Mr. Shaw will receive proper care."

Confidently staring him straight in the eyes, "Thank you very much Mr. Mallard, I was sure we could come to some kind of mutual agreement."

I left his office and headed back to Bobby. When I returned to Bobby's room, he was still in the same condition he was in when I left, even after my screaming at the nurses! I grabbed some linen off the cart in the hall and proceeded to clean him up. I must be totally truthful here, I was slightly afraid of catching what Bobby had, but I was not going to let that stop me from helping someone I loved very much. Two minutes after I finished, a nurse entered the room and asked me if I needed anything. I asked her to page Doctor Heddermen and have him stop in to see me. She said she would, and then she left the room.

Doctor Heddermen entered Bobby's room shortly after the noon hour and proceeded to examine Bobby who was in a semiconscious state. Afterward he turned to me, "Christina, have you had lunch yet?"

"No,"

"Why don't you take a break with me and we'll talk over lunch, my treat." I accepted his invitation and walked with him to the hospital cafeteria.

Over our lunch, I explained to Doctor Heddermen what had transpired that morning and how I felt about it. He said, "Christina, I think it's time you call me Robert." Then reaching across the table and taking my hand in his, he continued, "I heard the whole story ten minutes after it happened. I must ask you as a friend, to try not to get so upset with the reaction of the staff. Christina, please try to understand the situation the hospital is in."

"I can sympathize with the hospital's situation, but I do not agree with the way the hospital is handling the problem. We are talking about the lives of real people, not some inanimate objects which can just be thrown away and forgotten."

He replied with conviction, "You have every right to disagree with hospital policy, all I'm asking you is let the medical community deal with this disease."

I slid my hand out of his, "Robert, what is truly going on here with this disease? I cannot believe it's really only killing gay men. Common sense tells me that."

"Christina, I wish I knew. The plain truth is no one knows what is going on. All we know for sure is that people have been dying for the last two years from all types of opportunistic diseases. It appears to destroy the immune system in each of its victims. There have been thirty-two cases locally and all of them have been gay men. That's all we have to go on right now."

I shook my head with concern, "So what's being done about it?"

American Goddess

"The Center for Disease Control, along with private laboratories are working night and day to answer that question."

I sighed, "That sound's great, but it seems to me no one is telling the general population about this disease. I have heard nothing about it in the 'straight' press. The only ones talking about it at all are those in the gay press and the medical community."

"Christina, the nation is consumed right now with the Iran hostage situation. The last thing the President, or the public wants to hear, is a suspicion there might be a new disease killing people. There is another thing to consider, and that's the reaction of the general public to such a story."

With alarm, "Are you telling me, no one is willing to admit there is anything going on out there?"

He answered quite sincerely, "Until we know what it is, there is no scientific proof that there is a new killer loose on the general public. So yes, you're right. At this time, no one is going to admit to what the whole medical community believes to be true, in an official announcement. It could cause a panic and destroy careers."

My reply showed my alarm, "Oh my God! Robert, this is unbelievable. I guess the world has no choice, but to let you guys do your job."

As Robert walked me back to Bobby's room, I asked him, "Robert, please tell me the truth, how long do you think Bobby will survive like this?"

When we reached Bobby's door, Robert hugged me warmly, "I'm sorry Christina, but I don't think he'll last the night."

"Thank you, Robert, for being so candid with me."

I gowned up to enter Bobby's isolation room. When I walked back into the room, his breath was so labored, I felt compelled to call Jimmy, even though I knew how sick he was himself. When I called home, Carman answered the phone and within a moment put Jimmy on, and I said, "Jimmy, how are you feeling?"

He coughed to clear his voice, "I still have the chills and I can hardly talk, but I'll live. How's Bobby?"

Trying not to frighten him, "Jimmy if you're up to it, you should come over here."

"What's happening Christina?" he asked with fear in his voice.

"He's taken a turn for the worse, Jimmy."

Jimmy said nothing at first, then, "Okay, I'll be right there."

"Jimmy, have James drive you over here. I don't want you driving by yourself."

"All right, we'll be right over."

As I waited for Jimmy, I sat down on the bed beside Bobby and held his hand. I began to stroke his forehead, "Bobby, I want you to know how much your friendship has meant to me. You have touched my heart and I will always remember you." I started to cry, "Bobby, I'm sorry; I know you wanted me to help you and you believed I could, but I can't.

I wish I could, but I just don't know how to help you. Forgive me please." With that I kissed his forehead and just held Bobby's hand as I waited for Jimmy to arrive.

When Jimmy entered the room, I looked up at him and he just started to cry. He came over to me with his arms stretched out. I stood up to hold him, "Christina, I don't want to lose him."

Sadly, we both began crying, "Jimmy, I know baby, I know."

Jimmy looked down at Bobby and as we released our embrace, he fell to his knees beside the bed, laid his head on Bobby's chest and cried even harder.

My heart broke for Jimmy. I could feel his pain as I watched him cry for his love, "Bobby, oh my Bobby, I love you, I love you Bobby. Please don't leave me. I'm going to miss you. I need you Bobby. I need you. Please don't leave me. I can't make it without you."

As Jimmy pleaded, I could see Bobby open his eyes and gaze into Jimmy's eyes. As they looked at each other, Bobby took one last breath, and he was gone.

Jimmy cried horribly as he laid on Bobby's body. All I could do was to kneel down beside him and hold him as we both cried.

After what seemed like hours of crying there on our knees I said, "Jimmy, I'm here for you baby. I love you and we will make it through this together." Just then James entered the room and with his help, we finally were able to leave Bobby behind. No one said a word as James drove us home that day, because we had just lost another piece of **our hearts on that rainy day in August of 1980.**

CHAPTER 13

Two weeks after Bobby's funeral, the Ellesmere Building Tenants Association called an emergency meeting. Since 90% of the tenants were gay, the meeting was called to discuss this new 'gay epidemic'. Jimmy and I attended the meeting, which was held at 8:00pm on September 18th, 1980. Everyone in the building had the opportunity to speak. It was obvious everyone was on edge and that something had to be done.

American Goddess

Billy Williams the President of the Tenants Association said, "I have been trying to call attention to what is going on in the gay community with local-press and politicians, but no one is listening. It's like everyone is putting their heads in the sand on this one." He looked directly at me, "Ms. Powers, we here in the building, as well as the entire gay community, would like to ask for your help in this matter."

Billy lived on the same floor as Jimmy and me. We had become friendly passing in the hall, so I said, "Please Billy, call me Christina. Now, exactly what type of assistance would you need from me?"

He smiled eagerly, "We need someone with your kind of celebrity status, to help our voices to be heard and to find out what's being done medically and scientifically about this disease."

I walked over to stand at the podium, "Good evening neighbors. I understand exactly what you're asking and before I answer, please let me share some information with you. I have spoken with one of the top people in the medical field and I've expressed the exact same concerns to him which I'm hearing here tonight. I have been assured the CDC, along with private sector laboratories are working night and day on this thing. I was told if I were to raise the issue in public now, before anyone really knows what's going on, I could quite possibly cause a public panic. The medical field believes the backlash of such a panic would slow the progress of the scientific field, by causing them to divert more manpower to solving the panic, rather than finding the cause of these deaths. After my discussions and a lot of thought, I decided that the medical field is most likely correct in their assumptions. Now, after saying all this, I'm sorry, but at this time I feel I must remain silent on this matter. I believe we live in the greatest nation on earth, with some of the greatest minds in the world. I also believe we must first give the government and the scientific community time to work this out their way. I think we have to trust them, but I will stay on top of the situation. I want to know what's going on just as much as everyone else here, and I will. I can guarantee you all that!"

Once the meeting ended, Jimmy and I returned to our apartment. I went straight to the shower to clean off the day's work. After I dressed, I picked up the phone and called Detective Fred Ulrich, "Hi, Fred, this is Christina Powers, I haven't heard from you, so I thought I would check in. Are you any closer to solving the case?"

"Hi Christina, I wish I could say that I am, but I'm not."

"You're not telling me you've given up, are you?" I asked bluntly.

With a reassuring tone he answered, "No way, as a matter of fact I was out at the scene just yesterday."

"Why were you out there?"

American Goddess

"A few days after the fire, we found some tire tracks on your property. I had a mold made of the tracks and I finally learned more about the tires. So, I attempted to measure the width of the access road the truck took through the woods to enter your property."

"So, what were your findings?"

"I'm now sure we have the vehicle. So with any luck at all, it will lead me right to the arsonist."

"Fred, that's great news, I don't know how to thank you. Please keep up the good work and when you're done, I will have to think of a very special way to thank you."

We ended our conversation and I walked toward the living room. I was wearing my blue terry cloth robe and slippers, when I sat on the sofa beside Jimmy, who was in a tee shirt and tight-fitting jockey shorts, eating popcorn and watching the 1:00am local news. I reached for the remote control and flicked it off. Jimmy slapped my hand, "What's the matter with you? I was watching that.

"Jimmy, we have to talk."

He looked at me with concern, "OOH! That sounded serious, start talking, girlfriend."

I smiled a little, "Well, I think it might be. I think we should move from here."

Jimmy gave me a strange look, "What do you mean move from here? Bobby's still here with me, I can't move."

I took his hand, "Listen to me Jimmy, I have to be up front with you. I'm afraid to stay here any longer. I have nothing against the gay lifestyle, but until the world knows what's going on with this disease, I don't feel like living with six-hundred gay men. Common sense tells me this is not the healthiest place to be living right now, for either one of us. After all, we lost Bobby in this building."

Jimmy's eyes lit up as if someone had just turned on a light switch, "Oh shit! I never thought of that, what the fuck is wrong with me."

Bluntly I said, "The only thing wrong with you Jimmy is that you miss Bobby. I know that feeling better than anyone. That is why I don't want to take any chances of something happening to either one of us."

Jimmy put the bowl of popcorn down on the coffee table, looked at me very seriously, "You're right, so where do we go?"

As soon as he said those words, the phone rang. I looked at him, "Who would be calling us at this time?

"I don't know, pick it up."

"Hello, who's this?" sounding a little annoyed.

"Christina, its Tom Davies, from New York."

"Hi, isn't it 4am out there, what's up?"

"I'm sorry to be calling you so late."

I chuckled, "That's alright; we were only getting ready for bed."

American Goddess

"Forgive me, I'll let you go and call back later."

"Well, can you sum it up, quickly?"

"Sure. First, the building is complete, and we need you here in New York as soon as possible. Second, I have come up with some very interesting information I'm sure you will find it quite useful."

With interest I asked, "What is it?"

"I'd rather keep this under wraps until I see you in person. How soon can you get here?"

"I'll be there tomorrow," I answered in haste.

I hung up the phone, turned to Jimmy, "Well I guess I know where we're going."

He looked at me strangely, "Who was that?"

"It was our attorney, Tom Davies, and we're leaving for New York in the morning,"

"What about this place?"

"Screw it Jimmy, let's just get what we can out of here. I can't deal with this right now."

The next morning at our offices, I called Judy my Executive Secretary, her husband Mike, my Account's Office Manager and Ann Markel, who I had appointed Head Studio Coordinator for stage, lighting, and props into my office. Once they came in, I informed them Jimmy and I would be leaving that night for New York. I explained that we needed to open our new offices. I proceeded to promote the three of them to studio executives. I knew I could trust them all, so I left them in charge of my California operations. I also gave Judy and Mike 1% of Powers Incorporated Stock. I gave Ann Markel 2% of the stock and appointed them all a seat on my board of directors.

When Jimmy and I got off the plane in New York, all I had of my personal belongings were two suitcases and one singed bottle of champagne. When we reached our waiting limos, we had them take us to our suite on the 20th floor of the Plaza, in downtown Manhattan. I took the entire floor because I had a small entourage of hand-picked staff with me.

Friday, September 29th, I had made plans for Jimmy and me to meet with Tom Davies the next morning, at 9:00am in Milton, New York. We would be touring the new headquarters of Powers Incorporated. After that, we had scheduled a dinner engagement at the Turf Restaurant in the Kingston, New York, Holiday Inn. It seemed that Jimmy and I were being welcomed to the area by the Hudson Valley Business Association.

The following morning was a glorious one! The sun and the sky were so bright, they illuminated the day. Yet, there was no glare in my eyes as I drove Jimmy and me in our rented town car up the New York State Thruway, to the New Paltz exit, because I was slightly apprehensive over making this move. But thank God, my confidence returned the moment we arrived. The speed limit dropped to 20 miles per hour as soon as you entered the heart of Powers Incorporated, via the new four lane main thoroughfare. It wound its way five miles through the three main complexes on the banks of the majestic Hudson River. I was in awe of the landscaping. It was magnificent! There were flower gardens all along the roadway. Everywhere you looked, all you could see was nature. The towering pine forest was alive with the sounds of wildlife. There were two beautiful waterfalls in site of the main thoroughfare. As we passed each turnoff into one of the three main complexes you could not see a building through the trees until you reached it. This masterpiece of nature, landscaping, and modern building technology, which was finished down to my every wish was completed by Joyce Baggatta and her son Lonnie. They were the architects who helped make my dream come true when they drew up the plans and oversaw the building of my Empire.

Jimmy and I met Joyce and Lonnie at the main security house which was nestled in the center of the three main complexes. Joyce informed us Tom Davies would be delayed and would meet us at the Holiday Inn around 7:00pm. The two of them proceeded to take us on a complete tour of the complex. As we toured, I realized after seven-years and two-billion dollars, I had my Empire! It was a phenomenal feeling to behold what I had created and at that moment I knew I could have anything in this world that I wanted. Then, I thought, "You're next Frank! I did all this for one reason, for you to taste my revenge!" Immediately I felt a cold, hard, rush of hatred go through my soul, as I stood in the heart of this garden of Eden-like paradise, and thought, "I'm coming, you bastard!"

Later that afternoon around 6:30pm Jimmy and I checked into our rooms at the Holiday Inn in Kingston, New York. Ten minutes after I entered my room, the phone rang and it was Mrs. Sally Lou Schaffert-Brown, the President of the Hudson Valley Business Association. She welcomed me with warmth in her voice, as she told me of the evening's events. There was to be a welcoming meeting in the D-conference room of the hotel at 7:30pm; followed by cocktails at 8:30pm in the lounge for one-on-one meetings with local business leaders. Dinner would be from 9:15 until 10:00. Then back to the lounge for cocktails and dancing. She informed me she would be my personal guide for the evening and that Mr. Davies is in route. I thanked her and agreed to meet her in the lobby at 7:15pm.

As soon as I hung up the phone, I rang Jimmy's room, "Jimmy do we have any more of those peanut butter and jelly sandwiches left?"

"One, why?" He asked guardedly.

"Well you have ten minutes to dress and get your ass over here with half of that sandwich before we start this evening. Dinner isn't until 9:15 and I'm not taking any chances. I want something to munch on now."

Laughing he said, "I'll be right there, girlfriend."

American Goddess

Jimmy and I met Sally right on time and our greeting was overwhelming. She was a wonderful woman, intelligent, warm and witty. After our ten-minute personal introductions, she led us into the conference room. The place was packed with all the most influential businesspeople in the area. Sally opened the meeting by welcoming all the members of the Hudson Valley Business Association. After her little speech she said, "Now I would like to introduce the President and Vice-President of Powers Incorporated, Ms. Christina Powers and Mr. James Severino!" With that we headed up to the podium together, to a standing ovation.

Jimmy spoke first, "Hello, I'm James Severino, but please call me Jimmy, and as you know I'm the vice-president of Powers Incorporated. I thank you for your kind welcome. Now I would like to turn this mike over to the real wizard of Powers Incorporated, my boss and best friend, Christina Powers."

As Jimmy returned to his seat, I said, "Good evening everyone, I'm so thrilled by this gracious welcome to your beautiful Hudson Valley. I would like to say at this time, I truly look forward to joining everyone here, in creating a new financial Mecca in the Hudson Valley Region. I know with all of us working together, this region's economic growth will rival the worlds."

I received another standing ovation as I finished my speech. Then it was off to the dining room for dinner. I looked around for Tom Davies, but he had still not arrived. I began to become a little concerned. This was not like Tom, so I shared my concern with Sally who also knew Tom well, then asked, "Do you think you could have someone try to contact him for me?" She agreed, beckoned a young man to her and arranged it immediately.

Without hesitation Sally began to introduce us to as many people as she possibly could in half-an-hour. As we mingled, from the corner of my left eye, I saw him turn toward me. I recognized the smile immediately. His big brown eyes gleamed as he said, "Christina Powers, I know everything there is to know about you and I'm madly in love with you."

I gently hugged the man, who made love to me more than a year ago, "Lee Bradford! What a surprise. I had no idea you lived in New York."

He winked, "As I recall, we never got that far."

We parted our embrace, "So what do you do here in the Valley?"

With a smile that was now glowing, "I'm the President of Bradford Computers Incorporated. Our main offices happen to be right across the river from yours."

I smiled in my subtle, seductive way, "Well I guess since you know so much about me, maybe I should take the time and get to know you a little better myself."

His eyes lit up, "That can be arranged." All at once the light in his eyes dimmed, "I was truly sorry to hear of your recent personal tragedies."

American Goddess

"Thank you, Lee, I appreciate that," I replied with sincerity. "But please don't look so sad, I'm surviving."

Just then we were called to dinner, and Lee just happened to be seated on my right side at a beautiful garnished round table. Sally was on my left and Jimmy on her left, with a vacant seat for Tom Davies who was on Jimmy's left. Lee and I were getting along splendidly over our shrimp cocktails, when finally, Tom Davies showed up. He came to my side, greeted everyone at the table and apologized for his tardiness. He knelt down, so that his lips were close to my ear, "Christina, may I see you in private for a moment?"

"Sure."

We excused ourselves and I followed Tom to a private corner of the lobby, "I'm sorry I'm so late, but I was waiting to personally verify this information myself. First, just this afternoon I had my source present in a meeting which was held by Frank and all his sinister friends. The bill is finally finished, and they are going to hold off trying to pass it until they see if Ronald Feagan wins this November's election. If he does, they plan to bring their proposal to the Senate floor for a vote in April of 1981."

With curiosity, "What does the bill consist of?"

"I don't know that, but there is one man who might know. He is running for a Republican Senate seat here in New York in this November's elections. He also happens to be the most sought-after mind on Wall Street."

With excitement in my voice I asked, "Who is it?" as I thought, "Ah, a challenge!"

Lowering his voice just enough to heighten the suspense, "You happen to be sitting beside him tonight."

With a look of surprise, "Do you mean to tell me Lee Bradford is running for the Senate, and he's also the top man on Wall Street?"

Proudly he replied, "You got it, Boss!"

I kissed his check, "Good work Tom, you can expect a nice bonus for this one. Please, would you do me another favor?"

This beautiful, strong, intelligent, black man, looked at me through eyes of pure infatuation, "You name it Christina, and I'll do it."

"Great! I want to know everything there is to know about Mr. Lee Bradford." On that note, we returned to our table.

As I took my seat beside Lee, I mischievously thought, "This is too good to be true! I don't even smell a challenge! This one is going to be like taking candy from a baby."

Over dinner, Lee once again enchanted me with his brilliance, as well as his remarkable command of the English language. As we spoke, the fact that we were attracted to one another was once again beginning to flare-up between us, as we found ourselves remembering one very romantic night, not so long ago.

175

American Goddess

After dinner, Lee and I were dancing romantically in each other's arms, when, with a look of deep sincerity he said, "Christina, I have dreamed of a moment like this since our night together. You are truly the most remarkable and beautiful woman I've ever had the honor of meeting."

I gazed warmly into his eyes as he spoke these words, then seductively thanked him, "Lee that means so much to me coming from you. I think you're pretty special too." I kissed him tenderly, "I have remembered our night quite often myself."

We were arm in arm, as we walked off the dance floor, and when we reached our table after that dance, we could see no one else.

As Lee slid my chair out for me I asked, "Do you live around here, Lee?"

"I have a home in a quaint little town called Gardener."

"That sounds like a lovely town, are there gardens all around?"

"A few, would you like to see them?"

Devilishly I grinned, as I moved my head close to his to whisper, "That and much, much, more."

"Well, what are we waiting for?"

I laughed playfully, "For you to get around asking me!"

We informed those at our table that we were departing for the night and proceeded to walk out through the crowd together smiling all the way, which unbeknownst to us, became the talk of the rest of the evening, according to Jimmy.

When we reached Lee's car in the parking lot, it was a cute silver sports car, with red interior. As I buckled my seat belt I said, "This is a nice car Lee, what kind is it?"

He pulled out of the hotel driveway, "It's a 1980 Honda Prelude."

I looked at him strangely, "It's very nice Lee, but a foreign car? Couldn't that be politically embarrassing for you, considering I hear you're running for a seat in the U.S. Senate?"

He laughed, "When the American companies start building better cars, I'll start buying them again. It's my own little protest and I'm a man who stands on principle."

I smiled, "You've made your point quite well, I'm impressed," and we laughed.

When we arrived at Lee's home, it was an elegant, two storied old white farmhouse. As we got out of the car, a 'town car' pulled in behind us and Lee said, "I wonder who that is?"

I replied nonchalantly, "It's only my bodyguards; I pay them to tail me."

"Not bad!"

Then we entered his home. Our tour went from the front door to the bedroom where I proceeded to passionately rip his clothes off with one hand, mine with the other hand, while my lips were glued to his. It wasn't easy, but I was triumphant.

American Goddess

The rest of that night was spent in sexual and emotional bliss. It felt familiar, warm, and exciting to be making love to this man. The heat of our passion was so intense that Lee began to cry with tears of joy as he said, "Christina, I love you with all my heart. I have since my eyes first met yours."

With those words I melted, and I knew I would be safe from Frank in the arms of this powerful, gentle, loving man, and I found myself replying to his words of love in kind, "I love you too, Lee, I have also known that from the beginning."

After I told Lee that I loved him too, he went wild with passion. Our love making was phenomenal and we became one in the heat of our passion that night.

The next morning, we found ourselves on Lee's personal jet. We were heading to Las Vegas, to be wed that very day. When we returned to New York, we were newlyweds. It was Monday morning when I called a meeting of my staff in my suite at the Plaza. Jimmy almost fell off his chair when I introduced Lee to them all and announced that we were just married. Jimmy turned red as a beet as I began handing everyone in the room a list of assignments and said, "These are all the things I want done by December 10th, you all have detailed assignments and I'm leaving Jimmy in charge while I go on the campaign trail with my new husband."

That's when Jimmy interjected, with his jaws clenched tightly, "May I speak with you for a minute please Christina? **In private!**"

I followed Jimmy into the master bedroom, and he went off, "Have you gone off the fucking wall again? I can't believe you married him! What the hell is the matter with you?"

Quite innocently I replied, "First of all that was very rude Jimmy and second I'm in love with him. So now what's your problem?"

He looked at me like I was crazy, "Give up the act, **please** Christina, you're only kidding yourself. I spoke with Tom Davies the other night. I know how important this Lee character is to you. Can't you see you **did it** again?"

"What are you talking about, Jimmy?"

He shook his head, "It sounds awfully familiar Christina, it's the same reason you married Tony. Just because he was someone you could manipulate. Shit! It seems like I'm talking to myself here!"

"That's not fair Jimmy," I protested. "I have never judged your actions. I have always stuck by you and loved you, no matter what you did." I looked at him with hurt in my eyes, "I always thought you felt the same way about me."

"I'm sorry Christina it's just that you do this to me every time. You get us in over our heads with work, then you leave me a list of orders and off you go on another tangent."

I kissed him lovingly, "That's because I know you can handle it. I'm being called in another direction right now Jimmy, but I'll be back."

He returned my kiss and with that flick of his wrist said, "Go follow your dreams, Christina. I'll be waiting here for you because I love you, girl."

"I'm not going away, Jimmy, I will be coming in to help you. I just won't be moving into the new house on the complex grounds with you, but I'll still only be ten minutes away. I'm moving in with Lee and the campaign is only in New York State." We said goodbye and I was off with my new husband on the **New York State campaign trail**.

CHAPTER 14

On Tuesday, October 2nd, 1980, the day we should have left for our honeymoon, it was straight to the campaign trail with my new husband instead. Lee was an incredible man, and I was determined to make this relationship work. I truly wanted to be a good wife to Lee. I thought, "This wonderful, loving, gentle, powerful man loves me, and he deserves the best I can give him." Then my thoughts turned to revenge, "Besides, Lee doesn't know it yet, but he's going to be my ace in the hole against Frank."

You see, Lee was the owner of one of the most profitable corporations in the world, and he was one of only a handful of men who were wealthy enough and smart enough to defeat an all-out corporate assault from Salerno Incorporated. This little bit of information I discovered via a phone conversation I had with Tom Davies **from Lee's home,** the Sunday morning just before I proposed to Lee and swept **his ass off to 'Vegas'** to be wed.

It all happened like this. That Sunday morning after our night of love making, I climbed out of Lee's bed at 8:00am and went to find the kitchen so I could surprise him with breakfast in bed. As I was cooking, something told me to call Tom Davies at the Holiday Inn in Kingston, so I did.

Tom did not seem happy when he answered the phone with a groggy, "Hello."

But he perked up with my cheerful, "Good morning Tom. It's me, Christina! Sorry to wake you, but I just had a feeling I should call you."

Clearing his voice, he excitedly said, "Great, I was hoping you were going to come back last night."

"I had something to do; so, what's up?"

His voice held an air of urgency, "I received a call last night and discovered what the bill contains."

With a pleased excitement I exclaimed, "That's great Tom! Tell me, what does it say?"

"I'll sum it up like this," he began. "Right now, as the law stands, no corporation has to be listed on the stock exchange unless it sells stock to the public first. The other main provision in the law is that anyone can hold as much of a corporation's stock as they wish. This gives a holder of 51% or more of a corporation's stock, controlling interest in that corporation and the right to sit as the Head of the Board of Directors." Then he stopped, "Are you still with me?"

"I'm with you Tom, keep talking."

He spoke direct and clear, "The new law if passed will make every corporation with cash holdings of at least five-million-dollars, register on the public stock market. Then it will require that no one officer of a corporation be allowed to hold more than 49% of a corporation's stock, thus leaving no one officer, or stockholder, in total control of any corporation."

Through a voice of deep concern, I asked, "So knowing this Tom, what do you think Frank's up to?"

With a reply of disbelief, he continued, "It's so simplistic it's ingenious. Once he gets this law passed, you will be forced to scale down your personal stock to a holding of only 49%, which leaves you with only a 49% controlling interest of the corporation as well. Then he will attempt to acquire the remaining 49% for himself, with probably one of his puppets acquiring at least 2% of the stock, or as much as they can get, thus giving him controlling interest in Powers Incorporated. Then he could conceivably throw you out on your rear, leaving you humiliated."

Through intense anxiety I exclaimed, "Holy shit! Is there any way we can stop him?"

He sighed, "Well first, before the law is passed, make damn sure you give your stock to someone you can trust, because Salerno Incorporated has a cash holding of somewhere around sixty-six-billion-dollars. This gives him the financial power to convince most stockholders to sell. He also has been known to use other means of persuasion in the past. He is no one to play with. If he gets this bill passed Christina, he could crush Powers Incorporated in one day on the open stock market."

Feeling overwhelmed, I asked in desperation, "So what should I do?"

His reply was less than comforting, "First, I guess would be to try to stop the bill from passing. If you can't do that, then you need to be asking Mr. Bradford that question. He happens to be one of only a few men on Wall Street with the clout and smarts to stop Frank."

With a slight sigh of relief, "Thank you again, Tom. I'll take it from here but keep your eyes and ears open.

American Goddess

After that conversation I thought, "I do have a few Senators I could call on and it couldn't hurt to be married to one." So I proceeded to serve Lee breakfast in bed and I once again made passionate love to him. After which I proposed. Don't get me wrong. That's not the only reason I married Lee, but that is why I married him as fast as I did. You see, I knew all along I had a love for Lee. I also knew it could grow in time and I wanted it to. To be truthful, I was tired of fighting, and I was still afraid of Frank. I needed someone to love and take care of me for a change and I knew Lee was that someone; or I would not have married him. I also knew I could help him win his bid for a senate seat. Well, I was banking on it anyway.

When I joined Lee's campaign as Mrs. Bradford, he was six points behind his opponent, the incumbent Senator Joe Olympus. But within two weeks of our marriage and my joining Lee on the campaign trail, he was 10 points ahead of his opponent. Lee and I toured the state together, from the tip of Long Island to Niagara Falls. We campaigned in every city across the state, and the size of the crowds we drew was unheard of for a senate election. It was a wonderfully exciting experience to be on the campaign trail with Lee, because Lee was brilliant! He knew all the issues and he addressed them with finesse every time.

When he was finished wooing the crowds, I would take center stage and add my unique style and glamor into the arena. Lee's distinguished charms and the fact that the incomparable Christina Powers was now his new wife helped to attract the attention of the whole world to us as a couple. It felt great to be in a positive spotlight for a change. I got high on it!

In September I received a call for my good friend Eartha Kit who said, "Good morning Christina. I am calling to ask you for a great big favor. I have decided to run for office in Connecticut as the Democratic parties' candidate for the United States Senate. I know your terribly busy with Lee's campaign, but I was hoping I could convince you to join Barbara and I on October 1st for a fund-raising concert in Hartford. I could sure use the boost I believe the two of you could give my campaign?"

I laughed my reply, "I'm busy as hell girlfriend, but I'm sure I can fit it into my schedule, so count me in. Besides, it would be fun for the three of us to get together again."

With a great big purr, "Fantastic! I knew I could count on you and I promise I will not forget it."

I did fit the concert in on October first and the three of us had a blast. It was so much fun being with my best girlfriends again, and Barbara and I did give Eartha the boost in the poles she was hoping for and by 11 points. The very next day it was back on the campaign with Lee.

American Goddess

It's true that the entire month of October we worked night and day, but it didn't stop me from 'seducing' Lee, every chance I got. Being around Lee's powerful and brilliant energy all day long left me electrified all night long. Lee was proper with everything he did, even during our love making. I found myself having to be the aggressor every night, but once I got him started, he was a tiger.

One night after one such encounter, we were lying in bed together and Lee's body felt tense. I grabbed some hand cream, rolled him on his belly and began to massage his back. After a few minutes of this I asked, "Is this helping, Lee?"

He turned around to look up at me and lovingly replied, "It sure is, Christina! I love it, and I love you," as he ran his hand through my long, thick, black hair.

I leaned forward, kissed him softly, "I'm so happy you love me Lee, because your love has given me a reason to live again."

He had a glow in his eyes, "We make a great team together, you and I." Then he kissed me again, "One day I plan to be President of this country of ours and you will be the First Lady. Together we will make this nation greater than it has ever been. Christina, I truly believe our government needs to be run like I run Bradford Computers. That's why I decided ten years ago that I would make the Presidency be my life's goal, and now that we are together, I am more determined than ever to achieve that goal."

As he finished speaking words of love, I gazed tenderly into his eyes, "I do love you Lee and I admire you so much. I honestly believe that you will achieve that goal and I will be right beside you all the way to the White House. I promise." I kissed him, "Now you get some sleep. We have a busy day tomorrow."

He returned my kiss, "Goodnight," and rolled over.

As Lee drifted off to sleep, I started to do what became my nightly ritual. First, I spent one hour on my manuscript, then I would plug in my language tapes and for the next hour I would study a new language.

Then it came, November 4th, Election Day 1980 and by 9:00pm that night Lee was giving his acceptance speech to the cheers of the crowd, with me standing right beside him. He was elected senator by a whopping 62%, of the total vote. The celebration which followed Lee's speech was spectacular and the party was held at the corporate headquarters of Bradford Computers in Fishkill, New York. It was sometime around 11:00pm when Lee and I snuck out of the party and headed for Lee's car. Lee had decided his staff could handle the party from here; because he wanted to take me to his beach house in New Hampshire, for a one-week honeymoon.

As we drove through the village of Pleasant Valley on our way to the Taconic State Parkway just ahead of us in the sky, we spotted an exceptionally large object. I grabbed Lee's hand and with excitement said, "Pull over, I need to see this!" We both got out of the car and started looking at it. It slowly moved toward us and began to just hover over our heads.   It was completely silent with iridescent bright lights all around it.   I grabbed Lee's hand and said, "Oh my God Lee, what do you think it is?"

"I don't know but I think we need to get out of here, this is spooking me."

"No wait, it's beautiful! This is incredible! Do you think it's some kind of new military aircraft?"

Lee pulled me forcefully by the hand as he said, "Come on now!   I've worked with NASA for years and we have nothing that can do that!"

We climbed back in the car and as Lee drove away it seemed to be following us. That's when I started to get scared and I could feel my heart starting to pound. I looked toward Lee and he had a frightened look on his face which spooked me even more. Lee sped up to the entrance of the Parkway and hit the gas.

All of a sudden, I found myself standing in the center of a large silver room with 9 strange looking beings all around me. I became terrified and began screaming in fear! I looked for a place to run but they were all around me.   Then the largest one seemed to look right through me, with piercing black oval eyes and I heard, "Do not fear my child."

Immediately a since of calm came over me, and I asked, "What am I doing here and who or what are all of you?

Then I heard, "We are the head Council of the Federation of Extraterrestrial Beings who have been appointed to monitor and guide the human experiment. With great urgency we have brought you here Christina, to reveal ourselves to you and you along with a dire warring.   A Supernatural war has broken out in the heavens and a powerful force of evil darkness is gathering over your world as we speak. The Essence of all life has sent us to anoint you, 'Goddess' and give you the power to fight for the survival of humanity.   For it is 'You', who have been chosen to battle this darkness."

Fear and confusion, once again shot through my body as I asked, "How can I battle this darkness? I have no power to fight such evil!"

All at once a bright golden glowing being with four faces and four wings appeared right in front of me.   I fell to my knees in awe of such beauty and I heard, "Fear no longer my child, for I have guided and will continue to guide your steps. Now we will send you back to your mate and you will not remember any of this encounter until the appointed time."

As we pulled away from the aircraft I said, "Oh my God Lee, that nearly scared the breath out of me! Thank God it's not following us anymore! I thought we were about to be abducted by aliens!"

Lee grabbed his handkerchief, wiped the sweat from his forehead and said, "I don't know what the hell that was, but I thought I was going to shit my pants!"

I burst out laughing in hysterics until I could finally say, "You're not the only one!" Then he burst out laughing.

American Goddess

The rest of that trip, we spoke with renewed vitality of our future dreams. We were high together on Lee's victory, we laughed some more over not being abducted by aliens and our love was stronger than ever.

We arrived at the beach house sometime around 2:00am and we were wide awake. There was a brisk, cold, breeze blowing off the Atlantic Ocean, which felt clean and refreshing as we climbed out of the car and headed toward the house. When we climbed into bed that night, I placed my head on Lee's chest and began to softly nibble on his nipple. Then for the first time since our love making began, Lee became the aggressor. He gently placed his hand on the back of my head and began to forcefully guide my head down the length of his body until my lips reached the head of his wet, throbbing, manhood. I became so excited by his show of sexual aggression and manliness that I devoured him until his body became electrified. He held my head and rammed his hips forward, burying himself deep within the warmth of my longing lips. He screamed out in ecstasy as he exploded again and again flooding my sense of taste with his nectar.

Shortly after our love making, I felt that the time was right to finally question Lee on certain issues. So, as he held me in his arms I softly said, "Lee, I want to ask you something. Do you remember the bill I told you that Frank will be trying to pass in the Senate this year?"

He gently stroked my head, "Yes, I remember. Why do you ask?"

I positioned myself to gaze into his eyes and with curiosity asked, "Just suppose that bill passes and a corporation like Powers Incorporated tried to take controlling interest of Bradford Computers from you. What would you do?"

With a slightly arrogant tone, "First of all, Powers Incorporated couldn't orchestrate a corporate takeover of Bradford Computers, because it's not established enough to do so."

I gave him a cocky smile, "What if it was? What would you do?"

He chuckled, "You still couldn't do it."

"Why not?" I protested with frustration.

He laughed at me, "Because I wouldn't let you get away with it. I'd stop you first, that's why."

I gently bit his nipple, "You're still not answering my question smart ass. How would you stop me?"

"Okay! Okay!" He answered, as he pulled away from my teeth. He rolled over on top of me and proceeded to give me three scenarios of how someone might try to take over the corporation if the law were to pass. He told how he would stop each one. I listened ever carefully as he explained each maneuver, he would take to stop a corporate takeover. As he talked, I was amazed at how sharp this man's mind truly was.

American Goddess

The week we spent in New Hampshire together was the most romantic time I'd spent with anyone since Tony. We laughed, played, and had fun. It was as if we were children again, and we enjoyed one another as we basked in each other's growing love. Then with the blink of an eye, I realized one day, that it was working. I had finally overcome the devastations I had suffered over the past three years of my life, and I was excited to be alive again. I decided at that moment, Lee and I would truly live in the White House one day, and I was going to see to it!

As soon as we arrived back home, it was straight to work. We had two months to get things in New York settled with both our companies, before taking on the Washington lifestyle. We busted our buns together to get the job done. Before we started our new dual residency lifestyle, between New York and Washington, D.C., we knew everything there was to know in order for either one of us, to run the other's companies'. Lee was a genius at saving time, money, and manpower, in the way he ran Bradford Computers. I took every advantage of his expertise and implemented many of his corporate secrets straight into Powers Incorporation. Lee and I also decided to enter a joint business venture together, separate from our parent companies. I took two of my eighteen buildings and equipped them to produce computer components to supply Bradford Computers directly from our own subsidiary.

December 10th, we celebrated my twenty-fifth birthday by opening the new offices and home of Powers Incorporated to the business world. After two and a half months of hard work and two-billion-dollars in the red, my complex was 76% in use with a staff of six-thousand employees. We had films underway and records being produced in one of the main hubs. We had one hub strictly for producing computer components with research labs adjacent to the manufacturing buildings. I also decided to create a chain of corporate owned radio stations, which would link the entire country directly to me. There was no way my music would ever be taken off the air before its time again, and I was going to make sure of that. I knew that with my new business endeavors I could pay off the debt in two years. Then, I would see the real profits of my soon to be Mega Empire. This knowledge helped to make my party that evening the most exciting birthday party I'd known in years.

After my party, it was off to Washington, D.C., where Lee and I began to make ourselves familiar with the Capital region. We bought a modest, but elegant brownstone in Georgetown. We made it a point to get acquainted with a number of influential, political, operatives as we plunged feet first into the Washington scene. You see, I knew I had four months to muster all the support necessary in the Senate to offset Frank's expected assault, and I was wasting no time in getting that support. **NO MATTER WHAT THE COST!**

I worked us extra hard and it took us about two months to learn the Washington ropes. And when we did, we were great at it. Lee and I were racing the clock in an attempt

American Goddess

to be sure footed before April 1ˢᵗ, 1981, arrived, which would be the date when Senator Welm would introduce Frank's-sponsored bill to the Senate Floor for a vote. Senator Welm was only giving the senators one month to study the bill, which would be brought to 'the floor' for a vote on April 23ʳᵈ.

April 15ᵗʰ rolled around faster than we could imagine. Lee was scrambling around the senate floor all that day in a desperate attempt to estimate the final outcome of the vote. When Lee and I met at home that evening it was around 9:00pm. Just as we sat down for our normal late dinner, he said, "Well, I have a final count on next week's vote." My heart began to pound as I anxiously asked, "So, what is it?"

With a frustrated tone he continued, "With all our joint pull in both parties along with Eartha's vote, we are still down by one swing vote."

"One vote! It's that close! There must be someone's vote we can swing!"

Lee answered guardedly, "Tom Kenny's I thought, but when I approached him about it, he turned me down flat."

With a sense of optimism, I replied, "I know Tom, I met him a few years ago. I'll try to speak with him tomorrow."

Lee had a concerned expression, "I wish you wouldn't do that; he has a reputation with women."

I confidently chuckled, "Lee, you're talking to Christina Powers, there's not a man alive I can't handle."

He began to shake his head 'no' as he spoke in a demanding tone, "I know Tom too, and I don't want you to speak with him at all. It will look as if I sent you to him."

With a surprised expression, "Lee, don't be ridiculous. You know as well as I do what Frank will do to Powers Incorporated if this law passes."

Lackadaisically he cockled, "So what, I have more than enough for both of us."

I became instantly outraged by his chauvinistic reply and I showed it sharply, "Why you snob! What a selfish thing to say. I've worked my fingers to the bone to build Powers Incorporated and I'm not letting anyone take it from me! So I'm sorry if I blemish your ego, but I can't let this bill pass! Now, I am calling Tom tomorrow because he is a friend of mine, not because you are sending me. Even if you were sending me, we would be doing the same thing we have been doing since we got married, which I thought was working together to accomplish a mutual goal."

His attitude resembled Frank's as he shouted, "If you go, I will be very upset with you, Christina!"

I immediately stood up from my seat, "Oh really! Well, that's your choice, but I must do this and you, as my husband should understand that!" With that I stormed straight to the bedroom, grabbed his pillow, a blanket, threw them at him just as he reached the door, slammed it in his face and locked it.

American Goddess

The next morning, I called Senator Kenny's office and I was immediately transferred directly to Tom. He answered the phone, "Christina Powers, it's so good to hear from you. I've been hoping to run into you now that you're living in town."

With a pleasant tone I answered, "Well thank you, Tom. I'm sorry it has taken me so long to give you a call, but Lee and I have been very busy since we arrived."

"I know, I've been watching you from afar and I must say you're quite an impressive woman. You jumped right in the first day and made yourself right at home here in our nation's capital with no trouble at all."

"Now I'm impressed, I had no idea you were such a fan of mine."

He chuckled a little, "I've been your biggest fan since I first met you, Christina. Maybe even 'bigger' than your husband."

I chuckled first then seductively, "Tom that could be interpreted in many ways. But that is not quite why I called you. I really need to speak to you in private as soon as possible. Can that be arranged?"

With an excited tone he assured me, "I can arrange almost anything I want to, how about this afternoon for lunch?"

"That would be wonderful."

"Why don't you meet me at my private suite at the Radisson, suite 1210. Say promptly 1:30. Will that do?"

"That will do nicely Tom, I'll see you there," I answered, with a slightly seductive tone.

That afternoon as I rode the elevator to the 12th floor, I told myself, "Whatever happens here today, just remember its only business. As long as you can stop Frank, you do whatever you have to."

I wore a bright smile, as Tom answered the doorbell, to match my bright spring colored outfit. As I entered Tom's suite, I spotted one of my bodyguards standing by the elevator and I felt like I was being spied on instead of guarded, but I still gave Tom a big hug when I saw him.

Over our lunch, I told Tom exactly what I wanted from him and he was not surprised. As we finished our lunch he said, "Christina, your uncle would become quite upset if I did what you're asking of me."

With an air of confidence, "You're a big boy you can handle a little heat from Frank. He'll get over it the next time he needs your vote." I reached across the table, took his hand and seductively added, "Tom, this means much more to me than it does to Frank, and I promise I will remember the favor graciously."

His eyes lit up and I could see him start to sweat as he tried to calmly say, "Please allow me to inquire just how important is this to you?"

186

American Goddess

I looked him dead in the eyes, and turned up the heat with a sensual, "It's very important to me Tom, so let's not play any more games. If your appetite for me is worth your vote, then I will completely satisfy that hunger." Tom took me in his arms, and the moment he did I screamed in my mind, "Lord, God, forgive me!" Then, I proceeded to earn his vote, as once again I degraded my flesh to save my ass from Frank. I did not think of Lee once as I had political, animalistic sex with my biological uncle. I told myself, it's strictly a smart business agreement. The kind my men always keep. When I left Tom's office, I left with his vote, but I sure didn't feel like celebrating. I was sick to my stomach. 'Oh, by the way!' Tom wasn't as 'big' a fan as he professed to be.

That evening when Lee arrived home from work, he was definitely not himself. He acted as if he knew exactly what had happened. But I held my cool. He was not going to see the guilt in my eyes, no matter how hard he stared at me over that speechless dinner. I was a Hollywood Queen; I couldn't believe he even tried. No one has ever been able to read me unless I let them, and I was not letting him in my mind this time. I could tell by the way he was acting, if he ever found out, it would destroy us; so, I decided at that moment I would have to lie to him if he should ever ask. Finally, he spoke up, "So tell me, how did you make-out with Tom today?"

Nonchalantly I volunteered, "Very well thank you, he is going to give us his support." This time he asked point blank, "Did you sleep with him?"

I became offended, "Don't ever ask me a question like that again."

He stood up from his seat and yelled, "I can't believe this! It's true! You're nothing but a sick, painted up, lying, slut."

I leaped out of my seat and slapped him across his face with the might of my anger, as I viciously shouted, "Don't you dare speak to me like that! You knew how much that vote meant to me; so, if this was some stupid bet between the two of you, then you lose. And you think I'm the sick one! Well look again you egotistical prick. I can't believe a man with your character would place his wife in a position like that, and then call me the sick one for doing what I had to do to save my corporation. Lee, you would have let me lose everything just to save your ego. I think that's what's sick, not what I did!" I grabbed my bag and headed for the door.

When I reached it, Lee yelled with a demanding tone, "Where do you think you're going?"

I stopped, turned to look at him and sarcastically yelled, "Oh go fly a kite, asshole!" And I walked out.

Two days after my victory over Frank by the defeat of his bill on the Senate Floor, Lee and I were back together. We decided that our love would overcome our faults. Only Lee was never quite the same with me again. He refused to see his own part in the whole thing and he never truly forgave me. As for me, my image of Lee being my knight in shining armor faded fast. We still kept up the appearances of the happy newlyweds, at least for the public. Oh, we tried, but every time we had the smallest spat, he would throw it up in my face again.

We lived like this until November 13th, 1981. I could take the fighting no longer, so I decided to move back to our home in New York. I figured we needed some space and time to try to mend this marriage. Besides, my new manuscript 'The Innocence of Deceit' was finished and Powers Incorporated was also in need of a financial shot in the arm, so it was time to go back to work. I grabbed one bottle of champagne and it was back to New York, only by myself this time.

November 13th turned out to be another one of those days I would never forget, for many reasons. I got off the plane at 7:00pm that night at Stewart Airport in Newburgh, and the weather was cold to the bone and rainy. As soon as I entered the airport, I was met by Mickey Winslow. He was Lee's vice-president at Bradford Computers. He handed me an envelope, "Christina, Lee needs you to call him at this number from a pay phone before you leave the airport."

I opened the envelope and there was a phone number on a plain white sheet of paper and another with a list of accounts receivable. I looked up at Mickey, "What's this all about?"

With a mysterious tone he spoke under his breath, "All I know is I was to give this to you personally; then disappear." Then he looked at me as if I was stupid, "So you haven't seen me, understand?"

I looked at him as if he were an asshole, "Not really, but you can disappear now."

I headed for a phone booth, dialed the number and Lee answered with a mysterious nervousness to his voice, "Christina, is that you?"

"Of course, it's me Lee, what's going on?" I answered slightly annoyed.

Still with the nervous voice, "I had you call me on a public phone just in case my lines are tapped."

"Tapped, why would the lines be tapped?"

This time his voice began to shake, "Listen to me. I'm in a little trouble and I really need your help right now."

Immediately, I became concerned, "This sounds serious, what's wrong Lee?"

I could tell he was trembling, "I've just found out that all my financial records will be subpoenaed first thing in the morning by a Grand Jury, appointed by the Ways and Means Committee. They are investigating my personal and business finances and there is one item I can't afford to have them find. Christina, I have to be able to trust you completely before saying anymore."

With an annoyed baffled tone, I sharply reminded him, "Lee, this is me you're talking to; I shouldn't have to say any more."

American Goddess

Nervously he began, "Okay, I need you to go to my office at Bradford Computers. Go in my safe and take out the black leather binder. Take the binder and hide it until I ask you for it. Christina don't have anything in your hands when you sign in at the security office or going out. You will probably be questioned as to why you were there, so I am asking you to lie for me, if you're called before the Grand Jury." Neither one of us said anything for a moment, then he added, "Will you be able to do this for me?"

I swallowed hard, "Yes Lee, I will lie for you."

With a sigh of relief, "Thank you Christina you're saving my ass. Okay, there is a list of accounts in the envelope Mickey gave you. Take them and update the files in my office. This will give you a reason for having been there. I know it's a shabby alibi, but it will do. Then, hide the binder on your person and get out with it. Christina, before I give you the safe number, I'm asking you to trust me with one more thing?"

I answered reassuringly, "Lee, you don't have to say it again, I'm here for you."

With an obvious tone of self-shame, he continued, "Whatever you do, don't open the binder. It's something I don't even want you to know about."

With an uneasy tone and a feeling of apprehension, "All right, Lee. I'll do exactly what you ask." Then I hung up the phone and it was off to Bradford Computers.

I climbed into my rented town-car and drove through the downpour of that dark, cold, night until I reached the Corporate Headquarters where I proceeded to follow Lee's instructions to the 'T'.

As I drove through the rain with Lee's binder in my possession I thought, "If this thing is that hot, I can't hide it in my office. Where the hell am I going to hide this?"

I was on route 9W heading north from Newburgh to Milton, and the road was wet and slick. As soon as I left the city limits of Newburgh, the road seemed to become desolate and it was only 8:00pm. From out of nowhere a bright set of headlights began to blind me from behind and I thought, "What the hell is this asshole doing?" just as it rammed me in the ass end and my head jerked forward. My heart instantly began to pound as I received a second jolt. The vehicle started to pull up along-side of me and I heard, "Bang! Bang!" I screamed as my side window shattered.

I screamed again as I floored the car and swerved toward what I could now see was a large pickup truck. I smashed its front quarter panel with the rear of my car in an attempt to force it off the road. It crashed back into me as we both accelerated. We were reaching speeds of 80 miles an hour, as we rounded slippery curves and past other vehicles. We reached a stretch in the road where it became a four-lane highway and I pushed the-peddle to the floor! My blood was racing through my veins as this truck attempted to pull up alongside of me at 100 miles an hour. I turned to glance at it quickly and I could see the barrel of a large gun pop out of the passenger side window. I screamed and began to swerve the car from side to side. With fear in my eyes, I glanced down at the speedometer and even at 110, I still could not get away from this truck. Then, I caught the flashing of headlights in my rear-view mirror, so I slammed on the brakes and screamed as the car spun out of control. I struggled with the wheel until I finally regained control of the vehicle. I was shaking like a jack hammer as I brought the car to a stop. My heart froze again as I saw both the other vehicles whip around in the road ahead of me and start speeding right toward me again. I screamed in horror, "Oh God!" as I popped the car into reverse and spun around. I threw it in drive and hit the gas just as these two speeding vehicles slammed into the back of my car, causing the three vehicles to become wedged together as we all spun off the road.

I was freaking when we all came to a stop together. I grabbed the black leather binder, opened the door of my car and started to run away as fast as I could. Then, I heard someone holler, "Mrs. Bradford, get down!" I stopped running, turned to look behind me, and saw four men climbing out of the other two vehicles. One of the men from the pickup aimed a shotgun at me. I screamed in utter terror as I immediately threw myself onto the wet grass, trying not to be shot. Just as I hit the ground I heard, 'BANG' as one of the men from the car shot the man from the truck, just before he shot at me. The driver of the truck pulled a pistol from his pocket and began to shoot at the man who just shot his partner. As he was shooting, the other man from the car jumped out from what seemed like nowhere and landed on top of the man with the gun. I was shaking so badly; I could not move as I watched this take place right in front of me. I could see them fighting horribly, until finally the man from the truck was lying unconscious on the ground. When the fight was over, this man hollered over to me, "Mrs. Bradford, are you all right?"

I ran to the man who had just finished fighting for my life and I leaped into his arms crying. I was so shaking up, I could hardly think of what to do next. I managed to get a hold of myself with the help of this extremely handsome man and I was finally able to say, "I hope you guys work for me?"

The man holding me smiled and said gallantly, "Yes, Mrs. Bradford, we're part of that team of pesky shadows you have lurking in the background."

I kissed his cheek gratefully, "Well, I'm sure glad you were here tonight."

Confidently he replied, "I'm Michael Carr, I've been your chief security agent for six months now, and it's nice to finally meet you."

A little more relaxed I smiled, as I saw the lights of police cars coming down the road, "I'm glad you're in my shadows, Michael." I turned to them both, "You guys do your jobs very well. It's reassuring to know my money has been well spent."

Just as the Troopers pulled up, I slipped the binder under my clothing concealing it, and it was off to the State Police Barracks.

After we were questioned by the State Police, I called James to come pick us up. He took the three of us to the Powers Complex. As we drove, I thanked Michael and his

American Goddess

partner John once again for saving my life. I had James take us to the main garage and give Michael the keys to one of the corporate cars. As the two men began to climb out of the limo from the other door, I felt myself compelled to reach out and embrace Michael one more time, and in that one more embrace, I felt as if I never wanted to let go of this strong, handsome man. After our embrace, I thought, "I wish I didn't have to let this one get away." Then he was out of sight.

He was adorable. Every inch of his five-feet-ten-inch tall, one-hundred and seventy-pound, firm strong body, was all man. He had well-trimmed blond hair, beautiful blue eyes and a splendidly shaped face. His lips looked moist and hot, the kind that I knew could melt a girl's heart.

James turned to me, "Are you ready to go home now?"

"Take me to my office first James."

When I opened the door to my office at Powers Incorporated, I turned on the light, walked over to my desk, and sat down. I slipped the black leather binder out from under my clothing, at which time I opened it and there were some papers and a computer disk. First, I began to read the pages which had a list of top-secret government accounts with billion-dollar figures written next to each one. I made copies of the papers, after which I tried to access the disk, but it kept asking for a password code. I tried to copy the disk onto an identical one, and it seemed to work. I took the original papers along with the copied disk and placed them back in the binder exactly the way I had found them. Then I sealed the binder in a large envelope.

When I returned to the limo, I had the binder and three other envelopes. I climbed in and I told James to take me to the bus station in Kingston. As he started the car I said, "James, take this envelope and keep it in a safe place." I grabbed his hand before he pulled away from the curb and with a desperate tone, "You must never let anyone know you have this." Looking uneasily into his eyes, "James, the only thing I want you to do with this is to see that it gets to the FBI if anything strange should happen to me."

He looked at me with concern as he swallowed hard, "God forbid anything should happen to you Christina, but I will do exactly as you wish."

He took me to the bus station, where I had James rent two lock boxes. I instructed him to place the now sealed binder in one box and the other envelope in another. Then, I had him take us to Jimmy's. As we drove, I thought, "Holy shit! I can't believe Lee would actually do this. This is the kind of information people in the business world would kill for, but what's on this disk," I wondered. Then I thought, "God! I hope I get away with this one!"

James dropped me off at the front door of Jimmy's place around 11:40pm that night. He was living at the home I had built for him and myself on the grounds of the Powers Complex. We named it 'Executive House.' I was truly looking forward to seeing Jimmy and everyone else. Although I had been in touch with Jimmy over the phone on a daily basis, I had not seen him or any of my staff since my birthday. When Jimmy opened the door and I saw him, my heart was struck with fear. You see, the entire time from the day I went on the campaign trail with Lee to that very minute, I had not thought of, or even mentioned the 'gay plague' once. I pushed it out of my mind and totally forgot about it! It was as if it never existed until I saw how ill Jimmy was when he opened the door.

Jimmy looked terrible. He was thin and he had the same skin blotches on his face that Bobby had when he died. I immediately dropped my handbag and hugged him. I started to cry, as my heart pained, "Jimmy, why didn't you tell me?"

We were holding one another in the large open foyer of the Executive House, when Jimmy's voice began to break up, "Christina, I'm scared!" crying as his fear burst out from the depths of his soul, "I don't want to die! Christina, I still love life too much. I don't want to die! Not now! Not like Bobby did!" He became hysterical and screamed out, "Please don't let me die like I let Bobby die." Looking straight into my eyes as he cried out in anguish, "Christina, please kill me before it does!"

I grabbed him tight and with our pain and tears merging as one I cried and shouted, "No, God! Please don't take my Jimmy from me, too!"

I looked at Jimmy who now looked so much like Bobby did just before he died, that it was killing me. I screamed out again, but this time with anger, "No! God! No! This time I won't let you take him from me." From somewhere I've never touched before inside myself I felt a burst of 'Power' come over me. I shouted with authority as I placed my hands-on Jimmy's head, "I command you to be healed!" As I held my hands-on Jimmy, I could see a light beginning to glow from over our heads. I gazed up and the light was becoming brighter. As the light grew, I could feel the 'Power' of its pureness filling my body. The light and the feelings of awe and fear, all increased to an intensity which caused me to begin to shake and lose my balance causing us both to fall to our knees. The light grew so intense that I thought I was going to die from the pure 'Power' of this Heavenly Presence, and I screamed, "God! No! I can't take any more!" The light began to dim and a vision of a beautiful large glowing white figure with four faces and four wings appeared within the light and I heard, "I am an extraterrestrial being sent to you from the essence of all life. You Christina, have been chosen." Instantly it was gone.

I became filled with fear and was shaking to the core when Jimmy grabbed me, slapped my face with all his might and shouted, "Christina, snap out of it!"

When I began to come around, I said, "Oh my God! Jimmy, do you think that was God?"

With a frightened expression, "Do I think what was God?"

I looked at him as if he were stupid, "The light you idiot! What else?"

His face turned white, "I didn't see any light, Christina."

American Goddess

Then my face turned white as I exclaimed, "Don't tell me you didn't see that light, it was all over us!"

With an honest expression he replied, "I swear, Christina, I did not see anything, no less a light."

I shook my head in disbelief as I replied with an eerie tone, "This stress is either getting to me Jimmy, or I think I'm going mad." We got off the floor, walked over to the sofa, and fell asleep in each other's arms.

The next morning, I called my office and had a one hundred-thousand-dollar bonus placed in each of the pay envelopes of the two heroes who saved my life.

I thought of calling Michael Carr, but I decided that there were more important things to do then get involved with my own bodyguard right now, so I did not call.

When Jimmy woke up, he wiped the sleep from his eyes and said, "I'm starving, I feel like I could eat a cow."

I looked him straight in his eyes, "Maybe it has something to do with last night, Jimmy."

His eyes grew wide, "Oh my God! I don't know what to think Christina, but I do know I feel better than I've felt in months. Could it be?"

With a spooked expression, "Never mention last night again, all right?"

"Why?"

"Because I said so," slapping the back of his head, "Go ask Carman to fix us some French toast and bacon. I'm starved too." With that Jimmy went to the kitchen and I called Lee.

When Lee answered the phone, I told him about my little run-in with my two friends from the pickup truck, and of Jimmy's condition. I had him give me the number of the director of the CDC who was a friend of his. After which I said, "Lee, I truly do care for you. If you would just stop looking at your hurt, then maybe our love will survive."

With a sincere tone, "You know I want you here with me Christina, but I'm not going to try to force you."

"Let's plan on talking this out when you come home for Christmas." Then, we said our goodbyes and I hung up the phone. I picked it right back up again and called a Mr. Chuck West, the Director of the CDC. After we chatted for a few moments, I made an appointment to meet with him for the following afternoon.

I then called Dominick Giovannetti on his private line in Rome. When he answered the phone, I said, "Hi Dominick, its Christina. Dominick, someone tried to kill me last night and I'm not sure who, or why. Can you help me?"

His Italian temper flared his anger with a heightened sense of outrage as he said, "Tell me what happened!"

American Goddess

I told him what took place the night before, then I said, "My security man killed one of them and the other is in the Ulster County Prison. He swears he and his partner were just disgruntled fans out for fun. The police might buy that, but I sure don't."

He replied with an authoritative tone, "I'll see what I can find out from here and I'll get back to you."

With an appreciative tone, "Thank you again, Dominick, I knew I could count on you." With that we promised to see one another soon. We said our goodbye's and I hung up the phone.

I called Dominick because I knew that as far as Dominick was concerned, I was his very special mistress. He would not let anyone get away with trying to kill me and I knew it. I was also aware if it turned out to lead back to Frank, it could cause an all-out international underground war between the two most powerful 'Mafia' leaders in the world. But that was the chance I had to take. I had to know who ordered the hit on me. This way I could deal with them in my own way. As I was feeling this anger straight to my core, out of nowhere I once more thought about the light I thought I saw the night before and I thought, "I think I may be losing my mind!" I shrugged my shoulders to accompany my thoughts, "Oh well! I'll figure it out tomorrow!" With that it was off to the kitchen for breakfast. At least I hadn't lost my appetite.

The next morning on my office desk, I found an envelope from my insurance company, Allstate. When I opened the envelope, I discovered that their investigation into the fire was completed. There were also two checks enclosed. One was for the fire and the other was Joy's life insurance policy. They totaled thirty-two-million-dollars, and I just tossed them into my purse like pocket change. I was not ready to think about the past at that moment. I called all my best people into my office and put them to work on my soon to be fourth film, 'The Innocence of Deceit.' Then it was off to Atlanta, Georgia, and my 4:00pm meeting with Mr. Chuck West of the CDC.

I walked into Mr. West's office, exchanged greetings, sat down and I got right to the point, "Mr. West, please tell me exactly what is being done to stop this disease from killing more people?"

Bluntly he replied, "Mrs. Bradford, on the record I won't talk to you, but off the record I will."

I was surprised by his response, "Please call me Christina, and start talking off the record."

He began with a tone of urgency, "We think it is a sexually transmitted virus of some kind, but we have still not been able to identify any new virus as of yet."

I was taken back with his reply and it showed on my face, "If you know that it is transmitted sexually, then why has no one in the public been told about it yet, and what's being done to find this virus?"

Shaking his head in disgust, "You have to look at your current administration to find the answer to those questions."

"What do you mean?" I asked with a puzzled tone.

Sounding completely frustrated he answered, "The Feagan Administration has put a lid on all outgoing information from this place. It has also cut our budget so badly we can't even purchase the type of highly sensitive electronic microscope which is needed to even try to find the virus."

With a tone of shock, I swiftly replied, "Do you mean to tell me almost a year has passed since the elections and no one has made any progress at all toward finding this disease?"

His expression turned sad, "I hate to say it, but as long as it's only killing gays, the funding is not coming from this administration to find it."

Immediately I opened my purse, pulled out thirty-two million dollars in insurance checks, signed them, handed them to Chuck, "Use this to buy what you need. I'll make a deal with you; you find this killer and stop it. As for me, I think it's time to move some political mountains."

As I walked out of Chuck's office, I decided it was time to declare **war on this unknown killer**.

CHAPTER 15

The pace of the next few years was incredible! Between work, a long-distance marriage, my all-out attack on the government for not being truthful to the nation about this dreaded disease, my frequent FBI questioning and numerous days of sitting in front of a Grand Jury, I thought I was going crazy. When I wasn't in a Washington Court House, I was in an Ulster County Court House testifying against the man who tried to kill me. How I made it through those days only God knows. Not only did I go out on the limb with the Grand Jury for Lee, but I also put the financial holdings of Powers Incorporated on the line for him as well. The day the Grand Jury probe was announced Bradford Computers stock began to plummet. I had to personally guarantee Bradford Computers stockholders, Powers Incorporated would cover all losses which might result from any

195

negative publicity due to the Grand Jury probe. This was the only thing which kept most of them from panic selling. It was so intense; I hardly had any time to breathe. Whenever I tried to sneak off to collect my thoughts, I would be swamped by the press. As hard as I looked in those days for a place to find some peace, there was none to be found. I was being pulled in so many directions; I don't know how my nerves held up, especially since I chose not to fall back on my old friend, cocaine.

The only time I found any sense of sanity at all was when Lee and I were alone, which was not very often. You see, when Lee and I spent that Christmas together in 1981, just after the FBI began to come around, we had finally decided we were truly in love and that our marriage could survive anything as long as we continued to love one another. That Christmas, Lee was back to his wonderful loving self. He told me he was wrong and sorry for what he had done. He asked me to forgive him and I did the same. After that Christmas, I had my husband back and I knew it. He promised, together we will make it through the Grand Jury probe, and onto the White House. It was at that point we went from this warm, loving, Christmas, straight into the **Fires of Hell**.

Although the years between January 1982, and January 1985, were hectic, there were still some very good things happening. **First** and foremost, Jimmy's health slowly began to improve and with pressure from the American people, along with Lee and me, the 'gay plague' was finally given a name on January 4th, 1983. It was called, 'Acquired Immune Deficiency Syndrome,' 'AIDS' for short. Then, in October of '83, the AIDS Virus was discovered and shortly after a blood test to detect the HIV antibodies in the human body was developed.

Jimmy took the test on February 6th, 1984, and on February 16th, Jimmy and I both went to find out the test results together. To our complete amazement and relief Jimmy's test results were negative. As we hugged each other and jumped up and down with joy, neither one of us mentioned that night in November of 1981. We were just grateful for an answered prayer!

Second, my career was soaring. I had written and starred in three blockbusters, which I rode all the way to the bank. I also released six platinum albums and I had created my own cable television network called, 'Radio, Video, TV.' When videos first came out onto the market, I decided to record live performances and air them twenty-four hours a day over my new cable network. It was a long shot, but I was a gambling woman. My personal financial success helped Powers Incorporated get back in the black again. We managed to pay off our debts as I planned, but it wasn't as easy as I thought. By January 1985, our cash holdings had only grown to three billion dollars. But as I said, we were debt free.

Third, lucky for all of us, I found out in March of '83, that Frank had nothing to do with the assassination attempt on my life. According to Dominick Giovanetti it was not meant to be an assassination attempt at all. Dominick discovered Senator Tom Kenny was somehow aware that I was taking documents out of Lee's office that night, and he wanted those documents. Dominick also discovered it was Tom, who orchestrated the Grand Jury probe in the first place. It seemed he was trying to get even with Lee, for what, he had no idea. Dominick also said, "Christina, don't forget, we're talking about a famous U.S. Senator here, so think carefully before you tell me how you would like me to handle this delicate situation."

"Dominick, I love you and thank you for what you have already done, but I want to take care of Senator Kenny, **my way**. But as for this **pain in the ass** court trial, it's driving me crazy! I'm constantly being bothered with it. Is there anything you can do to speed this trial up somewhat for me?"

Without hesitation, "I'll take care of it tonight."

Quite sincerely, "Dominick, thank you again, and as soon as I can come to Rome to see you and thank you in person, I will."

The next day the man who tried to kill me was found dead in his cell and the trial was over. This was not quite what I meant, but it taught me to be extremely specific when it came to asking Dominick for favors.

Fourth, I received a call in June of `83, from Detective Fred Ulrich. He told me he had found and arrested the arsonist. Then he said, "He's a tough nut to crack, he's not talking. I'm trying to have him tried on first degree murder. Hopefully when he realizes he's going up for the next twenty-five-years, he'll accept our plea bargain and start talking. I'm sure he'll lead us back to Frank."

"Do you have any solid proof to connect Frank to the fire at all?"

Sounding determined he swiftly replied, "Not one bit, but I'm not giving up. I'll get this guy to talk, even if it kills me."

"Thank you, Fred, you're doing a great job and I'll be waiting to hear more."

Unbelievably on January 16th, 1985, the most drawn-out Grand Jury probe in history, finally dropped their investigation against Lee. When I heard that news, I thought, "Thank God! Now maybe my life can begin to return to its normal pace."

The press finally stopped hounding me and the stress created by this whole mess, which Lee pulled me into was gone for good. That was when I was finally able to breathe again. That night, Lee took me out for dinner to celebrate our victory over the Grand Jury probe. After dinner, we went home and the rest of that evening Lee was full of manly testosterone, as he obnoxiously gloated, from his personal triumph over Senator Tom Kenny. He proceeded to become aggressive in a way which was not flattering. I knew it was his way of showing me he was superior to Tom, and because I loved him, I allowed it to take place. I managed to make it through that night of tasteless sex, but I strongly protested the next morning. After that one outburst of aggressiveness, he was back to his normal laid-back approach.

It took about two weeks for the residual effect of the end of the Grand Jury probe to affect my life in a real way. Like breathing, eating, sleeping, you know, all those everyday things. It felt good to eat a large bowl of pasta again without having to eat a handful of antacids first, because my nerves were shot.

All of a sudden, like magic, I had some free time for me. I took advantage of that time and with half of it, I plotted and schemed my revenge on Frank; with the other half of that free time, I not only fought AIDS, I began to publicly fight every injustice I saw in the world. I was so loudly critical of the Feagan Administration and the reaction of our nation's response to human rights issues for all people and all nations, that the Republicans coined a phrase at my expense. They began to publicly call me, 'The Queen of the Bleeding-Heart Liberals' even though I was married to a Republican Senator.

By 1987, I was bad news in Washington. First, the Feagan Administration tried to hog-tie my mouth shut through Lee. When that didn't work, they tried to blacklist me throughout Washington. Needless to say, I was too visible and powerful for them to quiet me in the conventional ways, and after the Grand Jury I was squeaky clean, so they couldn't go from that angle either, so their only hope was Lee. Since that didn't work, Feagan and I found ourselves at a stalemate for the first few years of his term on every issue that I condemned his administration.

The tension I created between 'yours truly', and the administration, ended up becoming a personal battle between President Feagan and myself, for the public's approval rating. So, as he fought presidentially against me, I fought my way. I not only talked about the issues publicly, I contributed millions of dollars toward each one publicly. Then finally the public pressure which I rallied began to give me some leverage. This pressure caused the Administration to finally begin to bend a little. I became so good at burning the Administration I was nicknamed by the press, "Feagan's Wildfire."

Lee and I managed to be happy together until the summer of 1987, June 3rd, to be exact. That was the day Lee had me return the black leather binder to him. When I handed it to him, he said, "Tell me the truth Christina, did you open this?"

I looked at him innocently, "I did exactly as you requested, Lee."

With an air of relief, "That's good!" He kissed my forehead, "You really saved my neck by sticking with me, and I will never forget it. I thank you from the bottom of my heart."

I returned his kiss, "You're welcome Lee; just remember I did it because I love you."

Shortly after our exchange of the binder and our tender moment, Lee changed. The thoughtful, loving, concerned man I went through hell for, became a 'Doctor Jekyll'. The personality difference was unbelievable. At first, I wondered what I had done to provoke

American Goddess

this change, but I could not think of a thing. Then I thought maybe he knows I switched the discs. When I finally asked what was wrong, he acted as if I was imagining it. I put up with his verbal and mental abuse for a whole fucking year, just because I kept telling myself I loved him and I was not going to fail at this marriage. I had been a failure with my personal life for so long now I just had to make this marriage work.

On June 11th, 1988, Lee finally threw the straw on which broke 'this' camel's back. The scenario went like this. I had just finished shooting my sixteenth and most sensual film to date, entitled, 'Family Love Affair.' I was tired from work and I had not seen Lee in six weeks. So, I took the rest of the month off to be with him. That night, after six weeks of not being together, we laid in the bed naked with candlelight and soft music. Needless to say, I was feeling very amorous as I once again became the aggressor. To my amazement, as hot as I was that night, Lee couldn't get an erection. Believe me, I tried everything, and it stayed limp, so I said, "Do you feel all right Lee?"

With a disgusted tone he rattled, "I just don't feel like making love is that all right with you?"

I thought to myself as I laid there feeling rejected, "What the hell is this?" With that thought in mind I flew up out of the bed, grabbed my robe, covered myself quickly and shouted at him, "Screw you, Lee! I have had it! Do you realize who I am? I'm Christina Powers, a thirty-four-year-old sex goddess!" I was so mad I grabbed a book from off the dresser, threw it at him and shouted, "There is definitely something wrong with this picture! If I wanted, I could give every man on this planet a freaking hard-on, but I can't give my own, forty-eight-year-old husband one." **STEAMING** I stormed into the bathroom, got dressed, stormed back out to find him still lying-in bed just glaring at me. His superior expression made me even angrier, "Lee, I'm leaving and I'm not coming back. You will hear from my attorneys because I want a divorce." I took off my wedding ring, threw it at him and stormed out. I headed back to New York that very night.

The next morning, Tuesday, June 12th, I was having coffee in the kitchen, when Jimmy walked in and said with surprise, "What are you doing here? I thought you were in Washington?"

Over our coffee, I told Jimmy what had happened, and he leaped up into the air and shouted, "It's about fucking time! I have never said one word to you about him since you told me you married him. But now I can, and I'm gonna let you have it with both barrels! That guy is a fucking brainy, know-it-all, asshole. I will never know how you slept with that dweeb in the first place."

"Give me a break, would you please?" I answered defensively, "I'm feeling bad enough as it is. Do you think I'm happy my marriage broke up?"

Starting to laugh, "Christina, let me give you some news. Give it two hours of real thought and you'll be jumping for joy that your marriage **from hell** broke up." We both laughed, then Jimmy added, "Please do me a favor and don't get married to anyone without talking to me first!"

We laughed again and I promised, "You have my word on that one, but don't worry, I'm never getting married again. I've had it with this crap!"

Smiling, and **with the flick of that wrist**, he chirped, "If there is one thing I know, girlfriend, **you never say never**." Getting up from his chair, "I have to go to work; I don't get the luxury of staying home, like some of us do."

I chuckled, "That's right, I'm a slave driver. Now go make us some money."

Grinning from ear to ear he chortled, "Christina, I have a date tonight. His name is Tom LaChance. We're going out for dinner, then dancing at a local gay nightclub called, 'The Prime Time'. Why don't you come with us?"

I replied excitedly, "Are you kidding? You have a date? I wouldn't miss the chance to meet your first date since Bobby's death for anything. What time do you want me ready? And what the hell has taken you so long to date again anyway?"

He answered with a wink, "You, you bitch! Now that you've led me to Christ, I realized meaningless sex is not fulfilling. I figured if God wants me to have sex then he will bring the right person into my life. And this might be the one, so meet us here at 8:00pm girlfriend!"

"I'll be waiting!" I replied, as he kissed me goodbye and left the room.

After Jimmy left for work, I decided to take a walk outside. The morning was delightful, and I wanted to be part of it. I was once again back to my cut off blue jeans, tee shirt, sneakers, and it felt great. It was around 9:00am when I came back from my walk and I climbed right into my new Cadillac convertible and went riding with the top down. As I drove all around the Hudson Valley that day with the fresh spring air blowing through my hair, I realized Jimmy was right. I was free and it felt like a ton of weight had been lifted off my shoulders. This was going to be my time. I was not going to even think of having a man in my life. I was done with love and as I drove over the Mid-Hudson Bridge on my way into the city of Poughkeepsie, I could feel something in the air that morning. It was as if the day itself was telling me something wonderful was going to happen.

As I wound my way through the unfamiliar streets of Poughkeepsie, I found myself at a beautiful park right on the river. It was called Kale Rock Park and it ran along the river right under the bridge. As I parked the car, I looked up at this magnificent bridge, which towered the span of the river to connect the two mountains on either side. It was a beautiful sight to behold as the noon sun glistened on its silver arches. I climbed out of the car and started to walk the trail which ran along the riverbank. As I walked, I was daydreaming to the peaceful sounds of the waves slapping the shoreline. I began to focus my eyes on a man wearing a tight-fitting jogging suit. As he gracefully approached me, his firm muscles were rippling with every movement. I could not stop staring at his body. It was so sexy! With every step he took closer my heart began to pound, and it felt exciting. It was so exciting it was almost frightening. My body was beginning to quiver, and I hadn't even made eye contact yet. As we came within a few feet of one another, I timidly gazed up into his beautiful blue eyes and I was stunned! It was Michael Carr, my bodyguard, whom I had not seen since the night he saved my life.

I stopped dead in my tracks and with a pleasantly surprised tone exclaimed, "Michael! It's so nice to see you!"

His eyes lit up, "Mrs. Bradford! It's good to see you too. How are you?" Then he looked at himself with the sweat dripping from his brow, and apologetically added, "I'm sorry you're seeing me like this."

I smiled nonchalantly, "Don't be sorry Michael, and please call me Christina. Besides, I'm sure you're not working, are you?"

He chuckled, "Sure, I go to work like this every day! Don't you remember? I was sweating bullets the last time we met." He chuckled again, as he added, while pointing toward some townhouses, "No, I'm only kidding. I live on the other side of that hill over there."

I looked in the direction he pointed, "Are you in a hurry, do you have time to talk?"

"No, I'm not in a hurry. As a matter of fact, this happens to be the start of my two-week vacation."

With amazement I replied, "You're kidding, what a coincidence. I just started my vacation today as well."

"Well I'm just going up to my place to take a shower and have some lunch. Have you had your lunch yet?"

I answered with a friendly smile, "No I haven't eaten yet and I'd love to have lunch with you; so lead the way."

We talked about the weather as we walked to his home together. As we entered his three-bedroom quaint, clean townhouse, that overlooked the river and the bridge, I commented, "This is a very nice home you have here, Michael." Then I walked over to the glass doors which led out onto the balcony, gazed out at the splendid view, "Michael, I never took the time to truly thank you in person for saving my life; so, I would like to say it now, seven years later, thank you Michael."

He replied sincerely, "I would also like to thank you. If it were not for your kind generosity, we would not be standing in a debt free home right now." Then he placed his keys down on the big captain's desk, which was placed in the living room beside the brick fireplace, "If you don't mind I'll let you make yourself comfortable, and I'll go take a quick shower and remove some of this sweat."

I smiled warmly, "No I don't mind at all."

American Goddess

He smiled back as he turned to leave the room, "Great! Then I'll be back in a flash." I watched as Michael walked out of sight and I thought, "Holy shit! This man is incredible! Just look at how his tight, round, firm buns move as he walks. I can't believe I waited seven years to look at those buns again." He was hot! Then my mind wandered back to the night he held me in the pouring rain, just after saving my life, and I remembered how magical his embrace was that night and my body became warm with the memory.

As I walked around his home, I noticed there was a small home gym in one room and a library in another. When I walked into the library, I could not help but notice most of the books were on the subject of spirituality. There were some on God, Jesus, Angels, Heaven, life-after death, extraterrestrial encounters and understanding the spirit world. As I glanced through the books, Michael came into the room with a gorgeous skintight, pullover, short sleeve, navy blue shirt on with tight fitting, black denim shorts, white socks and Adidas sneakers. I found myself once again quite impressed with his beauty. He walked over to me as I glanced through one of his books, "Come with me, we can talk in the kitchen while I fix us a chef salad for lunch."

I followed him into the kitchen and offered, "Please let me help. I really can slice up a head of lettuce, no matter what you may have read about my cooking. It's all lies."

He laughed as he handed me a head of romaine lettuce and a knife, "Here you go! Now I am going to take your word over the Inquirer's and leave you on your own with this, so try not to cut yourself 'cause the proof is in the pudding."

I chuckled, "You're not only a chef, but you're a smart-ass too. I like that in a man." We both laughed some more, then I said, "Michael, may I ask you something?"

"Sure, ask whatever you'd like," He sweetly answered. "I'll be honest."

"I noticed all the spiritual books you have in your library. Are you a deeply religious person?"

He smiled boyishly as he glanced into my eyes and replied mischievously, "Yes I am, but not in the normal sense of the word."

"Ahh," I said suspiciously. "Now that was an interesting answer, what do you mean?"

As he was slicing up a tomato, "I believe in God with all my heart, and I try to live my life in a way which I feel is pleasing to God and that is usually how I please myself."

I looked at him strangely, "You must be a unique character then, because I've tried to live my life in the way the Bible says we should and it wasn't pleasing to me at all; as a matter of fact it almost drove me mad. I could not live up to God's expectations, no matter how hard I tried. I failed every time, which only made me feel worse, so I just gave up trying." I spoke as I tossed the lettuce into the bowl with Michael's sliced tomatoes, "Michael, I'm not putting you down when I say this, but I know in my heart there is no way any of us can keep the laws of the Bible, no less keep them and be happy doing it. It just can't be done, we're too imperfect not to fall into the trappings of certain sins no matter how hard we try, it's just not possible. That's why I have to disagree with you."

As Michael served the chef salad, "I respect your right to disagree with me, but at the same time I respectfully disagree with you. I'm not saying I'm perfect, all I'm saying is I try my best to follow my heart with everything I do. Since I believe I am one with God, then the desires of my heart will always lead me closer to God. But I think you have a more traditional Christian belief, which usually teaches fire and brimstone instead of love and forgiveness. If you look at God as a condemning heartless Father, then you're absolutely correct, not one of us will ever live up to the Christian world's teachings of what God expects of us as his children. That's because they put too much emphases on the sin, thus helping to keep people trapped in their sin. That's one of the reasons why I enjoy worshiping God in a corn field, better than I do in a church. I look at the earth, animals, trees, flowers, myself, and God differently than most churches do today. I believe I am part of it all."

With a doubtful tone, "Flowers and trees, I can see the beauty in them, but I can't see myself as being part of them."

He chuckled innocently, "I see it like this. When God created it all, he put his life force into every living atom and as long as God's life force is in that atom, that atom sustains life. Do you understand what I'm saying?"

I looked at him with amazement, "Yes I think I do, I never thought about it like that before, but I can understand the concept of it."

He smiled in a way which told me he was pleased, "So when I think of God, I think of myself and everything around me as being one with God. I try to live my life in harmony with the earth and every living creature, because if everything is from God and part of God, then I must respectfully treat everything and everyone with the same divine respect and love as I would myself."

In awe of his spiritual intelligence, yet at odds with it, "That sounds great, but it also sounds like you're saying you are God. Isn't that blasphemy? Didn't Jesus say there was only one God?"

With all sincerity, "Yes Jesus did say that, and that's exactly what I mean. Jesus taught there is only one God, yet he said, 'He was God' thus making Himself equivalent with God. Jesus also said, 'If I am one with God and you are one with me, then God lives within you.' I believe Jesus was saying we are all equal and divine in nature, meaning we are part of God the Father. So, whether we believe it or not, the unconditional gift of love Jesus gave us all when he paid the price for sin on the cross, gives us all the opportunity to have a love relationship with God, despite our sinful nature. Now, if God dwells within us; we are one with Him, which makes us divine beings despite ourselves. Once one reaches that level of spiritual understanding, sin will eventually lose its power over your life as you begin to move closer to Jesus' teaching and being Christ like." He looked at me with true passion in his eyes, "Don't you think if everyone would just stop looking at their sins and the sins of others, and start looking at themselves as being part of God, there would be a lot less judging of our neighbors and a lot more loving of our neighbors, as Jesus taught?"

I was surprised by his spiritual wisdom and it showed on my face, when with amazement I said, "That is so profound Michael, and incredibly beautiful. But I've found when I tried to live my life by the teachings of the Bible it put my entire life at odds with God's will. When I gave my life over to God's will, to do what I was told God wanted of me, which was to teach the will of God to everyone, those same church leaders who told me that, would never let me address the public alone because I was a woman. They said it would have been a sin. So as far as I'm concerned, I will love God in my way, and until I see the churches begin to bring the world together instead of dividing it, I will never become a member of any organized Christian group again."

He was surprised by my bluntness, "Well, you need to understand something about most Christian organizations and the Bible, and that is the Bible was written for a different time, place and people, with a lesser scientific mentality and spiritual knowledge. Churches are still stuck there. What really happened was that in time as mankind's knowledge and intelligence grew, so did his spirituality, and the churches ignored that. That's why I believe, as the soul of each of us departs from God to become a child, its goal is to bring our conscious mind and physical body to a higher awareness of our own divinity; which comes back to our own individual oneness with God. If we believe we are one with God, through Christ, Buddha, Allah or whomever one's higher power is, then our conscience, which is guided by the Essenes of God within us, is always there to guide our hearts on the choices we make in life; thus, we are given the ability to judge our own actions accordingly, and at the same time we're taught by Christ not to judge our brothers."

With that I interrupted, "How does anyone ever really know if they've made the right choices or not?"

He smiled like an angel and replied as if it were as plain as the nose on my face, "You know, if your choice brings you to a closer feeling of oneness with God. You will feel good about what you have done, and it will bring you eventually, to a higher awareness of your own divinity in God. That's when you will have the power to move mountains in your own life and others. So, if the churches choose to continue to teach us to look at ourselves, as weak failures in God's eyes, because we continually fall short of what they want us to believe is important to God, then that is what we will be, failures. But, if we look at ourselves as God sees us, which is a divine child or part of God's own essence, then we open ourselves to the mysteries of Heaven through God's eyes within us. But this knowledge only comes from true spiritual growth and the choices we have made throughout our lives."

"Whoa! That is heavy Michael. I never looked at God with such a broad aspect before. It's an incredible theory."

He gazed at me with sadness in his eyes, "That is all it will ever be to you Christina, until you allow yourself to touch a little bit of your own divinity."

"Please don't think I was putting you down, because I wasn't. I find what you are saying to be very enlightening; I just don't know how it all connects to my fundamental beliefs in Jesus Christ as being my God in Heaven, not in me."

He softly smiled, "First of all, I didn't think you were trying to put me down and I hope you don't think I was putting you down either. What I meant was, one day you will realize even though we all battle our own dark side and many times lose, you can still live as Christ taught. It is not our job to condemn the world or ourselves, it is our job to save the world in its sin, not from its sin, because if your faith is in Christ, then you know Jesus already did that. So, if we can see that, yes, God does reside in Heaven, but it is His life force which gives us every breath we take. When we truly realize that we will know God lives within us. Then sin will no longer be an issue in our lives. I believe once the human race as a whole stop looking at the sins and differences of others, and starts looking at their own oneness in God, then mountains will truly be moved."

"Michael that is beautiful, but how will the world ever reach the point of moving mountains, without Christ's physical presence?"

His eyes radiated wisdom, "Listen to your question, then try to think as I believe and answer the question yourself."

I thought for a moment, "Do you mean that because God lives within us, it will be the human race as a whole, who will make a heaven on earth and that Christ will not be coming from the heavens to take away the pain and tears himself."

Calmly he replied, "Not exactly. I believe the Christ will return someday. But until he does, we are the Christ every eye shall see and it's up to us to fight the battle against the darkness in our own lives, as well as in the world, not through condemnation, but through the unconditional love which Jesus has shown for us. Then one day, we will all dwell in the light of the Lord forever. But until He comes, we are that light and each one of us must use the light of God, which is within us, to light the path of love for others."

Once again, I was amazed and it showed on my face, "Michael, I can really relate to what you're saying, but it sounds like you're asking for a one world belief in God and I don't think the human race will ever reach that level of understanding."

With an alarmed expression he quickly replied, "No I'm not. I'm asking for a one world belief, which will allow for all beliefs, because I believe all faiths will one day lead the world to the truth Christ taught, which is, we are all one with God and God is one with

205

every living thing. So, if we don't start looking at ourselves as one with God, then we will not recognize the **evil one** when he begins to mislead the human race."

I chuckled, "Now you sound spooky."

Looking very seriously, "You can laugh, but some people believe that somewhere on this planet right now, is the living Anti-Christ. Many people across the world have received spiritual messages from the angels of God. Many of these angels speak of a demon, which has taken the form of a human, and is now rising in the world arena somewhere. No one will know he is evil until he strikes out. It is up to us to become aware of the power of our own divinity now, so we may stand strong against this **evil one** when he emerges. These spirit guides, or extraterrestrial beings as some people believe, say the human race as a whole is either coming to the true knowledge of our own divinity, or else we are coming to our own destruction on this planet. I believe these extraterrestrial beings come from a civilization far more advanced than humanity and are more aware of their oneness with God. But that may be a little too much to swallow over a chef salad. So, how would you like to go for a ride with me?"

I smiled, "You also believe in aliens with flying saucers?" Then I chuckled as I said, "Believe it or not, twice I thought I saw a flying saucer and it's still going to take a big gulp for me to swallow that one."

"I know it may sound out there to some, but don't you think our God is great enough to create other intelligent life forms? The Bible itself even speaks of flying saucers. In Ezekiel 1:4 it reads, 'I looked, and I saw a windstorm coming out of the north-an immense cloud with flashing lightning and surrounded by brilliant light. The center of the fire looked like glowing metal, descending from it came a god with four faces and four wings.'

As Michael spoke, a chill shoot through my entire body as I remembered the being, I thought I saw with four faces and four wings that night with Jimmy.

He continued with, "Also, in 2-Kings Elisha writes about what happen to him and Elijah by saying, 'there appeared a chariot of fire, and horse of fire, and parted us both asunder, and Elijah went up by a whirlwind into heaven. And I Elisha saw it and cried.' I also believe when Christ was taken up into heaven, he was also caught up by a chariot of fire or possibly it was a 'flying saucer', and when he returns it will also be in a 'flying saucer'. In Isaiah 66:15 it reads, 'Christ shall come with fire and with His Chariots' like a whirlwind, to pour forth His anger and rebuke upon unrepentant mankind.' When he does return it will be because one-third of the human race will be worshiping the Anti-Christ, the one who proclaims he comes in the name of Christian faith, but he will be the **evil one.**" I was shocked and it showed on my face as he asked with concern, "Are you alright? You look like you've seen a ghost."

American Goddess

I snaped myself out of it and said, "I'm sorry, that was just a lot to take in over lunch, and I think I'll figure this one out tomorrow, but that ride sure sounds great, let's go." With that we headed back out into the warm sunshine.

As we walked out of Michael's home that early afternoon I said, "I have my car in the park, do you mind if we take it?"

"Not at all, have you ever seen the Catskills on a beautiful spring day before?"

I looked at him with admiration in my eyes as we walked toward the car, "No I haven't, but I'd like to."

He smiled again, "Great, I have a family home up in Tannersville, which is a hamlet of Hunter Mountain. It's beautiful up on the mountain this time of the year would you like to see it?"

"I'd love to." I answered with an excited tone, "But only if you don't mind driving?"

He replied, with a boyish smile, "No, I don't mind at all."

I tossed him the car keys, and we climbed in. We drove out of the park and Michael casually waved to his two co-workers, who were on duty guarding me, as we drove past them, then he turned toward me, "Christina, I hope I haven't given you the wrong impression of myself. There happens to be a lot more to me then my spirituality. It's true I have a strong faith, but I am still learning every day, just like everyone else."

I slapped his leg in fun, "Don't become self-conscious on me now, I have been enjoying the real you."

Within what seemed like minutes, Michael was skillfully handling the curves of Route 23B, as we wound our way up the mountain. I was in my glory watching the beauty of the Catskill Mountains go by, as Michael told me how he, his parents, his one brother, and three sisters, all grew up on this mountain top. He spoke of his family life and growing up on this mountain, with such fondness I almost felt envious. Those were the kinds of memories I never had, but it was still wonderful hearing Michael's. He was actually charming as he shared some of his childhood antics with me, but the best was when he said, "I've got to tell you this one. One day when I was about five years old, my seven-year-old sister Jody was teaching my three-year-old sister Michelle and myself, how to ride a two-wheel bike. First, I held the bike for my sister Michelle and let her roll down the hill to where Jody was waiting to stop her and keep her from falling. Michelle did great, then it was my turn. Well I climbed on the bike, got my balance just like Jody told us to do and off I went. I began to pick up speed as I raced toward the place on the hill where Jody was waiting to catch me, and as I reached her, she screamed and jumped out of the way, letting me roll right past her. As I continued to fly down the hill, I realized Jody never told us how to stop the bike. So I went flying off the road, over an eight-foot embankment and landed face first into the ice cold creek at the bottom of the hill."

American Goddess

I laughed so hard when he told that story, I nearly wet myself, "I wish you had told me I'd be meeting your family; I would have changed first."

"You're not. No one lives in the house anymore; we only come up here to get away or on holidays. We all moved away after my father Joe passed away in 1976. I had a home built for my mom in a new development, near where my sister Jody and her family now live. It's in the village of Ravena New York, which is about forty minutes north of here."

With a smile of relief, "That's good, not that I wouldn't like to meet your family, I'd just like to dress for the occasion first."

Just then, we turned onto Carr road and drove up a winding, wooded driveway, until we reached a large three story white wooden colonial home. On the wood trim over the front porch were the words, The Dellwood House. As we climbed out of the car and headed up toward Michael's prestigious looking family home, I asked, "Michael, why is the house named Dellwood?"

He opened the gate to the white picket fence for me, "It was once a hotel called The Dellwood, back in the twenties. Some say the gangster Jack-Legs Diamond once stayed here with his mistress, Kiki Roberts. That was the big buzz on the mountain for years."

I laughed as we walked up the steps of the porch. Michael took me inside of this true country style home. He showed me his childhood bedroom, then we went up to the third-floor balcony and I could not believe how beautiful the view was. I took a deep breath of the fresh mountain air, "This is fabulous Michael." I pointed toward a bridge we could just see from our vantage point, which crossed the river, "What bridge is that?"

"That's the Kingston-Rhinecliff Bridge. That bridge happens to be more than 50 miles from here and we have the best view of it on the mountain top." He replied proudly.

Taking in the beauty all around me, "It must have been magical, to grow up in such a beautiful place."

He looked at me with fondness in his eyes, "It was." He grabbed my hand and as we stood next to each other gazing out over the horizon, "Would you like to take a walk to see the beaver pond? I think you might enjoy it."

I turned toward this extremely interesting and adorable man, "I would love to see it."

As we walked through the woods toward the beaver pond, Michael told me how he and his siblings would swim in the pond when he was a child, and how he and his whole family would come into these woods every Christmas Eve together to pick out their Christmas tree. As we walked, I grabbed his hand squeezed it gently for a moment, "Your family sounds wonderful Michael, now I'm sorry I'm not meeting them after all."

Just as I finished speaking, we reached a clearing in the woods and there it was! It was absolutely fabulous. It was a beautiful crystal-clear pond, nestled at the bottom of three large mountains. From off of one of the mountains, a small waterfall fed the pond on one side, and there was a large beaver dam on the other side, with two large beavers chasing their three babies all over the dam. Quietly we watched the five of these beautiful creatures playfully splashing together in the pond and I felt as if I were becoming a part of that peaceful display of mother-nature. It was truly a spiritually moving experience.

It was 4:00pm when we headed back to Michael's home in Poughkeepsie and by that time, we were both totally enchanted with one another. As we caught the Thruway in Saugerties I said, "Michael, I really enjoyed our afternoon together and I don't want it to end just yet. Would you please join me and some friends of mine this evening for dinner and dancing?"

He answered with an enthusiastic smile, "As long as I can go home and change first, I'd like that very much." With that he quickly glanced into my eyes and with a look of honesty questioned, "But I must ask one question first, before I accept. What will your husband think?"

I smiled, "I have asked him for a divorce. I plan to file for it on Monday, so it doesn't matter what he might think."

His whole body seemed to light up with his smile, as if his heart were suddenly filled with joy, "Wow! That's phenomenal news, and someone would have to kill me to keep me from going out with you tonight."

I chuckled as I felt myself compelled to reach out, take his hand, "I'm glad my bad news pleases you."

First, we drove to Michael's home, so he could shower and change. Then we went to my home, which was Lee's home in Gardener, where I showered and changed. From there it was off to meet Jimmy and Tom for our 8:00pm meeting at the Executive House. After we were all introduced, Michael suggested going to the Mariner Harbor Restaurant in Highland. Jimmy took Tom in his car and followed Michael and me in my car to the restaurant. When we arrived at the restaurant, we found ourselves right down on the riverbank. It was quite romantic with the lights of the City of Poughkeepsie glistening on the beautiful, peaceful, Hudson River. As we entered the restaurant, Jimmy and I immediately noticed the thirty-foot lobster tank. I looked at Jimmy and smiled, "It looks like we're at the right place."

He laughed, "Please don't try to eat a five-pound lobster this time. I almost threw up just watching you the last time."

We all laughed, and I added, "I'll stick to my normal three pounder this time, okay?"

The four of us had a lovely candlelight dinner that night as we dined in the shadow of the city. Jimmy and I approved of one another's dates and we both knew it without saying a word. We had grown to read one another quite well, and we knew we were both having the first good time we had had in years. After our meal, it was off to The Prime-

American Goddess

Time Disco, where I was going to dance for the first time in more than eight years. When I realized how long it had been, I was amazed.

When we pulled into the parking lot, Michael parked the car beside Jimmy's, and we all went in together. The four of us had the best time, and Michael turned out to be a great dancer. It felt good to be out on a dance floor again with the hot music and flashing lights. My sensual feelings were stimulated in a way I hadn't felt in years, as I watched Michael move so manly across the dance floor. I found myself deliberately trying to entice and seduce him with every move I made as we danced.

It was around 1:00am when Michael and I said our goodbyes to Jimmy and Tom and left them at the nightclub. When we climbed into the car Michael looked at me with a gleam in his eyes, "Would you like to go back up to the mountains with me tonight? It's a clear night and you would be amazed at how many stars you can see from out on the balcony on a night like this."

With a sincere tone and a sweet smile, "There is nothing I'd like more right now, then to be with you Michael."

He leaned over and kissed me gently, "Thank you, Christina." And it was off to the Catskill Mountains again.

When we arrived at The Dellwood, we went straight up to the third-floor balcony. Michael left me there as he went to fix two White Russians. I was caught up in the beauty of the starry sky when Michael returned with our drinks. We sat down side-by-side on a two person redwood recliner lounge chair. As we sipped our drinks, we were gazing out at this awe-inspiring view and feeling totally at ease with one another. Michael turned to me and said softly, "Christina, have you ever had an out of body experience?"

I gazed inquisitively into his eyes, "No I haven't. I have heard of the term before but I'm not sure what it means. Why do you ask?"

He smiled innocently, "Well, it's when you use your mind to allow your spirit to leave your body, so your spirit may soar anywhere in the universe you choose."

I laughed a little in disbelief, "It sounds like a wonderful fairytale Michael, but I don't believe it can be done."

With an air of confidence, he replied, "If I could prove to you it's possible, would you try it?"

I looked at him a little doubtful and smiled, "I'll try anything once."

He smiled again, only this time it was a mischievous smile, "Good! Then will you allow me to lead you into a meditation?"

I reached over and gently touched his hand, "I trust you enough Michael, to let you try."

He started with a soft, soothing, voice, "Then just lay back, close your eyes and begin to feel your body relaxing. Allow your mind to let go of all your concerns and fears. Now, take a slow deep breath filling your lungs completely. Very slowly, begin to allow yourself to completely exhale. As you continue to breathe like this, I want you to visualize in your mind's eye the light of God entering your body with each breath. Allow the light to totally fill your lungs and radiate throughout your entire being, so every single cell in your body is glowing with the white light of God and warmed with unconditional love. Slowly begin to fade deep within yourself, as your body becomes limp and free. Now, go deeper and deeper within yourself and when you're completely relaxed, I want you to open your mind's eye and look for me. I will be there waiting to help you."

I could no longer hear Michael's words, but I could still feel myself drifting deeper within myself. Somehow, I could feel my body become lighter as my spirit began to slowly rise. Within my thoughts, I could see my body lying beneath me and as I gazed at my physical being in awe, I felt a cooling touch on my back. I turned quickly to see Michael's silhouette floating right beside me. I looked around us at the stars as we weightlessly floated in the air together. What I was feeling at that moment was totally wondrous and spiritual. Michael then took my hand and I could hear his thoughts in my mind, "Come with me, Christina."

We began to fly through the emptiness of space together. It was incredible and we were truly soaring up toward the stars and straight into the heavens. In complete awe, I went to squeeze Michael's hand, but I could not apply pressure until I felt it in my mind. I gazed at him and noticed we were both glistening like gold star dust which seemed to follow us wherever we went yet keeping us connected to our bodies in some way.

He then put his arms around me, pulled me close to him in the heavens, and he began to kiss me. As he did, in my mind I could hear him say, "Christina, I have dreamed of making love to you like this and I have known our destinies would bring us here since the first moment our eyes met."

At that point, our spirits merged as one. It was phenomenal! I felt the scorching of our souls as our life forces mingled. It was pure heavenly ecstasy, and we became one as we soared through infinity together. There was no actual sexual contact between our physical bodies at all. It was the fire of our souls which became one in the heavens that night and yet, it was the purest feelings of ecstasy I had ever reached. It surpassed every feeling of love I had ever felt with anyone before. After what seemed like a lifetime of pure divine love making, Michael began to bring me back to the balcony and I could hear him in my mind, "I want you to very slowly re-enter your body now and when you're able to, slowly open your eyes. I'll be waiting for you."

When I opened my eyes, Michael was leaning over me and asked as I looked into his eyes, "Are you a believer now?"

With gratefulness I smiled, "Michael that was incredible!" I slowly ran my fingers through his golden hair as I pulled him close to me and feeling more love and passion then I had ever felt before for anyone, I kissed him, "Thank you Michael that was the most extraordinary experience I've ever had."

He returned my kiss, "I love you Christina, and I want you to be mine. I know we're meant to be together."

Somehow, I found myself saying, "Michael, I love you too and I want to be yours."

We embraced and Michael laid his warm body on mine. As he tenderly kissed my face he kept softly repeating, "Christina, I love you." He gently began to undress me and caressed my breasts with both hands as he exquisitely slid his tongue down to my naval, where he began to lick my entire body. My body was being stimulated to the point of melt down when he pulled himself back up to once again consume my lips in his. I reached down, took hold of his hot flesh and gently placed him at the quivering opening of my starving body. I placed the palms of my hands on his muscular buttocks and slowly began to push him just within me, as we devoured each other with our tongues. As we kissed, he plunged forward and I mounded in ecstasy, "Oh Michael take me." as our bodies caught up with our souls. The love we made that night was beyond words.

As we lay in each other's arms, I realized Michael was right. I truly believed I was part of God and I would continue to give my life, meaning my flesh and my soul totally to Jesus Christ's teachings, despite my sinful nature, until I reach that higher consciousness when I would know and feel my divinity in the essence of God. Somehow, I also knew I would spend the rest of my life with this man.

The next morning, I woke and kissed Michael until he awoke, "Michael, do you have plans for your vacation?"

He began to kiss me all over, "Nothing I can't change."

As I returned his kisses, "How would you like to hop in the car with me and just drive until we feel like stopping?"

He looked at me with wide eyes, "Let's go!"

We washed up, put our clothes back on, and hit the road, destination unknown. As we drove, we talked and talked. We talked about our lives, our dreams, our past lovers, and about God. One thing Michael said which struck a chord within me was how he sees the future, "Christina, I believe the earth and the human race is heading for a cataclysmic change. But after that, there will be a new birth, a new beginning in God, for the new earth and the new human race which will emerge from the ashes, will be superior to this old one. People will know what it means to live in the Light of the God, because the human race will truly be living after God's own heart. We will all finally understand that the Omnipotent God of the universe's Life-Force is within us and we are an extension of God. Then, we will learn to communicate through thought and all things shall be known. There will be no room for hatred and deceit, for all feelings and emotions will be open for all to see. Love, understanding, kindness, oneness, and true harmony will be the new way of life. One day families will live together as one, in unconditional love. Acceptance of each other's individual differences will be the natural way, not the exception. I know you have your doubts, but I believe then and only then will the human race finally be able to join the extraterrestrial community of worlds. "

With that thought I replied, "Michael that is beautiful. Now if it could only be true."

It was as if we were spiritually becoming one while we rode and talked for hours, of what our spiritual purpose might be. We only stopped driving long enough to eat, gas up, and use the rest rooms. We didn't stop to take a room until we reached St. Augustine, Florida.

We checked into a hotel at 11:00am on Monday, June 14th, and we went straight into the warm Jacuzzi, where we began a five-hour marathon of incredible romantic love making. After which we collapsed and we didn't wake up, until 10:00am on Tuesday, June 15th, and we immediately made love again, then it was off to the closest diner. We ate, and then hit the malls to do some clothes shopping. When we returned to the room, it was 6:00pm and I said, "Michael, why don't you shower first, and I'll call Jimmy. If we get in there together, we might not come out."

He chuckled, kissed me, "I'm going, but I'm gonna miss you."

I slapped his buns as he walked away from me, then I picked up the phone to call Jimmy.

When Jimmy answered the phone, he sounded concerned, "Where the hell are you? I haven't heard a thing from you since Saturday night."

Enthusiastically I answered, "Jimmy, Michael and I have driven to Florida."

Immediately he interrupted, "Let me get this straight. You're in Florida, with a man you just met, while your stupid husband is breaking my door down looking for you." Then he started to laugh, "Why am I not surprised, Christina? You will never stop amazing me no matter how long I know you. I guess that's one of the reasons I love you so much, girlfriend. So start talking, is he hot?"

I laughed at Jimmy's reply, then abruptly quibbled, "If you would let me speak, I'll tell you."

"Okay, who's stopping you?" He answered in only the way he could. I laughed a little more, then cleared my voice and with a tone of sincerity sighed, "He's a dream Jimmy, and I'm truly madly in love with him."

With a caring tone he blurted out, "Oh my God girlfriend, how you fall in love at the drop of a dime, I'll never know? Is it truly love this time Christina, or is he just another rebound?"

"Jimmy, I have never felt like this. Not even with Tony, or Johnny." I felt a hot flash shoot through my body when I heard myself say the name, **Johnny**. Then I thought, as Jimmy went on speaking, "Oh my God! I haven't thought of him in years, and just saying his name still makes me feel the effect his touch had on my life. Could I still be in love with Johnny?" Just then Michael burst into my thoughts and I realized, "Yesterday is gone with the wind. All I know is what I am feeling right now, today, and Michael, you're the one I'm dreaming of."

When I came back from my thoughts, I stopped Jimmy's babbling by saying, "Jimmy, Jimmy, Jimmy!" "What?" He screeched, as I said, "I don't care what Lee wants, just please don't tell him where I am. I also need you to do me a favor, call Lesley Stein and tell her to file divorce papers for me."

Michael and I spent eight glorious days in St. Augustine, and we were totally in love every minute of every day. We spent our time going to the beach, fishing, boating, water skiing, dancing, eating in restaurants and most of all love making. We were having a spectacular time which we wished would never end, but our last day did come. That night we walked from our hotel, to a restaurant recommended to us by the bellhop. It was located in the quaint Spanish section of town which was on the other side of a beautiful old draw bridge. After dinner, we each ordered pumpkin pie for dessert. As we ate to the wonderful sounds of the piano player, Michael took my hand, looked deeply into my eyes and placed a ring in my hand, "Christina Powers, will you marry me?"

I became so excited I dropped the ring right into my pumpkin pie. I started to laugh as I picked it up, licked off the pie, and with tears of joy escaping my eyes said, "Michael, yes! I will marry you." Then I slid it on my finger.

Michael immediately jumped up out of his chair and shouted, "Yes! I love you, my little Pumpkin pie." We both started to laugh and cry at the same time. Then, because everyone was looking at us, Michael shouted again, "She just said she'd marry me." Everyone began to applaud.

I was so happy; I went up to the piano player and asked him if he would play a song for me. I told him the song and he said he could. I took the mike, "Michael, I love you baby and I'd like to sing a special song to you."

The piano player began to play, and I began to sing, Karen Carpenters song, 'We've only just begun.' As I sang to Michael that night, I was singing from the depths of my heart and he knew it. After we left the restaurant, we began to walk arm-in-arm back to the hotel. When we reached the draw bridge, it began to go up. As we held each other and watched this bridge begin to rise, on that beautiful Florida night, I kissed Michael, "I wish I had told you the night you saved my life that I loved you, because I knew it then."

With his heart in his eyes, "I knew I loved you even before that night. But I guess all things happen in their own time."

The next day, we were on our way back to New York and we were determined to make a new life for ourselves together. We knew it was our destiny to be together. Michael summed up our feelings when he said, "I love you. These three words will change our lives forever and I promise I will always be here for you Christina, until the end of time."

I kissed him, "Michael, right here with you is where I want to stay. I thank God he has brought us together, and I know I will always love you."

As we spoke of our love and future dreams together, we totally forgot one thing Michael said, and that was, **"All things happen in their own time**."

American Goddess

CHAPTER 16

When we arrived back in New York, we went straight to Lee's home in Gardener. Once there, I proceeded to pack two suitcases, grabbed one singed bottle of champagne, and I was off to live with Michael in his Poughkeepsie town house. I was so in love with Michael and I wanted to be with him. I was tired of fighting the world alone and living all by myself without the affections of my true soul mate. Now that I had found him, I wanted to spend every minute of my life with him. I longed for just his slightest touch on my flesh. Michael had the bravest of hearts and the strongest of souls. He was the light of my life and the place I wanted to call home. He was the one man in this world I found myself living for, and I would lay down my life for the power of his love.

It was Monday morning at 8:00am when I asked Michael to leave his position with the security firm and come join me as my private, personal, bodyguard. He replied, "Let me have some time to think about it before I answer. But for now, I have to get back to work."

"Well after you clock in or whatever you do, just come in the house with me. You can guard me from in here."

With a chuckle he replied, "Christina, I haven't been assigned to your case in two years. They have me assigned to Donald Stump."

"Donald Stump! That arrogant chauvinistic Pig! You're kidding!" I replied, with alarm. "You mean to tell me I've had a false sense of security for two years now. I thought you were out there, somewhere watching over me."

Laughing, he kissed me, "Well Punkie, I have to go to work and I won't be home until Friday afternoon around 5:00."

With a disappointed tone I exclaimed, "Friday afternoon! Michael, I didn't know you were not going to be with me, how can I stay here by myself?"

He laughed again, "I love you Punkie, and I'll miss you like crazy, but for now I have to do my job. What else can I do?"

I held him tight as I kissed him, "I understand Michael, and I'll be waiting for you to come home to me." I watched him leave and I felt sad when I realized I was alone again.

Once he was out of sight, I grabbed a pen and paper, and began to write my feelings of love for Michael. By 2:00pm that afternoon, I had composed the lyrics to nine dynamite singles. Six of them, told my fans a different story of the feelings I'd had from my breakup with Lee, to my meeting and falling in love with Michael. Three of them were from the purest essence of my love for my Michael. I became so excited when I read my finished works, I climbed into the car and went straight to the studio, where I immediately put my favorite crew right to work on the melodies.

American Goddess

When I checked my messages at the office, there were eighty-two of them from Lee. According to Jimmy, Lee had come into his office twelve times, pleading with him to tell him where I was. Jimmy was adamant, "Christina, you're going to have to call him. He is half out of his mind trying to find you. The only reason Lee doesn't have a nationwide manhunt out looking for you, even after he received the divorce papers, is because your security people informed the FBI you didn't want to be found."

I lackadaisically replied, "What do you mean he's half out of his mind?" Just assuming Jimmy was over-dramatizing the situation.

But I became concerned when melodramatically he said, "Just what it sounds like. He was acting crazy, and he made no sense at all."

Becoming alarmed I asked, "When did you see him last?"

"He was here acting like a nut just this morning."

As soon as he said that I instantly thought of Tony and was hit like a bolt of lightning, with terrifying images of the last second, I saw Tony alive. With that, I dashed to the phone and began to dial Lee's number. Somehow, I knew something was horribly wrong. The phone rang ten times and just as I was about to hang up, I heard the line pick up. I waited for someone to speak, but no words came, "Lee, is that you?"

I heard him mumble, "Christina, I love you."

Then, I heard the phone drop and I screamed, "Oh God, no! Lee, answer me!" There was nothing but dead silence. I immediately slammed the phone down, dialed 911, and told the woman who answered, "My husband is lying unconscious in our home." Then I shouted the address and the woman said, "Okay ma'am, now I want you to stay on the phone with me, to make sure we find the right place."

I shouted at her, "To hell with you! I'm going to my husband!" I grabbed Jimmy's hand and shouted again, "Come with me. Lee is killing himself."

We ran out of the office and down the three flights of stairs to the parking level. When we reached the car, I hit the hazard lights then I hit the gas. We made the fourteen miles to Gardener in nine minutes, beating the rescue squad. I slammed on the brakes, throwing dust twenty feet into the air. When we finally stopped, we both jumped out of the car and ran to the front door. I tried to open it, but it was locked. Jimmy yelled, "Unlock the fucking door already!"

With a panicked tone I yelled, as I started to bang on the door, "I left the keys here. We'll have to break in."

That's when Jimmy and I both began trying to break down the door. After we almost broke our shoulders, I shouted, "**The hell with this**! Watch out, Jimmy!"

I ran to the car, which was still idling, threw it into drive and drove right through the front door. As I climbed out of the car and ran into the house looking for Lee, all I could see flashing through my mind was the blood-stained hands I had on that God forsaken night Tony took his own life. I screamed, "Lee! Lee," as I frantically ran through the house looking for him. I charged up to the bedroom with Jimmy right on my tail. When I flung open the bedroom door, my heart almost stopped. I saw Lee's lifeless body lying on the floor and I screamed again, "Lee," as I raced across the room to his side. I grabbed him and began to slap his face as I screamed and cried, "Lee! Wake up! Don't do this! Wake up Lee, wake up!"

At that moment, the paramedics came running into the room and began to try to resuscitate him. Jimmy grabbed hold of me as I cried desperately for Lee. Jimmy stroked my back, as I buried my shaking body into his arms. I whispered as I cried, "No Tony, no."

Jimmy whispered back, "I know, baby. I know. But this is Lee not Tony, and he is going to survive."

That's when one of the paramedics shouted, "Clear," as he used a defibrillator on Lee's chest. Then he shouted, "We have a rhythm here guys, let's move fast."

Jimmy drove as we followed the ambulance to Vassar Brothers Hospital in Poughkeepsie. All the way there, all I could do was pray for Lee to survive. When we arrived at the hospital, he was rushed straight into the emergency room. Jimmy and I answered their questions, then we waited in the waiting room for word on his condition.

After six hours of waiting on pins and needles, a doctor finally came out to speak to us. Without introducing himself he said, "Mrs. Bradford, your husband is in stable, but guarded condition in the Intensive Care Unit."

Distraughtly I asked, "What happened to him?"

"Your husband had a heart attack, brought on by alcohol and barbiturates."

With that news I immediately took on an air of authority, "I assume you are aware of how much my husband; Senator Bradford and I have contributed to this hospital. So, I will also assume you will delete the second part of that diagnoses from my husband's official record. I hope there is no need for me to express how disconcerting it would be to me personally to have this information made public."

Appearing nervous he quickly replied, "I understand perfectly Mrs. Bradford, and let me assure you that you have no need for concern."

I smiled courteously, "Thank you, doctor," as I moved his stethoscope, just enough to read his name plate, "Slater, I will see I do not forget your helpfulness in this matter." After our discreet conversation, we followed him to Lee's room.

Jimmy left when visiting hours were over, but I stayed with Lee all that night, just holding his hand. I felt so horrible every time I thought of Lee trying to take his own life because of me. As I looked at this man I once loved, my heart went out to him.

Sometime around 4:00am I gently kissed his hand as he slept. With tears in my eyes I whispered, "Lee, I do love you and I can't stand to see you hurting like this, but . . ."

American Goddess

As I spoke, he slowly opened his eyes, gazed up at me, gently squeezed my hand and in a half-conscious state said, "Thank you, God." He gently pulled my hand up to his lips and kissed my finger-tips, "Christina, as I swallowed the pills, I told God I did not want to live without you. I said to God if you want me to live then bring my Christina back to me. And here you are." After that, he drifted back to sleep. Needless to say, I never finished my sentence.

Later that morning, I called Michael's superior and asked him to inform Michael that I had to go out of town, and I would see him Friday afternoon when he returns home. He said he would give him the message as soon as we hung up. I did not know how I was going to handle this situation with Lee yet, but I sure didn't want Michael knowing that I was with him. I knew Michael would ask me to leave Lee and I just couldn't do that yet. You see, as Lee said those words, I realized I still had a love for him, and the fact I almost caused his death, ripped my heart apart. I had to help Lee through this, and I now also had to re-evaluate my own feelings of love, which I felt for these two men.

Lee was discharged from the hospital on Friday, July 3rd, and I was going home with him. I knew Michael would be coming home that afternoon, and I had still not said anything to Lee about Michael yet. In four days, I could not find one opportunity to tell him. It was 12:00pm when Lee and I sat down on the sofa in the living room of his Gardener home. We sat there speechless for the longest time. I was trying to get up the courage to tell Lee, I was in love with another man, and I couldn't stop loving this other man just because I still had a love for him. As I was having these thoughts, Lee turned to me and said, "Christina, I love you and I promise to never treat you badly again. I will give my life up for your love." He grabbed my hand, "Why don't we go get your stuff from his place before he comes home."

Instantly, I felt my face turn white, at the same time, I felt the blood draining from it, "Do you mean to tell me, I've been tormenting myself for four days over how to tell you, and you already knew?"

He slid over to me, "I didn't know how to say it, Christina. You're my wife and I love you. Let's not throw our dreams away. Together our love will take us to the White House. Think about how we will be able to help the people of our nation if we stay together. I offer you the power to really change the country for the better."

When Lee spoke of truly helping the people of our nation, my heart raced with a force I had never felt before. Somehow, at that very moment, I knew there was a higher purpose for my life. I looked at him and thought, "Could my destiny truly be with Lee?"

Damn it! I did it to myself again! **Without a second thought**, I leaned over, kissed Lee, looked deeply into his eyes, "I love you Lee, and I will go get my belongings right now. We will put this one behind us with all the others and head to the White House together."

American Goddess

I got up and went straight to Michael's town house; where I packed my belongings, grabbed one bottle of champagne and sat down to compose a **Dear John** letter to my beloved Michael. As I sat at the mahogany reading table in the library of his home, with the shadows of his essence all around me, all I could do was cry. The magnitude of my decision had engulfed my soul and my heart bled as I wrote these words.

"My Dear Beloved Michael, I am leaving you this letter, because I cannot speak these words to you in person. I must leave you; my destiny calls me in another direction. Michael, my love, my tears stain this paper as I tell you I can never see you again. I love you too much to ever look into your eyes and know our souls shall never soar through the heavens together again. Michael, remember what you taught me, crossroads have a way of leading us to our final destinies. Thanks to you, my beloved soul mate, the course I must take to reach my destiny has been revealed. I will love you through all eternity, my Michael. Forever yours, Love, your Punkie."

I kissed the paper leaving a deep red impression of my lips, and the pain shot right through my soul. My heart broke, as I gently placed the letter on the reading table. I placed my ring on top of the letter; picked up my belongings, turned and cried as I walked away from the most incredible lover I had ever known. As I drove away, I was completely enveloped in warm thoughts of Michael. I remembered our nights of pure unadulterated passion, our romantic talks and peaceful walks.

My heart ached as I pulled into Lee's driveway. I parked the car and climbed out, leaving my belongings still in the car. It was 5:00pm when I slowly walked up the sidewalk to the newly repaired front door. My eyes were still blood shot from tears of pain when Lee opened the door. Lee hugged me as I entered the foyer and said, "Where are your things?"

"I left them in the car, I'll take them out later."

He closed the door, and held me close to him, "Christina, I love you. I'm so happy you're home with me and I will never let you down again."

He began to gently kiss my neck as he nestled his erection against my waist. As he kissed me, I thought, "Is my destiny truly with this man I once loved? Is this the man I will spend the rest of my life with?" He kissed me deeply then he began to lead me upstairs to the bedroom.

As we reached the bedroom door I stopped, "I'm sorry, but I can't now Lee, so please don't ask me." I pulled my hand out of his and went back down the stairs. I went into the kitchen and poured myself a glass of orange juice.

As I sipped the juice, Lee entered the kitchen and walked over to me, "I'm sorry, Christina."

As Lee continued saying something, I felt out of place and I thought, "Oh God! Yes I still love this man, but it's not like the love I have for my Michael."

American Goddess

Then there was a knock at the door. Lee looked out the front window where he could see who was at the door. His face turned red with anger and he shouted, "What the fuck is he doing here?"

My heart leaped as I instantly knew it was Michael. I watched in horror as Lee dashed to the desk drawer and grabbed his gun. I ran to him and shouted, "Lee, no! Put that gun away."

Michael began to bang on the door as he shouted, "What the fuck is going on in there? Christina, open this fucking door now before I break it down."

I pulled the gun from Lee's hand and took out the bullets, "Stay here, I'll ask him to leave."

With my heart in my throat I opened the door, stepped out and looked into his eyes, "Michael, I told you I could never see you again." I started to cry, "Please leave now, Michael. I must stay here with Lee. My destiny is here with him."

He grabbed me and with tears in his eyes, "No my Punkie, you're wrong! Your destiny lies with me Christina, in my arms, not his."

I pulled myself from him, "Michael, listen to me. Lee tried to kill himself because I left him. I can't let that happen again." Then I turned, "Goodbye my love," as I walked back into the house, and closed the screen door. I watched as this powerful man I loved with all my heart and soul staggered away from me like a brokenhearted little boy.

I closed the door, leaned up against it and began to shake. Lee ran to my side and the moment he grabbed me; I heard the most heart wrenching cries my ears have ever heard.

"Christina! I love you! Please Punkie! I'm dying out here! Please save me!"

With pain shooting through my heart I screamed, "Oh my God! Michael," as I burst into tears.

I opened the door and Lee fell to his knees in front of me and pleaded, with tears pouring down his face, "No, Christina! Don't leave me! I love you, Christina!"

I shook my head and screamed, "Noooo! Stop this!" I ripped myself from Lee's clinging arms and ran out of the house and down the driveway. When I reached the street I was shaking, I turned back to see Michael leaning up against his blood red Saab convertible shaking as hard as I was. My heart pained from the sight of this beautiful man, suffering because of me. I ran back to him with tears of love in my eyes. I placed my hands on the shoulders of this beaten, brokenhearted man and sobbed, "Let's go home, my Michael."

He gazed up at me and his pain filled eyes began to glisten with a look of gentle, unconditional love. I gently helped him into the passenger seat of his car, "I'll be right back, Michael." He said nothing to me at all as I walked back toward the house. When I reached Lee, who was sitting on the sofa in a state of confusion I simply said, "Lee, I care about you, but I'm no longer in-love you with. My true destiny lies with Michael. I'm sorry, but I must leave."

I turned, walked out, and headed over to the car where my security guards watched this whole display of hysterics, and asked one of them to take my car and follow us. I went back to Michael's car, started it and headed for Michael's family home in the Catskills.

As I drove, I held Michael's gentle quivering hand and neither one of us said a word for the longest time.

Then somewhere on Route 299, between Highland and the Thruway entrance in New Paltz, Michael slowly placed my ring back on my finger and with a soft broken voice, "Punkie, will you marry me?"

I pulled the car over on the shoulder, took Michael into my arms and with tears of joy running down my cheeks whispered, "Yes, my love! I will marry you. And right here, right now, I pledge my undying, eternal, love to you my soul-mate." I looked right through his eyes, straight into the depths of his soul and whispered, "I will never leave you again my love, so gently close your eyes now and please take me as my spirit soars with yours."

With our bodies embraced as one, our spirits exploded with the passion of angels for what felt like a lifetime of ecstasy. The power of the love between us that night was beyond human explanation.

We pulled off the road around 6:30pm and we did not come back to our bodies, until we were abruptly drawn back, by the continual banging on the car windows by my bodyguards sometime around 10:00pm. I took a few minutes to compose myself, before pulling back onto Route 299 heading to the Thruway.

As we drove north, Michael had his head on my shoulder and at one point he said, "Christina, did you sleep with him?"

I squeezed his hand, "Michael, I love you with all my heart, you're my angel and the answer to your question is no. I did not sleep with him and I tell you right now, I am yours baby, body and soul. I also promise you I will never give you a reason to ask me that question again because we will always be together." He tenderly nestled his head into my breast, and he stayed there until we arrived at his family home in Tannersville.

We held each other up as we slowly walked to the house. When we entered it, we went straight up to Michael's boyhood bedroom. As soon as we walked in, Michael, took me into his powerful arms, drew me passionately into his all-consuming embrace and said, "You are my life force, Christina."

I looked up into his tearing eyes as his lips met mine with the power to enslave my heart for all eternity, and all I could say was, "I love you too, baby. I love you too."

He slid his tongue to my ear and softly whispered, "I love you my sweet Punkie, and I place my heart into your hands. Christina, I know I could face anything this cold world may throw at me, but life without you, would be a travesty." He gazed passionately into my eyes and with his heart in his hands, added with quivering lips, "Baby, please don't ever leave me again. I don't think my heart could take this again."

With the passion of undying love flowing through my being, I pulled his head back to mine and began to softly make love to his lips. Our physical passion that night had an aura of tenderness which neither one of us had ever reached before.

Upon our simultaneous explosion of ecstasy, Michael completely collapsed on top of me and we drifted off to sleep. The next morning, I woke up with my body so close to Michael's he was still buried deep within me. As soon as I kissed his lips, he instantly began to throb. My body flared, with the desire of pure love and we were thrust right into the fires of our passion again. After our exquisite encounter, I showered and dressed, then floated straight to the kitchen to fix my man his breakfast. This time, I was truly in love. Everything about Michael was beyond my dreams. I was just putting two plates of pancakes with bacon on the table, when my Michael walked into the kitchen. He was wearing blue jeans and a tight fitting, Italian tee shirt, which enhanced the beauty of his physique. He looked like an angel as he came toward me with open arms and I melted into his embrace.

After our passionate embrace, we sat down to eat our breakfast and Michael said, "If it's all right with you, I made plans for the day for us. I tried to call you last week to ask you about it, but you were out of town."

I mischievously smiled, "Whatever you would like to do will be fine with me, because I'm not doing anything without you."

He leaned over, kissed me and with an excited tone said, "Great! Then you will be meeting my family today. My mom is having a Fourth of July barbeque at her house at 1:00pm this afternoon. After that we have a honeymoon suite reserved on the 15th floor of the Omni Hotel in downtown Albany. I made sure our balcony would be situated precisely where we can see the fireworks go off."

I smiled, "That sounds wonderful, Michael." And we were off to Ravena, to meet my future in-laws.

As we drove to Ravena, I said with a slightly nervous expression, "Am I going to be meeting all of your family?"

"Don't be nervous you silly goose, my family will love you, and they'll all be ecstatic for us when we tell them we are going to be married."

He drove with the top down so I cuddled close to his shoulder, "I love you Michael, and I can't wait to tell your family with you. Do they know I'm coming?"

He casually replied, "No, I haven't said a word to any of them about you. It's going to be a complete surprise to them all."

American Goddess

The weather that day was made to order, as we basked in our love on the road to Ravena. When we pulled on to Magnolia Circle in the heart of the quaint little village, Michael took his arm from around my shoulder, "We're here, Punkie." Then he parked in front of a two-story colonial and we climbed out of the car and headed up the driveway toward his Mom's home.

As we walked toward the house, we passed another Saab in the driveway. As we did, Michael pointed to it and said, "That's my sister Jody's car. She's the one who turned me onto Saabs. She's also the star of the Dumpetts."

I looked at him strangely, "Is she a performer?"

He laughed, "No! Jody and my other two sisters, Connie, and Michelle would always take our father's old pickup truck to the dump every weekend. So one day, the three of them were all in overalls and on their way to the dump when I was coming into the house with some friends and said, "'There go the Dumpetts' and all my friends laughed. The next school day the whole high school began calling them the Dumpetts. The title stuck with them for the rest of that school year."

With that, I started to laugh, and I was in hysterics when Michael's mother opened the door. She gave me a strange look, as if to say, "who is this person laughing uncontrollably at my doorstep". Then she looked at Michael and after a few seconds of watching me, as I struggled to stop laughing, finally said, "Where did you get this hyena from?" and I really lost it. I felt like a fool, as his whole family came running to the front door, to see what the commotion was. If I could have crawled under a rock, I would have. I just knew they thought I was crazy. I could see it in their eyes. Finally, with some help from Michael, who had just stopped laughing himself, I was finally able to stop. But by that time, Michael's whole family was in the front yard, where I was just catching my breath.

No one had any idea where I even came from, no less who I was when Michael shouted into this commotion, "Since we're all here, may I have your attention?" Once everyone calmed down, Michael began with, "I would like to introduce my fiancée to all of you."

Their faces showed their shock, joy and surprise, as they all welcomed me with open arms into their loving close-knit family. His mother Tess turned out to be one of the most interesting women I had met in a long time and some of the 'mountain stories' she told were hilarious. His entire family was precious as well, from his oldest brother Jay, to the Dumpetts and straight to his niece, Mary. That day turned out to be wonderful and after our visit that Fourth of July, I knew I had finally been accepted into a loving family, which I could truly call my own.

We left Tess' home around 8:00pm and headed straight to the Omni Hotel in the heart of Albany, the beautiful Capital City of the majestic State of New York. We checked into the honeymoon suite under Mr. and Mrs. Carr, and the bellhop took us straight up to our suite on the 15th floor. When Michael opened the door, he picked me up, carried me over the threshold, and stood me up in the center of the room. He went to tip the bellhop, closed the door, turned and headed straight for me with an air of sensuality in every movement. I could feel myself beginning to melt with every step he took closer. As he reached me, we embraced into an explosion of light and sound from the open balcony directly behind us. That night we embraced in the shadows of the fireworks, which exploded over the beautiful Capital Buildings of the Empire State Plaza, in the heart of Albany.

The passion I felt with every kiss I placed on his flesh was electrifying. As the colors of the explosions filled the skies, the sparks united the flames of our souls.

Michael took my heart and soul, as he touched the deepest depths of my flesh with his. I screamed out in ecstasy, love, and passion, "Oh God! Michael! My love! Please, baby! Give me your child." And as he devoured my essence in the midst of the grand finale, I knew I had conceived my **beloved Michael's child.**

CHAPTER 17

Michael and I were happier than two people could ever hope to be. So happy, we decided to plan a wedding fit for royalty, just as soon as my divorce was final. Michael also decided to leave his position with the security firm after all. He made his decision on July 6th, 1988, as we walked hand in hand down Carr Mountain Road. It was a beautiful, sunny morning, and as we walked, I just stopped, and shouted with excitement! "Yes!" I turned to Michael with a gleam in my eye and added, "Let's go to the casinos in Atlantic City. It's only about a five-hour trip from here by car, and I haven't been gambling in years."

He kissed me in the midst of his amused chuckle, "You know, I have to take your job offer Punkie." He took me in his arms, shook his head, looked into my eyes and smiled, "Little girl, you need to have me around. You're just too damn impulsive for your own good for me to leave you alone for any more than ten minutes unsupervised." I laughed as we lovingly embraced, and it was off to Atlantic City.

American Goddess

On our triumphant ride home from Atlantic City later that night, I snuggled close to my angel and said, "Michael, I love you baby, and I don't want you to just come work for me, I want to give you half of everything I own. I'm not just giving you my love; I'm giving you everything I am. Baby, I want you to come run Powers Incorporated with me. It's ours Michael, and I'm praying with all my heart that you truly want to become part of my very existence. I know I can no longer reach my dreams without you." I moved up to kiss his cheek and with tender passion pleaded, "Please baby, I need to know the oneness we have in our souls can be obtained in the flesh as well."

He tenderly kissed my forehead as he drove, and softly said, "Punkie, I will go to the ends of the galaxy with you."

The way Michael said those words shot passion right through me. I became so excited I slowly unbuckled his pants, went down on him and lovingly began to ravage his flesh, as we sped north on the Garden State Parkway. It is totally amazing we survived that ride. I had Michael in such a state of ecstasy, he was screaming and humping with such force, the car was rocking. Our passion was so intense, by the time we both reached our points of ecstasy, we had to pull the car off to the side of the road and recuperate in each other's arms for ten minutes.

We laughed as we pulled away from the shoulder, because Michael said, "Whichever crew is on duty tonight, is going to have a lot to talk about tomorrow."

On Monday morning July 13th, Michael came into the office with me and it was straight to a prearranged board of directors meeting. I introduced Michael to all of my personal friends, and colleagues, all of whom, were personally appointed to their seats on the board of directors by 'yours truly'.

After Jimmy called the meeting to order, I stood up and addressed them like this, "Hi everybody, before we dive into business, I would like to introduce my future husband, Michael Carr." I turned to Michael who was seated beside me and said with a joyful smile, "Come on Michael, stand up and meet my family."

Michael stood up, "Hi everyone, I've heard so many wonderful things about every one of you that I feel privileged to be finally meeting such a highly respected group of people. I know you're all wondering where the hell did he come from, so I'll turn you back to Christina for that." Everyone was laughing as Michael turned the meeting back over to me.

I smiled as I stood up, "Well guys, not to anyone's surprise, I'm divorcing Lee. Just as soon as that divorce is final, Michael and I will be inviting you all to our wedding. I love him, gang! Now, I know I am going to embarrass him just a little, but that's because he's not truly aware of the relationships we all have in this room." I raised my right hand into the air with my fist closed and thumb up, "He's wonderful gang, and I know you will all love him once you get to know him. Now I am going to ask all of you to once again trust my judgment, because I am giving Michael 50% of everything I have. I would also like to make Michael Co-President of Powers Incorporated. This will mean, the ultimate decision-making power, will now lie with Michael, Jimmy, and myself. I believe the record shows at least 99% of my decisions have been on the mark since we all created our corporation. Well, I honestly believe this decision is the wisest one I have made to date, so out of courtesy of our camaraderie, I am putting my wishes up for a democratic vote. I also promise you I will abide by the majority decision." We finished the rest of our business and Michael was unanimously welcomed as Co-President of Powers Incorporated. From that day forward I began to teach Michael everything I knew about running a major corporation. I also began recording my next album entitled, 'The Power of Love.' I was so inspired by the power of Michael's love that I got right to work on my next screenplay entitled, 'Torn between Two Lovers.' I knew it was going to be hot! I had just lived it.

On August 6th, my marriage with Lee came to a mutually agreeable end. On that very day, Michael and I sent out five thousand wedding invitations. We set the date for December 10th, 1988, which would also be my thirty fifth birthday. Oh yes! Let me tell you. The press had a field day with this one. The headlines read, "**The Queen of Hearts, Christina Powers, Slays another One! Leaving Senator Bradford devastated, for the love of a man seven years her junior.**" The tabloids ran stories similar to this about my divorce, for the next month. It seemed my public was eating it up.

It was on August 12th, when I received a call from another very busy woman, whom I never got to see enough of; you guessed it. I answered the phone to this, "Shit girlfriend, can anybody keep up with you?"

I chuckled, "Well, I guess you received our invitation."

She laughed, "Don't you ever give that **cat** a rest."

I started to laugh, "No more than you do, smart ass!" When I stopped laughing, I added, "So how the hell are you, Barbara?"

She answered with a serious, "I'm fine, but if you're having a real wedding, then I'm guessing he is some stud-puppy."

With a purely sensual tone I purred, "The best, sister, the best!" We laughed, then she told me she would not miss my wedding for the world. We stayed on the phone for two hours, just talking like two silly schoolgirls, who were best of friends.

Barbara and I finished our conversation around 11:56pm. Just as soon as I hung up the phone, I turned my full attention to my Michael. He was doing paperwork through most of our conversation, but for the last ten minutes he had been lying on the bed beside me, and I had been massaging his erection with the soul of my foot the whole time. I did enjoy my conversation with Barbara, but after ten minutes of lusting for Michael's beautiful body, I lost all self-control. It didn't matter whom I was talking to with a man

227

like mine beckoning to me, I had to go. We made passionate love and fell asleep in each other's arms. After sleeping for I'm not sure how long, we were awakened by the ring of the phone.

Michael answered it, handed it to me as he said in a groggy state, "It's for you, Punkie."

I took the phone, still half sleeping, "Hello! Who's this?"

To my surprise I heard, "Hi Christina, its Barbara."

"What time is it?"

Her reply sounded quite serious, "Its 4:00am your time, sorry for waking you but this can't wait."

Sensing the urgency of her tone, I quickly sat up in the bed, "What's the matter, Barbara?"

Excitedly, she replied, "Hold on to your covers baby, because I've just discovered something you need to know."

I listened with a heightened sense of curiosity, "This sounds intriguing already. So what did you overhear this time?"

"Just this! Your dear Lee Bradford is getting ready to stab you in the back. He's joined forces with Frank to crush Powers Incorporated."

Shocked, I replied loud enough to startle Michael, as well as wake the dead, "Holy shit! Why that rotten bastard! Do you know what they're planning?"

Just as Michael sat up in the bed and started looking at me like, 'what the hell is going on' Barbara replied, "As a matter of fact, yes I do. Frank is having Senator Elms, resubmit the stock market bill for a vote in October of this year. Lee is going to help push the bill through, so President Feagan can have the pleasure of signing it into law, just before the November elections. The bill will go into effect on November 1st, 1988. After that, any corporation which falls under the guidelines of the new law will have to become compliant on or before midnight December 1st. This means Powers Incorporated will go on the public stock market at 9:00. Then on December 2nd, exactly at 9:30am, Bradford Computers and Salerno Incorporated plan to jointly attempt to take-over Powers Incorporated."

With that news I took a deep breath and exclaimed, "My God! You weren't kidding when you said I needed to know this. I won't ask you where you got your information but give that angel a kiss for me whoever it is."

"I will, but are you going to be able to handle this?"

I chuckled, then lackadaisically replied, "You know me, I'll always rise to a challenge. Thank you, Barbara, once again you're saving my ass, and I will never forget it. I love you, girlfriend."

American Goddess

We said our goodbyes and I immediately told Michael everything. I pulled out my personal phone book and called my attorney, Tom Davies at his home in Manhattan.

When he finally answered the phone, I said, "Tom, its Christina. Sorry to wake you, but I need you to cancel everything you're doing and get some information for me."

With a concerned tone he replied, "This sounds serious, just give me one minute, Christina."

The phone went silent for a few moments and when Tom came back on it he said, "I'm sorry Christina, please go on."

Feeling slightly suspicious I said, "Before I go any further Tom, I want to tell you something. I trust you, so if you're not with me then you'd better tell me now."

Sounding slightly offended he swiftly replied, "Of-course I'm with you, Christina! Have I ever given you a reason to ask me that question?"

Carefully studying the tone of his voice, I said, "Only one; what were you doing when you just left me on the line?"

He replied with a tone of sincerity, "Just going to the bathroom, boss lady."

I chuckled a little from my paranoia, "I'm sorry Tom, I'm just being cautious. I called because I need to have you come up to my office as soon as you can get here. When you come, bring me all the stats you can dig up on Bradford Computers, Salerno Incorporated and   Kenny Baby Foods. We have to plan some heavy-duty strategies."

Curiously he asked, "Can you tell me what this is about?"

My reply was blunt, "The sooner you get here, the sooner you'll find out."

"Okay, boss lady," he remarked with an assured tone. "I'll see you later this morning."

The moment I hung up the phone, I started to pace the bedroom floor. As soon as I did, Michael climbed out of bed and left the room. He returned with a cup of coffee, just as I reached my maximum state of thought and said, "I figured you could use this." I smiled appreciatively as I kissed his cheek, took a sip and went right back to pacing. As I paced my mind started to spin so fast and it wasn't stopping until I'd spun a web I knew none of them would escape.

It was 11:00am when Tom Davies arrived at my outer office and I had still not been able to organize my thoughts. As soon as Tom entered my office I said, "Tom, do you have what I asked for?"

He handed me three 12/14 manila envelopes, "All the financial dirt on the big three, are in those envelopes."

I took them from him intently, "Great! Come on and sit down with me for a few minutes, while I look these over." Then I looked at him, "Fix yourself some coffee, it's over there on the counter and I'll be right with you."

American Goddess

I buzzed my new personal secretary Terry Baggatta and said, "Terry, please notify everyone I will be ready for our emergency board meeting at 1:00pm." I handed the Bradford Computers envelope to Michael and the Salerno envelope to Jimmy.

I took the Kenny envelope as I thought, "This one was just for me! I didn't forget someone tried to kill me without meaning to, and since it's time for the payback, you might as well get yours now too." Then I said, "Dig me out all the information on cash holdings and I need to know who holds the majority of their stock." With that we went right to work.

By the time we were ready for the meeting, I had all the information I needed to begin to truly develop strategies. We all said our normal greetings when we entered the conference room. Then I got right to the point, "Okay guys, I called this meeting because Powers Incorporated is under siege. We are in a dire situation which will take the wits and cooperation of every single one of us in this room if we hope to emerge victorious from our upcoming battle." I took a sip from my orange juice then continued, "It's like this, Lee Bradford is going to help Frank Salerno pass his new stock market bill through the Senate." I filled them in on how they planned to achieve this, then said, "Now, depending on how much damage Lee has already done with other senators, I might be able to change Mr. Bradford's mind, thus once again, temporarily solving the problem until the next time. But I think there may be another way of handling this."

I began to slowly pace back and forth on the speaker's platform as I said, "I think if we let them pass the law, then we may be able to strike a sneak attack on both their corporations. But, before I suggest it, I first need to tell you if we go through with my plans and fail, then we may eventually lose Powers Incorporated."

Joe Cole stood up, "Christina, may I speak?"

"Please do, Joe."

"All I want to know is, will we finally get out from under the thumb of Frank Salerno? We go through this with him every year, and every year we go crazy trying to defeat this damn bill. So, if you have a plan you believe in then please tell us about it. I think it's about time we kick some corporate ass and take care of this problem once and for all!"

Everyone began to clap, so I said, "Okay guys, I said I had a plan. However, I didn't say it was going to be easy, but here it is. As it stands, if we were to go on the open market today our stock would be selling at sixty-two dollars a share. That's not high enough. When we hit the market, we have to be over one-hundred dollars a share. Now that point leads into this one: right now Powers Incorporated has cash holdings totaling sixty-three-billion dollars. Bradford has two-hundred and forty-four-billion dollars, and Salerno Incorporated has one-hundred and seventy-six-billion-dollars. This leaves us the financial weakling compared to our opponents. So the first thing we need to do is to increase our income substantially and fast. This will also bring up the value of our stock, and we will have to keep them up, as we try to knock our opponents' stock down. Now, I will handle the value of our opponent's stock come D-day, but I need you guys to bust some ass with me and build up our stock." 'Privately, I discovered Kenny Baby Foods had a cash value of seventy-eight billion dollars. I had to calculate all my figures to the penny if I were to be successful.' I continued; "First, we need to have the album ready to be released as soon as possible, like tomorrow. Second, we have two weeks to set up a six-month, seven day a week, nationwide concert tour, beginning in September." I turned to Jimmy and added, "Jimmy, I want my December 2nd, performance to be in Las Vegas."

That's when Joe interrupted, "A seven day a week tour, will the crowds come every night?"

Confidently I answered, "I haven't performed live in more than ten years Joe; they'll come. Once we announce the tour, our stock will begin to climb and once the cash from the concert tour begins to pour in, I think we'll be solving both our cash and stock problems at one time, but it has got to be a super-hot tour. So guys, you have got to make it hot. We are going to have to start finishing up the album tonight, because I will be going out of town for a few days, at the end of the week."

Anxiously Jimmy said, "You have two weeks to get in shape for a six-month concert tour, and you're going out of town for a few days?"

I shook my head at him disappointingly; then reassured them all, "In order for all of this to work, I have to. I'm not leaving you guys in a sinking ship. I know what I'm doing. So as soon as I come back, I'll start rehearsing."

It was straight to work and we worked all day long. When Michael and I arrived at our new home on the complex grounds, overlooking the river it was 1:00am. We walked in the door and went straight to the showers. Afterwards, we laid in bed together and Michael began to gently massage my shoulders as he said, "So where are we going?"

I turned to look him in the eyes, "Michael, there are some things about myself which I have never told anyone, and I've always handled things my way. But now I'm in a dilemma that I'm not sure how to handle." I looked up at him as if to say help me, as I struggled with my words.

Michael, seeing my distress took me in his arms, "Christina, I love you and if you're having a problem telling me something, then don't be, I will be beside you no matter what you've done."

I thought very seriously for one moment, "Michael, I've got to be truthful with you no matter what the cost. I have been the mistress to one of the most powerful mafia leaders in the world for years now. I have only slept with him twice in my life, but as far as he's concerned, I will always be his special secret lover. He lives in Italy and I need to go see him. He is the only man on this earth right now, with the power to help me."

American Goddess

Michael looked at me strangely, "Punkie, I can handle your past, but I hope you're not thinking of sleeping with him again?"

I pulled Michael on top of me, kissed him and replied, "Michael there was a time I would have just gone off and do what I had to do. But I can't do that anymore, that is why I'm telling you this. I need his help, but even if I come out of our meeting in a **box**, I will not sleep with him. I believe I can now make him understand that."

This time, Michael looked deeply into my eye, "I trust you, Punkie." Then he kissed me, "So when are we going; because I'm still coming with you."

I kissed him again, "Friday. But first we're going to Washington on Thursday."

With a curious look on his face he asked, "Why are we taking all these trips anyway?"

I answered cautiously, "Michael, I love you, but if I tell you and my plan fails, then I might be spending a few years in San Quentin."

"San Quentin! What the hell are you up to?"

My expression was more than serious, "Michael, the less you know about it the better your chances in a court of law would be, if it comes to that. So please don't ask me anymore."

"Fuck that!" He swiftly replied, "I want to know what you're planning before I decide whether we go through with it or not!"

With that remark I began to get a little hot under the collar, "Now just one minute, who do you think you're talking to? You're going to decide?"

"Hold on before you get upset Christina and look at it from my side. What if I just told you everything you just told me? What would you say?"

I thought about it for a moment, "Okay, Michael, you're right."

I told him every detail of my plan and he said, "That is pure genius and ruthless, besides. How the hell did you figure that out?"

I smiled deviously, "I'm a fucking genius, that's how. And I can't believe I just let you into my darkest thoughts."

With an amused look on his face he said, "Baby, I love you, and as devious as your plan is, I give you my blessings. I just hope no one gets hurt."

Don't worry no one will get hurt, except the three snakes." I looked very seriously into his eyes, "Michael, I hope you know I would never do this if I didn't have to, my hand is being forced."

Tenderly he kissed me, "I know that Punkie, and believe it or not, it makes me love you even more."

He kissed me passionately and we ended that night the way we've ended every night since we moved in together, in the heat of our passion. We just couldn't get enough of each other.

American Goddess

First thing I did the next morning was to place a call to Senator Tom Kenny. He would be my first pawn in our game of corporate chess. I told him I would be in town in two days and I needed to meet with him. We set an appointment for 1:00pm on Thursday, August 10th, at his office in Georgetown. My next call was to Dominick Giovanetti. I told him I would be arriving in Italy that coming weekend, and I desperately needed to see him. He told me to let him know when my flight would arrive, so he could have a driver waiting for me.   He also said he would cancel whatever he was involved in as soon as I arrived.

We ended our conversation, and I thought, "Dominick's assistance is absolutely crucial right now for my scheming to be foolproof. Now, if I can only talk him into helping me without the sexual favors, I'll be doing really well." Then I thought, "What if I can't control him?" With that I shrugged my shoulders and thought, "Oh well, I'll figure it out tomorrow." Then it was straight to work on the recording of 'The Power of Love.'

By Wednesday night we had finished recording and it was ready for mass production the next morning. After Michael and I tied up a few loose ends at the office on Thursday morning, we went straight to Stewart Airport in Newburgh.

On our flight to Washington, Michael and I were discussing our plans and I said, "Michael, I don't want you to be upset, but when we arrive at Senator Kenny's office, as well as Dominick's office, I will have to speak to them alone."

Immediately a strained look came over him, "Christina, I don't know that I can let you do that. Besides, I already know everything you're going to say."

I kissed him gently and with all my heart said, "Honey, I know how you feel about me doing this by myself, but just because you know everything, doesn't mean you can be present when I speak to these men. They must believe no one else knows what I will be asking them to do for me. I need to have their utmost confidence in my ability to pull this off, with no one knowing. Besides baby, I really am a big girl and I can handle myself quite well." He kissed me and reluctantly agreed.

When I entered Tom's office, I immediately gave him a warm embrace, just to remind him with whom he was dealing. After we exchanged greetings, he gestured to me to take a seat beside him on a large vinyl sofa. As I did, he gazed at me as if my presence alone made his blood begin to race to all parts of his body, as he said, "Christina, it's been so long and you're still as lovely as ever."

I softly smiled and graciously replied, "Well thank you, Tom. You're still looking quite good yourself. But this is not a social call, it's strictly business. I happen to have in my possession some information on a mutual friend of ours. I believe this bit of information would be very useful to a man in your position."

I knew I caught his interest, just by the way he tried to hide his enthusiasm as he casually said, "Christina, I have no idea what you're talking about."

American Goddess

I smiled again, but this time a little more sensually. Then I gently placed my hand on his upper thigh and seductively said, "What if I told you, if we worked together, we could politically, and professionally, slit Lee Bradford's throat."

Immediately the lights in his eyes said it all and 'I knew I had him.' With that, he grabbed my hand and said, "Just how do you plan to pull this off?"

I gently squeezed his hand and began to tell him my part, in my plan of revenge on our mutual adversary. I told him what I had and what I planned to do with it. A look of delightful wickedness grew on his face and he said, "It sounds too devious not to work, so what's my part in your little scheme?"

That's when I told him what I wanted from him, as well as exactly when and how I needed him to deliver.

After carefully absorbing and analyzing my every word he asked, "How can I be sure, I'll get what you say you can deliver, when you say you will deliver it?"

With utmost confidence I replied, "Tom, think about it. Do you really think I'm just out for personal revenge? Well I'm not. I want the world to know what kind of a thieving bastard Lee Bradford, truly is." With sincerity I stood up, took a few steps away from him, turned back and added, "Tom, you were right all along, Lee Bradford does need to be brought to justice for his crimes, and I'm the only person who can help you do that!"

With a look of sweet revenge in his eyes, and a smile on his face, "I'll do it!" he replied with enthusiasm.

By the time we finished our meeting, I had Tom drooling from the mouth, with just the anticipation of the thought, of the kill.

Michael romantically wined and dined me that night, and somehow in the midst of the beautiful city of Washington, D.C., we totally forgot our impending crisis and once again we were young lovers. This was the way we truly wanted to spend every moment of our lives, immersed in each other's love, not battling for our corporate survival against two evil men, who were so arrogant they believed they could destroy innocent lives at will just to obtain and maintain their corrupt POWER!

That night after love making, I laid in Michael's arms and thought, "I will let no man ever destroy me again, and may God forgive me, but if I have to, I will KILL THEM BOTH before they get a chance!" Then I drifted off to sleep in Michael's strong arms.

The next evening, we were both a little nervous as our plane approached Rome. I had just finished saying, "Michael, whatever you do, always treat Dominick with the utmost respect. You will see his presence alone commands it."

Before we knew it, it was 7:00pm Rome time and we were climbing into the limo Dominick had waiting for us at the airport. The driver told us we would be having dinner with Dominick at his mansion in the city, and off we went. Dominick was aware my future husband would be arriving with me. I didn't want to surprise Dominick with trivial things at our personal meeting. I also hoped this information would help to calm his appetite some. I knew it really wasn't going to hold any water with Dominick at all, but I was still glad Michael was with me.

When we entered the formal dining room, Dominick warmly embraced us both with a strong, Italian, bear hug. To my surprise, we were also meeting a small group of some of Dominick's very close friends, who had been anxiously waiting to meet me. After our cordial introductions, Dominick led us to the green dining room where we proceeded to have a wonderful dinner, with what seemed to be an older and more-gentler Dominick. He was absolutely charming, and he treated Michael more like a son, then the lover of his 'lover.'

Sometime after dinner that evening, as we all chatted in the informal golden living room, Dominick excused us from the rest of his guests' and led me to his private library. I winked at Michael as I left him with the others, then I took a deep breath as I followed Dominick.

As we walked, I began to pray in my thoughts. I was scared shitless! The last thing I wanted to do was to be forced to sleep with him in order to obtain his help." When he closed the library door, I swallowed my heart and thought, "Oh God! Help me with this one." With that, I turned to Dominick, went right into my performance and truthfully, but dramatically said, "Dominick, I'm here because I am fighting for my life, and I won't be able to survive without your help."

He hugged me gently and took me by the hand. My heart pounded like a jack hammer within me, as he led me to a love seat. Then he sat me down beside him and said, "Now calm down, you can ask me anything. If I can help, I will." He kissed my forehead and with sincerity continued, "Now tell me all about it and we'll decide how to handle it together."

I proceeded to tell Dominick everything, including my whole plan to remedy the situation. He was the only other person I told besides Michael, because when dealing with Dominick, one had to be totally honest.

He gave me a surprised look, "Do you really think you can pull this one off?"

I looked confidently into his eyes, "With your help, I know I can, Dominick. Once the smoke clears, I will only be battling Salerno Incorporated who will be weakened, but so will Powers Incorporated. Now if I could only come up with that one missing piece of the puzzle."

Dominick shook his head and smiled suspiciously, "I'm sure you're going to tell me what that piece is."

I took his hand and smiled, "I need one more board to pull out from under Frank's feet to make him unstable enough to fall with the rest of them."

Dominick stood up, pulled me into his arms and kissed me, "Christina, do you know what intrigues me the most about you?"

American Goddess

I smiled sweetly, "No, but I hope you will tell me."

With a loving expression, he kissed me again, "You are the most magnificent 'black widow' I have ever laid my eyes on." He began to lead me over toward a large sofa on the other side of the room, and as we reached it he said, "I can help you with Kenny, but as for Frank, I'll have to do some fancy side stepping when it comes to him, but I'll see what I can do." Then, he took me into his arms and began to passionately kiss me.

I gently tried to pull out of his clutches and with the deepest sincerity said, "Dominick, please listen to me before we go any further. I must tell you something."

He slowed his passion, and said, "I'm sorry Christina, I thought we were through talking, please continue."

Cautiously I replied, "Dominick, I do love and admire you with all my heart and I would never turn you away. But I must tell you, I am truly in love with Michael, and if I sleep with you it would kill him. Please, I love Michael too much to do that to him." I began to tear up as I grabbed his hand, "I'm begging you not to ask me to sleep with you."

His eyes began to tear with mine as he kissed me again, "I'm not a groveling man Christina, but if I hold you any longer, I will be. So please take my love with you and may God bless your future." He squeezed me gently, kissed me one more time as he looked deeply into my eyes, "I will always remember you Christina and I'll be cheering you on from the sidelines," as he slapped my ass, "Now get the hell out of here, before I change my mind."

With tears of joy and relief in my eyes I whispered, "I love you too, Dominick." Then I turned graciously and victoriously walked away.

On Monday, August 13th, it was straight into rehearsals for my just announced Ten Year Anniversary concert tour. The tour was scheduled to open at Yankee Stadium that coming Friday August 17th. That gave me four and a half days to get ready for the hottest concert I had ever given. I was a little rusty at thirty-five-years of age, but I still had it and once again the financial stability of Powers Incorporated depended upon it. As you know, the schedule was going to be beyond intense, but we had no choice if we were to be ready for D-day. I decided to hire a small army of security staff to accompany us across the country. I knew if any of my opponents got wind of my plans, there would be a good chance I might become the sight at the end of a sniper's barrel. And I sure as hell didn't want that.

When the morning of August 17th came, I found myself a little nervous, to say the least. All day long the pressure grew inside me. You see, I had still not heard from Dominick, and I had everyone I trusted looking for the last piece of my puzzle on Frank, **with no success**. I believed I could defeat Salerno Incorporated in an all-out battle, but if I had that last piece of the puzzle, I could do it with little or no bloodshed at all to Powers Incorporated. And to top my day off, I started to get my normal pre-performance jitters.

American Goddess

The show time was scheduled to begin at 9:00pm and by 8:00pm that evening I was freaking. I waited in my dressing room alone, trying to psych myself up for my performance. As I paced the floor, I glanced up at the clock on the wall and it read 8:15. I stopped pacing and headed straight for Michael and Jimmy who were taking care of some last-minute changes I had asked them to make on the stage props. When I found them, they were out on the stage and I could hear the crowds filling the auditorium just behind the curtain. I went straight to Michael, wrapped my arms around his neck and began to cry.

Michael lovingly embraced and tenderly said, "I love you Punkie, and you're going to be great tonight."

Michael kissed me as Jimmy walked over, "I told you she'd be crazy by show time." Jimmy wrapped his arms around Michael and me, "Listen to me guys, as long as the three of us stick together we can make it through anything." He kissed our cheeks, "Christina, when you go out there, you will be taking the strength of three with you. Now all you have to do is go in that dressing room and come out the great, Christina Powers."

I wiped the tears from my cheeks, kissed them both once and replied, "I love you two and you're both right." I slid out from between them, "Well I'd better go get ready." At that I swallowed hard, turned and walked back to my dressing room.

When I emerged, I was once again Christina Powers, the world's most famous and hottest sex symbol. And I looked like a **goddess** in my red satin skintight gown. The gown flowed down to just past my calves, with my famous slit up the middle, to show my million-dollar legs, red heels and silky clear stockings. I thought I was going to have to pick Michael up off the floor, when he saw just how beautiful his future bride could truly be.

In awe, he embraced me and bellowed, "I have never seen anything as radiant as you are at this moment." He kissed me passionately, "Take our passion for love with you and knock them dead, Punkie!"

I returned his kiss, "I love you too, Michael." It was at that moment, the lights flashed, signifying the opening act was finished and it was now my turn. I kissed Michael one more time, turned and walked over to get ready for my cue to go on stage. As I anxiously waited, I said a little prayer to myself.

I took a deep breath when I heard my cue and sensually danced my way out onto the stage, to the screams of one-hundred and fifty-thousand fans; all of whom actually had to fight for each one of their tickets. This was the biggest concert crowd to ever attend one performer's show and I immediately began to give them their moneys' worth. I went right into a medley of all my hottest past hits, straight into singing the singles from my new album, 'The Power of Love'. In between sets I stopped three different times to chat with the crowd. In the midst of the final chat, we were laughing and having a great time, when someone shouted out, "Christina! Please do 'Halloween in Hell' for us." As soon as he did, the crowd went wild with cheers and chants for 'Halloween in Hell'. When I was finally able to calm them down, I said, "Friends, I haven't sung a cut off that album since the night I lost my daughter, Joy. So please forgive me, but I must say no. You see, I promised myself I would never sing one of those songs again."

The crowd cheered even louder as they shouted, "We love you, Christina!" I stormed right into the rest of my performance and after being absent from the stage for more than ten years, I had them screaming in the aisles and my show that night was a smashing success!

The next morning the critics wrote, **"Christina Powers showed New York why she's the Queen! Her performance was spectacular!"**

We were full steam into our tour, when finally, on September 26th, I heard from Dominick!

I anxiously grabbed the phone from Michael's hand, in our hotel room in Atlanta, Georgia, when he said, "It's Dominick."

"Hi Dominick, I've been going nuts waiting to hear from you."

Chuckling at my anxious tone he replied, "Calm down little girl, I told you I'd get it."

With excitement in my voice I asked, "You got the piece I need on Frank?"

This time there was no chuckle, "First, I have Senator Kenny covered for you." Then he took on a serious tone, "Now listen, I don't want you going off the deep end, but here it is. As for Frank . . ." as he continued, he told me something which made my blood boil from the pain which shot straight through my soul.

"Dominick thank-you; I promise I will never forget what you've done for me. You've been my guardian angel for a long time now and I love you for it. As for what you just told me, **I will make it work**." We ended our conversation, and it was now time to begin to implement phase two of my counter strategy.

By the time the Senate passed Frank's bill on October 6th, I was well on my way to finally catching up with the two financial giants I would soon be doing battle with. My concerts were bringing in huge crowds every night and with no seat selling for less than one hundred dollars, the money was pouring in. When we added in the sales from the album, we were grossing a phenomenal ninety-million dollars a week, worldwide. Not only that, but I finally had Powers Incorporated in full swing and our grand total per week was reaching the three-hundred-million-dollar mark. I was jockeying into position as fast as I could, and our stock showed it. The value for one share went up to a hundred and two dollars on the market. We were doing so well, that by the time I decided to pay a visit to Lee, on November 30th, Powers Incorporated had a cash net worth of ninety-eight-billion dollars and rising fast! That fact helped me feel more then confident I would be victorious. But the best thing of all was as of yet, none of my enemies had any idea what was coming.

9:00pm on November 30th, I knocked on Lee's door at his home in Gardener. I knew he was home and I had plenty to say. I was looking particularly good and Lee was quite surprised when he saw me standing there.

As he opened the door, I casually said, "Hi, may I come in? I'd like to talk with you."

He gestured me in and as I entered, he arrogantly said, "Christina, come on in. Hmm, I wonder what brings you to my door." Then he gloated as he looked at me, "Maybe I should guess. Let us see, maybe you're here to grovel on **your knees, this time**. As a matter of fact, I'll bet you're thinking just maybe I can seduce and deceive Lee into saving my desperate little ass, just one more time before I destroy him again!"

I turned to him and with a disgusted tone reeled, "Lee, no matter what happened between us, I would have never betrayed you. The one thing you will never understand is even though we are no longer together you will always have a place in my heart, whether you want to be there or not, and I won't change the kind of person I am just to suit you." I took a step closer to him, looked earnestly into his eyes, "Even though that's all water under the bridge now, I still care about you and that is why I hate to say what I am about to, but Lee, you gave me no choice."

I told him what information I had on him and what I would do with this information, if he did not do exactly what I wanted him to do, when I wanted him to do it, and precisely how I wanted him to do it." I completed my instructions with a sarcastic, "Who's groveling now Lee?"

He turned so red I thought he was going to burst. He reluctantly agreed to my terms then said, "Do you destroy all your ex-lovers?"

I gave him a disappointed look, "Only the ones who betray me." I walked away feeling horrible for what I had just done, but as I drove away I thought, "Oh well, I'll figure it out tomorrow."

On December 1st, 1988, at 3:00pm Powers Incorporated became compliant with the new federal guidelines which governed the stock exchange. Powers Incorporated was now also, completely ready for our December 2nd showdown on Wall Street. When D-day arrived Michael and I were going over every detail for the one-thousandth time in our suite at Caesar's Hotel and Casino, in Las Vegas, Nevada, and it wasn't even 6:00am yet. I was so psyched I couldn't wait for the 9:00am bell to ring on Wall Street. We had the entire suite setup with computers and phone lines, so we could monitor every movement the stock market made. I also had a small army of phone operators who would be in constant contact with my hand chosen stockbrokers, all waiting for me to send them into action.

American Goddess

At 8:00am, Eastern Standard Time, 5:00am Pacific Time, I called Detective Fred Ulrich at his home in Los Angeles, California and said, "Hi Fred, its Christina Powers. I'm sorry to wake you, but I have to talk to you now."

He perked up, "You sound serious. Have you come up with something?"

With a positive tone I answered, "I sure have, Fred." I proceeded to painfully tell him what I had discovered. After which I asked him to keep this information to himself, until I called him later that morning. When I hung up the phone, I thought, "Finally all the pieces to my puzzle are in place, and I am more than ready to play the game with the big boys."

On December 2nd, at 9:00am, Eastern Standard Time, the bell rang on Wall Street. The market opened like this: Powers Incorporated, one-hundred and four-dollars per share. Salerno Incorporated, one-hundred and twelve-dollars per share. Bradford Computers, one-hundred and twenty-six-dollars per share, and Kenny Baby Foods, seventy-six-dollars per share. Frank's plan was to begin his joint corporate attack along with Bradford Computers, at 9:15am on Powers Incorporated. So I'm sure he was shitting when Bradford Computers waged an all-out corporate take-over attempt on Salerno Incorporated at 9:05am. By 9:15am I began to smile as I watched Salerno Incorporated shift gears from Powers Incorporated to a full-force retaliation against Bradford Computers. Their stock soared so fast that by 10:00am each corporation had committed more than twenty-five-billion-dollars cash toward the destruction of the other.

As I had counted on, by 10:30am Lee was showing all his might as he began to over-take Salerno Incorporated with a seventy-six-billion-dollar commitment. I knew Frank would be afraid to invest any more than seventy-five-billion dollars, even to save his empire. So, I made my first phone call to Tom. The entire stock market was going crazy as these two giants forced all the stock to begin to climb with them. Then, just as Frank was about to concede, Tom jumped into the game. Kenny Baby Foods offered to join forces with Salerno Incorporated against Bradford Computers, and they would divide up the spoils. Once again, just as I hoped, Frank jumped back into the game. I sat back and watched the markets go mad, as these three giants of the business world did battle. I watched in complete satisfaction as these three men committed most of their cash holdings into this battle. Finally, at 1:00pm Bradford Computers had committed two-hundred-billion dollars to the battle. Salerno Incorporated one-hundred and fifty-billion dollars and Kenny Baby Foods sixty-eight-billion dollars.

That's when I made my second call and once again it was to Tom, and at 1:05pm the United States Congress, announced a warrant for the arrest of Senator Lee Bradford, on the charges of conspiracy and espionage. Ten minutes later Bradford Computer's stock began to drop like a sky diver without his chute. At 1:20pm I made my third call, this time to Detective Fred Ulrich, and at 1:26pm an arrest warrant was issued for Frank Salerno, for conspiracy to commit murder. I was ecstatic by 1:40pm when Salerno Incorporated

American Goddess

stock began to drop almost as fast as Bradford Computers did. Then at 1:52pm I made my fourth call, this one was to Dominick, and at 2:11pm the CDC recalled two-million cases of Kenny baby foods for possible food poisoning. And guess what! Kenny Baby Food's stock began to plummet faster than the other two combined. The last minutes of the day, the stockholders of all three companies, scrambled to sell their plummeting stock with no buyers to be found anywhere. I laughed with a sense of pure satisfaction as I watched all three of these corporate giants begin to crumble.

By 2:30pm not one of them had enough capital left to save their own asses, no less try to take-over the corner drug store. So, at 2:35pm as each of their stock reached the lower double digits, I started shouting out orders left and right to my phone operators to start buying.

At that, I swept down and devoured the aftermath and by 3:00pm December 2nd, 1988, with the help of my colleagues, we had taken control of 79% of Bradford Computers, 92% of Kenny Baby Foods, and 96% of Salerno Incorporated. By 3:05pm the whole business world was reeling in the aftermath of my day of vengeance. By 3:15pm Eastern Standard Time and 12:15pm Pacific Time, I was on my way to the headquarters of Salerno Incorporated to claim the spoils of my victory, and to spit in Franks face. I could not wait to watch Detective Ulrich and the Nevada State Police arrest Frank for the murder of my baby. As our caravan headed to the headquarters of Salerno Incorporated, we drove through the worst storm front the Nevada desert had seen in ten years and my blood raced in anticipation with every mile.

When Michael and I arrived at Salerno Incorporated we came in with an entourage of staff to go right in and monitor all aspects of the corporation until I could formally take over.

As I walked down the hall to Frank's office I thought, "This is it! My moment of sweet victory, which I had fought sixteen years to achieve."

We reached Franks outer office and I was surprised to see Detective Fred Ulrich and the Nevada State Police were not there yet. But that was not going to stop me from throwing Frank the hell out of his own office.

I walked up to Carroll, Frank's long-time secretary, "Carroll, I'm sure you know why I'm here. Now where is Frank?"

Nervously, she answered, "Wait one-minute Christina, and I'll let him know you're here."

As Carroll began to buzz Frank, I barged into his office with Michael and three bodyguards right behind me, "Well Frank it's funny seeing you here in my office, I thought you'd be in jail by now."

In reply to my sarcastic words, he shouted out in rage, "Get the fuck out of my office right now, before I throw you out!"

American Goddess

With an air of superiority, I threw a fax of the final Wall Street count of the day's games into his face and viciously shouted back, "Looks like I win Frank, read them and weep, you bastard. Now get your ass the **fuck** out of my seat because the state police will be here any minute to arrest you, and I don't want to look at a baby killer any longer than I have to."

He seemed to calm down some as he replied, "I'll leave, but at least give me five minutes to talk with you alone before the police come. It's about your parents."

I looked at him with hatred in my eyes and with curiosity in my heart said, "For some reason I want to know what it is you have to say to me Frank, so I will grant you a private audience." I turned to Michael and my bodyguards and added, "Please give me five minutes with him alone and wait in the outer office for me."

Michael interjected with a suspicious tone, "Christina, I don't trust him, let me stay with you."

Sarcastically Frank asked, "Is this the new fiancée everyone is talking about? Funny, but he looks a lot like someone else we once knew, doesn't he, Christina?"

Angered by his innuendo I turned to Michael and with a forceful tone said, "No, Michael! Please wait outside! Besides, you'll only be on the other side of the door."

Michael shook his head reluctantly, and turned to Frank, "Okay, but I'll be right outside this door."

When they left, I said, "Okay Frank, start talking, your time is limited."

He stood up from his chair, "You think you have destroyed me, don't you?"

I smiled deviously, "I don't think so, I know so. So what's your point?"

With evil radiating from his eyes he answered, "My point is this, Christy. Your mother tried to destroy me once and I had her killed. Your father tried to destroy me, and I had him killed too. You just insulted me, and I had your child killed. So what makes you think you can do what a President couldn't do?" With that he pulled out a handgun, as he hit the button on his desk, which locked the large doors to his office. My mind and blood began to race as Frank pointed the gun at me, "What a shame it turned out like this for us, Christy. I would have loved you and given you the world. But now I have to kill you."

I looked at him with utter sincerity, "Before you pull that trigger Frank, I want you to grant me one last thing?"

I knew he could sense my desperation, "You're not in the position to ask for anything, but I'll let you speak."

I slowly began to sensually move toward him, "Frank, those doors are thick, and no one is getting in here too soon." As I reached him, I carefully brushed my fingers through his hair and very sensually said, "Frank, make love to me just once, before you take my life."

He took me in his arms, "This is what you needed sixteen years ago."

American Goddess

As he kissed me deeply, I kneed him right in the nuts as hard as I could, at the same time I grabbed the gun still in his hand, and as he yelled, "You fucking bitch!" I yelled, "Michael, Help! Help me!"

We began to fight for control of the gun as I continued to scream, "Help! Michael! Help!"

I screamed as our bodies smashed into the large bookshelves sending the books hurling to the floor, "Michael, help me!"

I could hear Michael banging on the door when the gun flew out of both our hands as we fought, and it landed on the desk. Frank grabbed me as I tried to run for the gun and flung us both to the ground. I could feel my breath being taken from me with Frank's weight landing right on top of me. I screamed and struggled to escape him as he reached for my neck with his hands. I had just made it to my knees, when Frank belted me right across the right jaw, knocking my head back against the corner of the desk so hard it split the back of my head open. I could feel the blood begin to rush down my back, as I struggled to catch my breath. Seeing Frank coming toward me on his knees, I sprang my knees back and with all my might pushed up with both feet, hitting him right in the chest. As he went flying over backwards, I climbed to my feet, grabbed the gun and ran for the door. Just as I reached the door Frank leaped at me and once again grabbed the gun as I held it in my hands, only this time it went off '**Bang!**' I screamed in terror, as I let go of the gun.

I watched in horror as Frank began to fall to the floor with blood gushing from his chest. Then **"Bang!"** came the second shot, this time I grabbed for my abdomen as the pain shot through my body. I began to stagger, then I fell to the floor with blood pouring from my open stomach. When I hit the floor, I could see the figure of a man and I could hear him talking to someone. I felt a cold feeling in my hand, and I began to fall backwards as if I were falling right through the floor. I kept falling back into the mist of a dark, bleak, nothingness. As I fell into this cold emptiness, I could see the spirit of my unborn child begin to leave my body. This gentle, soft, pure soul began to beckon me toward a speck of light in the distance.

This beautiful little spirit took my hand, and I instantly felt the bond of love only a parent could feel for their child. Joyfully I floated along with my child toward what was becoming a brilliant, bright white light. As we reached this magnificent light we were filled with the presence of the love of God. Just before we entered the warmth of the light a beautiful golden winged angel came to us. This beautiful being took my precious child from my arms and said, "It's not your time my child. You have much life to live yet."

Saddened I replied, "Then let me have my child."

This beautiful angel seemed to look through me as she said, "This spirit has fulfilled its destiny, but you haven't."

American Goddess

I cried out, "How could my child have fulfilled its destiny? It was never born!"
I heard, "You will understand in time my child."
Once she stopped speaking to my thoughts, they both began to fade away into the light, leaving me alone in the darkness. As they vanished, I desperately began to scream and cry, "My baby! I want my baby!" Then they were gone, and **everything went dark.**

American Goddess

CHAPTER 18

When I came out of that horrible darkness, I opened my eyes and the first thing I saw was Michael asleep in a chair beside my bed. All of a sudden, a sense of disoriented urgency came over me. I quickly gazed around the dimly lit room, then to the IV lines which led to my arm, and I realized I was in a hospital bed. When I tried to move, I felt a sharp pain in my stomach, and I moaned. As soon as I moaned, Michael's eyes popped open and instantly met mine. Like a flash of lightening, he sprang up from his chair and dashed to my side. He gently took my hand through the safety bars on the bed, softly kissed my forehead and with tears welling in his eyes gently whispering, "Christina, oh baby, I love you. I thought I had lost you. How do you feel Punkie, can you tell?"

I lovingly gazed back into Michael's tearing eyes, "I feel horrible Michael, what happened?"

A look of surprise immediately came over his face as he replied with concern, "Don't you remember what happened?"

I thought about it for a minute, "The last thing I remember is arguing with Frank, then everything went black."

Michael gently kissed me again, "Let's not talk about that now, its 4:00am we'll talk more later. Do you need anything for pain?"

With a groggy tone I replied, "No, I'm just tired, baby."

Michael gently slid the side railing on the bed down and carefully crawled in beside me. Very slowly, I laid my head on his chest, and as he gently held me in his arms' he said, "I thank God you're okay, Punkie. Now, lie still and just let me hold you." And that was the last thing I heard before I drifted off again.

It was some time around 7:00am when Michael was sternly ordered out of my bed by a large black nurse who said, "Mr. Powers! Get out of that bed right now! Don't you realize your wife is in a coma?"

Startled I lifted my head from Michael's chest and said as this nurse's mouth dropped open, "She looks like she means business, honey you'd better get out of the bed."

As Michael climbed out of the bed, she immediately came to me and began to take my vital signs as she said, "Welcome back Ms. Powers, we were all worried about you."

I looked at her earnestly, "I'm starving, may I please have something to eat?"

Giving me a big smile, "You've been unconscious for three weeks, you can't eat yet, but I'll have your doctor in here pronto."

She turned to leave the room and as she closed the door behind her, I turned to Michael, "What was she talking about? Have I been unconscious for three weeks?"

Michael sat on the bed beside me, took my hand in his, "Punkie, you really don't remember what happened?"

245

American Goddess

"No, Michael!" I answered nervously, "I still don't remember. Will you please fill me in on what's going on?"

Looking at me sincerely, yet tenderly, "Christina, you were shot. When the ambulance arrived with you here at the hospital, you were clinically dead. When they brought you into the E.R., the doctor wanted to pronounce you dead on arrival, but I started ordering them to resuscitate you, so they tried. Five minutes later, they got vital signs. Once you were stabilized, they took you right to the operating room, where they removed a bullet from your uterus." He gently held me, "We lost our baby, Christina."

I immediately started to cry, "God! Not our baby! I wanted to have our child so badly!"

Michael tenderly embraced me, "Christina, I just thank God they were able to save you. After the surgery, you were in critical condition for a week. I thought I was going to lose you too. My heart was breaking every minute you were in the intensive care unit hooked up to all kinds of tubes. They finally stabilized you enough to take you off the respirator, but you still wouldn't come out of the coma. The doctor who saved you in the O.R., a Doctor Sonne, thought the coma may have been brought on more by a mental trauma, rather than a physiological one, since physically you began to do better. But they still couldn't get you to come out of the coma, until you woke up this morning."

I was totally overwhelmed, and it showed on my face, "Michael, how did I get shot?"

Michael took my hand, "I was hoping you could tell me that. What can you remember about the fight you had with Frank?"

I shook my head, "All I remember is asking you to leave the room, because Frank wanted to tell me something in private. Somehow, we started to fight. Oh God! That's right! I remember! Frank pulled out a gun and we fought over it. I knew you were trying to get in, so I ran to the door and that's when everything went black. Oh my God! Frank must have shot me! Where's Frank, now?"

Puzzled Michael looked straight into my eyes, "Christina, Frank is dead! By the time we broke the door down two shots had already been fired. When we finally entered the room, you both had been shot and you had the gun in your hands. The Nevada State Police have been waiting for you to come out of the coma so they could question you."

All of a sudden I began to feel weak, "Michael, I'm not feeling too good. Please call someone I think I'm going to pass out."

Michael immediately pulled the call button out of the wall and within seconds, two nurses came running into the room. Michael told them I was feeling faint so one of the nurses put smelling salts under my nose and I began to come around. Just as I caught my breath, a distinguished looking tall man with graying hair, wearing a three-piece blue suit, walked into the room. When he reached my bed, the nurses backed off a little as this man said, "Hi, I'm Doctor Sonne, it's about time you woke up sleeping beauty."

American Goddess

I replied with a grateful smile, "Hi Doctor Sonne, I hear you had a hand in saving my life. I would like to thank you. Now I'd like to know what day it is and when may I eat?"

Doctor Sonne chuckled, then with a look of amusement said, "Today is Thursday, December 19th, and all you can have are clear liquids. We'll see how well you tolerate them, before we serve the fillet mignon. Now, I want you to rest for a couple hours, then I'm going to have the nurses walk you every four hours. We have to start building those muscles back up."

Gratefully, I shook his hand, "Thank you once again, but before you leave, I do have one more question."

"You may ask me whatever you need to."

With nervous concern I inquired, "Michael told me you had to take our baby because the bullet entered my uterus. All I want to know is, do I still have all my womanly parts?"

He shook his head sadly, as he spoke with a tone of authority, "I was going to wait to tell you this, but since you asked, the answer is yes. But Christina, your uterus suffered some severe trauma and I don't believe you will ever be able to bear a child again. I hate to tell you that, but that's my professional opinion."

I swallowed hard, "Well, I can at least thank you for being honest. Now I think I'll try to get some rest, before I have to go jogging."

After he left the room I turned to Michael, "Did you already know I could no longer have children?"

"Yes Punkie, I knew," he answered sadly. "But I was going to wait until you were feeling a little stronger, before telling you."

With anger in my voice I yelled, "That **fucking,** Frank! He deserved to die! This is the third child he took from me and now they're telling me I can never have children again!" My tears began to fall as I added, "I didn't mean that Michael, no one deserves to die. I just feel so sick inside. I wanted us to have a family so badly."

Michael held me oh so tenderly and with his voice full of compassion said, "Punkie, I love you no matter what! And even though we can no longer have our own children, we can still have a family. There is no reason we can't adopt."

I looked up at him through my tears, "I know we can adopt and God willing we will. I just wanted to bear your child, Michael. Now, we can never have a child of our own."

That's when Michael began to choke up, "Punkie, I love you more than life itself and there is nothing more I'd like then for you to bear my child; but, it's not the end of the world. So for now, let's get you out of this hospital, then we'll talk about how we'll have our family." As he finished speaking, Michael tenderly took my hand in his and held it until I fell back to sleep, which only took a few minutes.

Jimmy flew in from New York as soon as Michael called him, and he started to cry the minute we saw one another. Later that evening over my clear broth dinner, Jimmy filled me in on what transpired after my so-called death by saying, "Christina, it was crazy! 3:00pm that afternoon when the closing bell rang on the market, our stock closed at one-hundred and thirty-six-dollars a share. But the next morning, after the news hit you were shot and might not survive, our stock began to plummet with all the others. When Dominick saw what was going on, he called me and offered to help. He gave us a ten-billion dollar shot in the arm. After his generous loan, we were able to stabilize all four corporations, and right now Fortune 500 has declared you the most ruthless and richest woman in the world! Christina, thanks to your brilliant maneuvering, the size of the Powers Empire is now **second to none**." Then with pure excitement in his mannerisms he yelled out, "Christina, you have become the tenth richest person on this planet. Can you believe that? In thirteen years, you took us from a basement apartment in Rome, to this. You are truly remarkable Christina, and I thank God you're still with me, because girlfriend, I'd have to kill you if you left me." With that, I held my stomach to help control the pain, which shot through me the moment I started to laugh.

I quickly stopped laughing and asked curiously, "If Dominick gave us a ten-billion-dollar loan; how can I be the richest woman in the world?"

Jimmy laughed, then with that flick of his wrist said, "First girlfriend, no one knows where the money came from. Second, two days after you left Wall Street reeling, the Senate reversed the decision on Frank's Stock Market Bill; thus, leaving you the right to be the sole owner of the whole kit and caboodle. Do you realize what our holdings are now? We own an awful lot of stuff and now that we have moved in with stage three of your plan all four corporations are on their way back up. As a matter of fact, just today from the news of your recovery, our stock is back up to one-hundred and twenty-six-dollars a share. Not only that, but the Senate also passed a new law which states, 'all future multi-billion-dollar corporate takeovers must apply for Congressional approval first."

With that news, I asked the million-dollar question, "What happened to Lee and Tom after they lost everything?"

Jimmy smiled triumphantly, "Lee is once again fighting a Grand Jury Probe, but without the evidence you were going to give Senator Kenny, they still can't prove anything. As for Kenny, he went running home to his family with his tail between his legs. You really caused an-uproar this time, let me tell you."

Immediately a pleased expression lit up my exhausted face as I looked at Jimmy and Michael, "Well guys, that's great news, and I love you both with all my heart for being here for me, but I think I'd better get some rest now." I kissed them both and they left the room together.

The next morning, I had two poached eggs, toast and O.J. for breakfast and I devoured it all. Shortly after my second walk of the morning, I received a visit from a

American Goddess

Detective Jeremy Jones from the Las Vegas Homicide Division. After he introduced himself to Michael and me, he very bluntly said, "Ms. Powers, I just need to ask you a few questions on exactly what transpired the day of the shooting. Do you think you're up to it?"

I answered politely, "Yes, I think so. Go ahead and ask your questions."

He pulled out a pen and pad as he began, "What I need to know is how you both got shot?"

I shook my head in bewilderment, "I have been trying to remember as much as I can." At that, I proceeded to tell him everything I could remember about the fight, and after which I added, "I don't know how we both got shot, but I do know Frank pulled a gun on me and tried to kill me."

With a superior attitude he pressed on, "Well Ms. Powers, your story has a few things which don't seem to jive, so please try to remember everything you can. It would sure help us solve this case. I will be speaking to you again before you leave the hospital. Oh yes, please don't try to leave the state, or we'll just have to bring you back."

Curiously Michael asked, "Can you tell us what it is that doesn't 'jive', with Christina's story?"

He abruptly answered, "No, I'm sorry sir, I can't do that right now. I have to wait until all the evidence is in first." Then, he thanked us for our time, and left.

After he left Michael said, "I think we better call Tom Davies before you talk to him again."

With a concerned look I asked, "Why? Do you think I'm in some kind of trouble?"

Michael hugged me, "I don't know, I just didn't get a good feeling about the way he was questioning you. He acted as if he didn't believe you."

Feeling totally exhausted and overwhelmed, I sighed with frustration, "Then would you call Tom Davies and Lesley Steine for me? They're the two best attorneys we have."

Michael kissed me, "I think I'll go do that right now. Why don't you try to get some sleep before your next walk." He kissed me again and headed for the door.

As he left my room, I could tell he was concerned and I thought, "Oh, God! I pray I didn't kill Frank." I started to laugh to myself, "Oh well, if I did kill Frank, then he asked for it and if I didn't, I wish I had."

Finally, on December 24th, at 11:00am I was getting ready to be discharged from the hospital. I was going to be out of the hospital for Christmas, but I was still under a court order not to leave the state. Michael had just gone down to make sure the limo was waiting as close to the front entrance as possible, while I dressed in a two-piece, white business suit, with a knee length skirt, 'V' neck and matching jacket. We knew the parking lot was full of reporters, and fans. I also knew I had to face them, so I decided I wanted more of the sexy businesswoman look, rather than my standard superstar look. I was well aware my public was worried about me by the millions of telegrams and letters that were sent, all wishing me well. So I had to speak to them, but at the same time I wanted to make it as short as possible.

Michael and my sweet big black nurse arrived with a wheelchair to bring me downstairs and the nurse said, "Okay Christina, your ride out of this joint has come and I'm taking you to sweet freedom."

I happily took my seat, "Let's go, because I'm sure ready to get out of this place. Not that you guys weren't great, I just need to get out of here."

She laughed, "I don't blame you. You've been with us longer than most patients."

As we were getting ready to leave Michael said, "The place is mobbed worse than I thought it would be. There are camera crews from all over the world out there, all waiting to give the world just a glimpse of you." He knelt down in front of the wheelchair, "Punkie, are you sure you're ready to face them all? I can still get you out the back way."

I leaned forward and kissed him, "How do I look?"

He took a double take, "Great! I love the suit. Why?"

I smiled confidently, "Because I'm dressed to impress baby. So let's go do some impressing and get it over with."

He returned my kiss, "Okay, let's go get 'em, little girl." And off we went.

When we reached the hospital entrance, I climbed out of the wheelchair, opened the door, and with Michael and three bodyguards beside me, proceeded toward the large concrete staircase, which led down toward the front parking lot.

As soon as we came out from under the canopy which covered the front entrance, we hit the sunlight and were immediately swamped by the press and the clicking of their cameras. Then came the shouts of "We love you Christina," from my fans, who were being held back by Security Guards on both sides of the path to our limo.

From out of the crowd of reporters Connie Chuck yelled, "Christina, how are you feeling?"

I smiled, "I feel great! Don't I look it?"

She laughed, "You look as good as ever."

Kan Alh asked, "Christina, can you tell us how it feels to be so loved on Hollywood Boulevard and so feared on Wall Street?"

I smiled graciously as I triumphantly replied, "I love being loved on Hollywood Boulevard and I love being feared on Wall Street. So, I guess the answer is they both excite me."

Heraldo Saiviera shouted, "Christina, did you kill Frank Salerno?"

You know that saying, 'if looks could kill' well, if it were true, Heraldo would no longer be with us. Sternly I answered, "No! I did not kill Frank Salerno! Now, I think that will be enough questions, thank you very much Mr. Saiviera." Then I ended the press conference and began to head down the steps.

Just as I took my first step down, I watched in shock, as ten state police cars sped up to the front of the hospital with lights on and sirens blaring. It looked as if two-hundred state police officers jumped out of the ten cars, and they all came running toward me.

I thought I was going to die, when one of them said in front of the whole world, "Christina Powers, you are under arrest for the murder of Frank Salerno." Then, as he placed my hands behind my back and began to put handcuffs on me, he read me my rights. I was horrified as they led me away from Michael and straight through the shouts of the press and cries of horror from my shocked fans.

There I was, 'Christina Powers', "America's Sex Goddess" in handcuffs for the entire world to see and being carted off to jail!

When I arrived at the Las Vegas Court House and Jail, they took a mug shot, fingerprinted me, and put me in a holding pen until I could be brought to the judge for a bail hearing. I sat in that jail cell by myself, from 11:45am that morning, until 3:45pm. That's when Michael, Tom Davies, and Lesley Steine, entered my cell together. As soon as they did, I hugged Michael and said, "I have got to get out of here, or I will go nuts for sure."

Lesley hugged me, "Christina, I have been getting the run around all afternoon. The judge finally agreed to set your bail hearing for 4:30. What I could gather from my questioning is not too good. It appears Frank Salerno was well liked in this state. Everyone in political office, from the Mayor of Vegas to the Governor of the State of Nevada have been put there by Frank, and it sounds like they all want to see you hang for his murder."

I looked desperately at them all, "This can't be happening! I couldn't have killed Frank; I was shot remember. How the hell could I have killed him?"

Tom hugged me warmly and said, "As Lesley was trying to get a bail hearing, I was trying to find out what evidence they had to charge you with."

Anxiously I quickly replied, "What did you find out?"

He shook his head in dismay as he glanced at me, "Well to start, forensics shows Frank took the first shot fired from the 22-caliber handgun found at the crime scene. There were also gun powder burns on the palms of both his hands. This shows when the gun was fired, he was trying to take it from your hands. The second shot fired was at close range to you. The prosecution is going on the assumption; this is a failed, murder/suicide attempt." Then he took a breath, "To top it off, there are no other fingerprints on the gun but yours, and they still can't trace the gun back to its original owner, the serial number was illegible."

American Goddess

When he finished talking, my legs began to give out from under me, and I grabbed for Michael as I began to collapse. After he caught me, he helped me sit down on the small cot, and with a nervously excited tone asked, "Are you all right, Punkie?"

I slowly regained my composure, and with tears of fear filling my eyes pleaded, "Please guys, you have got to get me out of here! I know Frank had the gun, so if someone is saying mine were the only fingerprints on the gun, then they're lying." I stood up and with panic in my voice cried out, "Oh, God! Somehow, someone is trying to set me up!" Then, I turned to the three of them, "I'm afraid if they try to keep me here tonight, I might not be alive tomorrow!"

Michael immediately took my hand, "Christina, we have a bail hearing in fifteen minutes. No judge in his right mind is going to keep you in jail on Christmas Eve. Not with the world watching. It would be political suicide."

I looked dead in his eyes and with a fearful tone said, "Michael, you don't know this town like I do. If someone in high places wants me dead, the Las Vegas Jail is the place they would want me to be. Don't you see? If they're saying it was a failed suicide attempt, then there is a good chance you're going to find me hanging from a sheet in the morning."

Sternly, Lesley replied, "Christina, we are going to need you to be calm if we're going to get you out of this place. So please try to pull yourself together, and let's go see the judge before we all become hysterical." She then called for the guards and off we went.

The flashes of the press cameras were blinding as we reached the waiting area of the judge's chambers. I held my head high as I was led in handcuffs, by two female police officers past the furor of the press, straight into Judge Edward Homble's chambers, where I was taken to the defendant's chair, un-cuffed and asked to be seated. Michael took a seat behind me in the public seating section, as Lesley and Tom sat to the right of me at a narrow, six-foot-long table, which sat twelve-feet from and two-feet lower than Judge Homble's throne. Judge Homble was a gray headed, fifty-eight-year-old, right winged radical, who was appointed to his seat by Frank himself, and to add to my 'favor', he was a self-proclaimed bigot. The first thing he did was to order all the reporters out of his court room. He took one quick glance at me through condescending eyes and I knew I was in trouble. I watched in horror as he swiftly began to dispute both my attorneys' requests for bail.

After about twenty minutes of this, Lesley visibly frustrated said, "But Your Honor, my client just this morning, was released from the hospital. She is not physically capable of staying in custody. She also happens to be a World-Renown Figure, and she has no intention of breaking bail."

With that, the prosecuting attorney for the state of Nevada said, "Your Honor, I can bring witness after witness who will testify they heard the defendant state on numerous occasions she was going to kill Frank Salerno. Because of that, the state is seeking murder one in this case sir, and we also feel the defendant is more than capable of fleeing justice if she so desired. With these points in question, the State requests a denial of bail."

All at once, with a voice that thundered throughout the room, Judge Homble shouted as he slammed his gavel down, "The court hereby denies the defendant's request for bail. The defendant will remain in custody without bail until the completion of a trial by jury."

He stood up and began to step away from his throne and I shouted, "What the hell kind of bullshit is this! Do you know with whom you're dealing with my dear Judge Homble?"

In reply he shouted, "Counselor control your client, or I will hold her for contempt as well."

I felt fire in my eyes, and I knew for sure I was fighting for my life, so I shouted, "To hell with you, Judge! Do you really think I'm going to let you have someone put a noose around my neck and get away with it?" I shook my head, "It's not going to happen asshole. You should have looked really close at 'Christina Powers' before you decided to try to railroad me you stupid ass!" Two police officers once again handcuffed me and pulled me away as I shouted, "I'll be out of this place in two hours, Homble. And when this is over I'm coming after your career, you bastard!"

With anger in his voice, he turned to me, "Ms. Powers, I know damned well who you are and even you fall under the law of the land. So you're not going anywhere."

Even madder I shouted, "I am more than willing to come under the same law which governs us all your Honor, but I will not unjustly be prosecuted by **NO MAN**!"

By 5:10pm I was back in my dirty little cell, but I was determined not to stay there. I had Jimmy call Dominick, Michael call Barbara, and Tom Davies was trying to reach President Feagan himself. I figured among the three of them, someone would get me out of this place. Finally, around 9:45pm after the clamor from the crowds in the streets began to subside, I heard the sounds of footsteps echoing in the brick hallway. The sound was growing louder, the closer they came to my cell. My heart began to pound as thoughts raced through my mind, "Is this my way out or is this someone who is here to kill me?" When the sound reached my cell, I was stunned to see the vice-president of the United States, who was also the new President-elect, George Rush, standing on the other side of the bars.

Although I was shocked, I did not allow my face to show my surprise as I said, "George, it's so good to see you again."

George smiled sweetly, "Christina, it's wonderful to see you looking so well after your narrow escape. And you'll be happy to hear I have come to personally release you on your own recognizance." Then, the guard opened the door and out I walked through a back entrance with George, to three waiting limos. We climbed into his limo and off we went.

George and I had locked horns over political issues in the past, but as for our personal relationship, we had always treated one another with the utmost respect. Although I didn't always agree with George, I did however trust him; that is why I climbed into his limo without asking where we were going, or why he came in person. I was only glad to see him.

As we sped away from the courthouse, George said, "Christina, this is not just a one purpose trip for me. I have come to get you out of jail, but I have also come for something else as well. You happen to have something I would like you to give to me."

I smiled seductively, then innocently glanced into his eyes as I said with a chuckle, "George, I'm flattered, I didn't realize you cared so much." He began to blush, so I kissed his cheek and added, "All right I'll stop the joking, and be good now. So, how can I help you Mr. soon to be President?"

He wiped the perspiration from his forehead, "Woah! I almost forgot what I was talking about."

I smiled again as I took his hand, "You were about to ask me for something, and I was about to say thank you for rescuing me from that horrid place." I let go of his hand and continued, "If I can help you George, I will, so please go on."

Looking dead into my eyes and with a completely serious tone he said, "It has come to my attention you possess some very damaging information on Senator Bradford. Well, I am going to be blunt. I need that information."

I looked at him strangely, "Are you aware of what is contained in the information I have in my possession?"

Still with a serious look he answered, "I am well aware of the content, that's why I do not want this information made public. If this information is leaked, it could jeopardize the security of our nation."

I looked at him and wondered, 'How could this information jeopardize National Security?' as I said, "You're the President, George. Who am I to jeopardize our nation? You will have the one and only copy of this information in existence in two days and I will never speak of the matter again."

A look of relief came over him as he smiled, "That's a very wise decision Christina, and I thank you myself, and for the President."

When the limo arrived at my hotel, George took my hand and said, "I hope everything works out for you with the case, Christina. And if there is any way I can help you again in the future, please let me know."

I tenderly squeezed his hand as I softly kissed his cheek one more time, "Thank you George, and I wish you all the best with your 'Presidency' as well. I would also like to extend the same courtesy to you, if you should ever need my help in the future, please call."

I climbed out of his limo and was escorted by three secret service men to my suite at Caesar's Palace Hotel and Casino, which by the way, now belonged to me.

As soon as I opened the door I was greeted by the worried loving hugs of Michael and Jimmy. The first thing they both asked was, "What happened?"

Excitedly Jimmy said, "Tom Davies already told us George Rush was going to be bringing you home himself. What did he say?" I told Jimmy as much as I wanted him to know. Later that night while in bed, I told Michael everything which transpired between George and me.

At 9:30 on Christmas morning I was informed by Tom Davies, via a phone call that a jury would be picked after the first of the year, and the trial date was set for January 21st, 1989, at 9:00am. All that day Michael, Jimmy, and I tried to have a Merry Christmas, but none of us could get the murder trial off our minds. Then I got sad because Michael and I had missed our wedding; and to top it off, when we exchanged gifts around 7:00pm that evening, I didn't have one thing to give either one of them. So, I raised a toast with my tenth cup of coffee and said, "I wish the best to the two most important people in my life on this Christmas day. May I also say, please don't expect much from me this year, I was on vacation and it slipped my mind."

I began to laugh and as I laughed, Jimmy handed Michael a gift, turned to me and with the flick of that wrist said, "Sorry, girlfriend! We didn't think you were going to be with us this year, so we didn't get you anything either." With that we lost it! We laughed so hard; we all went running for the bathrooms!

I received a call at 10:00pm on Christmas night from Dominick Giovanetti. He was calling in response to Jimmy's call for help. When Michael handed me the phone, I said, "Dominick, thank you for calling, and thank you for saving Powers Incorporated. I'll never know how to thank you enough."

Dominick's voice cracked emotionally, "Christina, I'm just pleased you're still with us. After Jimmy told me what happened, I made some calls. I found out a few very interesting things. First, no one has tampered with the gun at the forensics lab. Somehow, between the time you were shot, and the time Michael broke into the room, someone either wiped off Frank's fingerprints and put the gun in your hand, or you had the gun all along little girl."

Urgently I replied, "Dominick, I swear I did not have that gun."

With a concerned tone he said, "Then someone is setting you up. I'll continue looking from my end, and I'll keep you informed. But we now have a wild card thrown into the works, which you're going to have to watch out for. It seems Anthony has taken control

American Goddess

of his father's position as head of the Salerno Family. Word on the street is he has blood in his eyes for you."

Frustrated I said, "Great! What's next, a round of machine gun fire as I'm driving down the road?"

"All I'm saying is increase your security, at least until I can try to get a handle on this." Then, with that deep Italian accent of his, "Abafangul girl, when you start shit, you really start shit."

I laughed a little, "Thanks for the vote of confidence."

As soon as I ended my conversation, I called Tom and Lesley, whose rooms were on the same floor as our suite and had them come in to meet with us right away. They arrived together at around 11:00pm and I told them, along with Michael and Jimmy, exactly what I had just learned from Dominick.

Tom said, "It could have been done. Lesley and I were at the crime scene just two hours ago, and there is a back entrance into Frank's office." He turned to Michael and added, "Michael, how long after the second shot did you and the guards break in the door?"

Michael scratched his head, "I'd say two minutes."

Tom snapped his fingers together, "That's it! Two minutes would have been more than enough time for someone who could have possibly been in the next room, to come in right after the second shot was fired. How long could it take for whomever to take the gun out of Frank's hand, wipe the prints off and place it in your hand? Except this time, the only prints on the gun would be yours. Then they could have slipped out of the room with no one seeing them."

"But who?" I asked with intensity.

He smiled confidently, "There can't be too many people with access to Frank's private entrance. All we have to do is find out who had that access, and then start eliminating suspects."

The next few months the craziness started all over again. I had so many psychological and physiological evaluations by the time the trial started, I felt like a guinea pig. Then once again the press was up my ass twenty-four hours a day, and once again I was going crazy. You'd think I would have handled the pressure better by now, but this time it was my neck on the line. The trial was delayed for weeks, as the attorneys from both sides, struggled to select an impartial jury. On April 21st, 1989, a jury was finally chosen, and a new trial date was set for May 2nd.

By the time the trial date came around, the whole world was anticipating the Frank Salerno murder trial, "Starring 'yours truly'!" My attorneys and I had been over every detail of my case, at least one thousand times, by the time we entered that Las Vegas

American Goddess

Court House, for the first day of what would captivate the entire world for eight grueling weeks of my life.

The prosecution for the state was District Attorney Samuel Perry. Sam was a short fat pudgy nosed, twenty-eight-year-old tiger, who was going to make a name for himself by frying my ass. Sam was playing for keeps and he came out swinging with both fists, with his opening statement to the Jury; as we sat in front of the, oh so humble, Judge Edward Homble, with the eyes of the world upon us.

Sam waddled up to the Jury Box with his hands behind his back, "Ladies and gentlemen of the Jury, the people of the State of Nevada intend to prove, beyond the shadow of a doubt, that the defendant, Christina Powers, is a calculating cold blooded killer, who ruthlessly planned the demise of her Uncle's fortune. Then, she took his life upon the news he would soon be in custody for the murder of her daughter. I must remind you now no matter what the circumstances, you must remember, no one is above the law. We cannot allow the driven passions of a grieving mother, to take the law into her own hands and commit cold blooded murder. We are going to show the defendant and the victim, have been consumed by a personal vendetta toward one another for the past sixteen years, which culminated with the murder of Frank Salerno and a failed suicide attempt by the defendant, Christina Powers. Now, I thank you for your time and I ask you to judge this case by the law, not by the emotional pleas you will receive from the Defense Counsel." Then, he nodded to the Jury, turned, and waddled back to his seat.

We had no proof of our suspicion I may have been framed, so we were forced to plead self-defense.

At that point, it was Lesley Steines turn. She was the one we chose to give the opening address for our side. She was a tall, slim, dark haired, thirty-six-year-old, Jewish girl from Queens. She had enough spunk and mental sharpness, to be the envy of most female attorneys, and I liked that. Lesley appeared more than qualified, as she confidently approached the jury, and she looked very professional in her custom made, dark blue designer suit.

As she reached the Jury Box she stopped, and slowly turned her head to gaze into each one of the juror's eyes, as she said, "Ladies and gentlemen of the jury, the prosecution made a very good point when he used the words, 'beyond the shadow of a doubt;' because that is the key to justice in our nation's judicial system. You must be convinced beyond the shadow of a doubt, that the defendant you are being asked to convict for murder in the first degree, is guilty of murder in the first degree. We, the members of the Defense intend to show there are too many shadows in the prosecution's case, to ever seriously consider prosecuting our client. The first question to be answered should be whether this is truly a murder case, as the prosecution believes, or was it actually a case of self-defense? We intend to show the court our client was brutally beaten by the so-called victim, before our client ever pulled the trigger on the gun which took the life of the man who was trying to kill her. Now, I would like to ask you individually and as a group, to consider this possibility as the trial proceeds. I also thank you all for your time and I ask one more thing as the evidence unfolds. Please remember, guilt must be proven beyond the shadow of a doubt." She nodded her head to the jury, walked back to her seat beside mine, and the trial of the century began.

From that moment on May 2nd, and day-after-day, there were numerous witness testimonies and cross examinations by the prosecution and the defense. The prosecution brought in every person who knew anything at all about my dispute with, and distaste for, Frank. And let me tell you, God knows, enough people knew. We spent the first four weeks of the trial just questioning personal character witnesses. I was so drained by the time the trial finally got around to forensic evidence; I hardly knew what the hell they were talking about. Lesley and Tom decided not to put me on the stand unless I could remember something more substantial. They felt I would give the prosecution more help, then I would be worth in my own defense. So I sat there day-after-day, all day long, just listening and watching as so much evidence piled up against me that eventually, even I was starting to believe I killed him. By the time the eighth week arrived, things were looking pretty bad for my case. It seemed no matter what angle we would take with the case, the prosecution kept coming back to their one hard piece of evidence, the gun with only my fingerprints on it.

On June 27th, at 10:00am we finally got around to the eight people subpoenaed from Salerno Incorporated who had access to Frank's private back entrance. Tom Davies called his first witness of the day, Kathy Brown, to the witness stand. Kathy glided to the witness stand, just like a perfect lady should. She raised her right hand and swore on the Bible with her left hand, to tell the truth and nothing but the truth so help her God. Kathy seemed somehow fragile looking as she climbed on the witness stand, but when she sat facing us and started her testimony, she became what she was, a lying, scheming bitch.

As I listened to her lying, I became angry and I thought, "Why you no good, bitch!" Then I thought, "Who are you to judge! You're looking at her is just like looking in a mirror!" After I chastised myself, I felt utter disgust for my own actions and I thought, "Dear God! Is there any hope for any of us here in this life?" As Kathy answered the questions to the best of her recollection, I closed my eyes and began to drift away.

As I drifted off into a dream state, I felt myself lifting out of my body. I began to gently float above the drama being played out in the court room. As I began to soar through the skies, I was praying for my memory to come back. As I searched through the stars looking for an answer to my prayer, I noticed a bright light glistening off in the distance through the darkness of space. I soared toward the warmth of the light with every drop of strength I had. When I reached it, I was greeted by a golden winged angel and I found myself in awe of her impressive beauty. As I gazed at her, she reached out and without saying a word took my hand and began to lead me into the white light. She took me to an enormous emerald mansion in the heavens, where she led me into a large diamond-glistening room. She placed my hands on a beautiful tear drop shaped crystal which was suspended in the center of the room. As I held my hands on that crystal, its reflection showed everything which happened that fateful day of Frank's death, like a TV screen.

When I opened my eyes, I was once again in the court room and I was stunned to see Anthony on the witness stand.

I caught my breath, stood up, pointed at Anthony, as Tom questioned him and shouted, "I remember it all now! You did it, Anthony! You cleaned the fingerprints off the gun."

Judge Homble shouted, "Order in the court! Counselor control your client," as Anthony shouted, "She's crazy! I don't know what she's talking about!"

Tom came to me, "Do you want a recess?"

"No! Put me on the stand now!" I demanded. "I remember what happened."

He nodded his head, "Your Honor, I am finished with this witness for now. At this time, I would like to call, Christina Powers to the stand."

You could hear a pin drop as I walked up to the witness stand, swore on the Bible and took my seat. Tom approached me, "Ms. Powers, would you please tell us in your own words what happened on December 2nd, 1988?"

I took a deep breath, "When I went into Frank's office with the others, I didn't expect to see him. When I did see him there, I began to order him out of the office. I told him the police were coming to arrest him for the murder of my baby and I couldn't stand to look at him anymore. Then, he asked to speak to me in private and when I accepted, I asked to be left alone with Frank for five minutes. As soon as everyone left the room, Frank pulled a gun out and said he was going to kill me. We began to fight over the gun and somehow, I got a hold of it. I ran to the door with the gun still in my hand, and Frank jumped me again. This time the gun went off and as soon as I heard the shot, I let go of the gun and screamed. As Frank began to fall backwards, he pulled the trigger of the gun, which was now in his hand and shot me. As I was falling, I saw Anthony come into the room through the back door. As I lay on the floor bleeding, Anthony took the gun from his father's hand, wiped it off and placed it in my hand."

With that Anthony immediately stood up and began to leave the court room. As he did Judge Homble sternly ordered him, "Mr. Salerno, please don't try to leave just yet. I'm sure the counselor will want to recall you to the stand."

Anxiously Anthony said, as a Court Guard approached him, "I don't know what she's talking about and I'm going to call my attorney."

American Goddess

Instantly I added, "There was also a witness to this scene your, Honor!"
Then in front of the eyes of the entire world, Kathy Brown stood up and shouted,
"Christina! I'm sorry! He said he would kill me if I told!"

Just as soon as she said those words, Anthony pulled the Court Guard's gun out of
its holster and shot, **"Bang!"** killing the guard instantly! He turned toward Kathy and in
the midst of the screams of the courtroom, '**Bang**' he shot again, hitting her right between
the eyes. I watched in horror as he took aim at me this time, '**Bang**' came a third shot only
this one came from a guard who shot Anthony dead. I screamed as I watched this
nightmare unfold in front of my eyes. I jumped off the witness stand and ran to Michael
crying hysterically.

My mind and body were totally numb when Michael and Jimmy helped me walk out
of that Las Vegas Court room on June 27th, 1989. As Michael pushed our way through the
midst of the frantic pace of the police and emergency medical crews, all I could think of
was Kathy and the horrible way she had just died. Then like a slap across the face, we
walked right into the press with their cameras and a million questions and I couldn't utter
a word. As stunned as I was from my emotional trauma, when we reached the madness
of the cheering crowds out in front of that courthouse, I emerged a **vindicated woman
and a national hero**.

That afternoon I was on the front pages of every newspaper in the world, and for
the next two weeks I had top billing on every news broadcast in the country. The
headlines read, **"Christina Powers, found innocent in the most dramatic court trial in
history."**

CHAPTER 19

As for the response of my fans to my personal triumph and tragedy, it was
overwhelming.   Once again, I received millions upon millions of cards and letters from
all over the world, all sharing their love and support.

Within two days of the trial, I received requests from every single woman's
association in existence, all asking me to address women's groups on how a woman can

achieve corporate success in a man's world.   I was also the main topic in every coffee shop, hair salon, gin mill, and grocery story in the nation.   The court trial turned out to be a publicity agent's wet dream, as my record sales and requests for personal appearances soared.   But, with the way I was feeling, I could not have cared less. I went into a state of depression immediately after Kathy Brown's funeral. The service was held three days after her death on June 30th in her hometown of Kittery, Maine.

You see, Kathy Brown's funeral turned out to be quite an emotional and awakening experience for me.   It was 11:00am when I stood beside Barbara on a rainy Maine day at the cemetery where Kathy was being laid to rest, I found out her war with me ended many years ago, when she apologized to me after our fight.

As we stood there in the rain listening to the eulogy, Barbara inconspicuously turned to me and whispered, "Christina, I know you're here because of what happened in the courtroom, otherwise you wouldn't be here."

I thought for a moment about what Barbara had just said to me, looked at her honestly and said, "You're absolutely right; I have hated Kathy for sixteen years, but when she stood up in that courtroom and said what she did, I truly forgave her for all of it."

Barbara took my hand squeezed it and replied, "I'm glad to hear you say that Christina, because there is a lot more about Kathy you don't know."

I looked at her with questioning eyes as I said, "Now that came from out of the blue! So what are you trying to say?"

Barbara tilted her head even closer to mine and in almost a whisper, "Kathy never wanted you to know, but she was the one who kept saving your ass from Frank."

My eyes grew large as I said, "Why would she risk her neck like that for me, and not tell me about it?"

Barbara gave me a look of disbelief as she answered, "Come on Christina don't tell me you really don't know?"

I was baffled and annoyed by her response to my question and it showed on my face as I snapped at her in a tone just above a whisper, "I really don't know what you're talking about Barbara, so if you have something to say to me, then for God's sake girl, spit it out. I'm not up to your guessing games today."

She let go of my hand and sarcastically snapped her reply back as everyone was beginning to take notice of us, "For just one reason Christina, she didn't trust you any more than she ever really trusted Frank. You know, sometimes I can't believe someone as intelligent as you can be so dense." Her voice level went up an octave, "Christina, because I love you, I'm going to be honest with you.   Don't you see over the years you have become just as vindictive as Frank was?   So please, for your own good, wise up and start looking at how you have been treating people.   Then reflect a moment on Frank and how he dealt with people, you may surprise yourself."

American Goddess

With that, Barbara turned to walk away and just as she did, Kathy's Mother caught us both off guard by appearing right in front of us.   She just stood there for a moment looking at us both with disgust in her eyes.   She cleared her cracking voice until she could finally say, "What kind of people are you two, arguing at my daughter's funeral? Don't either one of you have any respect for the dead at all?"   At that she placed her hands to her face and began to cry.   With compassion, I reached out for her and with all her might she slapped me right across the face and said, "You are just as evil as Reverend Timmy Swinebert says you are.   Now take your wickedness with you and let my daughter rest in peace.   Because I rebuke you!   You demon from hell!" Then she began crying hysterically.

I stood there stunned, looking at her for a moment.   Then I held my head up high as I turned and trampled through the mud past Kathy's angry and grieving family.   When I reached the limo, I climbed in and said as I started to cry, "James, get me the hell out of here!"

On the road back home, I was wishing Michael had come with me.   I had decided I wanted to attend the funeral alone, so I asked Michael not to come.   I also told him, I wanted to take the ride by myself, but he insisted James take me in the limo.   After my encounters with Barbara and Mrs. Brown, I was glad he did, because there was no way I would have been able to drive back home.   I was feeling so miserable after the two good blows I had just taken to my self-esteem that I would have never made it, and my tears showed it.

As we headed west on the Massachusetts Turnpike, I was reliving the drama which took place at Kathy's funeral, over and over again in my mind.   I wondered to myself, if I was as bad as they seemed to think I was.   With these thoughts racing through my mind, I brought down the partition between James who was driving, and myself in the back seat.   When the partition was completely down, I said, "James, may I ask you something?"   James gazed at me through the rearview mirror and said, "Of course, Christina."

I looked into his eyes through the mirror and with a sincere tone asked, "James, what do you think of me as a person?"

James smiled warmly, "Christina, I think you're the most incredible person I have ever met.   That's what I think about you as a person."

I managed half a smile, "Thank you James, but I sure don't feel incredible, I feel like a horrible person right now."

With a sympathetic tone he replied, "Christina, I saw and heard what Mrs. Brown did and said to you, so I do understand why you are feeling like you do, but it's not true.   I have known you for a long time now Christina, and all I can say is Carman and I love you. There happens to be a reason for that, and it has nothing to do with the overwhelming salary you pay us either." He shook his head as if to say, 'you should know this', "Christina, it's because of who you are as a person, and how you treat us as people. I guess what I'm trying to say is, you're real Christina. Carman and I have worked for other important people before, but not one of them was ever genuine. Not one ever truly cared how either one of us might be feeling from day to day. But not you, you treat us like family, not like servants. If there was ever any one person who I believed deserved to be treated like royalty, it's you. But instead, you treat us with the kind of respect there should be between a child and a parent, and we love you like one of our own daughters because of it."

My eyes began to tear from James' kind words, "Thank you again James, I only wish I felt the same about myself." My tears began to roll off my cheeks as I added, "Right now, I feel like the kind of person who just caused the **'deaths of three people'**. James may God forgive me, because I have allowed my desire for revenge to take over my every thought, until I not only destroyed Frank financially, but I took his life as well. I chose to build my life around my desire to have revenge on Frank, and what did it get me? Nothing but sixteen pain fought years, which ended up with just another trip to a cemetery, because I refused to forgive. James, how can I take pride in achieving something which no one will even care about, because none of it matters anymore?"

James handed me a tissue, "Christina, the whole world has stood up and taken notice to what you have accomplished in the past sixteen years, and believe me, it does matter to every person whose life has been touched by the good you've done. So please stop condemning yourself for something you had no control over and let yourself live again."

I used the tissue when James finished speaking and said, "I only wish it were that simple James, but it's not. Somehow, I am going to have to find a way to make up for all the hurt I've caused, or I will never get past this moment in time."

With a reassuring tone James replied, "Christina, I don't know how to help you, but I do know you will come through this tragedy just as you have in the past."

Sincerely I said, "James, thank you for answering my question, now if you'll excuse me, I think I'll rest until we arrive home." Then I closed the partition along with my weary eyes.

It was 4:10pm and still raining when we pulled into the underground garage of our home on the grounds of the Corporate Headquarters of Powers Incorporated. As soon as I entered the house, I called Michael who was at the office and told him I was home. I explained to him some of what transpired at the funeral, and mentioned I was going to try to keep my 5:00pm appointment with my new gynecologist, a Doctor Steven Hart. His office was in Poughkeepsie, so I had to run, but I would tell him more later that evening.   When we finished our conversation, I grabbed the keys to Jimmy's favorite white 1987 town-car and left for my doctor's appointment.

I inconspicuously entered Doctor Hart's reception room and signed in. When the receptionist read my name, she immediately took me to Steven's private office and told me the doctor would be in shortly. As soon as Doctor Hart entered the room, he reached out his hand to shake mine, and as I stood up from my seat he said, "Christina, it's so good to see you again. I have received your records from Doctor Sonne yesterday and I went over them all last night. So let's sit for a minute and I'll tell you what I know."

As we sat down, I said, "Steven, all I really want to know is what I can do to become pregnant again?"

He lifted his eyebrows discontentedly and said, "Christina, from what I could see from your files and from what Doctor Sonne has told me personally, I don't think you will ever be able to conceive a child again." I knew he could see from the expression on my face I was not pleased. Then he slapped his hands together and added, "But I will not know for sure, until I look myself. So why don't we do the examination first, then we'll talk more."

I tried to smile as I said, "Oh well!   At least that gives me something to hope for."

After the examination Steven said, "Christina, I must be up front with you. From what I could see, I would recommend a hysterectomy as soon as possible, just to make sure you do not accidentally become impregnated. Your uterus is so fragile; it would be life threatening for you to try to carry a full-term pregnancy. It would tear your uterus apart. So until you decide when to have the surgery, I'm putting you on oral contraceptives and I want you to take them."

With that cheerful news, I took a deep breath and said with utter frustration, "Oh well! I guess that's that, then. There will be no more children for Christina Powers. It looks like Frank will indeed have the last laugh."

Steven looked at me strangely then said, "This doesn't mean you will never be able to have a child again Christina, there is still adoption."

Sadly, I stood up and said, "Thank you Steven, I know you're right. I'm just not having a very good day today, so I think I'll go home for now and figure this one out tomorrow." I shook his hand and left his office with my heart breaking again.

After dinner that evening Michael, Jimmy, and I, went out on the back porch with our cocktails to watch the rain splashing on the surface of the river. As the three of us sat on lawn chairs watching the rain, I was sitting between the two of them, and sadly began to tell them what happened at Kathy's funeral. In an even sadder voice, I told them what Doctor Hart had said. Then with tears in my eyes, I looked at Michael and added, "Michael, I will never be able to bear your child."

American Goddess

Michael reached over and took my hand, "I love you Punkie, and I can live without having a child of my own. Why don't we try to adopt?"

I squeezed his hand as I sadly answered, "I know we can adopt, but that's not the point. I wanted to give you a child from your seed."

Jimmy took my other hand and said, "If you really want Michael's biological child that badly, then why don't you look into finding a surrogate mother?"

As soon as Jimmy finished talking, Carman came out onto the porch with the cordless phone and said, "Excuse me Christina, but Barbara is on the line for you. Would you like to speak to her?"

I reached for the phone, "Yes I would, thank you, Carman." Carman handed me the phone and left as I said, "Hi Barbara, how are you?"

"Not too good Christina," she replied. "But I still wanted to call you and tell you I'm very sorry for what I said to you this morning."

I brushed my hand through my hair and said with concern, "Barbara, I forgive you and I'm also sorry, but as for my reaction it was because I was shocked. You came out of nowhere this morning and I had no idea what you were talking about. Why in the world would you pick Kathy's funeral to start telling me how she helped me?"

I could hear Barbara's voice begin to breakup, "Christina, what you don't know is that I've been in a lot of pain since Kathy's death. Although you and I have been the best of friends for years' now, I have not been totally honest with you about myself." Starting to cry harder she continued, "You see Christina, Kathy and I had been secret lovers since the night you took Tony away from her at the Governor's Ball in Hawaii. So I not only lost my best friend, I lost my lover too."

I could feel her pain and my heart went out for her as I spoke with compassion, "Oh God!   Barbara, I'm so sorry. Why didn't you tell me? You could have trusted me Barbara. You should have known that."

Quickly she replied, "I know Christina, but I was honoring Kathy's wishes. You must be able to understand that?"

Sympathetically I answered, "I do understand Barbara, and once again I'm sorry, girlfriend. I only wish I'd known."

She stopped crying and said, "I'm sorry I never told you Christina, but I wanted to tell you before I leave the states tomorrow."

With a surprised tone I replied, "I didn't know you were leaving the country. Where are you going?"

Sadly she answered, "I'm heading for Israel in the morning to begin shooting the new screenplay Kathy and I wrote together."

With curiosity I asked, "Where are you now, Barbara?"

"I'm at my Manhattan penthouse. I'm leaving from Kennedy at 11:00am.

American Goddess

So I think I'll say goodbye for now Christina, because I'm really beat."

Not knowing what to say, I simply replied, "All right girlfriend, take care of yourself and remember I love you."

"I love you too Christina, goodbye."   She replied with a saddened tone.

When I hung up the phone, I thought to myself, 'I wish I could be there for her right now, I think she could use my company.'

I was in that state of mind for about a minute before Michael snapped me out of it by saying, "What's going on Christina, is Barbara all right?"

I placed the phone on my lap and answered, "She is still very upset over Kathy's death. I didn't know it, but they were best friends."

Michael leaned over, kissed my cheek and said, "Come on Punkie, let's go to bed."

He stood up, took my hand, and pulled my tired body out of the chair. We both said good night to Jimmy and headed for our bedroom.   When we entered the bedroom, we undressed and climbed right into bed together.   I was really very tired and not feeling romantic at all when Michael kissed my cheek, and gently began to stroke my nude body with his strong right hand.   As he began to stir my passion, I stopped him, "Michael, honey, I really don't feel up to making love tonight."

He kissed me tenderly, "I understand, Punkie.   Why don't we look at the calendar, and set a new date before we go to sleep?"

I looked at him strangely, "What date are you talking about?"   He lifted his eyebrows like, 'Duh' and said, "What date!   Our wedding date!   Remember?   We missed it, you were in prison."

I shook my head in disbelief and replied, "Oh God!   Honey, I can't think about a wedding date now.   I just lived through hell, came out of it to discover I can't even have your child, and you want me to start smiling and plan a happy wedding.   Well I can't work like that Michael; I need to sort through my feeling's some first.   Then maybe we can reset our date, so please don't start with me about it okay."

His face showed his surprise at my statement as he said, "I didn't mean to upset you, Christina.   All I wanted to do was get you thinking about something pleasant.   But it sounds like I may have made a bigger mistake than I thought when I heard you say, 'maybe we can reset the date'."   Then he turned his back to me and flicked off the light. I immediately flicked on my reading light, hopped out of the bed and began to get dressed.

Michael quickly turned back toward me and asked, "What are you putting your clothes on for?"

I turned to him and with anger in my voice, "You know what Michael, I can't handle this bullshit right now, so I'm going for a ride."

Michael hopped out of the bed, "Going out!   It's 11:00pm and its pouring out there, and you think you're going for a ride?"

American Goddess

I looked at him as I tied my sneaker, "Michael, I don't think I'm going for a ride, I'm going for a ride."

Michael began to slip on his pants as he said, "Well, I don't want you going for a ride."

I finished tying my other sneaker, stood up and said, "Right now Michael, I don't care if you want me going for a ride or not.   I'm going for a ride anyway.   I love you Michael, but you are really pissing me off right now.   Just who do you think you are, my boss? Well, I think it's time you get off your power trip, because you're trying to run my every move, and I'm getting sick of it."   Then I headed out of the room with Michael in hot pursuit.

When I reached the garage door, Michael grabbed my hand, "Christina, please I'm telling you not to go out there as angry as you are and leave me here alone to worry about you."

I pulled my hand out of his and sharply said, "Michael, don't do this to me.   Don't tell me what to do, because I'm going for a ride for my own mental well-being so now please excuse me." Then I walked back to Jimmy's Town car and drove away.

Ten minutes after leaving the house, I found myself on Route 87, heading south toward Manhattan.   When I reached the Harriman exit, I picked up the car phone and dialed our private bedroom number.

Michael picked the phone up on the first ring and anxiously said, "Christina, are you alright!?"

"No not really Michael. I've calmed down some and I just wanted to say I love you." I started to cry as I added, "Michael, I'm just feeling really bad right now.   I didn't mean all those things I said, I was just taking my frustrations out on you baby, that's all, and I'm sorry."

Tenderly he replied, "Don't cry Punkie, I love you too.   Where are you?"

"I'm on the Thruway heading south."

"Why don't you come home Punkie, and let me hold you," he answered anxiously. "I feel so empty without you being here, and I miss the hell out of you already."

"Michael, I miss you too, but I want to go spend a few hours with Barbara before she leaves tomorrow.   So I'll see you in the morning all right?"

Sadly, he replied, "Okay Punkie if that's what you want.   I love you and I'll see you tomorrow, just drive carefully."

"I will, and I love you too, Michael."   Then I broke the connection with Michael, and dialed Barbara's private number.

CHAPTER 20

She picked up on the tenth ring and sounded slightly incoherent when she said, "Hiii, who a, who is thisss?"

I answered with concern, "It's me Barbara, Christina.   Why are you slurring your words?"

"I'm, I'm a little tired Christina, that's all.   What a a a, time isss it anyway?"

"It's midnight and I'll be pulling into your parking garage in two minutes.   So wake up and call the security office, and tell them to let me in.   Then put on some coffee and I'll see you in ten minutes." I waited a few seconds for a response from Barbara, but none came so I shouted, "Barbara!   Can you hear me?"

A groggy voice answered, "Yes, I hear you."   Then she hung up the phone.

When I pulled into the garage of her building, I drove up to the security guard at the gate and said with a smile, "Hi, I'm Barbara's guest, and I'm hoping she just called to inform you to expect me?"

He smiled back, "Yes Ms. Powers, she just called.   You can leave your car here and we'll park it for you."

When Barbara finally answered the door, she reeked of alcohol and looked like hell. I walked in past her as she held onto the door for balance. I grabbed her, held her up with one hand, and closed the door with the other.   I hugged her and with compassion said, "I know girlfriend, losing someone you love is the worst hurt in the world."

I walked her toward the kitchen, turned on the dim stove light and sat her on a chair at the table.   Barbara sat there with her head buried in her curled-up arms on the kitchen table, as I proceeded to put on a pot of coffee.   As the coffee brewed, I took a seat beside Barbara, gently rubbed her back and said, "What did you mix with the booze, Barbara?"

She rolled her head toward me, "I've been snorting coke and gulping gin since 2:00pm this afternoon, and I feel like I'm dying."

I chuckled, "Well, you look like you're not far from it.   So we're going to pump you up with some coffee and have a heart to heart chat."

I got up and fixed us both the first of many cups of coffee that night.   We talked about our lives, our loves and where we hoped our futures would go.   Then I'll never forget it, it was around 1:15am when Barbara grabbed my hand and said, "Christina I have something of yours and I need to talk to you about it." Then she got up and went into her bedroom. When she returned, she had an envelope in her hand, handed it to me and said,

American Goddess

"I have had this for years, but I could not give it to you until now. Your real mother gave this to me two weeks before her death. I knew your real mother and father. Your mother was my best friend. When she gave me this envelope she said, "If anything should ever happen to me, please look out for my sweet little angel. And don't give this to her until you know she will be safe.'

I opened the envelope and inside was the original copy of my birth certificate. It read, "Mother: Norma Jean Montensel. Father: John Fitzgerald Kenny. Child: Christina Kenny."   I was shocked as I read it and thought, 'Oh my God! It's true! I am her daughter, and he is my father!'   Then I got angry and asked, "Why did you take so long to tell me this!?"

She took my hand softly, "Baby, your mother asked me not to tell you until I thought you'd be safe with this information."

I pulled my hand from hers angrily, "Why would she leave me with someone like Frank?"

Barbara Replied swiftly, "She left you with Frank because she was being watched by the FBI from the moment, she first met your father. When you were born, she was afraid that if the Kenny family discovered that you were John's child, they would have made you disappear. When your mother gave me this envelope, I didn't even know you existed. Marilyn told me that in 1953 when you were born Frank was her best friend and she trusted him. At that time, she knew he was the only one who had the power to keep you safe from the Kenny family. Christina, I was afraid to give this to you as long as Frank was alive. Your mother told me that after she sang happy birthday to your father on national TV, Frank became furious with her. When she returned to Frank's to see you, he asked her to marry him. When she refused, she told him that she was taking you and starting a new life. She told me that Frank went crazy as soon as she said it and wrapped his hands around her throat and nearly choked the life from her. When she came Frank told her she would never see you again if she refused to marry him. She escaped from his grasp and ran away from him as fast as she could.   That's when she came to me. That's when she gave me this envelope and left, and I never saw your mother alive again after that night. What she did Christina was save your life." Then she took my hand and added, "Look in the envelope again."

I started to tremble as I noticed a handwritten note with a photo of Marylyn Monroe and myself as a small child smiling at a child's tea party.   I could hardly breathe as I opened the note and began to read my mother's words,

"My beautiful Christina, I instructed Barbara, my longtime friend, to give you this letter in the event of my death. You see my darling daughter, I am your real mother and have spent all these many years watching you grow up, but afraid to approach you for fear that your father and his family would endanger your safety in some way. I met

your Dad at a dinner party, and we were immediately attracted to one another. In time we began a secret affair because your father was already married. He led me to believe he would leave the marriage for me. Only we discovered that his family and his father's political ambitions for your dad would not permit that to happen.   I had just discovered that I was carrying you, when your father stated that we could never be together and our affair would have to remain a secret, he said, "The world can never know."   At that moment, I became afraid to tell him about you. You see your father was a United States Senator and came from a very rich and powerful family. I knew they were capable of taking any action to protect their son's political aspirations and I had to keep you safe.

   I know the world will say that I was just another dumb blonde sex symbol, but I am far from that my sweet Christina.   I didn't tell anyone that you were born because I was afraid for your safety.   That is why I asked Frank to raise you.   I turned to Frank who was my friend because he was rich and powerful.   I entrusted him with you swearing him to secrecy.   I knew that he could protect you and also give you a beautiful home with anything that you wanted until I could come and take you away with me. Then, your dad ran for the office of President of the United States and won. All those years I never stopped loving him and when he became President, I knew I could never tell him about you or how much I still loved him. Even though I married several times, no one replaced him in my heart. When I finally reestablished a relationship with your dad, I thought he was going to walk away from everything for me; only I discovered that was not true.   It was then that the FBI began to watch my every move and I became even more paranoid about your safety.   When I turned to Frank, he betrayed me, and I learned that he was more interested in having me as his trophy wife then being your surrogate father. When he proposed to me, I was horrified and refused him.   He became terribly angry and tried to hurt me.   I ran from his house and was more determined than ever to make enough money with my next movie, so you and I could just disappear. Once again, I learned the hard way that the only person I could depend on was myself.   All those people in my life who I thought really loved me, did not.   They would leave me like my dad or were unable to love me like my mother who was sick, and all the rest just used me.

   I want you to know a little about me. All I ever really longed for was to be loved and wanted.   I never knew my dad, and my mom was too sick to take care of me.   I went from foster home to foster home until one day my mom came back for me. We were happy in our own little house, only not for long, because mom was once again hospitalized.   I ended up in an orphanage until a couple came and brought me to live with them. They were extremely strict and mean to me. Many nights I cried myself to sleep because I just wanted my mom back.

   If you are reading this letter my sweet darling, then you know that something terrible has happened to me.   I may not be able to tell you what, but I can tell you why. I am a threat not only to the Kenny family whose son is your father and the United States President, but now to Frank as well, who continues to harbor a great deal of resentment toward me, for refusing his marriage proposal.

American Goddess

Please know my beautiful baby girl, that you have always been the most important thing in my life. I love you with all my heart and soul. I know in my heart, that if you had the opportunity to know me, you would love me just as much as I love you. Not a moment has gone by without my wondering what you are thinking and doing. I have lots of photos of you growing up and I keep them in a secret place. Every night I take them all out and study each one carefully. I know every hair on your head, your laughing eyes, your little adorable nose and those beautiful little pink lips. How I long to hold you, how I long to kiss you, how I long to show you how much I love you. No matter what happens to me, please know that I never stopped loving you and will always be with you. I pray for you to have a far better life than I had; wherein, people will love, adore and shower you with tons of attention. One more thing my sweet angel, I beseech you not to ever reveal to the world whose daughter you really are. I fear they will come after you as well. Goodbye my sweet darling,

All my love, your Mommy"

In total shock I looked into Barbra's tear-filled eyes and with my heart pounding said, "That bastard Frank stole everything from my mother and from me!" I started to cry, "He stole me from my mother and my beautiful Joy from me; and now I'm being told I will never have a baby again! He kept me from my Johnny as the Kenny family withheld their Johnny from my mother! May God forgive me, but I am glad I was the one who finally stopped that evil monster! My mom was right, the world's perception of my mother was indeed that of a dumb blond sex symbol, but she was actually one of the most incredible women to have ever lived. I finally know the truth and I'm proud to be her daughter." I grabbed Barbara's hand, "Thank you Barbara, I finally understand myself, because I am so much like my mother. I now know there is truly a higher purpose for my life and I am more determined than ever to fulfill my destiny whatever that may be."

Barbara took me in her arms and we cried together until there were no more tears to shed. Exhausted and emotionally drained, we finally headed for bed around 4:00am that morning. I helped Barbara into her bedroom, switched off the light, kissed her forehead and said, "Now, let's try to get some real sleep and I'll wake you up around 9:00am, okay?"

She grabbed my hand and sadly said, "Christina, please lay with me? I don't want to lay here alone to night."

Lovingly I looked into her sad tearing eyes, "Sure move over."

I climbed into the bed, put my arm around her, and beckoned her to lay her head on my shoulder. As she did, she kissed my cheek and as she softly snuggled up to me she said, "Thank you Christina, you really are my best friend and I love you." Then she passed out. Even with everything I just discovered, I don't think it was five minutes later that I passed out and we fell asleep in each other's arms.

American Goddess

I think it was the sound of the rain hitting the patio doors which made me stir, and when I opened my eyes I shouted, "Oh shit!   Barbara, wake up!   It's 10:00am!"   We both flew out of the bed and I said, "Go shower quick and I'll call your driver and have him come pick up the bags."

All at once Barbara shouted, "Oh shit!" as she stubbed her toe on the dresser and began to jump up and down shouting, "Ouch that hurts!   Fuck me!   What a way to wake up!"   She hopped toward the bathroom and said as I laughed at her, "Stop fucking laughing you asshole and make me a cup of coffee to go, would you please?"

I shouted back, "Sure, sure, you're just like a man!   Sleep with them once and they think they can start telling you what to do."

As soon as the coffee started to perk, I called Barbara's driver and had him come up and take down her luggage. I called Michael at the office.   His secretary answered and told me he left at 9:45am.   I tried him at home and the answering machine picked up.   Then I tried his car phone and I heard Michael say, "Hello!"

When he answered the phone, I said, "Hi, honey it's me.   Where are you?"

"Hi Punkie, since I didn't hear from you I thought I'd take the day off too, so I'm on my way to my Mother's.   Where are you?"

"I'm still at Barbara's, but I'll be heading home in about an hour. What time do you think you'll be home?"

He hesitated for a moment, "I'm not sure Christina. I think I need some time to put my thoughts together before I see you. I have been thinking all night about the things you said last night, and if you resent my right as your lover to have a say in what you decide to do, then I think we may be coming to an impasse in our relationship.   Christina, if we get married then we are saying we belong to one another.   What that means to me is you and I are one, so I can't and won't do anything without considering you first.   I'm feeling marriage and oneness doesn't have the same meaning to you as it does to me, and I don't think I can live with the way you think it should be."

With that I took a deep breath and said, "Michael, if you think my marrying you means I must surrender my free will to your approval, then you're right, we do have a problem. Because I'll tell you right now, you're talking to Christina Powers and if you can't see by now that I don't do anything for anyone unless I want to, then you will never truly understand me.   Michael, no matter how much I love you, no one, not even you, will tell me, what to do!   So maybe we both need to rethink this relationship."

With a surprised and saddened tone he said, "That sounds like a good idea to me, so let's meet at home around dinner and we'll talk."

With a disgusted tone I said, "That's if I come home!   Goodbye, Michael."

I heard him yell, "Christina, wait!   Don't hang up!   What do you mean, if you come home?   Aren't you coming home?"

American Goddess

Sarcastically I answered, "Well you sound like you need some time, so I'm giving it to you."

Then for the first time since I met him, Michael raised his voice to me, "If you don't come home to me tonight, then I won't be there tomorrow."

All I heard at that moment was the pitch of his voice and I shouted, "Don't you ever use that tone on me. Oh shit! Forget it! I have to go now Michael, goodbye." I hung up the phone, poured myself a cup of coffee, sat at the kitchen table and started to quietly cry as I thought, 'What the fuck is it all about, and why do I bother trying anyway?'

As I sat there crying, Barbara came running into the kitchen shouting, "Where's my coffee, girlfriend?" When she realized I was crying, she came to me, put her hands on my back, nestled her head next to mine and said, "Christina, what's the matter?"

I turned to hug her and said, "I think Michael and I may have just broken up."

She looked at me as if to say 'what are you crazy' and exclaimed, "Come on, the two of you are made for each other. I don't know what the problem is, nor do I have the time to find out." She kissed my cheek and added, "Go to him and straighten it out whatever it is. Don't lose this one, Christina. Michael is a good man and he loves you. Now I have to go, so just lock up when you leave, and I'll call you as soon as I can." She grabbed herself a mug of coffee, kissed me goodbye, and as she ran out the door she shouted, "Next time we have to do dinner, girlfriend!" Then she was gone.

After Barbara left, I sat there thinking over what she had just said about Michael. I was trying to prioritize my life in my mind, and I realized Barbara was right about Michael. So I got up, walked over to the sink, rinsed my cup, grabbed my purse off the table and headed out the door.

Once I hit the car, I climbed in and I was on my way home. When I pulled out of the garage the rain slowly stopped and the sun was beginning to peek through the clouds. By the time I reached the Thruway, the sun had broken through the clouds in several places in the sky. Its beautiful golden rays were painting the sky over the mountains on the horizon ten different glorious shades of blue and pink. The sight of it was breathtaking, and it somehow helped me realize my going home to Michael was the right thing to do. The closer I got to the Poughkeepsie exit, the more my heart began to pound with the anticipation of a schoolgirl with just the thought of seeing him.

From out of the blue, I had a flash back and my emotions were filled with fear as I thought to myself, 'Oh my, God! I feel the exact same desperate feelings I felt the night I went racing to Johnny's home and found him in bed with Kathy.' I really started to sweat as I put my foot to the floor with the gas pedal under it and all I could think was, 'Would Michael do that to me? Would he cheat on me?' I shook my head and thought, 'No! Don't play this game with yourself Christina. I will choose to believe Michael's love is still stronger than that.   If I can't trust him, then we don't have anything, and I need to trust him.'   So I let up on the gas and continued home at a legal speed.

It was 2:15pm when I pulled into our garage and I almost started to cry when I didn't see Michael's car.   I parked and ran into the house hoping to find a note or a message, but there was neither. I began to pace the floor for a few minutes, until I thought of Tess. I headed for my address book and dialed Michael's mother's number.   I let the phone ring twenty times before I decided no one was home.   Then I thought of Michael's townhouse in Poughkeepsie and I began to dial the number. When the answering machine picked up, I started to cry as I said, "Michael, I know I'm a stubborn fool sometimes, but honey, I love you.   Please if you're there, pick up and tell me you still love me.   Please Michael, it's you I adore baby.   You're the one I live for Michael, and I forgot that baby." I got so scared I lost him that I started to sob, "Please I'm begging you Michael, pick up the phone baby, I can't live without you."

I started crying so hard I couldn't speak, and I heard, "I love you too, Punkie."   I turned around and leaped into Michael's open arms.

He held me as I cried, and with tears filling his eyes he said, "Oh, baby!   I'm sorry I hurt you.   I love you more than life itself and I will never chase you away from me again."   He picked me up, carried me into the bedroom, and proceeded to gently take me to heaven in a whirlwind of love, fire, and passion.

After our lovemaking I gently said, "Michael, I know how strong willed I can be, so I'll try my best to learn to be completely open minded to whatever you say in the future." I kissed his lips, looked at him cross eyed, and added, "Oh yes, by the way Michael, I also want to get married and bare your child more than anything in this world."

He laughed at the face I was making, kissed my nose and said, "Punkie, I love you, and I want that just as much as you do, but you know what the doctor said.   How can you still want to have my child?"

I looked seriously into his eyes, "Honey, we can do what Jimmy said.   I'm sure there must be some decent woman out there who would bare our child for us."

His eyes opened wide as he replied, "You mean a surrogate mother?"

"Yes!" I answered with excitement.

"But if we do that, then the child will only be mine biologically, and I would rather adopt than to have a child that you're not the biological mother of."

Kissing him all over his face I said, "I love you honey, and that is exactly what I'm talking about.   I have read where doctors at U.C.L.A. have taken the egg from one woman, fertilized it, and implanted it in the womb of another woman.   So don't you see? The child would still be biologically ours.   I can call Tom Davies tomorrow and talk to him about finding a suitable surrogate for us, if you agree?"

American Goddess

Michael's eyes lit up, "Well let's do it!"   He kissed me again, "Why don't we go out for dinner tonight to celebrate?   We can invite Jimmy to come with us if you like?"

"That sounds great to me honey, but I have got to hop in the shower before I go anywhere."

Michael kissed me again, "Okay, I'll see if Jimmy's home yet, while you get ready." Then I headed for the bathroom, as Michael headed for Jimmy's room.

CHAPTER 21

Over our seafood dinner at a quaint Country Inn called the Lobster Pond, in Wallkill, New York, we told Jimmy of our decision to have a child.

As we talked, a little girl no older than ten came up to our table and said, "Excuse me, but are you Christina Powers?"

I smiled and answered, "Yes I am, can I help you?"

Her eyes lit up as she smiled at me, turned to her parents, and said, "I told you it was her."   She turned back toward me and asked, "May I have your autograph?"

I smiled at her, as I pulled a 5-x 7 photo of myself out of my purse, signed it and said, "What's your name, sweety?"   "Kathy," she answered.

Still smiling warmly, I said, "Then I will write 'To Kathy, Love Christina Powers!' You know what Kathy; you're the first person to recognize me in public, in more than ten years.   How did you know it was me?"

She gave me a great big smile and said, "Your smile."   Then she thanked me and left.   Not two minutes later, I was saying 'hi' to everyone in this small country restaurant and before we knew it, we were in the middle of a family style dinner.   Everyone in the place began talking to one another as if we all knew each other for years, and it turned out to be a delightful dining experience.   The place is right off Route 44/55, if you're in the neighborhood stop by, you'll love it.   Tell them I sent you.

American Goddess

As Michael drove us home that night, I thought of the little girl at the restaurant named Kathy.   Then I realized how much she reminded me of Kathy Brown, and I thought, 'Kathy, wherever you are I want to thank you for saving my life.   I'll never forget the lesson you taught me on forgiveness.'

I was deep in my thoughts when Jimmy brought me back to the living, by saying, "I didn't have the chance to say it in the restaurant, but I'm really very happy the two of you have decided to find a surrogate.   I think it's a wonderful idea, and I can't wait to have a baby around again."   He began to rub my shoulders from behind me in the backseat and continued, "I also have some news of my own.   I met someone about three months ago and we have fallen in love."

I turned around in my seat, hugged him and smiled as I exclaimed, "Finally!   Jimmy! I thought you gave up on love.   Who is he?"

He kissed my cheek and said in a way I once heard a long time ago, when he first told me about Bobby, "Christina, his name is Richard Green and I adore him."

When he said the name, I thought for a moment, then said, "Gee Jimmy, that name sounds familiar.   Do I know him?"

He smiled mischievously, "No, you never met him.   But believe it or not, I actually met him because of you."

I looked at him strangely, "You did, how?"

"You had set up a personal tour of the recording studios for Richard and his fifth-grade class just before Easter.   Since you were involved in the trial, I decided to give the tour for you, much to the disappointment of the class, but Richard and I hit it off great and we have been dating since."

I kissed him again, "I'm so happy for you, Jimmy.   Now, when do we meet him?"

With an excited tone he replied, "How about tonight, I can have him come over for coffee?"

"That sounds great; do you want to use the car phone to call him now?"

Jimmy lifted his eyebrows, "No, I'll call from home.   I need to talk to the both of you first, and then I'll call him."

This time I lifted my eyebrows, "Now that was an opening for sure, and you know me Jimmy, I never pass up an opening.   Now start talking, what's wrong with him?"

He gave me half a smile, "There is nothing wrong with him Christina, it's me."

"You, what do you mean?" I said with a concerned tone.

Shaking his head, he replied, "We want to get married Christina, then we want to take a year off and go to Africa together.   The problem is I can't do that while I'm trying to reorganize and head operations of companies I never even heard of until we took them over."

American Goddess

I instantly slapped him in the back of the head and said, "Africa!   What are you nuts!?   Why the hell do you want to spend a year of your life in a backwards third world country that condemns your lifestyle?"

He looked at me like I had two heads, sat back in his seat in a huff and said, "For just that reason."   And that's all he said.

I looked at him as if he had five heads, "You're not making any sense Jimmy, I can understand getting married; but going to Africa, that's crazy."

Michael snuck in a word, "Punkie, you're not even listening to Jimmy.   Why don't you calm down and let him finish what he's trying to say?"

Jimmy pulled himself back up toward the front seat, "Thank you, Michael."   Turning to me he added, "Now will you please listen to me Christina?"

"Okay, okay, I'm listening.   So start talking and please make some sense this time."

He calmly began, "It's simple Christina, it's what we want to do!   There are hundreds of thousands of people suffering and dying from AIDS every day, just because no one is adequately educating them about the disease.   Not only that, but because of what is happening with the AIDS epidemic the fundamental Christians our getting the whole continent to turn against all homosexuals. They are actually putting them to death. Christina, I feel like I am being called to do this.   You of all people should understand that."

I looked at him with frustration on my face and said as I let out a deep breath accompanied by a sigh, "I guess I can't argue with that, now can I, Jimmy?   But you know I'm going to miss the hell out of you while you're gone.   Now tell me, when are you planning to do this?"

His eyes lit up, "We are going to be married on July 4th and then leave on the 10th."

Shocked, I replied, "This July10th!   Jimmy, I haven't been in the office since we took over three major corporations!   How in the world do you think I'm going to figure out everything you've done in only ten days?"

Michael grabbed my hand and said, "Christina, I'm right on top of it all with Jimmy, we can handle it and you can learn it."

I looked at them both as we pulled into the garage and said, "Well it sounds to me like you two have this all planned out already.   So who am I to try to stop you, I love you Jimmy, and I give you my blessing.   Now go call Richard, I want to meet my soon to be new brother in-law."

Within a half hour of Jimmy's call, Michael and I were meeting his new love, Richard Green.   Richard was a quiet, attractive, well dressed, forty-five-year-old, six-foot-tall man, with brown hair which showed just a touch of a receding hair line.   After my first glimpse at Richard, I winked to Jimmy in a way which indicated to him I was impressed with his choice.   Over our coffee Richard was overwhelmingly polite, friendly,

277

intelligent, and cordial. He seemed like the perfect man for Jimmy, but by the end of our splendid two hour get together, I realized there was one thing which concerned me about Richard, he seemed to have a slight tendency to be obsessive toward Jimmy. I noticed it with the little things. Since it didn't seem to bother Jimmy, I figured to myself, 'Who am I to judge, as long as Jimmy's happy. Besides, maybe that's what Jimmy needs in his life, someone to dote over him for a change.'

The next morning it was time to go back to work, and Michael insisted we have James take the three of us to work in the limo. So we did, and when we arrived James pulled up to the main building of our complex and as we climbed out, Michael handed me a long scarf and said, "Here, put this on over your eyes, Punkie."

I took it, looked at him like he was nuts and said, "What the hell do you want me to do that for?"

Jimmy jumped in laughing, "Oh just shut up and put it on. We remodeled the lobby to surprise you. So humor us a little, would you please!?"

I started laughing, "Okay, I'll do it. But Michael, you better not be going along with another one of Jimmy's stupid jokes, because I'll slap you both." Then I put on the blindfold and let them lead me to the main lobby.

When we entered through the large electronic front doors, Michael shouted, "Okay!" as he took off the blindfold to reveal my entire staff applauding me. Sitting in the middle of the lobby was a great big cake, and written on it was, "We love you, Christina! And welcome home!" I was shocked by it all. They had really pulled it off because I never expected it. It felt wonderful to be welcomed home by all my friends like that.

After our morning welcome home celebration, it was back to work. I mean heavy duty work, the kind I really didn't care for, but was very good at. There was no time for doing what I loved best, entertaining, and writing. Not this time! This time all my attentions were directed toward finding out what had been accomplished by all my staff under the close direction of Michael and Jimmy without my close supervision and direction.

Finally, after a six month delay due to a murder, it was now time to truly turn my corporate holdings, into a mega conglomerate. Not only did we jump into the corporate world feet first, but Michael and I also went full steam ahead with a very discreet nationwide girl hunt to find the perfect surrogate Mother.

American Goddess

It was on July 27, 1989, two weeks after the newlyweds left for Africa, that Michael and I had an interview with our first prospective surrogate mother. The interview was held at Tom Davies' office in Manhattan. Tom had researched every detail of the lives and backgrounds of twenty-five women, which he had personally chosen over hundreds of possible candidates.

Tom told us he felt one of these twenty-five women would make a suitable surrogate. The arrangements of our contract were to be kept strictly confidential at my request. I felt the world knew enough about me as it was, and for some reason, I didn't want my fans to know I could no longer conceive a child.

The terms of our contract would be as follows: Upon successful in-vitro fertilization, the surrogate mother would receive one-hundred thousand-dollars cash, with nine-hundred-thousand-dollars to follow after the birth. Tom Davies tried to convince me one-million-dollars was an exorbitant amount to pay for a surrogate mother, but I insisted I wanted the best money could buy for our child. The surrogate would also have to live on the premises with Michael and me; so, we could monitor every aspect of the surrogate's life during the pregnancy from her meals to her sleeping habits.

So, when Miss Joanne Naccarato entered the office with Tom where Michael and I were waiting, we already knew everything there was to know about her, without actually being inside her mind. She was a beautiful twenty-six-year-old law graduate, who had just passed the Bar Exam. She was from a respectable Italian American family and she had a higher than above average intelligence.

In response to one of the questions on the questionnaire Miss Naccorato stated, "My decision to become a surrogate mother was made out of my empathy for couples who are unable to bear children of their own, and being a surrogate 'for me', is an act of love and generosity."

She also wrote her initial decision to become a surrogate mother was truly first motivated by a desire to help, then followed by her own need for financial compensation. On another question she stated she intended to use the compensation for her services to pay off her student loans, and to help establish a law office of her own. We liked her responses to the questionnaire from all the rest, which made her our first choice on paper. Now it was time to see if she remained so in person.

Miss Naccorato was aware of the requirements of the contract for her services, but she was not aware of who was setting the requirements until she entered the room where Michael and I were waiting. Her face showed her surprise and shock when she recognized me. When she reached us Michael and I stood up to greet her with a warm embrace.   She hugged Michael, then me as she said with a big smile, "Oh my God, Christina Powers! I can't believe it's you! I was so nervous when Mr. Davies opened the door, but now that I see it's you, I feel so much more relaxed. I have got to be your biggest fan! I can't believe it's really you. Oh please forgive me for rambling on. I'm just so thrilled to think I might have the opportunity to be a surrogate for someone like you, Ms. Powers." Excitedly, she hugged me again and continued, "May I also say I would be honored to help a couple with your stature and reputation for helping others, to have a child of your own. Now I'll try to control my excitement and answer your questions to the best of my ability, under the circumstances."

Michael and I looked at each other and we both knew this was our girl. We fell in love with her sweet, jovial, disposition immediately. As we said our hellos, Michael indicated to me with his eyes, his approval. I knew Michael was right so I said, "Joanne, are there any questions you would like to ask us?"

She smiled again as we took our seats and said, "I know all I have to know about both of you, and like I said, I would be honored to carry your child for you, Ms. Powers."

I reached over, took her hand in mine and said, "When would you like to sign the contracts and get started?"

She shook my hand wildly with happy excitement, "Right now Ms. Powers, right now!"

Ten minutes later we had our surrogate mother and I was now more than ready to get the baby show on the road.   For some strange reason, I felt an overwhelmingly desperate desire, as if it were planted within my soul from a higher power to have Michael's child, and I was determined to fulfill that desire as soon as humanly possible.

On Monday, August 16th at 11:00pm, Joanne Naccorato moved in with us for a one-week trial.   We decided to take this time in order to give the three of us the opportunity to make sure; we still wanted to proceed with the implantation.   We were hoping in one week's time, we would know for sure whether she was truly ready to take on this tremendous, nine-month commitment for us.

As soon as we unpacked Joanne's belongings from her car, we took them straight up to her new bedroom.   After we dropped off her suitcases, I took her on a tour of our Hudson River mansion.   As we toured the mansion, I explained she was welcome to use any room she would like in the house, except the master bedroom of course.   Then I said, "Joanne, I hope you realize what the terms of our contract truly mean.   I want to make sure you are totally aware you can come and go as you please, but once you conceive, you will have two security guards assigned to you whenever you leave the mansion.   I hope you also realize you will not be allowed to have even one sexual encounter during the pregnancy.   Nor will you be able to take overnight outings without one of us being present."

280

American Goddess

As we arrived back at Joanne's room, she shook her head in agreement with what I was saying as she said, "I am completely aware of the terms of the contract, Christina. I also want you to know I understand and agree with the need for the stringent terms completely."

I smiled at her response, "I'm glad to hear that Joanne, because I know the terms of our contract are strict, but that is one of the reasons why your compensation is one-million-dollars."   As I walked to the door I added, "Now why don't you take a few minutes to settle in before lunch, and I'll meet you in the family kitchen, in say twenty minutes?"

She sat on the soft bed, bounced a few times, then said with a smile, "That sounds good to me.   I only have a few things to unpack and that will probably take me twenty minutes to do, if I don't get lost in the size of those bedroom closets first."

I smiled with half a giggle at her sweet attempt to be humorous then said, "I think you can handle it."   I turned, closed the door behind me, and headed toward the kitchen to see if Carman had found the new house menu, I left for her.   As I walked down the hall, I thought to myself, 'Oh, Dear God!   I pray we're not making a mistake.'   As I thought this I felt a cold chill go up my spine and I thought, 'All I ask you God is that you please let Joanne be the right one to carry our child for us!'

Over lunch I explained to Joanne the diet she would have to be on during the entire pregnancy.   Then I said, "Joanne, I hope I'm not making you uncomfortable by asking you all these questions.   I only want to show you that yes, this is going to be a wonderful experience for all of us, but at the same time I also want you to understand this is not going to be all peaches and cream either.   I want to remind you there will be no smoking, no drinking, and absolutely no drugs unless they're prescribed.   Like I said Joanne, I just want you to realize when you sign this contract; you will be actually surrendering your rights for many things to me totally until you've given birth."

Joanne took a sip of her milk, smiled and said, "Let me try to put your mind at ease, Christina.   I have read the entire contract and I am more than aware of the stipulations, and once again, I can live with them.   After all, you are paying me one-million-dollars, aren't you?"

I didn't particularly care for her little dig and I expressed it by saying, "Good!   Now that I know that you know, where I'm coming from, I will feel much more at ease placing my unborn child's life in your hands."

She looked at me very seriously and said, "I never looked at it in that light before." Taking my hand, she added, "Christina, I will give my life for your child if need be, so please try to dismiss any fears you may have over your child's safety with me.   I know the losses you have suffered with your children in the past, and I would never willingly endanger your child's life."

American Goddess

With tears in my eyes, I reached over the table to hug her and said, "Thank you Joanne, you truly are a remarkable person." I stood up as I added, "Would you like to take a walk with me?"

She returned my hug with tears beginning to well up in her eyes, and said, "I'd love to take a walk with you."

It was a beautiful, sunny, afternoon, and the river glistened like a rippling sea of shiny pennies from the sun's reflection, as we strolled along its bank together. When we reached the boat docks I said, "I feel like taking the motorboat out for a while, won't you please come with me?"

She jumped in the boat before I did, "You don't have to ask me twice, let's go!"

I laughed as I untied the boat, hopped in and said, "Ha! Ha! You're a girl after my own heart." Then I started it up and off we went.

As we cruised smoothly up the river toward Kingston, Joanne turned to me and asked, "Christina, may I be candid with you?"

"Of course, Joanne, I would expect no less," I answered sincerely.

She smiled mischievously and said, "I think you must be an absolute genius to have pulled off the most incredible, tri-corporate takeover in history. I have to tell you, I researched every move Wall Street took that day for my thesis, and I could not figure out how you could have pulled it off without some kind of advanced knowledge of what was going to transpire during that day. Won't you please give me just a clue as to how you did it?"

I started to laugh as I rode the wave off a passing boat, then said, "That will be the question of the decade for everyone on Wall Street and all I can say Joanne, is you're right. I am a genius."

She smiled at my answer, "When I look at all you've accomplished, I have to wonder. How did you get to where you are now without a college education?"

"Joanne, I'm surprised at you. This is America and throughout history most of your successful business entrepreneurs had no more than a high school education. What made them stand out was what they had to sell, and how they sold it. I just happen to have a talent the world loves, so that is what I used to help me arrive where I am today. But everyone, no matter who they may be, has the ability to tap into their own genius whether they have a formal education or not."

With a concerned tone Joanne asked, "Are you advocating continued education is not needed?"

I looked at her with a surprised expression, "No, not at all. I believe whole heartedly in higher education. All I'm saying is in my case, for me to reach my career goals; I didn't need a college education."

She shook her head, "Well then, how can you explain your business success?"

American Goddess

We had reached Kingston and as I began to swing the boat around, I replied, "Well, as for my business skills, they came from many hours of on the job training and a whole lot of personal intuition."

She put her hand on my shoulder and said, "Christina, I would love to put an application in with your company after the baby is born.   I would relish the opportunity to practice business law, under the direction of the 'Queen of Wall Street' herself."

I smiled, "Joanne, I'm sure we could use a woman with your skills on our team, and I can tell you right now the position will be there for you."   Then I thought for a second, scratched my head and said with a surprised tone, "Guess what!   It just so happens I have a staff and board of directors meeting tomorrow evening in Denver.   I'm going to be addressing one of the subsidiaries I recently acquired.   Would you like to join me for some hands-on action?"

Her eyebrows lifted with excitement as she answered, "I wouldn't miss it for one-million-dollars."

I laughed at her eager response as I said, "Great!   It's a date then."

We didn't say too much more on the way back, because we were both caught up in enjoying the beauty of the river.   When we arrived back to the mansion, we docked the boat and headed straight for the house.

Joanne and I were sitting on the balcony chatting, as a Hudson River Tour Boat passed by, and I noticed a group of passengers had draped a sign over the side of the boat which read, **"We love you, Christina!"**   When I saw the sign I stood up, walked over to the edge of the balcony and began to wave.   As soon as I did, you could hear the river come alive with shouts and whistles.   The Captain sounded the ship's horn, so I blew him a kiss.

Joanne walked over to me and said, "It must be an incredible feeling to know you're loved and respected by so many people!"

I turned my head toward her as I leaned on the railing and answered, "You're right! It is a wonderful feeling, but it can also be an enormous responsibility."

Just then Michael walked out and said, "Yes, it is my sweet, but you handle it with such finesse."   We embraced and I said with surprise, "Michael!   You're home.   We were having such a wonderful afternoon together I totally forgot the time."

He kissed me then said with a snicker, "Yeah!   Yeah!   Out of sight, out of mind, I know."   He turned to Joanne, "Welcome to our home, Joanne.   I apologize for not being here to welcome you when you arrived, but somebody has to work around here."

She smiled at Michael, "Thank you, and there is no need to apologize.   I've been in good hands."

Michael kissed me again and said, "Well if you ladies will excuse me, I'll go change."

American Goddess

I took his arm in mine and with my Mae West impression said, "Come on, big boy! I'll help you change into something more comfortable." Laughing I added as I dragged Michael away, "Make yourself at home Joanne, and we'll see you at dinner."

When we arrived at our bedroom, I immediately began to tell Michael what transpired between Joanne and me during the day. As I lovingly began to help him undress, I said, "Honey, I really think she is the perfect one to carry our child for us, but I don't want to influence your decision either. I just hope by the end of this week we both make the right choice."

Michael led me by the hand to the bed, where we laid down together. He kissed me tenderly and said, "Punkie, I love you and if you feel comfortable with Joanne, then so do I."

I kissed him back as I replied, "Michael, I want you to come to a decision based on your own feelings, not mine. Honey, I have to tell you as much as I want this to work, I'm still nervous about it. I don't know if I can handle losing another child."

He looked at me very seriously, "I know how you feel Punkie, I lost a child too, remember? I promise you I am taking this just as seriously as you are."

"I'm sorry Michael," I said with compassion. "I never really asked how you felt about losing our child."

He kissed me and said, "It hurt a lot, Punkie. The only thing that saved me was you coming back to me." He gave me a sexy smile, as he put his finger to my lips and added, "Shh, let's continue this conversation later." He passionately kissed me, and we melted into one another's embrace.

American Goddess

CHAPTER 23

Our dinner together that evening was lovely and as for Joanne, she was simply charming. She seemed to win Michael's heart over within minutes as she shared some of her childhood stories with us. When we finished dinner, we headed for the family room to continue our conversation.

As we got to know one another a little better that night, it turned out Joanne and Michael had many common interests. So much so that at one point they went into a ten-minute discussion over skiing, which I knew nothing about. I didn't mind being left out. I was just pleased to see Michael and Joanne getting along so well together.

As we talked, Carman entered the room with the phone in hand and said, "Excuse me Christina, Jimmy is on the line."

I thanked her, as I took the phone and with an excited tone exclaimed, "Jimmy! I have been waiting two weeks to hear from you. How the hell are you guys? Never mind that, where the hell are you guys?"

"Hi girlfriend," he answered in a not so cheerful tone. "I'm sorry I haven't called sooner, but we're in Ghana, and let me tell you, it's crazy here. Christina, you cannot believe what we are dealing with. There are hospitals full of people dying of full-blown AIDS and no one can do anything to help."

I didn't understand what Jimmy was saying so I asked, "Jimmy, if you're there to help, then how can no one be helping?"

With a disgusted tone he answered, "It's not that no one is trying Christina, there just happens to be a civil war going on here. It appears the warring factions are not letting medical and food supplies through to the needed areas."

When Jimmy said these things, I became even more concerned over his safety. So I said, "It sounds dangerous Jimmy, are you sure you're doing the right thing by staying there?"

285

American Goddess

With a tone of pure compassion, he answered, "I know I am Christina, but Richard and I can't do it alone. We need your help."

With a surprised tone I said, "My help, how can I help?"

His reply sounded more like a plea, "Just by making the world aware of the travesty which is taking place here.   Somehow, we have got to get the warring factions to allow the supplies through.   From what I gather, it's actually the national government, which is stopping the supplies, so I think if you could pressure Congress into threatening to cut aid to the Ghana Government, then maybe they will let the supplies through."

I answered reassuringly, "I'll tell you what Jimmy, you send me positive proof of what is going on there and I'll do everything I can to help from here."

"Thanks', Christina.   I knew I could count on you."   Relaxing his tone, he continued, "So tell me, have you found a surrogate yet?"

I chuckled then said, "Why don't you give me a number where I can reach you.   I'll call you back later and tell you all about it."

"I don't have one," he answered.   "But if you have to go, I'll call you back tomorrow."

"That sounds good Jimmy," I answered.   Then I continued with a tone of concern, "And for God Sake's, please take care of yourself!   I love you and I would be devastated if something were to happen to you."

"I love you too Christina and I'll talk to you tomorrow night."   I hung up and rejoined Michael and Joanne's conversation.

Later that evening after Michael and I retired to our room, I told him what Jimmy had said.   Then we climbed into bed together where Michael took me into his arms, kissed me, smiled and said, "Punkie!   I don't think we could find a better surrogate then Joanne, if we looked for twenty years.   So as for my vote, she's got it."

I hugged him with excitement and said, "Oh God, Michael!   I love you, and I can't wait to have our baby in my arms."

Michael climbed on top of me, looked deep into my eyes and passionately said, "The only thing that could make my heart happier right now is for us to set our wedding date."

I smiled and lovingly replied, "Why don't we call your mom and ask her to set everything up for us again?   Tell her to set the date for
Thanksgiving Day.   I think we have a lot to be thankful for."

He kissed me passionately and said, "Christina, I love you Punkie, and I have never felt happier or more complete then I do at this very moment."

I returned the kiss and we lovingly indulged in one another's anticipation and excitement for our future family.

American Goddess

The next morning, Joanne was accompanying Michael and me, to Denver on a trip that was strictly business. On the plane to Denver Joanne sat quietly beside me as Michael, my staff, and I, all worked on a last-minute review of our proposal. As I read through the pamphlet Michael had prepared to hand out to all the staff of Salerno Sodas, I turned to him and said, "Michael, we state in here we have the financial records for Salerno Sodas for the past ten years and we compare them to the five-year financial records of Catskill Mountain Soft Drinks, so where are the figures?"

He grabbed the handout from me as he answered, "I had them on a separate sheet which was to be included in the pamphlet. Don't tell me they're not there? I shook my head as I said, "You can look for yourself honey, but it's not there."

He looked for Terry Baggatta my senior secretary, who was on the other end of the cabin working on the pamphlets and shouted, "Terry! Would you come here, please?"

She walked over to us, "What's up?"

Michael looked up at her and asked, "How come the sheets with the financial figures are not in the handout?"

She smiled and said, "Don't worry about it; I'm on top of it right now. The printing room accidentally left them out, so we're inserting them by hand."

Michael smiled, "Great job Terry, I'm glad you caught it."

I smiled and said, "Well in that case gang, I think we're all set."

My entourage and I arrived at the headquarters of Salerno Sodas at 10:00am, where we went straight into a prearranged board meeting. After Michael, Tom Davies, Joanne, and I, were introduced to everyone by the current president of the company Paul Barer, we took our seats.

Paul stood up and said, "Ladies and gentlemen of the board, now I would like to formally turn this meeting over to the new owner and top shareholder of Salerno Sodas, Ms. Christina Powers."

Everyone in the large conference room applauded as I took the mike and said, "Good morning and once again I would like to thank you for your kind welcome. Now the first thing I would like to say is that the final proposal which most of us in this room agreed upon concerning the future of this company, has been drawn up in a pamphlet form. Right now, my people are distributing copies to all the staff in the plant. I want to make sure everyone involved is totally aware of our plans before putting it to a vote this evening.

American Goddess

Now if anyone has any questions, this is the time to ask." After answering several questions, I continued, "Now if there are no more questions, I would like to take a walk through the plant to meet the staff before I address them this afternoon."

We left the board room at 11:00am and went straight into the heart of the two-thousand employee, soda producing and distributing plant.   Once there, I began to personally introduce myself to every employee I could.   As I shook their hands, I offered a copy of our pamphlet to those who had not yet received one and said, "All I ask is you please read and come to a complete understanding of my proposal before you make your decision for this evening's vote."

After a two-hour tour of the plant, it was off for a 1:30pm luncheon with the head union representatives, which led right into a 3:00pm meeting with the entire union membership.

I was scheduled to address the meeting at 4:40pm, which was shortly after the opponents of our proposal addressed the assembly.   The union representatives present included all the members in the main plant, along with seventy truck drivers and the three-hundred employees, who manned the thirty distributing centers based throughout the West Coast.

Finally, my turn came to speak, and I was introduced to the members by Paul Barer. When I took the podium, I was welcomed by a hardy round of applause.   After the crowd settled down, I smiled and said, "I thank you all for your warm welcome, I also thank you for giving me this opportunity to address the issues before this evening's crucial vote. Now, I would like to come straight to the heart of why I am here today, which is to try to save a dying company.   My hope is after you have read our proposal on eliminating the production of Salerno Sodas, as well as overhauling and modifying the entire plant, so it can be smoothly transformed into the West Coast branch of Catskill Mountain Soft Drinks, you will see that our proposal is the proper business decision to be taken under the circumstances.   When I'm finished speaking here tonight, my hope is to have convinced you all, our terms are generous so that you will all vote yes on our proposal. The reason I am making these proposals is because, since Powers Inc., acquired Salerno Inc., we have discovered Salerno Sodas has been steadily losing profits during the past five fiscal years.   As you can see by the figures, we have in our handout, if left to its present management course, Salerno Sodas will be filing chapter eleven within two years.   Now if you take a look at the profit figures shown for the past five years of Catskill Mountain Soft Drinks, you will see there is quite a difference.   Our intent is to combine the two companies into one major soft drink company, which will truly be able to compete with the big guys.   We plan to have the transformation of Salerno Sodas, into Catskill Mountain Soft Drinks, completed by the end of the first year.   This will be stage one in a three-stage plan to turn this company around in only two years.   As you can see by the figures, this transformation will cost an initial investment from Catskill Mountain Soft Drinks, of thirty-six-million-dollars. Now as for stage two of our proposal, it's true that during this time our proposal calls for a two-year salary freeze, accompanied by a two-year hiring freeze. But I give you my word right now, if you agree to tough it out with us, then at the end of the two years this company will be in the position to give a 30% across the board salary increase, to every employee! We also promise the company will provide a comprehensive health care plan, which will include full dental coverage to every fulltime employee. As for stage three of our proposal 65% of the top management responsibilities will be transferred to our New York office; thus, saving eighteen-million-dollars a year in top management salaries."

Someone from the audience shouted, "How can you be so sure you can deliver after only two years?"

I looked in the direction the question came from as I said, "Very good question, and I was just about to come to that. What makes me sure we can turn this company over in such a short time, is because even though Salerno Soda is losing revenue, it still has a firm hold in the Central and Western corridors of the country. This fact, accompanied with its distribution centers, trucking, and Salerno Soda's shelf space availability, all make the company worth salvaging under a new label. On the other hand, Catskill Mountain Soft Drinks is basically an East Coast phenomenon at this time. But, if we can pull that East Coast success into the Central and Western markets where Salerno Soda is now losing business, then I believe we can combine the two companies, into one mega profit making, soft drink, powerhouse. I also feel if we take this path together, then by the end of the two years we will be ready to carry it to the International Markets."

I stopped to take a sip from my soda cup and added, "Now that I've summed up our proposal for you, I encourage everyone here for the benefit of us all to vote yes. Oh yes! I think I should mention one more thing, and that is concerning my opponent's proposal, which was submitted by the current management. I hope everyone here can recognize a pipe dream when they see it." With that I gave them all the thumbs up and added, "Now that I've said my piece, I would like to thank you all again for your time." Then I turned the platform back to Paul Barer, who was looking visibly frustrated by my remarks to his proposal, as I returned to my seat in the midst of another round of cheers.

After my address, thank God, we were finally served our lunch. We mingled with the members as we impatiently waited for the results of the vote. By the time the eight o'clock hour rolled around, the final vote was tallied, and our proposal had received a 92% approval.

When the winning proposal was announced I once again took the platform and said, "I just want to thank everyone for their vote. Now together, we can swing our plans into action for a brighter financial future for us all." I waved goodbye to them all as I shouted, "Great job, guys!   And may God bless us all."

Later that night on the flight home, Joanne took a seat beside me and said, "Christina, I have got to tell you, you were amazing today. That was the most exciting business experience I have ever had." She shook her head in astonishment and added, "The way you handled that crowd, with such confidence and finesse was incredible.   Do you realize you would make an excellent political candidate?   Have you ever considered running for a public office?"

I looked at her and started to gently chuckle as I said, "With my life history being an open book, who would vote for me?"

She put her hand on my shoulder as she replied, "I'm serious Christina, I think you would make an excellent senatorial candidate and most of all, I think you could win."

Michael who was sitting on my other side, jumped into the conversation rather quickly by saying, "Please! Don't give her any more ideas; we have enough to do as it is."

Joanne took her hand off my shoulder and said, "Oops, I'm sorry! It was just a thought. Just the same, I had a wonderful time today and I learned a lot. I must admit the pace of this learning experience itself, was what I truly enjoyed most about the day."

I replied with a smile, "Well if you're still with us next week, then you will be more than welcome to accompany us to the West Coast for a few days.   We have three more corporate meetings which will be quite similar to todays. In addition, I am hosting two AIDS benefits next week; one in L.A. on Thursday night, the other in San Francisco on Friday night. If you really enjoyed today's pace, then I think you're going to love next weeks."   I smiled, patted her hand and added, "The only reason things are not so hectic this week is because of your stay with us."

She sat up in her seat, looked at us both very seriously and bluntly asked, "If your lives are so busy all the time, then how do you plan to find the time to properly raise a child?"

I smiled at Michael, then I turned to Joanne and answered, "That is a very responsible question and I'm glad you asked it.   It shows me you truly care about the welfare of the child you might carry." I took Michael's hand and added, "It's because we have a plan Joanne, which includes our wedding this coming Thanksgiving Day. Our plan places us on a strict time schedule for the next eight months. If things do go as planned, by the time our baby arrives we will have completely overhauled every company acquired from our corporate takeovers. By then our other partner will have returned from his hiatus, to take over my duties and assist Michael, while I stay home to raise our child."

She smiled and said, "I'm sure the two of you are going to make excellent parents and I hope I'm the one to help."

I smiled back at her with warm sincerity, "I hope so too, Joanne."

American Goddess

CHAPTER 25

By the time Friday had arrived, the three of us had made our final decision.   So at 9:00am that morning we entered Tom Davies' office in Manhattan, and we were more than ready to officially and legally sign our surrogate contract. After signing, it was straight to Poughkeepsie for a 1:00pm appointment with Doctor Hart for our first attempt at in-vitro fertilization. Doctor Hart told us if all went well, we would know in six to eight weeks what sex our child would be.   Then he added, "But we must be realistic, there's always the risk Joanne could abort at any time between the implantation and the first three months."

Joanne had to remain in a supine position for two hours after the procedure; so, by the time we finished everything, we didn't end up arriving back home that evening until after 6:00pm

We were so excited over our experience when we entered the family room talking; none of us noticed the 12 X 12-inch package addressed to me, which was sitting on the coffee table right in front of us. Carman entered the room and said, "Excuse me, but dinner will be ready in ten minutes. Oh, by the way, there's a package for you on the coffee table, Christina."

I looked down, laughed and said, "Thanks Carman, if it had teeth it could have bitten me." I picked it up and added, "It's from Jimmy. That was quick. Let's eat first and I'll open it after dinner."

After dinner, the three of us went back to the family room with our coffee, where once again I picked up the package from Jimmy.   Michael and Joanne were still speaking as I proceeded to open the package to find a video tape, with a note taped to it. I carefully removed the tape from the note which read, **"Christina, this tape has all the proof you will need to back up everything I told you over the phone. As you will see for yourself, the government troops are clearly ambushing convoys of food and medical supplies shortly before they reach the refugee camps, which are in the rebel held areas**

American Goddess

of the northeastern hill country. The government justifies their raids by saying the convoys are carrying weapons to the rebel outlaws, which are held up in the jungle. Christina, this tape proves without a doubt, there were no weapons found during this raid and the troops still destroyed everything the convoy was carrying. Hold on to your seat girlfriend when you watch this, because three innocent Red Cross Workers lost their lives in this ambush. Please, do what you can, and I'll call you soon. Love you guys, Jimmy and Richard."

After reading this note to myself, I read it to Michael and Joanne. Then I plugged the tape into the VCR, and we proceeded to watch in horror as all the atrocities Jimmy spoke of, graphically appeared in front of our eyes.

As soon as I caught my breath I turned to Michael and said, "Honey, would you please make two copies of this tape for me and I'll be right back? I have to make a phone call."

I then went to my in-house office and proceeded to place a direct call to President George Rush on the private number, which he gave to me personally. The phone was answered by a recording which instructed me to leave my name and number, so I did. Not ten minutes later I received a return call from the President himself.   When I answered the phone, I heard, "Hello am I speaking with Christina Powers?"

I quickly answered, "Yes George, it's me. Thank you for returning my call so quickly." He answered in a sweet soft voice, "You're welcome, Christina. Your calling is a pleasant surprise. It's nice to hear from you. So is this a personal call or business?"

I cleared my voice and proceeded, "I wish it were personal George, but it's not.   I really need to speak with you in private as soon as possible. Is there a possibility that it can be arranged?"

This time he cleared his voice then said, "I think it can be arranged, but first let me ask you something.   Does this have anything to do with the matter we once discussed?"

"No George, nothing at all," I answered reassuringly.   "This is more of a human rights issue which I believe you should be made aware of before I go public."

Then I proceeded to inform him of what I had discovered and that I had a video tape which proved what I was saying.   By the time we finished speaking, we had arranged for a 1:00pm luncheon date for the following afternoon.   George wanted me to meet with him at Camp David.   He said he would arrange for my transportation by the U.S. Air Force from Stewart International Airport, in Newburgh, New York.

When I hung up the phone, I sat there for a moment and thought with curiosity, 'Why would he still be so concerned over the information I had on Lee Bradford? I know Lee had scammed the government for billions of dollars, but without knowing what was on the original computer disk, which by the way was still in my possession, I had no idea how he did it. Better yet, what's the real reason George is still so concerned about covering up this crime?' I turned my head to gaze at the small flag I kept in my office and

292

American Goddess

I wondered, 'How can allowing a financial crime against our nation go unpunished, be in the best interest of our national security?'

With that thought, I put my finger to my lips and said in a soft voice, "Hmm, I think it's time to do some investigating of my own." So I called Tom Davies and arranged for a dinner date for that following evening at 7:00pm. We agreed to meet incognito at the Mariners Harbor Restaurant, in Highland, New York.

After my conversation with Tom, I rose from my seat, turned off the light and returned to Michael and Joanne, who were still in the family room. When I entered the room, Michael handed me the copies of the tape he made and said, "Was that 'The President' returning your call?"

"Yes," I replied. "I'm having lunch with him tomorrow."

Michael shook his head in amazement as he smiled at me and said, "You're not kidding, are you?" He kissed me and continued, "Why don't we call it a night and you can tell me all about it upstairs."

I returned his kiss then said, "That sounds good to me, because I'm going to have a busy day tomorrow." We said our goodnights to Joanne and retired for the evening.

After Michael and I snuggled comfortably together in our bed, I kissed him and proceeded to inform him of all I had scheduled for the following day, including my dinner date with Tom. I told Michael I wanted to speak with Tom after meeting with the President. The only thing I didn't tell him was the real reason I wanted to meet with Tom. I felt the less he knew about what I knew, the safer he would remain if something went wrong. When I finished telling him about my conversation with the President, I said, "Honey, I hate to leave you alone tomorrow, especially since we planned to spend the day with Joanne, but you saw the film. I have to do something."

He gently kissed me and reassuringly said, "I understand, Punkie. I just don't know what I'm going to do to entertain Joanne all day tomorrow. I was counting on you for that."

I smiled and said, "Oh, I think you'll be able to come up with something."

He began to playfully kiss my nose as he asked, "What time do you think you will be getting home tomorrow?"

I started to feel myself becoming distracted by his kisses as I answered, "Probably not until after 10:00pm." I kissed him passionately and added, "Now shut up and make love to me," and that was all I had to say.

American Goddess

CHAPTER 26

At 12:45pm, on Saturday, August 21ˢᵗ, I exited an Air Force helicopter at Camp David, and I thought, 'Would you look at this, I'm really at Camp David.' As I was escorted to a private luncheon with President Rush himself.

The first five minutes of our conversation was quite casual. Then I got straight to the point when I said, "George, I hate to jump right into the reason I'm here, but I must." I handed him a copy of Jimmy's tape and continued, "This tape shows Ghana Government troops destroying medical and food supplies."

I reached across our small table, took his hand in mine as I looked him straight in his eyes and with anger in my voice added, "George, this tape also graphically shows the brutal execution style murders of three innocent Ghana Red Cross workers. What is taking place there George is horrendous, and the fact America is supporting this government is an atrocity." Releasing his hand, I continued, "I'm sorry I don't mean to be so dramatic. It's just that when I think of what is taking place over there it angers me and breaks my heart at the same time."

This time George took my hand in his as he comfortingly replied, "There's no need to apologize for caring, Christina. Sometimes it's incomprehensible the human race can be so vicious. When I witness human behavior like this, I wonder how we've made it this far."

As he spoke, I pulled my hand from his, took a sip of water and said, "Well, now that you know what is going on my first question is, how can we stop it?"

He put his hand to his chin, rubbed it a few times as if in thought, then said, "This is going to have to be handled through diplomatic channels. I'll arrange for a personal conversation with the Prime Minister of Ghana this afternoon, and I promise you the supplies will get through." Then he momentarily squinted his eyes precariously as he looked at me and added, "Christina, you mentioned something over the phone about taking this information public. I don't believe that would be a wise thing to do at this time. So I'm going to ask you not to go public with this information." I was surprised and bewildered by his request and I knew it showed on my face. When he realized by my expression, I disagreed with him, he looked very seriously into my eyes and added, "The only reason I'm making this request of you is because if this information becomes public, it could jeopardize American security interests in the region."

I shook my head in disbelief, "Don't you think that if our security interests bring us to the point of allowing human rights atrocities to take place, then it's time to rethink our foreign policies?"

American Goddess

He was visibly taken aback by my sharp response to his reasoning as he said, "It's not as simple as all that, Christina. There are regional conflicts taking place throughout Africa, and we can't stop them all."

I slightly shook my head in amazement by his statement as I said, "That may be true George, but that doesn't mean we cover up murder and allow the perpetrators to go free, because we can't stop them all. You and I both know, if you stand by idly watching as injustices take place throughout the world and do nothing to expose and stop them, than we are no better than those committing these crimes."

The expression on his face showed his frustration with my rebuttal when he said, "Christina, I can't stop you from going public with this tape if you insist. So, I will be blunt with you and tell you something which must be kept strictly confidential. I want you to realize what the most likely outcome of going public will be." With a look of firmness, he sternly added, "If you go public then Congress will be forced to cut American funding to the current Ghana government. If that happens, then the American backed Ghana Government will be toppled by the Communist Party of the Republic of China. China happens to be secretly backing the rebel outlaws who are trying to overthrow the Ghana Government. America can't afford to allow the Communist Party of the Chinese Government to get a foothold in the region, and this is why the information you have **must be kept from the public.**"

I was once again surprised by his statement and I showed it by saying, "My God, George, this is becoming more unbelievable every time you tell me something. The last I heard America had good relations with China, and now you tell me they're trying to undermine our stability on the African continent." I gave him a look of total amazement and added, "I'll just assume the Chinese have expansionism on their minds and that's why you want me to sit on this."

He sighed with a sense of relief as he smiled at me and said, "I'm glad you understand the delicacy of the situation."

I almost laughed at him, but I managed to stop at a smile as I said, "I understand where you're coming from totally now George, but I respectfully disagree with you." I shook my head as I continued, "Furthermore, I'm afraid I can't put a lid on this one; it's already out of my control. The tape is now in the hands of the top brass at CBS and to top that, I will be appearing on the Barbara Water's National News Program this Monday night to show the tape to the country."

His face turned white as I finished speaking and with a disappointed tone he said, "I wish you hadn't done that before speaking with me."

In an attempt to be comforting, I once again took his hand in mine and said, "George, I'm truly sorry I jumped the gun on this one." I shook my head with disgust, looked him straight in the eyes and added, "When will the leaders of the world stop playing all these top-secret international games of deceit with one another, and start working together to make the world a safer place to live?"

He smiled with sincerity as he gently squeezed my hand and said, "Only God has the answer to that question, Christina."

My reply was adamant, "That may be so, but I believe if one nation truly stood up for freedom, truth, and justice for all, then perhaps it could be accomplished."

He grinned almost to the point of laughter as he said, "Christina, I would never have believed you to be so naive on international matters.   I only wish it could happen that easily."

I felt a slight sense of indignation by his assumption at my beliefs, which he obviously saw as unrealistic, and somehow naive.   I quickly calmed my gut response to rebuke him and said, "George, if there is one thing I've learned in my life it is that with hard work and determination anything is possible."

He gave me a surprised look and said, "That's a very noble concept Christina, I only wish it were true." Then he gazed at the time and added, "Christina, you are a lovely woman and even when we disagree, I always enjoy our chats.   But now I'm afraid I must end our visit."   Smiling he continued, "I have some damage control to get underway, thanks to you."

I smiled and said, "Well at least I think I can help you out with the domestic end of the damage control."

He looked at me with interest as he asked, "And just how do you propose to do that?"

I smiled deviously and replied, "If you arrange for me to address a Senate Hearing with my evidence before I break the story on Monday night; then, it will look as though I have your backing.   It would also save face for our foreign policy and your administration."

He thought about it for a minute then said, "You know, it just might work."   With a deep sigh of relief, he added, "Be prepared to address Congress the first thing Monday morning, and I'll take care of the rest." With that, we said our goodbyes and it was back to the helicopter. It was 6:00pm, when I climbed from the helicopter back at Stewart Airport.   Just before I entered the terminal buildings, I deliberately turned back and sensually waved goodbye to the seven very charming and attractive members of my wonderful, military escort.   When the valet driver brought my car, I climbed in and decided that due to the time I would head directly for my dinner date with Tom Davies. As soon as I pulled away from the curve, I picked up the car phone and placed a direct call to a personal friend of mine, Steven Bock who just happened to be the President of CBS.   You see, I had to arrange to be on the Barbara Water's show for that coming Monday evening, before George discovered my on the-spot bluff.   After hearing as much of the details I carefully chose to share with Steven, he was more than willing to cover my back.   He told me he would have Barbara call me personally later that evening, to go over all the arrangements for the interview.   After I thanked him, I cut our connection and thought, 'Why you sly fox, you! You just pulled one over on the President. I can't believe I actually did that and with such finesse.' I laughed out loud as my thoughts continued, 'Maybe I was Mata-Hari in a past life.'

Tom and I sat at a very secluded table in the back of the restaurant where we could speak privately.   While we ate, I said, "Tom, first I want to thank you for meeting me here on such short notice.   As you know, I would not have asked you to drive up here if it weren't important."

He gazed across the table at me with admiring eyes and said, "Christina, you don't have to thank me, I'm more than happy to help whenever you need me."   Smiling he continued, "Besides, that's one of the reasons you keep me on such a hefty retainer isn't it?"

I smiled and said, "No Tom, it's actually because you're such a brilliant sweetheart. That's why I keep you hanging around."   I reached across the table and gently patted his hand as I said, "Tom, the reason I asked you here happens to be profoundly serious.   I am asking for your help because you're the only person I trust to handle this very delicate situation."

The excitement grew on his face as I spoke and he looked at me with a gleam of anticipation in his eyes as he said, "I just love when you give me these interesting assignments, they always turn out to be quite challenging and I never know for sure where we're going to end up when we're finished."

I smiled devilishly as I said, "I do come up with some doosies though, don't I?   And I think this one has the potential to top them all.   Now let's get serious.   I want you to find some pieces of a puzzle for me and I don't want you to let anyone catch onto what you're trying to do.   I know somewhere there is a connection to be found between Lee Bradford, George Rush, NASA, and The Challenger Disaster, and I want to know what that connection is."

His eyes almost popped out of his head, as he took a deep breath and said, "You don't think the two of them actually had something to do with The Challenger Disaster, do you?"

I looked at him very seriously and replied, "If you say that too loudly you might get us both killed and no, that's not what I'm saying. All I want you to do is find me the connecting pieces and I'll put the puzzle together."

He shook his head in disbelief and said, "You got it, boss."

We had time for one quick drink after dinner, then I was finally on my way home to Michael. I walked in the door at 9:45pm and had just enough time to say hi and kiss Michael before taking a phone call from Barbara Waters. Barbara and I went over the details of the interview until midnight.   When we finally had the outline for the interview completed, she said, "You know Christina, I have been trying to get an exclusive interview with you for years."   With a conniving tone in her voice she continued, "Steven seems to think you're between a rock and a hard place on this one, and that you may be willing to consent to a candid interview with us, as a way of showing your appreciation to the network."

When I finished laughing, I said, "You sure have a way of saying what's on your mind Barbara, and I guess that's more than fair."

As soon as I hung up, the phone rang again, and I was back on it talking with Jimmy. And as soon as I heard Jimmy's voice, I said in our joking tone, "You know I have to tell you, you're some piece-of-work girlfriend.   You leave me here running around the country like a chicken without a head, trying to organize a mishmash of corporate mumbo jumbo, then you have the gall to ask me to do you a little favor in Ghana."

We both started to laugh, as he said, "I gather you've received my list of demands."

After I stopped laughing, I filled him in on the day's events; then, I said, "Jimmy, I wish you were home. You can't imagine how much I miss you. I haven't crashed on the sofa with buttered popcorn since you left."

With a sad tone to his voice he replied, "I miss you too girlfriend, but I couldn't come home now no matter how much I might want to. Christina, someone has to do something on this end, because you're not going to believe what I've discovered this time." He proceeded to tell me with a tone of anger just how the Ghana government was spending the American Foreign Aid it was receiving. By the time we finished our conversation it was 3:12am and I headed straight for the bedroom. Michael was sound asleep when I climbed into the warm bed with him. I was so tired when my body hit the mattress that I kissed Michael's bare back and passed out.

The next morning, I was awakened at 7:00am by a call from the President. After the call I headed for the kitchen and a much-needed cup of coffee. Over breakfast I told Michael and Joanne what transpired between the President and me at our meeting. Then I continued to fill them in on my new schedule for that afternoon and the following day, beginning with a 2:00pm meeting this afternoon with the Speaker of the House, in Washington, D.C. After which, with a sympathetic tone I added, "I'm sorry about this guys, but I have to do something to help stop this madness." I looked at them optimistically and added, "Maybe we can find the time to do something fun together while we're on the West Coast this week."

Joanne perked up and said, "Well, our day wasn't quite as exciting as yours, but we did have fun.   We took the boat all the way to Albany, and that was the first time I ever saw the New York State Capital from the viewpoint of the river.   I've got to tell you, it's even more of a beautiful city from the water."   She reached across the table to where

Michael was sitting, gently took his hand in hers and continued, "I also have to thank you for asking Michael to take me. Your husband is a gracious tour guide."

I smiled sweetly as she talked, because I realized I was consciously timing how long she held Michael's hand.

When she finished speaking, Michael nonchalantly pulled his hand from hers and said, "I'm glad you had a nice day Joanne, I did too." He looked at me as he said, "What time are you leaving today?"

I lifted my eyebrows in dismay and said, "As soon as I clean up and change, honey."

With that, I finished eating and went to take a shower. As I washed, I was sure Michael was going to be coming in any second now to make passionate love to me, but he never did. When I was ready to leave, I came down to say goodbye and I couldn't find them anywhere. I looked out the opened back patio doors, to find the two of them splashing in the pool together. I walked over to them, gave Michael a kiss goodbye as he climbed out to meet me, then waved to Joanne who waved goodbye from the pool, and it was off to the airport.

CHAPTER 27

When I arrived in Washington, I went straight to my 2:00pm appointment with The Speaker of the House, Senator Edward Kenny. The appointment was at his downtown office, and I felt quite uncomfortable to say the least. After all, I did steal one of the family companies from him. Not to mention, humiliating him in front of the entire country. So when I opened the door to his office, you can understand why I was slightly perspiring.

American Goddess

He rose from his seat like a true gentleman as I entered his office and very calmly approached him. When I reached him, I stretched out my hand to shake his as I said with a friendly tone, "Edward! It's nice to see you." I lifted my eyebrows to help flatter him and continued, "You're looking well. I'm pleased to see you've recovered so nicely after our unforeseen corporate collision."

I could feel his masked hostility toward me as we shook hands, and when we released our handshake he graciously said, "Christina, it's wonderful to see you as well, and thank you for your thoughtful concern over my welfare." He gestured to me to take a seat as he added, "Please make yourself comfortable, this is going to be a long night."

As I sat down, I thought, 'Well that wasn't too bad, I've experienced worse.'

After we exchanged a few more casual comments Edward said, "Well, I think we should get down to business before the committee arrives. I need to explain to you the procedures involved in addressing Congress. A six-member Senatorial Committee including myself has been chosen by the President to head the hearing of your case tomorrow morning. That committee and I will be questioning you this afternoon so we may decide ahead of time, which way to lead the questioning at tomorrow's Congressional Hearing."

I looked at him and sighed as I said, "I knew I had to prepare for this, but I didn't realize it was going to take all night."

When I finished speaking, four Republican Senators entered the room and I had had a run-in with each one of them over some human rights issue in the past. Then to add insult to injury, I was almost visibly shocked when I saw Lee Bradford enter the room. At that moment, I realized everyone in that room had a personal vendetta against me for one reason or another. I smiled as I thought, 'Touché, George Rush! You knew this payback was going to be a bitch.' I slightly shrugged my left shoulder as I thought, 'Aaa, I'm a big girl, I can handle it. Yeah! As long as no one tries to shoot me that is.'

As soon as everyone sat down it was straight to work. My grueling hours of answering questions finally came to an end around 9:30 that evening. As everyone got up to leave the office, Lee stood up, turned and walked away from me without even saying goodbye, and he hadn't even said hello. As a matter of fact, the only time he acknowledged me at all was when he had no choice. As I watched him leaving, I felt compelled to say, "Lee, are you really going to walk out that door without even acknowledging me?" He didn't even look back and I thought, 'How could I have loved that man for all those years and never truly knew what kind of man he really was?' Then I brought up the rear as we left and headed for my waiting limo.

The moment I entered my suite at the Hilton, I phoned room service and heard a masculine voice say, "Good evening, Ms. Powers. This is Pierre Collins, head of in-house accommodations. How may I be of service to you this evening?"

American Goddess

I was impressed by his sense of accountability to the customer; so, in a very commanding, yet provocative tone I replied, "By accomplishing two tasks for me Pierre, as swiftly as possible.   First, I would like a large serving of linguine with white clam sauce, accompanied by toasted garlic bread, tossed salad with Italian dressing, grated Parmesan cheese and a chilled bottle of Chianti.   Second, I would like a Sudanese language study guide.   The language guide I want you to deliver to me personally no matter what time, even if you have to wake me, I want it tonight!"   Then I hung up the phone and started to laugh as I thought, 'If this guy pulls this off on a Sunday night at 10:00pm I'm stealing him from this place.'

After I stopped laughing, I figured it was time to call home. I dialed our bedroom phone first and when Michael didn't answer I called the house phone.   When Carman answered the phone, we exchanged greetings, and then I asked for Michael. She said, "Hold on Christina, I have to bring the phone out to them."

With curiosity I said, "Where are they anyway?"

From between the sounds of scuffling shoes and heavy breathing I heard her say, "In the pool."   When she reached the pool, I could hear Michael and Joanne laughing between the sounds of splashing water.

When Michael answered the phone, he said, "Hi, Punkie! How are things going down there?"

I was tired and irritated by his good-natured greeting, so I answered with an air of irritation, "Not as smoothly as it sounds like it is there.   I can't believe you're still in the pool."

He laughed as if I were making a joke and said, "We haven't been in the pool all day. We only just came back from the camp house in the mountains.   Now stop fooling and tell me how you made out."

I sighed and said, "I'm too tired honey, I just wanted to tell you I love you, and miss you, before I call it a night."

Michael replied with a loving tone, "Okay Punkie, I love you too.   Now I want you to get some rest, and know I'll be with you in spirit tomorrow."

After I hung up the phone, I headed straight for the shower.   Ten minutes after my shower there was a knock at my door.   When I answered it, there was an extremely attractive young man standing behind a room service, meal cart and he said, "Good evening, Ms. Powers.   Here is the meal you requested, as well as the Sudanese Language Study Guide you asked for."

I took the guide out of his hand to examine it. When I confirmed its authenticity, I smiled and said, "Pierre Collins, I'm truly impressed. That's why I would like to offer you a position as one of my personal secretaries starting at three times your current salary." Needless to say, he accepted my offer on the spot.

American Goddess

The next morning, I was dressed like a female business tycoon should be, when I entered the Halls of Congress. Promptly at 9:00am, I formally introduced myself to the members and proceeded to address the U.S. Congress in a Congressional Hearing. At one point in the midst of my five-hour address, after the viewing of the tape, I began to condemn the Ghana Government for allowing their troops to commit such monstrous, human rights violations. As soon as I knew I had everyone's attention I said, "I believe the citizens of the United States must call upon the United Nations to take swift action in investigating the murders of these three International Red Cross Workers."

Then I began to answer their questions, right up till we broke for a one-hour lunch break at noon. The moment I stepped out of the door, I was swamped by reporters, who became quite disappointed when I said, "Sorry gang, but I promised 'Waters' the exclusive on this one."

As soon as we returned from lunch, I proceeded to condemn the Ghana Government for their disgraceful mismanagement of the American Foreign Aid they were receiving, and then said, "I am at this very moment gathering further evidence which will show just how wealthy the Ghana Government Officials are, while their citizens live in deplorable conditions. It's no wonder the people of Ghana are joining the Rebel Movement to overthrow the government." At that point I took a sip from my water glass because the place was getting hot. I knew I was now treading in dangerously forbidden waters, so I cautiously continued by saying, "Ladies and gentlemen of Congress, please don't misunderstand me, I'm not advocating abandoning the Ghana Government completely. All I am saying is that America, as the leader of the world in foreign aid grants to Third World Countries, should have in place a much better monitoring system. I believe if a nation agrees to accept aide from America, then that country should be held accountable to the American people on how they spend that aid."

With that, Senator Elm stood up and said, "Ms. Powers, that sounds like a wonderful suggestion, but how in the world do you expect America to monitor all the nations who receive grants from the U.S.?"

I looked at him confidently and replied, "Senator Elm, I'm surprised at you. All we have to do is establish an international financial investigating committee, and then send them traveling the globe doing just that. And I could not think of a better place to get them started than in Ghana. I believe if we make an example of Ghana; then, we just might begin to curb this type of activity throughout the world."

I'm pleased to say the Senator had no rebuttal, and by the time my address was completed, I had convinced 72% of the members to openly condemn the Ghana Government and to call for an investigation of our financial dealings with them. When I left the hearing that afternoon, I left to a round of applause; and it was straight to the airport by 3:30pm, where I boarded my corporate jet and headed for New York City.

American Goddess

During my 9:00pm nationally televised interview with Barbara Waters, I showed the world the tape that Jimmy had sent to me. I answered some questions which led me right into telling the world just how I believed the situation should be handled. Not ten minutes after the interview and before I could even leave the CBS Studios, I received a call from Jean Fitzpeters, the American Ambassador to the United Nations. She called to invite me to address the U.N. Assembly, at 11:00am the next morning, and I graciously accepted.

When I hung up the phone, I handed it to Pierre Collins, who was standing behind me waiting for something to do and said, "Here Pierre, for your first assignment book me a suite at the Plaza, we're staying in town tonight." He anxiously took the phone from me and went right to work.

As soon as we arrived at the Plaza, I called home to inform Michael of my change in plans and that I would be home just in time to leave for our business trip to the West Coast. After we finished our conversation, I talked with Pierre for around an hour about his expected duties. After which I showered, changed and began to study the Sudanese Language of Ghana before calling it a night.   I found the language to be very similar to the Bantu dialect used in the Union of South Africa, which I studied only two years' prior. So my studies that night turned out to be less strenuous then I had expected, and I was glad. I had enough to do without trying to learn a totally new language in a few weeks, because for some reason I knew I was going to need to know this language.

The next morning at precisely 11:00am, I found myself addressing the United Nations Assembly. When I took the podium I said, "I truly thank you all from the bottom of my heart for inviting me to speak here this morning especially since the reason I'm here is to ask for your international assistance. I believe that the United Nations has truly become the international symbol of peace and cooperation throughout the world that its founders intended it to be. That is why I find myself here, because this is the only organization on the planet with the power, to profoundly influence the world's governments into giving all people the dignity of basic human rights. These rights which we cherish must belong to every child born on the face of the earth, or no nation will ever experience true peace. This is why we cannot sit idly by, as dictatorship style governments brutally massacre thousands of their citizens and force hundreds of thousands more to flee into refugee camps, where they are left to starve because the government is cutting off all supplies from international assistance. I am asking the World Community to say no to Ghana. We must send in an international peace keeping force, accompanied by an international committee to investigate all human rights violations." At that point, I looked around at the reaction I was getting and added in a very serious tone, "If we don't act now, then millions of innocent people will die. Please do not let that happen! Not when it's in our power to do something to stop it, before we see any more atrocities such as the horrible ones, we've witnessed on the video tape I've shown the world." I received a round of applause.

When everyone quieted down the lead speaker of the U.N. Assembly stood up, and said, "Ms. Powers, I would like to thank you from the World Community for so graciously addressing the assembly on such a delicate matter. Right now Ms. Powers, I promise you and the citizens of the United States, the International Community will not stand by and watch as these atrocities continue. Furthermore, let me also say we will put your suggestion to a vote this afternoon. Ms. Powers, on behalf of the International Community, I would like to make a counter request of you, which is if we agree to follow your suggestions, would you consider heading the International Human Rights Committee on behalf of your country?"

I was on the spot and I knew it. In that moment I thought, 'Oh my God! I don't have time to go running off to Ghana to do this now' Then I got angry and I thought, 'Why you, bastard! I'm standing here in front of the whole world; how can I say no?' Knowing everyone was waiting for my response, I smiled as I stood up tall and said, "Sir, I would be honored to serve the World Community in such a distinguished capacity." When I finished accepting the position, I received a standing ovation. I swallowed hard as I took my seat and thought, 'Shit, Jimmy! Six-thousand miles away, and you're still pulling me into these things! You just wait till I get my hands on you.'

Not ten minutes later, the resolution to send an International Peace Keeping Force, along with an International Human Rights Committee, headed by 'yours truly' to Ghana, was voted on and passed with 96% of the vote. I was thrilled and horrified at the same time over the vote, but I only showed my enthusiasm to the world.

By the time I arrived home, I only had one hour to pick up Michael and Joanne and get back to the airport. So when I entered the family living room at 7:00 that Tuesday evening, and found Joanne lying on the sofa with a low grade fever, 'you know me,' I became a little concerned to say the least.

When I asked her where Michael was she said, "He went to the drug store to pick up some Tylenol."

The moment she finished speaking, Michael walked in and said, "Here I am now." He came to me, kissed my cheek and continued, "Hi Punkie, I've missed you. Joanne's not feeling well and we were out of Tylenol, so I went out for some."

He opened the bottle, handed it to Joanne, and I said, "You can't take that. If you're running a fever your body could be rejecting the baby." I picked up the phone as I said, "I think we'd better call Dr. Hart before we do anything."

As soon as I got him on the phone and filled him in on our situation he said, "Listen, I'm just leaving the office now, so why don't I stop in and check on Joanne at the house."

I thanked him, hung up the phone and said, "Dr. Hart will be here in a few minutes."

American Goddess

After Dr. Hart's examination he said, "I can't say for sure what's causing the fever, but it may be a sign your body is rejecting the fetus. I would suggest you stay off your feet for a few days. Make sure you get plenty of rest, drink plenty of fluids, and only Tylenol for the fever. I want you to call me immediately if you have any discharge, or if the fever goes past 101."

I had ten minutes before I had to leave, when Dr. Hart left, so I took Michael's hand and said, "Honey, I think it might behoove us to have you stay home with Joanne, and I'll take this trip by myself."

He agreed with me then said, "I don't know when we're ever going to spend some time together."

I shook my head, "You haven't heard anything yet."

He looked at me strangely, "What happened now?"

I kissed him, waved goodbye to Joanne and said, "I'll call you and tell you all about it later, because I have got to leave." Looking at them both I added, "Take good care of our baby, okay guys, and you'll be in my prayers, Joanne." I kissed Michael once more, turned and headed for the airport.

After my intense four-day business trip, combined with two charity dinner fund raising benefits, I returned home exhausted, only to discover I would be taking the next four weeks of planned business trips by myself as well.   Not five minutes before I arrived home, Dr. Hart had decided to put Joanne on complete bed rest. So, I spent one loving night with Michael and the next morning I began a four-week business trip, which started on September 1st, in Miami, Florida.

My personal staff and I had already completed our corporate studies on all the companies we had acquired and arranged to meet with on that trip. I wanted to personally introduce myself to all the staff and assure them I had every intention of keeping and modernizing their companies.   I told them if we worked together, we could all move into the twenty-first century as leaders in a world market.

On October 1st, which was two days before I was to return home, I received a call from the Secretary General of the United Nations.   He informed me I would need to be ready to leave for Ghana to join the International Human Rights Committee on October 6th.   Two days later, I had the glorious opportunity to spend several days helping Michael cater to Joanne's every whim before taking off for Ghana, even though Michael had arranged for her to have around the clock nursing coverage. I swear in the month I was gone; I think Joanne forgot every word in the English language except 'Michael'. If Michael and I had six hours alone before I left, it was a lot.

Then at 6:00pm, on October 6th, Michael took me to the airport for my 7:00pm flight to Ghana, and I did not plan on returning home until November 18th, which would be only one week before our wedding day.

American Goddess

Just before I boarded my corporate jet, Michael took me in his arms and said, "I don't know how in the world, you talked me into allowing you to go into a war-torn country."

I smiled, kissed him and said, "It's because you love me and you know in your heart I'm doing the right thing."

He shook his head and with a look of concern replied, "I do know you're doing right by going, I just can't stand letting you go alone."

I lovingly gazed into his warm sad blue eyes and said, "I love you honey, but we both know you have to stay with Joanne and try to keep on top of the corporate monster we have created. Besides, I won't be alone I'll have my staff with me. You already know I've arranged for the jet to be kept at the airport, so if you need me, I will be able to leave right away."

He gently hugged me and said, "I know all that Punkie, I'm more worried about you being alone so far away, without me being there to protect you."

I kissed him and tried to comfort him by saying, "Honey, please try not to worry, I'll be fine. Jimmy will be meeting me at the airport with the American Ambassador. How dangerous can it be?"

Tears came to his eyes as he said, "Christina, I don't know what lies ahead for you over there and that scares me. But I do know somehow God's hand is on your life. So wherever God is leading you, keep trusting in your Guardian Angels to guide your steps." As both our tears began to fall, he kissed me passionately and softly whispered in my ear, "You're my precious Punkie, and I will keep my thoughts on you every second we're apart."

As we embraced Julie, my flight attendant interrupted us, "Excuse me Ms. Powers, but the captain has said we must leave now."

I felt an empty feeling come over me as I pulled away from Michael's embrace. I wiped the tears from off his cheeks with my fingers and said, "I miss you already my love, and I will call you as soon as I'm able."

He kissed me one more time and said, "Be safe Christina, Please!" I returned his kiss then quickly walked away. As I boarded the jet, I blew him a kiss. I stepped back as Julie closed the door, and like the blink of an eye he was out of sight, and I was off to Ghana.

American Goddess

CHAPTER 28

I wobbled as if I had rubber legs when I exited the Jet in Accra, the Capital City of Ghana, at 1:00pm on October 7th. I was surprised to be welcomed by a large group of cheering fans, some holding large signs reading, **"We love you, Christina!"** As my feet touched the ground, I was greeted by a group of armed soldiers, who proceeded to escort my staff and me through the crowd and into the airport terminal. When I finished going through the security gates, I headed down the hall and my heart was filled with excitement the moment my eyes caught Jimmy's. We rushed to one another with open arms and with the exuberance of little children leapt into a wholehearted embrace. In the midst of our loving greeting, I whispered into his ear, "I'll get you later you, shithead!"

He started to laugh and whispered back, "I figured, you would." I hugged Richard as Jimmy continued, "Christina, let me introduce you to the American Ambassador to Ghana, Diana Frangella."

I greeted her then off we went to the Princess Hotel. Our entourage had a military escort which led us through the incredibly, beautiful, tropical like paradise, of the Capital City of, Accra.

I was amazed by the obvious wealth of this city, so I turned to Jimmy and said, "I'm surprised Jimmy, I half expected to see a war-ravaged city here. This place is far from it."

Jimmy shook his head and said, "I know and so are its sister cities, Secunda and Takoradi. But you go only five-hundred-miles inland and the government is forcing hundreds of thousands into starvation camps. The most barbaric thing about it is all the refugees are the true black native Ghanaians, while the ruling party is completely white. The only blacks you will see in the cities are laborers, who are bussed in from the surrounding slums."

I looked at the Ambassador and said, "Diana, how in the world has this type of racial bondage been allowed to go on?"

She looked at me sadly as she answered, "This civil war between Prime Minister Kwame Nkmah's troops and the rural population in the northeastern hill country has been going on since the ruling party took power in 1957."

I was angered by my own ignorance to this suffering and asked, "What about the U.N. Security Council's Resolution on human rights? Doesn't that apply to Ghana?"

With a sense of frustration, she answered, "Ghana has been a political time bomb for America for years now, and no one was willing to talk about it. It appears the

American Goddess

American policies of the fifties haven't changed toward Ghana, since the then, Leader of the House, said to Congress, 'after all, they're only ignorant savages, aren't they.'"

I was shocked by her bluntness and it showed as I said, "What you're telling me is if I hadn't brought this to the world's attention, Ghana would still be considered a valued member of the United Nations. That blows me away! If our government knew this was going on, then you can't tell me the U.N. had no idea these atrocities were taking place."

She looked at me dead serious, "That's exactly what I'm saying, Christina."

I shook my head in disbelief and said, "If I've done my homework correctly, the current Prime Minister, Kwame Nkmah, is the son of the former Prime Minister."

She smiled as though she was impressed and replied, "You're right and the war has increased since he was elected to succeed his father in '79, and he has won every election since."

As I listened to her words, I thought, 'My God! Somehow I've got to put a stop to this madness.'

Shortly after the noon hour, I checked my staff and myself into the entire 20th floor of the Princess Hotel, which was located directly across the Boulevard from the Prime Minister's Palace. When we entered the suite, Diana informed me I had a 3:00pm meeting with the International Human Rights Committee, in the conference room of the hotel. She said, "They are anxiously waiting for you to inform them on how you intend to lead this investigation."

I looked at her with a surprised expression, "Are you telling me no one from the U.N. Security Council has a game plan for an investigation?"

She turned my surprised expression into her own and with concern in her voice said, "Yes! We were informed you would be advising the committee on how to proceed with the investigation. As for the advisors from the Security Council, they're all with the British and French, Peace Keeping Forces, in Togoland, which is four-hundred-miles north of here in the interior of the country."

I shook my head in dismay, smiled and said, "Don't worry about it Diana, I'm on top of everything." as I thought, 'Oh well! I'll figure it out later.'

As soon as we settled into the suite, I picked up the phone and dialed the Prime Minister's private number. Diana was asked by the Prime Minister's Personal Secretary to see that I received the number. He also requested she inform me the Prime Minister would like for me to call him personally as soon as I was settled. So, with the answering of the phone by Prime Minister Kwame himself, I proceeded to dive headfirst into the entangled web of the Ghana political nightmare, as soon as he said, "Hello, Ms. Powers. Thank you for calling so promptly."

American Goddess

Courteously I replied, "Good afternoon, Prime Minister Nkmah. I would also like to thank you for your private number. It is reassuring to know I will be able to reach you at any time during the investigation, if there should be a need."

With a wonderful use of the English language and a tone which was not very appealing he said, "Ms. Powers, let's understand one another right off. I am not pleased with your presence in my nation. The only reason I am contacting you at all, is because it was requested of me to do so by the U.N. Security Council, and I agreed. Now, I would like to request your presence at a 7:00pm informal dinner this evening at my personal residence here in the Prime Minister's Palace. I would like to know in advance exactly what your plans are for this Human Right's Investigation."

I quickly responded with an authoritative tone of my own, "I'm very pleased you will be cooperating with the investigation, I'm sure you will assist me in any way possible." Just as quickly I changed to a friendly tone as I continued, "I would also be honored to have dinner with you this evening to inform you of my intentions, while I'm here in your beautiful nation." We ended our conversation on a friendly note and it was right to work.

As soon as I hung up the phone, I went back into the living room where Jimmy, Diana, Richard, and Pierre, the young man I stole from the Washington Hilton, were relaxing, and called them all into an on-the-spot conference.

When I had everyone's attention, I said, "Pierre, would you please take out the map of Ghana for me?" I opened the map and continued, "Now Diana, please point out and circle all the hot spots for me? I'll need a brief background on them all." She looked at me with a bewildered expression, so I added, "You know, the ones where the crimes have been committed." As she circled the hot spots, I began to come up with my game plan for the investigation.

We worked until 2:45pm, at which time we proceeded to the Conference Room for our luncheon with the eighteen international members of the Human Rights Committee. As Diana introduced us all, I was quite pleased with myself because I could actually speak to them in their own individual languages. After our lunch, I walked up to the platform and said in English, "Ladies and gentlemen, I would like to say it has been a pleasure meeting every one of you, and as pleasant as this meeting has been, we mustn't forget the gravity of the circumstances which brought us here. Starting tomorrow morning, we will all become incredibly involved in a highly sensitive situation. But I will not be overwhelming any of you this evening. All I will ask for tonight, is that everyone try to enjoy the amenities of the Hotel and get your bearings. I will be having dinner with the Prime Minister this evening, and I will fill you all in on our conversation tomorrow morning at 8:00am, so please enjoy yourselves until then."

It was 6:30pm when a military escort arrived at the door of my suite to accompany me to the Prime Minister's Palace. I was led to the Prime Minister's Office where he was waiting for my arrival. He rose from his seat as I entered the room and impatiently stood there, as I slowly walked the thirty paces toward his large desk. He was a tall, distinguished looking man, in his early fifties, with a stern expression. When I confidently reached him, we graciously exchanged greetings and with sophistication and charm, I quickly put us on a first name basis. I was wearing an off-white Giavani business suit and I made it a point to come across as the beautiful angel who, with a hard hand, would help salvage his crumbling nation. The Prime Minister was dressed in a formal presidential style, black, three-piece suit. He tried to present himself as sophisticated royalty, but he was so taken by my physical appearance that it showed through the eyes of his royal facade, just like any down to earth, red blooded, American male, that I'd ever met. The minute I spotted that look, I knew he was going to end up being putty in my hands!

As Kwame and I chatted, we earned a little respect for one another and what was supposed to be a very formal private dinner, turned into a very informal one. After our cordial dinner, Kwame invited me into his private study, so we might be more comfortable as we discussed our business. I agreed and proceeded to walk with him to his study. As we sat in two side by side, Queen Anne chairs gazing out over the beautiful Gulf of Guinea, Kwame smiled warmly at me and said, "Christina, I must tell you as much as it displeases me to have you in my nation for the reason you're here, it has still been a great pleasure meeting you. May I also thank you for joining me for dinner this evening, because I have discovered for myself you are truly the beautifully, enchanted woman your reputation proclaims you to be."

I smiled with a slightly flattered expression and replied, "I would like to thank you Kwame, for your gracious compliment and I'm pleased to hear it, because my feelings are similar." I then boldly and gently patted his hand, as I gazed into his eyes and with a soft smile added, "Maybe now that we are a little more comfortable with one another, we should consider the reason I'm here."

He nodded his head diplomatically and said, "I agree completely Christina, and my first question is exactly how you intend to proceed with your investigation?"

I turned toward him as I gracefully swept my fingers through my hair, then settled it back in place with a quick shake of the head and said, "First, I would like to proceed by having the International Human Rights Committee travel into the interior of the country, to eight different regions where Human Rights atrocities have been reported. I would like to get them started on the investigation as soon as possible, and I would also like for you to instruct your military to cooperate with the requests of the committee completely."

As I was speaking, we were interrupted by a house servant who entered, poured us both a glass of white wine, and then slipped away as quickly as she appeared. I took a sip of the wine and continued, "The second thing I would like to do, is come straight to the point with you personally on just where you are leading your nation. You and I both know you're up against a wall now that the world's eyes are upon you. Now as I see it, you have one of two choices to make for your nation's survival. You can either end this civil war and unite your whole nation or continue with this brutality. Now if you will bear with me just a while longer, I will give you the outcome of the latter, first. If you ignore the U.N.'s warnings to put an end to this civil war, your nation will suffer great sanctions from the International Community. Once this happens, the rebels will become a mighty opponent, backed by the Red Communist Party of China, and I can guarantee the International Community will not come to your aid. You see, the plain truth is Ghana is just not strategic enough for the West to risk a war with China, thus giving China a strong hold in Africa and at the same time enslaving your nation forever."

He was visibly irritated by my bluntness and it showed as he replied, "Well, that sounds like a morbid prediction." Lifting his eyebrows with curiosity he added, "So what is your prediction with my first choice?"

My smile was brilliantly seductive as I answered, "Now on the other hand, if you are willing to rightfully embrace more than three quarters of your population into the mainstream of your Nations' society, then your Nation's future will be quite bright and I will help assure that."

He stood up, reached his hand out to me and said, "Please come with me for a moment, I would like to show you something." He proceeded to lead me through the palace to an open balcony which gazed out upon the Capital City. He waved his hand out toward this splendid city and said, "Do you see all this wealth? If I were to do what you propose, it would be turned into a slum in two years anyway, because that's when the next election rolls around. So, as I and all the residents see it, we have no choice but to continue fighting this civil war."

I embraced his shoulders and with honest sincerity in my voice said, "Kwame, it doesn't have to be like that. You can begin to turn this Nation around just by industrializing the interior of the nation. What you need to do is show the rural population you are truly going to help supply them with the opportunity to make a better life for themselves and their families. Once you treat them with common human dignity, they will become an asset to your nation, not a threat."

He looked at me in dismay and said, "Christina, that's impossible. First, most of them are savages, who can't even live among themselves. Just look at their own tribal wars and then you tell me they can live in peace with us."

I shook my head and said, "Kwame, you're still living in the past and you don't even realize things are changing in the interior of your nation. Can't you see how over the last three years the tribes have begun to band together with the Chinese to wage an all-out attack on the Capital? If they can band together against you, then they are a little more

311

intelligent then you give them credit, and one should never underestimate one's opponent." I looked at him with deep sincerity and continued, "If there is one thing I've learned in our meeting this evening, it is that deep inside, you are not an evil man. I also realize for myself you honestly believe you have been doing the right thing for your nation."

He smiled and said, "I'm happy to hear that Christina, because I'm truly not the ruthless dictator you've led the world to believe me to be." His expression became helpless and my heart went out to him as a fellow human being, as he humbly said, "My dilemma is I cannot see how to overcome all the obstacles my nation faces."

I gazed at him with compassion as I replied, "If you will allow me to Kwame, I will stand by you and help you guide your nation with dignity, into the twenty-first-century."

I could see his overwhelming feelings of frustration rising from within him as he shook his head, "Christina, I wouldn't have a clue as to where to start."

I smiled and said, "That's because you're too close to the situation to see the big picture. All you have to do is what I've said, and that is to bring life to the interior of this nation. Start by industrializing the war-ravaged areas. Bring business there, bring roads, electricity, hospitals, running water, and build health safe communities for the people. Show them your government genuinely wants to change. Treat them like you really care. Apologize to them and help them understand why you thought you were doing the right thing."

He looked at me with a slight sense of relief and asked, "If I do that do you really believe they will listen to me?"

I answered him with the utmost sincerity, "Yes I do! And I will tour your nation with you, and together we will convince your people this is the right path to follow." I took his hand as I continued, "I promise you right now Kwame, I will personally bring manufacturing plants into the needed areas, and I will also help bring other American Corporate sponsors to your nation." He still had an unbelieving look so I added, "Kwame, all we have to do is create a business-like plan, which you can implement over a four-year span."

His eyes widened as he said, "Four years! The people would never give us four years to turn this nation around, and I will be voted out of office in two years. Then it will all end up in the hands of the Communists anyway."

I released his hand with frustration and thought, 'how can I convince this man this is his only answer?' Then it came to me and with excitement I said, "All we have to do is stipulate in a peace agreement that your government must have four years to implement your plans before the next election." I smiled with even more excitement as I continued, "The best part of that is it will put international pressure on the rebels to agree with this peace accord; thus, taking the pressure off your government."

American Goddess

He looked at me with total amazement and said, "If you can prove to me we can convince the rebels to go along with your plan, and you give me six years to complete the task, then I will accept your offer."

I hugged him with excitement and said, "God bless you Kwame, because with courage and dignity you have chosen to do the right thing for your people."

The next morning, I put the International Human Rights Committee to work throughout the countryside in pairs, accompanied by the U.N. Peace-Keeping Force. Kwame and I, along with my staff, began a thirty-six-hour marathon to compose a peace treaty that would be favorable for all concerned. Let me tell you that was not an easy task, but we did it! At the same time, I requested the U.N. arrange for immediate peace talks to be held among all the chiefs of the interior tribes with Kwame Nkmah's Government. Kwame had finally agreed to all the changes I proposed for his government and a wonderful peace treaty was ready to be presented at the peace talks. After our marathon, Kwame made a personal request to the U.N., asking the Security Council to allow me to mediate the peace talks, as the official representative for the United Nations. Their reply was they could only do that if I were an 'Official Ambassador to the U.N. The moment President Rush heard this news, he immediately appointed me an 'Official Representative for the United States of America, to the United Nations'.

The next thing I knew, I was overseeing the peace talks in two different African dialects, to the eyes and amazement of the entire world. At 10:00pm on October 16th, a national peace treaty, which declared each of the twelve tribe leaders, governors of their respective regions, which were to be renamed states was signed. At noon that day, all the governors who signed the treaty, along with the Prime Minister and I began a nation-wide tour to explain to the citizens exactly what the treaty meant for them. And as all this was transpiring in Ghana, back home the headlines read, **"Christina Powers has proven to be America's 'Angel of Peace!' as she helps bring harmony to a war-torn nation!"** Or **"America stands proud as one of her own, Christina Powers helps bring peace to a racially divided nation!"** The peace treaty was ratified on November 5th, and two hours later I put into motion, my prearranged plans to begin to turn this nation into a profit making, free society for all its citizens.

Despite the pace of those few weeks, I tried to stay in touch with Michael as much as possible. With each conversation I could tell Michael was becoming more and more concerned over Joanne's health. It seemed she had experienced the spotting of blood on three occasions and she was still on strict bed rest. Even though I heard Michael's concern, I couldn't allow myself to become caught up in his fear of losing our child, so I chose to bury myself even further into the task at hand. Then, two days before I was ready to return home, while I was touring the nation with the Prime Minister, I received a message to call home immediately.

American Goddess

So, at 9:06pm on November 16th, when Michael informed me in a devastated tone that Joanne had miscarried our child, I was so far away from the immediate impact of the reality of our child's death, that I could not even feel the emotion of pain my Michael was experiencing. When he finished crying all I could find myself able to say was, "I will be home as soon as possible."

Then I said my goodbyes to the Nation of Ghana, without attending the Prime Minister's planned ticker tape parade for me, took the only ten minutes Jimmy and I had alone together the whole time I was there, to say a sad goodbye, and at 11:57pm I was on my way **home to Michael.**

CHAPTER 29

Due to the early blustery, winds and snows, of an icy Nor'easter, I was not able to enter the front door of our home until 2:00am, November 17th, 1989. The house would have been quiet, except for the howling of the winds as they roared through the river valley. The bursts of air which crept through the walls with each gust, gave me a cold chill as I made my way to the master bedroom. I was careful not to disturb Michael's sleep, as I quietly opened the bedroom door. The room was dimly lit by the glow of the alarm clock and a small plug-in night light, which enabled me to tiptoe through the room, past the bed and into the bathroom. Once in, I turned up the heat and quietly showered. Afterward, I slipped into my robe and returned to the bedroom without turning on a light. When I reached the bed, I slipped off my robe and laid it on the chair bedside the bed. I gently pulled down the covers and softly slipped into the bed with Michael. My body

314

American Goddess

became cold as soon as I disrobed, so I slowly began to snuggle to Michael's warm bare back. The second my body touched his, the fires of my passion began to heat from within. My desire for Michael rose until I found myself slowly beginning to stroke his body, in an attempt to wake him already aroused. He slowly began to come out of his deep sleep. When he realized I was lying behind him, he turned to me and instantly took on a broken-hearted expression, as he desperately clung to my breasts and began to weep like a little boy.

As he softly wept in my arms, I slowly stroked his head and tenderly whispered, "I'm here my love, I'm here. Everything will work out now that we're back together again; I promise you it will, Michael." As I lovingly spoke these words, he slowly gazed up at me and with tear filled eyes cried,

"I've failed us, Punkie! I've lost our baby. I can't understand how you could go off and help save a nation and I couldn't even help keep our baby alive."

My heart broke as I held him tight and at that moment, I felt the pain of his devastation and the shame of his perceived failure. My tears began to flow with his. I wanted so much to comfort him, so in a gentle and assuring voice I said, "Michael, honey, don't do this to yourself. You did everything humanly possible to prevent this from happening, I know you did! But you know as well as I do, sometimes no matter what we do we can't prevent or change anything from happening."

He slowly shook his head as he stopped crying and with disgust in his voice said, "I know you're right Punkie, but it's still killing me that we lost another baby."

I tenderly kissed his forehead as I lovingly replied, "I know it hurts Michael, I feel the pain too, but I promise you we will try again, and we will have our baby."

At that, his eyes filled with tears again as he cried in anguish, "No we won't Christina because Joanne has decided she can't go through this again and she's leaving in the morning." Then his voice became weak with a tone of defeat as he continued, "And Punkie, if Joanne will not carry our child, then I don't want to go through the whole ordeal again. I just don't think I can handle it."

I held him close to my heart and with all the love I felt for him said, "Just lay still in my arms and try to get some rest my love. I love you honey, and I promise you things will be clearer in the morning." With that, my heart ached for my love, as I gently rocked him in my arms.

When he finally drifted off to sleep, I thought, as I listened to the cold wind outside our window, 'Dear, God, why do you keep taking my babies from me? Are you still punishing me for the abortion I had? I was young when I did those things God! I didn't realize how precious a baby's life was. Nor did I realize how much I would end up wanting to have a baby of my own. God I'm sorry, I know what I did was wrong. My soul is scarred for life because of what I've done, haven't I suffered enough? Help me!

American Goddess

I can't and I won't deny Michael a child of his own, and even if it kills me, I will bear him his child.' I lovingly gazed at my sleeping beauty and thought, 'Michael, I want your child my love, more than anything I have ever wanted in my life, and I will give birth to your seed, I vow I will.' After I thought these things, a sense of peace came over me, and I was finally able to join Michael in his restless sleep.

The next morning after a warm welcome home by James and Carman, Carman, served us a delicious French toast breakfast. But, as Joanne, Michael, and I, sat there hardly saying a word, it was apparent I was the only one who appreciated our meal. I quietly ate my feast while waiting for one of them to say something. Finally, I could take the silence no longer so I said, "I know this has turned out to be an incredibly sad situation for all of us, but that doesn't mean we shouldn't talk about it. I think if we talk about how we're feeling then maybe we can walk away from this not feeling so devastated."

Joanne turned to me and in a very harsh tone said, "How do you know how Michael and I are feeling? You weren't here all those hours I layer in that bed, trying to prevent my body from rejecting the implant. Michael and I went through it alone and we cried alone when I had the miscarriage. So please don't sit there with your all-knowing and uncaring attitude, and tell me I'll feel better if I talk, because I'm talking, and I still feel like shit."

I quickly tried to understand where this was coming from before getting angry. So, with a calm steady voice I replied, "You're absolutely correct Joanne, I wasn't there. But that doesn't mean I'm not feeling the same loss you are. It doesn't mean I don't understand what the two of you have lived through in the past three months either. What I'm trying to say is, I do know what you went through and I love you for what you did. I also want you to know, even though you weren't able to give birth to our child, I will still see you receive the rest of your compensation. I also understand why you feel like you can't do this again and whether you can believe it or not, I can accept and agree with your reasons. I just don't want you to leave here hurting because I do care about you."

The moment I finished speaking, Joanne stood up and walked out of the room without saying another word. As she did, I could feel a sense of desperation come over Michael as he quickly rose from his seat and went after her. I immediately followed and when I reached them, my heart pained as I watched Michael grab Joanne by the arm and pleaded, "Please Joanne, I'm begging you to reconsider! We will give you two million-dollars if you will please bear our child for us." Tears welled up in his eyes as he continued, "Joanne, why can't you see you're the only hope we have of having a child. If you don't carry our child then we won't have one, because I will not do this again. I could never have another woman carry our child for us, not after knowing you."

American Goddess

As I helplessly watched Michael pleading with Joanne, for the first time in my life I felt inadequate as a woman, and that thought, at that moment, almost stole the pride I had in being a woman away from me. As I stood there feeling like this, I knew Michael had no idea what he was saying was killing me. Watching him plead with another woman for a child, made me want to scream out, "Michael, I will bear our baby!" But I couldn't, because I felt something was not right with this picture. As I watched them standing there together, I struggled to understand the obsession they seemed to have toward one another, and I began to feel very uncomfortable with the whole situation.

As soon as Michael finished pleading, Joanne began to cry as she said, "Michael, I love you and Christina very much, and I would love to give you both the baby you desire so badly. But look at it from my perspective because there is no way I can handle another week of bed rest, and you're asking me to stay in bed for nine months. I just can't do it, not even for ten-million-dollars."

That's when I jumped in with a sharp tone, "Michael, she's right! Now stop making this so hard for all of us and let her leave in peace."

Joanne looked at me with angry eyes as if to say, 'Who are you to speak to him like that.' Then she gazed warmly into Michael's eyes and said, "Michael, because I think you are truly a caring man and would make a wonderful father, I will bear your child for you, but only if you use my egg." With that statement, she smiled, turned to face us both, and continued as if she was also speaking to me, "This way you will both have your child, because I will surrender my parental rights to you Christina, as soon as the baby is born." Once again looking directly into Michael's eyes she added, "Michael, I'm sorry, but this is the only way I can be sure my body will not reject the fetus again."

Michael looked at me with a glow of pure excitement, joy, and relief then said, "Maybe this is the answer to our prayers, Punkie. I know the baby will only be mine biologically, but it will still be ours."

He could see the stunned look on my face, so he hugged me and with the most sincere voice I've ever heard said, "Christina, I love you with all my heart baby, and I would never consent to anything without your approval. But honey, before you answer please know what I've just realized, this may be the only chance I'll ever have of carrying on my father's bloodline."

I stepped back from him, looked into his loving eyes and I wanted to scream, "No, Michael!" But instead I said, "I think it is a wonderful idea too, Michael." We joyfully embraced as I said these words and all the while I was wanting to say, 'Even though I don't want a child like this, I won't keep you from having your own child. I can't bring myself to cause you anymore pain and disappointment than you already have suffered. I love you Michael more than anyone I ever loved before.' Only I kept these words to myself.

317

American Goddess

After our warm embrace, Michael dragged us to the bar, popped open a chilled bottle of champagne and began to pour three glasses. I smiled as we began to celebrate our decision that morning, but as I smiled, I wondered to myself, 'Will I be able to love this child even though it will not be mine?' As we talked, I really began to look deep within myself for the answer to my question. I looked at how happy Michael had become and how pleased Joanne seemed to be over the fact she could help after all, and at that moment, I truly realized just how much this child meant to Michael and I thought, 'Yes! I know I will love Michael's child, no matter who the biological mother is.' When I came to the awareness of just how much I would do for Michael's love, I was able to come to terms with the idea of having a child in this manner, and as soon as I did, a sense of peace came over me.

Two days later, we were back at Dr. Hart's office to request his assistance in our new adventure. After Joanne's physical, Dr. Hart advised us we needed to allow Joanne's body time to heal properly before proceeding. He felt she might be ready to conceive without a high risk, by her February cycle. So we set our sights on February 1st, 1990.

When we returned from our doctor's visit, I whole heartedly invited Joanne to become a permanent guest in our home, until after the birth of our child. I also felt it only fair, to give Joanne her million dollars and Michael promised another million after the birth of his child. We had also arranged for a new contract to be signed among the three of us, which stated Joanne could never admit to being the birth mother. I wanted this stipulation because I was still terribly ashamed of my infertility. So much so I actually dreaded the thought of my fans ever finding out that the **'Christina Powers'** couldn't bear her own husband's child. Once we signed our contract, Michael and I were once again filled with joy and anticipation for our future family.

American Goddess

When November 25th, 1989 arrived, the news cameras were flashing at the worldwide, headline stealing, wedding of the two happiest people on the planet.

After we said our wedding vows that Thanksgiving morning, I closed my eyes to kiss Michael and as we kissed, I became the proud wife of this beautiful man. As soon as we ended our wedding kiss, we gazed into each other's loving eyes and at that moment, for the first time in my life, I knew I was a failure, because I could never bear Michael's child. At that realization my eyes began to tear, and my feelings began to spin so fast, I couldn't tell if I was crying because I was happy or because I felt like an empty shell of a woman. In that moment, I went on autopilot as all my thoughts began to ricochet through my mind until they stopped on 'Frank'. Once again, I became able to concentrate on one thought, 'How in the world did I allow my hatred for Frank, to grow so evil that I will be paying for it for the rest of my life?' My mind and heart went deeper into my higher consciousness as my thoughts continued, 'As God is my witness, I will never allow hatred to consume my life again!'

Instantly I felt myself being lifted from years of hard heartedness and a glorious, strange feeling of harmony and oneness came over me toward every living creature. Finally, I understood what Michael once told me about how he knew he was one with God. I came to this realization as I talked with my new mother in-law, Tess Carr. As we spoke, a cool gentle breeze brushed my shoulder and I heard a soft voice whispering behind me, "Christina, strength comes forth from those who truly tap into the power of their own divinity. Remember this." I turned so quickly I startled Tess and to my surprise, no one was there.

When we left St. Patrick's church, in that quaint little town of Ravena, New York, there were thousands of people lining both sides of the main street. As we drove past them, they threw Red Roses at the fleet of horn blowing limos, which not only held the wedding party, but the guests as well. As Michael and I waved to my fans, the press caught it all with their cameras, for the whole world to see!

After the reception Michael and I flew to Key West, Florida for a one-week honeymoon. We spent the whole week in Barbara's secluded, oceanfront, beach house, which she so graciously offered to us as a wedding gift. That week we spent alone together was a beautiful dream come true for the both of us. Finally, after all we lived through since the night Michael proposed to me, we were legally husband and wife. Throughout that week we spent our days walking the beach for hours planning our future family dreams, and every night was spent in the loving intimacies of our oneness. Our honeymoon was the most incredibly romantic experience I had ever known. When it was time to leave our heavenly bliss, we took with us dreams enough to last a lifetime. So, on the flight to New York when I picked up a pen and paper to turn my thoughts into lyrics, I had a lot to write.

We returned home on December 4th, and on the next day it was right back to the office.   While I was in Ghana, Michael managed to stay on top of the business, while taking care of Joanne, but he still had to cancel six pre-arranged business trips, which were the first things I began to reschedule when I sat at my desk.

As I was going through my appointment book that day, Pierre {who had now become a full-fledged staff member of my personal team} buzzed me on the intercom and said, "Good morning Christina, and welcome home. I have dozens of messages for you, when would you like to go through them?"

I answered with a humorous tone, "Why don't we do it now Pierre, because I'll have managed to give us plenty to do by this afternoon."

I began to prioritize my return calls in my normal manner, as Pierre read through the messages in the order they arrived.   As Pierre spoke, I was balancing at least twenty thoughts through my mind at the same time and I came to an abrupt stop when Pierre said, "Then you received a call on your personal business line, from a woman who said she was an old friend.   She said her name was Mary Everett and she asked that you return her call as soon as possible."

When I heard her name, I instantly thought, 'Johnny!   Something terrible has happened to Johnny.'   I took the number from Pierre and said, "Would you please excuse me for a moment, and I'll buzz you when I'm ready to continue."   He nodded his head and left the office.   As soon as the door closed behind him, I picked up the phone and dialed the number.

When Mary answered the phone and realized who was calling, her voice took on a tone of urgency as she said, "Christina! Thank you for returning my call.   I've been waiting on pins and needles to be able to talk with you."

With concern I answered, "What's wrong, Mary?"

In reply she said, "Christina, I know we truly don't know one another.   And I'm sorry to contact you like this from out of the blue, but you once told me if I ever needed anything and you could help, that I should feel free to call you.   So that is what I am humbly doing, because I am in great need of your help."

As she talked, I found myself wanting to scream at her, 'Well, what is it? Is it, Johnny? Is he, dying? Has he, died? Just stop beating around the bush and tell me!'   Instead I answered with a comforting tone, "And I meant it, Mary, so please feel free to do just that and ask me whatever you need."

American Goddess

She sighed with a sense of great relief and said, "Thank you Christina, but I was hoping we could speak in private.   If you could only find ten minutes to meet with me, I will drive to New York tonight."

As she continued, I could not hold back my curiosity any longer, "Please just tell me is anyone ill?"

She answered calmly, "No, everyone is well.   This is more of a private matter."

I relaxed my tone and said, "Mary, I have a business trip I am scheduling right now, which will take me right to Richmond, Virginia.   What if I plan it for December 7th, which is only two days from now? I can stop by your home and save you the trip up here."

With a secretive tone she replied, "Wednesday will be fine Christina, but would you mind if I meet you for lunch somewhere.   I feel funny saying this, but I really don't want John knowing I've called you."

I was taken aback by her mysteriousness and I let it be known by saying, "I find it slightly disconcerting that you feel you need to be secretive about our meeting."

She quickly answered, "Please don't feel that way. My reason for the secrecy is to save the man I love from some personal embarrassment. That's all."

By the time we finished talking, we had made plans to meet for a 1:00pm luncheon at The Old Country Inn, which was located in the heart of the historic district of 'Old Richmond Town.'

After setting up the scheduling for a three-week business trip throughout the country, Michael and I decided since we were now three months behind in our plans to revamp our entire holdings, that it would behoove us to have Michael take care of things at our corporate headquarters, while I handled the business trips.   We had plenty of reliable people to leave in charge, but I still felt better knowing Michael was at the helm. So when I left at 4:00am on the morning of December 7th, to continue whipping my new corporations into shape, I was not planning to see Michael until he met me in Richmond for my thirty-sixth-birthday on Saturday, December 10th; then it's off to Mississippi and I did not plan to see him again until I returned home on Christmas Eve.

When I arrived in Richmond it was straight to a board meeting, where I immediately began to work my magic on its members.   But the whole time I was captivating my audience, I was watching the clock.   In the back of my mind, all I could think about was my rendezvous with Johnny's wife.   When we finally broke for lunch, I swiftly made my way to the limo and it was off to the Old Country Inn.   When I entered the restaurant, I recognized her immediately, even though I had only seen her once in my life, for only two minutes.

She rose from her seat when she noticed me approaching and as I reached her, she warmly embraced me and said, "Christina, it's so good of you to meet me like this, I know you're a very busy woman."

American Goddess

I thanked her as we took our seats then said, "It's nice to see you Mary, you're looking well."

She smiled with apprehension as she replied, "Thank you, you're too kind; but I know what time and working on the farm for the past fifteen years have done to my youthful looks.   As for you, you still look like you're twenty-years old.   When I look at you, I have to ask myself, how do you do it?   I have watched your career and I know you have not had an easy life either, but it doesn't show on you at all."

I finally broke into the middle of her rambling, {as a waitress stood at our table impatiently waiting to take our order} by saying, "I think we should order now, so we won't be disturbed while we talk."

She giggled with surprise, then like a light switch turning on, she saw the waitress standing there and exclaimed with a southern twang, "Oh my, I didn't even notice you there."

Over lunch she went on about her family, the farm, her parents, John's parents and she continued with this litany of her life history, until I finally said, "Mary as much as I'm enjoying our conversation I do have to leave at 2:00pm.   So if you need to speak with me about something in particular, then I think we should do that."

She smiled with embarrassment as she replied, "I'm sorry I'm rattling on, I do that when I'm nervous."

As she continued babbling on and on without saying anything, I thought, 'Holy Shit! This is who Johnny married! You poor thing.'   Then I thought, 'On the other hand, this is what you deserve for not coming after me.'

Finally she caught my attention when she said, "Christina, I don't know how to say this without just coming out with it."

At that point I had heard enough nonsense, so I abruptly said, "Mary, I'm a very busy woman so would you please get to the point."

Once again, I embarrassed her and when she gained her composure she said, "Okay! It's like this Christina; the last five years have been pure hell for us financially.   It has become so bad we are at the point with the bank, if we don't pay them in full by the first of the year, then they will foreclose on our farmhouse.   And I know if that happens, it will kill whatever life is left in John."   She looked deep into my eyes and spoke from her heart as she continued, "I would never have come to you for help if I had anywhere else to go.   The only reason I'm here is to try to save my husband, and if he knew I came to you for help his pride would never let him accept it."

She spoke her words of love with such passion that as a devoted wife myself, I felt her concern for Johnny in my heart.   So I took her hand and said, "Of course I'll help, Mary.   How much do you need?"

American Goddess

She squinted her face as she timidly squeaked out, "Three hundred-thousand-dollars. We have two-hundred-thousand-dollars, but the bank will not accept it. They say we must have the whole amount, which is five-hundred-thousand-dollars."

I smiled at her gently and said, "I know how banks can be, I was in your position myself once." Then I opened my purse, took out my checkbook and wrote out a check for five-hundred-thousand-dollars then said, "Please except this gift Mary, and see that the bank gets paid. I want you to keep your money and take the family on a vacation."

She became so excited she nearly knocked my water glass into my lap, as she reached across the table to hug me. With tears in her eyes, she smiled enthusiastically and replied, "Thank you Christina, I will never forget this!"

I kissed her cheek and replied, "I'm glad I was able to help, and don't worry I will never tell a soul of our meeting." Then I deliberately looked at my watch as I continued, "Oh my! Look at the time. I'm sorry to cut this short Mary, but I really must be leaving now." We embraced once more and I walked away thinking, "I would have never lasted all those years on that farm."

After our lunch, I went straight to work for the next two days on corporate negotiations. I did not have final approval for all my proposals, until 9:00 pm that Friday night. As I walked out of my last board meeting in Virginia, I was totally surprised when I saw Michael standing beside my limo in a black tux, holding a bouquet of Red Roses.

When I reached him, he lovingly hugged me and boisterously said, "Happy Birthday, Punkie!"

My body immediately became rejuvenated and alive with feelings of joy, as Michael kissed me. With a gleaming smile I replied, "It's not my birthday yet silly, but I'm surely glad you're here."

He kissed me romantically and said, "Well, I thought we might usher your birthday in together."

I returned his kiss, "That sounds wonderful, but why the tux handsome?"

He opened the car door and beckoned me to climb in. As we climbed in, he instructed the driver to take us to the hotel. He turned to me and said, "I placed a new gown in the suite for you, so all you need to do is get ready and leave the rest of the evening to me."

I smiled with sheer delight, then with a slightly seductive tone replied, "OOO! Michael! This sounds like it's going to be a fun and romantic evening. And I love you for thinking of it."

When we arrived at the suite, I disappeared into the bedroom for one half hour. When I reappeared, I was dressed to kill. Michael gazed at me with pure manly pride as I approached him. Then he kissed me gently, took my hand and off we went.

American Goddess

Michael proceeded to take me on the most romantic evening I had in a long time. We started with a candlelight dinner at a quaint little Italian restaurant, in the heart of the 'Old City.' From there, it was ballroom dancing in a 1930's style dance hall. After what seemed like hours of lovingly holding one another, as we rhythmically floated on the dance floor, Michael treated me to a romantic, 2:00am horse driven, Hansom Cab ride. As our buggy took us around the beautiful buildings of the wonderfully historic city of Richmond, Virginia, we were beginning to anticipate the end of our evening. Then right in the midst of this exquisite moment in time, Michael sweetly asked me to close my eyes and hold out my hand. When I opened my eyes, I was holding a small, velvet covered, heart shaped pillow, and in the center of it was a beautiful twenty-four karat diamond angel pendant! When I saw it, I immediately hugged him as I said, "Oh Michael, it's beautiful and I'm going to put it on right now! Thank you, my love."

I slipped it on my neck chain and as Michael snapped it back on me he said, "I love you more than life itself, Christina." With that, he held me tenderly until we arrived back at our hotel.

When we returned to our suite at 4:00am the morning of the 10th, we wasted no time in fulfilling our passions. We continued in our love making until we welcomed the rays of the morning sun through our bedroom window. That night was incredible and from the time we woke up twelve hours later, straight through to the end of the weekend, Michael treated me to more of the same. Our loving weekend ended Sunday the 11th, at which time Michael returned home and I returned to the hectic pace of my business travel.

CHAPTER 31

American Goddess

After thirteen days of triumphant corporate maneuvering, I returned home on Christmas Eve to spend a wonderful Christmas at home with Michael and Joanne. The three of us continued to spend almost every minute of the rest of that week together. During that week Joanne became so persistent in her efforts to make herself and the upcoming procedure the center of attention that by the time New Year's Eve rolled around, I was ready to throw her ass out the door.

By the end of that week, I wanted to say to Michael, 'Forget it! I'll adopt before I put up with ten more months of this crap.' However, for the love of my husband I chose to remain silent.

But, when Jimmy called on January 1st, 1990, to wish us a Happy New Year, let me tell you, he got an ear full the minute he shouted, "Happy New Year, Girlfriend! It's your long-lost lover boy! How the hell are you?"

I snapped back my response, "Lousy, that's how I am! And how many times do I have to tell you to call me? You didn't even call me for my birthday."

He lovingly snapped back, "Bullshit! I called, but you weren't home. Now stop your nonsense and tell me why you're so miserable?"

At that, I proceeded to take the next hour, to tell him exactly how I felt about this baby plan after spending only one week watching Joanne doting over my husband. I also expressed my new concern over taking business trips and leaving her alone with him.

Jimmy tried to reassure me I could trust Michael and that it would all work out for the best. But for some reason, I was not comforted by his words, so I said, "Well, at least you will be home to help me in July. Hopefully, things will calm down some by then."

It was with that statement; he cleared his voice in a disturbing manner and said, "Oh Shit, Christina! I forgot to tell you. Richard and I won't be leaving for home until August 3rd. Richard's parents are having their thirty-fifth wedding anniversary on August 1st, and they've invited us to come. So we are now going to be leaving Ghana on July 4th, for Kuwait instead of America. Richard wants us to spend one month with his family in Kuwait before we come home."

With a surprised tone I replied, "Kuwait! What are his parents doing in Kuwait? I thought he was from New Jersey."

Jimmy laughed as he said, "I know what you mean. We've been together for six months, and I didn't find out myself until two weeks ago. It appears his father works as an adviser to the Kuwait Government, and they have been living there for the last six years."

I replied with a sigh of relief, "Well, at least it's only one month. I think I can hold on that long."

American Goddess

Jimmy laughed at my words at first, then all at once he took on a sad tone, as he said, "Well, I better get off the phone before he comes looking for me. I swear, sometimes he drives me crazy. Christina, the man is always up my ass."

I asked with concern, "Don't tell me you guys are having problems?"

He lowered his voice disconcertingly as he said, "I won't tell you we are having problems because I hear him coming. We'll talk about my troubles next time, okay?" On that note, we lovingly said our goodbyes and I returned to Michael, who I found in the living room watching TV with you know who.

The next morning, it was back to work, only this time it was Michael who went on the road, while I stayed home with Joanne and the home office. During that time, I decided to take advantage of my free evenings, which gave me the opportunity to finally get back to the recording studio. Just the thought of singing again was enough to take my mind off the Joanne situation, and I definitely needed to be distracted. Besides, since the day Michael and I returned from our honeymoon, I had written the lyrics to twelve incredible songs. Nine of them were love songs straight from my heart to Michael's, and three spoke of my dreams of one day knowing total peace on earth. Six I planned for ballads, the other six to burn up the dance floor, and I knew they were going to please my begging fan clubs. This soundtrack was going to be hot and I couldn't wait to get it ready for release. So from the moment Michael left on January 3rd, 1990, I buried myself into my work, which didn't bother me at all, because as I said, it kept me away from Joanne and at the same time, it kept my mind off missing Michael, who I did not plan to be seeing again until January 31st.

The whole month Michael was away, we talked on the phone every night at 11:00pm, and every night I wanted to tell him how I truly felt about our plans to have Joanne carry his child. But every time we spoke, the baby was all he could talk about, so once again I bit my tongue.

On January 30th, one day before Michael was to return home, I received a certified letter from the Nobel Institute in Norway. I quickly opened the envelope to discover that the Nobel Awards Committee had unanimously voted to award me, the 1989 Nobel Peace Prize, for my gallant efforts in helping bring an end to a thirty-two-year, civil war in Ghana. The notification also informed me that because I was a last-minute entry for 1989's annual award ceremonies, which I had already missed because it was held on December 10th, the committee had decided to hold a special ceremony in my honor on February 10th, in Oslo, Norway. It also graciously stated the Committee was hoping I could be present to accept the Nobel Peace Medallion in person. At the end of the note was a contact number and I was asked to confirm whether I would be available to accept in person or not, by February 1st. With excitement and pride, I immediately called to accept their gracious invitation to appear in person.

American Goddess

I was so excited the rest of that day and I could not wait to share my incredible news with Michael. Finally, around 7:00pm, I decided to call it an early night. I wanted to get home, get comfortable and call Michael early that evening. When I arrived home, I was still quite excited about calling Michael, so I headed straight through the house on my way to a quick shower. As I approached the doorway which led into the family room, on my way to the master bedroom, I could hear Joanne talking on the phone. Something told me to just eavesdrop on her conversation for a moment. So, I did, and to my surprise, within one minute of listening to one side of this conversation, I knew she was talking to Michael. As I listened, she was saying, "Oh Michael, I am so excited to be able to carry your child, and the closer it gets to the procedure the more excited I'm becoming."

She was silent for a moment, then in response to something Michael said, she said, "Thank you Michael, very much, and I love you for saying it. You are the most thoughtful and romantic man I have ever known and if you weren't married, I'd sweep you off your feet."

With that, I wanted to burst in and start screaming obscenities, but something held me back. Instead, I walked in as if I had just arrived and said, "Hi, Joanne. How was your day?"

She instantly took on a surprised, yet cool look, as she calmly said, "I'm sorry but I have to go now, thanks for calling," Then she swiftly hung up the phone, turned to look me dead in the eyes and said, "Christina, you're home early. What happened, the place burn down?"

I smiled and in a joking, tone said, "No smart-ass, I just wanted to make it an early night tonight" I added with sincerity, "I'm sorry if I interrupted your conversation; was, it anyone I know?"

She smiled innocently as she answered, "That's all right, it was only my mother and I'll call her back later."

I showed no reaction to her **bold-faced lie**, as I said, "Well I'm tired Joanne, so I'm going to bed. I'll see you tomorrow." I walked out of the room and headed for the shower.

My mind was a complete blank when I hopped in the shower, but as soon as the water hit my body, my mind went wild and I thought, 'What's going on here? Why is he calling her? Why did she lie to me? Are they falling in love? Oh my God! Have they been having an affair!?'

When I regained my composure, I was once again able to concentrate on details and facts, instead of jumping to conclusions due to jealousy and rage. I calmly finished showering and headed straight for the phone. As I dialed the number, my first question was going to be, "Why are you calling, Joanne?" Then I thought, 'No! Let me give him a few minutes to see if he starts playing her game.' So as soon as he said, "Hello." I said, "Hi honey, it's me."

With a concerned tone he answered, "Punkie! Where have you been? I was starting to get worried."

"What do you mean?" I asked innocently.

"I've been trying to find you for an hour now. I called the office and Pierre said you left early. Then I called home and Joanne said you weren't home yet."

I felt an inner sense of great relief as I nonchalantly replied, "You must have just missed me, but I'm surprised Joanne didn't tell me you called."

His voice became calmer as he said, "It probably slipped her mind."

With an emphasis on my words I said, "Slipped her mind! I saw her hanging up the phone when I walked in."

He chuckled and said, "Don't be so hard on her she's just a kid."

I began to choke, as I said, "Just a kid! Michael, she's only a year younger than you. If she's just a kid, what does that make you?"

He laughed again, so I changed the subject by saying with pure excitement, "Oh by the way, I have some great news, Michael! I found out this morning I have been chosen to receive the Nobel Peace Prize."

I proceeded to fill him in on all the details and when I finished speaking he calmly said, "That's wonderful news Punkie, and you deserve it." His tone became excited as he continued, "Oh God Punkie, I can't wait to get home tomorrow! I feel like I did when I was a little boy and I knew Christmas was coming the next morning. I would get so excited I couldn't sleep, and I would be on the edge of the bed all night long waiting for the morning. Punkie, I can't believe just the thought of having our own child is driving me nuts with anticipation."

I answered with a disappointed tone, "Oh boy! I thought all this excitement was over me."

Once again he laughed like a little boy who could only think of one thing as he said, "Christina, that's a given and you should know that, but we don't have a baby every day you know."

"I know," I answered lovingly. Then I added, "By the way, how did today's vote go?"

I heard him take a deep breath as he replied, "I hate to tell you this, but it didn't go in our favor."

With a shocked tone I said, "What! How could they defeat our proposal, Michael? You've been working with them for three weeks now. Can't they see our plans are the only way they're going to survive the competition of the changing markets?"

With a sigh of disappointment, he answered, "I'm sorry honey, I guess I'm just not as good as you are at winning people over."

American Goddess

I felt bad I snapped at him so I said, "Don't worry about it Michael, it's not the end of the world, and I think I can fix it."

I guess I didn't comfort him enough because with a very defensive tone he sharply replied, "Please don't patronize me, Christina! I know you're wonderful at everything. And let's face it; I just can't deal with people like you do."

Feeling frustrated, I sighed and said, "I'm sorry, but I wasn't trying to be patronizing. I just didn't want you to be upset over it, because we can decide what to do about it when you come home."

He quickly changed the subject and talked about the baby, until I could take it no more and finally I said, "Honey, I love you, but I need to get some sleep. We can talk more about the baby tomorrow." Then we said our goodbyes and I hung up the phone feeling slightly slighted, to say the least.

When I laid my head on my pillow that night I thought, 'I don't believe him! I just told him his wife has received the phenomenal honor of being awarded the prestigious Nobel Peace Prize, and in two hours of conversation all he could say about it was, 'That's wonderful!' He is so obsessed with having this child, he's becoming totally thoughtless.' That's when I started to really lose my temper and I thought, 'No matter how much I love you Michael, I'm not going to stand for this shit! We are going to be doing some heavy duty talking when you get home later today! If you think you're going to act like this the whole time she's pregnant, you got another think coming.' As much as I hate to admit it, I allowed myself to fall asleep with these angry thoughts.

The next morning when I awoke, I made a conscious decision not to become irrational. I decided I would try harder to understand Michael's position, so that when we talked, I hoped to have had a good idea of how to approach the subject without hurting his feelings. I realized I had to handle the situation in this manner, because I certainly didn't want to be misunderstood. This was too touchy a subject for that, and I knew it.

When Michael entered my office at 4:00pm the next afternoon, he was gleaming from ear to ear. The moment he reached me, he began kissing me with a childlike enthusiasm, as he exclaimed, "I love you Punkie, and just think, before we know it, we'll be having a baby! And as he rambled on I thought, 'This is going to be a bigger challenge than I **ANTICIPATED!**'

After our loving embrace, he kissed me passionately then said, "Hi, sexy! How would you like me to rescue you from this mad house for the rest of the afternoon? Maybe we could take a ride up to the Catskills, and I'll treat you to a romantic dinner."

I kissed him back and sincerely said, "Now that sounds like a proposition I can't refuse." I grabbed my coat and off we went.

It was 4:10pm when we left for what I hoped would be a wonderfully intimate afternoon. I figured this would be the perfect time to talk with Michael about my

329

concerns, but he talked so much about having the baby, that I still could not find the appropriate time to bring the subject up. We didn't return home until 11:00pm that night and believe it or not, the whole time, Michael never said another word about the news I received from the Nobel Institute. When we did enter our home that night, I watched in total amazement, as Michael and Joanne instantly climbed up each other's butts like two love birds, the minute they laid eyes on one another. And at that moment, I knew we were heading for trouble.

The three of us talked about the baby until midnight, at which time I said, "Well it's been a long day and I think I'm ready for a quick shower and a warm bed." I turned to Michael as I continued, "Are you ready, Michael?"

He gave me an incredibly sexy wink and said, "Why don't you take your shower and I'll be up in a minute."

I smiled, kissed his cheek and replied, "Okay sexy, I'll meet you in bed." I said goodnight to Joanne and left them alone.

After my shower, I climbed in bed feeling quite amorous and waited for Michael. As I lied in bed, I found myself waiting and waiting for Michael. As I waited, I once again started to lose my temper. Michael finally entered the room at 1:30am and he went straight into the shower. At 1:45am he climbed into bed, snuggled up to my back and began kissing my neck. The moment I felt his lips touch the back of my neck, I sat up in the bed and all my self-control and how I would handle this situation, went right out the window when I sharply said, "You've got a lot of nerve! I'm sorry, but I can't keep quiet any longer! Do you actually think I'm going to make love to you after the way you've been treating me?"

A shocked look, come over his face as he said, "What do you mean, the way I've been treating you? I don't know what you're talking about. Didn't we just spend a wonderful afternoon together?"

With that, my voice rose an octave as I said, "I cannot believe, you! How can you not know what I'm talking about, Michael?"

He shook his head in frustration, "Well, if taking you out for a romantic dinner is treating you bad, then I'll never know how to please you!"

At that point I climbed out of the bed, turned the light on, headed for my dressing room and began to get dressed.

When Michael realized I was dressing, he came flying into the room and demanded, "And where do you think you're going at two o'clock in the morning!?"

I looked at him as I brushed my hair with dramatics and replied, "I have got to get out of here before I say something we may both regret." He grabbed my arm forcefully, "You're not going anywhere unless you tell me what this is all about!"

American Goddess

I ripped my arm out of his grasp, grabbed my purse, looked him dead in the eyes, and with real anger in my voice, said, "You've just pushed me over the edge Michael, because no one talks to me like that, not even you!"

This time his voice became panicky as he said, "Please, Punkie! Don't walk out like this without telling me how I've made you so angry. That's not fair to me at all."

His words struck my heart, so I took a deep breath to calm myself, "Michael, it blows me away to think you could hurt my feelings like you have, and not even be aware of it." Then like a child, my eyes began to tear as I continued, "Do you even realize I told you, I was going to be honored with a Nobel Peace Prize and all you said was, 'That's wonderful'! And you haven't said another word about it since. All you talk about anymore is the baby. All I hear is the baby this or the baby that. I'm to the point of being sick of hearing about the baby and she hasn't even conceived it yet."

His face showed his sincerity as he said, "Oh God, Punkie! I'm sorry! I had no idea I was acting that stupid."

I gazed into his eyes and with tears in mine, I replied, "That's just my point Michael, and I don't like it. Can't you see you're so obsessed with having your own baby, you've become totally consumed with it?" I took a deep breath and thought, 'If I'm going to let him know how I truly feel about Joanne, then this is the time to do it.' So I dove right in as I continued, "Another thing I don't like is the coziness you and Joanne seem to have together. I have got to be truthful, Michael. This whole baby thing with Joanne is starting to worry me. I don't trust her anymore. I know she's falling in love with you, and if she thinks she can find a way to have you, she'll try."

He gazed at me with an unbelieving expression and said, "Christina! You're my Punkie, and I love you. I would never knowingly give you any reason to worry about my faithfulness to you. And as far as my friendship with Joanne, that's all it is." He took me in his arms and kissed me and as I reluctantly surrendered to his charms, he continued, "Punkie, Joanne is a good person and she's not falling in love with me. The only reason it might appear as if we're, 'so cozy', as you so eloquently put it is because this is just as exciting for her, as it is for us. Don't you see she is doing such a wonderful thing for us, that I don't know how to adequately thank her."

I looked into his eyes and proceeded to tell him how Joanne had lied to me. Afterward, he looked at me sadly and said, "I don't know why she would lie to you and that concerns me. But as for trusting her to fulfill her contract with us for our baby, I'm more than certain she will."

I gently hugged him comfortingly, as I said, "I hope you're right, Michael." We made our way back to the bed where we tenderly made love before drifting off to sleep in each other's loving embrace.

CHAPTER 32

Two days later on February 2ⁿᵈ, the three of us were back in Doctor Hart's, office, where Joanne was artificially inseminated with my husband's seed.   Doctor Hart told us we should wait two weeks to see if she has conceived, so he gave us an appointment for February 16ᵗʰ. The day after the insemination, I was back in the recording studio finishing up what would be my first new album in more than two years, which I entitled, 'One Voice, One World and Love Enough for All.'

I stayed in the recording studio sixteen hours a day, because I wanted it ready for release the day, I would receive my Nobel Peace Prize.   While I was burning the midnight oils in the recording studio, Michael was back to handling our corporate headquarters, and Joanne.   After much deliberation, we decided it would behoove us financially, to have Michael continue to man the main office, while I would resume our now, four months behind business schedule, on February 17ᵗʰ.   I didn't care for this plan too much, but we really had no choice.   Michael just could not handle that side of the business.   He was a behind the scenes man and we both knew it.   Finally, on February 7ᵗʰ, we completed the entire soundtrack, plus six videos to accompany my first six planned releases. On February 8ᵗʰ, Michael and I were off to Oslo, Norway for my Nobel Peace Prize acceptance.

At 10:00am, on February 10ᵗʰ, 1990, in front of the eyes of the world I received the prestigious Nobel Peace Prize.   As the chairman of the Nobel Institute presented me with the Medallion of Peace he said, **"My dear Ms. Powers, it brings great pleasure to the Nobel Institute, to bestow the honor of the Prestigious Nobel Peace Prize to such a**

American Goddess

deserving candidate.   Your work in Ghana has proven to the world that all races can learn to live together in peace and harmony.   The Nobel Peace Prize is the way the world is saying thank you, Christina Powers, for the tremendous strides you've made in, helping to bring the light of peace to a war-ravaged nation."   He placed the peace medallion around my neck, as tears of pride welled up in my eyes.

Afterward, I kissed his cheek and said to him, "Mr. Chairman, I would like to thank you, and all the notable members of the Nobel Institute Committee, for this distinguished honor.   And may I say that I have never felt prouder of my accomplishments than I do at this very moment."   At that point I gave a speech of why I believed, there was no reason why the whole world should not be able to live in peace. I added, "Now I would like to thank everyone in my own very special way.   I have written the lyrics to a new song which was inspired by my experiences in Ghana.   Now if I may, I would like to sing that song for the first time, right here, as my gift to everyone listening?"

Just then the curtains behind me opened to reveal my entire orchestra and to the applause of everyone in the auditorium, I began to sing the first release off my new soundtrack to the entire world through the cameras of the media.   I entitled this single which I wrote as a ballad, 'Love Grows in the Arms of Peace.'   My performance was captivating, and the song was so filled with emotion, and the entire audience cheered for five minutes.

When I walked off that stage, Michael embraced me, passionately gazed into my eyes, and with pure love said, "You are the most remarkable person on the face of this planet, and I am proud to tell the world you are my wife." He kissed me with enthusiasm and added, "I love you, Punkie!"

The next day, I was praised by world leaders in the headlines all over the globe, for my wonderful contribution to peace in the world.   And to top it off, the Pope himself said in a public statement, **"Christina Powers has proven herself to be a beacon of light in the midst of man's darkness."**

Even President Rush, at a news conference that same day, praised the Nobel Institute for their choice by saying, **"Christina Powers has earned the right to be called America's 'Angel of Peace.'"**   He also informed me, as well as the entire country, he was going to honor me with the Achievement of the Year Award for 1989, at the White House on March 1st." He ended his news conference that day with, **"I hope and pray that the work Christina Powers has done in Ghana, will be a call to all nations to stand against human rights violations, whenever and wherever they may occur in the world."**

When we arrived back home at Stewart International Airport, on February 12th, we were totally exhausted and just wanted to get home.   But, to our surprise we were welcomed by thousands of cheering African Americans, and the cameras of every news station across the country.   We walked through the crowds shaking hands and receiving grateful hugs all the way.   Then finally, after a short news conference we headed for home.   Joanne greeted us both warmly with open arms when we entered the front door, and for the next four days the three of us got along wonderfully whenever we were together, although most of that time Michael and I spent working on my up and coming business trips.

On February 16th, with great anticipation, the three of us went to Doctor Hart's office to see if Joanne had conceived.   Not five minutes after her blood test, the three of us were crushed when the test result came back negative.   Doctor Hart set up another appointment for March 3rd, to try again.   Only this time, I would not be accompanying them.   I would be in Dallas, Texas securing another one of our new companies.   After that, I was beginning a six-month business tour, which included periodic charity benefits, and addressing student bodies in as many universities as I could.   I was now considered a scholar on human rights and peace, and I wanted to take my message of peace for all mankind to the youth of America while the current mood of the country prevailed.   So when February 18th, rolled around, once again I was sadly kissing Michael goodbye, because we would only be seeing one another periodically.   To our dismay our visitations would remain this way, until all our planned business trips would hopefully be completed by August 1st.

While I was away, Michael and Joanne's second attempt on March 3rd was also a failure, and they had to reschedule the procedure for April 4th.   They would not know the results of the third insemination until April 18th, which happened to be one of the weeks I planned to be home with Michael and do my work from the main office.   In the midst of my business trips and personal appearances, my popularity soared and so did the sales of the soundtrack 'One Voice, One World and Love Enough for All.'   And the single, 'Love Grows in the Arms of Peace,' stayed at number one for fifteen weeks after its worldwide debut in Norway.

I arrived back home on April 18th, in just enough time to accompany Michael and Joanne back to Doctor Hart's office.   This time we left cheering because Joanne had finally conceived.   As soon as Michael heard the words that he was going to be a father, his eyes lit up like a plane's headlights.   He took Joanne in his arms, swung her around in the air and shouted, "We finally did it, Joanne, and I love you for it!"   He then grabbed me and shouted, "We're going to have a baby, Punkie!   Isn't that the best news in the world?"

I kissed him and with joy in my voice said, "It sure is the best news Michael, and I love you."

Doctor Hart gave Joanne an appointment schedule for her to keep, which included an appointment for a sonogram to be taken on July 5th.   As soon as I could, I changed my business plans so I could be home for the sonogram, and the rest of that week the three of us spent walking on cloud nine together.   Joanne treated me with such respect and love that week that without realizing it herself, she put all my fears to rest.   Then on April 23rd, I was back on my business trip schedule.

When I arrived back home on July 3rd, I was only planning on staying five days before resuming my business trips.   The three of us spent the Fourth of July at my mother in-law's annual barbecue. We were having a wonderful day right up till 7:00pm, when without asking me first, Michael proceeded to inform his entire family of my infertility and how Joanne was carrying our child for us.   After the initial shock wore off, his family congratulated us on the baby.   Then, with open arms, my in-laws welcomed Joanne into the Carr family, almost as if she were Michael's second wife.   As Michael's family lovingly welcomed Joanne with hugs and kisses, her face lit up like a bride on her wedding day.

When my mother in-law turned to congratulate me, she looked at me sadly and whispered in my ear, "I know it must be a disappointment for you not to be able to bear children any longer, but no matter how much you wanted a child, you should have never talked Michael into having a child in this manner.   It's wrong."

I whispered back, "Tess, I respect your opinion, but as far as I'm concerned, you're mistaken.   As for your son, he's a big boy with his own mind, and no one can talk him into anything he does not want to do."

Ten minutes later I came down with a headache and I asked Michael to take me home.   That's when he and Joanne complained we would miss the fireworks if we left now.   So, first I apologized for causing them to miss the fireworks; then, I insisted we leave.

As soon as we climbed into the car, I lost all my self-control and proceeded to blast Michael for telling his family.   He was speechless as I said, "How could you tell them without consulting me first, especially since you knew I didn't want anyone knowing!?"

When I finished my tantrum, all Michael could say was, "I'm sorry Punkie, but you said you wanted to keep it from your fans, I didn't think that meant keeping it from my family too."

I shook my head in frustration and replied, "Well, if you knew me as well as I thought you did, you would understand why I didn't want anyone knowing, not even your family."

Just then Joanne snapped at me from the back seat, "Christina, I don't know why you're acting like such a child.   You didn't really think you could hide your infertility from Michael's family, did you?   Besides, no one said anything derogatory, everyone was happy for us."

I didn't even turn to face her when I said, "Joanne, this has nothing to do with you, so please keep your opinions to yourself."

American Goddess

Michael turned to me and said, "Christina, there's no reason for you to take your frustrations out on Joanne.   And if you plan to continue this tirade, then please save it until we're in private."

This time I didn't even look at Michael when I said, "That's the most intelligent thing you've said in months Michael, and you won't hear another word from me."   After that no one said a word the rest of the way home.

Later that night in the privacy of our bedroom, the first thing Michael asked me was, "Why in the world did you snap at Joanne like that?"   I guess I didn't answer him as quickly as he would have liked, because he sarcastically added, "You don't even know why, do you?   Do you realize you talk about me being obsessed, but you're the one who's obsessed?   You're so jealous Joanne can give me what you can't; you're distorting everything I do and say.   Now I'm going to ask you to stop acting like the child this time, because if you don't get a hold of your own insecurities, you could mess this up for both of us with Joanne.   I'm surprised she's not packing to leave right now."

I looked at him with an expression of total disbelief, "Why you stupid ass!   All this time and you still don't know what I'm all about."   I shook my head in disgust as I continued, "Now let's go to sleep Michael, because I'm just too tired for any more of this tonight."   Then I rolled over and ignored every word he said from that point on.

He became so frustrated that I would not answer him that he climbed out of the bed and began to get dressed. As he walked out of the room he said, "I'm going for a ride, and maybe I'll be back by morning."

As the door closed behind him, I decided I was not going to allow myself to feel anything at that moment.   I didn't want to give him the satisfaction of seeing me upset. But needless to say, I didn't get a moment's sleep that night, and as for Michael, he didn't come in until 5:00am that morning.   I was so angry with him that when he climbed in the bed; I climbed out.

Michael and I were still not on speaking terms when we entered Doctor Hart's office later that morning, at 11:00am with Joanne.   Remarkably, that whole morning we were both able to keep Joanne from sensing our hostilities toward each other.   Doctor Hart personally escorted the three of us to the sonogram room and proceeded to perform the procedure.   First, he moved the screen so we could all watch as he videotaped the fetus. Then he proceeded to explain to us exactly what we were looking at.   When we could actually see the baby moving in the uterus, my heart melted as my eyes teared, and I instantly fell in love with that little fetus.

With these feelings flowing through me, I drifted close to Michael, took his arm in both my hands, squeezed it tightly, and with tears of joy in my eyes, said, "That's our baby.   Michael, I'm sorry I've upset you honey, because I love you more than life itself."

At that he lovingly took me in his arms and with a gleam of joy in his eyes said, "I love you too, Punkie!" Then we turned our attention back to the fetus on the screen.

American Goddess

The procedure only took ten minutes and when it was finished, Dr. Hart handed me the video tape with some snapshots he took of the fetus. I passed the snapshots to Michael to see, who passed them to Joanne. After Joanne looked at them, I watched as she opened her purse and casually slipped them in. At the moment she snapped her purse shut, I knew all my fears would soon be my reality. So in a calm voice I asked, "Joanne, why did you put those snapshots in your purse?"

She snapped at me like a rattlesnake as she shouted, "For God's sake Christina, I'm giving you my baby and I can't keep the fucking negatives? What the hell is wrong with you?"

As she hatefully spit these words at me, Michael's eyes almost popped out of his face with anger toward me as if to say, 'How could you dare!' So I quickly apologized for being so insensitive to her feelings and when I finally stopped her from crying, I said, "You're absolutely right Joanne, and I want you to keep these photos."

She wiped her alligator tears with a tissue as she replied, "I'm sorry if I was overly emotional, it must be the baby." She turned toward me as she continued, "Thank you for the snapshots, Christina. I'm glad you can see that because this is not your biological child, the snapshots should come to me. I also feel I deserve to have the tape as well. After all, I am allowing you to raise my child, aren't I?"

In reply to her cruel statement, I handed her the tape with a reassuring smile and said, "Joanne, you're welcome to the tape as well. I want you to know I do realize what you're doing for us and once again I thank you for it."

She hugged me gratefully as she replied, "Thank you Christina, now would someone please feed me? This fasting when you're eating for two doesn't make any sense at all."

I turned to Michael and nonchalantly said, "Honey, why don't you take Joanne for a bite to eat and just drop me off at the office? I have too much to do before leaving tomorrow to go with you guys." And that was what he did.

American Goddess

CHAPTER 33

When they dropped me off, I went straight for a company car and took off.   As I drove around that day, I was feeling so hurt by what had transpired that I had no idea how I was going to handle it.   I wished I could just run away and never come back, but I loved Michael too much for my own good, to be able to just walk away from him and the baby.   At the same time, I wanted to be as far away from Joanne as I possibly could.   I knew one more outburst from her could push me over the edge, and I feared for her life if that should happen.

It wasn't until 6:00pm, when I finally calmed down enough to pull into the driveway of our home. As I reached the house, I could see Joanne frantically throwing her suitcases into the trunk of her car, with Michael trying to take them out.   I quickly stopped the car right next to the action and when I jumped out, to my shock, I found Joanne crying hysterically, and Michael pleading with her not to leave.

I immediately stopped their struggle over a suitcase, by shouting, "What the hell is going on here?"

Joanne threw her suitcases into the trunk, slammed the lid and started to walk toward the driver's door.   This time, I grabbed her arm and demanded, "I asked you a question, and I expect an answer before you go anywhere."

She pulled her arm out of my hand and with hatred in her voice shouted, "You really want to know what's going on?   Well your husband and I have been having an affair for months now.   We've spent every night together when you were out of town, and now that you're home, I'm not good enough anymore."

Michael instantly grabbed my arm, looked dead into my eyes, and with panic in his voice said, "She's lying, Christina!   I swear I've never slept with her.   She just tried to seduce me and when I refused, she went nuts.   She started screaming at me yelling, 'You told me, you loved me!'"   I trustingly gazed back into his eyes and soothingly replied, "I believe you, Michael."

That's when Joanne tried to slap my face.   I blocked the slap, swung her arm behind her back, pushed her up against the car and shouted, "Don't you ever try to do that again or you will find yourself at the bottom of the river.   Now you have a contract with me, and you are going to keep it!   So please calm down and start talking!"

I let her go and she screamed at me, "I'm leaving, and you can't keep me here.   I don't care how many threats you issue."

I shook my head in dismay as I said, "You're right again Joanne, I can't keep you here.   But if you leave, you will be breaking a contract with me and no one does that and gets away with it."

338

American Goddess

She opened the door of her car, climbed in and shouted, "Fuck you, Christina Powers, and you can shove your contract up your ass because neither one of you will ever get this child now." Then she started the car and sped away.

As she drove away, Michael took me in his arms and pleaded, "I swear to you again Punkie, I never slept with her."

I squeezed his hand reassuringly and said, "Michael, honey, you don't have to do this, I know you're telling the truth." What Michael didn't know was that after 'the phone call incident' back in December, I had the house wired. I wasn't going to leave them alone again without being sure there was nothing going on between them. But I didn't need to tell him that, I preferred for him to believe I just took his word for it.

As soon as we went into the house, I immediately had a tail put on Joanne. Then, I called my attorney Tom Davies, and informed him of our dilemma. During our conversation, I discovered the only way we could get the baby from Joanne now was through the legal system. Afterwards he added, "But if you're going to fight her for the baby, you'd better do it now before she takes off."

There was no way I wanted to go public with this headline, but I had no choice. So, with a completely disgusted voice I said, "Go ahead and do whatever it takes. I'll just have to learn to live with this one too, I guess."

Two days later, the whole country knew I was infertile, and in the middle of a custody battle with the surrogate mother of my husband's child. To top that off, Joanne took her distorted version of the facts to the tabloids, and they had a field day at my expense.

Michael became so distraught over the situation, he was put on antidepressants, which left him almost unable to function, no less take care of business. So once again, I put my business trips on hold and on July 15th, 1990, I dove headfirst into the hottest custody battle in American history. And let me tell you, everybody had something to say about it. Even the Pope himself, who only a few months earlier had praised me publicly for my peace efforts, released a new statement saying, **"Christina Powers is suffering at her own hand for trying to have a child in an immoral and sinful manner."**

To that I was compelled to issue a public statement of my own, saying, **"I believe the Pope and the Christian community should read their Bible a little closer before passing judgement based on it. Because if I correctly recall Abram's wife Sara, had the Egyptian slave girl named Hagar, bear Abram's child for her, because she was unable to conceive herself. After that God blessed the child and Sara, He didn't condemn them."** But all they heard were their own little naive words of condemnation.

As the court battle heated up, so did the battle between Michael and me. Little by little, it became quite evident Michael was blaming me for what transpired among the three of us. But it all came to a head on July 27th, after one particularly bad day in court, where Joanne superbly portrayed me as the 'wicked witch' who caused it all. When we arrived home that evening, I was feeling totally defeated. But I guess that didn't matter

American Goddess

to Michael, because as soon as we entered our house he finally blew-up at me and said, "If you hadn't opened your month like you did the night we left my Mother's house, none of this shit would have ever happened."

I burst out in sarcastic laughter as I said, "I think you'd better take the blinders off Michael and see things for what they really are. I'm not what caused this at all! I told you before we went through with the procedure, I feared something like this might happen; but no, you wouldn't listen! You had to have your own child whether I was part of it or not. And because I listened to you, our private lives are once again an open book and I've been humiliated in front of the entire world. Thank you very much! So don't you dare stand there and tell me it's my fault. Now wise-up and stop trying to blame me because we're both at fault here and the sooner you realize that the sooner our relationship will improve." I tried to hug him and his body became rigid; which made me even angrier, so I pulled away and said, "Michael, I will do everything in my power to bring your child back to you, but I will tell you right now, as long as she is the birth mother, that child will never be part of me."

With that harsh statement he looked at me and started to cry like a baby, "I'm so sorry, Christina! I'm feeling so confused, I don't know what I'm really feeling anymore."

I held him with compassion and softly said, "I'm sorry Michael, I didn't really mean that. I love you and it will work out for the best; I promise you it will."

The next morning on Friday, July 27th, it was my turn to take the stand. Upon the first question, I proceeded to strategically, yet gracefully tear her story to shreds **so badly** that by the end of the day, we were sure we were going to win the case. At 2:00pm the Judge called for an adjournment until Monday, August 1, at 10:00am. Michael and I both had a feeling of confidence that whole night and right up till 2:00pm the next day; when, I received a call from the tail I had on Joanne, informing me that she gave them the slip.

With that news, I hung up the phone and within ten minutes I had every police officer in the state, unofficially looking for her. We frantically searched for her that whole weekend! But to our dismay, no one saw her again until she entered the courtroom with her attorney, on the morning of Monday, August 1st. As soon as Joanne's attorney approached the bench, he informed the court that his client aborted the fetus in question, at 7:00pm on July 30th, and after viewing the official medical records, our courtroom custody battle came to a devastatingly abrupt end. Especially for Michael, who went into a deep depression the moment he heard the news. As we walked out of that courtroom, the press charged us.

Michael turned to me with tears in his eyes and said, "I have to get out of here, Christina."

I took his hand and replied, "We don't have to make any comments at all. We can just get in the limo and take off." And that was exactly what we did.

American Goddess

When James pulled into the driveway, Michael looked at me and sadly said, "I can't go in yet.   I think I'll just take the car and ride around for a while."

I grabbed his hand as we climbed out of the limo and with concern asked, "Why don't you let me come with you, Michael?"

He looked at me as if he were going to cry again as he answered, "I need to be alone right now, Christina."   He pulled his hand from mine, walked to his car, and drove away without saying another word.

At that, I went in the house and straight to our room, where I laid on the bed and cried my eyes out for several hours.   I was not only living through the death of this child, but I was reliving the deaths of all my babies.   I decided not to go anywhere for the rest of that day because I wanted to wait for Michael at home.   I waited from 11:00am that morning, {on pins and needles} until he finally called me from his Mother's home in Ravena, at 11:40pm that night.   He told me not to wait up, because he was not sure when he would be coming home.   So with a sad voice I said, "Michael, please come home honey, I really need you here."

His voice cracked as he replied, "I can't yet, Christina.   I have to figure out how to deal with this cruel blow."

I nearly pleaded, "Michael, listen to me, honey.   I'm your wife and I love you so much I would die for you if it would take the pain away, but it won't.   The only way we are going to come through this is if we do it together, honey.   So please come home to me?"

With a bit stronger voice, he replied, "I'll be home Punkie, I promise.   I just need a little more time by myself."

I sighed and with a small sense of relief replied, "All right, my love.   Just please be careful and come home to me safe."   We finished our conversation by saying, "I love you."

Not five minutes later, I received a call from Jimmy, and as soon as I heard his voice I exclaimed, "Oh thank God, it's you, Jimmy!   You won't believe what happened today."

His first words back to me were, "With you girlfriend, nothing would surprise me." I filled him in on all the details and he reassured me, "Just hang in there two more days girlfriend, and I promise I'll be home for good.   Then as you would say, 'we will figure it out together'."

With that news, I took a deep breath and said, "I hope so, because if Michael doesn't come through that door soon, I'll be weaving baskets, so you'd better come home in two days."

As Jimmy started to laugh, a sharp squeal came over the line and we lost our connection.   I tried to redial the number he gave me for Richard's parents, but I couldn't get through.   Then I laid my head on the pillow and as I waited for Jimmy to call me back, I fell asleep.

CHAPTER 34

It was shortly after 2:00am when I was startled awake for, I heard Carman's panicked cries as she banged on my bedroom door yelling, "Christina!   You have to get up!   It's urgent!"   I flew out of the bed fearing the worse had happened to Michael.

I opened the door in a flurry, grabbed Carman's shoulders, and with fear in my voice shouted, "Where's Michael, Carman?"

With the panic of your typical older Italian woman, she shouted back at me with her hands shaking, "It's not Michael, Christina!"   At that, she put her hands to her face and cried, "Dear God, Christina!   It's our boy Jimmy!   Something terribly dreadful has happened!"

I looked at her strangely and asked, "What are you talking about, Carman?   I was just talking to Jimmy two hours ago and he was fine."   She grabbed my hand with the force of a halfback as she said, "You have to come see for yourself."   With that she dragged me into her attached servant's quarters, where James was riveted to a news broadcast on CNN.

Immediately I took a seat beside James and asked with a concerned tone, "What's going on, James?"

He turned to me with an expression of horror and replied, "At 1:00am, five-hundred-thousand Iraqi forces, with hundreds of tanks and heavy artillery, swept across the Kuwait border.   They say the fighting is fierce and the Iraqi Air Force has destroyed the Kuwait International Airport."   Then, he shook his head with shear concern as he

American Goddess

continued, "That means Jimmy is probably a fugitive in hiding already, and if they find him they may kill him."

I became glued to the TV, as well. A deep sense of great fear came over me for Jimmy as I watched and listened to the blow-by-blow details of the invasion, live on CNN. The three of us watched TV like until 3:42am that's when the announcer said, "Our unofficial sources state that the Sultan and his family escaped into Saudi Arabia minutes before the Capital fell into Iraqi control."

I was so horrified by what I was seeing and hearing that I knew I had to do something. So I got up and dialed President Rush's private number. I paced for the next twenty minutes praying the whole time for Jimmy's safety as I waited for a return call.

I grabbed the phone on the first ring to hear George say, "Christina, as much as I enjoy them, I don't have time for one of our quaint chats right now. So please make it quick."

I answered him just as swiftly, "I can't make this one quick George; not when my dearest friend's life is at stake. George, do you remember my business partner Jimmy Severino? Well he is somewhere in Kuwait at this very moment, and I'm sure you're aware of what's taking place there! What I want to know is what are we going to do about it?"

He cleared his voice and said, "I'm sorry Jimmy got caught up in this Christina, and I promise you I'm going to do everything possible to get him out of there safely. My staff and I were working on how to respond to the crisis when you called."

Once again, I was swift to respond, "Have you talked to Lussein to see why he is doing this?"

His voice was not optimistic as he answered, "Lussein is desperately trying to save his own political ass, that's why he's doing this. I have been trying to prevent him diplomatically from invading Kuwait for months now, and he has ignored my every attempt to meet with him personally. I'm already at the point of deciding where and how many American troops to send over there."

With that statement my heart shot up to my throat because I realized he was about to throw our nation into another 'Vietnamese-style' conflict. So with a sense of desperation in my voice I said, "Please forgive me George, but if you send American troops in now, you'll be making a big mistake. Please listen to me. This is not America's war. This is a transgression against the statutes of the U.N. That means this problem belongs to every free nation on earth, not just us. This must be handled through the U.N. Security Council, or it will end up looking as though America is trying to rule the world. If we go through the U.N., then we'll have the backing of the entire international community.   Once we do that, Lussein won't have a prayer of staying in Kuwait."

I could tell by his voice, I had caught his interest when he said, "That sounds great, but if I do that; then, we will have to turn large numbers of American troops over to the control of the U.N. and our Joint Chiefs of Staff would have a real problem with that scenario."

I answered with complete optimism in my voice, "This is true George, but you're the President of the United States, and you can sure as hell tell the U.N. that you want American generals in control of all American troops."

His voice was very clear when he said, "Do you really think we can rally the whole world into storming the deserts of Kuwait?"

"Yes I do, George," I answered assuredly.

With a respectful laugh he said, "I thought you would say that and I'm sure if anyone could, it would be you. So I'll make a deal with you Christina; if you will be my mouth piece to the world, then I will hold back our military response and do it your way."

Without a second thought of anything I replied, "When and where do you need me, Mr. President."

Quite relieved he answered, "The sooner you get to Stewart Airport, the sooner I can have a military escort bring you here."

I hung up the phone, told Carman to pack my suitcases, and I headed for a shower. As I dressed, I thought, 'Oh my God!   I'm forgetting about Michael.'   I sat down and wrote him a note explaining what happened and where I was going.   I also told him I loved him with all my heart, and that I would be home as soon as I could. I placed it on Michael's pillow and headed out of the room.

As I was coming down the stairs, James entered the foyer and said, "The car is packed and ready to go whenever you are, Christina."

I grabbed my briefcase from the hall closet, "Pull the car around front would you please James, and I'll be right out."   I grabbed a mug of coffee to go from Carman's shaking hand, kissed her cheek and said, "Keep us in your prayers, Carman."

I headed for the front door and as I opened it, Michael was standing there getting ready to open it himself.   Instantly his expression turned to one of surprise when he saw me dressed, and he asked, "What's going on?   Better yet, where are you taking off to at 4:30 in the morning? I thought you were going to be waiting for me?"

I drew him tightly and passionately to my body, kissed him gently and lovingly said, "Michael, honey, I don't know if you've heard, but there's a war going on in Kuwait.   I have already talked with the President and I have to leave for Washington, D.C. right now. I left a note on the bed for you explaining everything."

American Goddess

He pushed himself out of my arms and in a loud, angry, voice he screamed, "You're what!?   You can't just kiss me then tell me there's a note on the bed and walk out the fucking door!   You told me to come home!   You told me we would get through this together!   How could you be leaving me now!?"

I felt his pain so deep within my soul that it threw my emotions into a state of confusion, and I started to cry as I pleaded, "Michael, please don't do this to me now.   I love you honey, with all my soul and I know how much you're hurting, but I still have to go, can't you understand that?"

With a plea of his own he shouted, "I'm hurting, Christina!   Really hurting!   And now you're tearing my heart apart even more.   You told me you needed me!   I finally got my head together enough to come home to you, because I need you as much as I thought you needed me, and now you're telling me you have to leave?"

I grabbed his arm and cried, "Please Michael, you have got to listen to me and understand!"

He only shook his head in disgust as he exclaimed, "Understand what, Christina? That you don't give a fuck about me!"   Then, he turned his face away from me.

I grabbed his jaw and turned his head to force him to look at me, "Listen to me!   I love you, but I have got to go, Michael!   Jimmy's life is on the line here, that's what I want you to understand.   Don't you realize that hundreds of people are really dying, and I have to do something to help stop it?   Now, please, just kiss me goodbye Michael, so I may leave knowing I have your blessing."

He turned his head out of my hand and angrily said, "No, Christina!   Because if you can walk out that door on me now, knowing how much I need you; then, I won't be here when you get back.   I just can't take this shit anymore, no matter how much I love you!"

He began to walk away from me and as he walked away I shouted, "Fine then, Michael!   Once again we'll have it your way!"

I was so angry at him for not being reasonable that when I slammed the door the glass panels shattered.   I looked back to see Michael angrily staring at me through the broken glass and I thought, 'Thank God they're not mirrors!   I sure as hell don't need any more bad luck.'

As James pulled out of the driveway that morning, I put my feelings on hold and dove headfirst into what would soon be known to the world as, **"Desert Storm!**

American Goddess

CHAPTER 35

When I arrived at the White House, I was escorted by security guards straight to the Oval Office. I was greeted by the President, who with his all male staff, stood up as I entered the room. I held myself tall and confident as President Rush proceeded to introduce me to the Vice President, the Joint Chiefs of Staff, and the Secretary of Defense. Our introductions were formal to say the least and the aura in the room was thick, so thick it was quite apparent at least to me, my presence was not appreciated by everyone in the room. So, I immediately attempted to cut through the bad vibes by saying, "May I say it is an honor to be in the same room with so many distinguished gentlemen, and I humbly thank you all for allowing me this opportunity to express my feelings concerning this crisis."

At that we took our seats. Then George turned toward me as he said, "Christina, I have shared our conversation with everyone in this room and we've been brain-storming since. Most of us have come to the conclusion that your suggestion to go totally through the U.N. with this crisis is the best way for America to proceed. That's if it can be done."

Vice President Pigeon interrupted with an attitude which was strongly adamant and slightly hostile as he said, "Pardon me Mr. President, but before we go any further with this, I must strongly protest. Lussein is a mad man, sir! If we delay our military response, he'll take it as an open invitation to send his troops right into Saudi Arabia. Then you won't have to worry about getting the U.N. involved, because that will do it nicely."

I was taken aback by his willingness to jump into a military conflict, so I looked directly at him and said, "How can you be so anxious to throw American troops into a war alone, when this is not just our responsibility? Yes, we are a superpower, but we're not God of this earth. We are one nation, and there are other counties who must accept their responsibility for protecting the welfare and freedom of all nations. That's the reason why the U.N. was established."

Directing my words toward George and the others, I continued, "Gentleman, we must go through the U.N. Security Council and do this with the cooperation of its members, or this will explode," then turning to George, "in 'your face' Mr. President."

With a little more irritation to his voice, the Vice President, in an attempt to intimidate and humiliate me said, "Please listen to me Ms. Powers, because I know what I'm talking about, and obviously you don't have a clue. This is not Ghana and you will never convince the U.N. members to commit troops against such an awesome opponent. Do you realize Lussein has the second strongest military power in the Middle East? And the time we waste with diplomatic bullshit, will only give Iraq more time to dig into Kuwait."

His condescending remarks angered me, so I tried a little intimidation of my own when I said, "I think 'you're' the one who's not seeing the entire picture here Mr. Pigeon. Can't you see those are the exact reasons the U.N. is the answer?   Don't you realize if we take on Iraq without the U.N.'s full support, then you will be inviting the Russians, as well as the Chinese, to confront us over the Middle East?   Now, if you would just stop being so bullheaded and listen for a change, you might understand what I'm saying."

Frustrated, he slammed his fist on the table and nearly shouted, "I understand exactly what you're saying, Ms. Powers!   I also understand you have a personal friend in Kuwait, and I'm telling you he may not survive if we wait.   Do you realize how long it will take to get the world's military support on this?"   Then he shouted, "Iraq has already overthrown Kuwait!   If we lose any more time, it will not only be too late for Mr. Severno, it will be too late for Saudi Arabia as well."

With that slap in the face I stood up and forcefully said, "Mr. Pigeon!   That was totally uncalled for, unprofessional, and I expect an apology.   And please don't you ever speak to me with such disrespect again."

That's when George cleared his voice deeply and the moment he did, Mr. Pigeon began to apologize.   I accepted his attempt to be civil by once again taking my seat. Then, with a much calmer tone of my own I replied, "Before I answer your question Mr. Vice President, I have one of my own.   How can you be so sure Iraq is going to invade Saudi Arabia?"

He looked at me as if I were an idiot and with a tone of contempt replied, "Ms. Powers, if he gains control of Kuwait and Saudi Arabia, then he can hold the industrial countries of the world hostage, because the world relies on these two nations as its primary source of petroleum."

As soon as he finished speaking, I stood up, turned to look at everyone in the room, and very calmly said, "If you were all listening to the Vice President's words, you should now realize under the circumstances he just described, going through the U.N. is the only legal way for the United States to handle this situation. Under International Law, Iraq is threatening the security of many nations, not just ours. These are the reasons why I believe it will only take a few hours to rally the world's support against Iraq."   Glancing at my watch I continued, "And I could be in New York to address the U.N. Security Council by 11:30am to do just that, if I left now."

Just then the Secretary of Defense, Mr. Breaner joined the conversation by saying, "Mr. President, I agree with Ms. Powers completely.   We have to go to the Security Council to ask the U.N. to condemn the Iraqi invasion, anyway, so why not try to get our allied nations involved on the military end of this as well.   Besides, I think a military action of this size would sure as hell pass congress a lot faster if they knew we weren't footing the entire bill alone."

Mr. Mickie, the Chief of Naval Operations, spoke up, "My only problem is if we do a joint military response through the U.N., then we will be putting substantial numbers of American forces under the guidance of the U.N. Security Council."

I confidently spoke up, "Sir, there is no nation on the face of the earth more capable of handling a military action such as this, than ours, and I'm sure the U.N. Security Council will look to America for strategic guidance on how to proceed with an invasion, if it comes to that. But, it is still our responsibility as a member of the U.N., to do everything possible diplomatically, to prevent this from escalating to that point."

George stood up and said, "All right, let's not waste any more time. We're going through the U.N. all the way with this one and that's my final decision." Then he looked at me as he continued, "Christina, I'll call for an emergency meeting of the Security Council right now, if you're ready to go?"

I looked at him proudly, smiled confidently, and answered, "I'm past ready, Sir."

He smiled at my enthusiastic answer and replied, "I thought you'd say something like that. Now if you will head to New York for me, I'll have a fax waiting for you on what issues I want you to discuss, and the ones I want you to stay away from. I also want you to keep in close contact with me. I need to know every response you get from individual countries. Clear?"

I stood up, shook his hand firmly and answered, "I'm on my way, Mr. President." Then I said my goodbyes to everyone, and out the door I went.

I arrived by Presidential chopper on the roof of the U.N. building at 11:04am, and as soon as I got off the chopper, I dialed the number to Michael's handheld cellular. When there was no answer, I called the office for him.

Lucille Karatzas, his secretary answered and told me, Michael said, 'he had to leave town and he was leaving Ann Markel in charge.'

I immediately had her connect me to Ann's office, and when she answered I said, "Ann, tell me what's going on and how come Michael isn't there?"

With a confused tone she answered, "I'm not sure Christina, I thought you knew. Michael called me this morning, told me you had to go to Washington and that he had to leave town. He left me in charge and told me if anything comes up I can't handle that I should call you, because he would not be available to be reached."

Sadly I asked, "Ann, did Michael leave you anyway for me to get a hold of him?"

With a hint of concern in her voice she answered, "No I'm sorry Christina, he didn't. But I could tell he was hurting really badly over the abortion of his child. Christina, is there anything I can do on a personal level to help you guys through this?"

American Goddess

I answered quickly, "Yes Ann, there is.   If Michael calls please tell him I love him, and I need to speak with him."

We finished our conversation, just as I reached Jean Fitzpeters office, the American ambassador to the U.N. As soon as I opened the door, she handed me an envelope and said, "Hi Christina, this just came in on the line from the President for you.   You better read it fast we only have a few minutes before the Assembly gathers."

We talked for another ten minutes as I scanned through the fax.   Afterward, I was once again off to address the U.N. Security Council, on a matter which I saw strictly as another violation of human rights, thus falling under the jurisdiction of the U.N.'s Statutes.

As I waited to be called to address the U.N. Assembly, I found it difficult to place my thoughts of concern for Michael on the back burner of my mind.   Which, for a moment caused me to completely forget even where I was, when I heard my name called as the speaker introduced me to the Assembly.   I quickly regained my composure as I confidently approached the podium. I greeted the Assembly casually, and then proceeded to call for the world to condemn Iraq's aggression and demand Iraqis' immediate withdrawal from Kuwait.   I was so dramatically convincing that by 1:00 that afternoon, that's just what the U.N. did.

The next day the headlines read, **"Christina Powers once again leads the band wagon for the Rush Administration, only this time it's against Saddam Lussein's invasion of Kuwait!"**

The only problem was Iraq ignored the U.N.'s demands and proceeded to do exactly what the Vice President predicted and began to move thousands of troops to Kuwait's border with Saudi Arabia.   So, on August 3rd, 1990, I was on a two-day trip to six European nations, to try to convince them to stop all international trade with Iraq.

Then it was back to New York, to address the U.N. on the 6th, at which time I helped convince the U.N. Security Council to declare an economic embargo against Iraq.   Right after I finished addressing the Security Council, I received a message from the President asking me to come directly to the White House.   I said I would and by 1:00pm, I was on a military flight back to Washington, D.C. The entire time we were in the air all I could think about was Michael.   It had been four days now and I had not heard a word from him, even though I had left numerous messages on his pager for him to call me.   I wondered how he was and if he had listened to the world news.   I hoped he had the opportunity to see for himself what I was doing.   Maybe then, he would realize I had no choice, but to leave him like I did.

As I sat there thinking over the loud roar of the chopper's blades, my eyes began to tear and I thought, 'Oh God, I miss him so much!   Won't you please bring him back to me Lord, I promise I will never leave him alone and hurting again.   I need his love and strength so badly right now and I know he needs mine, so please send him home to me.'

349

American Goddess

All at once, I was abruptly snapped out of my thoughts as the chopper bounced at least twenty feet on landing, leaving the remains of my stomach in my throat. My nervous system was so upset after that shock it took me several minutes just to unbuckle my seat belt. When I finally stopped my shaking, I looked up to see the crew nonchalantly laughing as if it were a common occurrence. So I shook my head at them as I said, "Next time I want Air Force One." With that, I exited that noisy monstrosity laughing along with the guys.

The next thing I knew, I was once again being escorted by White House Security to the Oval Office. When I entered President Rush immediately rose from his seat to greet me with a warm embrace as he said, "Christina, thank you for coming so quickly." He gestured for me to take a seat as he continued, "Please make yourself comfortable. I've asked you here because we are approaching a very delicate stage with our U.N./Iraq operation. You see, I will be announcing to the U.N. tomorrow, the United States will be sending troops to the Persian Gulf to defend Saudi Arabia from a possible attack by Iraq. I will also be asking for the members of the U.N. to form a military coalition under the guidance of the U.N., and then authorize that coalition to use force to carry out the embargo against Iraq. Now, I've spoken to the leaders of all the member nations with veto power, and the only problems we have are the Chinese and the Soviets. Neither country is willing to allow the U.N. to use force against Iraq. I have already been warned by both nations' leaders if we use force, then it could escalate the situation rather quickly. Now as I see it, the only way we can pull this off is if we keep the human rights issues at the core of this crisis. This is where you come in, because I'm hoping with your help, we will be able to convince both nations not to use their veto power against the formation of a coalition."

I lifted my eyebrows with concern as I said, "It sounds like it's already a crisis." I shook my head in dismay and added, "I'll do whatever I can to help George, just name it."

He grinned from ear to ear and said, "I'm glad you're on my side, because you're a little dynamo lady."

I smiled graciously and replied, "Why thank you Mr. President, I'm pleased you noticed. Now how may I serve my country?"

We both smiled at that one, then he said, "I have a great come back for that, but since I'm a gentleman I'll get right down to business. I would like you to leave this afternoon for Moscow. I have arranged for you to meet with President Gorbasoff tomorrow morning. I would like you to convince him, and the Soviet People, in only three days that this invasion is a violation of human rights, and as a member of the U.N. they must support the Security Council to stop this atrocity. After that, I'll need you to take three more days and do the same in China. I've heard you speak both languages fluently, I hope that's true?"

American Goddess

I was overwhelmed by his request, but I chose not to show it when I said, "I really need to stop by my home first, do I have time to do that?"

He put his hand to his chin as he replied, "Not really, Christina.   If you're going to make the meeting with Gorbasoff, you will need to leave now."

He handed me a large envelope from off his desk and continued, "Here is an outline of our strategies and goals for the embargo.   I would like you to give a copy of each to both leaders, as a show of good faith."

With that, I took a deep breath and said, "Oh Well, I guess National Security must take precedence over the heart every time."   I smiled, took the envelope and added, "So how do I get there?"

Within ten minutes of our conversation, I was on a military jet to the Soviet Union. Eight days later I returned to Washington a victorious woman.   I had gracefully charmed the citizens of both nations, and I received a verbal promise from their leaders, that they would not veto the formation of a U.N. coalition.   After that, I had two days to go home before heading off to the Arab countries of Jordan, Libya, and Yemen, who opposed the involvement of non-Arab nations on Arab soil.   George hoped I could use my powers of persuasion on them as well as I had on my last mission.

While I was home, I tried to get in touch with Michael over the phone, but I decided not to look for him. I figured if he truly loved me he'd come home on his own.   I only went into the office twice and for one hour each time.   Thank God for Ann Markel, because I couldn't concentrate on work if my life depended on it.   All I did in those two days was mope around the house hoping Michael would return my calls, but he never did.   On the 20th, I was off to my mission in the Middle East, where I was able to at least convince Jordan, Libya, and Yemen, not to join Iraq in fighting against the coalition, if it should come to that.

I returned home just in time to accompany the President, as he addressed the U.N., and on August 25th, at 11:00am the U.N. Security Council passed a resolution to allow enforcement of the embargo by military means.

Before retiring to our suites that night, President Rush and I celebrated our U.N. victory over a private drink in the lounge, of the Plaza Hotel in Manhattan.   As we toasted one another he said, "Christina, words cannot adequately express my gratitude for your help with this crisis, and your efforts have proven the U.N. truly has the ability to play a leading role in world affairs.   I know that's the purpose the U.N. was created, but because the world is so diverse, it's still something I never thought would become a reality."   He took my hand in his as he continued, "You truly are a remarkable woman Christina Powers, and I'm impressed by how much you really care about people.   If you should ever desire to get into politics with the Republican Party, I'll support you all the way."

American Goddess

Starting to laugh I said, "Thank you kindly George, but you can keep the politics. My life is crazy enough as it is, so I certainly don't need to add the responsibility of a public office to it. Oh by the way, since we are speaking of hectic lives, I must tell you I have to do something to slow this pace of mine. George, now that things seem to be on the right track, I need to ask you to send me back to my civilian life. I have a husband I have not seen since the day this started, and I need to find him."

He graciously brought my hand to his lips, gently kissed the back of it and said, "I will definitely miss your presence on this Christina, but I understand your circumstances completely. I have a wife at home I hardly see also."

Shortly after that, I kissed his cheek as we said our goodbyes and off I went. I decided not to stay in the city that night. Instead I drove the four-hour trip to Michael's family home in the Catskills, in the hope he would be there. I was missing him just too much and I could no longer wait for him to come to me.

I arrived at the mountain house at 1:00am, and my heart began to pound with excitement, when I saw Michael's car in the driveway. I quickly parked and as I opened the door to climb out, my body began to shake, and I thought, 'What if he doesn't want to see me?' Then I remembered the night I went after Johnny and I thought, 'What if he's not alone? Oh my God, what if Joanne is with him? What do I do? What do I say?' I immediately, yet gently slapped myself across the face and chuckled as I thought, 'Just stop this you asshole, before you talk yourself right out of going in.' Shrugging my shoulders, my thoughts continued, 'Oh well! If she's with him I'll react tonight and figure it out tomorrow.'

With that thought, I pulled out my key to the front door and headed for the house. When I opened the door, I could hear the sounds of a CNN news broadcast on the TV, so I slowly walked toward the living room. When I entered it, the light from the TV helped me see Michael sleeping on the sofa, completely dressed in shoes and all. I walked over to the sofa and kneeled down beside him. I noticed he hadn't shaved since I left, and the growth of his beard looked mighty good on him. I just watched him sleeping for a few minutes; then, I began to slowly kiss his forehead. He was startled by my first kiss which made him jerk up quickly. He looked at me, and with a surprised tone said, "Punkie! What the hell took you so long?" At that, he pulled me into his arms and began to kiss me passionately.

As we melted into one another's embrace, I slid my hand behind his head, pulled him close enough to whisper in his ear and said, "Michael, my love, I've lived and learned a lot throughout my years on this planet, and I've always known I could face anything life threw at me. But over this last month, I've discovered you are so much a part of me, that I am an empty shell of a woman without you. So I am asking you now Michael, please come back to me. I love you with all my heart, and I need you desperately."

American Goddess

Gazing lovingly into my eyes as he replied, "Christina, honey, I love you and I'm sorry we both had to go through this. But after you walked out on me like you did, I couldn't just return your calls like nothing had happened. I hate to admit this, but more than anything I had to be convinced you really love me, Punkie. So I gave you the time you needed to decide for yourself how much I really meant to you. As for me, I needed you to show how much you loved me, by coming after me." Then he held me tightly and added, "Punkie, I love you and I thank God you came back, because my soul has been slowly dying every second I've been without you."

My heart melted, as I lovingly said, "Let's not ever do this to one another again."

We kissed with the passion of angels in love and proceeded to gently disrobe each other. As we made love that night, I kept from Michael the fact I had gone off my birth control the day I left for Washington, D.C. We shared in the passions of our flesh until dawn that morning, and at the height of our love making Michael screamed out in ecstasy as he forcefully bore himself within me. As I felt his explosion, I prayed in my thoughts, 'Please God, let me conceive his child this night.'

Later that morning, I fixed us a lovely little breakfast and as we sat down to eat I took Michael's hand and said, "I love you baby, and thank you for last night, you were incredible."

He kissed my hand, smiled devilishly and replied, "I didn't get there alone."

I smiled back and it hit me like a flash, so with excitement I said, "Michael! Ann is doing a fine job handling thing, and while the rest of our business trips are still on hold, why don't we spend all of September up here together? We have some lost time to make up and, in more ways, than one."

His face lit up with love as he replied, "There is nothing I would love more, than to spend an entire month alone with you."

He led me back to the bedroom, slipped off my robe, laid me on the bed, spread my wings with his thumbs, and began to devour my essence with his warm moist lips. He drove me to the point of actually pleading with him to plunge deep within me. The moment he did, my emergency code rang on my pager and we chose to ignore it. He went wild as he loved me with every ounce of his strength, and my body screamed with ecstasy as I took every explosive inch of him.

When I did finally answer the fourth emergency ring, to my surprise I discovered it was President Rush, and the first thing he said was, "Christina, I have some bad news for you. It seems Jimmy has been taken hostage with a number of foreign diplomats in Kuwait. Lussein has ordered these hostages moved to military and industrial sites throughout Iraq. He is using them as human shields to discourage attacks by coalition members."

American Goddess

I gasped loud enough to alarm Michael who was sitting beside me and said, "Oh my, God! No, George! Not Jimmy! What are you going to do about it?"

With a hint of urgency, he replied, "I'm going to try and force Lussein to release them through international pressure. That's why I am calling you. I don't know how you did it, but you seemed to have created a good personal rapport with the Arab nations of Jordan, Libya, and Yemen. This fact could prove to be quite useful, because the only way we are going to have even a slim chance of obtaining the release of the hostages, is if these nations put pressure on Lussein. Now I am going to ask you to visit them again and convince them to pressure Lussein for the release of all the hostages. I thought you would want to be the one to try to convince them, especially since Jimmy is one of the hostages."

I looked at Michael with tears in my eyes as I said, "Mr. President, I will call you with my answer in ten minutes."

I hung up the phone and proceeded to tell Michael everything. Afterward I said, "Michael, all I will say is I feel I must go, but if you'd rather I let the President send someone else, knowing Jimmy's life is on the line; then, I will call the President and tell him to find someone else."

He looked at me sadly, "Well I guess you better not unpack." And not two hours later I was on my way back to the Middle East.

CHAPTER 36

The next month, I spent hopping across the Arab Nations of the Middle East like a jack rabbit, and on September 29th, I was the first Westerner since the invasion, to have a personal conference with Saddam Lussein in Baghdad, the Capital of Iraq. When I arrived at Lussein's palace, I was escorted to his office by several high-ranking Iraqi military officials. As I was led in, I could see Lussein standing by some large windows

American Goddess

on the opposite end of the room, and from the moment our eyes met I began to study him. I had heard so many conflicting stories about the man that I had no idea how to handle him. So once again, I was playing it by ear, and you know how I hate doing that. As we greeted each other with a bow, I thought, 'Shit! What am I worried about? He's just another man.' At that I smiled at him softly and laughed to myself as my thoughts continued, 'I'll probably end this war in ten minutes,' and the first words out of his mouth were, "You are an imperialist pig, Christina Powers, and if I hadn't vowed to my fellow Arab brothers I would negotiate the release of the hostages with you, I'd have you assassinated right on the spot! If you hadn't gotten involved, I would be ruling OPEC already. Now please keep these things in mind before you attempt to use your trickery on me."

I was so completely taken aback by the ruthlessness of his tone that for one moment, I, 'Christina Powers' was speechless. I quickly changed gears, realizing I needed a new approach, so I removed the smile from my face, and in his native tongue firmly said, "Somebody had to stop you, because what you're doing is wrong."

His response to my answer was even more hateful as he growled, "You have not stopped me **WOMAN**! You've only succeeded in slowing me down."

I took a deep breath and tried another angle by saying, "King Lussein, if we continue to hurl insults at each other, we'll never accomplish anything. So may we at least try to be civil as we discuss the reason why I'm here?"

He put his hand to his chin as he silently studied me. Then all at once, he slapped his hands together loudly, and shouted, "Everyone leave us!" And the room cleared in seconds.

When the room quieted, I turned to Lussein and said, "King Lussein, you mentioned negotiating the release of the hostages with me. But I have come to ask you in good faith, to show the world you are not the barbarian everyone believes you to be, by letting me take these individuals with me when I leave. I believe if you do this, you will gain some support from the International Community. Then if you will air your grievances with Kuwait to the U.N., maybe together in the harmony of worldwide brotherhood, we can come to an acceptable settlement between your two nations."

He looked at me sternly and said, "How would you like me to address you?"

I proceed to stare him down, because I refused to allow him to intimidate me with his evil eyes, and the second he looked away, I answered his question with a firm voice, "You may call me, Christina."

In response he lifted his eyebrows with amazement; then, turned and walked over to his desk. When he reached it, he invited me to take a seat, at which point he outright refused to release the hostages, and he promised Iraq would never submit to American pressure. After three grueling hours of trying to reason with a nearly unreasonable man; I finally convinced him to at least allow me to see the hostages. By 9:00pm that evening, he was personally escorting me to where the hostages were being held.

The moment Jimmy saw me he leaped from out of the group of hostages and landed right in my arms. He clung to my breast like a baby nursing and began to cry. I tried to nonchalantly hold him like a stranger as I whispered in his ear, "Jimmy, try to be cool, I don't want them to realize we know each other." I began to pat his head as I very loudly said, "I understand how you feel sir, and I promise the international community is doing everything possible to obtain everyone's release."

Jimmy jerked his head from my shoulder and with a petrified look said, "Doesn't the fact you're standing here, mean we're going home?"

I was fighting back my tears and Jimmy knew it when I said, "I'm very sorry sir, but King Lussein is refusing to release anyone at this time." I looked at them all and added, "Folks, I know this is a horrendous ordeal you're living through, but I give you my word we will not stop trying to obtain your release. So, I must ask everyone to please be patient with us and remain strong."

The second I stopped talking Lussien slapped his hands together and immediately his guards came between Jimmy and me, and abruptly ended our visit. I was quickly ushered out of the room, without even being given the opportunity to say goodbye. It happened so fast I was stunned.

The next thing I knew, I was on my way to the airport, and all the way I tried my best to convince Lussein to release the hostages. As I spoke with this man, I felt like I was talking to a wall. Just before I was helped out of Lussein's limo I turned to him and said, "King Lussein! Please listen to me. I don't want to play games with you, so I'm going to be blunt. The world realizes what you stand to gain from annexing Kuwait. First, you will have acquired Kuwait's oil wealth, plus Iraq eliminates a two-hundred-billion-dollar debt to Kuwait. Second, you become a major power in OPEC." As I spoke, I put my hand to my chin, and with a slight touch of sarcastic humor added, "And would you just take a look at the increased access your Naval Forces will have to the Persian Gulf."

I slowly changed my approach and as my words intensified, so did the expression on my face. I gently shook my head and with conviction said, "The people of the world will not stand for this. I'm telling you the international community will truly do battle against you and for one reason only, what you're doing is morally and ethically wrong. Won't you please reconsider and release some of the 'steam in this pressure pot', by releasing those innocent people?"

I could tell I was getting through when he slowly lifted his eyebrows, shook his head and in a calm voice said, "You have proven to be everything I was told you would be, and you have given me much to think about." He slapped his hands again, and I was immediately escorted to my waiting jet.

American Goddess

October 2nd, I was back in Washington, D.C. for a six-hour debriefing with the President and his advisers.   From there, it was onto a one-hour international news conference, and finally by 6:00pm that evening, I was in the air and on my way home to Michael.   As I tried to make myself comfortable on the jet, I grabbed the phone to call Michael.

He answered the phone with a hopeful, "Christina, is it you?"   The moment I heard his precious voice, and knowing I would soon be with him, brought tears of joy to my eyes, which flooded forth from a fountain of pure love for my man.   With a tone of absolute sensuality, I said, "Hi, baby.   It's your Punkie, and I'm longing for your touch."

I received quite the erotic response, "Well I just happen to have something throbbing, and it's longing to touch you too!"

I sighed, "Aaa," and with my famous May West interpretation replied, "I can't wait big boy.   I should be landing at Stewart by 7:00pm, meet me with that gun in your pocket fully loaded and I'll help you fire it."

With a tone of pure excitement, he answered, "I'll be there baby."

As we talked, I began to feel slightly dizzy, then nauseous.   Ten minutes after we ended our conversation my nausea turned into lower abdominal cramps.   By the time we landed the cramps became so intense, I could hardly walk off the jet.   I managed to make it through the airport, and when I reached Michael I nearly collapsed in his arms. He grabbed me to hold me up and with a concerned tone said, "Christina!   Baby, what's wrong?"

I grabbed at my abdomen and cried, "I don't know Michael, I started feeling sick to my stomach on the flight, and it's been continually getting worse."

He proceeded to help me to the car and when we reached it, I doubled over in pain and I cried out, "**OH GOD, MICHAEL**! Something's wrong!"

Swiftly he lifted me up, placed me in the car seat, and as he climbed in he said, "We're going to the hospital right now."

He hit the gas pedal and the moment he did, my lap filled with blood as I began to hemorrhage.   I grabbed Michael's arm and cried, "Honey, help me!"

I heard him say, "Oh my God!   Baby, hold on!"   And that was the last thing I heard before losing consciousness.

American Goddess

CHAPTER 37

I woke up two days later at Vassar Brother's Hospital in Poughkeepsie, with Michael once again sitting beside my hospital bed. I glanced over at him, managed half a smile and said, "Well how was that for an exciting reunion?"

His blue eyes and glorious smile brightened up the dimly lit room, as he gracefully came to my side. Taking my hand gently in his, and looking deeply into my eyes, he lovingly said, "You're going to be the death of me yet, Punkie."

We both managed a smile, then he gently kissed my painfully dried out lips, and in a soft voice said, "I love you Punkie, and I know why you did what you did. I only wish you would have talked to me first Christina, before risking your life for me."

I looked at him with a completely bewildered expression, as I mustered up the strength to say, "What are you talking about, Michael?"

He gave me a surprised look and proceeded to inform me that I had just had a miscarriage and nearly bled to death. As he spoke, a horrifyingly sick feeling came over me. I put my hands to my face and cried, "Oh God! **Michael no**! I can't believe I let myself become so caught up with trying to obtain Jimmy's freedom, I completely forgot I deliberately tried to conceive our child."

All at once a fear hit me from deep within my soul, so I squeezed Michael's hand with all my strength, and with intensity in my words I asked, "Did Dr. Hart perform a hysterectomy on me?"

He shook his head as if he were disappointed by my deep concern over the welfare of my uterus, and it showed in his voice as he answered, "Dr. Hart told me after the surgery he wanted to perform one on you, but since he didn't deem it a necessity to save your life, he elected not to risk your wrath. He asked me to help convince you to have a hysterectomy done as soon as you recover. So Punkie, I'm asking you to agree to the surgery right now, for your own safety." Then he slowly dropped to his knees and with a look that told me he was truly troubled said, "Punkie, how could you endanger your life like this without talking to me first?"

I explained I had forgotten to take my pills when I left for the Middle East, then I added, "I remembered as we were in the heat of our passion and I didn't know how to stop things to bring it up. I also wanted to have your child."

He kissed my hand and with half a smile replied, "I can understand everything you just said, but I'm still having a problem accepting it. I thought neither one of us would ever do anything involving our personal lives together, without discussing it first. Don't you see that keeping something like this from me is just the same as if you were purposely deceiving me?"

American Goddess

I looked at him sadly, realizing what he was actually saying and said, "Michael, honey, I wasn't keeping this pregnancy from you, I didn't know myself.   So that's why I never thought of it as lying to you, and I promise you I will never keep anything from you."

His smile was loving and sincere as he said, "Please, Christina! Never deliberately put your life in harm's way again.   I love you so much Punkie, it would kill me to be without you."

I took his hand in mine, brought it to my dried lips, kissed it once and said, "I love you too, Michael."

Michael looked open heartedly into my eyes and with complete integrity said, "Punkie, I need to know something.   I have not kept one thing from you since the day we met, can you say the same?"

I gazed back at him confidently and answered, "Yes Michael, I can say the same." After that I continued to reassure him, I have always told him everything, all the while knowing I had just lied to him.   As I spoke, I thought, 'Michael, I wish I could tell you everything, including all my fears.   But I have been betrayed and hurt so badly in the past, I do not know if I can ever completely trust anyone again, even you my love.'   These words I kept to myself as Michael kissed my cheek and laid his head down on the pillow beside mine.

The first thing I did the next morning was spend twenty minutes listening to Dr. Hart and Michael, trying to convince me to have a hysterectomy.   After their plea, that it was for my own safety, I politely said, "No!"

With frustration in his tone Dr. Hart responded, "Why are you being so obstinate, Christina?"

"Obstinate," I snapped back.   "That's spitting in the wind, isn't it Dr. Hart?   I will say this but only once more, this is my body and I will decide what is best for it."

He looked at me as if I had slapped his face and said, "You're absolutely correct Christina.   Please forgive me, it's only because I'm your physician and I care."

I could see in his eyes I had hurt his feelings, so I took his hand in mine and said, "I understand that Dr. Hart."   And in that moment, I could feel through his hand the anger of his soul begin to fade, and I realized this incredibly handsome young man, was desperately in love with me. So I released his hand to keep his knees from forcing him to the floor.   I could sense he knew I had discovered his secret, so I continued as if I hadn't, by saying, "I also want you to know I respect your opinion Robert, not just because you're my physician, but Michael and I, consider you a close family friend as well."

He smiled with a sigh and said, "Well then maybe you will at least listen to this.   I don't want you going back to work or traveling anywhere for the next month.   That's when I want to see you back in my office."   With that, he gave us both a warm friendly handshake, and gracefully left the room.

American Goddess

The next morning as we left the hospital, we were surprised to say the least, when a mob of reporters charged us. Especially since Michael assured me, he kept a lid on this one. But to my dismay, it appeared someone from the hospital staff had informed the press twenty minutes before my discharge, that I was a patient in the hospital and that I had a miscarriage. I was horrified and humiliated as I openly dodged questions like, "Christina! With all the children who need to be adopted in this world, why would you risk your own life to have a child?"

Thank God for Michael, because I froze up so badly from that question, I could hardly move. Michael rescued me by swiftly ushering me into the limo. The second we climbed in he shouted, "James, take off!"

James sped away and he did not stop speeding until he finally lost the paparazzi. After our escape, James drove Michael and me to the Catskill Mountain family home, with enough supplies to last a month.

Michael gave Ann Markel full power over our entire empire for that month and told her not to call us unless the world was about to end. He was so determined to keep me from running myself into an early grave, that for the entire month he was my 'knight in shining armor', as well as my servant boy. And let me tell you, I loved every minute of it!

On November 5th, Dr. Hart gave me a clean bill of health put me back on the pill, and the next day it was back to work. When I saw how well Ann had handled the helm of Powers Incorporated, I called her into my office to meet with Michael and me. When she entered the office, I invited her to be seated and said, "Ann, I can remember when you, Jimmy, Bobby, Joe Aiello and me, all worked together on my first U.S. tour back in the seventies, and you have been a loyal employee ever since. That's why I want you to know I think very highly of you as a friend, as well as an employee, and as an employee you have proven yourself to be more than capable. Because of this, Michael and I would like to offer you the position of fourth executive vice president and increase your salary to five-million annually." With a joyful smile, I reached for her hand as I continued, "Congratulations Ann, you deserve it."

She hugged me and with tears of pride said, "Christina, I don't know how to thank you." She hugged Michael with sincerity and added, "Thank you for giving me the opportunity to prove myself, Michael."

He happily returned the hug as he said, "You don't have to thank me. I thank you for doing such a great job." When Ann went back to her office that day, her feet were not touching the floor.

Although we were back at the office, it was not work as usual. Michael insisted we begin delegating much more of the top brass responsibility to others, which gave us more time to be together as a couple. Michael delegated so well that by November 13th,

American Goddess

we had everything running fairly smoothly, including our marriage. Yet at the same time, I always had a sick feeling inside, because I would never allow myself to forget Jimmy's plight for one moment.

On the evening of the 17th, as Michael and I watched the evening news together, Tom Brokoff said, "The President announced today he would be visiting Saudi Arabia, November twenty-first, through the twenty-second, to celebrate the Thanksgiving holiday with American troops deployed in the Kingdom of Saudi Arabia as part of Operation Desert Shield."

The second he finished speaking Michael watched with amazement, as I grabbed the phone like a possessed woman and began to punch the numbers. As soon as I heard the beep of the answering machine, I excitedly said, "Hi George, its Christina. Please call me on my private line as soon as possible."

At that, I put down the phone, turned to Michael almost breathless and exclaimed, "I can't believe this, honey!"

He looked at me strangely and with bewilderment in his voice said, "What are you talking about?"

Just then the phone rang, so I quickly grabbed it and said, "I hope it's you, George?"

He chuckled as he answered, "You'd better make this one quick too Christina, because you caught me in the middle of preparing for my trip."

With excitement I said, "Take me with you, George!"

Sounding slightly confused he asked, "What?"

I answered quickly, "You heard me right. Take me with you. I want to perform for our troops. I think it would aid in your task of building morale, by showing them every American is behind them on this, not just the government?"

With a disappointed tone he said, "I can't take you with me. Saudi Arabia law forbids live performances of any kind on their soil."

I slightly wined my response, "Come on, George! You are the President of the United States, and they're American troops. I find it hard to believe you cannot convince King Fehd to allow it. After all, their law also forbids foreign troops on their soil, doesn't it?"

I was calling his bluff on that one, because I had no idea what Saudi Arabia law stated. But by his momentary silence, I knew it was a good guess; then, he said, "I'll tell you what Christina, I'll do it if you do one for me?"

I thought to myself, 'Here we go!' As I said, "Name it, George."

He cleared his voice and said, "I want you to be standing beside me with your full support when I announce my bid for re-election in January."

I started to laugh then I controlled myself and said, "That's a good one, George."

With that he said, "You're laughing at me! I can't believe you!"

American Goddess

I quickly replied, "You know I love you George, it's your party I'm not too fond of. But my answer is still yes."

He laughed, "Great! I'll see you here on the 19th."

After we said our goodbyes, I placed the phone down on the coffee table, turned to Michael with a smile of pure excitement, and before I could utter a single syllable he shouted, "What the fuck do you think you're doing? Call him right back and tell him you're not going!"

I was taken aback by his outburst, but I still answered calmly, "Honey, I have to go."

He snapped back, "I don't care what you think you have to do. You're not going!"

I tried to make him understand by saying, "Michael, there is something telling me I have to go."

He shook his head with utter frustration, and in an extremely angry voice said, "You've got to stop this, Christina. I know you're upset over Jimmy, and so am I, but you're driving yourself mad with this. Can't you see you're killing yourself?" His voice began to calm as he took me in his arms and continued, "Punkie, I'm just worried about you. You almost bled to death on me only a month ago, remember? I can't let you go charging off to Saudi Arabia to perform, when you're not even totally recuperated yet."

I looked at him sincerely and said, "Michael, my health is fine, so please listen to me and try to understand. I know that for some reason, I'm being guided there, and I must go."

With that statement, he pushed me out of his arms and shouted, "Guided! Are you a nut!? You are being guided all right, by your own obsessions, and if you don't pick up that phone and make that call, then I'm washing my hands of you. If you don't give a damn about yourself, how can you expect me to give a damn about you?"

This time I lost it, so I shouted back, "Nuts huh! I must be nuts, to live and breathe for someone like you."

He began to laugh sarcastically as he shouted, "That's why you're always so willing to drop me on a dime and take off. Shit Christina, this is a marriage and it's meant to be a mutual partnership, that means we're supposed to discuss this stuff, remember?"

I flung my hands in the air and shouted, "I can't take this anymore, Michael. I'm tired of you trying to run my life. You're my husband, not my master. So if you want to walk out the door go ahead and walk."

I could see the fire in his eyes as he yelled, "You know what? That's just what I'm going to do!"

My own anger flared with his as I answered, "If you do Michael, don't expect me to come after you!"

He shouted back, "Do us both a favor this time and don't bother!"

American Goddess

He stormed out of the room and as I watched him go I thought, 'What the hell are we doing?' So I quickly went after him, grabbed his hand as he reached the front door and said, "Michael, wait a second please."

He pulled his hand from mine and angrily replied, "Christina, I don't give a damn anymore!" Then he slammed the door in my face and walked out.

I stood there speechless, not totally believing what had just occurred, and feeling completely bewildered thought, '**Oh Well! I'll figure it out tomorrow!**'

CHAPTER 38

I gave Michael two days to cool off, and on November 16th, I thought, 'All right Michael, that's long enough.' I figured he should be a little less obstinate and a little more reasonable by now, so at 9:00am that morning my search began with a phone call. As I guessed, Michael did not return my call and since I didn't have time to play games, because I was leaving on the 19th, I called my security firm and asked them to locate his whereabouts for me. I told Frank Rossi, the Director for Powers Security, all Michael's normal hideouts, and I expected he would be found in a matter of hours. But to my dismay, Frank never called me back until 9:00pm that evening. When he did, he informed me Michael was nowhere to be found, and the search would take a little longer than anticipated.

The longer it took to find him the more concerned I became. So, at 8:00am the following morning I decided to call my mother-in-law, who unbeknownst to me, absolutely could not manage to rise and function before 10:00am. She wasted no time informing me of that fact when she answered the phone with a groggy, "Hello, who is this?"

"Good morning Tess it's Christina," I said with a slight hint of urgency.

Sharply she asked, "What time is it, Christina?"

"8:00am I apologize for waking you, but I really need to speak with you."

With the sincerity of an angel in her tone she replied, "Christina, it takes me ten minutes just to get moving in the morning, so please don't ask me to solve your family problems before 10:00am, okay?" And all I heard was {click} as she hung up the phone.

As I stood there holding the phone with my lower jaw touching the floor, I thought, 'What the hell was that?' I proceeded to work my thoughts into a fury as I paced through the house for the next two hours wondering, 'Where the hell are you, Michael? I know you love me asshole, so why are you being so damn stubborn. Oh my God! This man has a power over me that's frightening.' My mind went wild like this until finally the 10:00 a clock hour came, and I hit redial. The phone was answered on the third ring and I heard,

"Good morning Christina, and don't ask me where he is."

"That's not fair Tess," I protested vigorously, "Michael's my husband, how can I not want to find him?"

Just as forceful she replied, "Well, from what I have seen and heard, you've nearly destroyed my son. Now from a mother's point of view, if your son had been swept up by a worldly woman as yourself, and you watched as she broke his heart time after time; then, he finally comes to his senses and tells you that he never wants to see this woman again; then, this woman calls you and wants to know where your son is, I wonder if you would wonder, is she coming to finish the job? What would you do?"

I answered her with an air of integrity, "After having met the woman in question I would hopefully be capable of looking past the hype which precedes her, and still be able to make a clear decision on the woman's true intent toward my son."

With integrity of her own she simply replied, "Then you will understand when I refuse to answer your question. Now, I am a seventy-six-year-old woman Christina, but I will still fight to protect one of my children. I'm going to do just that by saying goodbye, I have much too much to do for an old lady as it is, and I certainly don't need this worry."

"Please! Tess! I'm begging you don't hang up!" and I heard (Click). With that I slammed the phone down feeling totally frustrated and I began to cry.

The next morning over my first cup of coffee, James brought in the local newspaper the Poughkeepsie Journal. I took two sips from my cup, as I unrolled the paper. I took two more sips as my eyes caught the headlines and the moment they did, I choked so hard, I showered the article with coffee. Once I caught my breath, I quickly wiped off the paper and in big bold print it read, **"Michael Carr, the husband of our local celebrity Christina Powers Carr, has hired the law firm of Lafarge and Han of Middletown, New York to file divorce papers against his famous wife."**

My first response was shock, then anger, and after finishing the article I thought, 'Christina, what are you worrying about?   This can't be a true story.   You know Michael loves you.   He's a reasonable man when he's calm.'

Just then the doorbell rang and not two minutes later, Carman entered the room with a certified letter from the law firm of Lafarge and Han.   I ripped it open and sure enough, there were divorce papers inside.   I stuffed them back in the envelope and ran for the shower.   I was dressed and on my way to Tess's house with letter in hand, in only twenty-two minutes, and I was looking hot to boot.

As I drove through the sleepy village of Ravena, I remembered how the main street was lined with people the day of our wedding and I thought, 'Michael, there is no way you're getting away from me, I love you too much you pain-in-my-ass.'   At that I pulled into Magnolia Circle and proceeded with determination to my mother in law's home, only this time I was not laughing when she opened the door.   I was dead serious, and it was my turn to show it when I said, "Tess, please listen to me because I don't have much time. I have got to find Michael!   I love him Tess, and I do not want a divorce.   I know if I can only see him, I could convince him of that."

She looked at me with disbelieving eyes and said, "To do what Christina, say hello for ten minutes then leave him again?   Do you realize you will be out of the country on your first anniversary?   How do you think that is making Michael feel, knowing you would rather be in Saudi Arabia on your anniversary then with him?"

I gently touched her hand as I said, "Tess, what Michael is refusing to see is if by my taking this trip I am able to save even one life, then that's worth giving up every anniversary for the rest of our lives.   I know if I could just speak with him, I could make him see that.   Tess, I love your son, my husband, more than life itself, but he has got to understand the lives of thousands of innocent people are at stake.   I would be less than human, if I did nothing to help try to bring a peaceful conclusion to this crisis."

She looked at me and as tears welled up in her eyes said, "He's at his sister's camp house in a town called Indian Lake, in the Adirondacks.   I misjudged you Christina, and I am deeply sorry I did.   I know if you talk to Michael he will understand, he loves you just as much Christina, I know he does."

I opened the door all the way so I could hug her, and with tears of relief in my eyes I said, "Thank you, Mom.   I know I have never said it before Tess, but I do love you." And for the first time since the day I met her, she returned my hug with an open heart. She gave me directions to the camp and sent me on my way with God speed.

American Goddess

CHAPTER 39

After spending two hours driving around the back roads of Indian Lake, I finally found the driveway which led up to a quaint little cabin, nestled in the woods, with Michael's car parked at the end of it. I climbed out of my car, walked to the door and knocked. Michael answered the door and the moment our eyes met, I wanted to leap into his arms, but the look of disgust on his face and the tone of his voice, forced me to conceal my true feelings, because the first thing he said was, "What are you doing here? I thought we agreed not to come after one another."

At that I shook the divorce papers in his face and forcefully said, "What is this Michael, a plea to get my attention? Well you have it! And I'm here! Now, would you please stop this nonsense and listen to me, I know you don't really want a divorce and neither do I."

"I'm not pleading for anything, Christina." He answered sarcastically.

"Then what is this all about, Michael? Is it just to keep me from going because you think I'm rejecting you? You know I love you with all my heart, how can you truthfully stand there and honestly think to yourself that I am putting you second, especially since you know world peace is at stake."

With a look of deep sincerity in his eyes and a voice to match he said, "Christina, I told you. If you go to Saudi Arabia again, we're finished, you told me you were going, so there's your divorce papers. Since you're here, please just sign them and be on your way."

I looked at him, started to laugh at his performance and said, "Don't expect an academy award Michael, and please don't expect me to sign these papers. I'm telling you again Michael, I love you and I know how difficult being married to me has been. I also understand why you're so upset, and that's why I'm not going to give you a divorce."

He nearly became irate as he shouted, "Would you fucking listen to me for once! All I want from you is a divorce! Damn it, Christina! I don't want you or all the bullshit that comes along with you. Don't you get it? I don't want anything that will make me think of you even once, including your precious empire. Just let me leave with my self-respect and dignity." Tears came to his eyes as he continued, "My heart can't handle this life with you any longer Punkie; you're destroying me."

I felt the pain of his heart, so I reached out to comfort him with all my love, and as my voice cracked I said, "Michael, please honey, listen to me, I'm not trying to hurt you, I love you. Don't you remember, Michael? You're the one who told me you knew God had a higher calling for me in this life. After knowing that, how can you now ask me to

American Goddess

turn from that calling, when I finally realize I'm truly hearing it?" Passionately I grabbed his hand and with fear in my voice, "Michael! I don't know why I must go; I only know I must!"

With his strong firm hands trembling, he grabbed my shoulders and with a voice as hurting as a little boy lost, said, "I know that Christina. I also know you are my soul mate, and even though my love for you springs forth from the depths of my being, if you go for whatever reasons, we will not be together in this lifetime. Christina, I am constantly filled with fear for your life when I'm not with you, and I can't deal with it anymore. So as much as it's breaking my heart to say this I must, if you're still planning to be on that jet in the morning, then sign these papers before you leave and I will know we're just not meant to be. But if you choose to stay here with me, I will rip up those dammed divorce papers and love you with all my heart every day of my life."

My tears began to flow like a fountain as I looked at him and pleaded, "Michael, Honey! I love you, but I can't stay. Please, just let me do this one more thing, and I promise you, I will never leave you again."

He dropped his hands from my shoulders, and with a tone of utter frustration said, "One more thing! Never again! How many times have I heard those words before!? Don't you mean until the next time and the time after that!? Well I can't, and I won't, be the man behind the woman, Christina. I just can't, so at least you can let me keep whatever self-respect I have left and grant me this divorce."

This time 'I' was the one to become irate, and it was apparent the moment I opened my mouth, "You, bastard! You totally refuse to give an inch, don't you?" I stomped my foot with pure anger as I continued, "Well, I'll tell you what you stubborn male, you're my husband, and if you think I'm going to let you walk away from me that easily, you have another think coming!" I ripped the divorce papers into pieces, threw them in his face and shouted, "If you want your freedom from me that damn bad, then you better find a reason that's going to hold up in court because you're going to have to fight me for it. Now dammit Michael, listen to me! I have something I must do and I'm going to do it! I want you to take some time to get your head together, and I'll expect to see you at home when I get back." I grabbed the door handle and shouted, "This time, I think I'll slam the door in your face!" (Crack!)

At that I turned away, stormed to the car, threw it into drive and flung gravel thirty feet in the air all the way to the main road.

At 6:00am the next morning, I forced thoughts of Michael to the back of my mind as I boarded Air Force One with the President and the First Lady. To my surprise it was off to Paris before Saudi Arabia. The President invited me on behalf of himself, and President Gorbasoff of the Soviet Union, to attend as their personal guest, the history making summit being held to mark the end of the cold war. Our twenty hours in Paris were the most exciting hours for true global peace, the world had ever seen, and I was elated to be part of it.

We left Paris at 10:00pm on the 20th, and headed for Jidda, a city on Saudi Arabia's Western Red Sea Coast. This time on Air Force One, we were joined by National Security Adviser Brent Scowcroft, Gen. Norman Schwartoff, and four senior bi-partisan leaders of Congress: Senate Majority Leader George J. Nikcall (D, Maine), Senate Minority Leader Robert J. Zole (R, Kan.), House Speaker Thomas S. Boley (D, Wash.) My friend Senator Eartha Kit (D, CT) and my ex-husband, House Minority Leader Lee Bradford (R, N.Y.). Needless to say, neither one of us was pleased to see the other, but we did manage a civil greeting.

As this cheery group talked in the main cabin I thought, 'God, I pray Michael and I don't end up like Lee and me.' I thought some more, 'Oh Shit! This is the way all my relationships end up.' At that, a chill of fear shot through me as my mind began to race with thoughts of losing Michael forever. Just before the verge of insanity, I hit the brakes of my mind and thought, 'Stop it! Our souls have soared through the heavens together our love could never end like the others.'

Sometime around 2:00am on the flight to Jidda, as all the guests dozed in the dimly lit main cabin, George came to me and touched my shoulder as he whispered in my ear, "Christina, Sorry to wake you, but I'd like to speak with you alone in the conference cabin now, if I may?"

I woke quickly as he spoke, nodded my head 'yes' in response to his request, and quietly followed him into the conference cabin. As we made ourselves comfortable, he softly smiled as he said, "Finally, we have the opportunity to talk. I need to fill you in on the rest of our agenda and what we can expect to pop up next."

I chuckled with total sensuality as I said, "Oh yeah!"

He turned as red as a beet and started to laugh as he struggled to say, "You know what I mean."

I stopped laughing and with a girlish smile said, "Yes, I know what you mean George, I just couldn't pass that one up." I continued with eagerness, "Now please tell me, what's next? You know how I hate being kept in the dark; I have this phobia over leaping into bed before I know what's in it."

He smiled that famous ear-to-ear smile and replied, "You're a bad girl, Christina Powers!"

I gave him one of my own famous smiles and with an emphasis on my Texan accent said, "Oh stop George, you know you love it. Now stop fooling around and start explaining!"

From that point on our conversation became serious as he said, "The first thing on the agenda when we arrive in Jidda, is a 9:00am meeting with King Fehd and Sheik Jabir

American Goddess

Al-Ahmad Al Sebah, the exiled Emir of Kuwait. From there we have a 1:00pm luncheon with Saudi Arabian and Kuwait dignitaries, until 4:00pm. Then we will begin a two-day, whirlwind tour of four different U.S. Military sites in the region. Our schedule is set up so we first meet the troops with handshakes and autographs; then, we'll have a quick Thanksgiving meal with them. Afterward, I will give a short tough anti-Iraq speech, turn it over to you, and you can wind up our visits with a half-hour performance at each site. The preparations for our visits are already complete, so all you and your crew will have to do is jump up on the platform when I introduce you."

Impressed, I smiled and said, "Great! It sounds like you've covered all angles."

He lifted his eyebrows as if he thought he was overwhelming me and continued, "Do you think you can handle this schedule?"

With an air of confidence and a slight chuckle I replied, "Without a doubt, George."

He slightly blushed as he said, "Please forgive me. For a moment I forgot with whom I was speaking. Now maybe we should try to get some sleep before this day starts, I think we've covered everything."

He gazed around the room aimlessly, as if he were forgetting something, then finally said, "Oh yes! There is one thing I neglected to tell you. In order for me to get the approval for your mini concerts, I had to agree ahead of time that you would grant King Fehd's son, Prince Mohammed Fehd a private meeting with you. King Fehd told me personally his son Mohammed has been obsessed with following your career. He claims to be your biggest fan."

I found myself intrigued by the news of this request, so I said, "A Prince, huh! That's interesting, what do you know about him?"

"Just that he's heir to the Saudi throne, and the vastest fortune on the face of the earth."

"You're kidding! What else do you know?"

He smiled mischievously, "Christina, I heard about the divorce; don't tell me you're looking already?"

"No, George, I'm not, I'm thinking of the bigger picture," I answered devilishly, "what if you thought a prince was after your wife?"

He started to laugh then said, "You're too much, Christina! I guess that's why I enjoy your company as much as I do."

I winked with a seductive smile, "I enjoy your friendship too, George. Now will this Mohammed suit my needs or not?"

He shook his head and with a big smile answered, "Well if your goal is to make Michael stand up and take notice, then you picked the right guy. He's a thirty-six-year-old genius, who graduated top of his class at Harvard Law. From what I hear, he's the most sought-after bachelor in the world."

American Goddess

With wide eyes I said, "Whoa!   It sounds like I'll be meeting my male counterpart instead of a fanatical fan."

"All you have to do is meet with him sometime during our luncheon; then, you can sing your heart out on Saudi soil."

With that I yawned then said, "I think I can handle the prince, George, as long as I can have a little sleep first."   He chuckled then we said good night and I passed out the minute I hit my seat.

The next morning, we received the most incredibly intense military escort to the King's palace that I had ever witnessed.   Everywhere the eye could see, there were armed soldiers guarding the entire route of our motorcade, through this incredibly beautiful and wealthy city of oil sheiks.   When we reached the palace, everyone in the President's entourage were swiftly ushered from their autos straight into the main greeting room of the palace.   From there, those of us who were attending the meeting with King Fehd and Sheik Jabir Al-Ahmad Al Sebah, were led from the group and into the King's private chambers.

The four-hour meeting which followed proved to be deplorable as Sheik Jabir showed us graphic photographs of Iraqi atrocities in Kuwait.   Immediately after the meeting, George held a news conference where he strongly condemned Iraq and called for the United Nations Security Council to pass a new, anti-Iraq resolution by the end of the month.   He also assured the world that any differences between the U.S. and the U.S.S.R. on Persian Gulf policy were extraordinarily small compared to our mutual commitment to see an emboldened withdrawal of all Iraqi troops from Kuwait. After the news conference, we joined some of the most powerful men in the Middle East for lunch in the formal dining.

Shortly after lunch, George stood on the platform at the head of the room and began to address those present.   As he did, six heavily armed soldiers came to me and asked me to accompany them to the prince's private chambers.   I looked at their weapons; then, I looked at George feeling a sense of apprehension.   I guess he sensed it too, because he winked at me in an attempt to ease my concerns.   At that I smiled, and proceeded confidently and fearlessly, following my escorts to a prearranged rendezvous with the prince.   As I walked in the center of my six towering guards, through a large hundred foot long, thirty foot tall and wide, oval shaped corridor, I looked with astonishment at how this entire palace was lined with detailed solid gold trimmings, and I thought, 'Oh my God!   The wealth in just this one corridor could probably put an end to world hunger.' I got a quick cold chill as my thoughts continued, 'What an incredibly vulgar waste of wealth and at the same time it's mighty enticing.'

At the end of this massive corridor hung two large, fifteen foot oval shaped African redwood doors, with the family crest molded on each door, and you guessed it, they were in solid gold.   The doors opened into the large, pearl white, and purple, hexagonal shaped chambers of the prince.   The ceiling was a solid gold dome, with six golden hexagon chandeliers, dropping twenty feet from the ceiling, to illuminate the center of the room, where stood a large throne.   Seated upon the throne some one hundred feet ahead of me, was the most beautiful man I had ever seen.

As I glanced at him in his golden attire I thought, 'This man's physical beauty rivals my own, while his strength and wealth towers that of mine.   Whoa!   This is exciting!'

He looked to be a six-footer, with deep Arabian brown eyes.   I could just see the edges of his jet-black hair, peeking through his hand-woven golden turban.   He was gorgeous!

The moment I stepped into the room a feeling of apprehension came over me, and my heart rate increased with every step I took closer.   As these unexplained feelings swept my emotions, I felt myself wanting to run out of the room.   I mentally slapped myself across the face and thought, 'Pull it together girl before you pass out on the spot. He's just another man.' As I reached the foot of his throne, I swallowed hard, took a deep breath and thought, 'I don't know what's going on here, but whatever it is you can handle it Christina.'

As I curtsied, I kept my smile cool and calm, just like the perfect performer I was born to be, in an attempt to conceal my true inner anxieties.   Our eyes met with intensity as I completed my curtsy.   He rose from his seat and gracefully approached me with his hand stretched out.   Taking my hand in his, he brought it to his lips and never letting his eyes leave mine once, he kissed the back of my hand with such passion, that I felt it in the core of my being.   When he opened his mouth, the words flowed forth like a chorus of angels as he said, "How honored I am to have the incomparable Christina Powers, curtsy before me.   And I must say your beauty is more radiating in person, than any likeness of you could ever hope to capture."

I thought, 'Whoa!   You called that right,' as I replied, "Your words are too kind Prince Fehd, but I thank you just the same."

He smiled gracefully, "Modesty in a woman with your physical attributes is a precious rarity, which is refreshing."

He was attempting to immediately sweep me off my feet, and I knew it the moment he said, "I have adored you from my first glimpse of you, and now that I've kissed your hand, I will not rest until I make you mine, body and soul."

I stepped back, put my hand to my chest, caught my breath and said, "You certainly don't waste time beating around the bush, do you?"

He gently took my hand and with excitement said, "Come with me my love, I must show you something."   I slipped my hand from his and began to walk along beside him as he spoke.   He continued to speak words of his undying love for me, like lyrics of my own songs as he led me on a tour through the palace.

I was nearly enchanted by this man's charms by the time we reached the roof of the main towers of the palace, which overlooked the entire city.   He gently held my hand in his again as we stood there gazing out over the sun glistened rooftops, which like a mirage, gave the city the sparkle and appearance of pure gold.   I looked at this powerfully bewitching man, in the middle of this awesome setting, and I found myself spellbound by his beauty and charisma.   At one point as we spoke, his eyes seemed to look right through me with such clarity, I began to feel a strange connection with him.   I felt myself drifting into every word he said. Then he took me in his arms and kissed me so passionately, I thought I'd melt.

I felt myself almost helplessly being utterly devoured by this man's ferocious appetite, right up until he said, "Your destiny Christina Powers, is to be my bride and bear my son; the son which will one day rule the world from the throne of Persia."

With that statement, I put up the stop sign by gracefully slipping out of his grasp and saying, "Slow down, Prince Fehd!   I'm flattered, but I'm a married woman and I cannot accommodate your needs."

I could see sadness come over his face as he replied, "Christina, if you were mine, I would be so empowered by our union, I would catch the light from a star to adorn your bridal gown."

It finally dawned on me he was serious, so I said, "Forgive me Prince Fehd, but I must ask you to please take me to the President's luncheon now. It's getting late."

Then all at once, with force he grabbed my hand, pulled me back into his arms, and with passion to his words said, "If you marry me, I will stop Lussien tomorrow."

I knew I had to try to handle this situation on the humorous side, so with a chuckle I said, "Oh really.   What makes you think you can do what no one in the world has been able to accomplish?"

He started laughing only his laugh was frightening, and when he stopped laughing his face took on an evil expression and with viciousness said, "You really don't know who I am yet, do you?"   He squeezed my shoulders to the point of pain and laughed as he shouted, "You don't even realize who you are yourself yet!"

I became more then concerned when I looked into his eyes and realized there was nothing but black space behind those deep Arabian brown eyes, so I quickly said, "You're absolutely right, Prince Fehd!   I don't know what you're talking about, and at this point I don't really care to know.   All I want you to do is let go of my arms and stop hurting me before I start to become upset."

American Goddess

In response to my demand he applied more pressure to my arms, and with anger in his voice said, "You don't have a choice Christina, because you were born to be mine. Your destiny lies with me, and together we shall conquer and rule the world."

All at once he began to bodily drag me to the edge of the tower as I shouted, "What are you doing?   Please let go of me, Mohammed, you're scaring me!"

When we reached the edge, he forced me to look over the side as he said, "Do you see all this?   If you marry me and bear the child we have been pre-destined to bring into this world together, I will give it all to you."

Realizing I was in the hands of another Arabian madman I said, "It's beautiful Mohammed!"   Then I turned my head to gaze romantically into his eyes and continued, "You would really give all this to me?"

He slowly released his tight grip as I gently kissed his lips, and the moment I could slip out of his hands I did.   And as I backed away from him I said, "You don't want to give it all to me Mohammed, I'll only give it to the less fortunate souls on this planet anyway."

He lunged for me, grabbed my neck and I could see the hatred flare in his nostrils as he shouted, "Jesus Christ, Christina!   You're just like him, and if you refuse to unite your gifts with mine, then you will die the martyr like him as well."

I pushed him off me with all my strength and shouted, "What the hell is this, the twilight zone!?   Well if it is all I can say is I don't know who you're comparing me to, but I can tell you I'm not like anybody you've ever met.   So you better keep your hands off me."

As fast as lighting, he grabbed my hand and this time he flung me up against the chains which held one back from falling to their death and shouted, "If you don't agree to marry me right now, I vow one day you will be on your knees pleading for your life at my feet!"   Then his eyes radiated unquenchable evil as his voice thundered, "Remember this, Christina Powers!   I will be standing as the divine ruler in the temple of Solomon, when I have you beheaded!"

My anger seemed to give me the strength of ten men, as I once again pushed him off me and screamed, "You're a **sick fuck,** Mohammed!"   Then, I took off running toward the elevator we came up on, as he yelled, "Come back here now Christina! You don't understand! We belong together!" He came running after me, and when I reached the door to the towers I slammed and locked it just as he reached it.   I finally found the elevator and when I reached for the down button my hands were shaking so badly I could hardly push it.

I had myself somewhat composed as I swiftly exited the elevator on the main floor of the palace.   I immediately began to search for the dining room where the President was and as I walked down a large corridor, I could see two armed guards approaching me from up ahead. From behind me I heard the prince yell, "Guards, retain her at once!"

American Goddess

My heart almost stopped when I realized I was trapped in this corridor and all I could do was pray in my thoughts, 'Dear God! Please get me out of this country alive and in one piece!'

I struggled to keep my composure as Prince Fehd reached me.   To my great relief he gently took my slightly trembling hand and said, "Christina, my sweet, you're heading in the wrong direction."   With a smile that could tame a lion he added, "Please allow me to escort you?"

At that, he led me back to the dining room where the President was, and proceeded to carry on amongst his father's guests, as if nothing had happened.

I watched his graceful transformation back to the charming man I first met, and I thought, 'My God!   This man is scary!   He's a better performer than I am.'   From that point on I stuck to George like glue.   I actually feared for my safety with this madman still in the room.   Finally, that long bizarre afternoon ended around 4:00pm when the President took his entourage, via a convoy of helicopters, to our first military site about two hundred miles inland.

On the flight, George turned to me and said, "Why don't you tell me what it is?   I know something is wrong!   You haven't left my side since you came back from your meeting with the prince."

I gazed at him and with an obvious look of concern on my face and said, "George, we think what Lussein is doing is mad, but mark my words, the world hasn't seen anything like it's going to see when that fruitcake takes over his father's throne."

His expression was one of complete surprise, "You can't be talking about the same Prince Mohammed Fehd I know."

I shook my head as I replied, "The one and only.   Let me tell you, he's U.S.D.A. certifiably insane."

His face reflected my concern as he said, "Man!   The implications of that are frightening."

I lifted my eyebrows, "Tell me about it!   I just experienced it firsthand."
"What happened?"   He asked with curiosity.

"Nothing worth repeating; all I ask is that you keep a close eye on my back while we're here."

He laughed and said, "Well I guess he's not going to be replacing Michael too soon."

Feeling much more relaxed I allowed myself to laugh at George's attempt to be humorous and said, "Not if my life depended on it!"

I finally felt completely relaxed the moment I was back in my element, surrounded by cheering fans.   I'm sure the fact they were all armed American soldiers, had a lot to do with my confidence level.   When I took the stage to perform, the first live performance on Saudi soil in its history, I was deliberately so seductively hot I could almost hear Prince Fehd's ancestors turning in their entombed temples. The desert had been brought to life by the cheers of the young Americans for whom I performed that night, and when I took my last bow, I blew the crowd kisses as they chanted, "We love you, Christina! We love you, Christina!"

When I finally quieted them down, I said, "I love you too! And from the depths of my soul, my thoughts and prayers shall be on each and every one of you, until the moment you all return home safely. I also vow to continue to work hand-in-hand with the President, to bring a peaceful end to this crisis. But I know in my heart if Lussein forces a confrontation with you guys; he'll regret it for the rest of his life." At that the cheers rang out and I shouted, "I love you, and may God bless you all!" I waved goodbye as I walked off the makeshift stage, in the seemingly barren and tranquil Saudi Arabian desert.

With all the encores, I ended up performing that night my show went twenty minutes past my half hour allotment. When I did finally leave the stage, I discovered the President and his immediate entourage were forced by time restraints to depart ten minutes prior. He had left three choppers for my staff and me, along with those who stayed behind, with instructions for their pilots to take us to the next military site when the show was over.

As we were being escorted to the choppers, I asked the sergeant if I might be allowed a few minutes to freshen up before taking off, and of course she said yes. As the others went to the choppers the sergeant led me to a makeshift latrine, which was about three hundred yards from the parked choppers. I had been washing the sweat off for about five minutes, when I heard the sergeant yell, "Ms. Powers, I'm going to have to ask you to please pick up the pace a little; we need to be on our way."

The sergeant was a tall muscular black woman and I was not about to challenge her; so, I yelled back, "I'll be right there, Sergeant Dexter!"

Not two minutes later I emerged feeling much cleaner and I said, "Thank you sergeant, I needed that and I'm ready to go!"

She smiled, "You're welcome Ms. Powers, but we'd better hurry."

We proceeded with a gentle but steady side-by-side trot through the open spaces of the desert toward the choppers. Our path was well lit by a bright full moon and we could clearly see the others standing by the chopper, as we approached. When we reached the halfway mark between the latrine and the choppers my heart almost stopped, as a pack of ferocious sounding desert wolves appeared from out of nowhere, cutting off our path to the choppers. We both simultaneously stopped dead in our tracks, the moment we spotted them. I looked at the growling pack of wolves, then at the horrified face of Sergeant Dexter and said, "I hope they're part of security?"

American Goddess

"No, they're not!"   And the moment she spoke, a big black one who seemed to be the leader stood out with a ferocious howl.   Sergeant Dexter pulled out her gun to shoot and it jammed.   She turned to me with a look of horror and shouted, "How's your running legs!?"   And at that point, they began to charge us. I let out a blood curdling scream when I realized the black one with the sharp fangs had his eye on me. Everyone around the choppers came running toward us and from out of the corner of my eye; I saw the black one lunge for me as I started to run back to the latrine.   I screamed in terror as I ran, knowing at any moment I would soon be feeling the sharp fangs of this beast on the back of my neck. From behind me there was a horrendous explosion {BOOM} and the force of it threw me flying at least twenty feet forward, and I landed headfirst into the sand.   I quickly turned and I could see flames bellowing hundreds of feet into the air, directly over the spot where the choppers were parked.   In the midst of the sound, flames, and heat, I looked frantically for the black wolf and his pack, and to my astonishment, with the entire sky lit up there were none to be found.

My body became filled with fear as I looked back at the burning chopper and realized, one minute sooner and I would have been in those flames. I gazed up into the heavens, feeling completely humbled before the throne and power of God, and I thought, 'Thank you, Lord Jesus!' It was at that moment, I felt my mortality and realized "God must truly have a higher calling for my life, this time around!"

Remarkably, not one person was killed in that explosion, which was eventually declared a mechanical defect.   But that is not how the reporters, whose lives were saved because they ran to my aid, put it.   The headlines read, **"Dramatic Wild Wolf Attack on Christina Powers' Life remarkably saves the lives of passengers and crew alike, from the ill-fated military helicopter, which exploded in the Saudi Arabian desert!"**

Of course, I shook the experience off like it was nothing, and twenty minutes later I was in the air and on my way to completing the tour with the President.   But underneath my cool exterior the rest of that trip, I was a frightened little girl just longing to be safely home and in Michael's arms.

Finally, at midnight on November 23rd, 1990, we were landing back home in America on the Presidents' private runway, in the great city of Washington, D.C.   When I exited that jet, I was so glad to be back on American soil, that I knelt down and patted the pavement.   After that I shook my head, looked up at the President and the First Lady, who were watching, and with a relieved smile I said, "There's no place like home!" I stood up, still looking at the two of them and continued with a chuckle, "I must thank you both for the most incredibly exciting trip I have ever taken in my life.   But thank God, even the most sensational adventures must end and now I shall say adieu.   I'm sure I have a husband at home desperately awaiting my arrival."   I winked at the First Lady and added, "After all, he did almost lose me you know!"

American Goddess

She smiled at me and with utter charm said, "I'm sure you do, Christina! He'd be a fool not to be." We said our goodbyes with genuine sincere hugs and kisses, and as they headed toward the terminals, I headed for my private jet which was waiting to take me home.

CHAPTER 40

I pulled into the driveway of our home at 3:00am on the morning of the 24th, which also just happened to be our first wedding anniversary. When, I entered the house, it was quiet and dimly lit, so I swiftly made my way to the master bedroom without making a sound. I opened the bedroom door with my heart in my throat, totally expecting beyond a shadow of a doubt, to find Michael lying in the bed. When I discovered he was not, I was completely crushed. I couldn't believe he wasn't there, and I thought, 'He had to know I was almost killed! How could he not be here, waiting for me? Dammit, it's our anniversary, Michael.' I shook my head as my heart pained and my thoughts continued, 'I even wired you to let you know when I would be home Michael, why aren't you here?' The awakening effect of that thought caused me to lie across the bed and begin to cry. My mind went on, 'Could it be he truly means what he's been saying?' At that, my personality seemed to split, and I don't have a clue as to what happened to the real me from that point on, as my thoughts took over, 'Wait just a minute, Christina! He couldn't have known you were coming home, the Michael you know would be here. Stop kidding yourself, he's a man and all men show their true colors sooner or later! You've always known you could never really trust anyone, so why are you so shocked? Now stop it! He didn't get my wire and I know he didn't! Michael's not like the rest!' I somehow snapped myself out of that moment of madness; then, confidently grabbed a tissue, wiped off my face, blew my nose and proceeded to page Michael.

American Goddess

I woke up six hours later at 8:16am, still waiting for a return call. By 10:00am no call had arrived, and that's when I decided to call my mother in-law. When Tess answered the phone, her voice perked up the moment she realized I was on the other end, and she said, "Christina! Thank God, you're home safe."

First, I thanked her then I asked if Michael was there. Her tone seemed to sadden as she answered, "No honey, he's not here. He was here the morning we heard the news bulletin that you had nearly lost your life in a fiery helicopter explosion. The minute the story ended, he grabbed his coat and started to walk out. I tried to stop him, and he told me to let him go because he needed to think. Christina, I haven't heard from him since and he never received the telegram you sent, it's still sitting here on my counter."

I thanked her again; then, told her I would be staying home the rest of the day to wait for Michael and that if he should call her, to please have him call me. We said our goodbyes and I spent the rest of that entire day, just waiting for Michael who never came or called. After a night of feeling extremely sad, I decided it was time to put Michael out of my mind and go back to work. After some hoopla from my staff when I entered the main building, I went straight to my office. I sat there for the first twenty minutes not doing anything. I slowly began to go through my messages, but I was still not really caring about what I was doing. All I could think about was Michael. I missed and wanted him so badly, and the pain was so intense, I felt as if someone were to look at me in the wrong way, I'd just start crying. As I felt these things I thought, 'Michael, please come home. I feel so insecure and confused since my trip to Saudi Arabia. Honey, can't you feel in your soul how much I'm hurting?' I softly shook my head as my thoughts continued, 'You've just got to come home, I need you!' At that point, Pierre, my secretary buzzed me and said, "Christina, there is a courier out here with some legal documents for you to sign."

"Send him in Pierre," I answered disconcertingly.

A tall Hispanic man entered my office and said, "Good morning Ms. Powers, I'm sorry it's under these circumstances, but it's a pleasure meeting you."

I thanked him as I took the large yellow envelope, he handed me. I opened it and inside were divorce papers from Michael's law firm, with a note clipped to them asking me to sign and return them with the courier.

I picked up my pen and wrote, **"If your client wants these papers signed, then he'd better bring them in person."** As I thought, 'You want to play games Michael? I'll play games with you!' I slipped the papers back in the envelope and handed it to the courier. From that point on I became angry, and I allowed that emotion to fuel my energies. And when I was completely juiced and fuming nicely, I decided I'd better dive headfirst into my work, realizing I needed a diversion from thinking about Michael and I needed it fast. I resumed going through my messages, only this time with real fervor, and I stopped when I came to one which read, "Tom Davies called, says he has some puzzle pieces for you."

I quickly dialed his number and I said with enthusiasm, "Hi Tom, how many pieces did you find?"

He proceeded to rattle off a list of interesting things, but nothing seemed to make any sense. As he talked, a shiver shot up my spine as my eyes spotted the next name and number on my message list. So I thanked Tom for the good job, asked him to keep up the good work, and it was quickly off to the next message.

As I dialed the number, I glanced at the message again which read, "**John Everett called, urgent personal matter. Please call ASAP!**" As the phone rang, I thought, 'You're making this call without thinking about it first!' "CLICK" 'You better think about it first! This is Johnny, you're calling.'

I took a deep breath and thought, 'All right Christina; you can handle this like an adult. Now just pick that phone back up and proceed with this call as if it were to any business associate.'

At that, I took one more deep breath and hit redial. I could feel my heart rate increasing with every ring and on the fifth ring I heard a woman's voice say, "Hello!" For a moment I couldn't speak. "Hello! Is anyone there?" Came a second reply.

I cleared my voice, "Excuse me, I had something in my throat."

"Who's this?"

"It's Christina Powers, is this Mary Everett?"

Her voice instantly became panicked, "Christina! I'm so sorry John called you. He found out I lied to him; so I had to tell him the truth."

With a reassuring tone I replied, "It's nothing to be upset about Mary, take a deep breath and tell me what happened?"

She took that breath and did just as I feared, took off like a jackrabbit with a story that zig-zagged just as fast, "It happened like this! I told John I won the Lottery for five-hundred-thousand-dollars and that I took the money to pay off the bank. He believed my story up until two weeks ago, when he looked at our savings account for the first time since I paid off the loan. When he saw we still had our original two-hundred-thousand-dollar balance, he came to me and said,' Mary you told me you won five hundred-thousand and paid off the bank with it, is this true?' I told him yes and he said, 'Well, then you should have only received about three hundred and fifty-thousand-dollars after taxes. The rest of the money I assumed came from our savings, but I see you haven't even touched it. Now start talking and tell me where you got the money!' So I had to tell him the truth. Once I told him the money was a gift from you, he became irate and demanded I tell him how I got in touch with you, so I gave him your number."

American Goddess

When she finally finished talking, I said, "Don't worry about it Mary, I'm not upset and if John wants to talk about it with me, I'm more than willing to listen to what he has to say. Is John there now?"

"No, but he will be coming in from the fields at noon for lunch. Can I have him call you then?"

"That will be fine Mary, tell John I'll hold off going for lunch until I hear from him." I said a quick goodbye and thought, 'No big deal,' as I went right back to work.

At 12:00pm on the nose, I received a call from Johnny whose first words were, "Christy, I mean Christina. It's John Everett. How are you?"

"Hi John, I'm fine, how are you?" I answered nonchalantly.

"I've been better," he answered abruptly. "And that's why I'm calling you. I need to speak with you about this loan you gave Mary."

I quickly interrupted, "John, it was a gift not a loan. We were friends at one time, remember?"

With a tense tone he replied, "I remember. Just the same, I'd still like to speak with you in person if I may. I'll be in Manhattan on December 8th, and 9th, for business, I should be free sometime after 10:00am on the 9th.

If I took the ride up to your office in Milton, I could be there around 12:00pm, is there any possibility you could meet with me then?"

Casually I answered, "Hold on John, while I check my schedule." I took a few moments just to keep him waiting then said, "That would be fine John, and since it's the noon hour, why don't we do lunch while we chat." "Thank you, Christina and lunch sounds good." he replied with a more relaxed tone.

I gave him the directions to my office and told him I looked forward to seeing him after all these years. Our goodbyes were casual to say the least, but I was still intrigued by the thought of seeing him alone for the first time, since the day I threw him out of my bedroom, almost seventeen years ago.

At 3:00pm that same afternoon, I finally received a call from Michael, and as soon as I heard him say, "Christina, why are you playing games? Can't you just sign these damn papers, so we can get on with our lives?"

I thought, 'Up your's, buddy!' but very calmly and business like I said, "I'm not playing games with you, Michael. I want this divorce just as much as you do, especially since I've realized what a jerk you really are. To think, I once thought you loved me, but you don't even have a clue as to the meaning of that word. Michael, you know as well as I do, I don't have time for you anymore, so if you want me to sign your papers, meet me here at my office on December 9th, at 2:00pm!" I said these things, all the while thinking, 'we'll see how much you want me to sign those papers when see me walk in with Johnny on my arm.'

With a high pitch in his voice he responded, "December 9th! I'll be there in ten minutes!"

`"Don't bother!" I quickly replied, "I won't be here, I'm leaving in two minutes and I won't be back until the 9th."

With sarcasm he snapped, "Where are you going now?"

With just as much sarcasm I answered, "I don't think that's any more of your business Mr. Carr. I must leave now, so if you want your papers signed, then you better be here for our appointment, or you might have to wait months for that signature!"

He shouted, "Wait one minute, Christina!"

I deliberately cut him off real fast, by saying, "I've got to go, Michael! Till the 9th." (CLICK!) And that was the end of that. I sat there at my desk with a smirk on my face bright enough to light up Time Square at midnight, and I thought, 'Well, since my loving and reasoning sides haven't reached you, maybe the bitch in me will.' Then, I thought, 'Now to set this trap just right! But first I'd better get out of here.' I got up from my desk, quickly gathered my stuff, and headed out the door before Michael could get to me. I figured it was now his turn to wonder where I was for a change, and I hoped it would help him see he would be throwing away the best thing that had ever happened to either one of us.

As I ran out of the office I turned to Pierre and quickly said, "I have to get out of here before Michael comes. So do me a favor, rent me a villa on the French Riviera for the next week, and only page me if something urgent comes up, otherwise wait to hear from me. Oh yes! Make sure you tell Michael I had to leave town to help an old friend who's going through a divorce." At that I was on my way out the door, and as the door closed behind me I thought, 'That story should do nicely for starters with setting a good trap, and a great suntan couldn't hurt either.'

CHAPTER 41

American Goddess

When I entered my office on the morning of December 9th, 1990, I was tanned to perfection and dressed to the max, for today would be 'Dday', in my ongoing saga of love with Michael.   And just as I anticipated, 12:00pm on the nose, Johnny walked into my office.   He was dressed in a distinguished looking three-piece black pinstripe suit and besides the signs of a little roughness around the edges from the years; he still had that twenty-four-year-old smile.   We gazed at one another with childlike fear in our eyes and smiles on our faces, as we both stood there momentarily speechless.

As he approached me, I could see he was struggling to keep his composure, so to help ease both our discomfort from this stressful meeting, I stood up from the seat at my desk to greet him with a fearful yet relaxed handshake.   With a warm friendly smile I said, "John!   It really is good to see you after all these years."   I looked straight into his eyes with complete sincerity, "You look as if the years have been good to you John, I hope that's true?"

Keeping his composure, he smiled gently as he answered, "I can't complain Christy, but I can see they haven't been as good to me as they have to you.   You're looking just as beautiful today as you did the day we met."

"Thank you, John.   That's nice to hear, especially coming from you," I answered with a cheery smile. "Now I hope you brought your visa card, because you're taking me to the best seafood joint in the area, and I'm starving."

He chuckled with that same boyish grin I instantly remembered so well, as he said, "Don't tell me you still have that ferocious appetite?"

I smiled graciously, "I guess some things never change, so let's go eat.   I have my car, do you mind if I drive?"

He shrugged his shoulders, "Not at all."   And off we went to Marine's Harbor in Highland, New York.

When we arrived, we were immediately escorted to my favorite table which, overlooked the beautiful Hudson River, the majestic Mid-Hudson Bridge, the glistening city of Poughkeepsie, and of course, Michael's Townhouse.

As we were seated, I looked at John and said, "You're going to love eating here the food is great; I know, I'm their best customer."

He smiled, "I like the view!"

"I know that's the other reason I like it here so much."

"Do you know what you're having yet?" He asked innocently.

"Nope!"   I answered as the waitress handed us our menus.

We both opened up our menus and as we looked through them, he glanced over his at me and said, "Would you care for some champagne with your lunch?"

American Goddess

As I gazed back at him, I struggled unsuccessfully not to burst out laughing. But of course, I did, and when I could speak again, I said, "No, John! I like vegetable juice with my lunch, remember?"

After he stopped laughing, he said, "Now that you mention it, I do remember something like that."

With childlike curiosity I replied, "After all these years I have got to ask you, what is it with you and champagne with your lunch?"

He gave me that southern boy look that could melt butter and said, "When I was a boy my mom took me to see the movie 'Lunch at Tiffany's', and as I remember all the sophisticated people were having champagne with their lunch. So, I thought it was the proper thing to do when having lunch with a sophisticated woman."

I smiled, then chuckled at his charming answer, "You're too cute, John! But I think it was 'Breakfast at Tiffany's', and they were most likely drinking grape juice, not champagne." With that we laughed some more.

Over our luscious seafood lunch, I discovered what I automatically assumed would be a difficult encounter was actually turning out to be quite an enjoyable one. As we ate, we talked about things which took place in our individual lives over the last seventeen years, as if our bond of friendship had never ended. He told me he and Mary had raised a happy family of five children on their farm together, and that he hasn't missed the ball playing at all since he was forced to retire, due to an arm injury ten years ago. I told him how hectic my life has been of late, but that I also had high hopes things would someday settle down.

At one point in our conversation, he looked sincerely into my eyes and said, "I have watched you from afar for years now, and I'm completely amazed and totally impressed at the way you have led your life." He took my hand as he continued with gentle passion, "The memories I have of the two of us, are still some of the most precious memories I hold. I often wonder what our lives would have been like if we did reach our dreams together." Realizing what he had just said, he swiftly let go of my hand and in a soft embarrassed tone added, "Shit, Christy! I'm sorry! I didn't come here for this. I came to give you a check for two-hundred-thousand-dollars." He reached into his pocket, took out a check, and handed it to me as he continued, "I would like you to take this and set up a payment plan with me, so I can pay you back the rest of the money."

I handed it back to him, "I've already told you John, it was a gift, I can't take this and I would consider it a slap in the face if you were to insist I take it. Please don't do that to me John, I gave it from my heart for someone who will always have a special place in it."

American Goddess

He looked at me with his mouth hanging open.   Catching himself, he closed his mouth and said, "I guess I can't argue with that."   He tore up the check as he continued, "If there is ever anything, I can do for you Christy, please don't hesitate to ask."

I smiled and said, "As a matter of a fact John, there is. First, please call me Christina. I haven't been called Christy in years and it sounds strange.   Second, when are you heading back home?"

"Tomorrow morning; why?"   He asked curiously.

At that, I told him what I wanted him to know about my situation with Michael. Then, I added, "It's just this, John.   Tomorrow happens to be my birthday and if Michael doesn't take me out for dinner tomorrow night, I don't want to spend it alone, and there is no one else I'd rather spend it with than you.   But only if Mary gives her okay."

He smiled at me, "I'd love to take you for dinner on your birthday and I'm sure Mary won't mind.   After all, we never did get the chance to go dancing on your birthday, did we?"

"No, we didn't!"   I answered matter-of-factly.

"So when will you know if you will need an escort or not?"

I smiled mischievously, "Shortly after we return to my office.   Michael will be meeting me there at 2:00pm and I'm going to ask him to take me out then."

He glanced at his watch then exclaimed, "2:00pm!   Christina, its 1:45 now!   We'll never get back before 2:00pm!"

"Don't be too upset John.   I had no plans on being there when Michael arrived."   I smiled again, only this time it was a devilish one as I continued, "I was hoping I could convince you to escort me arm-in-arm back to my office.   I think it might give Michael something more to think about, before he asks me to sign those papers again."   I squinted as I added, "Do you mind?"

He chuckled, "So you want me to help you make him jealous, do you?" With a playful wink he continued, "I'd be honored to play the other man for you, Christina."

I stood up, kissed his forehead and with excitement said, "Okay my new partner in crime; let's go pull one off."   And off we went.

We entered my office arm in arm at 2:15pm and just as I planned, Michael caught the whole sensitive scene.   And believe me; I made sure it looked good.   I had an adoring look on my face as I clung to Johnny's arm, pretending to be on cloud nine as we strolled in chatting.   Michael was sitting in my outer office talking with Pierre as we approached. With an act of genuine surprise, I pretended to just notice Michael, only three feet before reaching him.   Putting my hand to the right side of my face I said, "Oh, Michael!   I totally forgot about our meeting."

He immediately stood up, taking notice of Johnny's closeness to my person and said, "I'll bet you did!   Who's your friend?"

384

American Goddess

At that I took front stage, "Where are my manners?"   Turning to them both I continued, "John Everett, I'd like you to meet my husband, Michael Carr."

I released my hold on Johnny as he reached for Michael's hand and said, "It's nice to meet you Michael, and I've got to tell you, you have one incredible wife.   A word for the wise, I wish I'd never let her slip out of my hands when she was mine."

Michael snickered as he smiled and said, "Maybe you were wiser than you think."

Johnny rubbed his hands together and said, "Well I think that's my cue to leave." He kissed my cheek and added, "Thanks for lunch it was great."

I gave him a peck on the lips then said, "Thank you, I love those two-hour lunches. Now don't forget.   I'll call you tonight to let you know about tomorrow."

With a cute wink he replied, "I'll be waiting."   I walked him to the door, gave him one more hug to tighten my snare, and off he went.

When the door closed, I turned and began to walk back toward Michael as I asked, "Do you have your papers?"

He handed me an envelope, "Yes I do, Christina.   Now how about signing them?"

I gestured to him to lead the way, "Let's go into my office, so I may read them first."

I took my seat as I opened the envelope and gazing up at him impatiently standing there I said, "This may take me some time Michael, so why don't you try to make yourself comfortable and sit down.   After all, we did share this office not too long ago and, in more ways, than one as I recall."   He just ignored me and continued to stand there.

After deliberately leaving him standing there for several minutes as I slowly read the two-page document, he shook his head in frustration, "Can't you just sign it!?   You know damn well what it says!"

With anger I sharply focused my eyes on his and snapped back, "We've spent several years together in love and you can't spare me ten minutes now!"

That's when my act fell apart and tears slowly began to escape from my eyes as I added, "Did you ever really love me at all, Michael?"

I could see his huge muscles straining as he fought to hold back his tears while saying, "Don't do this to me, Christina!"

"Don't do this to you!   You're the one who wants this damn divorce, not me!   Do you realize tomorrow is my birthday?   Is this really the birthday gift you want to give me?   I can't believe this from you, Michael!   I thought we were one!"

"Oh please!"   He shouted, "Don't sit there and tell me you don't want this divorce, or you would not have spent the last two weeks helping your divorced friend. And I'll bet money it's that asshole ball player.   What did you think, just because you never told me anything about him yourself, I didn't know he existed?   I always knew he was once your lover.   The fact you never told me anything about him, told me you still loved him.

American Goddess

Especially since we told each other about all the rest of our past lovers, but I still noticed how you conveniently left him out of the stories you shared."

I quickly reached out and grabbed his hand, as I wiped the tears from my face with my other hand and said, "Michael, honey.   Please, let's not turn this into another fight."

He pulled his hand out of mine, "Then sign the damn papers, let me vanish out of your life, and we will never have to fight again, Christina!"

I could feel my blood beginning to boil as I clenched my fist, "You stubborn Irish are all the same, **Stubborn**!" Once again, I ripped his divorce papers up, and as I threw them in his face I yelled; "Now I really mean it!   If you want a divorce then you're going to have to fight for one, because you know me, I like to do things the hard way."

He shouted, "That's the whole problem with us, Christina!   You think you're my husband.   Well if you want to wear the damn pants in the house, then you go right ahead and wear them.   But I give you my word, as long as you insist on wearing the pants, no matter how much I love you or how much it breaks my heart, they will never be my pants again!   So I guess if it's a fight you want, then a fight it will be!"

I took a deep breath and struggled to calmly say, "Michael, why won't you understand I wasn't trying to wear the pants in our relationship when I went to Saudi Arabia.   I had to go and now that I'm back I need to talk with you about what happened to me over there.   Don't you realize I was almost killed when I was there, and when it happened, I immediately called you, but you never called me back!   How do you think that made me feel?"

He slammed his fist down on my desk with such force he nearly frightened the life out of me as he shouted, "I can't listen to this!   I asked you not to go! I begged you not to go! I tried ordering you not to go! None of that meant enough to you to keep you from going then, so none of this is going to keep me from divorcing you now!"

I felt the pain of his words shoot through my heart and the only thing I could do was scream, "Get out!   Get out!   The longer I look at you the madder I'm getting, you stubborn asshole!"

For one moment I could see my Michael coming through in his eyes, as he reached out for my arm, with his true feelings showing on his face. Catching himself he stopped just before touching me, and as if in slow motion turned and gently walked away.

As I watched the door close behind him, I slowly sat back in my seat feeling totally dazed by what had just transpired, and once again all I could do was cry.

Later that evening after my third White Russian, I picked up the phone and dialed Johnny's number.   He answered the phone with a cheery "Hello!"

My reply was a groggy, "Hi, Johnny.   Oops!   I mean John.   It's Christy.   Oops, I mean Christina."

"You sound as if you're two sheets to the wind.   Are you all right?"   I immediately started to cry, and the moment I did he said, "I guess it didn't work out."   And I cried even harder.   "Don't cry Christina, he'll come around."   He said with a reassuring tone. I blew my nose and with a drunken whimper cried, "No he won't!   You don't know Michael, he's more thick-headed than I am."   "Are you going to be all right?"   He asked with concern.

I thought about his question for a moment then replied, "No John, I don't think so. I don't think I'll ever be all right again."

He gently chuckled then said, "That's the alcohol talking, not the Christy I know, oops, I mean Christina."

I gently laughed finding humor in his oops and said, "I'll bet you've charmed a number of the ladies on the side, you little devil you."

"Ha!   Not me!   I learned my lesson a long time ago."   He answered assertively.

"I'm glad to hear that, John.   So tell me, what did Mary say about our date?"

     "She was fine with it."

"Great!   I'll pick you up at your hotel around 5:00pm tomorrow evening.   Now before I pass out, I'm going to say goodnight.   I'll see you tomorrow."

He chuckled again, "Don't tell me I'm getting the bum's rush for turning your tears into laughter."

"Like I said, I'll see you tomorrow!   I'll thank you properly then, now go to sleep because you're going to need your rest for this date."   On that note, we ended our conversation.

CHAPTER 42

I wasn't planning on going into the office on my birthday and it's a good thing, because I couldn't have dragged myself out of that bed before noon, unless the house was on fire.   When I did get up, I headed straight for the medicine chest and nearly choked on three aspirins as I struggled to get them down.   It took me another hour and four cups of coffee before I could even climb into the shower.   I felt a little more like a human when I returned to the kitchen for a cup of Carman's chicken and rice soup, which I requested with hopes it would help settle my stomach.   I took my last sip of soup around 2:10pm; then, I headed back upstairs to prepare for my trip into Manhattan and my date with Johnny.   By 3:40pm I was dressed to impress and, on my way, out the front door.   When I opened it, I was stunned and excited at the same time to see Michael reaching for the door with his key.

His face lit up with amazement when he saw me standing there, and with a tone of delight he exclaimed, "Wow!   You look phenomenal."   His expression and voice immediately changed to one of suspicion as he continued, "Where are you going dressed like that?"

I finally struck a chord of jealousy, and my face couldn't conceal my pleasure as I smiled and said, "You know it's my birthday Michael, and I told you I was not going to spend it sitting in this house alone."   As I continued, my voice took on an air of curiosity, "So what are you doing here?"

Without any detectable reaction at all, he answered, "I've come to pick up a few of my things."

I chuckled and sarcastically said, "Well that's great!   After all this time, you pick today to come get your stuff."

With a slight sense of his own sarcasm he replied, "Yes!   Do you mind?"

As a feeling of disappointment came over me, I sadly answered, "No I don't mind, come on in."

He entered the house and I followed him as he headed up to the bedroom. I watched as he took out his black tux with all its accessories from the closet and laid them on the bed.   At that, he started to unbutton his shirt, and as my body temperature began to climb, I asked, "What are you doing?"

He knelt down, untied his shoes, then gazing up at me with that look that slays me he answered, "I'm going to take a shower, get dressed, and take you out for your birthday."

My heart leaped with joy as I softly said, "Really, Michael?"

He slipped off his pants and in his already bulging, 'Fruit of the Loom,' he beckoned me to him as he said, "Really, Punkie."

I went to him like a quivering love-struck damsel in distress, longing for the touch of her gallant knight in shining armor.   When I reached him, I stood in front of him gazing longingly into his eyes, and softly said, "I'm here, Michael."

He put his arms around me and as he gently pulled me to him, he said, "Happy birthday, Punkie."

American Goddess

My tears began to flow, and with every quiver of my body, I melted deeper into his powerful arms. I could truly feel our souls reuniting as he held me, and I whispered, "I love you, Michael, and if you come home, I'll take off the pants."

He kissed me in the way only he could then said, "I love you too, Punkie."

He swept me off my feet and carried me into the bathroom. Our lips were one as he placed my feet on the floor, then slipping off the rest of his attire he began to massage his groin against mine as he masculinity said, "Come join me in the shower. You have a lot to catch up on."

I nearly overheated on the spot by his forceful command, and as I covered his face lovingly with baby kisses I said, "Just let me take this outfit off, make a quick phone call, and then I'm all yours."

He pulled his head back from mine and said, "A phone call now! What's so important about this phone call it comes before making love to your husband?"

I shook my head as I placed my right index finger horizontally across his lips and said, "It's not, Michael, and your right, I don't need to make it now."

I watched helplessly as his excitement dissipated and he said, "Well who is it you have to call, your baseball player?"

I stroked his shoulder as I carefully said, "Yes, Michael. He's waiting for me to pick him up, but he can wait forever for all I care. It was out of courtesy, I automatically thought to call, and that's all."

He backed away from me and said, "I must be nuts to think you could ever put me first in your life." He shook his head as he pushed past me and continued, "Get out of my way! I've gotta get out of here before I throw up!"

As he proceeded to get dressed, I pleaded, "Michael, don't leave me. Please, I'm sorry I upset you honey, but honestly I wasn't putting anything or anyone before you."

He jammed his feet into his shoes and said, "Save it for someone who believes you, like your lover boy."

I became so infuriated by his comment I actually hauled off and slapped him right across his face as I shouted, "Why you creep! If you want me to go to him that bad, then I will!" I headed for the bedroom fireplace, where I grabbed one singed bottle of champagne from off the mantel and dashed out of the room.

As I did that, Michael grabbed his stuff from off the bed, and came charging behind me. When I reached the driver's door of my car, I heard Michael yell, "I hope you have a great birthday, Christina!"

I opened the car door and yelled back, "Don't worry I will!" I slammed the door and proceeded to burn rubber all the way down the driveway.

American Goddess

CHAPTER 43

When I arrived at Johnny's room in the Newark, Holiday Inn, I was carrying a bag with an eight-piece bucket of Kentucky Fried Chicken extra crispy, with all the trimmings in one hand, and in the other was a seventeen-year-old singed bottle of champagne.

Johnny was wearing a black tux when he opened the door, and he had a bouquet of roses in his hands. And guess what? There were two dozen red ones with one white one in the middle. He gazed at me standing at his door with my chicken in hand, and started to laugh, so I said, "Well are you going to invite me in, or would you rather I'd stand here so you can keep laughing."

He gestured me in as he controlled his laughter enough to say, "I thought I would take you out for a fancy meal, and you come to my door looking like a million, with a bucket of Kentucky Fried Chicken."

I smiled as I unpacked our meal and said, "You got that right! So I hope you're in the mood to lick your fingers." I handed the champagne to him and added, "Would you put this on ice for us please?"

He took it from me and said, "This looks like it's been through a war, are you sure we should drink it?"

I turned to him with a mysterious grin as I fixed our plates and said, "Yes! Now please chill it and I'll explain why after dinner."

At that he headed for the ice machine, and by the time he returned, I had the small table in his room set for a romantic chicken dinner for two, with candlelight to boot.

We chatted as we ate, and after our meal I took the champagne bottle out of the ice, handed it to Johnny and said, "There is only one person in this world who may open this bottle, and that's you, but before you do there is a little story I need to tell you first. The singed champagne bottle you hold in your hands and are about to be asked to open is the same bottle of champagne you gave me the day we met at the Tavern-on the-Green."

His face took on a look of complete surprise as he gazed into my eyes and said, "You really kept this all these years, and you want me to open it tonight? Wow, Christina! I'm truly moved and honored by this. Now that you've shared that, I need to share something with you." At that, he unbuttoned his shirt to reveal the chain he had around his neck with a ring on it and said, "I know you remember this ring! You're the only other person besides my grandmother who has ever worn it, and it hasn't left my neck since the day I received it back from you in the mail."

American Goddess

I softly smiled as I said, "And I thank you John, for sharing with me, that's sweet of you and it really means a lot to me to hear that.   Now would you please do the honor of opening this bottle, so we may both finally find out what it tastes like?"

He stood up holding the bottle, braced it between his arms and as he slowly pushed up on the cork with his two thumbs he said, "May the shadows of our once fantasy life together, live on in our memories forever."   "POP!"   Then, he poured two glasses and as he handed one to me he added, "The toast is on you."

I smiled as I clicked my glass to his, "To memories!   Good and bad."

As I slowly took my first sip, feelings buried seventeen years ago came rushing to my consciousness like a flash flood in the deserts of Nevada.   And as I watched him sip his, I began to feel myself wanting to be touched by him, and I thought, 'What the hell are you getting yourself into now, Christina?   Don't forget you're both married.'   At that I said, "Hmmm!   Not bad after all this bottle has been through."

Taking a second look at the bottle he said, "I guess this must have survived your tragic fire."

Sadly I replied, "You're right, as a matter of fact it was one of only a few things which did survive that fire."   I took another sip from my glass and let my emotions show when I said, "John, since we're being open with our feelings, I wonder if you would tell me something?   Why did you send me the roses with the 'ditto' note, the night I preformed 'The Love I lost', and yet you never called me after Tony's death?   Did the words on that note truly come from your heart?"

I could see in his eyes he knew my question was coming from a place of great pain; then, he gently took my hand in his and said, "Christina, with all my heart I didn't just want to call you, I wanted to come running to you.   But I couldn't!   When you recorded 'The Love I lost' Mary was three months pregnant with our second child.   When she saw you sing that song to me that night at the concert, she became distraught and she cried for days.   The night I heard about Tony's death, I had to make a choice to be there for one of you.   She was my wife and carrying my child, what could I do?"

I gently squeezed his hand as I said, "Thank you for being honest with me, John."

He slowly shook his head as he replied, "You know what I don't understand is after knowing how Mary has feared you for years, how could she come to you for that loan?"

I let go of his hand, smiled, and said, "It's because she's madly in love with you, you big jerk."

As I spoke, he refilled our glasses and when I finished, he handed me mine and with the look that once captured my heart said, "Let's make this one to new memories!" We drank to his toast and as we put our glasses down he slowly leaned toward me still gazing into my eyes and added, "I love her too, I guess that's why we are still together, but my love for her never compared to what I've felt for you since the first instant our eyes meet."

The moment he stopped speaking, he leaned closer and softly began to kiss my lips.   I felt myself slipping into my passion as I slowly began to surrender to memories of powerfully embedded feelings.   All at once realizing what was happening, I caught myself and went for the quick save by slipping out of his embrace and excitedly saying, "Do you know what I would like right now?"

He gave me his southern country boy smile and very seductively said, "I hope it's the same thing I do."

With playful force I grabbed his arm, pulling him up from his seat and said, "For us to go dancing at the Plaza Ballroom, just like we once did."

Gallantly he replied, "If that's what my lady would like, then that's what my lady shall get."

With that, off we went and as we walked toward my car I thought, 'Man-oh-man! That was a close one.'

We arrived at the Plaza shortly after 10:00pm, and you should have seen the heads turn and the tabloid cameras flash, when the two of us walked in together. Marcel the head Maître' immediately came to us with open arms and a big smile.   The moment he reached us he said, "Christina!   John!   I can't believe this!" He gave us both a warm, hardy, Italian hug as he continued, "My heart is filled with joy, seeing the two of you walk in here together again!"

I smiled graciously, "Thank you, Marcel, it's good to see you as well.   Is there any chance we could have our old table?"

He smiled his answered, "Of course you may!   Even if I have to throw someone out.   Just give me one moment and I'll be right back."   Within two minutes Marcel was happily escorting us to our table, then the second we were settled he took our drink orders, and off he went.   I glanced into Johnny's sparkling eyes as from the vantage point of our balconied table we watched the orchestra play and all the enchanted people dance on the open dance floor below us.

Within moments Marcel returned with our drinks and when Johnny picked his up, he gazed romantically into my eyes and said, "May I offer a toast to the most beautiful woman in the world on her birthday.   Happy birthday Christina and may-you be blessed with many, many, more."

"Why thank you John, that's quite the toast."   I replied with wide eyes.

He smiled, "Don't be so modest.   I know you've been People Magazine's choice for most beautiful woman-of-the-year, thirteen times in the last fifteen years."

American Goddess

With a look of surprise, I said, "You're kidding! I didn't know that." As I thought, 'Yeah, I know! I lost in `85 to Princess Diana, and then again in `88 to Kim Bassinger. Can you believe that? Kim Bassinger!'

At one point during our conversation, I smiled softly as I gently touched his hand and said, "You showed me something, now I'd like to show you something." I unfastened my necklace, the same one he gave me in the dugout so many years ago and I continued, "Do you remember this? Well I haven't spent a day without this around my neck since you gave it to me in the Dodger's dugout."

He took it from my hand and said, "I always knew our love would somehow last for all eternity." As he examined my chain he added, "Where are these other pendants from?"

I took it from him and as I showed him each one I said, "This Heart pendant came from my best friend in the entire world, Jimmy Severno, and inside it reads, **"Your A fucking Genius! Love Jimmy**!" I held out the medallion next, "See this! It's of a golden goddess standing on top of a flaming ball of fire. She is breaking the cords of gold which bound her to the inferno. I found this on a white-water rafting trip in Lake Tahoe with my late ex-husband Tony. But the strangest thing about this believe it or not, is the fact that I buried it over Tony's grave, and the day I buried my daughter Joy, I found it lying on top of the headstone. I took it home, washed it and I've had it on ever since." As I touched the last one, I added, "And this dainty little guardian angel here was a gift from my Michael."

Smiling he replied, "Christina, you're a sentimental romantic, just like I am." Just as he said that the orchestra began to play 'Johnny's Love,' and when Johnny heard it his eyes lit up as he asked, "Would you please give this dance to me? I requested it because our memories would not be complete without it." I gracefully accepted, and he escorted me to the dance floor.

As we danced the memories of dances past brought tears to my eyes and when Johnny saw I was tearing up he held me tight and said, "I must call you Christy one more time. I need to tell Christy I love her with all my heart. Christy, I have regretted hurting you like I did, every day of my life since you told me to leave."

He brought his hand to the back of my neck and slowly began to move his head toward mine as we danced. The moment his lips met mine, he was ripped out of my embrace by a crazed Michael, who belted Johnny so hard, he went flying into the wall twelve feet from us. Michael shouted, "You bastard! Until the divorce is final, she is still my wife, and if I catch you touching her again, I'll kill you!" Cameras were snaping all around us and as they flashed Michael turned to me and with a tone of hatred shouted, "Thanks for giving me grounds for divorce!" He turned and began to walk away.

American Goddess

I followed him saying, "Michael, it's not what it looked like! Not really!" Right in the middle of all the sophisticated people I grabbed his arm, swung him around to face me, and sharply added, "You're not going to just walk away from me like this! We need to talk!"

He pulled his hand out of mine, "Oh yea! Watch me!" And at that he turned and continued to walk away leaving me standing there looking like a fool.

I stamped my foot in frustration; then, turned around to see Johnny standing beside me holding an ice pack to his nose. I looked at him and exclaimed, "Oh my God! Are you all right?"

"I'll live" he answered, and while looking at all the on lookers he added, "The shows over folks, you can mind your own business now."

I took his hand, "Come on, I think we better get out of here."

When we arrived back at Johnny's motel, I parked next to his room, leaned toward him and said, "This was certainly an interesting evening, and I thank you for it very much."

He smiled as he replied, "Well at least you got a reaction from Michael. Maybe not the one you wanted, but it was sure a doosie."

I started to laugh as I stroked his arm once gently then said, "I'm sorry for laughing, but if I don't think about this as something funny, then I'm going to start crying again, and I'm tired of all the crying I've been doing lately."

He took my hand and passionately said, "Christina, please come in with me. I want to make love to you again so badly I can taste you." All at once he began to lean toward me with the look of love in his eyes.

I put my hands up to stop his approach, "John, I'm in love with Michael, and no matter how enticing your offer may be, I can't make love with you. I may do a lot of things behind Michael's back, but I can't and won't cheat on him." I gently kissed his forehead and continued, "I thank you again John, for an incredible evening, but I have to go now. I still have a long ride ahead of me."

"I'm sorry, Christina," he said apologetically. "I was thinking with my heart instead of my head. I hope I haven't put a damper on our evening?"

I smiled warmly, "No John, you haven't, but it's already 2:00am and I'm really very tired."

"Well if you must go would you please wait until I get in the room? I didn't know it at the time I rented here, but I heard this is a gay neighborhood. The last thing I need tonight is to be arrested for punching somebody out."

I assumed he was kidding, so I chuckled and said, "Sure, I'll wait big boy! Now get going." Finally, we said our goodbyes and I was on my way home.

394

American Goddess

CHAPTER 44

Of course, the press had a field day with my latest public escapade, and the headlines on the front page of the next mornings 'New York Post' read, in big bold print, "It looks like Christina Powers is up to her hips in dueling men once again!" When I unfolded the paper I was horrified to see a full-page, color photo of my unflattering, shocked, expression, which the camera caught so well of the three of us, and Michael's now famous punch that I wanted to go into hiding. And that was just the start of my day. My next humiliating experience took place only twenty minutes later, the moment I sat at my desk and answered my private line. When I picked it up, I was hoping for Michael, but instead I heard Johnny's wife, Mary Everett say, "I should have known better then to trust a woman like you. John is my husband and a Christian family man, why would you seduce him and destroy us in one night."

"Wait just a minute now Mary, and listen to me," I protested. "It was nothing at all like the papers put it."

"No miss big shot, Christina Powers, you wait! I don't care to hear what you have to say, I know you could talk your way out of a crocodile pit. So you just listen to me and stay away from my husband, or you will see just how tough we country girls can be." "Click!"

I thought, 'Was that really the same little mousey woman I know? My God! Is it me? Could I really have some kind of strange effect on people, or is everyone going nuts?'

The next incident came around 10:00am, when Michael walked into my office escorting a process server, and without saying a word she placed an envelope in my hand. The two of them turned around and walked right back out. I opened it to find a summons to appear in the Ulster County Court House for divorce proceedings at 9:00am on February 28, 1991. I placed the summons on top of a pile of papers, placed my head on my desk, and as tears slowly fell, I thought, 'Okay Michael, I give up, you win. I don't have the heart or energy for this. I'm so tired of the heartache, I can't even think about trying to fight you anymore.'

As I sat there with my head on my desk feeling utterly depressed, Pierre buzzed me with an extremely nervous voice and said, "Christina! The President is standing out here, and he would like to see you now!" Quickly I grabbed a tissue, wiped my eyes, and headed for the door thinking, 'What now!?'

When I opened the door, I wore a big smile, and immediately invited him into my office with a warm embrace. As we sat down, I looked at him with a suspicious expression and said, "It's good to see you George, but I know damn well this isn't a social call."

He smiled, "Once again you're absolutely correct, this is not a social call. I'm here in person because I'm hoping my presence will make it impossible for you to turn down my request."

My eyes opened wide as I said, "Don't tell me you want me to go back to Saudi Arabia, because if that's it, you've wasted a trip. There is no way I'm going back there George, and you know why."

"Well that's good, because that's not what I need you to do." I sighed as I exhaled and said, "I'm glad we got that out of the way, because nothing you might ask could be that bad."

His face took on a strained look as if the pressure of it all was getting to him, and he said, "Actually it's a lot worse than that, Christina. As you know, the U.N. Security Council has given the coalition members permission to use all necessary means to expel Iraq from Kuwait if Iraq does not withdraw by January 15, 1991. So, as you can see, it is imperative we free the hostages before that date. I have been frantically trying to reach Lussein personally since the U.N. made that announcement. Finally, I had a private phone conversation with Lussein at five o'clock this morning, and in his own very convincing words he said, "I will agree to release the hostages only if Christina Powers comes in person, and on her own private jet to take them out of my country."

My initial reactions to his words were split right down the middle to either extreme. I was elated to think of Jimmy and all the hostages coming home, but I was mortified to think I had to go get them. It took a few moments to let it all register; then, I looked at him without hiding any emotion and said, "Why me?"

"He says he trusts you."

"What's to stop him from keeping me with all the others this time?"

He began to shake his head with utter frustration and answered, "Honestly Christina, nothing. If he wanted to have you executed the moment you walked off the plane, he could. That's why it's tearing me apart to ask you to do this, but if I want the hostages out alive; then, I have no choice but to ask you to take this chance with your life."

Realizing he was right, I looked him straight in his eyes, and with my own frustration showing asked, "What is it I'd have to do?"

He gave me his famous Texas smile and said, "That's my girl! I knew you would go. All you have to do is fly over there in your corporate jet, with our military pilots in civilian clothing at the controls in the cockpit; then, personally take possession of the hostages from Lussein. He will be waiting at the Baghdad Airport for you; then, the air force pilots will bring all of you to a U.S. Military base in Germany.

American Goddess

"When is this trip scheduled?" I asked calmly.

"That's the other reason I'm here. I wanted to escort you to the airport personally right now."

I shook my head as if I were shaking off a punch to the jaw, and with a stunned tone said, "What!? Now!? George, my personal life is turning into a shamble at this very moment, and you want me to get up and leave? Can't I at least finish my workday and make some personal phone calls?"

With a bleak expression he replied, "The time is also being dictated by Lussein, and he's only giving us thirty-four hours. He said, "It's now or never."

I ran my fingers through my hair from my forehead back, shook my head again, and sighed, "Well, I guess we had better leave then."

Feeling almost as if I were being kidnaped myself, I was ushered out of my office and down to a Secret Service escorted by a convoy of limos. As I was climbing into the President's limo with him, out of the corner of my eye I noticed Michael standing on the curb watching us leave. I stopped, turned to George, and said, "Give me one minute." I climbed back out of the limo and began to run toward Michael. The moment he saw me coming he turned and began to walk away. I stopped dead in my tracks, turned around and as I headed back to the limo I sadly thought, 'Goodbye, Michael.'

CHAPTER 45

We landed in Baghdad at 5:00pm 'their time' the next afternoon, and when the doors opened; all I could see was a large military presence all around the plane. And guess what!? There was no sight of any hostages or King Lussein. As I stood there at the open door a group of forty or so armed Iraqi Soldiers approached with the staircase for the plane, and when it was in place an obviously high-ranking officer came up the steps and in Arabic said, "Ms. Powers, King Lussein would like for you to accompany me to the palace."

American Goddess

I turned to Todd Deyo, one of the out-of-uniform lieutenants and said, "Todd, this is not what was to transpire, what should we do?"

He shrugged his shoulders, "I don't think you have any choice but to go with him, Ms. Powers."

I really became concerned, and it showed on my face when I said, "Couldn't we just take off?"

He looked profoundly serious, "Only if we want to be shot down before we ever leave the ground."

I shook my head, "Oh well! I hope I'll see you later." At that, I turned and proceeded to leave with my armed Iraqi Military Escort.

When I entered Lussein's Palace, I was escorted to an extravagantly decorated dining room, and as we entered the room my escort said, "Please make yourself comfortable the King will be with you shortly."

He closed the door leaving me standing there alone. I looked around the room and noticed the table was set with flowers and candles. It was a ready-to-go romantic dinner for two. The soft sounds of a romantic rhythm came through the sound system, and putting two and two together I thought, 'Oh God! Don't tell me Lussein has 'the hots' for me too!'

I walked over to the window to gaze out, and as I stood there, I heard the door open from thirty feet behind me. I turned around with a friendly smile and was stunned and horrified to see Prince Fehd dressed in all his princely attire walking right toward me. I was so taken aback by his presence I could feel my adrenalin immediately rushing through my veins. I quickly scanned my thoughts for the appropriate response to this potentially deadly situation. So with a strong, calm, smooth, motion I began to head toward him as well. With a confident seductive lifting of my eyebrows, I hid my fears behind an expression of pure surprise and said, "Mohammed! What in the world are you doing here?"

He reached me with a smile, gently took my hand, and as he lovingly gazed into my eyes said, "I told you if you married me, I would bring an end to Lussein's occupation of Kuwait. The freeing of the hostages is just my way of showing you, what I can and will do for your love, Christina."

I was floored by his statement, and my face couldn't hide that emotion as I said, "I don't understand this! How can your father be fearing an invasion from Iraq, if you have the power to convince Lussein to withdraw his troops from Kuwait? This makes no sense to me at all, and it compels me to ask, how is this possible?"

Beginning to lead me by the hand toward the table he said, "Come with me my love, and I will explain it over dinner. I hope you are hungry. I took the liberty of having all your favorite dishes prepared."

American Goddess

I took my seat as he filled two glasses with white wine. When he was seated, he looked straight into my eyes and said, "It's actually not that hard to understand. Lussein and I have been faithful brothers in Islam all our lives. We respect and honor one another with such a divine love that we would do anything for one another."

Still not understanding I asked, "If there is such a great love between the two of you then why is he threatening to invade your nation?"

He was swift and to the point with his answer, "Because he despises my father and Sheik Jabir for betraying their Islamic roots and embracing the demons of the Western World."

Still confused, I shook my head in disbelief, "If you know all this, then why don't you try to mediate a peaceful solution between the three of them?"

He answered with an air of true sincerity, "I've tried to reason with both my father and the Sheik, but they refuse to listen and in doing so they've sealed their fate. Now, I can do no more to interfere with their destinies."

"But aren't you interfering now by freeing the hostages?"

"Yes, I am, and for one reason only, to show you I would interfere with fate if it brought your love to me. Nothing else on this planet would make me interfere with my brother's destiny but you, and that's because you are my destiny."

At that moment the most incredibly enticing, garnished, sea food smorgasbord was brought into the room. There were lobsters, shrimps, oysters, fried flounder and squid. I mean it was all there and on separate platters ready to eat. It smelled so good I thought, 'Well since this could be your last meal Christina, you'd better take advantage of it.' So I dug right in and as we ate I said, "You're a strangely intriguing man Mohammed, and for the life of me I can't figure you out. You tell me you're having Lussein free the hostages to prove your undying love for me, yet you nearly threw me to my death at our first meeting. Maybe I should ask you to tell me what you would think of someone with such erratic behavior?"

He smiled and said, "Forgive me for my foolish outburst at our last meeting and let me assure you no harm would have come to you that day. My assumption you would have realized by now whom you truly are was premature."

I looked at him strangely, "Why do you speak in riddles? You compare me to someone I don't know, and then tell me I'm just like him. You tell me I should realize I'm your destiny, when I know I'm not. You tell me I'm going to bear your child and I know I can't. Mohammed, listen to yourself for a minute and you will realize I'm not the woman you think I am. Didn't you just say you hated the demons of the Western World? Well according to your Islamic beliefs, I must be the epitome of those demons. I could see it now, a woman of the world who openly flaunts despising any male dominated society, marrying the Prince of the Islamic faith. I don't think so."

American Goddess

He lovingly took my hand and said, "I know what you are, and I don't understand it myself, but I do know you were destined to be mine.   Now, I will tell you how I know this to be true. It is because I am the rightful Prince of Persia, the direct descendant of Ishmael, the son of Abraham and Hagar. You are the direct descendant of Isaac, the son of Abraham and Sarah."

Struggling not to laugh, I nearly choked on my last bit of lobster as I said, "You're really in outer left field now, I know there's not a drop of Jewish blood in me."

Still gazing lovingly into my eyes, I knew he was unconvinced as he brought my hand to his lips, kissed it, and said, "If you're finished with your meal I'd like to show you something?"   I slipped my hand from his, "I'm finished."

He took my hand back as he said, "Come with me then."

He led me into a massive library, where he proceeded to go through a large old book of Islamic Prophecies.   Finding what he was looking for, he handed the book to me and said, "You read Arabic, read it for yourself."

I took the book and glancing to where he was pointing began to read, "**At the time of the alignment of all celestial bodies within your solar system, the king's daughter shall rise to power, and she shall be known to the world as the 'Angel of Peace'.   This one is the mother of the Messiah, who is the daughter of the king and the descendants of Abraham.   Her power is in her tongue of many languages, and she alone shall marry the true heir to the throne of Solomon and bear him his first male child.   The child she brings forth in the wilderness shall be the pure descendant of Adam's seed, and he represents the true returning of the Prince of Peace.   He alone will finally usher in the Heavenly Millennium of paradise on earth foretold by the prophets.**"   As I finished, I closed the book and said, "I'm not usually this bad with puzzles, but I still don't get the connection."

Looking at me as if I were an imbecile he said, "You, Christina, are that woman! The one the world calls the 'Angel of Peace', and I am the rightful heir to the throne of Solomon."

I shook my head in total disbelief and said, "You really put all this together just from a newspaper article which called me the 'Angel of Peace?'"

Taking the book from my hands, he placed it on the shelf.   He turned back toward me, and taking me in his arms, he lovingly said, "That is not the only reason my love, you are rising to power in the world whether you realize it or not.   The alinement of the planets spoken of in this prophecy will take place in May of the year 2000, and you are also fluent in many languages.   I know everything there is to know about you.   I have always known in my heart; you would one day be my bride and bear me my son. Together through peace, we shall conquer the world and give it to our son, who will lead all peoples into a millennium of peace on earth."

American Goddess

I had to push hard to get out of his loving embrace as I said, "Please, Mohammed, not so close, I like my space. I have got to say for someone who supposedly knows so much about me, then how come you overlooked the fact I can no longer bear children. Doesn't that put a damper on your theories as to whom you think I am?"

He was slowly coming closer to me with a very hungry look on his face as he said, "I know about your injury. If you let me, I will teach you how to heal your wounds from within. You can tap into the divine power, which is yours, and I know how it's done. Then, you will be able to bear our child. The secrets of God's power are at your disposal Christina, it lies within."

He was still slowly continuing to walk toward me as I backed away. Putting my hands up to slow his descent upon me and thinking quick I said, "You're not listening Mohammed, I just told you I can no longer bear children."

I could see in his eyes he was beginning to become upset with my resistance when he said, "You're the one not listening! You already have the power to heal yourself."

As my back reached the wall I said, "Well, I hope I can grow back a uterus then, because that's what it's going to take."

His face became as white as a ghost. He took a deep breath, while hovering over me shouting, "What are you talking about!?"

That was the moment I knew I was heading for trouble and I thought, 'God, please help me out of this one!' As I said, "I nearly lost my life last year in an attempt to have a child. While I was unconscious, the doctors had to perform a hysterectomy on me in order to save my life."

His eyes became red with anger. With one hand, he took my left shoulder and flung me with such force, I went flying into a bookshelf sending the books toppling on top of my head. Laying under a pile of books I heard him yelling, "This can't be! I thought you were the one!"

As I looked up from under the books, I could see he was coming to give me some more, so just as he reached down to grab me, I pushed up with my legs knocking him into another bookshelf. I scrambled to my feet, went running for the door and of course it was locked. I turned quickly to see where he was, and he was coming right for me. I screamed out with all my might, "Stop this, Mohammed! This is **madness**! Help! Someone help!"

He put his hands around my neck and began to try and chook the life out of me. I kneed him right in the nuts and pushed him over backwards. I ran to an open window and tried to climb out. He grabbed my waist and flung me against the wall. Looking around quickly, I spotted two swords mounted on the wall. I grabbed for the sword which hung on the wall about four feet from me. When I had it, I swung around as fast as lightening just in time to hold its sharp point right at his throat.   He stopped dead in his tracks and as I backed him into a bookshelf I shouted, "Get it together or I won't hesitate to use this! I'll do it right now you crazy bastard!"

Suddenly, Lussein with twenty guards, burst into the room and shouted, "Mohammed, if we take her life now, we will be destroying all our future plans.   Calm down my brother and know one day you will have your revenge. Besides, I already told you she was not the one.   Now leave her alone and let her go back to her demon possessed nation where trash like her belong."

The thought of Lussein's prediction at that moment, nearly made me cut Mohammed's head off right on the spot.   It took all my self-control not to lunge forward and plunge the blade right through him, but I thought, 'It's not worth it Christina, he's just an evil man.'

Within moments Mohammed calmed himself down and with his angelic voice said, "I'm sorry if I hurt you, but your news was devastating, and it made me upset."

Still holding the sword to Mohammed's neck I looked toward Lussein and said, "You told the President you would release the hostages to me, now I'm tired of fooling around here, so please release them and let us leave at once."

With a deadly serious look in his eyes, he said, "If you give your word you will not tell anyone that Mohammed was here, you may leave now."

I smiled and reassuringly said, "You've got a deal!"

He clapped his hands, turned to his guards and shouted, "Take Ms. Powers to the airport immediately."

"Wait just a minute," I demanded.   "I'm not going anywhere without the hostages."

Lussein walked right up to my face while I still held the sword and said, "You really are a gutsy broad."

Without blinking once I replied, "Thank you!   I'll take that as a compliment, now please bring out the hostages."

He smiled and his smile seemed to hold a slightly detectable glimmer of admiration as he said, "It's all right to go with the guards Christina, the hostages are already boarded on your jet and waiting for you."

Looking into his eyes, I knew he was telling the truth; so, I thanked him as I handed him the sword. Then I turned and confidently proceeded to walk out of that room holding my head held high with an air about me, as if I had total control over this insane situation and not thinking of losing my composure the entire time.   But inside, I was a frightened little girl.

American Goddess

We arrived back at the Baghdad Airport precisely at 9:00pm, and when I boarded the jet the cheers of two-hundred and twenty-six freed hostages filled the cabin. As Lieutenant Todd Deyo locked us in, I asked, "Is everyone here?"

He nodded his head and with a pleased smile said, "Everyone Ms. Powers, thanks to you. Come on let's take our seats and get the hell out of here before he has a change of heart."

With wide eyes I answered, "You got that right!"

As I followed him to the front of the jet, I received warm hugs and kisses from everyone. I returned their greetings in kind, but the one person I really wanted to see was nowhere in sight. Finally, when I reached my seat at the front of the plane there he was. My, Jimmy! Sitting curled up like a little mouse on the seat next to mine, with Richard seated on his other side. The moment he saw me, he gazed into my eyes with those big, sad, browneyes of his, and reaching his arms out to me he said, "Christina, hold me!"

I embraced him as I took my seat and said, "It's all right Jimmy, I'm taking you home." I buckled us both up, and neither one of us uttered another word. I just held him gently in my arms all the way to Germany. We arrived at an American Military base shortly after 3:00am, and all the hostages were quickly ushered into the infirmary. Jimmy and the others had to stay in Germany a few days for physicals and debriefings. I had to leave immediately for my own debriefing with the President back in Washington, D.C.

After my short but emotional goodbyes to Jimmy, I was back in the air. I did not get off that plane until 8:00am on December 14, 1990, and I was greeted by the largest gathering of reporters I had ever seen. They proceeded to swarm me like killer bees as I tried to walk through the airport. They were shouting questions at me, "Christina! How are the hostages? Were they harmed in any way?"

Now being joined by the Secret Service who began to lead me toward a group of waiting limos, I quickly responded to the question, "The hostages are in good spirits, and as far as I know no physical harm has come to any of them."

One of the reporters shouted, "Christina, why was your mission to Iraq kept from the public until now? And what were the terms for the release of the hostages?"

Reaching the limos with my presidential escort I answered, "I'm sorry, but I haven't given the President my debriefing yet; so, I'm afraid the answers to your questions are going to have to wait."

I climbed into the waiting limo and off we went to the White House for a six-hour debriefing. Afterwards, the President and I gave a joint forty-five-minute news conference; then, it was off for a celebration dinner at the Washington Hilton with George and all of D.C.'s top brass.

American Goddess

With all the hoopla being in my honor, you would think I'd be at least interested, but all I wanted to do was go home.   And as much as I wanted to get up and walk out of that fancy dinner, I did not.   I was not able to leave for home until 11:00pm.

CHAPTER 46

I walked into the house at 2:14am on December 15th and headed straight for the bedroom.   I started to undress as soon as I entered the room and while kicking off my shoes, I hit the message retrieval button on my answering machine.   The first message 'BEEP' was from my mother-in law and in an obviously upset tone she said, "Christina, it's, Tess!   It's now 2:00pm and I'm calling from Albany Medical Center.   Michael's been in an awful car crash.   He's in surgery right now, so please get here fast." 'BEEP'

My heart was in my throat as I waited for the next message 'BEEP'.   The next two messages were from Johnny and the fourth 'BEEP' was from Tess again, "Christina! Where are you?   It's now 8:00pm, Michael is out of surgery, but he's in critical condition and unresponsive.   He needs you Christina, now more than ever.   He's been mumbling your name, so if you really love him please come now!" 'BEEP' and that was her last message.

It was 2:30 in the morning when I dialed Tess's number, and as soon as she answered I shouted in a panicked voice, "Tess, it's, Christina!   How is Michael?"

"Calm down Christina, he's doing fine now.   He came around at 1:00am on the 13th and thank God he's been improving remarkably since."

With a sigh of relief, I said, "Thank God is right!   I would have been there for him Tess, but I had to leave the country and I couldn't tell anyone."

"I know, we saw you on the evening news with the President.   I am really very proud of you for what you've done Christina, and I know Michael is too.   If only you could have seen his face light up when he saw the news broadcast."

"What room is he in?"   I asked anxiously.

"625 but visiting hours aren't until 10:00am"

American Goddess

"Thank you Tess and God willing I'll see you at the hospital in the morning." We said our goodbyes as I put my shoes back on and the minute, I hung up the receiver, I dashed back out of the house, and at 2:45am, I was on my way to the Albany Medical Center.

I arrived at the hospital at 3:30am, and I had to convince a security guard that I was truly Christina Powers. He insisted on escorting me up to Michael's room. I quietly opened the door so not to wake him; then, I slowly closed it behind me and tiptoed to his bedside. Tears began to flow down my cheeks, as I came closer to Michael and noticed his entire head was shaved while the top portion was wrapped in bandages. As I knelt down beside his bed, I softly started praying, "God, please let him be all right."

As soon as I spoke these words, I could see his eyes slowly opening. When he realized I was there he gently smiled, then began to force himself out of his sleepy fog. I took his hand in mine, kissed it and said, "Michael, my love. I'm so sorry I wasn't here for you, but I'm here now. If you will only take me back in your arms just once, I know we will never leave each other again."

He gazed down at me, stared straight into my eyes and with the most loving, tender look he had ever given me, said, "Punkie, my love for you comes from the deepest essence of my soul. And I'm truly very proud of you for what you've accomplished, and for who you are as a person. But no matter how strong or proud my love for you is I vowed to myself I would never allow you to place me second in your life again. So for my own mental health, I am going to keep that promise to myself by asking you to leave right now."

I instantly masked the devastating pain his words brought to my heart, under an emotionless expression. I gracefully rose from my knees and just as quietly tiptoed back out of his room without uttering another peep. Somehow, I managed to hold back my tears of pain as I walked through that hospital, but there was no way I was keeping them back the moment I sat in my car. I stayed in the hospital parking lot for two hours crying before I could compose myself enough to drive away.

It was 8:00am on the 15th, when I finally collapsed in my bed, clothes and all, and I did not get out of that bed until the same time the following morning. When I returned to my office that morning, I told Pierre not to disturb me as I started right where I left off, following up with messages. I decided it would be wiser to return all business calls first this time, then the personal ones hoping maybe this way I could accomplish something. I didn't get around to making that first personal call until 2:30 that afternoon, and it was to return the twelve messages from Johnny, each one sounding more concerned than the other. As I dialed the number, I noticed it was a local exchange and as soon as he said, "Hello!"

I said, "Hello, yourself! Where are you? This is an in-state number."

American Goddess

With excitement he said, "I was wondering that about you myself until I saw you on the news the other day.   You sure know how to get around.   One minute you drop me off at my motel, the next you're returning from a Middle East trip no one knew you were on."

I laughed, "I know how well I get around, but what about you?
What are you doing back in New York?"

"I'm in Tarrytown.   I've been here since Mary and I split up."

"What!   What happened?"   I asked with a surprised tone.

"When I arrived home the day after your birthday, Mary accused me of cheating on her.   I denied it and she threw me out.   I went back two hours later and persuaded her we did not sleep together.   She asked me if I wanted to sleep with you and when I told her the truth, she threw me out again.   So, I came to my secret hide away, my condo here in Tarrytown and like I said, I've been here ever since."

"That is ridiculous, what's wrong with her?   Do you have any plans for tonight, John?"

"Not one."   He answered sadly.

"Well then why don't you come over and I'll take **you** for dinner this time. Then we can talk in person."   He agreed and we made a date for him to meet me at my office at 6:00 that evening.

Just as punctual as ever, Johnny entered my office right on time, and as we were leaving, I stopped at Pierre's desk and said, "Pierre, I won't be in tomorrow.   I am going to be picking Jimmy up in the morning at the airport.   I'll probably be in the following day."

"Christina, would you mind if I come in late tomorrow myself?   I'd like to come to the airport with you and the others in the morning, if I may?   Jimmy and I really hit if off well when we were in Ghana together last year, and I'd like to be there to welcome him home."

I replied with a smile, "Sure you can.   I'm sure Jimmy would appreciate your being there.   Why don't you come to my place at 7:00am? A few other close friends are meeting me there at that time and you're more than welcome to join us."

With a curiously delighted smile he thanked me, as I handed him a note and added, "Open this in ten minutes, and I'll see you in the morning."

I turned my full attentions toward Johnny with a seductive smile and in my best May West interpretation jokingly said, "Well big boy! Let's rock and roll; this night is on me."

We went to my place first where I changed into Christina Powers the sex symbol, and immediately proceeded to take Johnny out on the town.   Oh yes!   The note I left with Pierre read, "**Pierre, around 10:00pm tonight I will be in Albany at a gay night club** called LONGHORN'S. What I want you to do is call News Channel Ten in Albany and ask for anchorwoman Angela Hamilton. Tell her I will be in town and if she meets me at Longhorn's at 10:30 tonight, I will give her an exclusive. Then, call our radio station in the area it's 'Fly 92' around 10:00pm. Tell them to announce I am at the nightclub and that I'm going to perform a surprise mini-concert for my Albany fans." I had the evening planned right down to the smallest detail, and I started it out by taking Johnny for a romantic dinner, then to Longhorn's. As I parked the car, Johnny noticed two men walking into the club together holding hands. He quickly turned to me with a nervous look on his face, and in a sarcastic tone said, "Is this a fag bar?"

I gave him a strange look, "John! Don't tell me you're homophobic!"

His tone and expression quickly calmed as he answered, "No, not at all! It's just that I've never been in a gay club before. I'm telling you, I'll freak if some guy tries to hit on me."

I laughed, "Don't be an asshole, John! You're with Christina Powers. Do you really think any one of these guys is going to be looking at you with me here? Get real! Tonight, in this place, I'm the only one who's going to be 'hit on'. So put your fears away, leave all your prehistoric views of gay men out here in the parking lot, and let's go have some fun."

"Why are we going to a fag bar anyway?" He asked like a frightened little boy.

I answered firmly, "First, it's just a gay club, not a fag bar and no one is going to attack you. Second, you will not have any competition. Third, I have personal reasons for being here tonight."

He took a deep breath and said, "Ok, just don't leave me alone."

Climbing out of the car, I started to laugh at him again as I added, "Now please Stop fooling around, John! I know you're more liberal minded then that, or at least I hope so."

At that, we proceeded toward the entrance. As soon as we walked into the club, I immediately sat Johnny at a table with a drink and proceeded to take center stage. I went up to the owner, Phil Jackowski, handed him a background tape of my music and asked him to allow me to do a few numbers for the crowd. Breathlessly, he agreed and as he readied his staff and the crowd for my performance, Angela Hamilton from News Channel Ten entered the club. I quickly walked over to her and said, "Angela, hi! Thanks for coming."

With an excited smile she replied, "Christina, it's so nice to meet you and please don't thank me. I should thank you! I can't wait to find out what this is all about."

"I'm going to be giving a small surprise performance here tonight, and I've invited you because this performance is my way of announcing to the Capital Region, my intentions to purchase properties in the City of Albany. My plans are to one day build a

American Goddess

major new recording studio right here in your town, and I'm hoping the citizens as well as the city leaders will welcome Powers Inc. into the 'All American City' with open arms."

We went right into a live interview and just as we finished, a crew from Fly 92 entered the club. The crew began to set up a connection to their main station; so, they could start broadcasting my performance live, right on the spot. When their connection was completed, I proceeded to give the D.J. who introduced himself to me as 'Sugar Bear' a quick live on-air interview. Ten minutes later, I had that city in such an uproar that everyone and their brother knew I was in town and partying my tail off with the legendary ballplayer, John Everett. Before I knew, the club, as well as the entire city was mobbed with people and traffic. When I started to sing at 11:00pm that Thursday evening, I made sure I was loud enough for Michael to hear me six blocks away in his hospital bed.

After my mini-concert, I proceeded to dance the night away with Johnny and everyone else in the club. Of course, I orchestrated my latest public display for just one reason. I wanted to hurt Michael just as much as he hurt me, and I figured what better way than to be throwing a party right outside his hospital bedroom window with my ex-lover.

The night was so hot, and the city so busy, I didn't get Johnny to his car until 4:30 in the morning. As I waited for him to exit my car, he leaned over kissed my cheek and said, "Christina, I had a great time tonight. Thanks for taking me; I needed the change and being with you felt like old times. If I'm not being too bold, I hope you felt it too."

I smiled warmly as I replied, "I had a great time too John, it was fun. I know we really didn't get to talk about your situation with Mary very much, and I'm sorry about that. But I'll tell you what. I'm having a small welcome home dinner party for Jimmy and Richard tonight; so, if you come over around 7:00pm, I'll make it up to you by finding the time to talk privately after dinner."

He gracefully accepted my invitation, kissed my cheek once more and out he climbed. As I watched his still very muscular body climb into his car, I thought, 'My God he looks good! And if I think about it, underneath all the true reasons for this evening, I ended up really having a great time with Johnny.' As he left for Tarrytown and his bed, I took a quick shower, grabbed a cup of coffee and headed for the airport.

American Goddess

CHAPTER 47

I was accompanied to the airport that morning by Pierre, James, Carman, Joe, Ann, and a group of other friends from work.. We were met there by a large group of reporters, who were also waiting for Jimmy's arrival. We waited anxiously holding our welcome-home signs and I'll never forget the feeling of relief I felt seeing my best friend in the entire world, safely exit that plane. I became so excited I started to cry. Neither one of us holding back any longer went running toward the other like two excited little children on Christmas morning. In front of the eyes of the world, we leaped into a loving, enthusiastic, embrace.

Jumping in the air with our arms around each other Jimmy shouted, "Oh God, girlfriend I love you! Thank you, Christina! Thank you!"

My tears of joy flowed again as I replied, "I love you too, Jimmy! And I'm so glad to see you home!" In the midst of our hug, I looked behind him then added, "Where's Richard and his parents?"

Breaking from my embrace he answered, "They're coming in on a commercial flight."

I Looked at him strangely and replied with concern, "Why?"

"I'll tell you about it later," he murmured in a lower tone. "I don't want to ruin this moment."

I nodded curiously, "Okay."

At that, he turned to me with his own expression of curiosity as he asked, "Where's Michael?"

I started to laugh as we began to walk toward the others, "I'll tell you about it later, I don't want to ruin this moment either."

His face took on a shocked look as his mouth dropped open, but it was too late for him to allow anything to come out, because we had just reached the cheers and embraces of the others.

Believe it or not, that entire day turned into one big party. Friends were coming in and out of the house from the moment we pulled in at 10:00am, right up until our private dinner party at 7:00pm. That's when I told James not to allow any more visitors. I wanted to keep dinner formal so besides Johnny, I had invited only our closest friends. And for some reason, I wasn't surprised when Jimmy added Pierre to the list by inviting him to come back for dinner. But I asked no questions, figuring they could all wait until Jimmy and I finally had our time together. Still, we ended up with thirty guests for a joyful, heart-warming, dinner that evening, filled with toasts to Jimmy and me, along with lots of thanks to **God**, for Jimmy's safe return home.

American Goddess

Shortly after dinner as we gathered in the bar Carman entered, walked over to Jimmy and said, "There's a call for you on Christina's private line.   You can take it in the den."   He thanked her, excused himself and headed out.

I quickly went after Carman and asked, "Carman, who called on my line for Jimmy?"

She turned to me with a sad face, "Christina, it's Michael.   He asked me not to tell you it was him."

I thanked her and headed straight for my office to do some eavesdropping. Just as I picked up the receiver, I could hear Jimmy saying, "I cannot believe this, Michael! Why in the world do you want a divorce if you still love her?"

"It's a long story Jimmy, and I'm sure she'll tell you all about it as soon as she can."

"Well at least let me tell her you're on the phone, I don't care what happened between the two of you, I know that girl loves you and she'll want to talk to you."

Michael's reply was harsh, "You think so, huh!   Tell me one thing, is he there?"

"Is who here?"   Jimmy asked with a confused tone.

"The ballplayer.   That's who."   Michael replied adamantly.

"Uh uh uh, uh no."   Jimmy stuttered.

"You're a pisspoor liar, Jimmy."

"He can't mean anything to her, Michael.   I've only known him for a few hours, but I can already tell he's a jerk just by his phony handshake."

"It's like this Jimmy; I can't afford to care anymore, so if she wants him, she can have him."

Confidently Jimmy replied, "Come on, that doesn't sound like the Michael I know. Where's the man who once told me, 'If anybody can tame her and keep her from killing herself it's me, and I'm going to succeed.' Don't you remember telling me 'that', the day Frank Salerno's murder trial ended?"

"I remember!   But Jimmy, I'm telling you, there's no one who can save that girl from herself, and I just can't keep trying anymore or she will be the death of me.   Jimmy, just take care of her for me because she needs someone looking after her more then she knows.   Now, get back to your party and I'll see you when I get out of this damned hospital."

Sadly Jimmy replied, "I'll say all right for now Michael, but we're not done talking about this I promise you."

They said their goodbyes and I sat there hurting so badly, I just couldn't go back to the party. I had Carman make my excuses for me, while I headed for a hot shower.

It was 12:10am when Jimmy finally came climbing into bed with me and proceeded to prop himself up on three pillows, with a big bowl of buttered popcorn and

American Goddess

two bottles of Catskill Mountain Cola. He began to nudge me as he said, "You better get your ass up and start talking right now, before I dump this bowl on your head."

I sat up quickly, "Don't you dare dump that bowl! I've been dying for your popcorn."

He laughed, "All right, shithead! I know you were on the phone and I know why you didn't come back down. Now, tell me what's going on with you two?"

As we munched on the best popcorn, Jimmy had ever made, I told him everything that happened. When I completed my story, Jimmy turned to me shaking his head and said, "Whoa! That's a tough call. On one hand, I can't believe Michael would be so stubborn, especially since **my life** was on the line. But if I look at it from his point of view, I can totally understand. The problem here is neither one of you are right nor wrong in this situation. You guys are just going to have to get through this and go on."

I chuckled, "Tell him that! He's the one who wants a divorce." Seriously, "I'm not talking about just him; I mean you too. If you really want Michael, what are you doing with this John guy?"

"He's just a friend!" I protested.

"Just a friend! A friend who happens to be throwing Michael for a loop and his presence sure isn't helping matters any. Besides he's not just a jock, he's a jerk jock. That's the worst kind."

"I was going to bring that up to you. I don't think you are being fair to John. He really happens to be a great guy."

Sarcastically he replied, "Christina stop kidding yourself! I'll bet underneath that country boy smile lays a KKK member. I could see it the minute he looked at me."

I started to laugh then quickly changed the subject by saying, "That's enough about me. What happened with Richard?"

Sadly he replied, "Let's just say he was no Bobby, and I don't think anyone ever will be."

"Well something must of caused the breakup. After all, you spent sixteen months with him!"

"I did love him until he became a possessive, manipulative, neurotic fruitcake. He got so bad; I was afraid to go to sleep at night worried he was going to murder me in my sleep. I just couldn't take it anymore; so, I broke it off the night before we were to leave Kuwait."

I shook my head in amazement, "Wow, I guess it's true, you never really do know anyone until you live with them. Now for my next question, what's up with you and Pierre?"

Innocently he replied, "Why whatever do you mean? "

I chuckled, "You know what I mean!   I can see something brewing there, I know you too well, Jimmy."

"Ha!   Ha!"   Jimmy replied, "I think he's a nice guy, that's all."

"You're right he is, but is he gay?"   I asked with curiosity.

"Yes!   You didn't know that?"   He answered with a surprised look.

"No!   When did you find out?"

"The minute you first introduced him to me in Ghana."

"Well then go for it Jimmy, he's a doll."   I said approvingly.

That's when Jimmy took my hand, brought it to his heart and said, "Do you know what I would really like?"

I squeezed his hand, "No Jimmy, I don't know, but I'm sure you're going to tell me."

He smiled mischievously, "I would love to spend Christmas and New Years in 'P-town', with you and your secretary before having to face life's responsibilities again."

I smiled back, "I think I can arrange that.   Would you like me to call my secretary and inform him to be ready for a business trip in the morning, or would you like to call him for me?"

He kissed my cheek with his buttery lips, hopped up and said, "I think I'll go call him right now, and you better get some sleep girlfriend, it's starting to show around the edges."

And as he went for the door, I went flying for the mirror yelling, "Where?   I don't see anything!"

CHAPTER 48

American Goddess

We arrived back home from our Cape Cod holiday on Saturday, January 6, 1991. The three of us had a wonderful time together the entire two weeks we were there, unless I was left alone for more two minutes. That's when I would begin to think about Michael and end up crying. I would insist the two of them go have fun and they did, while I like a damned fool stayed in my oceanfront room crying my eyes out. I missed Michael so much, especially that Christmas. I called my mother-in-law, only to become more depressed when the message I received from her was, "He's out of town Christina, and unavailable to all of us."

After that message, I was able to push thoughts of Michael away, at least until New Year's Day. I was so upset Michael didn't call me back the night before, after I left him three urgent messages, that I spent the entire day blowing off steam jogging for miles on the wind frozen beaches of the Cape. So needless to say, when I did finally enter the front door of my Milton Home, I was really glad to be back. At least now I could begin to bury my pain, by diving headfirst back into my work.

Jimmy and I decided to take the rest of that weekend before plunging into my work, by spending it alone, just the two of us. We stayed home and talked about everything that happened to both of us while we were apart. He told me how awful it was for him to be held against his will, not to mention frightening. As for me, I told him how scared I was for him and how glad I was that at least for him the ordeal was now over. I went on to tell him all my thoughts and feelings. We talked about Michael and our crazy love/hate relationship. Jimmy talked about his relationship with Richard and how he watched it fall apart.

At one point, I told him about my wish to someday adopt a great big family with Michael, and that's when I started to cry as I sarcastically said, "I can't believe this, Jimmy! Me! The so-called, great Christina Powers can't even keep her husband!" Throwing my hands up in disgust, I continued, "Look, world! The Sex-Goddess of the twentieth century! Ha! Ha! I would not know how to keep a man if my life depended on it. What the hell is my problem, Jimmy? Why can't I hold onto a man?"

He chuckled as he answered, "Christina, I love you and you're the best friend anyone could ever have, but you're also like a wildfire burning everything in your path. No man, not even Michael has been able to control your flames, and I don't think anyone ever will unless you let them."

Seriously I asked, "So what are you telling me, am I a hopeless cause in the love department?"

"No! Why don't you try thinking about what I said before you jump to conclusions?"

I thought for a moment, "You're right! I am too overbearing sometimes, but I don't mean to be. Life just seems to dictate my response to certain situations. Like you being in Ghana for instance, or the business.   It's nothing I do on purpose, so what can I do about it?   Stop caring and let it all fall apart just to please Michael?   Well if that's what it takes, then I'd rather be alone."

"That's not what it takes," he replied. "And that's not what I meant either.   What I'm trying to say is, if you let Michael know he is first in your life, he'll come back to you."

At that I kissed his forehead, "Well Jimmy, I think it's a little too late for Michael and me, but I'll keep it in mind for the future."

Our weekend went on like that until 8:00am Monday morning rolled around.   It came so fast, it felt like we never had any rest at all.   But all the same, when Jimmy and I entered our prearranged board meeting at 9:00am that morning, we were full of energy and ready to tackle anything.   And for the next five hours, everyone in that room went through an entire review of every aspect of Powers Incorporated since the day Jimmy left.   It was 1:00pm when our review ended and without a breather, I went right into action and started giving new orders.   In that entire time, we had one ten-minute coffee break at 11:30am and I did not have us break again for lunch until 3:00pm. That is when I entered my office to find a certified letter, from the Grammy Awards Committee of the National Academy of Recording Arts and Sciences.

Jimmy and Pierre were standing beside me waiting to go for lunch, as I quickly opened the letter to discover my latest soundtrack, 'One Voice, One World and Love Enough For All' had received a phenomenal total of fourteen different Grammy nominations.   And the single, 'Love Grows in the Arms of Peace' had eight of those nominations all to itself.   I was so excited by the letter I leaped into the air shouting, "Yes!   Yes! Fourteen nominations!   Can you believe it, fourteen!" I shoved the letter in Jimmy's face and continued shouting, "Look, Jimmy!   Look!"

"Wow!   Christina, this is great news!"   He shouted back with enthusiasm then continued, "Did you read the rest of this?"

"No, I stopped at the fourteen nominations.   What does it say?"

"It goes on to read, '**Ms. Powers, we the members of the Grammy Awards Committee, would like to invite you to co-host the awards ceremony this year with Barbara Goldstein, as well as perform your single, 'Love Grows in the Arms of Peace.' The ceremony will be held in L.A., on February 27, 1991.   Please reply by January 20, 1991'."**   Jimmy hugged me wildly shouting, "You go, girlfriend!"

Pierre then joined the celebration by shouting, "Congratulations, Christina! And your lunch is on me!   Now, may we please go eat?"   We all started to laugh as we headed for lunch and for the first time in weeks, I was feeling great.

Shortly after returning from lunch, I called to accept the Grammy Awards Committee's invitation to co-host the ceremonies.   I also agreed to arrive in L.A. for rehearsals on February 15, 1991.

American Goddess

After that call I thought I'd better return Johnny's many calls, and as soon as I said, "Hi, John, it's Christina."

He said, "I swear you must be the vanishing woman, so what secret mission were you on this time?"

I laughed, "I'm sorry, John, I was on a much-needed siesta with Jimmy, and we decided not to tell anyone where we were."

"Well thanks a lot! Do you realize I've been waiting three weeks to talk to you, and you've brushed me off each time?"

Remembering what Jimmy said to me about not letting any man control my so-called flames I said, "John, if you will please let me take you out for dinner tonight, I promise we'll talk."

"That sounds great shall I pick you up after work?"

"How about 7:00pm, my place?" I replied.

"I'll be there." He answered with enthusiasm, and when we said our goodbyes, I sat for a moment thinking, 'I really do need to learn to be more considerate of man's feelings. The problem is I don't readily trust men unless they're gay, then I feel right at home with them. I guess it's because gay men don't look at me as a woman who must be conquered into submission.'"

Later that evening when Johnny picked me up, I wore my helpless little girl look, so as not to intimidate him. He took me to the Capri Restaurant in the town of Port Ewen for dinner and dancing. Over dinner, we talked about his breakup with Mary and how much he missed his children.

As we talked, he gently took my hand in his and said, "I have to be honest with you and myself, Christina. The only reason I married Mary was because I was on the rebound from our breakup. She was my high school sweetheart and I was hurting so badly, I jumped into her arms without thinking twice. So now that I've finally admitted this to myself, I decided to file for a divorce. We go to court in March."

I was saddened and strangely pleased at the same time, but I refused to show my emotions as I replied, "Is Mary aware of your true feelings, John?"

"She is now," he answered. "I told her last week just before having my attorney file for the divorce."

"How did she take it?" I asked with sincere concern.

"Not too well, she started to cry, then said, 'I've always known your love for her was strong, but I still allowed myself to believe I could make you forget her.' I told her my decision to file for divorce had nothing to do with you. I simply said, 'We just can't keep living this lie together.'"

With a deeper sense of concern, I asked, "How are your children handling this?"

American Goddess

"Not too well right now, but they'll get used to it. Children are like that." Just then, the band began to play 'Johnny's Love.' Johnny lovingly gazed into my eyes and said, "Do you think we can try dancing to my song again, I'm pretty sure Michael's not here to punch me out this time?"

I smiled and gracefully accepted his invitation. We were having such a good time we never noticed it began to snow, and by the time we were ready to leave there was already six inches on the ground and still falling steadily. Our ride home that night was slow going to say the least, and at one point the storm became so intense, we had to pull off the road to wait for it to let up. As we sat in the car watching this beautiful snowstorm, I turned to Johnny and softly said, "John, you've told me so much about how you were hurting after our breakup, but you've not mentioned once why you slept with Kathy Brown. I've waited a long time to hear the answer to that question, because it was that discovery which caused me to abort our child." With tears now filling my eyes I continued, "Would you please answer my question now? I don't know why after all these years, but I really need to know the answer."

With tears now welling in his eyes as well, he said, "It was because I was a fool. Kathy came to my home not twenty minutes before you did that night. She told me in a very persuading way if I were to sleep with her, then she would see to it Frank let you out of your contract. So foolishly I believed her and thinking I was doing something for you, I agreed."

"For me!" I replied with shock. "Didn't you think about how I might feel if I were to find out? You must have known I'd be devastated once she told me, and she would have if I hadn't discovered the two of you together myself. And when I did find the two of you together, why didn't you come after me then? You had the card from the flowers I gave you, telling you I was pregnant. Didn't you realize how devastated I was when I saw you sleeping with Kathy?" My voice rose as I cried out the pain, I hid for all those years until I was shouting with anger, "You should have known it might have caused me to have an abortion?" I opened the car door and as I began to run into a blinding snow squall, I stopped turned back and screamed, "Why didn't you come after me, Johnny? Why?"

Johnny ran after me yelling, "Christina! Wait! Come back here!"

I was so upset; he had to tackle me into a snowbank to stop me from running. Once I hit the snow, I pushed him from me crying, "Please don't, Johnny? Just leave me be."

I was freezing and covered with snow when I stood up, took a deep breath and just started to cry. And once 'again' my tears fell for all my babies. The pain I felt that moment went so deep, my body began to tremble, and I knew it had nothing to do with the weather.

American Goddess

As I cried in the midst of that blinding, snow squall, Johnny took my hand and with his tears falling as hard as mine said, "Christy, can you ever forgive me for the hurt I caused you all those many years ago?   I realized I was the reason why you had the abortion.   I came to your penthouse on the night of your birthday to ask you to forgive me, but your place was empty.   I looked for you for months.   I even went to Barbara's home thinking you might be there, but she told me she had no idea where you were. Shortly after that I went back home, where I ran into Mary."

As he cried, I gently pulled him into my arms, and we cried together like two babies. I tenderly stroked his head as I softly said, "Oh Johnny, if you had only come that morning, I would have been there and I would have forgiven you then, as I forgive you right now."

Gazing into my eyes he passionately said, "Christina, I love you.   I've always loved you and I will always love you."   He moved his lips to mine and softly began to kiss me as he continued to whisper, "I love you. I love you.   Please tell me you still love me angel?"

Feeling lonely and vulnerable, I felt myself drifting into his loving, gentle, kisses. I allowed myself to slip deeper into his advances, as his warm tongue slid to the back of my cold neck.   As his kisses grew in passion, memories of our lives together began to flood my mind.   I could feel my desire rising as his hands began to caress my longing breasts.   As my temperature grew, all those dull faint feelings of love I once felt for Johnny, rushed to my consciousness.   So much so I wanted to cry out 'Johnny, I love you too!'   But just as I opened my mouth to speak, thoughts of Michael held my tongue. It was at that moment, I abruptly put a stop to this unfolding fantasy by saying, "Johnny, please don't!   Let's not rush into something we both might end up regretting, because as long as we're both still married, we can't take our relationship any further."

Still holding me in his arms, "You're right Christina, but I promise I will court you as long as it takes, if you well allow me?"

I smiled sheepishly, "I'd love to be courted by you, Johnny."   And that's exactly what he did.

American Goddess

CHAPTER 49

That month went by so fast that before I knew, it was 5:00pm on Sunday, February 14th, and I was packing for my trip to L.A., the following morning. I'm sure the fact Johnny came 'a-courtin' every single night, had a lot to do with how fast the time went. He was determined to spoil me with flowers, gifts, and most of all, his full attention, and I must say, I was genuinely enjoying it all. And boy the tabloids enjoyed it too; they had a field-day with this one! Headlines read, **"Christina's new Love Triangle! Who will hope to win her heart this time around?"**

Thank God for Johnny and my intense work schedule, I was able to stay so busy, I hardly thought about Michael or the tabloids. And Johnny's ability to treat me like a queen, helped keep me so content and happy, I began to feel free without Michael breathing down my neck, and I thought, 'Gee! Now that I think about it, Michael was always trying to tell me what to do, wasn't he?' Shrugging my shoulders to accompany my thoughts, 'I'm probably better off without him in my life anyway. Besides, who needs a man who is always trying to control you? Not me!'

As I was convincing myself of my newfound happiness, Jimmy on the other hand never ceased to remind me of how miserable I truly was, by telling me how happy Michael seemed to be living back in his Poughkeepsie Townhouse. But there was no way I would admit to Jimmy I might be unhappy. Especially since he had visited Michael several times since his discharge from the hospital, and he refused to tell me even one thing said between the two of them.

As I finished packing for my 'Grammy' trip, Jimmy entered my room, gave me a peck on my cheek and said, "You're only going to be gone for twelve days and already I miss you."

I returned his kiss, "That's sweet Jimmy, and I'm going to miss you too, but you're coming to the award ceremony, aren't you?"

"I wouldn't miss it for the world!" He cheerfully replied.

He appeared too happy for some reason, so with a tone of curiosity I asked, "Where did you go anyway? I was looking for you at breakfast and Carman told me you left before 8:00 this morning."

In response to my question Jimmy looked at me strangely and said, "I told you Pierre and I were going ice fishing with Michael today."

I shook my head in a confused way as I responded, "I'm sorry it truly slipped my mind."

American Goddess

"Sure it did!" Jimmy laughed. "You don't really think I'm going to buy that one, now do you?"

"I really don't care what you buy, Jimmy." I snarled with indignation, "So did he ask about me?"

His smile was mischievous this time and his answer was blunt, "As a matter of fact he did. He asked when you were planning to leave for L.A."

My curiosity took hold as I suspiciously asked, "Why did he want that bit of information?"

Jimmy's smile gave me the impression he was up to something, and his cocky answer to my question confirmed my suspicions something was up,

"He wants to make sure you're nowhere in sight when he comes for his stuff."

"He what!?" I shouted! I took on an air of dominance as my voice cooled, "Does he really, now? Well you tell him for me if he comes anywhere near this place without me being here, I'll have his ass thrown in jail."

Jimmy protested strongly, "That's not right Christina, they are his things!"

"I don't care, Jimmy, and don't you dare let him in here while I'm gone either, or I'll be after your hide along with his." I demanded.

He sighed sarcastically then snapped back, "Well, when can I tell him to come then, Miss Prima-Donna?"

"When I'm going to be here!" I snapped back. "I want to make sure what he takes out of here is his."

"Well since your leaving in the morning, why don't I call him and tell him to come tonight?"

"No, Jimmy! After how he hurt me you expect me to make this easy for him? Well I'm not. Besides, I have a date tonight with, Johnny."

At that, Jimmy's fangs came out as he hissed, "Oh! You're calling him, Johnny now! Wasn't that your pet name for him? What is wrong with you, girlfriend? I can't believe you could choose that phony asshole over Michael. It just doesn't make sense to me, or do you really want this Johnny?"

Losing it I shouted back, "Who the hell do you think you are passing judgment on Johnny!? And if you would open your eyes, you'd be able to see Michael left me, not the other way around. He wanted this divorce because he is a stubborn, bullheaded Irishman, and now he can have it! Because I sure as hell don't want him anymore, not after he hurt and humiliated me like he did in his hospital room." That's when I started to cry and with my tears flowing off my cheeks I harshly ordered, "You may inform, Mr. Carr I will be returning on the 25th, for one day, and he may come that afternoon at 1:00pm to get his things. I will be here to allow him access to his belongings. Oh yes! If he doesn't make it on the 25th, there won't be another chance because I will have already thrown his belongings into the Goodwill box. 'Capiche!' Jimmy!"

He stood there speechless and dazed for a moment, then as meek as a kitten he replied, "I'm sorry, Christina! I don't want us to be fighting also. It's just that I can't stand to see the two of you apart like this, especially since I know you two belong together. What I don't understand is why can't you see Michael is the best thing that's come into your life, since Tony's death?"

I wiped my eyes with a tissue as I turned toward Jimmy and replied, "I know you're right Jimmy, but I've tried to make Michael come back to me. He's refused and I've given up. So now, for the sake of my sanity, may we please drop the subject of Michael?"

With a frustrated tone he answered, "I don't like this one-bit Christina, but I will honor your wishes."

I smiled, "Thank you Jimmy and I apologize for my outburst, it was uncalled for and you didn't deserve it."

"That's all right." He replied with a smile. Taking on a curious tone he continued, "The Grammy Awards Ceremony is going to be held on the 27th this year, so why are you coming home on the 25th?"

"I'm only coming home for that one night. It's Johnny's birthday and I promised to spend it with him. Now would you get out of here so I can get ready."

"If I must!" He whined as he left me to get dressed.

Johnny looked like a knight in shining armor in his black tux, as he stood at my front door that evening, and that southern boy smile he wore was enchanting, to say the least. As I greeted him, his eyes lit up the night when he saw me in my low cut, black silk, evening gown, "You look absolutely gorgeous tonight, Christina." He said as he gently pulled me into his arms. "I know you said we must remain friends until our divorces are finalized, but I can't help myself. I'm so madly in love with you I want to shout it from the rooftops."

At that he kissed me with such passion I was left breathless, and as I began to return the passion in his kiss I heard, "Ahem! Ahem," from behind me, "Excuse me!"

I turned to see Jimmy standing behind me with his hands folded while tapping his left foot, "I'm sorry, Jimmy. Did you want something?" I asked with a slight touch of sarcasm.

"I just wanted to know what time you plan to be home tonight. You're leaving in the morning, remember?"

I chuckled my reply as I led Johnny by the hand, "Don't wait up 'mother-hen'." And off we went.

American Goddess

As we drove off, I took Johnny's hand in mine and said, "You're spoiling me, and I'm going to miss this while I'm away."

"I'm glad!" He replied with a gentle squeeze to my hand.

"So where are we dining tonight?" I asked with curiosity.

With a mysterious expression he answered, "Since you're leaving in the morning, I planned something extra special for tonight."

"Hmm," I replied with a smile. "This sounds like an interesting evening already."

We chatted as we drove and before I knew it, we were parked at a lover's lane over-looking the city of New Paltz, from the top of Mount Minnewaska. Once Johnny turned off the ignition, he climbed out of the car, went to the trunk and returned with a blanket and a picnic basket. He then laid the blanket on the hood of his car and called me out into the cold, now snowy weather, for dinner on the hood of his car.

I looked at him as if he were insane and said, "You want to eat dinner here?"

"Yes! Come lay on the hood and look at the stars with me."

"But there are no stars, Johnny!" I protested, "And this has got to be the coldest night in twenty-years."

"Come on, I'll keep you warm." He insisted as he rubbed his hands together.

Reluctantly, I agreed and took a seat beside Johnny on the hood of his car and thank God at least that was warm. Johnny produced a bottle of champagne and a bucket of K.F.C. I started to laugh as I kissed his cold cheek and said, "You're too much! And this is great, Johnny. Thank you for thinking of it."

Johnny was so suave and debonair as he served dinner and drinks that night that I didn't mind the cold at all. After our meal, he raised his glass and said, "I'd like to make a double toast tonight. First, here's to the most incredible woman I've ever known. Second, here's to the new Assistant Coach of the New York Mets, as of 10:00 this morning."

I hugged him with excitement as I exclaimed, "Congratulations, Johnny! I didn't know you were after that position, why didn't you tell me?"

"Because I wanted to make sure I could nail the position on my own merit, not on your recommendation."

I hugged him again, "I understand completely Johnny and I'm so happy for you."

With that, somehow our hug became an embrace, then gazing into my eyes he said, "Being up here with you tonight reminds me of the night we planned our future together on the balcony of your penthouse, do you remember?"

Lovingly gazing back into his eyes, I replied, "How could I forget that night Johnny, it was one of the most precious nights of my life. Just remembering it brings tears to my eyes."

American Goddess

"I love you, Christina!" He said as he began to gently kiss me. All at once, he pulled himself out of my embrace and reached for his neck chain. Taking off his grandmother's ring, he took my hand and as he held the ring over the ring finger of my left hand he said, "Christina, will you say you will marry me as soon as our divorces are finalized, so I may place this ring back on the finger where it truly belongs?"

With tears of joy streaming down my frozen cheeks I shouted out, "Yes, Johnny! I will marry you!"

Immediately he pulled off my wedding band, and he slipped his grandmother's ring on my finger, and as tears welled up in his eyes he said, "This time this ring shall stay on your finger, and we will spend the rest of our lives together. I promise you this Christina."

With that I kissed him passionately, and we just held one another in a loving embrace as we watched the snowflakes falling, until I could take the cold no longer.

It was 2:00 am when Johnny returned me to my front door. We kissed once more and promised to meet back at my home at 3:00pm on the 25th, which would be Johnny's 42nd birthday. We gave each other one last longing look, kissed and simultaneously said, "I love you."

He just smiled gently, turned and walked away. I stood at my open door watching him leave and I felt like I was floating on cloud nine. I was in love again when I closed that door and headed for my room. Unfortunately, I was intercepted by Jimmy's keen radar, and before I could close and lock my bedroom door, he had one foot in it.

I tried to push harder on the door hoping he'd pull his foot out and go away, but of course he didn't. Instead he yelled, "My foot's in the damn door you stupid ass! Now open this door so we can talk girlfriend before I have to slap you."

I opened the door to let him in and as I started to undress, I said, "Well come on in! You might as well climb in bed with me, or neither one of us is going to sleep tonight."

Looking at me strangely he said, "Aren't you going to shower first?"

I laughed as I answered, "I didn't work up an ounce of sweat tonight and I'm too tired to bother."

All at once, "Ahhh! No! No! It can't be!" Jimmy screamed. "Don't tell me that's his grandmother's ring you told me about, on your finger?"

"Calm down, Jimmy, and I'll explain."

He gasped as he softly said, "I'm calm girlfriend, now start explaining."

"Okay, now I will tell you just one time and please no questions tonight. Johnny has asked me to marry him and I've accepted. Now goodnight." And I turned off the light.

American Goddess

Everything was quiet just long enough for me to think I got away with it. Then all of a sudden, the light came on, "Are you, nuts!? You're not even divorced yet and you're already engaged! I can see some old patterns emerging here, that's for sure."

I interrupted, "I thought I told you no questions?"

"I'm not asking you anything smart ass! I'm telling you!" His voice calmed as he continued, "I've listened to you, now it's only fair you listen to me. Agreed?" I nodded 'yes' and he went on, "Good! First thing I want to say, if you genuinely love this John then I will have no choice but to accept him as a part of our family. All I ask is that you search your soul on this one, because I think it's a 'biggie' for you right now."

I looked at him with bewilderment as I sarcastically exclaimed, "I have no idea what you are talking about, Jimmy. So if you're trying to say something profound, at least have it make sense."

He hugged me gently and said, "Oh God, what did you do with this girl? She's so wise, yet so dumb." Grabbing my shoulders, he continued, "Christina, just make sure you're really ready to give up on Michael before you go running off with your Johnny. I wouldn't want you regretting something you may still have the power to change."

I kissed him tenderly, "Thank you, Jimmy. I guess that's one of the reasons I love you so much. You never cease to give me something to think about."

I flicked off the light, "Now go to sleep."

"I love you too, Christina."

"Shh! Goodnight."

"Goodnight."

Not four hours later, Joe along with my orchestra and me, were on our way to L.A. And thanks to Jimmy I had a lot to consider. But after arriving in L.A. and only spending ten minutes with Barbara, I forgot everything Jimmy said. As a matter of fact, I was so caught up in feelings of joy just from seeing Barbara, that as we sat on her living room sofa talking after rehearsals that night, I forgot about Jimmy completely.

That was until Barbara said, "Christina, I love you, and I want to really talk to you now from one friend to another."

"All right!" I eagerly agreed with a smile.

"I was on the phone with Jimmy last night and he told me everything that's been going on with you and your men. And I've got to tell you, we're both very concerned about you, so won't you please tell me what's really going on?"

My smile vanished as I replied, "I don't believe him! Why did he have to call you?"

"He didn't," she answered. "I called you last night and Jimmy took the call. I asked him if there was any truth to all the rumors John was back in your life. And you know Jimmy, that's all it took, and he was telling me everything."

American Goddess

"Yes I know Jimmy," I said with a smirk.   Taking on that air of confidence I present so well I continued, "Barbara, let me put your mind at ease.   You know me, and I'm telling you I have it all under control."

A bright smile appeared on her face as she replied, "Enough said!"

As our conversation went on, I thought, 'Boy that was a close one! I don't have a clue as to what the hell I'm really doing!'

The two of us had our Grammy presentation roles down pat within the first week and it was 'fooling around on the set time,' from there on in.   We hammed it up so much that second week, that every night another goofy story of the two of us fooling around on the set of the Grammys hit the evening news.   This was the kind of news coverage I didn't mind, and the public loved it.   Before I knew it, the 25th of February came and I was back in my Hudson River Valley home, waiting for Michael to show up for his belongings.

I waited without Michael showing up, until the clock hit 1:05pm. That's when I immediately stormed up to his closet and began packing his belongings for the Goodwill truck, as I bitched to myself, "Why you, bastard!   I can't believe you could hate me so much you won't even face me to get your things."   I could not hold back my tears as my thoughts continued, 'Why, Michael?   Was I really so terrible?' I went for the phone, picked it up and started to dial his number.   'Ding dong!   Ding dong!' went the doorbell and my heart stopped.

I just dropped the phone, quickly wiped the tears from my face, and hurried for the door knowing I gave James and Carman the day off.   When I reached it, I took a deep breath as I grabbed for the doorknob, then exhaled as I opened the door to find Michael standing there, looking like the perfect Marlboro Man in his cowboy hat, blue jeans, and red plaid, flannel shirt.   He nodded to me and said, "I'm sorry I'm late, I was held up crossing the bridge."   As I stood there speechless, he looked at me strangely, "Is it still all right to get my things?"

I snapped out of whatever it was holding my tongue to say, "Yes it's still all right, Michael, come on in.   I was just packing some of your things myself."

He followed me up to what once was our room and went straight to work packing his belongings.   I sat on the bed watching him for a few minutes before breaking the silence, "I tried not to disturb your stuff, so you should find your things where you left them."

While on his knees in the closet he glanced up at me, "Thank you, I appreciate that."

While I had eye contact, I couldn't help but ask, with a flair of sincerity, "So how have you been, Michael?"

Looking back down at his packing he answered, "Well, thank you."

American Goddess

With a cheerier tone I added, "How's Tess doing?   I've been so busy I haven't had the chance to call her."

I heard from the closet, "Fine."

I let a few more minutes pass before saying, "Is it going to kill you to talk to me Michael?"

"No, Christina, it's not going to kill me, there's just nothing to say."   He abruptly answered.

"Nothing to say!   Michael, I'm still your wife, how can there be nothing to say?"

Closing his last suitcase, he said, "I think I have everything, so I guess I'll see you Friday morning at the courthouse to finalize our divorce."

I stood up as he began to leave the room and said, "Is that all you have to say, Michael?"

He turned to me with a tear in each eye as his strained voice cracked, "I hope your new husband can make you happy, Christina.   Cause God knows I never could."

"That's not true!" I protested only to be interrupted.

"There's nothing left to say, Christina, except goodbye."   Turning away from me, he headed toward the door as he continued, "Now I really have to go."   With that I helplessly watched him walk out of my life and with him went part of my soul.

I just sat on the bed without moving or even thinking until I heard the slight beep of the alarm, which indicated the opening and closing of the front door.   It was only then that I thought to go after him, but by the time I reached the front door, he was pulling away.   I gazed longingly as his white Mercedes coup convertible, vanished into the snowy, wooded, scenery and I remembered a song I once sang to Johnny, 'The Love I Lost.' and I thought, 'I was wrong, Michael.   You're the love I'll never forget.'

My thought was interrupted by the appearance of Jimmy's car coming up the driveway.   He parked quickly then ran up to where I was standing with a desperate look on his face.   Knowing that look all too well, I immediately became alarmed and it showed in my tone when I said, "What's wrong, Jimmy!?"

The panic in his voice confirmed my fears as he answered, "Where's John, Christina?   It's an emergency!"

"He's not here yet!" I answered quickly.   "Why?   What happened, Jimmy?"

He nervously replied, "His son John Jr. called your office number.   He said he tried to call here but couldn't get through."

"What did he say," I asked anxiously?

"He said his mother is in the hospital on her death bed because of a suicide attempt.   He went on to say he came home from school to check on her because of the deep depression she was in that morning, and he found her in the bathtub, with both wrists slit."

American Goddess

"Oh God, no!" I cried in horror, and putting my hands to my face I exclaimed, "What has my reckless behavior caused now!?"

"Don't you dare start that now!" Jimmy demanded. "If you try blaming yourself for this, you're only going to make this entire emotional mess worse for John when he gets here."

I looked at him strangely and snidely remarked, "Since when are you so worried about Johnny's feelings?"

"Since I heard the anguish in his son's voice." He snapped back sarcastically.

Feeling the fool, I replied, "I'm sorry, Jimmy! I shouldn't have said that. I don't know why I keep jumping on you?"

"I do," he replied sadly. "It's because unconsciously you and Michael are both blaming me for your breakup."

Before I could even analyze my thoughts for a suitable reply to Jimmy's remark, Johnny pulled up the driveway and we both headed for his car. As soon as I reached him, I calmly explained what had happened. I could see the anguish taking over his expression as I told him of Mary's condition; so, I gently kissed his cheek and said, "I'll have my crew fly you to your family right now."

He looked at me with confused eyes, and with the fearful voice of a little boy who was being forced to face the unknown said, "Will you come with me?"

I gazed at him tenderly, "You will have to do this on your own, Johnny. I'm afraid my shadow over your life has caused your family enough pain, and I'm the last person any of them needs to meet right now." I held him tight for a moment, then turned to Jimmy and said, "Jimmy, would you please drive Johnny to the airport while I arrange for his flight?"

Jimmy agreed as Johnny protested, "Won't you at least come to the airport with me?"

"No, Johnny." I replied weakly, "I can't right now, but I'll be waiting to hear from you. So please call me when you know something." He looked so sad as he climbed into Jimmy's car and without either one of us saying another word; I watched as they drove down the driveway.

When they were out of sight I turned and quickly walked back into the house, where I immediately called Pierre and had him arrange for Johnny's flight to Virginia. As I hung up the phone I thought, 'God, please help Mary come through this.' Then I thought. 'What's wrong with me, Lord? Why do I destroy everyone I care about?"

As I sat there at my desk, I morbidly began to chuckle to myself as I solemnly thought, 'Oh Well! Game's over and it looks like you lose all the way around once again, Christina.' Then all at once it hit me like a lightning bolt sparking an explosion in my mind and I thought, 'Not yet, you haven't! You still have one more chance to win

American Goddess

this game lady and you better make it good!'   With that thought in mind, I reached for a pen and paper and began to turn my feelings into lyrics.

I had been writing for only twenty minutes before Jimmy entered the house and yelled out, "Christina!   Where are you?"

"I'm in my office!" I yelled back continuing to write.

Jimmy entered my office and as he approached me he said, "I thought you'd like to know the crew was ready when we arrived, and they took off immediately."

"Thank you, Jimmy."   I replied still not breaking my concentration as I continued to write.

He leaned over my shoulder and with a curious tone asked, "What are you writing?" And all at once, came that oh-so-familiar, melodramatic screech, "Ohhh no! What on earth are you doing now?"

I turned to him calmly, "What's it look like I'm doing, Jimmy?"   I knew from his expression he immediately took offense and I thought, 'Oh God!   Here we go.'

As he shouted, "It looks like you're getting ready to make a damn fool out of yourself again!   Don't you remember what happened the last time you sat down and wrote a song to that asshole?   Don't you realize what kind of power you hold in the position you're in right now?   His wife just tried to kill herself, his children are devastated, he's half out of his mind, and you're writing words like that to sing for them all to hear!   Think about what you're writing, and the harm those words could do."

I fired back, "Damn it, Jimmy!   You don't even know what you're screaming about!   So if you're not going to at least be helpful, then please just shut up and let me finish what I'm doing!"

With indignation he snapped, "What!   I don't know what I'm talking about!   How could you say that?   For **God sake**, wake up girlfriend, don't you remember your late husband Tony!?   He died because you had to sing a song to your precious Johnny once before!   What do you want to do, kill a few more innocent people?"

Struggling to keep my composure I stood up, grabbed him by his shoulders and calmly said, "Jimmy, for the first time in months I know what I'm doing.   So would you please just trust me?   Trust me and help me because I could sure use your help right now."

He shook his head in frustration, and gently smiled as his eyes began to radiate the kind of love that only comes when you can trust someone with your life.   From those emotions he softly said, "What do you need girlfriend?"

I joyfully kissed his cheek and with excitement answered, "I need you to help me create the most beautiful symphony ever written to accompany these lyrics."   Then, showing him my almost finished product with great enthusiasm, I completed my sentence with, "and we only have two hours."

427

American Goddess

Wide-eyed, he gazed at me and said, "I don't know how I let you talk me into these things, but let's do it!"

Just like the old days, we sat down together and worked the magic that made our music famous. Not twenty-four hours later we were in our L.A. studios with my personal crew, putting it all together from stage props to the color of my eye liner. I was determined even if it killed us all, to have everything perfect for the following nights live, world-wide, broadcasting of the Grammy Awards Ceremony. And after thirty-six grueling sleepless hours, we emerged with a masterpiece.

CHAPTER 50

It was 6:00am February 27th, when we completed several, nearly perfect rehearsals. Gazing at a crew of totally exhausted, yet jubilant people I proudly said, "Great job, guys! Now let's get some sleep and meet me in the backstage setup area of the Grammys at 2:00pm. We'll have to start early, we have almost as much to do setting up for the change in tonight's performance, as we did getting this song ready."

Their faces went white, and as they all gazed in shock at me. My orchestra leader Joe Aiello came out from the speechless crowd of professional performers to say, "Christina, I mean no disrespect, but this is the Grammys you're talking about. Everyone is expecting us to perform the Grammy nominated song, 'Love Grows in the Arms of Peace' tonight. What you are asking us to do is unprecedented, and I'm not sure we can go along with it."

Jimmy jumped in to add, "Not to mention the legal ramifications, or the fact that your professional credibility is on the line."

Pondering their opposition momentarily and realizing they were absolutely correct, I turned toward them all and said, "We're all friends here, so I'm going to be

428

American Goddess

honest. I know what I'm asking you to do for me is historic. But I swear, this means so much to me, I'm willing to stake my reputation on it. So now, I'm asking you all as my friends to help me pull this off!"

Jimmy yelled, "I'm with you, girlfriend!" and simultaneously his sentiments were echoed throughout the room.

That evening's Grammy Awards Ceremony was incredible! Barbara and I were so captivating as the hostesses, we kept the audience filled with the excitement of each moment. With six Grammys already awarded to me for the soundtrack, 'One Voice, One World and Love Enough for All' before it was even my turn to perform my number, it certainly appeared the night belonged to me. I became so high and confident with each triumphant, self-gratifying, moment of that night; that, I pranced on and off that stage, glowing and gloating like I was the **superstar of superstars**. That was until I received my cue to prepare for my performance. For it was at that moment, I remembered humility and fear, and I thought, 'Oh God! Please don't let this backfire on me.' Leaving the stage to Barbara, I rushed off to get ready. Jimmy was pacing nervously when I reached my dressing room. But as usual, in the pinch, he pulled it together and quickly helped me begin to dress in the costume we created only hours earlier. As Jimmy slid the glittering, silver, elastic straps, of the sandal woven silver ankle boots, over clear sheer stockings and attached them to a black bridal garter, I climbed into my skin tight, all lace, silver satin gown that hugged my feminine curves to just past my knees, and of course there was my famous slit up the front. Sewn to the gown were diamond studded hands, which cupped my breasts and held them in the most flattering position. While Jimmy and I did our part, Ann Markle removed the golden turban scarf I wore that evening, to reveal the hidden, one-thousand, individual, strands of diamond braids, which cascaded down the elbow length of my full bodied, dark black, hair. And when topped off with the perfect makeup, I looked like a **goddess** as I headed back to the main stage.

Three minutes later, I was taking a last-minute deep breath as I listened for Barbara's cue for the curtain rise. My heart was pounding as I heard Barbara say, "Ladies and gentlemen, as you are aware, my co-host tonight is a woman of many talents, but one of them I know to her dismay is not the ability to stay out of the tabloids. Have you all read of her latest dilemma? The poor dear girl has suffered the embarrassment of having two, extremely attractive men, publicly brawling over her affections. Well, I don't know about you, but I wouldn't mind a dilemma like that for myself!" Once Barbara had them laughing, she continued, "And now, without further ado, I would like to introduce my dear friend and co-host to perform the Grammy nominated best song of the year, 'Love Grows in the Arms of Peace.' Ladies and gentlemen, please welcome the incomparable, **Christina Powers**!"

American Goddess

The cheers rang out as the house lights went down.   While the curtains went up, the stage lights shone on me to cause my attire to flareup like the sparks of a comet's tail soaring through the heavens.

"**Da-da-dumm-di-de-dumm!**" Began the orchestra with an unexpected thunder and as the violins rose in unison with an unfamiliar melody, so did the sudden sharp squeals of the now shocked on-lookers.   As the sounds of their displeasure echoed throughout the auditorium, flowing from my heart came the sounds that could subdue the gods as I began to bare my soul in song to the world.

First, the tempo started smooth and soft, then slowly began to build as I sang, "**I was standing at the door, with tears in my eyes, when you walked away from me, vanishing like a ghost, into a hazy mystery.   Leaving me only, lonely and lost!   Did you ever care, to count the cost?   Now since you've been gone, like my troubled history, I'm living in shadows of solemn misery.   But yet I wonder is there a way to make you see, this love of ours is destiny!   Then echoes of love ring out in my mind, causing past passions to flair, burning in me everywhere, just to leave me longing and bare, with no one to care.**

Now I've waited at home, but you wouldn't phone, you've been playing a part, which has wounded my heart.   Cause like a fool, I was thoughtless and cruel, never thinking of what you went through.

Now I know!   Oh yes I know, it was our love, that was meant to grow.   So I've tried every day, in the most simple way, to say I love you and ask you to stay.   But with each failed attempt, I've driven you further away.   Further and further away.

With my arms rising to accompany the heights of my vocals, "**Now I cling to the memories of passions which once was our love, for the 'thunder, the lightning', that crashed up above.   For the wonders, of the heavens, your touch has revealed, and for the fires, of the love, your steps have concealed.**

That's why I'm singing a plea, oh baby sweet baby come home to me.   Darling I fear, without you my dear, this lifetime will crash and burn in despair, leaving us both so empty and bare, with nothing to spare, till neither one of us will be able to care, anymore."

At this point the tempo slowly drops off, then begins to climb once again and so did the passion of my voice, "**Or was this just a game of love lost!   Leaving broken hearts to be tossed, and memories of dreams, floating away on streams!   Like shattered bits, of our past lives revealed, blown by the whims of the winds as we sailed, and it scattered our futures till we had to break free, leaving only the remnants of what was to be.**

So baby... sweet baby..., say once for me, now and forever, this just can't be!   For where once abound love endless and true, now only dwells pain, reserved for the fool.   My soul cries in despair, with each moment you're not here, cause I know in my heart, we must never part.   For it's not destiny, for us to be free, so I'm saving my love, for what I know will be, your love in this lifetime forever with me.   Chorus: Forever and ever with me.

I pleaded with my body shaking as I reached for the sky with my voice,

American Goddess

Oh baby... sweet baby..., bring your love home, and promise oh promise never to roam, for I'll always be here, forever to care.   Forever and ever, to care.

At that point, the symphony takes over like 'thunder and lightning' as the lights and my body movements accompany the rhythm in perfect harmony, to spin a web of passion in an attempt to hypnotize the entire audience.   Dramatically everything stops.

This time I lead the tempo of the orchestra's rhythm, as it climbs to the range of my vocals, **"Now I'm lying in bed, with thoughts in my head, I'll fight for the right, to live for the light. The light that is shone, when only you're home.   So baby... sweet baby..., forever and ever come home.** accompanied by chorus: **Forever and ever come home!"**

Or we'll play these love games, time after time, forever and ever, till I make you mine. {**"Chorus: Forever and ever!   my love!"**} `Cause you' re the spark in my heart, the flame of my soul, and I know the power, of the love we share, can conquer the darkness and the pain that dwells here.   So baby...., sweet baby...., won't you come home, bring your love too, take all I am, this whole lifetime through, forever and ever, never to part, forever and ever come unbreak my heart.

Although you say when it's over, one must let it die and never, ever, dare to ask why!   But I refuse to see, our love will not be, not when it's as strong, as the forces of the sea.   `Cause together there's still, mountains to climb, the source of infinity, together we'll find, and the secrets of divinity are yours and mine when we leave our bodies behind.   Then meet in the air, souring high in the sky, where two become one spirit, body and soul, on the wings of our passions, filled with dreams still to grow. Soaring higher and higher, {**"Accompanied by chorus: Forever and ever my love!"**}

Now the tempo of the rhythm begins vibrating the auditorium, **Oh baby... sweet baby...,** why can't you see, destiny calls your love back to me.   That's why I won't waste a breath, or shed a tear, if it won't bring your love, near my dear.   For our hearts are pure, and our souls are free, so won't you come dance, a heavenly dance with me. Above the universe, come climb and see, beyond the hands of time with me.   Where the light we find, will help you see, this love of ours is meant to be.   That's why for your love, there is no shame, so if I must, I'll take all the blame, to bring you back to me, with feelings so free, forever and ever free for me.   {**"Accompanied by chorus: Forever and ever my love."**}

Now tears flow down my cheeks as I muster all my strength for the finale, **Oh baby...baby..., sweet baby...** won't you come to my door, and lay with me, just once more, to taste my love, from its core.   {**"Chorus: Forever and ever."**}   Then I know you'll be mine, and together we'll shine!"   {**"Accompanied by chorus: Forever and ever my love!"**} I know there's no way, I can force you to stay.   But I'll put it all on the line, to try and make you mine.   That's why I'm singing a plea, oh baby... sweet baby... come home to me, where we'll forgive and forget, as we soar like the angels and never regret. {**"Accompanied by chorus: Forever and ever we'll never regret our love!"**}

I strip away pride, as I vow to stay by your side, now and forever your bride. {**"Chorus: Forever and ever my love."**}

American Goddess

Cause there's no mountain of stone, nor a tower of steel, can stand in my way, when I know what's real. Yes I am bold, I've faced bitter cold, but if life's lived without you then our stories untold. So baby..., sweet baby..., save me please save me and don't let our story grow old. My heart is down on one knee, and I'm singing a plea, oh baby sweet baby come home to me, and promise oh promise never to flee, forever to care and always be here, forever my love. Now I'll be waiting at home, for you all alone, preparing a place, for you in my space. Where I'll show you a life, without all the pain, where love abounds, despite the rain. For in your eyes I see visions of futures to grow, alive in the heavens forever we'll go, where the stars, in our eyes, forever will glow and the light, of our love, forever will show.

Together we'll sow, the seeds of our love and together forever we'll watch from above. Forever and ever I'll give you my love. Forever and ever my love. {"Slowing tempo. Echoed by chorus."}

Now I'm singing a plea, where I'm begging you please, bring your love home to me. {Now slowing to nearly a whisper} Forever and ever! Michael, my love!

When I finished singing, the roar of the crowd was deafening. They loved my performance so much; I was given a standing ovation through eight curtain calls. Three of them were before the broadcasts commercial break, with one still continuing when the cameras returned. Finally, Barbara calmed the audience down enough to say, "Bravo! Christina! That was fabulous, but we wanted last year's nomination, not this year." And the audience signaled their approval!

At that point, Barbara came back with, "Now, to present the award for best song of the year, please welcome Elizabeth Tayler and Michael Jackson."

Jointly they read the nominees, then Elizabeth opened the envelope and announced, "And the Grammy goes to Christina Powers, for 'Love Grows in the Arms of Peace.'"

As the cheering rang out again, I ran onto the stage from behind the curtains, took the Grammy, kissed Elizabeth, then Michael. Turning to the mike I said, "Thank you so much for this evening and your appreciation. Now I just want to say thank you to everyone who helped make this song what it is and ask for your forgiveness for not performing 'Love Grows in the Arms of Peace' tonight. But this was my last chance to touch the heart of the man I love. So now, I'm going to take these precious gifts that were so graciously given to me this evening, and I'm going home with love in my heart." Looking straight into the camera I added, "'Cause Michael, my love. I'm praying you're going to be there." With that, I blew kisses and waved as I said, "I love you, America! God Bless! And thank you again!" I walked off the stage leaving them cheering.

American Goddess

CHAPTER 51

It was 1:00am Pacific time when our flight left L.A. for Stewart Airport, and the whole world knew I was hopefully rushing home to Michael's arms.   My emotions were raw, and my energies depleted from exposing my soul with such passion, it was all I could do just to get on the jet.   Once seated, I placed my head on Jimmy's shoulder and stayed that way almost the entire flight home, without speaking for hours.

As I laid there with Jimmy gently stroking my head, I prayed, "God, please let him be home?   Because if this doesn't do it, nothing will, and you know how much I love him.   God, I miss him so desperately, I'm honestly afraid I won't be able to live with the pain, if he's not.   So please let him be home when I get there."

But I found no solace, nor comfort in that prayer, because I still feared Michael's seemingly unbendable Irish pride could keep him from coming home to me.   Then I decided I'd rather think of Michael being there, and the moment I did, my mind went wild with thoughts of passion.

As I envisioned my thoughts, I began to take notice of the movements of the aircraft which seemed to have been in a circling pattern for quite some time.   I glanced at my watch which read 9:00am Eastern Standard time and I thought, 'We should have landed by now?'

Curiosity took over as I sat up, reached to lift the window cover so I might glance out and just as I did, my new pilot, ex-lieutenant Todd Deyo opened the cabin door and said, "Excuse me Ms. Powers, but there has been a slight change in our landing plans."

"Is everything all right with the jet?"   I asked in haste, as I quickly stood to my feet.

"The jet's fine Ma'am, it's the weather."   He replied calmly.   "Snow has been falling heavily over the region for hours now, and the tower at Stewart has rerouted all traffic to LaGuardia.   So I'm afraid your arrival home will be delayed for quite some time."

"What!?"   I snapped with frustration.   "I'm not waiting another day to get home! Are we over the airport right now?"

He was surprised by my angered response and I could tell as he cautiously answered, "Yes, Ma'am."

Studying his eyes I asked, "Todd, are you capable of landing this craft in a blizzard?" Without blinking he boldly replied, "Yes, Ma'am!"

I smiled at him confidently, "Good!   Then let's go get you clearance."

Jimmy wore a stressed expression as he followed us into the cockpit and watched in silence, as I had Todd radio the tower.   Once he had the chief traffic controller on the radio, Todd handed the extra headphone to me.

433

American Goddess

I clumsily put it on and said, "Hi, this is Christina Powers, with whom am I speaking?"

"This is Chief Controller Colonel Jeff Roberts, Ms. Powers.   How may I help you?"

"Well Jeff, you could have a runway opened for us so we may land."

A polite yet firm voice replied, "I'm sorry Ms. Powers, but it's been deemed unsafe at this time.   That is why your pilot has been ordered to proceed on a new coordinate."

To that I simply replied, "Jeff, forgive me, I'm not normally this abrupt, but if you don't have a runway cleared for us in ten minutes, then I will see that the President hands me your career on a silver platter by this evening.   Capiche!?"

Without a crack in his voice he replied, "Completely Ms. Powers, and you may inform your pilot to prepare for decent."

With a pleased tone I replied, "I thank you Colonel Roberts, and I will see that the President thanks you for me as well."

Todd smiled with amazement as he looked at me and said, "You might want to buckle up, this may be a slippery landing."

I studied his eyes once more, "You can handle it, can't you?"

With a confident nod he answered, "Sure thing, Ma'am."

I chuckled and said, "Great, then we'll go make ourselves comfortable, and Todd, please call me Christina.   I prefer that to Ma'am, 'cause I'm sure not as old as the word implies."   Then I nudged Jimmy whose mouth was on the floor and continued, "It will be fine, Jimmy.   Now come on, let's go put our heads between our legs."

A nervous laugh began his come back, "Why, so we can kiss our ass's goodbye?"

"Don't panic I'm only kidding."   I replied with a chuckle.

He shook his head and said, "I know you want to get home, but don't you think you might be pushing it."

I smiled devilishly and said, "When have you ever known me not to push it, Jimmy?" Then turning to my flight crew, I continued, "Now do a good job boy's, 'cause I need to get home."

I reassured Jimmy with a confidant rustling of his hair, as I buckled him in and said, "God willing we'll be down safely in ten minutes, so try not to worry."

"Thanks, that helps a lot!"   He replied with a nervous look, "I should have stayed at the party with everyone else."

"What?   And miss all this fun?   That's not like you, Jimmy."   I said with a smile as the jet began its descent.

We were doing fine, even laughing as our ears popped on the descent, that was until the tires hit the pavement and Jimmy screamed, "Oh God!"   as the jet immediately began a dramatic zig zagging slide down the runway.

It wasn't two seconds before both of us were screaming out prayers as we were forcefully thrown from side to side in our seats for what seemed like an eternity, before finally slowing to a jerky stop. Realizing the danger was over I swallowed my heart, turned to Jimmy who was as white as a ghost, and started to laugh.

As soon as he caught his breath, he slapped my shoulder and shouted, "You think that was funny!?"

"No, just ironic!" I answered still laughing, "That little ride made me realize I love life too much to give up on it, even if Michael doesn't come home."

Once unbuckled, I went right into the cockpit to congratulate my crew on a job well done, then I said, "Now would someone please open that door so I can go home."

The moment I saw the intensity of the blizzard we were walking into, I grabbed Jimmy's arm for strength and with a hopeless expression said, "He's not coming back, Jimmy."

"Yes he is, Christina." He answered with a big confident smile.

"No, he's not, Jimmy." I insisted with tears welling in my eyes, "Strangely, I've come to see the weather as the ultimate forecast of things to come in my life. And this storm is telling me to give it up girl, `cause you don't have a chance in hell of him coming home!"

Jimmy squeezed my shoulder as we walked toward our warmed car and said, "Girlfriend, I know how much Michael loves you, and I know he's going to be there. So stop torturing yourself and I'll have us home in thirty minutes."

I kissed his cheek, "I hope you're right Jimmy, but the weather hasn't lied to me yet."

At that point, we reached the car and began to creep our way through the storm. As Jimmy drove, I pulled an envelope out of my purse, addressed it to Johnny, slipped his grandmother's ring in and had Jimmy stop at the first mailbox. I wrote nothing because there was nothing that needed to be said. Then, as I placed Michaels' ring back on my finger, I thought, 'Whether you come home or not Michael, I will never take this ring off again.'

Jimmy's thirty-minutes turned into an hour and thirty-minutes, before we pulled up to the house. As the large garage door began to open, my heart instantly pained. I turned to Jimmy with tears now streaming down my cheeks and cried, "His cars not here, Jimmy."

Jimmy looked at me before pulling into the garage, and said, "Well his car may not be here, but look who just stepped out onto the front porch."

I turned quickly to see my beautiful man coming toward our car. My heart filled with excitement as I screamed, "Michael!" At that I jumped out of the car without my jacket and dashed through the snow toward him.

My sad tears instantly turned into joyful ones, as I leaped into his arms still screaming, "Michael! Michael! I love you! I love you, baby! I love you! Thank God, you're home!"

American Goddess

"I love you too, Punkie!" He shouted back as he lifted me into his arms. Gazing deep into my eyes he gently continued, "I love you more than life itself, and I'll never leave again, not even in 'death'."

He kissed me with such passion that our souls were instantly whole again, and I knew he was home for good.

I clung to his neck as he held me like a babe in arms and carried me toward the house. When we reached the door, he opened it, and charged up the staircase leaping three steps at a time.

He didn't slow his pace until we entered the bedroom, where he kissed me deeply as he laid me on the bed and softly whispered, "Don't move, Punkie." Then he proceeded to undress.

I watched in loving awe, as this god in the flesh tossed his clothing to the floor one piece at a time. Finally, he dropped his last garment, and with the look I'd die for, returned to begin gently undressing me. I couldn't help but to lavish kisses all over his chest as he slipped the gown, I still wore from my Grammy performance off my shoulders to expose the now hard nipples of my firm, bare, breasts. As he leaned over to slide the gown from my hips I longingly and softly stroked the rest of his masculine body.

Slipping my last stocking off, he snuggled next to me and with a gentle air of dominance said, "Christina, you're my wife, and I'm proud to tell the world how much I love you. All I ask is that you let me be your husband, not just someone who waits at home."

"Oh, Michael!" I cried as I gazed into his eyes, "I love you, and I'm so sorry! I was blind and foolish Michael, but I'm not anymore! I want you to be my husband Michael, and I'm going to learn how to be your wife. I promise!"

Sliding his leg over mine he said, "Before we go any further, are you still on the pill?"

I lifted my head to kiss him passionately, and lovingly gazing into his eye's said, "No, Michael. I stopped taking them when we stopped making love."

He smiled peacefully and said, "I have a condom, let me get it."

I gently grabbed his hand and with loving conviction said, "Before you do, Michael, I need to say something. There is only one thing that could make my life totally complete right now, and that would be to conceive your child." Taking on an air of certainty I continued, "Please hear me, Michael? I have prayed and meditated nightly for weeks now, in an attempt to heal my body. So that if by the grace of God destiny brought us back together, then I would be able to carry our child. I know in my heart, Michael, that your seed will grow in me and I'll not only give birth, but I'll live through it as well." At that point I couldn't stop my tears as I continued, "Please, Michael plant your soul in mine so we may give birth to an angel."

American Goddess

He kissed me with joyful wonder and said, "I love you and I feel it too, Punkie!   Deep in my soul, somehow, I know you are healed!   So with all my love I will give you my seed, and just like you sang, we'll watch it grow together."

From that moment on we were swept up in a whirlwind of pure passion and unconditional love. I was in heaven, as over and over we shared our love, and we didn't break our embrace until Jimmy came banging on the door shouting, "Hey guys!   It's 7:00pm and you have got to get up now! It's urgent!"

As I said, "What is it Jimmy?"

Carman fixed all your favorite 'aphrodisiacs' for dinner, and it will all be ready in twenty minutes.   So would you guys like to be served dinner in bed or would you prefer to join me in the dining room?"

I lifted my eyebrows as I looked at Michael and with a seductive smile said, "The menu sounds inviting, but I'll leave where we eat, up to you."

He returned my seductive smile with one of his own as he replied, "Let's go down and eat, then I can carry you back up again.   That was fun!"

I nibbled his nipple then said, "Aw, now I can't wait to go down, just for the trip back up."

"Bang, Bang," came the second round of knocks as Jimmy shouted, "Do you guys hear me?"

"Yes." Michael replied, "We'll be right down, Jimmy."   Then we quickly showered and headed for the dining room.

As soon as we entered the dining room, Carman ran to us with tears in her eyes, hugged us both and said, "God has answered my prayers by bringing the two of you together again!   Now come sit and let me serve you the first dinner of your new lives together."

I kissed her and said, "Thank you my sweet Carman that was beautiful."

Then Michael added, "Won't you and James share our meal with us tonight?"   Her face gleamed as she gracefully accepted.

We took our seats as Carman ran for James and our meal.

Jimmy entered the room with Pierre and a handful of newspapers, took his seat beside mine and with an excited tone said, "You guys are not going to believe today's headlines.   Listen to this one, '**Only Christina Powers could pull off the controversial substitution of a Grammy performance and be given a standing ovation**.' Or this one, '**Christina Powers' daring Grammy performance last evening, establishes her as the icon of the twenty first century, as millions of worldwide viewers immediately swamped their local radio stations with requests for the song the callers themselves called, 'Michael My Love'.**' Can you believe this response from your fans?"   Jimmy continued, "It's phenomenal!"

American Goddess

Michael and I were both shocked as headline after headline repeated the same sentiments.

After reading the articles I looked at Michael with a concerned expression and said, "We need to really talk Michael, because this is scaring me."

He leaned over to kiss me, "I'm here now Punkie, and you don't have to worry about anything tonight, except me.   We'll deal with the world tomorrow."

I was truly comforted by his words when I returned his kiss and said, "You're right Michael, because there's one thing I've learned, everything else is secondary to us."

Pierre now sitting next to Jimmy jumped in, "Christina, I've never seen anything like it.   I watched the Grammys in our main auditorium with about 200 other employees and the entire place was stunned when you started singing a different song, but one minute into it they were all crying and loved it.   You are truly loved by so many people Christina and I love you too my friend."

"Thank you, Pierre that was sweet."   I leaned over kissed his check then Jimmy's, "and it's good to see you two together.   I'm so happy for you both."

Just then, Carman entered the dining room with a feast fit for two kings.   When our meal was complete Michael did exactly as he promised, swept me off my feet and carried me back to our boudoir, where we continued exactly where we left off.

It was 4:00am when I slipped out of Michael's sleepy embrace and tiptoed through the dimly lit bedroom to the master bath.   When I returned, Michael was sitting on the edge of the bed, and as I approached, he beckoned me to sit next to him.   I submissively took my place beside him and he gently drew me into his embrace.   I snuggled to his chest as he tenderly said, "I love you Christina, and it's now my turn to say I'm sorry.   I know I wasn't there when you needed me either, I guess I was afraid to hear what you had to say.   So Punkie, if you're up to telling me what happened in Saudi Arabia, I'm up to listening."

I held him tightly as the frightening; bizarre memories of that trip and the one that followed came flashing back.   It was at that moment I finally felt safe enough to show the fear I truly felt, and I began to weep as my body trembled from the images exploding in my mind.   I told him about Mohammed and how he nearly took my life three times. Then I said, "It was so awful Michael; I remember every second of it. First, he tried to throw me off a roof top, then he tried to blow me up in a helicopter, and the last time I saw him he tried to kill me barehanded. I had to hold a sword to this throat to stop him. It happened in Iraq when I went to free the hostages.   He led me into a massive library, where he proceeded to go through a large old book of Islamic Prophecies.   Finding what he was looking for, he handed the book to me and said, "You read Arabic, read it for yourself."

I took the book and glancing to where he was pointing began to read, "**At the time of the alignment of all celestial bodies within your solar system, the king's daughter shall rise to power and she shall be known to the world as the 'Angel of Peace'.   This one is the mother of the Messiah, who is the daughter of the king and the descendants** of Abraham.   Her power is in her tongue of many languages, and she alone shall marry the true heir to the throne of Solomon and bear him his first male child.   The child she brings forth in the wilderness shall be the pure descendant of Adam's seed, and he represents the true returning of the Prince of Peace.   He alone will finally usher in the Heavenly Millennium of paradise on earth foretold by the prophets."   As I finished, I closed the book and said, "I'm not usually this bad with puzzles, but I still don't get the connection."

Looking at me as if I were an imbecile he said, "You, Christina, are that woman! The one the world calls the 'Angel of Peace', and I am the rightful heir to the throne of Solomon."

I shook my head in total disbelief as I replied, "You really put all this together just from a newspaper article which called me the 'Angel of Peace?'"

Taking the book from my hands, he placed it on the shelf.   He turned back toward me, and taking me in his arms, he lovingly said, "That is not the only reason my love, you are rising to power in the world whether you realize it or not.   The alinement of the planets spoken of in this prophecy will take place in May of the year 2000, and you are also fluent in many languages.   I know everything there is to know about you.   I have always known in my heart; you would one day be my bride and bear me my son. Together through peace, we shall conquer the world and give it to our son, who will lead all peoples into a millennium of peace on earth under Islamic rule."

I had to push hard to get out of his loving embrace as I said, "Please, Mohammed, not so close, I like my space. I have got to say for someone who supposedly knows so much about me, then how come you overlooked the fact I can no longer bear children. Doesn't that put a damper on your theories as to whom you think I am?"

He was slowly coming closer to me with a very hungry look on his face as he said, "I know about your injury.   If you let me, I will teach you how to heal your wounds from within.   You can tap into the divine power, which is yours, and I know how it is done.   Then, you will be able to bear our child.   The secrets of God's power are at your disposal Christina, it lies within."

He was still slowly continuing to walk toward me as I backed away.   Putting my hands up to slow his descent upon me and thinking quick I said, "You're not listening Mohammed, I just told you I can no longer bear children."

I could see in his eyes he was beginning to become upset with my resistance when he said, "You're the one not listening!   You already have the power to heal yourself."

As my back reached the wall I said, "Well, I hope I can grow back a uterus then, because that's what it's going to take."

His face became as white as a ghost.   He took a deep breath, while hovering over me shouting, "What are you talking about!?"

American Goddess

That was the moment I knew I was heading for trouble and I thought, 'God, please help me out of this one!' As I said, "I nearly lost my life last year in an attempt to have a child. While I was unconscious, the doctors had to perform a hysterectomy on me in order to save my life."

His eyes became red with anger. With one hand, he took my left shoulder and flung me with such force, I went flying into a bookshelf sending the books toppling on top of my head. Laying under a pile of books I heard him yelling, "This can't be! I thought you were the one!"

As I looked up from under the books, I could see he was coming to give me some more, so just as he reached down to grab me, I pushed up with my legs knocking him into another bookshelf. I scrambled to my feet, went running for the door and of course it was locked. I turned quickly to see where he was, and he was coming right for me. I screamed out with all my might, "Stop this, Mohammed! This is **madness!** Help! Someone help!"

He put his hands around my neck and began to try and chook the life out of me. I kneed him right in the nuts and pushed him over backwards. I ran to an open window and tried to climb out. He grabbed my waist and flung me against the wall. Looking around quickly, I spotted two swords mounted on the wall. I grabbed for the sword which hung on the wall about four feet from me. When I had it, I swung around as fast as lightening just in time to hold its sharp point right at his throat. He stopped dead in his tracks and as I backed him into a bookshelf I shouted, "Get it together Mohammed or I won't hesitate to use this! I'll do it right now you crazy bastard!"

Suddenly, Lussein with twenty guards, burst into the room and shouted, "Mohammed, if you take her life now, you will be destroying all our future plans. Calm down my brother and know one day, you will have your revenge on this temptress from the depths of hell. Besides, I told you she was not the one, now leave her alone and let her go back to her demon possessed nation where trash like her belong."

The thought of Lussein's prediction at that moment, nearly made me cut Mohammed's head off right on the spot. It took all my self-control not to lunge forward and plunge the blade right through him, but I thought, 'It's not worth it Christina, he's just an evil man.'

Within moments Mohammed calmed himself down and with his angelic voice said, "I'm sorry if I hurt you, but your news was devastating, and it made me upset."

Still holding the sword to Mohammed's neck I looked toward Lussein and said, "You told the President you would release the hostages to me, now I'm tired of fooling around here, so please release them and let us leave at once."

With a deadly serious look in his eyes, he said, "If you give your word you will not tell anyone that Mohammed was here, you may leave now."

440

American Goddess

I smiled and reassuringly said, "You've got a deal!"

He clapped his hands, turned to his guards and shouted, "Take Ms. Powers to the airport immediately."

"Wait just a minute," I demanded.   "I'm not going anywhere without the hostages."

Lussein walked right up to my face while I still held the sword and said, "You really are a gutsy broad."

Without blinking once I replied, "Thank you!   I'll take that as a compliment, now please bring out the hostages."

He smiled and his smile seemed to hold a slightly detectable glimmer of admiration as he said, "It's all right to go with the guards Christina, the hostages are already boarded on your jet and waiting for you."

Looking into his eyes, I knew he was telling the truth; so, I thanked him as I handed him the sword. Then I turned and confidently proceeded to walk out of that room with my head held high and an air about me, as if I had total control over this insane situation and not thinking of losing my composure the entire time.   But inside, I was a frightened little girl."

When I finished telling Michael everything I started to cry again as I clung to his chest.

Michael rocked me in his strong comforting arms until I cried it all out.   Michael was listening intently as I told him the whole nightmarish ordeal. He looked baffled by the time I finished speaking then said, "My God, I could shoot myself for not being there for you."

"Don't say that, Michael, you're here now and that's what counts."

He kissed me gently, "What do you think it all means?"

I hid nothing of myself as I gazed into his eyes and said, "I'm not sure, honey.   But something tells me I'll be hearing from Mohammed Fehd again, and that thought leaves me spooked."

"Don't be."   Michael said angrily, "Because I'll kill anyone who tries to harm you!"

I hugged him again, "I love you Michael, and believe it or not, I know I'll always be safe with you beside me."

Then gazing into the open thoughts on his face, I could see there was one more thing that needed to be settled.   So I tenderly took his hand in mine and said, "Michael, baby, I don't want to keep anything from you ever again.   So if you will allow me, I'd like to tell you about my past relationship with John Everett."

He looked lovingly at me as he said, "Just for the record please answer two things for me, then I'll never mention it again.   Did you sleep with him since we've been together, and do you still have feelings for him?"

441

American Goddess

I kissed his cheek as I proudly said, "The answer is no baby, to both your questions." Squeezing his arm as I continued, "Michael, I've only loved and longed for you since our first kiss."

He sighed then smiled as he said, "I was pretty sure of the answers, but it's sure good to hear them from you." He kissed me passionately, then gently rubbing my belly added, "By the grace of God, we have the union of our love growing inside of you right now Punkie, and I know we're going to have our family."

He took on the sincerest expression I'd ever seen from anyone as he continued, "Christina, I want to take you and our child away from here. I want us to have a normal life without all the craziness. I guess what I'm asking is for you to give it all up for me." As tears welled in his eyes, "Can you do that? Can you give it all up for a family life with me?"

"Yes," I cried as I wrapped my arms around his neck. "Oh Michael, my love, I would put a match to it all and watch it burn, if it brought our souls together for all eternity."

His face lit up with joy as he said, "Then let's start by leaving Jimmy in charge for a year or so this time, while we go start our family. We could tell him at breakfast and be on our way by lunch."

I was surprised by his spontaneity, so I chuckled as I said, "Michael, if you want to leave now and never come back, then I'm ready. Because I'll follow you to heaven or hell, and all you have to do is lead."

"Oh Baby, I love you! You just made me the happiest man on earth." He said these words as he laid me back onto the pillows, and once more began to fill me with his essence. The love we felt as we made love after the conversation of that morning had a divine power to it that was beyond words.

Later that morning over breakfast, Michael informed a now stunned Jimmy of our immediate plans to leave, then said, "Jimmy, I'm not sure how long we're going to be gone or where we'll even end up, but I do know it's our turn to find a life. So we're just leaving it all in your hands until we know for sure what we're doing."

Jimmy looked sad as he replied, "I understand guys, and I'll take care of everything, because I know this is the best thing for both of you." He started to cry, "It's just that I'm going to miss you guys. You're my family and we've been apart for so long already."

I hugged him and said, "Jimmy, we're not leaving you, just the madness of this lifestyle. You will always be my brother and welcomed into our home wherever we live."

"That's right!" Michael added, "And like I said Jimmy, it's not forever and we'll let you know what's going on with us when we know."

Still sad, but at least smiling he murmured, "I love you guys, and I hope you find the happiness you both deserve. All I ask is that you don't forget me."

I laughed, "Forget about you. That's impossible, Jimmy."

American Goddess

We all started to laugh, then Michael stood up and said, "Now that that's settled, I'll go make some travel arrangements."

"So you do know where you're going." Jimmy interrupted. "Well at least tell me where you're headed?"

Michael smiled mischievously as he said, "Don't worry about where we're going right now Jimmy, I want to keep it a surprise for my wife." He kissed me and added, "I'll be back in a few minutes then we'll get out of here."

"Already," I said with a surprised tone. "Shouldn't we pack some things first?"

He smiled again and said, "Carman already packed for us and James is putting the suitcases in the trunk of the car right now. I've also called our head of security Frank Rossi and he is working on getting us out of here without the press finding out."

I kissed him back and said, "You're not wasting any time are you?"

Jimmy interrupted again, but this time his voice was panicked, "Wait, what about the song? Michael, we have millions of fans wanting to buy that song, you can't take Christina away without recording it first."

"I didn't know it wasn't recorded." Michael answered, then turning to me with a look of frustration, "Christina, if we stay for that we may never get out of here."

I thought for a minute then said, "I got it! Jimmy, have a recording and a video cut from the tape of the Grammy performance to release to the public as a single. Title it, 'Michael My Love.' Then feature it as the lead cut on a greatest hits' soundtrack. Just don't include any of the cuts from the 'Halloween in Hell' soundtrack."

"That's a great idea." Jimmy said with a big smile, "I could have it ready in no time that way." Then with the flick of that wrist he added, "Just like I've always said, you are a 'fucking genius', girlfriend!"

Michael was still standing next to me when he said, "I think I'll go make that call before something else comes up."

And just as he said those words, Carman entered the dining room with the cordless phone and said, "Excuse me Christina, but the President is on the phone for you."

"What now!" Michael said with disgust.

I took his hand reassuringly, "Don't panic Michael, let's just see what he wants." I took the phone from Carman and said, "Hi George, how are you?"

"I'm great now that Kuwait is liberated, and the ground war is over. But how are you? Did Michael come home?"

I chuckled with a sense of relief, "Yes, he did George, and it's sweet of you to call and ask."

"Well, you only happen to be the second hottest story in the headlines, and the last report I heard, neither one of you showed up for the divorce proceedings. And since I was calling anyway, I thought I might be one of the first to find out for sure." At that,

443

his voice took on a tone of sincerity as he continued, "You're a good friend Christina, and Barbara and I are very pleased for the both of you."

I felt honored hearing words of friendship coming from our nation's leader, so I gracefully replied, "I thank you again, George.   It means a great deal to me to be considered your friend.   Now I don't mean to rush you, but let's get to the other reason for your call, because Michael and I were just on our way out the door as you rang."

He chuckled, "We're not ones to waste time beating around the 'bush' are we?"

"You got that right!"   I laughed, as Michael rushed me with his hand gestures.

"Now, for the other reason for my call; I would like to bestow the Distinguished Citizens Award upon you, during tomorrow night's Presidential address to Congress and the nation.   I also plan to take this occasion to announce my bid for reelection.   I hope to have you standing beside me at the news conference to follow, so you may throw your full support behind my reelection bid at the same time."

"I'm more than honored George," I said with surprise.   "But I'm not sure I can make it.   Let me have you speak with Michael; he's handling my schedule now."   I handed the phone to Michael who was motioning, 'no, no,' with his hands as I whispered, "You have to talk to him Michael, because I don't know what to say."

Michael took the phone with apprehension, "Hello Mr. President, how can we help you?"

The next thing I knew, we were on our way to Washington for dinner with the President and First Lady for that very evening.

To our surprise that evening's dinner included not only the President and First Lady, but also every Republican politician and foreign dignitary in Washington.   Only Michael and I were not aware of this fact until we entered the dining hall, and the entire dinner party rose to their feet applauding.   Then, as we were led to the President's table, we were greeted by everyone we passed with warm smiles, handshakes, and words of admiration.

This only intensified when we reached the President who raised his glass to us and said, "Dear Friends, I would like to make a toast tonight to a woman, who in her young life span has gone from being called the 'queen of bleeding heart liberals' to the 'angel of peace'."   Smiling he continued, "Well now it's my turn to coin a phrase at your expense Christina, only this time I bestow it upon Michael as well.   Here's to 'the most passionate couple on earth'.   Bravo Michael and Christina!"

We drank to the toast and were cheered again, "Bravo Michael and Christina!"

After dinner, we were formally invited by the majority of the foreign diplomats whose citizens I helped release from Iraq, on behalf of their nation's leaders to visit their countries.   Michael and I were overwhelmed by the reception we received that night, and it didn't end there.   For the next evening, after the President's address we were given another standing ovation.   Only this time, it was by all of Congress broadcasted on national TV, when with Michael beside me, I received the Distinguished Citizens Award for my contributions in freeing the multinational group of Iraqi hostages. At the informal news conference/celebration which followed, the President once again grandstanded Michael and me, as he announced his bid for reelection.

Immediately after his announcement he turned the podium over to Michael and me both by saying, "Barbara and I have invited our dear friends, Michael and Christina Powers Carr, to share their thoughts with us this evening. So now I'd like to turn all attention over to the Carr's."

Everyone applauded as I moved to the mike still holding Michael's hand and said, "Good evening friends. And it truly has been a good evening, especially for Michael and me. That's why we'd like to say a special thank you to the people of this great nation of ours for your love and support. We'd also like to thank the President and First Lady for giving us this glorious evening. Now I'd like to come to the other reason I'm standing here tonight and that is to throw my full political support behind the President's bid for reelection. Believe me; I don't take this endorsement lightly either. I have come to this decision from having worked side-by-side with the President and seeing first-hand how he deals with our country and world issues. I believe he has proven himself to be a great leader, and that is why I am able to say, George you have earned my vote."

With that I received a standing ovation. That evening, we were catapulted as a couple into the political spotlight by the arms of the entire Republican Party as they embraced us whole heartedly. Let me tell you, 'the smellier stuff' was flowing so thick that night, that even my ex-husband, Senator Lee Bradford invited Michael and me to a party in the President's honor, at the Republican Party's New York Headquarters in Manhattan. Michael took all this attention quite well, that was until the President came to us privately and said, "Michael, I'd like to have you and Christina join me at one more campaign banquet tomorrow evening."

Michael didn't even look at me when he said, "I'm very sorry Mr. President, but Christina and I are leaving for our second honeymoon right at this very moment, so I'm afraid we can't make it to any more gatherings."

George looked at me with a surprised expression and said, "But Christina, I was counting on your support. That's why I've already made a public announcement that the two of you would be accompanying me to tomorrow night's banquet."

I smiled mischievously, "Good try George, but I'm sorry you took the liberty to do that without discussing it with us first. Like Michael said, we were just leaving, so I'm afraid you're going to have to make our apologies for us." I kissed his stunned cheek, hugged the First Lady, took Michael's hand and said our goodbyes as we swiftly made our way through the crowd.

American Goddess

It wasn't until we were sitting comfortably, snuggled in each other's arms and in the air that I said, "So where are you taking me anyway?"

He smiled mischievously and answered, "First tell me, how long it will be before we know for sure if you're pregnant?"

"Probably another twelve days.   Why?"   I asked with interest.   "What does that have to do with where you take me on our second honeymoon?"

"It's only because I don't want you to over-do it, that's all."

"Okay smarty, but you still haven't answered my question, where are we going?"

"Well I wanted it to be a surprise, but I guess I can tell you now.   It was the strangest thing.   The minute we decided to try and have a baby again something told me to prepare a family tree for our child.   So I thought what better way than to go back to the countries of our forefathers to make one.   That's why I've planned two weeks in Ireland to find my side of the tree, and another two weeks in Italy to find your side of the tree."   Smiling with excitement he added, "So what do you think?"

I was speechless realizing for the first time that I have never told anyone, not even Michael who my true parents were.   His smile turned into a frown as he said, "Gee!   I thought it was a good idea."

I still said nothing, not knowing how to answer him until with a very concerned look he said, "Christina, what is it?   You look as though you've seen a ghost."

Gazing up into his eyes with intensity I said, "I have Michael, and it's a ghost from my past."

With a wondering look he asked, "I don't understand what you're saying, what ghost from your past?"

I slipped out of his arms so I could sit up and look directly into his eyes as I said, "Michael honey, do you remember I told you that I was keeping no more secrets from you?"

His expression went from wondering to concern as he calmly said, "Yes."

"There is one more thing about myself that I have never repeated to a soul since the moment I heard it.   I guess it's because I never really wanted to face it myself, so how could I talk about it?"

Michael knew I was struggling when he took my hand and said, "Punkie, I will love you no matter what ghosts may haunt you.   I thought you realized that by now?"

I smiled, "Yes Michael, I do realize that, and I know there's nothing that we can't conquer together."   Kissing his cheek, I continued, "That's why finally, I know I have the courage to face what I'm about to tell you."   At that, I proceeded to tell him everything Frank Salerno said to me that awful day so long ago. Then I told him that Barbara gave me my birth certificate and a letter from my true mother after Frank's death.

Michael was overwhelmed by my revelation and with a look of wonder the first thing he said was, "Oh my God, you are the daughter of a king."

446

American Goddess

"What?"   I said with nervous surprise.   "Why would you say that?"

He shook his head with concern, "The first thing that came to my mind was that nut Mohammed's, prophecy."

Looking at him intensely I asked, "What do you think it means, Michael?"

"I don't know Babe, but something tells me the answer lies somewhere in Ireland."

"Ireland!   Why there?"   I asked with a baffled expression.

"Don't you see, this changes things."   He said with wide eyes, "We've known I've had a full-blooded Irish heritage all along, and now we know your father was also Irish. So all we need to do is discover your mother's true bloodline and I think we'll find our answer."

I shook my head with a confused look, "I think you lost me.   What does my mother's heritage have to do with Mohammed's prophecy?"

"I don't know, but something tells me we'll find out when we know more about your true mother's bloodline."

American Goddess

CHAPTER 52

Our two weeks in Ireland turned out to be quite interesting as we discovered many similar thing's about our forefathers. For example, on Michael's side the Carr's were both from the same village as the Kenny's on my father's side were. But the most interesting of all, was our discovery that my mother's biological father could have been a man named John O'Hara, who's family also happened to originate from the same Irish town and if that were true, then I would also have an Irish heritage.

The afternoon we made this discovery we were in the hall of records in Dublin, and I turned to Michael with a bewildered expression and asked, "Michael, what do you think it all means?"

He smiled gently, "I think it means that Mohammed was wrong, it's not his child in the prophecy, it's ours."

I looked at him strangely, "I still don't get it. What does the fact that I'm Irish and not Italian have to do with Mohammed's prophecy? I'd have to be Jewish to fit his prophecy." Then I laughed out loud, "You can't think the Irish race could be the true lost tribe of Israel, do you?"

He answered with a profoundly serious tone, "I think anything is possible. Furthermore, I think God is telling us that it is our baby who is destined for great things."

I kissed him, smiled and said, "I am sure of that, Michael, without a prophecy. What I'm not sure of, is weather I'm even pregnant or not yet."

He laughed, hugged me and replied, "Well why don't we go back to the hotel and use that test kit you bought, so we can finally find out."

I kissed him again and with a sexy smile said, "Let's go for it big boy." And off we headed for the motel.

I came out of the bath holding a test strip in two fingers, and as I reached an anxious Michael I said, "Keep your fingers crossed, honey."

"How does it work?" He asked intently.

"We wait two minutes and if it turns red then it's a go, but if it turns blue then we keep trying."

We were breathless as the color began to take on a greenish tint, then to our dismay it turned utterly blue, and as soon as it did, Michael whined with disappointment, "Oh no!"

I threw the strip away, hugged him, and said, "It's all right, honey. It will turn red; I know it will." Then I slipped my hand into his pants, "And we'll just keep trying until it does."

American Goddess

He kissed me, swept me off my feet and as he headed for the bedroom he said, "You can bet your sweet buns on that, little girl!"   When we reached the bedroom, he placed my feet on the floor as his lips engulfed mine. He released his hold of me and gently commanded, "Dance for your Daddy and take those clothes off."

I immediately preformed for him the way only I could, and the last garment stripped was his bikini brief. I found myself on my knees in front of the man I loved, and I began to devourer him with every drop of my passion.   In perfect rhythm I lusted and longed for each thrust he gave me.   As I looked up into his eyes he said, "I love seeing you in that position baby. You are so beautiful Christina. Oh yea...make love to your Daddy baby girl."

We were nearly to the point of ecstasy when he stopped our dance and gently lifted me from on my knees and placed me on the bed.

"Oh baby." I moaned as he began to gently caress my breast.   I felt so much love for him that I surrendered totally to his slightest touch and as his lips surrounded my engorged nipple my body became electrified.   "Take me Daddy, I'm yours." was all I could say as we became one.   And for the next three hours he seduced me with his every movement.

It was 9:00pm when we decided to wash and go for dinner, and as we strolled hand in hand, through the historical streets of 'Old Dublin' I said, "Now that we have our family trees, what would you like to do next, Michael?"

He put his arm around my shoulder and said, "I've been thinking about that.   And I think that since we're in Europe anyway, we should try to visit as many of the nations whose leaders have invited us.   They all want to thank you formally for helping free their citizens and I think it's only right that we go.   At least until you've conceived; and we can check that every couple of days.   This way, we still get to be together and we can enjoy Europe at the same time.   What do you think?"

I kissed him with excitement and said, "I think it sounds great, baby!   I've wanted us to be able to go away like this forever."   The next morning, we were making arrangements to visit the heads of state throughout Europe beginning with England.

We arrived in London on March 17th, 1991, and we were treated like royalty, even by members of the royal family themselves, including the Queen.   She made me an Honorary British Citizen for my gallant efforts in obtaining the freedom of thirty-six British citizens.   It was incredible, everywhere we went the people of England greeted us with cheers as they held signs which read, **"We love you Christina and Michael!"** And the headlines read, **"America's first couple; 'Christina and Michael Powers Carr' are welcomed with opened arms by all of Britain."**

We stayed two weeks in England then it was off to France for two weeks.   Since I still hadn't conceived, we decided to take our traveling to Italy.   From there it was off to

American Goddess

Spain, Greece, Germany, Switzerland, Russia, Romania, India, China, South Korea, Japan and in September we ended up in Australia.

Everywhere we went the reaction to us as a couple was the same, warm and loving. It seemed that as the fame of 'Michael My Love' spread, so did the mystique of our relationship. It was as if the whole world decided to place us as a magical couple on top of an international pedestal to be admired and idolized. The treatment we received was so overwhelming and enticing that we became perfect at playing the part of America's royal couple.

We arrived in Australia on September 7th, at 9:00pm, to a hero's welcome at the airport. We were taken by an official government escort to our hotel in beautiful downtown Sydney. As we checked in, Michael grabbed the usual pile of telegrams waiting for us at the front desk and we headed to our suite. After settling in I began to open the telegrams.

With the first one I opened, I turned to Michael with a nervous tone, "Oh no Michael, it's from him."

"From whom?" He asked as he walked toward me.

"Prince Mohammed Fehd," I answered. "Listen to this, '**Dear Christina, I see you have successfully salvaged your pitiful marriage. What a shame to waste such energy and passion on a common peasant, when you could have had a god. At least your foolish actions have proven to me that you are definitely not the woman I thought you were. Once my eyes were opened, I was finally able to find my true queen. That's why I took as my bride the daughter of King Sada of Syria, Princess Jasmine on August 25th of this year. I know she will bear the child I foolishly hoped would be ours, but I also know she will never fill my heart with the passion I felt just from kissing your hand. So regretfully, I must now say goodbye to my dream of you Christina, for it's time to fulfill my destiny. I also know I will always carry the pain of an unquenched flame within my soul for you my love. Forever, Prince Mohammed Fehd.**" "Can you believe this," I said shaking my head?

"Well at least it sounds like we won't be hearing from him again."

I chuckled, "I hope she gives him three hundred kids to rule the world; that ought to keep them busy for a while." At that we laughed it off.

But what transpired the following morning took the laughter away. It was 10:00am September 8th, when we took our seats with Australia's Prime Minister Mark Amentia, to view the extravagant parade which was held in honor of our visit. That morning Sidney was alive with the sounds of marching bands and shouts of admiration and love, for their adored visitors, 'Christina and Michael'.

As I sat there watching thousands of people cheering as they passed by, 'suddenly' it hit me, and my eyes were opened as if for the first time since we left Ireland. The awakening frightened me as I realized Michael and I were unconsciously becoming sanctimonious, as both of us were being sucked into the vacuous powers of international

American Goddess

idolatry.   And the speed at which we were catapulting toward our world image of some god like couple, was so phenomenal that I thought, 'Oh my God!   We're becoming just like Mohammed; thriving on the admiration of the masses and the power that comes with it, instead of thriving on helping the masses and the satisfaction that comes from it.'

At that moment, with that thought, I caught sight of an old gray-haired woman wearing shredded rags.   I watched as she began to slowly make her way across the street, right through the marching bands toward us.   As she came closer, I could see pain in her eyes with every step she took, and my heart went out to her.   She walked right past the Prime Minister's security guards and began to climb up the twenty or so steps toward where we were seated.   I was surprised no one stopped her, but I said nothing because I could not take my eyes off this pitiful woman.

I just sat there staring and when she reached me, she took my hand in her withered one, looked straight into my eyes and with a weakened voice said, "Christina my child, there appeared a great wonder in heaven, a woman clothed with the sun and the moon.   And under her feet and upon her head a crown of twelve stars.   And she-being with child cried, travailing in birth and pained to be delivered.   And there appeared another wonder in heaven and behold a great red dragon, having seven heads and ten horns and seven crowns upon his heads.   And his tail drew the third part of the stars of heaven and he did cast them to the earth."

Then she pointed one shaky finger at me as she continued, "And then the dragon stood before the woman who was ready to be delivered, to devour her child as soon as it was born.   And she brought forth a man child, who was to rule all nations with a rod of iron and her child was caught up unto God and to his throne.   And the woman fled into the 'mountains', where she hath a place prepared of God that they should feed her there a thousand two hundred and threescore days, at which time war shall breakout in heaven and it shall spill over onto earth.   But do not fear for God is with you my child."

With that she let go of my hand and as I began to shake, the medallion I found so many years ago with Tony, began to burn my skin.   At that split second, I quickly pulled the medallion from my chest, as I nervously turned to Michael, grabbed his hand and said, "Michael, listen to this woman!"   I turned back and my heart froze with fear for she was gone.   I looked at Michael again only this time I was as white as a ghost and I said, "Michael, something's wrong!   Please get me out of here!"

Instantly, without even asking me what was wrong, he made our excuses and had us swiftly escorted back to our hotel.   As soon as we entered the room Michael closed the door behind us and said, "What is it, Punkie?"

I clung to his chest for strength and answered, "Michael, something is telling me that our rise in popularity is a trap to keep us from having a child.   And as long as we

451

continue to stay on this course, I will never conceive our child." Then I looked into his eyes with fear in mine and added, "Michael, did you see that old lady?"

"What old lady?" He answered with a confused look.

A cold chill shot up my spine, "The one who was talking to me right in front of you."

He held me tight as he answered, "No Punkie, I didn't see or hear anyone."

I pulled out of his arms and proceeded to tell him what she said to me, and when I finished I said, "Honey, I don't know what's going on here, but I know I'd feel much better if we were home."

He had a curious look on his face when he said, "I think you're right we should go home. Only I think home should be our Catskill 'Mountain' House."

I hugged him and with a sigh of relief said, "Oh Michael, I love you! I feel a sense of peace already, just knowing where we're going."

He kissed me lovingly and excitedly said, "So do I, Punkie! Why don't we make our excuses and leave now?"

"Could we, Michael?" I asked eagerly.

"Sure we could."

"Great, then I'm going to go to speak with Frank our security chief, I'll be right back." I went right to Frank's makeshift office and when I walked in I said, "Frank, I want to speak with you in private. Michael and I want to go back home. Frank, I would like to ask you to arrange it so that we can enter the country without anyone finding out. Do you think you can arrange it?"

This beautifully handsome six foot tall man looked at me through eyes of pure adoration as he said, "Christina, I don't just consider you my employer, I respect you immensely and I consider you one of my best friends. I would do anything for you my friend. And I can assure you that no one will know you're back in the states."

I hugged him, "Thank you, how soon do you think we can get home?"

He smiled reassuringly, "You start packing and I'll start calling." And not two hours later **we were on our way home.**

American Goddess

In an attempt to avoid the fanfare, we decided not to tell anyone, except Jimmy and the proper authorities that we were returning home. Believe it or not at 1:00am on September 9th, 1991, we entered the country without one reporter finding out, thanks to my security chief Frank Rossi. Inconspicuously, we made our way through the airport and headed straight for our waiting car. Like two emotionally exhausted and mentally bewildered children, we drove off into the darkness hoping to find a place to hide and reflect. As we drove up the winding path of 23A to Tannersville and our mountain top hideaway, I took Michael's hand and said, "Michael, look at how beautifully the stars are shining tonight."

He brought my hand to his lips, kissed it and said, "Whoa, the sky really is bright! I can't remember seeing a night this bright since I was a child growing up on this mountain." Glancing my way with a relieved smile he continued, "And let me tell you Punkie, it sure feels good to be on familiar ground again. How about you? Are you feeling any better?"

I smiled my reply, "I feel like the weight of the world has been lifted off my shoulders, just from knowing we'll soon be home." In a serious tone I added, "But honey, I still cannot get that old woman out of my mind, and for the life of me I can't figure it out. Then I thought, if it really was a message of some kind, then why can't I understand it?"

"I've been thinking a lot about what she said." Michael replied softly. "Now I'm not sure, but I think I may have read something similar to her words in the Bible. When I get a chance, I'll take a look and see if I can find it. But as for making sense of it, maybe she was telling you the world's attention was like a beast. After all, she did come just as you realized we were being caught up by all the glorified notoriety, didn't she? So maybe she was saying this beast was somehow keeping us from having a child."

With a mysterious tone I said, "That's funny! I thought the same thing, but I dismissed it thinking it couldn't be that simple."

Just then we pulled into the driveway of Michael's family house and joyfully he said, "We're finally home, Punkie!" With that, we climbed out of the car and headed hand-in-hand toward the house.

Halfway up the walk I stopped, wrapped my arms around his neck and said, "I love you, Michael." Then I kissed him and added, "Maybe now that we're home, we'll be able to start our family."

He returned my kiss passionately, "I don't think we should waste one more minute getting started either." I laughed, then with a seductive smile shouted, "Last one on the porch has to undress the other." Then I took off running as I continued shouting, "With no hands!"

He charged after me and leaped into the lead just as we reached the porch. I jumped on his back shouting, "No fair! You have longer legs then I do."

I was still on his back laughing and nipping at his ear as he tried to open the door while twisting his head and saying, "I'm going to get you if you don't stop."

We entered that lonely, quiet mountain house with love, laughter, and renewed anticipation for our future family. The house was chilly when we raced in, so I quickly started making hot cocoa, while Michael built a fire in the bedroom fireplace. I had two buttered English Muffins to accompany our cocoa when I entered the bedroom. But as soon as I saw Michael through the fire-lit room, lying on the bed with nothing on, I knew we were not about to eat English Muffins. So, I placed the tray on the nightstand then slowly moved between the bed and the fireplace where I very seductively began to undress for my man. When there was nothing left to remove, Michael reached his hand out to mine. As I took hold of his hand, he pulled me into the bed and began to tickle me till I was laughing so hard, I was begging him to stop. When he did stop, he placed my hand on his now firm muscle and with a sexy smile said, "It's all yours Punkie, tonight and every night for as long as you can get it up."

"Wow, all mine," I replied with a big grin. Then figuring it was now my turn I added, "Good, then you won't mind if I break it off." I began to playfully squeeze his pride and joy as I laughed, "Tickle me will you, I know how to get even."

"Stop, Christina stop," he pleaded from between his laughter.

I let go and said, "Oh poor, baby! Do you need me to kiss it and make it all better?"

"I couldn't think of anything I'd like more." He replied with a sweet grin.

We found ourselves feeling so comfortable and free from being home, we spent the rest of that wonderfully romantic night, lovingly and playfully becoming one. Our love was so deep and peaceful that we both knew we were moving mountains, and two weeks to the date, the test strip I held confirmed I was pregnant. We looked at each other with our hearts in our eyes as we watched the thin strip quickly turn red. With tears streaming down our faces, we leaped into each other's arms screaming. I grabbed his hand and shouted, "Come with me!" I pulled him out the back door and began running into the sunshine toward the clearing in the back yard, which gazed out over the valley and the river below. When we reached it, I shouted, "Thank you, God! Thank you!" Then I leaped into Michael's arms still shouting, "Watch out world, because Michael and I are having a baby!"

Michael swung me around once and shouted, "Yahoo! My baby's having a baby!" Setting my feet on the ground, he lovingly gazed into my eyes, "I love you, and Punkie I don't think I could ever be happier than I am at this very moment." He kissed me deeply, then with tears in his eyes and a broken voice, "Thank you Christina, for loving me enough to bring me to my senses.   Since we've been back together, I can't remember what life was like without you."

I kissed him, "Michael, I love you and I'm so happy I could tell the world."

"I know how you feel Christina, but I think we shouldn't tell anyone until the baby's born."

I looked at him sadly, "You're right.   Damn Michael, we can't tell anyone."

He smiled, "Well one thing I do know we have to tell my Mom, Jimmy and Pierre or they'll never forgive us."

My face lit up again as I said, "We also have to call Barbara Goldstein, she is my step-mom remember.   And Eartha would kill me if I didn't tell her. Why don't we ask them all come for dinner tonight, then we can tell them together?"

"That sounds great!   You know they're going to be shocked."

I laughed then said, "To say the least.   Come on, let's go call them now."   And off we went back to the house like two happy carefree children, anxious to share our good news with the people closest to us.

Barbara and Eartha couldn't make it, but the rest did.   That night after dinner Michael and I ended up joyfully telling Tess, Jimmy and his new lover Pierre our good news.   They went wild with excitement for us at first, especially Tess.   But immediately after the enthusiasm of the moment passed, it was Jimmy who voiced the first concern by saying, "This is fabulous news guys, but aren't you putting yourself in danger?   I thought you weren't going to take that chance again, especially since you nearly died the last time."

Tess interrupted at that point with a powerful, "Oh My God!   Lord Jesus, Mary and Joseph!   Do the two of you know the chance you're taking?"

We both smiled with overwhelming joy radiating on our faces as Michael very calmly said, "Listen guys, we know this may seem extreme.   But what you don't know is both of us believe in our hearts that through the power of prayer and meditation, Christina has tapped into the essence of her oneness with the divine power of God. While in these meditative states of oneness, we believe she was able to heal her own wounds from within."

They were all speechless until Tess rose from her seat, came to hug us with open arms and said, "I love you both very much and knowing you both like I do, I know if you truly feel this strongly about this, then so do I.   But to play it safe I am going to be coming up here to help you as much as I can, Christina.   I may be seventy-seven, but after 10:00am I can still help with the chores.   For some reason God still keeps a lot of life in these old bones and I don't like wasting it."

American Goddess

I hugged her, smiled and said, "Thank you, Tess. I'm sure as time goes on your help is going to be more than just welcomed."

At that, Jimmy and Pierre echoed her sentiments with warm embraces until I said, "Come on guys, let's go on the deck for dessert; I made cheesecake."

"Cheesecake, that's my favorite." Tess replied cheerfully as she rose from her seat.

"Mine too!" I answered as I headed for the kitchen.

"Punkie," Michael interrupted, "Why don't you take everyone to the deck and let me get dessert?"

"I'll help!" Pierre added as he followed Michael into the kitchen. As they went for our dessert, Tess, Jimmy and I headed for the deck.

As we took our seats Tess lovingly took my hand, "I'm so excited that another Carr child will be carried to term in this old house. Did you know I conceived and carried all my children to term in this house?"

"You're kidding!" I said excitedly, "Oh please tell me Tess, where was Michael born?"

She started to laugh then said, "Oh my heavens! I haven't thought about that day in years. Michael was born in Benedictine Hospital in Kingston. Do you mean I never told you the story of Michael's birth?" "No, you haven't," I replied eagerly.

She smiled and said, "Oh God! You're going to love this story Christina, because that Michael of ours did things his way from day one. I was at the hospital in labor with him for twelve hours and then the labor just stopped. I stayed in the hospital two more days with no pain at all, so I was discharged. Joe, Michael's father started to take me back home and when we made it to the top of the mountain I went back into labor. Joe took off flying back down the mountain and was pulled over by the troopers, who ended up giving us a police escort all the way to the hospital. When we got there the doctor had already left and Michael was not about to wait, so he was delivered by a nun named, Sister Genevieve Clare." "Oh, No," I roared as we all started to laugh.

Just then Michael and Pierre appeared with our dessert. Michael glanced at me tenderly as he began to set the patio table and said, "What are you guys laughing about?"

"You" I chuckled, "Mom was just telling us the 'NOW' legendary story of your birth. It seems you've been a stubborn pain in everybody's ass since the day you decided to grace us with your presence." At that we all laughed.

Michael still gazing at me shook his head with a smile and said, "Normally I'd lambaste you for that one Punkie, but your smile right now is worth all the laughs in the world at my expense. Because you've never appeared more beautiful to me then you do at this very moment."

American Goddess

I began to feel flush by his words when I shyly said, "Oh Michael, that's so sweet I think I'm going to cry." And like a blubbering idiot I did just that. Only the tears flowed so hard that I started to laugh as I tried to say, "I'm sorry, it was just the sweetest thing anyone ever said to me."

Michael knelt down beside me slightly laughing, "I think I better watch what I say to you for a while." With that, we all laughed some more.

From that night on the three of them made it a point to be with Michael and me as much as possible during the entire duration of my pregnancy. It started with them spending the weekends with us. Then in
November they came to fix us Thanksgiving Dinner and stayed the whole week, which wasn't too bad; but when they came in December to spend Christmas week with us and didn't leave until the end of January, they were beginning to get on our nerves. But they meant well, so we said nothing.

In February of 1992, I was nominated for three Grammys, so we decided to take the week before the ceremony to spend it alone with Barbara at her Malibu home. We enjoyed one very relaxing night with Barbara, and the next morning Jimmy was at the door with Pierre and Tess. They wanted to surprise us and they sure did, by spending the rest of that week with us. At least Tess got to go to her first Grammy Ceremony, where I just happened to win three more Grammys for 'Michael My Love.' But the worst came when the three of them got together and decided that since my June 16th, due date was closing in; I shouldn't do anything strenuous for the rest of my pregnancy. So on May 1, 1992, forty six days before my due date they all moved in with us. "To help." As a matter of fact, I was being helped so well, that by June 6th, I cracked. The night before I was so uncomfortable that I didn't fall asleep until sometime after 5:00am, which was bad enough. But when a loud noise startled me awake later that morning, I decided I had, had enough help! So still not feeling well, I flew out of the bed and dashed toward the kitchen, holding my big round, sour belly all the way. When I reached the source of the noise, I found the four of them sitting around the table laughing. About what God knows, all I know is I didn't like it at all and I wasted no time in informing them of that fact when I shouted, "What the hell is wrong with the four of you? Are you trying to scare the baby out of me?" Directing my words straight at Tess, Jimmy and Pierre I continued, "And you three! I thought you came to help me, instead you're driving me nuts!" Now including Michael, I added, "All I hear from the four of you is, don't do that Christina you might hurt yourself, or go lay down Christina you need your rest. Do I look like an invalid to you people? Well I'm not!"

Jimmy stood up and calmly replied, "Well, what is it you'd like from us then, Ms. Prima-Donna?"

I gave him my 'don't mess' look and said, "Since you asked so nicely smart ass, it would be nice to have the four of you off my back for just ten minutes."

"Well!" Tess snapped with indignation as she stood up, "If this is the thanks we get for caring enough to disrupt our whole lives for your welfare, then I think I'll leave for more than ten minutes." And she started to walk away.

Realizing how I just spoke to the people I loved most in this world, I quickly said, "Tess, please wait! I didn't mean what I said to any of you. I love you all and I do know how wonderful you've all been. So won't you all please forgive me and ignore what I said."

She came over to hug me, "I had five children and I remember what it's like."

Then Michael wrapped his loving arms around me and added, "Would you like us to leave for a while so you can have some free time?"

I smiled softly, "No, honey. What I'd like is for you to take us all to Pizza Hut for lunch." Turning to the rest of them I continued, "Who's up for pizza?"

CHAPTER 54

We spent the rest of that beautiful sunny June day driving around the countryside. We had lunch in Albany, dinner in Catskill and didn't get back home until 8:00 that evening. I was so tired when we did get home, I headed straight for the bedroom and in minutes I was fast asleep. Only once again it didn't last. I found myself awake at 1:00am and this time my belly wasn't just sour, it was bursting with pain. I grabbed Michael's arm and shouted, "Oh shit! Michael, wake up! I think it's time!"

He flew out of bed and in ten minutes we were all on our way to Benedictine Hospital in Kingston, N.Y. I was checked in at 1:45am and as far as I was concerned, I was already in full blown labor, but to my dismay I was wrong, because the pain only increased as the night grew longer.

It was 4:00am when I was offered a spinal, but I refused. I was just as determined to keep my wits about me through this pain, as this child was determined to keep causing the pain. Michael held my hand through every joy filled tear of that very painful labor.   Finally, around 11:30am, I squeezed his hand extra hard and screamed, "Oh God!   It won't be long now."

He wiped the beads of sweat from my brow, kissed my forehead and said, "You can do this Punkie.   Just hang in here with me and we'll bring our baby into the world together."

I chuckled as I cried, "I'm doing just fine, Michael.   This is the purest pain I've ever felt and I wouldn't miss it for the world.   Ouch!"   And at 11:50am, on Sunday, June 7th, 1992, I thankfully heard the first cry of our beautiful new baby.   We both started to cry the minute the doctor handed us our five-pound thirteen ounce, blonde haired, blue eyed, baby boy.   My heart was filled with untamed wonder and joy, as I held our precious bundle of love.   I lovingly gazed at Michael who was gazing at his new baby with an expression of divine love on his face, and I thought, 'Thank You, Lord Jesus for granting our prayers and I vow to be the best mother I can possibly be.'   Michael gazed up at me and the second his eyes met mine, we both knew this was the happiest moment of our lives. I recovered so quickly; I was back in my private room with the baby by 1:35pm.   When we settled in the room, I took Michael's hand and said, "Would you like to hold your son?"   He looked at me with frightened eyes and replied, "He's so small.   I won't hurt him, will I?"

"No, silly" I chuckled. "Just cuddle him gently in your arms and he'll be fine."

Michael took him and the moment he did his face lit up like a Hollywood Premier as he said, "Christina he's beautiful and he's our little angel."

I watched in pure delight as Michael tenderly held his son and I was grateful to God I was able to give my Michael the son for which he so desperately longed.   We had ten minutes alone with our son, before the happy trio came tiptoeing in and as soon as they laid their eyes on him he won their hearts.

"God bless him!"   Tess said with tears in her eyes, "He is the most precious little thing I've ever seen."

As for Jimmy, he started crying before he saw the baby and it only got worse when he did see him.

Pierre came to hug me and said, "I'm so happy for you boss lady, that's one beautiful baby you just gave birth to."

I kissed his cheek as I replied, "Thank you Pierre, that was sweet and just in case you're not aware of it, I'm very happy you've joined our family.   You and Jimmy seem to be meant for each other, and I'm so glad I had something to do with bringing the two of you together."

Just then Doctor Hart entered the room with a slight tap on the door and a big smile, "Well how's that little man doing?"

"Great, Doc."   Michael gleamed back still holding our son.

American Goddess

Doctor Hart patted Michael's back, "I'm glad to hear it. Have you decided on a name yet?"

Michael turned to me, "I think we've chosen Tyler James, right honey?"

Just as I opened my mouth to answer, Tess said, "Tyler, I thought you were saying Taylor?"

I looked at her with pleasant surprise and said, "Tess, I never even once thought of the name Taylor, but I love it. Michael let's name him Taylor James Carr."

Michael turned toward Doctor Hart as he gazed down at the bundle still in his arms and said, "Welcome to earth, Taylor James Carr. I'm your Father, and my name's Michael." Now pointing at me, "You see that angel in the bed over there? Well she's your mother and her name is Christina." Kissing his forehead, he continued, "Taylor, my boy, there is nothing in the world more precious to either one of us then you little guy. I love you son, and I will always be here for you."

Tess kissed Michael's cheek then said, "Let me hold him please." With a proud smile, Michael handed Taylor to Tess, "Here's your grandson, Nanny."

With tears in her eyes she took Taylor, "He's an angel, Michael." When Jimmy finally managed to stop crying, he hugged me and said, "Great job, girlfriend! He's such a little doll and I'm so happy you'd think he was my son."

I kissed his cheek, "I love you, Uncle Jimmy."

We walked out of the hospital at 10:00am on June 9th, to the largest gathering of international reporters I had seen since my joint news conference with the President. The first thing Taylor James Carr did, on the front steps of Benedictine Hospital, was to meet the world. There had to be more photos taken of the three of us that morning then was taken of me all year long. We gave the world a fifteen-minute view into our private lives, and then we were helicoptered to our Milton home. From there we eventually managed to slip out of the Powers Compound, and we headed right back to our mountain hideaway. It was 6:00pm when we reached the driveway of our home and to my surprise the parking lot was full of cars. I turned to Michael nervously, "Oh no! The Press found us."

"Relax, Punkie!" Michael replied with a calm smile. "It's your in-laws. Since we never told them you were pregnant, they asked to come up tonight to surprise you with a baby shower and meet Taylor at the same time."

My adrenaline stopped flowing as I smiled with relief, "That's nice honey, but Taylor's sleeping and I didn't want him getting too much attention just yet, so if they start to get out of control I want you to say something, all right?"

"All right, but if you're uncomfortable, you can say something. They're your family now too you know."

American Goddess

"I know, it's just that your siblings think I'm nuts as it is; I don't want them thinking I'm a bitch too."

Starting to laugh he said, "Punkie, I don't care what they think because I know the real you." Then he kissed me and we headed in.

The family gathering that night turned out to be quite nice. Especially since I discovered when Michael's siblings weren't busy passing judgement on me, they were actually fun to be with. But the best was all the wonderfully, thoughtful and creative gifts Taylor received from his new family. It was the closest experience to a family of my own I had ever known. The love they bestowed on Taylor and I truly made me feel welcomed into the Carr clan. Of course, they all doted over Taylor, but not too much, and everyone had the chance to hold him including Michael's sixteen-year-old niece Michelle. But the best thing happened when Michael's eldest sister Carol was holding Taylor. She was rocking him in her arms as she walked him back and forth between the living room and dining room. During one of her trips she stopped in the living room where we were all sitting and said, "He's falling asleep Christina, should I put him in his cradle?" The minute she said cradle, Taylor opened his eyes, looked straight into hers and started to frown. Carol's face took on a shocked expression as she said, "This kid's is a freaking little genius!" Laughing, she turned toward Michael, "Little brother, I have a feeling your son is going to show you firsthand just what you put Mom and me through when you were his size."

At that Tess joined the laughter then said, "God help you Christina, if Taylor is half the Democratic spirit Michael was."

I stopped laughing then said, "Tess, chances are Taylor's going to outdo even Michael's childhood reputation and probably by leaps and bounds."

When it was time for everyone to leave I lovingly asked Jimmy and Pierre to leave with them. I asked Tess to stay on with us for the rest of the week. I told her it was because I wanted to draw on her years of experience, but the real reason was I knew it would have broken her heart if I asked her to leave then. And the look on her face as she vowed to help us as long as we needed, said it all. That look, at that moment, was filled with such unconditional love that it went straight to my heart and I knew there would always be a place for her there.

I fed Taylor and had him sleeping nicely by 10:00pm. The three of us spent the next two hours just watching him sleep. It wasn't until midnight that Tess looked at us and whispered, "We better get some sleep before he's ready to eat again, or none of us will be sleeping tonight."

With that she left our room and not two seconds later Taylor was ready to eat. Guess what? Tess was right! None of us did sleep that night, but not for the reasons Tess thought. It was because every time Taylor would fall asleep, one of the three of us would start poking him to make sure he was still breathing. We were so bad that it was the three of us who ended up keeping Taylor up all night, and as for that first night, Tess's years of experience turned out to be quite useless. She was so worried Taylor would slip out of her once strong arms that she was afraid to do anything for him except hold him in the rocking chair and only after she was already seated. But it was not until Michael asked her to help us change Taylor's diaper that I knew I was in trouble.

Michael was holding Taylor on the changing stand and while I removed his diaper he said, "Mom, hand us one of those diapers please?" Which I thought was strange since they were two feet from his hand, but I said nothing. Then, Tess put her hand in the diaper bag, but she did not hand us a diaper. She had her back to us as we waited, so we could not see what was taking so long. Finally, Michael said, "Just hand me one diaper, Mom. That's all."

Her reply was, "These damned fool new diapers, I never saw such a thing." We turned around and Tess had taped both her hands together with one diaper. Michael started to laugh as he grabbed the diaper from her hand; "Give me that Mom and stop fooling around, you silly gooses."

Taylor was now crying as he laid there still waiting for the warmth of a diaper so I said, "Come on guys, where's the diaper already? He's getting cold."

"Hold on it's coming," replied Michael. When I gazed at their reflection in the mirror, I was dumbfounded, for now the two of them where taped to the same diaper and struggling to break free.

I picked Taylor up to stop him from crying, grabbed a new diaper from the other side of the bag their hands were taped to and laughed as I said, "Taylor, honey, whatever you do don't take after your father's side of the family; I'm getting a feeling the whole bunch of them might be silly geese." With that, Michael and Tess both burst into laughter.

We were all so tired when we finally fell asleep that morning, that no one but me heard the banging on the front door. I nudged Michael who was unconscious, looked at the alarm clock and thought, "8:00am, who the hell would be here now?" The banging started again. I climbed out of bed, threw on my robe and headed for the door. When I opened it, Jimmy was standing there with a big smile and a pile of newspapers. I shook my head, "Come on in, just try to be quiet. We only fell asleep an hour ago." As we walked to the kitchen I continued, "What are you doing here this early anyway?"

He placed his bundle on the kitchen table and started to make a pot of coffee as he said, "I wanted to see my nephew, is that all right with you?"

I smiled, "Of course it's all right, smart ass. It's just that I've been seeing you so much lately, I'm wondering if you're keeping a close enough eye on our little empire."

American Goddess

"Don't you worry about our empire girlfriend, everything's just fine. You just worry about taking care of your precious family. Now I don't want to hear any more about where I should be today, because no matter what you say I'm spending the day with Taylor. Besides, Pierre can watch things by himself for one day."

I laughed as I took two cups from the cupboard, "So what's all the papers for?"

"I stopped for coffee on my way up here and yours', Michael's, and Taylor's photos were on the front page of every paper on the rack, so I grabbed every copy of each newspaper they had. I thought it might be nice for Taylor to someday read what the world had to say about his birth."

I chuckled, "What's he going to do with the rest of them, wallpaper his walls?" I poured our coffees, took a seat beside Jimmy, picked up the New York Times and started to laugh as I said, "Get this Jimmy! '**Christina Powers defies medical advice, as she once again dares to stare into the face of death, to give birth to her now famous son, Taylor James Carr!**' Can you believe that?"

"You think that one's bad!" Jimmy laughed, "Listen to what the Post wrote, '**Christina Powers now adds miracles to her list of achievements, as she gave birth to her new son, Taylor James Carr.**'

I laughed again, "I can't believe they actually printed this stuff."

"Oh wait!" Jimmy interrupted. "Here's the Albany Times Union, '**Christina and Michael bask in their love as they proudly introduce their beautiful new son, Taylor James Carr to a cheering public'.**"

"Wow! That was really sweet," I said. "I think I'll drop the reporter a card." That's when Taylor started calling.

Tess stayed with us for the rest of that week, and there wasn't a moment that she didn't spend doting over Taylor. She adored him and it warmed my heart to see what a loving grandmother Taylor truly had.

As for Jimmy and Pierre, they came up every night after work and of course Jimmy brought a new stuffed animal with him each time. The only difference when Jimmy and Pierre came up for dinner that Friday night was Jimmy informed us they were staying for the weekend. We didn't argue, we knew better, and I was actually glad they did because we ended up having a great time. It was around 10pm Friday night when we all decided to retire for the night. I woke up at 1am and could not fall back to sleep; so, I thought I'd go wake Jimmy and ask him to make some of his famous buttered popcorn. I made my way to the room he and Pierre were sleeping in, and when I opened the bedroom door I was surprised to find Jimmy standing on the bed with a huge erection and his legs spread eagle directly over Pierre who was laying on his back beneath him totally nude saying, "Oh baby, you are my Colossus of Rhodes!"

I started to laugh so hard and the moment they realized I was there, Jimmy screamed, lost his balance and fell off the bed hitting the back of his head on the dresser as Pierre frantically tried to cover himself.

American Goddess

"Oh my God!" I shouted as I ran to Jimmy's aid struggling not to laugh. "Are you alright?"

Holding the back of his head he yelled, "Ouch that hurts! What the hell is wrong with you girlfriend, did you forget how to knock?" He then looked up at me and started to laugh, "My fucking genius is back. What great idea did you get this time?"

That's when Michael came charging into the room yelling, "What the hell's going on?"

I looked at the three of them and started to laugh so hard I almost couldn't get the words out as I said, "I just wanted to ask Jimmy to fix me some of his famous buttered popcorn."

Pierre joined the laughter as he wrapped the sheet around his waist, hopped out of the bed and said, "Great idea Christina, that's just want I was about to ask Jimmy to do when you entered the room." Turning to Jimmy he continued, "Is our popcorn ready yet?"

Jimmy, now putting on his shorts added, "Great, now I have two fucking geniuses to deal with." He looked towards Michael; "Come on Mike, let's go fix our geniuses some popcorn or neither one of us is ever going to get some sex tonight."

We all laughed some more as we went downstairs and ate two big bowls of the best buttered popcorn in the world. But the best thing that happened that weekend came after our Sunday night dinner, when Michael brought out six cupcakes with a birthday candle in each one and said, "These are to celebrate Taylor's first week's birthday. Now we're going to sing happy birthday to Taylor and as we blow our candles out, we can make our own special wish just for him."

With a surprised expression I said, "That's beautiful, honey."

After our little party, Jimmy said, "This was a great idea Michael, why don't we throw Taylor another birthday party next weekend?"

"I'll tell you what," Michael replied with a gentle smile. "Why don't we all plan to spend next weekend together?" When everyone agreed Michael added, "Listen up guys, Christina and I have to ask all three of you to stay home this week. We need some time alone, just the three of us, all right?"

Reluctantly they all agreed and when they left that night, it was actually the first time Michael, Taylor and I were alone together, since Taylor's birth. It was such an incredible experience being alone as a family that night, that all Michael and I could do was lovingly bask in the wondrous feelings of parenthood. We were both so happy we couldn't keep the smiles from our faces if we tried, especially since every little movement Taylor made gave us another reason to smile. As the days passed that summer, we had to be the happiest little family in the entire world.

Every time Michael picked Taylor up, he glowed with a divine love for his son and wife. As for me, I was finally a Mom again and somehow the precious gift of

American Goddess

motherhood made me feel complete as a woman and a wife.   I finally had my angel and what an angel he was.   He would sleep all night long and he never cried unless he was wet or hungry.   He was such a happy baby and every smile he gave me told me so.   He wrapped my heart around his tiny finger a little tighter with every smile, especially when I would sing to him.   I sang a new song to him straight from my heart every time I would feed him.   He was the only person in the world who could get me to start singing with a smile, and his smile radiated the deepest feeling of unconditional love I had ever known.   As for his little birthday Parties, well they became a weekly occurrence with cake, wrapped presents and all the party favors.   The five of us loved Taylor so much that he just became the center of all our lives.   If Michael and I had let them, Tess, Jimmy, and Pierre would have moved in with us for good.

American Goddess

Our lives' were going along wonderfully that summer right up until September 22nd, 1992; until Jimmy called me at 11:00am and said, "Christina, I just received a call from President Rush, who asked me to please have you call him as soon as possible. He sounded as if it was urgent and he said for you to call him on his private line."

I thanked him then told Michael who said, "Whatever he wants, you talk to me before you say anything, all right?"

I smiled as I answered, "Yes, sir." Then I picked up the phone and proceeded to dial the President's number. When he answered, I said, "Hi, George, Jimmy told me you called and he said it sounded urgent. Is something wrong?"

"Thanks for calling so promptly Christina; I've always appreciated that in you. Now to answer your question, yes there is something wrong and I'm calling to ask for your help."

"What is it?" I asked with concern.

"Christina, I've been slipping in the polls steadily over the last three months and its dramatic enough to cause me great concern. That's why I'm now asking you and Michael to come with the baby and make a cameo appearance at the Republican Convention in Dallas tomorrow night. It's the last night of the convention Christina and it needs a shot in the arm. I believe if you were both to endorse my campaign while holding Taylor in your arms; then, the tide of the election could be turned back in my direction."

With a surprised tone I answered, "George, I'm flattered you think Michael and I have that much influence with the American public, but I really think the voters are going to vote on the issues, no matter what we may say."

"Are you kidding, Christina? Right now, the three of you are America's most famous family. The American people love you and all the public opinion polls show that you are the most trusted public figure since President Kenny. I'm telling you people will listen to what you have to say Christina, especially if the two of you back me as a family. Won't you please help me? All I'm asking is for you to read a two-minute speech at the convention, with Michael holding Taylor beside you. Christina, you know I'd do anything for you and I'm only asking for one night out of your time."

"Listen George, let me speak with Michael and I'll get back to you."

The moment I told Michael the details of my conversation with George, he outright refused by saying, "There is no way I'm parading my family on national television to support him, especially when I have no intentions of voting for him myself. Christina, can't you see from the last time we had to deal with him that he is just trying to use us?

466

American Goddess

On the outside the man comes across like a great guy, but I do not trust him and if I don't trust him there's no way, I'm going to publicly support him."

"Michael, I agree with you completely and if I hadn't given my word, I'd support his reelection campaign, I would have never done so in the first place.   But since I did give my word to support him, I feel obligated to go.   So, for the honor of my word honey, I'm asking you to allow me to go by myself to do this one more thing for him."

He shook his head and said, "I've learned not to fight with you when you're right Punkie; so, if you really want to go then your family is coming with you.   Just don't expect Taylor and I to take center stage with you when you read whatever 'bull' it is he wants you to pawn off on the public."   The next morning the three of us were on our way to the Republican Convention in Dallas, Texas, which also happened to be George's hometown.

It was 7:00pm when we entered the convention hall with the President's immediate party and as we walked to our seats, we were cheered by the crowd so loudly, the noise had Taylor crying in seconds.   I was able to calm him down as the stadium quieted, then we proceeded to sit through two hours of Republican indoctrination.   The first half hour went to the vice-president who touted the Administration's achievements over the last four years.   The next speaker was Republican Majority Leader, my ex-husband Lee Bradford.   Lee spent an entire hour virtually spouting out the trustworthiness of the current administration and the faithful determination of the Republican Party to steadfastly stand for the morality of the American family.   By the time Lee finished his speech, I was nearly nauseous and that's when Reverend Truewell took the podium. The good Reverend took the next fifteen minutes to praise the virtues of the return of family values in the United States.   He dedicated the next fifteen minutes on rebuking the evils of the Democratic Party, by starting with their plans to allow gays in the military. After that he condemned them as well for their refusal to overturn Roe v. Wade. Incredibly I was able to hold my anger until he said, "What will they want next, for us to recognize the rights of homosexuals to marry and adopt children.   That's not the type of family God wants raising our children, and as long as the Holy Bible say's in Leviticus 20:13, 'If a man lies with another man, they are an abomination and shall be put to death.' we must never allow the evils of the Democratic Party to prevail."

He proceeded to sum up his sermon with a prayer for victory and that's when the announcer said, "Ladies and gentlemen, to introduce the President we have invited some special guests here tonight.   So without further delay, I'd like to welcome America's most popular family, Christina, Michael, and Taylor Powers Carr."

Cheers filled the stadium as Michael grabbed my arm and said, "Damn it Christina, I told him Taylor and I weren't to be announced with you, and I'm not taking him up there."

American Goddess

I looked desperately into his eyes as I pleaded in a whisper, "Michael, Please, come up there with me or I won't be able to do this."

"No!" He grunted back.

I pleaded again, "Michael, I need you! Please do this for me, not for him?"

With that he took Taylor from my hands as he stood up and with anger in his voice said, "I'm only doing this for you, so let's get it over with." And off we nervously headed toward the podium.

We were both smiling as we stood before the cameras and my smile immediately turned into a look of horror, as I glanced at the monitor in front of me which read, "Good Evening, America! I must first say that Michael, Taylor and I are honored to be here tonight. We have come as an American family to give our full support to the President's bid for reelection and the Republican Party's Commitment to uphold the honest Christian family values of all-American citizens." I just stood there speechless. I could not bring myself to say anything, no less read those words.

Michael brought me out of my momentary coma with a nudge to my arm and the moment I regained my composure I said, "Please forgive me, but in good conscience I cannot read the words on the monitor." I quickly turned behind me, toward where George was seated and looked him dead in the eyes. Then I turned back toward the audience and with disgust in my voice added, "I'm sorry George, but after having listened to such hypocrisy, I must withdraw my support for your campaign."

That's when the delegates gasped from shock and little did they know I was only getting started, "What gives any of you the right to think you can dictate American morality? Do you all really believe having some puffed up preacher stand here on National TV advocating the hatred and discrimination of millions of innocent people, is truly the type of leadership our country needs? Well personally I don't think so. I think we're looking for real leadership, the kind that will bring our nation together not divide it."

Everyone there was still gasping for breath when Reverend Truewell grabbed a mike on the other side of the stage and said, "You're no longer welcomed here, Ms. Powers! You have blasphemed the Holy Word of God, by calling my scripture reading hypocrisy, so please leave."

"I'm leaving sir!" I answered with my head held high, "But not because I've blasphemed anything. It's because I'm getting sick to my stomach from just being here. Can't you see that you're the one who is the blasphemer? How can you proclaim the love of Christ in one breath, and then condemn your brothers in another breath? You quote death from a book you call Holy and you ignore the fact that Christ died on a cross to free us from the sin that you and that book, are so willing to chain us all back up to. Reverend I've searched my thoughts while you preached from your Holy Bible, and for the life of me; I couldn't find one Holy Word in your entire sermon."

American Goddess

With indignation he shouted, "How dare you question my knowledge of why Christ was crucified, especially when it's evident you have no idea what Christ died for?"

Calmly I replied, "Reverend, I'm not going to argue scripture with you or defend my statements, because until people like yourself understand that all Christ wants from us is to follow his example, and not the laws of the Old Testament, then it would do no good."

With that he screamed at me, "Are you now telling me to disregard the Bible, which everyone knows is the Holy Word of God?"

Still holding my composure, I answered, "I don't think you should just disregard the Bible reverend; I think we should throw it away!   Along with all the negative concepts that come along with it, like prejudice, hatred, bigotry, and murder.   Can't you see that the world would be a much better place if we just followed Christ's teachings of unconditional love and nailed the rest of the book back on The Cross where Christ intended for it to go nearly two thousand years ago?"

At that everyone began to boo me, and the good reverend lost it all together as he started to shout, "The entire world knows you're nothing, but a harlot and you dare to preach to me?"

That's when Michael grabbed the mike and said, "Sir, if I weren't a gentleman, I'd make you eat those words, but since I am I'll take my family and just leave.   And Sir! For your own good, I hope you can be civil enough to keep your crude remarks to yourself."   Then he put the mike down, took my hand and said, "Come on honey, let's get out of this God forsaken place."

The reaction of the spectators was pure anger.   We were booed and sneered at so badly as we headed out of the auditorium, that even the President himself could not calm the crowd down fast enough.   And that wasn't the worst, for when we tried to leave the building the mob outside began throwing bottles and stones at us.   Michael quickly closed the door and ushered us back to the security office to seek help.   When we were inside, I turned to Michael and said, "I'm sorry, Michael.   I had no idea people would react like this when I said what I did, but I was so angered by the stupidity of their doctrine that I had to speak out."

He hugged me reassuringly and said, "Don't be sorry Christina, if you hadn't said something I would have."

Just then the President entered the room and in an angry tone said, "The mob out front has become so unruly, the Governor has had to call in an extra hundred and fifty Riot Control Officers.   It will probably take half the night to quiet the damn city down. What the hell were you thinking?"

American Goddess

"Hold on Mr. President." Michael interrupted. "If you would like us to continue this conversation, then please speak in a civil tone, because there is no reason for you to speak to anyone like that."

"Well excuse me, Mr. Powers," George snapped back sarcastically. "That's because you're not the one who's Presidential reelection chances, have just been blown to hell on National TV." With that he took two deep breaths and after calming himself for a moment he shook his head as he looked at me and added, "I could have gracefully accepted the public withdrawal of your support from my campaign, but how do I publicly accept your all-out assault on the entire Republican Platform?"

I returned his steady gaze with a look of sincerity and said, "George, I don't know if you can understand this, but I was compelled to say what I did."

Without blinking he replied, "Your security chief has your helicopter waiting on the roof to take the three of you safely to Houston. I'm afraid you'll have to fly out of Texas from there. It seems there's already a mob waiting for you at the Dallas Airport, with protest signs which read, **'Death to the Fag Lovers!'** And **'Let's keep the Bible and nail Christina Powers to the cross!'** So I think it would be wise for you to leave town now. There's an armed guard waiting in the hall to take you to the roof." Then, he turned to walk out and when he reached the door he turned back and added, "Oh by the way Christina, I don't know if you can understand this, but I'm now compelled to publicly destroy you." And with that he exited the room.

It was 10:00 the following morning when our jet taxied down at Stewart Airport and we were greeted by another large gathering of protesters. Only this time, they were divided into two groups, with half of them cheering a chant, "Way to go, Christina! That's why we love you!" The other half was booing a chant, "Down with the Anti-Bible fagot lovers."

As we exited the plane, we were ushered by thirty or so, New York State Police Officers past the crowd and straight into a beehive of reporters. They shouted questions as we walked past and in the midst of this madness I turned to Michael and said, "Michael, if I don't make a public statement right now in defense of my actions, it will look as though I'm ashamed of what I said."

He stopped us dead in our tracks and said, "Well you better start talking to them then. Because I'll be damned, before I'll let the world think you're anything but proud of what you said." He shouted to the reporters, "If you will all just calm down and ask your question's one at a time, then we'll be more than happy to answer them." Right on that spot, we began to hold a mini press conference, while Taylor fell asleep in Michael's arms.

The first question asked was, "Christina, some of your critics are saying you have disgraced yourself by what they see as a deliberate attempt to sabotage the President's reelection campaign, and the reputation of the Republican Party. Would you care to comment on those charges at this time?"

"If the critics you speak of, think making a stand against injustice, wherever it may be found is disgraceful, then as far as I'm concerned, their opinions are worthless. And as for the validity of the insinuation that my actions were premeditated to sabotage the President, or the Republican Party's reputation in any way, is absolutely ludicrous."

"Christina! Christina!" Asked the hungry mob of reporters until I took the next question by pointing, "Christina, the world's Christian community is up in arms over your controversial statements that the world would be a better place without the Bible and it should be thrown away. At this time would you care to respond to their outrage, as well as shed further light on what you meant when you said and I quote, 'The Bible should be nailed back on the cross where Christ intended it to be in the first place?'"

I smiled at the young reporter then gently said, "My words weren't meant to be taken literally. I spoke as Christ himself might have, in a parable. What was meant by the parable had nothing to do with crucifying the Bible. I was simply stating when Christ died; He took the penalty of sin and the laws of sin to the cross with him. I'm just so sick of the spiritual leaders of today, thinking it's their responsibility to continue to keep the world enslaved to the laws of the Bible's Old Testament. Especially when they should be freeing the world from the laws of the Bible and the knowledge of sin that comes with it, like Christ taught us to do. For didn't Christ himself say in Matthew 15:9, **'But, in vain they do worship me, teaching for doctrines of man.'** Christ also taught in Matthew 7:1, **'Judge not, that ye be not judged.'** The reason I said what I did is because history has shown us that man has been using the laws of the Bible and all the Sacred Books to justify war, prejudice and murder for centuries now, and all in the name of God and through the laws of The Old Testament, New Testament, Torah and the Quran. Well I think it's time we stopped all the judging and leave the job of conviction and self-judgement up to the Spirit of God. For Christ didn't tell us to follow the laws of the Old Testament, because He fulfilled them when He also said in Matthew 26:56, **'But all this was done, that the scriptures of the prophets might be fulfilled.'** He said again in Matthew 28:20, **'Teaching them to observe all things whatsoever I have commanded.'** Not the Old Testament's commandments. What Christ commanded can again be found in Matthew 22:37-40, **'Thou shalt love the Lord thy God with all thy heart and thou shalt love thy neighbor as thyself. On these two Commandments hang all the laws and the prophets.'** And that is why when I heard an entire political party advocating conformity to one belief, it reminded me of the Nazi Regime, and I had to speak out." "Christina! Christina!" They pleaded again so I pointed and said, "I'll answer one more question."

"Christina, do you plan to support the Democratic Party's nominee for President now that you've withdrawn your support from the President's Campaign?"

American Goddess

I gave a big smile for that one and said, "I think I'll try to stay out of the political scene from now on. Besides, American citizens are smart enough to see past all the smoke screens of both Parties and come straight to the heart of the issues for themselves. That's why I have full confidence the voters will vote with their hearts and minds just fine without my help. Now I'd like to thank everyone for keeping the volume down so Taylor could remain sleeping. It's not many news conferences an infant can sleep through and as a family, we deeply appreciate it." At that, we headed for the limo and our State Police Escort to our Milton Home.

Before that interview, I was ridiculed by a majority of Americans', who felt I crossed the lines on freedom of speech and good taste by my actions. After that interview, the opinion polls began to change and no matter how hard the entire Republican Party from the President down tried to slander my character they failed. It appeared that the majority of American citizens now overwhelmingly approved of my public chastising of the President and the Republican Party. It took about two weeks for things to settle down enough for us to sneak back home to our little piece of heaven in The Catskill Mountains. That's when we decided to put the whole nightmarish ordeal behind us and get back to the business at hand, which was simply to live our lives' as loving parents.

CHAPTER 56

Cherished so much was the precious gift we had prayed so hard for, our beautiful new baby boy, Taylor James Carr, that we made a conscious choice to finally free ourselves from the complications of the world and the insanity that accompanies it. We didn't even appear publicly when the President angrily blamed me for his loss in the election and thanks to the great work of my Security Chief, Frank Rossi our true whereabouts were never discovered by anyone. As far as the world knew, we were hiding out at our very secure home on the Power's Complex Grounds in Milton, N.Y., but in reality we were in the mountains learning to live a normal family life and loving every second of it. From that time on we devoted our full attentions to Taylor, who was developing into a unique little individual right in front of our eyes. Before we realized it, the days turned into weeks and the weeks into months, and raising Taylor turned out to be the most rewarding aspect of our entire lives. Unbelievably, the eternal love we already had for him somehow grew deeper with every breath we took together. He was so loved and lovable that Michael and I knew there was nothing in this world we wouldn't do for our Taylor. Those sentiments were not just ours either, because Tess, Jimmy, and Pierre were just as devoted to Taylor as we were. The five

American Goddess

of us loved him so much that we continued to celebrate his birthday every week for the rest of that year. It wasn't until after his first birthday party that I insisted on cutting the mini birthday Party's down to once a month. The poor little guy's room was becoming so filled with the gifts he was brought every week; it was either cut the Party's or build an addition. I opted for the Party's figuring it would be less strenuous then an addition.

Taylor was a remarkable child to watch grow and he never ceased to amaze us. He actually spoke his first word on his sixth month birthday and of course it was, "Dada." I laughed when he said it and said, "Oh well! I guess Mama will have to settle for second." The next morning over breakfast, I was talking with Jimmy as he spoon-fed Taylor and to the surprise of us all, Taylor reached out to Jimmy and said, "Meme."

We all stopped everything we were doing and when he said it a second time, I leaned my head next to the highchair and said, "Meme! What about Mama?" At that moment he stuck his little tongue out at me and went, "Blppppp" splattering baby cereal right in my face and when he topped it off with a great big grin I lost it. I started laughing so hard I almost fell off my chair. Needless to say, from that day forth, Jimmy became known as Meme.

The following weekend he stunned us all again with his mastery of the English Language by calling Tess, "Nana." Then on December 19th, 1992, he woke up crying at 2:00am and as I rocked him in my arms he gazed his sleepy eyes up into mine, and with the sweetest voice I ever heard said, "Mama." I looked down at my angel as he struggled to keep his eyes open, and the happiest tears I ever cried began flowing from my eyes. Surprisingly before his seventh month, our little genius had mastered four words.

By his tenth month Taylor was taking his first steps and talking like a toddler. He also turned out to be an advanced child athletically and was running around the house like a trooper by his first birthday. He was so clever that at eighteen months he realized he was the center of our lives, and from that moment on it took him no time to figure out how to get around every one of us. The child was so good with getting his way he could persuade us to do almost anything for him, like racing rocking horses across the living room floor, or marching behind him in single file around the coffee table while playing his harmonica. He would have Jimmy, I mean Meme, behind him rattling his key chain. Pierre was next clinking two spoons together. Then came Dada clanging two pot lids like cymbals and I had to follow up the rear singing Old Macdonald, while Nanny sat in the middle of this marching band around the coffee table. He loved to play and he could turn anything we were doing into a game and have us all laughing hysterically in seconds.

It was hard for all of us not to spoil him by bringing him some little toy every time we went out because he loved getting surprises so much; it was worth a little spoiling.

American Goddess

His face would light up every time he opened a gift, but the brightest face of all shown when he came downstairs on Christmas morning 1993, to find a large gift wrapped in red Christmas paper, with golden ribbons and bows all over it.   He started opening it very slowly at first, but when he saw there was a shiny white, Volkswagen Convertible just his size hidden by the paper; his face outshone the Christmas tree.   He began to tear the paper off so fast and wild, that the automatic camera couldn't snap the picture's fast enough.   By his second birthday he was driving that little buggy so well, that Michael and I had to jog just to keep up with him.

At age two and a half our loveable little man, learned that if he didn't get something when he wanted it, he could demand it by throwing a little tantrum.   That was a trying six months for all of us let me tell you.   But we got through it and by age three he realized negotiating for what he wanted worked better than the tantrums.   By three and a half our little monkey was working computer programs better than I could.   He actually taught me how to pull up the phone on the computer and make a call while still working on his program.   He said and I quote, "I had to call Nanny to say goodnight, but I wasn't finished with my program yet, so I figured I'd do them both at the same time."

I was amazed at his statement, so I kissed his cheek and replied, "I love you, my monkey punkie doodle, and I swear you're a little genius."

By the time he turned four our little angel was holding intellectual conversations with us as if he were twelve years old.   He loved words so much, he would pick out every new one he heard and if he discovered a word that caught his fancy like "Stupidity," you heard it over and over again accompanied by laugher.   This would continue until he understood exactly how to fit the word into as many sentences as he could possibly think of.

Taylor was not only a sweet loving little genius, he was also the most tenderly emotional child I had ever known.   Once we found a bird nest laying on the ground with four little blue eggs in it.   He picked it up and when he noticed two of them were broken, he started to cry so hard I had to promise to try and save the other two eggs just to calm him down.   We ended up taking the nest with the two unbroken eggs home with us to try to hatch them under a light bulb.   The eggs hatched two weeks later and the next thing we knew Taylor had two robins' following him everywhere he went.   Then there was the incident when we found a trapped field mouse that we had to set free.   When he decided he wanted a dog, we were immediately off to a pet shop where amongst thirty or so puppies he instantly spotted a little ball of white fur and said, "That's the one Dad! He loves me."   He picked the little Bichon up then turned to Michael and I and smiled as he said, "His name is Pettoe and he wants to come home with me."   So of course,

American Goddess

Pettoe came home with us. Then, he and his two little buddies from down the road Andy, and A.J., would chase Pettoe all over the house.

I always thought I knew the meaning of hard work, but no work I had ever done compared to cleaning up after Michael, Taylor, two birds and a puppy. Between being a mother and a wife, came all the cooking and cleaning. It didn't take me long to realize one had to be a super woman to be a good mother in the nineties, and I wasn't even holding down a full-time job like most mothers were doing. Even with all the work I only had to see Taylor smile once a day and it was all worth it.

Everything we did was done as a family, and Taylor was never left out of the decision making. It got to the point any time Michael or I had to go out of the house without him; we had to inform him of our entire itinerary. If by chance either one of us were heading to the office for the day, we weren't going alone. Taylor would start crying with such dramatics to come with us, it would have broken our hearts not to have taken him. After the third crying bout over wanting to come to work with us, we decided the obvious solution was simply to just take him. Once we got there, it would only take two minutes for his shyness to dissipate, and then he went straight to work running the show and captivating the hearts of all our employees. Of course, he would immediately claim Jimmy who was now being called 'Meme' by everyone, as his business partner and within ten minutes the two of them would be working on some major project that Meme would dream up, while Michael and I held board meetings in the same room. I guess it was acceptable to our business associates because no one ever complained about the background noise provided by Taylor and Meme. After a while we thought it was great having Taylor attending our meetings with us. It was actually quite nice being able to keep an eye on him at the same time. After all, he and Meme would play through the meetings anyway, so how could it hurt? It never even crossed our minds he could possibly be taking in the details of each meeting. But on June 11th, 1996, we discovered that was exactly what he was doing, when he came up to me after what was a very stressful board meeting, where I had given hell to the entire top management of one of my subsidiaries and said, "Whoa, you're so cool Mom. It was pure genius the way you handled that meeting."

I looked at him with wide eyes and with a big smile said, "Why thank you, honey." Then I picked him up, kissed his cheek and whispered, "You're the real genius in this family partner, and don't you ever forget it."

Michael, Taylor and I had to be the happiest family on the face of the earth and our family included Nana, Meme and Pierre as well. This happy little boy was so much the center of all our hearts that we shared equally in Taylor's love whenever we were together, and he had more than enough love to go around. Taylor had a way of making every day come alive with new and exciting challenges. He filled our lives with so much love and made those days truly the happiest and peaceful times of my life.   Only as everyone knows, all good things must come to an end, and ours ended very abruptly at 10:00 am on July 1st. 1996.

CHAPTER 57

Michael and I had just sat for a meeting with our attorney Tom Davies, who unknowingly brought with him; along with a number of documents to be signed, the final missing pieces to our ever-deepening puzzle.   I signed where needed then passed the documents to Michael for his signature.   As Michael signed the documents, I began going through the latest puzzle pieces.   I was carefully examining the information gathered by Tom when I noticed a date on a government contract which was signed by Lee Bradford.   The date was March 18th. 1979, and all at once it hit me and I thought, "That's the same date I met Lee and if I'm not mistaken it's also the same date of the last entry on the disc I switched on Lee."

With this in mind I took the disc from my safe and for what had to be the hundredth time, I inserted the disk into my computer.   Once I confirmed the date I thought, "I must have tried a thousand different passwords, it couldn't be that simple, could it?"   At that I typed in Christina and for the first time in seventeen years I was granted access.   As the information saved on that disc appeared on the screen, I was shocked to see detailed diagrams of NASA's Space Shuttle.   Then all of a sudden on the bottom of the screen appeared the words: 'To access top-level clearance files' type in your six-digit password.' As I pondered what this meant I thought, "Oh well, give it a shot."   So I typed in 'Powers' and sure enough, the computer responded.   After a second look just to make sure my eyes weren't deceiving me, I shouted out in a disgusted tone, "National Security my ass!   The bastard was just covering his own ass."

Michael and Tom immediately stopped what they were doing and at the same time anxiously said, "What is it?"

I had a look of shock on my face as I gazed up at them both and said, "Only proof of the most horrendous crime ever to be perpetrated against the American people." Their faces turned white as they realized the implications of my discovery.

After filling them in on exactly what shocking bit of information we had uncovered, the three of us began to agonize over how to proceed from this point.   The first half hour we tossed around the pros and cons over whether revealing this information to the nation at this point, would really be in America's best interest or not.   Especially since two of the people involved, were now running for President and vice-president on the Republican ticket.

As we brain-stormed, Tom spoke up, "Let me play devil's advocate for a moment." Looking straight at me he continued, "Christina, I hope you realize if you do expose this conspiracy, you will be opening up a can of worms that has the potential of coming back to haunt us all. There are also a lot of fanatics out there who might want to make us all the targets of an assassin's bullet for exposing this."

I knew exactly what he was saying, so I looked at them both very seriously and said, "I think we have a responsibility to see justice prevails whenever a crime is committed, but I'm not sure I'm willing to go to the point of jeopardizing any of our lives for my beliefs."

With frustration Michael shook his head at me and said, "Damn Christina, I don't know either! Part of me says we have to come forward with this evidence and the other part say's to just forget it and let sleeping dogs lie. We're not just talking about the three of us you know; we could be putting Taylor in harm's way as well."

That's when Tom said, "The other thing to consider is how high up the political ladder this goes, we don't even know if there is anyone, we can trust to tell this to."

Michael's face showed the anguish of our dilemma as he added, "If we don't even know who we can trust to tell the truth to, then I'm not sure how to handle this."

With that we were at a stalemate. Taylor who was playing with Jimmy on the other side of the room, came over to us with a look of pure innocence on his face and from out of the blue said, "Mom, you told me I should always tell the truth and if I make a mistake or do something wrong, I should never be afraid of telling you no matter what it is. Well I think if these men are afraid to tell you what they did, then you need to let them know it's all right to tell the truth." I smiled at him lovingly as he looked at Michael and continued, "And Dad, if you don't know who to tell the truth to, then why not just tell everyone the truth, like you told me I should always do?"

Michael snatched him up into his arms and said, "You're right Taylor, that is what I said and that's exactly what we are going to do." Then he kissed Taylor as he placed him down and continued, "I love you Taylor, and you're the best son in the whole world. Now I want you to go and play with Meme while we finish our meeting." As Jimmy led Taylor back to their playing, Michael turned to me and said, "We have to go public with this, Christina."

I smiled my approval, then taking on a determined expression I said, "You're absolutely correct Michael, we do have to go public and it must be done swiftly and strategically."

American Goddess

Once the decision was made to go all the way to a congressional hearing with this, I figured the safest way to proceed would be by covering our own ass's right from the start.   So the first thing we did was have numerous copies made of all the documented proof I had obtained over the years, which collaborated my allegations.   Once that was completed, we calculated the time we could have each copy simultaneously hand delivered to their destinations and came up with 6:30pm.   Each copy was then sealed in separate briefcases and by 1:10pm on their way out of our office by individual couriers. As soon as word reached us that each courier was safely in the air and on their way to their prospective recipients, I called for a press conference to be held at Powers Inc. for precisely 6:30pm that evening.   The rest of that afternoon was spent frantically brainstorming over how to present my case to the American public, without appearing guilty myself.

At that point, Tom convinced me that I would have to alter my story just a bit to cover up the reason I chose to release this information the first time which happened to be the same day of my Wall Street incident in order to protect myself and my family. Otherwise I stood to incriminate myself for 'Insider Trading.'   After reluctantly agreeing it was time to put our story together.

It was only two minutes before confronting a conference room full of reporters, which I realized by sheer coincidence our 6:30pm news conference just happened to correspond with the major networks national news broadcasts.   So when I stood before those reporters and their cameras, I knew once I started speaking, they would have my image beaming live into the living rooms of the entire nation.   That knowledge caused my voice to crack as I said, "Good evening' {cough!}   Please excuse me."   I cleared my voice, smiled and continued, "Let me try that again."

With that, a friendly laughter filled the room which immediately caused me to relax, just enough to proceed with confidence as I said, "First, I'd like to thank you all for coming and I promise this won't be boring.   Next, I respectfully request you refrain from all questions or outbursts, until I have completed my entire statement."   I stopped for a sip of water then continued, "Now that, that's out of the way we may begin. As I speak there will be copies of documents passed out to each one of you.   These copies are exact duplicates of files, which have been sent to the President and the heads of the FBI and CIA.   These files hold documented proof of the allegation I am about to make of conspiracy and treason, against our nation by top officials of our own government."

American Goddess

Instantly the room became filled with shouts of questions from the shocked reporters as they all scrambled to be the first to go live.   Once I regained control of the press conference, I continued by saying, "If you will recall, on November 14th, 1981, there was a congressional hearing called to investigate the current Republican Vice-Presidential Candidate, Republican Majority Leader, Senator Lee Bradford.   This investigation was ordered by the Ways and Means Committee six months after Senator Edward Kenny, made allegations of a conspiracy between the then, Head of NASA, Dan Pigeon and the President of Bradford Computers, Lee Bradford.

The charges alleged that the current Republican Presidential Candidate and Former vice-president Dan Pigeon, had conspired with Lee Bradford for financial kickbacks, before ever awarding the entire computer manufacturing contract, for the space shuttle to Bradford Computers.   Bradford Computers was awarded this astounding, one hundred-billion-dollar, government project in 1975, and since Senator Bradford once worked for NASA as one of the main designers on NASA's own computer programs, Senator Kenny had many questions he wanted answered, concerning possible improprieties.

In an attempt to head off an investigation, Dan Pigeon still heading NASA at the time, then canceled the Bradford Computers contract and awarded it to Peach Computers and Victory Technologies.   At the time Senator Kenny made his accusations, I was married to Senator Bradford and knowing him, I did not believe it possible for him to be involved in a conspiracy.   However, because Lee Bradford miscalculated the response of his fellow Senate members, I discovered differently.

Since the contract between NASA and Bradford Computers had been canceled, Lee never expected a congressional hearing to be called; thus, when it did it caught him off guard.   Fortunately for the Senator, news of the hearing came to his attention the night before it was made public.   He was informed that a Federal Marshal was to arrive at 8:00am the following morning to seize all of Bradford's business and personal financial records.   That very night certain documents, along with a computer disc belonging to my now ex-husband Senator Lee Bradford, came into my possession. Lee told me the documents were for a secret new computer he was designing, and he asked me to keep them in hiding until he needed them.   I did as he asked and after he was cleared of all charges from the Congressional Hearing, he asked for them back. I thought it odd and I became concerned I may have inadvertently helped conceal evidence of a crime, so I made copies of everything before returning them to Bradford. I had no idea what these documents contained, because they were in a seemingly undetectable computer-generated code, but I knew I had to decode the message if I was ever to know the truth."

American Goddess

With that I thought, 'God, forgive me,' as I proceeded to lie through my teeth to cover my ass'. I honestly had no idea what the code meant until I finally deciphered the first line which was simply one word, Christina. When I loaded the disc and typed my own name into my computer, I found myself entering NASA's top-secret main computer through a built-in back door. This discovery was made on December 1st, 1988, when I obtained ownership of Bradford Computers. The following day I informed Senator Kenny of my discovery. He immediately called for a second Congressional Investigation of Senator Bradford, only this time it was on charges of treason and espionage. Before I could get copies of these documents and the disc to Senator Kenny, I was nearly killed by a gunshot wound. The investigation was then placed on hold, until I was well enough to come forward with my evidence. Only the very night I was released from the hospital, I was requested by the then, newly elected President George Rush, to turn the evidence I had over to him. He informed me the information I had would become a threat to national security if it was made public. He wanted me to turn the true documents over to him and turn a phony set of documents over to Senator Kenny. I did as the President requested and gave him what he believed was the only copy of these documents and the disc in existence. Then I turned the phony documents over to Senator Kenny and the following day Senator Bradford was once again cleared of all charges.

After turning the evidence over to the President, I never mentioned it again. I decided instead to begin doing some very subtle investigating of my own. I then acquired the assistance of my attorney Tom Davies, who for the last eight years persistently gathered the puzzle pieces to what was clearly unfolding into some sort of political conspiracy. Then at 10:00am this very morning the puzzle was finally completed, and I understood the gravity of the crime committed against our nation and her people. The folders you have received contain dated, documented proof of a conspiracy which spans three decades. It began in 1972, when President Richard N. Bixion signed an Executive Order that officially started NASA's Space Shuttle Project. He then appointed his nephew Dan Pigeon who had just graduated from Yale University to head NASA's new Space Shuttle Project. Once settled into his appointed position, Dan recruited a brilliant young computer scientist, who also recently graduated from Yale, for a top position on NASA's new computer design team. That young man was Lee Bradford and the team which Bradford headed only six months after joining NASA, was given the mission of upgrading NASA's entire computer network. This team then built the computer and the program which enabled NASA's computers to create a precise computerized design of the spacecraft, needed for the President's new Space Shuttle Project.

American Goddess

The upgrades of NASA's computers were completed on September 10, 1973, and work on the computer design for NASA's new Space Shuttle began two days later. NASA records show the computer design for the new spacecraft was completed by the same group of NASA Scientists, headed by Lee Bradford in December of '74. Shortly after, in January of '75, Lee Bradford resigned from NASA and immediately established Bradford Computers Incorporated.   Then in June of '75, NASA began awarding contracts to build the new Space Shuttle.   That's when Bradford Computers received a twenty year, one hundred-billion-dollar government contract to build all the computers NASA would need for its Space Shuttle Program; thus, in one day, turning Bradford Computers into the largest computer manufacturer on the face of the earth.

My next astonishing discovery came upon the examination of every aspect of Bradford Computers.   For the six years that Bradford Computers held NASA's shuttle account, the company was purchasing all the electrical components for the computers from Westly Electronics.   Then I find out Westly Electronics was a front corporation actually owned by Dan Pigeon himself.

Needless to say, both men made a fortune between the years of 1975, and 1981. But that all came to an end the moment Senator Kenny called for a Congressional Investigation.   Only their greed did not stop there, because Bradford and Pigeon were not about to give up their lucrative arrangement that easily.   So they had to devise a way around Congress before an investigation could be voted on.   Once they decided on a course of action, they had vice-president George Rush delay the vote for the 1981 hearing, while Pigeon and Bradford publicly cancelled the contract between NASA and Bradford Computers, stating: 'The fact that Senator Bradford was a former employee of NASA was simply an oversight on NASA's part.'

While this was being done publicly, Lee Bradford, who was the top computer scientist in the field at the time, was secretly slipping into NASA's mainframe through his own private back door.   Once in NASA's computers, he planted a virus which would without detection, slowly disable every computer system for the Shuttle Project that was not manufactured by Bradford Computers.   His next move was to switch the computer design for the O-rings on the shuttle's solid rocket boosters, with a flawed design.   He knew under the right conditions of cold weather during a launch, the flawed O-ring design would fail, allowing hot gasses to leak out of the boosters through the joints.   Flames from within the booster would then be able to stream past the failed seals, causing the spacecraft to disintegrate into a ball of fire.   From that point on, they sat by watching and waiting, as time after time NASA suffered numerous computer system delays and shutdowns.   Then on January 28th, 1986, their waiting ended with the Challenger Disaster.

American Goddess

After the Challenger, all shuttle missions were halted, while a special commission appointed by then, President Feagan determined the cause of the accident. The commission which was also headed by Senator Lee Bradford said, 'NASA's decision to launch the shuttle was flawed, due to an inferior computer monitoring system. The system failed to alert top-level decision-makers, of problems with the joints and O-rings, or the possible damaging effects of cold weather on them both.'

After that Shuttle Designers, with help from Bradford Computers, made several technical modifications, including an improved O-ring design and the addition of a crew bail-out system. The commission's findings then helped justify Dan Pigeon's decision in May of `87, to once again award Bradford Computers the entire shuttle contract. After discovering all this, I realized the only reason George Rush wanted to conceal this crime, was simply to cover his own back. He knew if his vice-presidential choice was caught up in a conspiracy against NASA, it would have crippled his administration before he was even sworn into office.

Now, if you will compare the O-ring design which is dated Jan 15th, 1979, which I received from Lee Bradford in `81, to the design which the Commission **headed by Lee Bradford** submitted to NASA after the Challenger Disaster, you will find they are one and the same. My Fellow Americans, all the evidence I've presented is why I am now publicly accusing Republican Senator Lee Bradford and Former Vice President Dan Pigeon, of the calculated destruction of the Challenger Spacecraft and the cold-blooded murder of the Challenger's seven member crew."

From that moment on, we were plunged into a four-month nightmare which nearly consumed our every thought, as we were deluged with questions on a daily basis. It was awful! Between the White House, the FBI, the CIA and Congress, I was going nuts. But worst of all were the press, for they were ruthless with their persistent questioning. The world's eyes were on us with such intensity that it was impossible to shield Taylor from the madness.

Finally, at 2:00pm on November 3rd, 1996, the whole unbelievable ordeal came to an end with the sentencing of Lee Bradford and Dan Pigeon to 'life without parole'. As we made our way from the courthouse to the limo after the sentencing that day, we were swamped by the press and their questions as they shouted, "Christina! Are you satisfied with the verdict?"

I knew I had to respond to their questions so I stopped and said, "I am pleased with the verdict, but at the same time dismayed with the reality that trusted leaders of our nation could actually perpetrate such a violent act, for the purpose of financial gain."

I pointed to the next reporter who asked, "Christina, with the election only a day away, how would you rate the accomplishments of President Baxter's Administration?"

I answered, "I believe he is doing a good job for our nation, but I'd feel much more confident in his ability to get things done, if I saw a little less rhetoric and a lot more action.   The fact there is still no Comprehensive National Health Care Program, or how quickly the President folded on the issue of 'Gays in The Military' leaves me disillusioned, to say the least."

The next reporter asked, "Christina, what are your views of the new Republican Presidential Candidate, Businessman Donald Stump?"

I nearly laughed at that one, but I managed to keep it to a smile as I replied, "The concept of running our nation as a business is just the kind of radical change I believe our nation needs, but I think we should have someone a little more mentally stable to implement such a dramatic overhaul of our government."

He came back with, "That's quite a controversial statement, especially since Mr. Stump has already proven his ability as a successful businessman."

"Maybe so, but you asked for my opinion and I gave it to you."

The young reporter was swift with his follow-up, "Are you saying you could do a better job?"

I answered with an air of confidence, "Without a doubt!   Now it's already been a long day, so I'll take only one more question."

"Christina, if you can't find one virtue among the field of candidates; then why don't you consider running for office yourself?"

That's when I started laughing as I answered, "I have enough to do already with raising a four-year-old, **BUT I'LL THINK ABOUT IT.**"

American Goddess

CHAPTER 59

We thought once the verdict was in we'd go back to our secluded lives, so immediately after that interview we left Washington, D.C., and headed for our home on the Powers Complex in Milton, N.Y.   From there our plans were to wait a few weeks for things to cool down, and then sneak back to our mountain hideaway; except once again fate stepped in with her impeccable timing and changed our plans completely.

For you see the day after the trial ended, just happened to be November 3, one day before the 1996 Election Day.   That morning as Jimmy, Michael and I read the papers over breakfast; we were actually amazed by what we read.   The front-page headlines hardly had anything to do with the upcoming election at all.   It seemed the whole world was so consumed with the trial, the verdict, and my participation in both, that it became the story everyone wanted to read about.   Of course, the headlines featured 'little old me' as a national hero, with captions like the New York Times ran, "**Christina Powers topples corrupt government officials with her own style of justice.**"   It went on to read, "**Then she says she is contemplating running for the White House herself in the year 2000!**"   Or like the one the Post ran, "**After exposing the crime of the millennium Christina Powers answers, 'Without a doubt.' when asked if she could do a better job heading our nation than the current Presidential candidates.**"

I could see by the look on Michael's face he was not pleased with the headlines insinuating that I may run for President in 2000, but he let it pass without even one comment.

That was until Jimmy looked at me with excitement on his face, in his eyes, and radiating from his voice as he asked, "Christina are you really thinking of running for the White House in 2000?"

"No!"   Michael answered sharply.   "She has no plans to run for the Presidency. The press took her statement out of context, that's all."   Then he looked at me with concern in his eyes and asked me point blank, "You're not really thinking about running, are you?"

I answered with a reassuring smile, "No, Michael, I'm not.   I have more than enough to do just taking care of you and Taylor, so I sure don't need to add running for President to my list of things to do."

Jimmy obviously didn't sense Michael's irritation to the subject when he popped out with, "But just think Christina.   You could be the first woman President of the United States.   I know you would make a great President and look at all the opportunities you would have to make life better for all Americans."

Again, Michael answered for me with, "Jimmy, did you or didn't you hear her just say no?"

"Yes, but..." Jimmy tried to answer again.

Michael trying to put an end to the discussion said, "I don't want to hear another word about Christina running for the White House.   You got that Jimmy?"

I think Jimmy got the picture when he snapped 'that wrist' at Michael and said, "Well, you don't have to get nasty about it, Michael.   I was only trying to say I think Christina would make a great President, that's all."   "You're right Jimmy, she would be an excellent President, but she's still not running."

At that point the conversation was dropped, but little did we know it wasn't going to be the end of the subject, for the next morning when we went to our local firehouse in Milton to vote, there was a large banner stretched across the front of the building which read, **"Christina Powers for President in 2000!"**

There was also a large group of reporters just waiting for our arrival, and the first question asked was, "Christina, are you going to run for the Presidency in the year 2000?"

I replied with complete sincerity, "I have no intentions of running for the White House, so I'm afraid there's no story here guys."

We voted, and then headed back to the limo, and on our way home Michael took my hand in his and said, "Punkie, this is starting to concern me.   I know you have a way of getting caught up in things, but this is the Presidency of the United States we are talking about.   Do you realize how something like this could change our lives forever?"

I kissed his cheek softly and answered, "Yes, honey, I do realize what it would do to our lives and Taylor's.   That is why you have my word, I will never run for the White House and I promise you, so please try not to worry about it anymore.   All right?"

He kissed my hand and with a sense of relief said, "I'm so glad to hear you say that."

Just then, my cell phone rang and I answered by saying, "Hi, how's Taylor?"   Fully expecting to hear Jimmy's voice and instead I heard,

"You go, girlfriend!"

"Barbara, is that you?"   I asked, pleasantly surprised.

"Of course, it's me, sister."   She answered with excitement.   "I just heard you're going to run for the White House in 2000, and I want you to know I will back you all the way."

"Barbara," I tried to interrupt.

"Christina, you know I'm the President of the League of Women Voters and I promise you, I will start a grass roots' movement right now to get your name on the ballot as the Democratic Party's nominee for President in 2000."

"But Barbara!"   I tried again.

American Goddess

"Oh my God, I'm so excited. I can't believe this. It's like a dream come true for me. Christina, I'm flying in tonight so expect me for dinner. We need to talk because I'm willing to grovel for a position on your cabinet."

I finally interrupted by shouting, "Slow down, Barbara! Before you go tallying up the votes you need to know I'm not running for President. I don't know where you heard I was, but it's not true."

"Please don't tell me that," Barbara whined. "I was just about to orgasm, and you go and tell me it's not true."

"Sorry to burst your bubble baby, but there is no way I'm running for the White House."

With a saddened tone she replied, "Can't we even discuss this?"

"There's nothing to discuss Barbara. I do not want to be President. But you're still more than welcomed to come for dinner."

"What? It's been two years since I've seen my nephew; of course, I'm still coming for dinner. I should be there around 7:00pm. Oh shit, I have to run, I'm needed back on the set, but we'll talk more when I see you tonight. Ta ta for now, girlfriend, love ya."

"Love you too, Barbara."

Throughout my conversation Michael was listening intently, and when I placed the phone in its cradle, he turned to me with a painful look on his face and said, "It's starting already, isn't it?"

At first, I laughed, but Michael failed to see the humor in it so I smiled confidently and replied, "Barbara wants to be my running mate. Can you believe this? She said she'd love a position on my cabinet and has invited herself over for dinner this evening to talk to both of us about it."

Michael shook his head, "That's just what I meant, before we know it, everyone and their brother is going to want you to run for President."

I laughed again then said, "It's only Barbara, Michael. You know how radical she is; besides, I've already put a stop to it so don't worry."

He kissed me and with a big smile said, "Don't worry, huh! I've heard that before my love, and the more I hear you say it, the more I know there's something to worry about."

Laughing again I said, "You know you're right! Maybe we do have something to worry about."

"Just being married to you is enough to worry about, please don't give me any more grief!" He exclaimed with a smile.

"You should worry, smart ass!" I answered with a sexy wink, "I'm the best thing that's ever happened to you."

American Goddess

He playfully began to tickle me as he said, "You're a pain in the tuckus, that's what you are, but you're worth it."

CHAPTER 60

We were laughing like two fools when James pulled the limo up to the front door of our Milton home.   As soon as we climbed out of the car, Jimmy came bursting out of the house with Taylor, and with the excitement of a schoolgirl said, "You guys are not going to believe this, but Reverend Jessie Jensen called, and get this, he wants to speak with **you** about possibly joining your campaign!   Can you believe it, Jessie Jensen? He's a legend in his own time, and he wants to join your campaign, Christina! Girlfriend, doesn't that tell you something, like maybe you should at least think about it?   I took his number and told him I'd have you return his call as soon as you came in, so you need to call him right away Christina, he's waiting!"

I took Taylor out of Jimmy's over excited grasp and said, "You should have just told him it's not true; then, I wouldn't have to call him at all now, would I?"

Then I kissed Taylor and said, "Did you miss us, honey?"

"No Mom, I was playing with Uncle Jimmy."   He answered with a smile.   Then he cupped his little hands together and whispered in my ear, "Mom, are you going to be the President?"

I kissed his cheek as I chuckled, "No honey, I'm not going to be President."

He gave me one of his heartwarming smiles and said, "That's good Mom, because I don't like it when you have to be away from me."

"Aaa honey, I love you and I don't like being away from you either baby."   I answered lovingly.

"Ha, little man!"   Michael interrupted as he reached for Taylor, "Come over here and give your dad a huge hug."

Without warning Taylor leaped from my arms into Michael's and said, "Don't worry Dad, Mom's not going to be President, I am."

Michael smiled at Taylor and replied, "That's great news, Taylor."   Then he looked at me as he continued, "And Mommy is going to call the good reverend right now and tell him that, aren't you mom?"

I kissed both their cheeks and said, "I sure am, guys!"   And off I went.

American Goddess

Reverend Jensen was disappointed that I was not going to run for office, but he handled it gracefully.　Barbara on the other hand was far from graceful.

She started in on us immediately after dinner that evening and when Michael and I outright refused to even discuss my running for office with her, she slapped her hand down on the table, and with frustration in her voice said, "Why are you both being so damned obstinate?　Can't you see you are the perfect candidate?　Please guys, just listen to me for one minute, if not for your own sake, then Taylor's.　Christina, our world is in deep shit as we head into the twenty first century.　If we don't do something drastic to change things right now while we still have time; then, we might as well light a match to the dreams of our children. The earth won't last other hundred-years if the human race continues the course that we're on."

"Ouch!"　I said interrupting.　"That was below the belt."

"You left me no choice, but to be blunt."　She replied firmly.　"How else can I make you see how desperate the situation really is?"

"We know things aren't perfect in the world Barbara," Michael interrupted.　"But that doesn't mean Christina has got to run for President in order to make a difference."

Just then Taylor sat up and said, "Aunt Barbara, why do you think the world won't last a hundred more years?"

Barbara smiled gently at Taylor, "That's a very good question, honey.　The reason I'm so concerned is because the human race as a whole is polluting our planet so much, scientists believe if we don't begin to take care of the earth and stop polluting it; then, the earth will no longer be able to sustain human life in another hundred years."

At that point I got up from my seat, "I think we've heard enough on this topic for tonight, besides it's Taylor's bedtime." Glancing over to Michael I continued, "Why don't you take everyone to the family room and check on the election results, while I get Taylor ready for bed."

He agreed and once Taylor completed his round of hugs and kisses, we headed up for bed.

CHAPTER 61

Taylor was unusually quiet during his bath that evening, and every time I'd ask if there was something bothering him, he would slap my arm forcefully and say, "Just stop talking, Mom!"

American Goddess

After the third slap, I figured I'd better stop talking before my arm turned black and blue.   I knew what he was upset over, and I wanted to comfort him, but I also knew I couldn't force him to talk about it either.   So after his bath, I tried small talk, "How was your dinner, honey?"   For my efforts I received another slap. "I said stop talking, Mom!"

"Hey, what do you think I am your punching bag?"   I caught the hint of a smile, so while he was trying to put on his PJ's, I tried a little tickling.

He pushed me away and said, "Please stop, Mom," with such intensity I nearly started to cry for him right on the spot.

I dropped my hands and said, "Aaa!   I'm sorry, honey.   I promise I'll stop talking right now."

I said nothing more until he gave me a strange look and shouted, "Well, are you going to read my story tonight or do I have to do that for you too."   I fought back my laughter and immediately started reading chapter six of, **The Lion, The Witch and the Wardrobe**.

After story time was over, Taylor looked up at me with sad eyes, quickly wrapped his precious little arms around my neck and said, "I love you, Mom."   Then he laid his head on my breast and in a soft gentle tone asked, "Mom, what is pollution?"

Feeling relieved he was finally opening up, I smiled and lovingly answered, "Pollution is a foreign substance which can cause something clean like fresh air and drinking water, to become impure and unsafe to breath or drink.   It's usually a by-product of mankind's own ingenuity, which simply means we create pollution ourselves."

Still wearing a sad face, he again gazed into my eyes, and with a confused tone said, "I don't understand, Mom.   If pollution is really hurting the earth like Aunt Barbara says it is, then why does everyone continue to make pollution?"

I held him tenderly as I tried to answer my four-year old's seemingly innocent question, "It's a little complicated honey, and I don't know all the answers myself, but I'll try to explain it.   I think the biggest reason is because as individual nations, we really don't know how to live and compete in an industrialized world economy, without causing pollutants."

He looked up at me with the expression of a little genius brainstorming and enthusiastically said, "I got it, Mom.   All we have to do is learn how to stop polluting ourselves; then, we can teach everyone else how."

I hugged and kissed him, then said, "That's a brilliant idea honey, and we can start working on the problem first thing in the morning if you'd like, but right now we need to say our prayers so you can get some sleep."

American Goddess

He kissed me, then we both knelt beside his bed and he said, "Dear God, please bless Mommy, Daddy, Nanny, Meme and the whole world.   And please help Mom and me learn how to stop polluting, so we can teach everyone else.   I love you God, and please bless Baby Jesus, too.   Amen."

I kissed his forehead as I tucked him into bed and said, "Goodnight sweetheart, and have only pleasant dreams my love."   Then, I began to softly sing a lullaby and as I watched my little angel drift off to sleep, I found myself feeling totally humbled by the innocence of this wondrous child's uncorrupted intelligence.

American Goddess

When I entered the living room everyone was glued to the TV as Dan Rather was tallying up the final numbers for the 1996 Presidential Vote.

I quietly took a seat beside Michael and said, "Remind me later and I'll tell you what he said, he was so cute tonight."

Michael, smiled as he replied, "Isn't he always?"

I nodded my head in agreement and asked, "Who's winning?"

"Dan's about to tell us now." Barbara answered, as she turned up the volume on the TV's remote to hear Dan, say, "With all the votes in, it now appears that for the first time in American History, with 52% of the vote, the Republican Party Candidate, Donald Stump, will be heading to the White House for the next four years. I have a special note here tonight. During our CBS voter poll, we discovered that if Christina Powers had been in the race for the White House this evening, she would have swept the election with a whopping 68% of the vote. Now that's a statistic I'm sure all three political Parties are going to have to take notice of."

Just then Barbara clicked off the set, turned to Michael and me, and said, "I told you! For God sakes Michael, please talk some sense into this girl."

Michael shook his head, "Don't think I'm going to help you Barbara, I don't want her running for President any more than she does."

Barbara sighed in frustration as she said, "Can't you guys see how serious the world crisis really is right now? Dammit guys, the human race is hurdling toward self-destruction and no one is really even willing to admit it, no less make the hard decisions which need to be made in order to solve the problem. I'm telling both of you that if people like us, who have been given so much in this lifetime don't do something to stop the destruction of the human race; then, no one will, and one day it will all go up in flames."

With my own frustration I asked, "Well if you're so sure things are all that bad, then why don't you run for President yourself?"

Her eyes lit up as she replied, "I would in a heartbeat if I thought I could win, but even as popular with the public as I am, my name doesn't carry the clout yours does girlfriend. Christina, the majority of Americans love and trust you, they've seen you in action and they know what you've accomplished. They also know you're respected and feared by the world's leaders and that's something even our current President can't claim. These are just some of the reasons why you would make a great President. Christina, our nation needs the kind of strong leadership skills you alone possess."

American Goddess

"Barbara, please stop." I interrupted. "I'm not running for President and that's final, but I will try to become more active in social programs, and I will be more vocal on environmental issues. This I promise!" On that note, we ended the conversation.

I've always called for strict environmental controls on all my corporate holdings. But the next morning before I even served breakfast, I discovered that Taylor was determined to see just how well Powers Incorporated held up to his pollution test. By the end of the day, we had gathered all the statistics needed to make a fair judgment on the clean-up performance of Power's Incorporated, and according to Taylor, we failed miserably, even though we led the world's industries in environmental improvements.

His answer to the accomplishments of our overall improvements in reducing pollutants was, "We have to figure out how to stop all polluting right now Mom, or it's still going to kill our planet."

Once again, I was amazed by his intellect and all I could say was, "You're right honey, we do."

In response to my answer, he looked at Michael and me as he raised his hands to his cheeks and said, "How are we going to figure this one out, guy's?"

We all started to laugh, and I answered, "I don't know honey, but I guess it's one we'll all have to figure out together, won't we?"

From that day on Michael and I set all the brawn and brains of Powers Incorporated into coming up with answers to our pollution questions. I wanted documented proof of all known pollutants, their causes and their effects on our environment. I also wanted solid solutions on how to stop the pollutants and reverse their environmental damage. For the next two months while we were diving head-first into the environmental issues, we were also besieged by every special interest group across the nation, all wanting to support my candidacy for President. I continued to gracefully decline all the support and after a while the clamor began to subside.

Finally, on March 1st, 1997, we were able to quietly sneak back to our mountain hideaway. With us we had six large boxes of pollution statistics to study. Michael and I studied those statistics for the next two weeks with Taylor looking over our shoulders the entire time. And the more we learned the clearer it became to the three of us that Barbara was right, we are in deep shit!

For the next few days, we thought about what we had learned so far. The true facts were so overwhelming we didn't know what to do, but no matter what steps we took, running for President was not going to be one of them. Or so we thought. But the events which took place on March 16th, 1997 had the power to change the course of our futures forever.

American Goddess

That morning began with Michael and me lying in bed openly discussing our findings when Taylor surprised us by entering our room unannounced. Then, he slowly began to walk toward us wearing a saddened expression on his face. When he reached the bed he said, "It doesn't sound like there's much chance of solving this one, guys."

Michael, snatched him up into his arms and said, "Don't look so down little Punkie, there's plenty we can do."

"That's right," I added as I began to tickle him. "You just watch your Mom and Dad in action." With that, Taylor leaped into my arms and shouted, "I'm glad to hear that, Mom. I just learned to do a handstand and Uncle Jimmy said if I practice; I could be in the Olympics someday." Then, he jumped off the bed and shouted again, "Watch me, guys!"

As we watched our little monkey laughing and playing, 'confident' that his parents would solve the world's problems, we knew somehow, we had to make the peoples of the world see just how contaminated our planet really is. Then, maybe together humanity could make the changes needed to save the future for our children; a future, I only just discovered would be riddled with toxic death from all corners of the globe, if we don't begin to act now.

After breakfast that morning, the three of us headed into the office to brainstorm with my top environmental people. I wanted to know all the options to determine the best way to proceed with our mission to clean up the earth, before going public.

Just as our meeting began, Pierre came to me and handed me a note which read, **"Christina, President Donald Stump is on the line for you."**

Looking at him strangely I thought, "The President, what could he want?" I thanked him, excused myself for a moment and headed to my office to take the call in private.

When I reached my desk, I picked up the phone and with a tone of curiosity said, "Hello, Mr. President. This is Christina Powers. How can I help you?"

"Please Christina, call me Donald." He replied in a casual tone, "I've known you for so long, I feel as though we're old friends."

"Well thank you Donald, that's very kind of you." I answered with sincerity.

"Christina, forgive me for taking you from your meeting, but this call is more of a personal matter concerning a dear friend of yours. We thought it best for you to hear this directly from him yourself. As we speak, I am also connected via a satellite to Saudi Arabia. Mohammed, are you able to hear Christina?"

"Yes, Mr. President quite well," replied a voice I recognized instantly. "And I thank you for your assistance."

"You're welcome," Donald answered. "Now I'll get off the line so you may break the news to Christina in private."

American Goddess

With that the President hung up and left me to speak with someone I knew to be a mad man.

"Good morning, Christina my friend," he began very properly. "This is your 'brother in spirit,' Mohammed Fehd. My call is to inform you personally of the deeply sad event which has taken place this very night in the Holy City of Mecca. My father, King Toudia Fehd has passed over to great Allah in the Seventh Heaven."

"I'm sorry to hear of your loss Mohammed," I facetiously remarked, "But why would you think I would want to hear this news from you personally?"

With a sincere tone he answered, "I would think you would, because I still believe we are two spirits with one destiny my sister. And I wanted you to know of my father's passing before I tell my people and the world."

"Well, soon to be King," I replied sarcastically. "I thank you for this revelation, but neither your father's passing, nor your taking his throne, has any interest to me at all. So I'm afraid you've wasted a call. Now I'm very busy, so I really must say goodbye."

"Please Christina, don't be so hasty! I have not called to harass you. I guess I deserved that after the way I behaved at our last meeting, but I was hoping we could be civil enough to put that all behind us. I need you to know Christina that I have learned much from watching your life unfold over the years, and it has changed the way I am looking at the world these days. I just wanted you to know when I take the throne of the wealthiest nation on earth; I will be dedicating the address I've written to my nation and the world, to you, Christina Powers."

I was taken aback by his statement, so I interrupted by saying, "Let me see if I understand this, Mohammed. I think you are trying to tell me I've made some kind of a positive impact on the way you're looking at life these days. I find that hard to believe."

He chuckled with a tone of sophistication then said, "More than just a positive look my friend. You have helped me to reach the true power of my own divinity, when you gave birth to your little miracle, and I want to share this knowledge with the world as you do. This is why I think you will find my address this evening remarkably interesting."

Relaxing my sarcasm somewhat I said, "I'm still not sure I understand the message behind this call Mohammed, but I will try to watch your address just the same. If nothing else, you've at least piqued my curiosity."

"That's wonderful!" He roared with enthusiasm. "CNN will be airing my address live to the world in the morning. You should be able to view the broadcast on your local station at 8:00pm your time this evening. I'm sure you and your family will find what I have to say very enlightening."

"I will be watching Mohammed, now I really must say goodbye."

"So must I my sister, for my destiny is beckoning. Now I wish you well till we meet again, Christina."

After that call I took Michael aside and filled him in on my conversation with Mohammed. As soon as I finished speaking Michael looked at me with a confused expression and said, "What do you think this is all about?"

I shook my head and answered, "I haven't got a clue honey, and I'm not going to worry about figuring it out either. Besides, I'm sure we'll know more by the time he finishes his address, and we'll deal with it then. We have real things to deal with right now, just ask Taylor."

Michael smiled as he replied, "You're right and if we don't get back to work soon, we're going to hear about it." With that we shrugged Mohammed off.

CHAPTER 63

The rest of that day, I went through the motions like any other day, acting as if I was in control of everything, but in reality I couldn't have felt more helpless than if I were a little girl lost in the wilderness. All I could think about was my conversation with Mohammed and how frightened I really was of this man. Finally, the day ended, and it was time to head home. Since I was concerned over what we might be hearing that evening, I asked Jimmy to come spend the night with Taylor, so Michael and I could watch Mohammed's address without Taylor's presence. Jimmy agreed, and when we arrived home, I quickly served dinner then sent Taylor and Jimmy off to play in Taylor's room, while Michael and I got ready to watch CNN.

8:00pm came slower than I thought it should, but when it finally arrived, we found ourselves glued to the TV set the moment Mohammed took center stage. His appearance on the TV was awesome. He glistened like an angel in all his kingly attire, and he moved with such majesty as he took his place on his father's throne, that he resembled a god incarnate.

As I watched him take his place I thought with a chuckle, "I should have taken him out when I had the chance."

Once Mohammed was settled, he began his address by mourning the loss of his father, then by touting the former King's achievements over his lifetime.   After a more than honorable eulogy to his father's memory, he spoke of his father's dreams for his nation.

Then he said, "Now as I take my place as king of our great nation, I know I have much to do if I want to see my father's dreams for our people come true.   This is why I thank Allah this is a Godly people I am commissioned to lead into the future, and we must never forget the great strides our beloved king has made for our nation and our people.   We must also never forget King Toudia's desire to achieve total peace in the Middle East.   And not just for Saudi Arabia, but for all the rest of the Middle East as well.   Because of my father's dream I find myself determined to lead Palestine along with all her Arab brothers, into a true peace with the Jewish state of Israel."

He began to remove the crown of gold from his head as he rose from his throne. Then he knelt down and as he placed his crown on the floor he said, "I do this as a symbolic gesture to show all men I am their equal."   Then he rose to a standing position and continued, "Words of great wisdom which have come from a woman I have learned to honor and respect, have only recently helped me to believe that such a peace as my father dreamed of for the Middle East, is truly possible.   The woman I speak of is known to the world as the 'Angel of Peace,' and that woman is my sister in spirit, Christina Powers.   Christina, I'd like to thank you right now for the great lesson of unconditional love you have taught me.   Without your insight in the ways of the Almighty, I may have never realized that the power of Allah's love resides within us all. For as Christina has said, it is time to stop passing judgment on our fellow man, and start loving them for the good that is innately instilled within all of us, instead of hanging onto all the hate and bigotry of a time that's best forgotten.   This is why I will be inviting the leaders of Israel and Palestine to meet with me in the Holy City of Mecca, to discuss and hopefully sign an everlasting Peace Accord.   A Peace Accord that will begin a new legacy of love between the Arabs and Jews, which I know will have the power to conquer the legacy of hatred left to us by our forefathers."

Michael and I looked at each other with stunned expressions as he spoke.   We actually found ourselves speechless by what we were hearing.   And much to our surprise Mohammed was only beginning to blow us away, for his next sentence was, "It is time for Arabs and Jews to look past the hatred taught to us in the Bible and the Koran, and begin looking toward a peaceful future.   For once we can move beyond the doctrine of hatred; we will be able to see we are all equal in the eyes of God, whose eyes are yours and mine.   Now to show to Israel and the world, that the Arab people mean what we say, I will list just a few of the proposals I will bring to the peace talks with Israel.   First, Saudi Arabia will promise to pay twenty billion dollars in Western currency, to the government of Israel to relinquish the occupied territories in the West Bank and the Gaza Strip, to the Nation of Palestine.   Second, we will pledge another twenty billion dollars in Western currency to the government of Palestine, along with economic advisors to help establish Palestine, as a viable democratic nation.   Third, I will ask the people of Palestine to relinquish all their historical claims to the Holy City of Jerusalem and honor the right of the Nation of Israel to keep Jerusalem as their Capital City.   In turn, I will request that Israel freely open the doors of the City of Jerusalem to the unimpeded movement of all Arabs in a city which the Arab World also reveres as Holy.   Fourth, if a peace accord is signed as I believe it will be, then Saudi Arabia will remove the Islamic Temple and also pledge as a gift to the people of Israel, another twenty billion dollars to rebuild the temple of Solomon to its original glory, and on the original site King Solomon had it built over six thousand years ago.   Fifth, I will personally pledge to work hand-in-hand with the Nation of Israel, until its leaders have signed peace accords with all the nations of my Arab brothers.   Sixth, I know in order to finance the peace I hope for in the Middle East, Saudi Arabia will have to pull large amounts of cash reserves from the banks of Western Nations, as well as, liquidate most of our holdings in these nations.   Because of this I also pledge to help offset any harmful effects to the economies of the West, by purchasing all the needed supplies from these Western Nations to rebuild the nations of the Arab world.   Then one day all of my Arab brother nations will become thriving members of the world community.   As I have said, these are only a few of the proposals I will bring to peace talks with Israel, and I'm hopeful that these along with the rest of my proposals, will help us all to finally realize a true peace for the Middle East in our lifetime.   The legacy I want to leave my five-year-old son is one of peace and life, not hatred and death.   I now want to thank all of you for taking time to hear my ideas on how to establish world peace, and I pray Allah may bless the futures of us all."

The moment the commercial came on I clicked off the set, turned to Michael, and with complete exuberance said, "I can't believe this!   This is wonderful news, Michael.   Do you realize what he just did?   He paved the way for real peace in the Middle East, and he thanked me for planting the seeds of peace in his heart.   This is too good to be true."

Michael motioned with his hands for me to lower my voice as he said, "Calm down before you have Taylor in here."

I lowered my voice to say, "I'm sorry honey, I'm just so excited."

American Goddess

Michael hugged me joyfully and said, "Why don't we go outside to discuss this, before we end up having to explain to Taylor why his Mom's bouncing off the walls."

I playfully kissed his cheek several times then said, "Good idea, handsome.   I'll go get our coats while you let Jimmy and Taylor know were going for a walk."   He patted my buns as I turned from him and said, "Hurry back ya little screwball."

We strolled arm in arm along the mountain roads that evening, and in our hearts, we felt a new sense of hope for Taylor's future.

As we walked, I lovingly squeezed Michael's arm and said, "Michael, I feel so pleased with myself that something I've said or done has caused such a remarkable change in that man's life, and I truly believe he has the ability to accomplish what he's set out to do."

"It's something to be proud of Punkie.   You have helped to create the largest movement toward peace on earth the human race has ever known.   Now, all we have to do is get him to join us with cleaning up the planet, and we'll be set."

With that statement I stopped walking, hugged Michael with enthusiasm and said, "That's a fabulous thought Michael, and I'll bet we can get him to help us too!"

Just then Michael shouted with excitement as he pointed toward the northwestern sky, "Look, Christina!   I think we are seeing the first visible sighting to the naked eye of Comet Hal-Bop.   Isn't it beautiful?"

I gazed in the direction of the comet and with a sense of awe said, "Oh my God! It's breathtaking, Michael."

We found ourselves captivated by the wonder of the comet, and with my eyes still fixed on this awesome sight I said, "I wonder if the Christmas Star   shone with such splendor when it lit up the skies over Bethlehem.   Do you realize it was nearly two thousand years ago, when that star brought the good news of the birth of Christ?"

Michael turned to me and in a purely spiritual way said, "Isn't it appropriate that this comet should appear over the earth on the same evening King Mohammed would announce his plans to rebuild the Temple of Solomon."

In a flash, icicles shot up my spine, as echoes of a vow once made to me came rushing to my consciousness.   "Remember this, Christina Powers!   I will be standing as the divine ruler in the Temple of Solomon when I have you beheaded."

Fear shot the words from my mouth as I shouted, "Oh my God!   Michael!   He's planning to use his wealth and power to manipulate the world in the name of peace, and he's doing it all just to gain his own ultimate evil goals."   With horror radiating from my eyes, I looked at Michael and continued, "Michael, his true goal is to annihilate the Jewish race from the face of the earth, and rule the world from his throne in the Holy City of Jerusalem."

"Wow!   Slow down!"   Michael strongly protested, "If that were true, why would he thank you for opening his heart to peace?"

American Goddess

I looked at Michael as if he were stupid and said, "Can't you see the bastard is trying to use the world's faith in my reputation to gain their trust in him. Michael don't you remember the vow he made to me concerning the Temple of Solomon?"

Michael's face instantly turned white and when he caught his breath he said, "Holy shit! Do you really think he's capable of accomplishing his goals?"

I shook my head and answered, "He most likely has the secret backing of the entire Arab world. I definitely think it's a possibility."

Just then Michael gazed back toward the heavens and in a curious tone said, "I still don't understand how he could hope to conquer the world. Especially if he's giving most of his wealth to Israel."

I thought for a moment as I joined Michael in gazing up at the stars and replied, "Sixty billion dollars is nothing to a man like that. He has vast holdings all over the world, especially in the United States." Then it hit me! I grabbed Michael's arm with brute force and excitedly said, "That's it, Michael; he plans to slowly undermine the economies of the west by transferring his financial and industrial holdings throughout the world to the Arab Nations. All he has to do is get the ball rolling in the name of peace, and the West will be unwittingly sucked into his plans without revolting once. I'll bet the moment he sends the economies of the world into a nosedive; he'll be attacking Israel from within her own borders. The only thing I can't figure out is whether he's hoping I don't figure this out, so he can use me in his plans, or if he's openly challenging me to a sick chess game with the world's nations' as our pawns!"

This time Michael had the look of fear as he said, "Is there any way we can stop him?"

I shook my head in bewilderment and replied, "I don't know, Michael. I just don't know."

I honestly believed Michael and I prayed for guidance that night harder then we'd ever prayed for anything in our entire lives. We were both frightened by the future we saw unfolding for humanity, and the foresight we held of things to come only broke our hearts. We knew if nothing was done right now to change the course the human race was on, then there would be no future for any of our children. Needless to say, with the apprehension we felt that night neither one of us could sleep. It was 3:00am when I rolled out of Michael's arms and said, "Honey I'm going to go for a walk, I need to clear my mind."

"Do you want me to come with you?"

I kissed his cheek, "No babe, I feel like I need to be alone. Do you mind?"

He gave me a hug as he answered, "Not at all, just stay close to the house ok."

"I will, don't worry."

American Goddess

Then I grabbed my jacket and headed out into the cold night. As I walked down the road all I could hear in my mind was Mohammed's vow to me. "I will be standing as the divine ruler in the temple of Solomon when I have you beheaded!"

As these words echoed through my mind a bright light lite up the sky and began to slowly move toward me. I looked up into the light and I could see it was some kind of flying object. There was no sound at all as it stopped moving and just hovered about 30 feet above me. I froze, but not in fear, in awe as the bottom of the object opened and a figure began to descend toward me on a cloud. It stopped about 10 feet from me, and I could see it had four faces and four wings. All at once I could hear a voice that rumbled like thunder, **"Do not fear my child. I am the Goddess Shiva, the destroyer of worlds. Only through destruction can new life emerge. The essence of all life, 'I am that I am', has sent me with a divine message.' Judgment approaches for the annihilation or salvation of the human experiment. You Christina have been chosen for this battle. Remember the teachings of the Christ, 'Overcome evils dark hatred with the light of the power of unconditional love.'**

Then this deity began to ascend in the cloud back toward the spacecraft and I cried-out, "Wait! Please wait! I don't understand! What do you want from me? Please! I'm begging you! Don't leave! I don't know what to do!"

It looked down at me as I yelled and I heard, **"You will be visited again my child but remember you must follow your heart."**

Then the bottom of the craft closed and within seconds it was gone. A cold chill came over me and all at once a memory of being taken up into a spacecraft many years ago hit me and I thought, "This must be the appointed time I was told I would remember! What the fuck! Could this really be happening or am I losing my mind?"

I just stood there in a state of shock for the longest time until I was finally able to compose myself enough to go back inside, but I did not say a word to Michael about what had just happen. I just climbed in bed and snuggled close to him until I finally fell asleep.

All of a sudden, I found myself on my knees on a beach in the middle of the night, crying in anguish from the pain of confusion and fear. With tears streaming from my eyes and my face buried in my hands, I yelled out, "God, why have you been tormenting my soul like this?" At that moment I heard a loud voice say, "Look up!" As I did, I saw a streak of light shooting across the sky and from its tail appeared a beautiful angel. I watched in awe as this heavenly being dressed in a shining white gown with black wavy hair, piercing blue eyes and wings sparkling gold, began to descend from the sky towards me. She hovered just above the sand, reached her hand to mine and said, 'The Essence of all life has heard your cries my child, now take my hand and come with me.' I took her hand and instantly we were in the heavens and I could see an entire world stretched out beneath us. She waved her free hand over that world as she said, "See what the Spirit of God will reveal to you." I looked back down, and I could see below me a beautiful planet and it was divided into nations of all types and colors of strange looking creatures. In the middle of these nations one nation stood out, and

in the center of that nation a huge dark green scaly beast with five heads, ten arms and a thousand hands crawled out of a hole in the ground on its belly like a snake.   It was so hungry that it began to search wildly all over that nation for something to eat.   Then spotting some seemingly plump creatures it began grabbing them with all its hands and shoving them into each of its mouths mercilessly.   It ate these creatures, stripping their flesh to bones, and then it threw the bones into a huge pile.   When there was none left to eat, it lifted its heads and seeing there were more seemingly plump creatures in all the nations around, it summoned two other beasts just like itself.   The two new beasts began to slither from out of holes which appeared in two smaller nations.   The first to completely emerge was black and the other orange.   These three beasts then stretched out their hands together and began to eat the seemingly plump creatures in the nations throughout that world. Then I saw another nation far away with stars shining bright all around its borders.   When the creatures of that bright star nation realized what the beasts were doing, they joined forces with the creatures of the other nations of that world and together they killed the three beasts. Then they divided the beast's conquered nations among themselves and saved the rest of the seemingly plump creatures from being eaten.   All the creatures having pity on the seemingly plump creatures gave them a nation of their own far away from where the beast first crawled out of the hole and there was finally peace in that world.   Only the beasts were not really dead.   In a little while the green beast once again crawled out of a new hole in the ground in another nation not far from where it first appeared, and it was even bigger and uglier than before.   This time it had eight heads and two extra arms with hands bigger than the other thousand hands.   In one of the large hands it held a hammer and in the other a sickle.   With the smaller hands it grabbed ahold of the creatures in that nation and when it had them all it reached out and grabbed the creatures of the nations all around it and held them tight.   I watched in horror as the two big hands began to slash and pound the creatures of those nations until it turned bright red with their blood.   Then it looked all around that world and when it spotted the seemingly plump creatures all gathered in one nation, its hunger for their flesh arose again.   The beast then summoned forth the black beast from a boiling black tarry hole in the ground of a nation right next to the nation of the seemingly plump creatures.   This beast reared its ugly black head and roared like a lion so loud that every creature in that world heard it. Then it lunged towards the seemingly plump creatures to devour them, but this time the seemingly plump creatures fought back and when the creatures of the bright star nation vowed, they would fight with the seemingly plump creatures the black beast retreated in fear.   These two beasts being so blood thirsty tried again to reach out and devour the seemingly plump creatures; only this time from over the bright star nation appeared a large silver screen and from that screen leaped a beautiful white stallion carrying a large creature dressed in white with a silver star on its chest.   This white creature rode on the stallion to a city on a hill where it grabbed the hand of a godly creature dressed in purple garments.   Together they shouted, "We come in the name of God," and began to chop the thousand hands from off the once green beast now red from the blood of the creatures it held and they freed the nations and the creatures that beast held so tightly.   The red beast, remembering how the bright star nation defeated it once before, retreated again and it appeared to all the creatures that there would now finally be peace again in that world. The red beast seemed as if it were going to be a friend of the bright star nation and the godly creature in the purple garments; but the black beast wrapped itself in golden garments similar to that of the godly creature.   The black beast disguised in golden garments was furious with the creatures of the bright star nation for stopping it from devouring the seemingly plump creatures, so it struck the heart of the bright star nation with four huge bolts of lightning, as it proclaimed to all the creatures of that world, "I've come in the name of God."   The creatures of the bright star nation were wounded terribly, but they united and began to fight the black beast in the golden garments pretending to be godly.   This angered the two beasts so much that they released spirits of darkness on the bright star nation tormenting its creatures with division, fear, hatred, and murder.   The creatures of the bright star nation became confused by what was happening to their nation, but they continued to fight the black beast wearing the golden godly garments. As they fought the red beast being frustrated with great anger caused by the bright star nation summoned the orange beast.   In fear I watched as a horrific cesspool of poisonous toxins appeared right in the heart of the bright star nation.   The orange beast was even more repulsive then the red and black beasts and it arose with the stench of the cesspool all over it.   The orange beast being cunning concealed itself with white garments similar to those of the creature who once appeared over the bright star nation on the white stallion and it plotted secretly with the other two beasts.   Then the orange beast began to roam all over the bright star nation deceiving and dividing the creatures as it pretended to be one of their godly creatures and a friend of the seemingly plump creatures.   The orange beast was so deceitful and shrewd it convinced the creatures to choose it to be their leader and to fight for them against the black beast in the golden garments.   As soon as the orange beast was in control of the bright star nation it openly took the hands of the other two beasts and they sunk their fangs into the heart of that planet and started to suck it dry of its life-sustaining blood.   Then the three beasts began blowing thick poisonous black phosphor smoke from their mouths. Beginning to die, that planet started to shake painfully, and the winds roared as the planet tried to survive the plundering of the three beasts.   The creatures of all the nations started to get sick and die as the poison began covering that entire world.   When the creatures of the bright star nation realized their new leader was truly one of the beasts they started to shout," lock the beast up!"   Only now the beast had so much power that it stripped the creatures of all their rights to object. Then it took off the white garments revealing its true putrid smelling hideous orange beastly identity.   When the godly creature in purple garments in the city on the hill saw what the orange beast had done it called all creatures to unite and fight against the orange beast.   All three beasts became enraged and together they went to the city on the hill and they tore the godly creature to pieces in the center of the city so that all the creatures would see.   Many of the creatures revolted and began to fight against the three beasts, but their power was too strong; and they tortured and killed any creature that dared to challenge their rule.   Young and old, rich and poor, none were spared. Then the red beast which summoned the black and orange beasts remembered the seemingly plump creatures and its craving for the taste of their flesh arose ferociously. The three beasts realizing they had finally defeated the creatures of the bright star nation, decided they could now freely eat and strip to the bone the seemingly plump creatures once again. As I watched, the three beasts became one hideous monstrous beast, and it began to drag one third of the nations of that world towards the nation of the seemingly plump creatures to devour them. From within the nation of the seemingly plump creatures stood up a large creature wearing a silver robe with millions of tiny stars shining as bright as the heavens all over it. This creature shouted so loud that every creature in that world could hear it yell, "Stop! We will not give one more drop of our blood to feed the beast!" Every creature in that world began to tremble as they begged the beast to stop, only the beast refused, shouting back, "Your flesh and the flesh of your children are mine to feast on and I alone shall rule this world from the throne of your fathers!" and it kept heading towards the nation of the seemingly plump creatures. As the beast reared up to pounce on the seemingly plump creatures the large creature in the silver starry robe lite a fire over the head of the beast so big, that it consumed all life in that world. In shock, I began to cry out hysterically, "NO! NO!" Then I turned towards my angel guide and shouted, "Why have you shown all this to me?" With tears in her eyes she looked at me and said, "Because what you have been shown is the evil trying to destroy your world as we speak, but this is not the will of God, the true Essence of all life." She then waved her arm up toward the heavens as she said, "Look." I looked up and saw a multitude of beautiful tiny lights dancing all around a light so bright that I had to look away. Then she turned back towards me as she said, "The lights you see are all the pure innocent souls of the children yet to be born, that will not be born, if you allow the human race to continue on the path it is on now." With my heart breaking and my mind stunned I shouted, "Me! What can I do?! I'm no one!" She smiled at me gently as she replied, "Fight this evil! Show them they can change the future of the world if they come together in the spirit of Christ and 'God' the Essence of all life's Power of Unconditional Love." I screamed at her in frustration, "How! She pointed one finger towards the earth and said, "You have been given the power Christina. Only you can save the human experiment." Then she just vanished.

I woke up quickly with fear in my heart and I just held on to Michael even tighter until I finally fell back to sleep.

The next morning as we surfed the web, we knew our fears were well founded. The front pages of the newspapers across the globe all shouted the praises of King Mohammed Fehd to the entire world, with headlines like the one the London Times ran, "Saudi Arabia declares King Mohammed Fehd their 'King of Peace' as he takes the throne of the wealthiest nation on earth!" Better yet, listen to the one the New York Post ran, "King Fehd, the first man to be called the 'King of Peace' since Christ himself!"

After reading these headlines I turned to Michael, and with disgust in my voice said, "He's a devil in sheep's clothing, just waiting to pounce. He's good too. He disguised himself as the perfect King of Peace last night and that was just his first address to a world audience. I've learned enough about the male psyche to know if you give a man like that time unchecked, he'll slit your throat from behind the first chance he gets."

I think in that moment, Michael realized the situation we found ourselves in was more urgent, then our dreams for the quiet life ever could be. Because the minute I finished talking, he looked at me with anger in his eyes and said, "We have no choice, Christina. For Taylor's sake we have to stop him."

I gently ran my fingers through his hair and with a mischievous look in my eyes replied, "I know we do Michael, and we will."

His angry expressions turned wild as he asked with an aggressive tone, "What do you have in mind, hired assassins?"

I started to laugh then said, "Michael, that's the problem with the typical male response to a perceived threat, you guys always think violence is the answer. What do you want, a murder on our hands? Besides, there is not a hired assassin in the world that would even get close to him, no less kill him. The only way we can stop him is to beat him at his own game."

Michael's wide expression took on a nervous one as he asked, "So how do we do that?"

I looked at him lovingly, realizing he really didn't know the answer and said, "There are three things we need to accomplish if we even hope to have any chance of beating him. First, we are going to have to triple this year's expected earnings for Powers Incorporated and send our stock through the roof. We have to be more than just financially sound in order to take up some of the slack when he starts pulling the rug out from under our nation's financial feet. And the only way we're going to accomplish that, is if I go back to work and work harder than I've ever worked in my life. Second, I have to make him believe he's pulled the 'wool over my eyes' as well. Then, maybe I can undermine some of the popularity he holds with his nation's citizens by hitting him where he's most vulnerable."

Michael looked at me as if he really didn't want to know the answer to the question he was about to ask, "What's the third thing?"

I shook my head sadly and said, "I'll have to become President of the United States." I can't even describe Michael's expression. You had to be there.

CHAPTER 64

American Goddess

After breakfast that morning we gave complete charge of Jimmy, to Taylor, if you know what I mean. Then Michael and I spent the rest of the morning discussing exactly how I felt we should proceed with our mission to get King Mohammed Fehd before he gets us. As serious as the plotting was, it still only took us till just before lunch to agree on our course of action. Before our lunch break with the kids, I called our attorney Tom Davies and security Chief Frank Rossi to ask them to come for dinner that evening. We wanted to tell Jimmy, Pierre, Frank and Tom, of our plans as soon as possible, because we knew we were going to need their assistance and right away! We also wanted them to be the only other people on the face of the earth to know what the world would soon be facing from King Fehd, and what we planned to do to stop him.

We said nothing about our decisions to Taylor until just before bedtime prayers that evening. The three of us were sitting on the edge of his bed when Michael looked at Taylor very seriously and said, "Taylor, my boy, your Mom and I need to discuss something with you."

Taylor gazed lovingly into his Dad's eyes and with the happiest little voice said, "Meme and I knew you and Mom were figuring out how to clean up our planet Dad, that's why we didn't disturb you guys when you were working."

We both laughed as we kissed his cheeks, then Michael continued, "You guys were right and that's why we need to talk. Taylor, your Mom and I have learned in order for us to try and clean up the environment, we both have to go back to work."

"What about me?" Taylor interrupted with wide eyes. "What can I do to help?"

I smiled as I answered, "Well honey, you're going to get to come with us. I'm going to put you and Meme in charge of figuring out how to let the children of the world know what to do to help clean up our environment. Your Dad and I have also decided to let you appear in a film with me. What do you think about that?"

His face gleamed as he replied, "Wow! When do we get started?"

I wrapped my arms around him proudly and answered, "Tomorrow morning my little man, but there is still one more thing we need to talk about."

He looked at me curiously and said, "You look sad Mom, what is it?"

I smiled softly, "Honey, going back to work and letting everyone know we're in an environmental mess will help, but if we really want to make changes; then, your Mom will have to run for President."

His expression seemed to glisten as he smiled and answered, "I know Mom, the golden lady in my dream last night already told me you would run for President, and I'm happy because she said Dad and I are going to help you."

I was amazed by his reply, so I kissed his cheek and said, "I'm glad you're happy honey, now I want us to keep this a secret among just the three of us until the time is right. Okay?"

"All right, Mom," he answered joyfully.

American Goddess

I kissed him again, "I love you, Punkie Doodle.   Now let's say our prayers and get some sleep, we have a busy day tomorrow."   After he said his prayers, we tucked him in and headed back down to Jimmy, Pierre, Frank and Tom.   It was time to do some recruiting.

The six of us spent the rest of that evening intensely planning each step we would have to take to reach our goal.   Tom's mission was to find every holding King Fehd and his possible allies held throughout the world, and to do research on every move all of the Arab nations made politically and economically over the last ten years, and from now on.   And just for curiosity's sake we decided to check out China too.   We needed to know just who else was in on Mohammed's plot, and how they might be secretly maneuvering together to collapse the economies of the west.   Frank's mission was first to guard Taylor with his life whenever Michael or I couldn't and to increase our security force into the size of a small army.   I put Jimmy and Taylor on a project to come up with the best way to help the children of the world become more aware of our current environmental problems.   At the same time, teach the things they can do individually and collectively to help stop the destruction of our world.   Pierre was to mind our little empire.   As for Michael and me, well, we had some money to make and fast.

After our discussions, I decided to call Mohammed on his private line.   I placed the call on the speaker phone so everyone could listen in.

The moment Mohammed was on the line I began our conversation with excitement in my voice as I said, "Mohammed, its Christina.   I am calling to thank you for your kind words, and to let you know your speech has touched my heart in a way I never thought possible.   The things you said brought tears to my eyes, and I want you to know I'm more than honored, that you thanked me for helping to open up your heart to forgiveness and unconditional love."   I then changed my tone to one of true sincerity and added, "My only regret Mohammed is that you didn't understand my heart when there was a chance for us to be a couple."

His voice actually sounded sad as he replied, "I also hold that regret in my heart Christina, for I realized with the remarkable birth of your son, it was you who was meant to be my bride and bear my son.   I've asked myself time and time again why we're not together or why I was kept so blind, for so long.   But then I think, who am I to question the wisdom of Allah?"

"I don't know the answers either Mohammed."   I answered sympathetically. "What I do know is you've finally found your way into my heart, and if there is anything I can do to help you achieve the peace you and I both dream of, please don't hesitate to call me."

American Goddess

His reply seemed almost genuine, "I will be addressing the U.N. assembly next February, Christina, and I would cut off my left hand just to have dinner with you once more."

I chuckled a little seductively, and then said, "I'm flattered Mohammed, but that's not necessary because I would love to have dinner with you."

We ended our conversation by setting a date for dinner for February 28th, 1998. When I hug-up the phone, Michael turned to me looking very irritated, and with a slightly jealous tone said, "I know you had to sound convincing, but did you have to sound so damned sensual too?"

Jimmy and I started to chuckle at Michael's response, then I tenderly kissed his cheek and said, "Don't get jealous on me now Michael, because I'm going to need to use every trick in the book against this character, if we even hope to have a chance of beating him. And getting him to believe he has a chance with me has got to be my first angle."

Tom spoke up, "Christina, are you sure this guy is really trying to deceive the world? He sounded pretty sincere to me."

"I was thinking the same thing," Frank added.

"So was I," Michael joined in.

I looked at them all with an unbelieving expression and said, "Have you guys ever seen me scheming this hard for nothing? Besides, all he has to do is come up clean when we start digging, and we'll back right off." Then, I lifted my eyebrows in a discerning way and continued, "So are you guys, with me, or not?"

They answered simultaneously, "Of course we're with, you!"

I smiled confidently and replied, "That's good, because I don't think I'm wrong about Mohammed's true motives. Now I think we'd better get some rest, there's a lot to do tomorrow."

The first thing we did the following morning, March 18th, 1997, was to dive headfirst into our assignments. Three months later we were preparing to release my first film in over fifteen years. I entitled the film, 'The Slaying of the American Knights.' The story was about a single mother who worked for the Governor of New York State. The thrills began ten minutes into the film when the heroin, 'yours-truly', stumbles upon a conspiracy between the Governor and three high ranking state officials, to conceal how they knowingly allowed the state's largest chemical and plastics manufacturer, to dump millions of supposedly leak proof barrels of toxic waste into the Hudson River. The barrels that lined the bottom of the river from the mouth of New York harbor to the Port of Albany were slowly leaking toxic death to the entire state. From there the story unfolds with her secret search for proof of what she knows and what she goes through to bring that proof to light.   The film had just enough action, drama, love, and suspense to be a major blockbuster, and with Taylor as my little co-star, I knew it couldn't fail.

Released with the film was a ten-cut soundtrack entitled, "Follow Me to Utopia." The title cut was a ballad which invited the whole world to follow me as one family into a loving, free, and unpolluted future.   The second cut was a souped-up contemporary dance hit entitled, "Self-annihilation."   It told how through great hatred, bigotry, and pollution we were destroying ourselves and our earth.   It also allowed me to show the world that even at forty-three, I was still the Goddess of the dance floor.

My little co-star and I began promoting our new film with zeal before the editing was even completed.   We started by appearing on every talk show in the country, and like magic, Taylor stole the hearts of the nation.

When we appeared on the nation's leading talk show, Taylor immediately stole the spotlight with his big smile as he looked at me and enthusiastically said, "Wow, Mom! We're really on the Orpah Gunthry Show."

The audience immediately began to laugh and after we discussed the film, Orpah looked at Taylor and asked, "So tell us Taylor, did you like making a movie with your Mother?"

He smiled again and replied, "It was great, but the best thing is that my Mom made the movie because I asked her to."

Orpah smiled at him curiously and with a surprised tone said, "You did!   Why did you do that?"

Still smiling Taylor answered, "The reason the film is plotted around an environmental disaster is because I asked my Mom and Dad if there was anything the three of us could do to help save our planet.   They told me the only way we could make a difference was to get involved, and the film is one way we're trying to do that.   My Mom, Dad, Uncle Jimmy, Nana, and all our friends have become members of Green Peace and The Save the Earth Brigade.   I'm also working to establish a worldwide environmental awareness television network, which will be geared toward a younger audience."

It was apparent Orpah was taken aback by Taylor's intellect when she took a deep breath and said, "My goodness!   Wouldn't you rather be playing at the park like most four-year-old children do?"

Taylor looked at her sadly as he hugged my arm and answered, "Mom, Dad, and I use to play all the time and I miss that, but we know if we don't do something to stop the pollution today, then there won't be a world for anyone to play in tomorrow."   With that Taylor received his first standing ovation.   He got his second two days later on the Josie O'Hara Show.

American Goddess

CHAPTER 65

The film was ready to go on June 3rd, which was calling it close, because we had already arranged to premiere the soundtrack along with clips from the film on June 5th, with a Thursday night blowout concert extravaganza in L.A., and it was being broadcast live on CBS.   We premiered the film in New York on Taylor's fifth birthday Saturday, June 7, 1997.   Afterward, with a birthday cake and presents, we turned the film's premiere into a city-wide birthday party for our Taylor.   The first weekend out the film grossed a-record ninety-two million dollars nationwide and sales of the soundtrack were beginning to soar.   Our success was so phenomenal that by July 1st, we were grossing billions in the world market, our stocks were skyrocketing, and to top it all off I began a five-month fifty city concert tour.   My popularity was so high; I filled stadiums to capacity as we worked five cities a week, two concerts a night.   And with each performance, I would set aside twenty minutes to have an open conversation with the audience about our environmental crises.

The concert tour ended on December 8th, 1997, and in only nine months we had more than reached our financial goals for that year with whopping corporate earnings of two hundred and sixty-nine billion dollars.

The time flew by so fast that before we knew it, it was February 28th, 1998, and I found myself reluctantly leaving a very nervous Michael behind, as I left for my rendezvous with King Mohammed Fehd at the Saudi Embassy in downtown Manhattan. While heading toward the city that night, I found myself feeling frustrated and uncertain over following through with my mission of international espionage, and sabotage, because with all the information Tom had gathered over the last eleven months, we still had no solid proof Mohammed was doing anything underhanded at all.   I guess it was simply pure gut instinct, which compelled me to launch that orchestrated evening of adulterated deception.

The moment James drove the limo through the heavily guarded gates and into the courtyard of the Saudi Embassy, a cold chill of fear came over me and I thought, "Dear God, please give me strength, because I'm really scared, and the last thing I want to be doing right now is looking this guy straight in the eye to try to convince him that I even like him, no less love him."

Just then James pulled the limo to an abrupt stop right in front of the embassy, and the moment one of the armed guards opened my door, I swallowed hard, and immediately became Christina Powers, the most seductive woman on the face of the earth.

American Goddess

Of course, I exited the limo with my right leg first, allowing just enough flesh to show through the slit of my turquoise gown, to heat the frigid February temperature at least 20 degrees.   Then to fan the flames, I very slowly and provocatively emerged from the limo radiating sensuality with my every move.

I was not at all surprised to see the King standing at the curb looking better then Omar Sharif could have ever hoped to look.   The second we made eye contact I gave him one of my famous winks.   With that, pure passion flared up from the depths of his dark brown eyes to the rising bulge in his pants, and instantly I knew I could handle King Mohammed Fehd.

Once I reached him, I slightly curtseyed then very femininely offered him my hand, which he appropriately kissed then released as he passionately said, "Christina, my love, you're more captivating at this moment; then, the most enchanted angel in the heavens, and I must admit that by merely standing in your presence, I'm finding myself actually feeling humbled by just a glance of your wondrously bewitching beauty."

I smiled graciously and seductively replied, "It is a pleasure seeing you again your majesty, and I thank you for your charming flattery, and it was quite the compliment."

He smiled adoringly as he reclaimed my hand and warmly said, "I feel as though I've waited a lifetime for this evening, so won't you please allow me to escort you to the dining room?"

Still smiling I gently squeezed his hand and replied, "I wouldn't want it any other way."

Mohammed poured on the charm as he romantically lead me arm-in-arm through the embassy, and as we spoke with voices of mutual admiration, visions of almost being thrown off a roof by this man began flashing through my mind and I thought, "Oh shit! You better keep your cool Mata Hari and dismiss these thoughts, 'cause if he senses just the slightest hint of fear you might as well kiss your ass goodbye."   With that in mind I jumped right back into my role with, "Mohammed words can't express how pleased my heart is over the incredible contributions you are personally making toward world peace.   And the way you have been able to leap over the numerous obstacles your organized peace talks have encountered, is an astonishing tribute to your own brilliance, and the love you hold for all humanity.   What I can't understand is why Israel outright refuses to bargain on the Jerusalem issue?"

He shook his head as he replied, "I don't understand it either.   All they have to do is agree to allow Arab citizens free movement in the city of Jerusalem, and we could sign the most promising treaty for peace the world has ever known."

The moment he finished speaking, I lifted his hand to meet my lips, then tenderly kissed it just once and said, "I told you over the phone, you have found a special place in my heart Mohammed, and if there is anything I can do to help you get your peace treaty signed, please don't hesitate to ask."

He smiled softly and with a gentle voice replied, "Thank you for sharing that Christina, because knowing I'm in your heart, fills my heart with joy." He said those words with such sincerity that as we walked on I thought, "My God, could I possibly be wrong about this man?"

Just then we reached the dining room, where Mohammed turned to me with the cutest smile and said, "I hope you brought your famous appetite, because I had a feast fit for a king and queen prepared."

Our dinner arrangements were more than just fit for royalty, they were obviously ordered to be as romantic as possible, with a candle lit table, flowers, champagne, and soft music. When we reached the table Mohammed very gallantly, pulled out my chair then proceeded to pop the cork from a champagne bottle.

He poured two glasses to the rim, handed one to me, and as we toasted, he said, "I raise my glass to the most incredible woman I've ever met." I smiled graciously as we sipped from each other's glass. Then I gave him the sincerest look I could muster and replied, "My sentiments are mutual."

He looked at me with admiration in his eyes and said, "I want you to know I've seen your latest film, and I found myself quite impressed with the message your film carried. So I decided to have a tape of your concert performance sent to me, and I was even more impressed by the crusade you have begun to save our planet's environment." He took my hand in his and added, "Christina, I believe if we joined forces for peace and a cleaner environment, then the two of us could actually save this planet."

My eyes lit up the room as I squeezed his hand and excitedly replied, "Oh, Mohammed. I was hoping you would feel that way, because I wanted to talk to you about doing just that."

He looked at me inquisitively and asked, "What did you have in mind?"

I stood up from my seat, then taking his hand in mine, I knelt beside him and said, "Just this Mohammed, in two weeks I will be taking my concert on an international tour, and I'm doing it because I want to bring my environmental message to the entire world. The only obstacle keeping me from accomplishing my goal is the League of Arab Nations, because all of them, including Saudi Arabia, have denied my request to perform a live concert in your nations."

"I know of the request you made," he interrupted. "The reason your requests were denied, is because it is forbidden by Muslim law to allow any type of public performance to take place in our nations at all."

This time I interrupted with a look of delight, "Mohammed, please just hear me out! Besides going on an international tour, I have also arranged for my first concert which is scheduled to take place in Israel on March 15th, to be televised live to every nation on earth. Except of course for the Arab Nations; they also refused to air my concert.   Now what I'd like to propose is that you as the leading member of The League of Arab Nations, use your influence with your Arabian brothers, and convince them to allow me to perform in their nations."   Immediately he pulled his hand out of mine, and for one split second I caught that old familiar look of pure evil anger radiating from his eyes.

Then just as fast he plastered a patronizing smile on his face, and with a chuckle said, "That's preposterous, Christina.   Don't you realize what you're asking me to do is completely unheard of in the Arabian world?"

I stood to my feet and calmly replied, "Frankly, Mohammed, I'm disappointed with your condescending attitude.   Don't you realize what you're asking Israel to do is completely unheard of as well?" Looking him straight in his eyes I added, "Please tell me how you expect Israel, the Western world, and myself to truly believe the Arabian world is honestly leaving the ways of the past behind, if your nations won't even allow your citizens to view a live performance on their own television sets?   You said you already seen my performance; how can you still say no?   You know how important this message is for the survival of our planet. "

His eyes opened wide with that little bombshell, then he began shaking his head again as he looked at me curiously and said, "You know, you may be right."

I jumped right on that one as I knelt back down and excitedly said, "Just picture it, Mohammed.   You and I standing together in the Holy City of Mecca, beaming our images to the entire world as we proclaim our mutual desire for world peace and a cleaner environment."

I could see the wheels turning in his head. Then all at once he embraced me lovingly and said, "I'll do it!"

When I left for home that evening, I took with me the knowledge that on March 14, 1998, I would once again be performing a live concert on Saudi soil.   Only this time, the entire Arabian world would be watching!   As James drove me back to our home on the Powers Complex, I thought, "Oh well my dear Mohammed, I guess soon enough I'll know for sure if you're truly sincere, or if you're as full of shit as I think you are."   Just then we pulled into the driveway and three very anxious men came running out to greet us.

The first thing I said with a presumptuous smile and a devious look in my eyes was; "Mission accomplished, guys."

American Goddess

For the entire two weeks before leaving for Saudi Arabia, I tried desperately to convince Michael to stay home with Taylor. That way he would have at least one parent with him in case our plans backfired. But he and Frank outright refused to allow me to go on this mission alone. And to tell you the truth, when we got off the plane at the Mecca International Airport, and I saw all the armed guards waiting to take my entourage and me to the king's palace, I was more than happy they were with me. Mohammed was more than cordial when we arrived at the palace, especially to Michael.

He seemed to be sizing Michael up with every look as they talked, and at the same time he almost totally ignored me, which was fine until I heard him say, "Christina has informed me you will all be leaving for Israel right after her performance tonight, but I was hoping I could persuade you and your wife to stay over as my guests and leave in the morning. This way you and I might get to know one another a little better."

I didn't even give Michael the chance to open his mouth before I interrupted with, "Mohammed, I've already explained to you my itinerary is planned right down to the very last minute, so why would you think my husband could change it?"

He looked at me as if I were totally out of line then turned to Michael and said, "Does your wife always speak for you?"

Michael politely answered, "Only when she's running the show, and this happens to be her show."

Mohammed turned back to me, "Won't you please accept my invitation to stay the night, Christina?"

I smiled sincerely and answered, "We'd love to stay Mohammed, but to be honest with you the reason we can't was meant to be a surprise for you."

He looked at me curiously, "You're leaving immediately after your performance is a surprise for me? I don't understand."

This time I smiled mischievously, "I guess I can tell you now. I have an 8:00am meeting with Prime Minister Guron of Israel tomorrow morning, and after tonight's concert I'm sure I'll be able to convince him to sign the Peace Accord with Palestine."

His expression showed his approval as he excitedly replied, "You're truly a remarkable creature, Christina, and you never cease to amaze me."

I chuckled confidently, "You haven't seen anything yet. Now I'm going to ask you gentleman to excuse me while I make sure everything is set for tonight's performance."

When I walked out on the stage that night to perform the first live performance ever to be viewed by the Arabian nations and televised worldwide, I was not surprised at all to see an audience composed of fifty thousand male chauvinist pigs. I proceeded

American Goddess

to give them a one-hour show that went down in history. Immediately after my performance I invited Mohammed to join me on stage, where we jointly proclaimed our desire to achieve world peace and a clean environment for all.

Once I had Mohammed and the entire audience agreeing with my every word, I knew it was time to drop my bombshell. So, I enthusiastically grabbed Mohammed's hand and said, "Thank you so much my friends and I want to say a very special thank you to King Fehd for inviting me to entertain for everyone this evening. I love you all and I want to say that King Fehd and I see a future world where women are treated as equals throughout the world.". For it is time woman all over the world unite as one unbeatable force to fight against oppression, chauvinism, discrimination, and the brutality that is perpetrated against us by what has always been a male dominated world."

Immediately Mohammed pulled his hand out of mine and walked off the stage as the entire, stunned, audience began to boo and jeer! Only I wasn't finished yet.

I deliberately stood there and shouted over the screams of, "Stone her! Stone her!" With, "what type of people is it that will proclaim their desire for world peace, and yet continue to enslave their mothers, sisters, and daughters?"

That's when the cameras went off and the heavy curtain came down right on my head knocking me to the floor. When I stood up, I could hear the objects which were being thrown by the audience hitting the outer side of the curtain, and before I could even get my balance, Mohammed ran toward me grabbed my arm and began to drag me off the stage.

Once we were backstage, he flung me up against the wall and shouted, "That was not a wise move you stupid bitch!" He raised his fist and just before he struck my face, Michael leaped on him with such force they both went flying into the orchestra pit. I screamed in horror as guards tackled Michael from all directions and began to beat him with Billy clubs.

Mohammed turned and started heading toward me with fury in his eyes and just as he reached me Frank came out of what seemed like nowhere and landed right on top of Mohammed.

Without a second thought I smashed a violin over one of the guard's head, grabbed his gun, fired it twice in the air, then lunged toward Mohammed and shouted, "The next shot is right between your King's eyes!"

Mohammed instantly looked me in the eyes, and knowing I meant it, he shouted, "Guards, cease immediately!" Once they stopped beating Michael and Frank, Mohammed ordered, "Now bring them up here!" Then turning back to me he calmly continued, "If you pull that trigger Christina, none of you will get out of this country alive."

American Goddess

Looking as ruthless as the devil himself I coolly replied, "I don't want to kill you Mohammed, but you're not going to kill my husband either. And I know you don't want the entire free world after your ass for killing me, now do you?"

He instantly turned the charm back on and said, "Please forgive me for my outburst, but you really should have discussed your views on equal rights for women with me before making such controversial public statements to the Arab world. Do you realize the amount of heat I'm going to get from Arab leaders for what you've done?"

I placed the gun down and said, "I'm sorry Mohammed, but if we're going to work together for a brighter future, then I had to know that future also includes the liberation of women as well."

When we were finally safely in the air, I looked at Michael and Frank who were obviously still very shaken up and started to laugh so hard I nearly fell out of my seat.

They both looked at me as if I were nuts, then Michael threw his pillow at me and said, "You were nearly killed, I have two black eyes, your whole crew was scared to death, you almost had to shoot the fucking king, and you're laughing!"

I finally composed myself and smugly answered, "We may have taken some lumps tonight, but it's nothing compared to the lumps he's getting from his Arab brothers right now. As a matter of fact, I won't be surprised if Muslim women all over the world are marching for equal rights as soon as the sun comes up."

Frank started to laugh as he said, "Did you see the look on his face when you started shooting? I thought he was going to shit in his pants."

With that the three of us began laughing and when we finally stopped, I sarcastically said, "Step one in our mission to get the king is accomplished, step two is yet to come."

The next morning the free world was raving, the Arab world was ranting, and Mohammed was scrambling to hang onto his strong hold by releasing a public statement which read, **"I am in complete agreement with Christina Powers' desire to liberate the women of the world. But we in the Arab world realize that such a dramatic change cannot take place overnight."**

While he was very nicely covering his ass, I was preparing to set stage two in motion. Only stage two didn't go as well as I had hoped. When I tried to persuade Prime Minister Guron that Mohammed was not to be trusted, he looked at me in a condescending way and said, "Ms. Powers, just because King Fehd is not willing to bring the Arab world's view on women's rights into the twenty first century tomorrow; does not mean I'm going to cancel the most promising peace talks we've ever held with our Arab neighbors."

With that slap in the face I stood up and angrily said, "Why you arrogant asshole. I'm telling you he's plotting against your Nation's people, and you think I'm trying to sabotage the peace talks because he's a chauvinist pig."   His mouth was just about to hit the floor so I added, "And if you're stupid enough to sign his peace accord, then you deserve everything you get."   I turned, walked to the door and slammed it on my way out.

From that day on I dove into the rest of my six-month world tour, and while I was doing everything possible to stay in a positive public light, so was my adversary. Mohammed had worldwide attention as he played the perfect king of peace.   He was so good at playing peacemaker that on September 3rd, 1998, the day we returned home and the same day Tom Davies confirmed our suspicions that the Arab nations were conspiring with the nation of China to undermine the economies of the West, the nations of Israel, Palestine, and Saudi Arabia were signing an historic Peace Accord which would take twenty years to implement completely and it also gave Mohammed everything he wanted.

That night we began calculating the current rate at which Mohammed's plans were proceeding and we figured that by the year 2027, he could have his temple completed and be ready to bankrupt the West at the same time.

So the next morning I got Barbara on the line and said, "Hi, Barbara, would you please do me a little favor?"

"Sure, what is it, Christina?"   She answered.

I very calmly said, "Have the League of Women's Voters help me get on the ballots across the country for President of the United States?"

And you know what she said, "**YES!!   YES!!**"

American Goddess

After my talk with Barbara the night of September 3rd, 1998, I turned to Michael, Jimmy, Pierre, and Frank, who were sitting with me, and looking at them with the most earnest expression, said, "It really starts now guys!   Because this isn't just a race for the Presidency, this is a race for all humanity!"   My heart went out to them, as they gazed back at me with the expressions of four frightened little boys.

Then Jimmy, with full dramatics seemed to sum it up for all of us, when he grabbed my shoulders and nervously said, "Oh my, God!   Christina, this is scary shit!   Why is all this happening?"

Sadly, I shook my head, "I don't know Jimmy, but I do know this game Mohammed is forcing us to play is for keeps, and we have got to win it!"

With that, Michael hugged us both, as he pulled Pierre and Frank into an embrace of five, and said, "By the grace of God and the power of God within us, we will win."   Then we proceeded to humble ourselves before the throne of God, like the five little children we truly were.

When we finished praying, Michael looked at the rest of us as if he were ready to leap into the lion's den, then while pulling up his sleeves he eagerly said, "Well, what did Barbara say?"

I smiled at Michael's willingness to get started, especially after knowing how he once felt about the subject.   Then I slightly chuckled, as I answered, "She was screaming 'Yes, Yes,' in such a frenzy, I thought she was going to have a heart attack. I didn't get it all, but I'm quite sure she said, she'll be flying in around 7:00pm tomorrow night, and don't forget to have dinner ready!"

Barbara showed up at our door for dinner as promised, and this time she brought Eartha and three colleagues from the League of Women Voters.   After Barbara introduced Mary, Vicky, and Tanya, to Michael, Taylor, and me, she said, "Christina, we've come together to formally invite you on behalf of the League of Women Voters, to announce your candidacy for President to the country, at our annual convention next month in Washington, D.C.."

Then Eartha said, "I'm with you Christina all the way and I know the entire Democratic party will be too, once they know your running."

Smiling I replied, "I thank you ladies very much, but before I can accept your gracious invitation, I would like all of you to know exactly where I stand on the issues first."

Barbara returned my smile with a big one of her own and replied, "Well then start talking girlfriend, `cause we're here to listen!"

American Goddess

I hugged her warmly and answered, "I think it can wait until after we have dinner." With that we all began to laugh, as I led them to the dining room for one of Carmen's famous lasagna dinners.

Immediately after dinner, Michael and I invited the five of them into the den. For the next five hours I proceeded to fill them in and answer their questions on exactly where my campaign would stand, on as many of the issues we could possibly cover in one evening.

Once all the main topics were discussed, Barbara began shaking her head. Then looking at me as if I were out in left field, she said, "Girlfriend, are you getting in the race to win it, or is this a joke?"

I looked back at her as if she were the crazy one and answered, "Of course I want to win, I'm not running for President because I have nothing better to do!"

Shaking her head again she replied, "Well then you better tame your rhetoric a little. If you give the Republican and Independ Party's ammunition like that to use on you, then you're not going to have a chance in hell of winning this thing!"

I started to chuckle with a slightly sarcastic tone as I answered, "I don't believe this. You're the one who convinced me that dramatic changes had to be made to save our world, and now you're telling me my language is too strong!" Flinging my hands in the air I added, "Well then, what is it you want from me?"

"Christina," she calmly began. "I agree with everything you've said, and I also believe in being radical. However, if you use your campaign as a forum to try and persuade the American public, we need to make all these changes within the next four years, then you will lose for sure."

With that statement I rose to my feet and said, "Barbara, I have no desire or intention of 'sugar coating' the issues for anyone. If I am going to be President of our Nation, then everyone is going to know exactly how I plan to lead us out of this mess. Now all I want to know from the League of Women Voters is, will you back me or not?"

The five of them looked at each other with bewildered expressions for a moment, then Eartha answered for them all by saying, "All the way to the White House, girlfriend."

I smiled confidently and replied, "Great! Then I graciously accept your invitation to announce my candidacy for President, at your national convention next month."

It was sometime around 2:00am, when I was finally able to get them to stop asking their questions, and because of the hour, Michael and I insisted on Barbara, Eartha and the girls spending what was left of that night, in the guest rooms, instead of heading for a hotel as they planned. Realizing they were being politely told it was time for bed, they reluctantly agreed to stop talking about my candidacy in order to get some sleep. But of course, the first topic over breakfast later that morning was my candidacy for President. Right after breakfast, we held another meeting to discuss my candidacy, and how 'The League' might play a role in helping me get my campaign off the ground.   Only this time I had Jimmy, and my Attorney, Tom Davies join us.

We made many decisions that day on how we would proceed with getting my name on all fifty ballots, as the Democratic Party's Candidate for President.   But our first decision was to keep my intentions secret until after I addressed the League's Convention, on October 16th, 1998.   By 6:00pm our plans were finalized and ready to be put into motion.   When Barbara and the girls left for L.A. that evening, their mission was to inform every woman's group across the nation that Christina Powers would be addressing this year's convention.   As for the seven of us, Michael, Jimmy, Pierre, Frank, Tom, myself, and of course Taylor, well we were going to have to 'bust some butt', if we wanted our campaign ready to go into full swing as soon as I made my speech to The League of Women Voters.

Not ten minutes after everyone left our home that evening, I received a call from my dear friend Mohammed, who called to say, "Christina, my love.   Did you like the way I persuade Prime Minister Guron to sign my peace accord, even after the spectacle of your dramatic, futile attempt to convince him not to sign?"

I immediately grew angry by his superior tone, and nothing was going to make me bite my tongue this time, as I sharply answered, "If you were standing in front of me right now Mohammed, I'd slap your arrogant face!   Does that answer your question?"

Seemingly unscathed by my harshness he calmly replied, "Forgive me Christina I truly didn't call to gloat.   I'm calling because I'd like to sign a peace treaty with you.   I know you were very upset after our last meeting, but that doesn't mean I'm not willing to try and help relax my Arabian Brothers' views on women's rights."

I quickly and sarcastically replied, "Oh really, Mohammed.   Why haven't you stopped the way your Arab Brothers have been brutally crushing every women's movement that has risen up in your nations since my concert?   The whole world knows, the moment they attempt any type of public display of unity at all, military troops disperse them."

He answered with a slight chuckle, "These things take time Christina, I can't change the views of the entire Arab World by myself overnight.   That's why I'm calling for your help."

"My help!"   I answered with a shocked tone.   "What is it you would like from me this time Mohammed, to persuade these women to humbly submit to their oppressors?"

He took on that familiar tone of sincerity as he answered, "I'd like for you to come visit the women's movement your covert activity has spawned and help me persuade them the changes they are calling for must come slowly, and without all this civil disobedience.   Additionally, once I have everything running smoothly between Israel and Palestine, which I hope will be sometime around September of 1999, I'd like to invite you to accompany me on a trip to Russia, Switzerland, and China. I believe if we work together on the second stage of my plan to achieve world peace; then, we could persuade the Switzerland banking establishment to help Saudi Arabia, in financing and then signing the first peace accord ever, among the Russian Republics, China, and the entire Arab World."

Just the thought of a Peace Treaty being signed between those nations brought chills to my spine, and I found myself no longer able to keep up the charade as I viciously replied, "Why you evil, beast! You're setting the world up for the battle of Armageddon and you're actually pleased with yourself, aren't you? Well if you think I'm that stupid that I'll unwittingly help you get away with this, then you've got another think coming!"

He started to laugh as he replied, "I figured you'd catch on sooner or later Christina, that's why I'm going to ask you one more time, right now, to leave your family and marry me. Then you can rule the world with me as my Queen."

I nearly choked with that one as I snapped back my answer, "You really are a **sick fuck,** Mohammed. How can you honestly believe you'll get away with this?"

His laughter at my words radiated pure evil, as he ruthlessly replied, "This is my destiny Christina, and there is nothing anyone can do to stop me."

I was so angered by the expression of his wickedness that I shouted, "You Monster! Enjoy your laughter while you still can, because I promise you Mohammed, I'm going to wipe that smirk right off your face!"

He stopped laughing with that statement, and snapped back, "How dare you presume to make idle threats against me and believe you'll get away with it. Especially when you're nothing more than an insignificant little woman with a big mouth! After your fiasco with Prime Minister Guron, do you still really think there's a man on this planet that would ever truly listen to what you have to say?"

With that slap across the face of every woman on earth, I really lost it!

And I'm sure the anger of any woman ever insulted by the condescending attitude of a male chauvinistic pig, echoed in my voice as I shouted, "I'm going to make you eat those words, you repulsive scum bag!"

His portentous interruption was sinister to say the least, as he shouted back, "If you attempt to interfere with my plans one more time Christina, I won't wait for my Temple to be completed, because I'll come kill you myself tomorrow!"

With a superior tone of my own I replied, "You just try coming near me once, you asshole and I'll broadcast the tape I just made of this conversation on every television station across the globe. Then you'll see just how quickly the plans of **mice and men** can fall apart!"

American Goddess

With that blow to his intelligence he angrily replied, "You release a tape of this conversation to anyone, and you can kiss your son goodbye, because I'll come after him instead of you."

I saw flames as I screamed, "Don't you dare threaten my family, because I'll castrate you myself, you bastard!   And if you don't want anyone to hear what you truly have to say to the world, then I suggest you stay the **fuck** away from my family.   If I so much as catch the slightest scent of your stench anywhere near us, then you can kiss your plans to rule the world goodbye, because I'll obliterate you from the face of the earth!   And Mohammed, if you truly learned anything about me from watching my life unfold as you have said, then you know I don't make idle threats!"

I slammed the phone in his ear, turned to Michael who was listening the whole time, and with **fire** in my eyes said, "I'm more determined to win this race and get that sick bastard, then ever before!"

American Goddess

After that call, we wasted no time getting our act together. Before the day of the convention, we managed between the six of us, to set and keep four hundred and forty six appointments with top female and male business and government leaders throughout the country, whom I believed felt as strongly about the issues we face today, as I did. I made arrangements to go abroad for the month of August 1999, to visit the leaders of Russia, Switzerland, China, Germany, France, Italy, Turkey, England, and South Korea. Not only did I have to become President, but I had some catching up to do on the international scene as well if I was going to beat Mohammed at playing his own game. As for Barbara, Eartha and 'the girls,' well they wasted no time either, and when October 16th, 1998, rolled around, I found myself mentally preparing to read the most powerful speech I had ever written, to the largest group of women in history to ever attend a convention held by The League of Women Voters. There were eight hundred thousand women of every race, creed, and color from all across the nation, who besieged the Capital that day, and they all came just to hear what I had to say. Of course, along with the girls came the reporters, who had over the last three weeks created enough speculation over why I was appearing at the convention that year, to cause Vice-President Mike Larson to call me personally and ask, "Christina, is there any truth to the rumors you may be interested in running for a public office?"

I simply answered, "If you didn't hear it from me, Mike, then it's not true."

The next thing we knew, his wife Karen Larson had personally invited herself to address the convention, and with a little arm twisting from the White House, her address was purposely slotted to come just before mine. I was a little surprised Barbara gave in as readily as she did, but I didn't see the sense in pushing the issue if she wasn't, so we let Karen go first.

Due to the size of the expected crowds, the convention was moved from the Convention Hall, to the Washington Monument. Seated in the front row we could hear Karen quite well as she told the League's Members, at least ninety-seven reasons why, President Stump and her husband Vice-President Mike Larson should be given four more years in the White House.

As she was finishing up her speech, I was unconsciously squeezing Michael's hand so hard, that he said, "Ouch! What are you trying to do, break my hand?"

I loosened my grip and answered, "I'm nervous, all right."

Taylor hearing this pulled my other arm down toward him until he could wrap his little arms around my neck to whisper in my ear, "Don't be nervous Mom, Dad and I are here."

American Goddess

A tear came to my eyes as I lovingly returned his embrace, and softly replied, "Thank you my little love. I feel better already."

Just then I looked up at the platform to see Barbara taking the podium from Karen to boisterously say, "Ladies, without any further delay, let's just welcome Christina Powers to the podium!"

I rose from my seat when their cheers filled the fresh autumn air, and as I climbed the steps to the platform I thought, "Oh well! Here goes everything." When I reached the podium I hugged Barbara warmly, then turned to the largest audience I had ever addressed in my life and said, "**I thank you for a truly heart felt welcome my sisters; and I am honored that every one of you actually dared to brave this phenomenal Washington traffic, just to hear what I have to say.**"

With that a loving laughter echoed throughout the park. Then raising my fist in the air, I enthusiastically shouted, "**Way to go, ladies!**" The laughter immediately turned into cheers of self-worth, so I encouraged our moment as united women, to bask in the glory of our self-pride, by applauding the crowd and the cheers rumbled like thunder.

When we composed ourselves, I continued by saying, "**And I must add, my heart is also filled with a great sense of pride in knowing that among we woman nearly two hundred thousand brothers with kindred spirits have come to celebrate a common bond, the desire to truly obtain equality for all, and in our lifetime!**"

This time as the cheers rang out a sense of true oneness with my fellow human being exploded within my spirit, and in that instant, I knew that our souls were linked together by a divine force with an omnipotent plan for the human race. That knowledge seemed to fill me with an overwhelming sense of power, and confidence, which radiated from my very core, as I continued, "**I know there are men in the world today who state that civilization and the earth we inhabit, have become so barbarically corrupted and poisoned, that our generation has lost the desire to create a better world for future generations, because they see no way for the human race to survive anyway. Well, what I'd like to say to those men, after standing here and feeling the power of women united in body, and spirit, to make sure there is a brighter future for our children, is get with the program guys!**" And the cheers rose again!

When I was able to continue, I said, "**I'm going to take a moment now to share a personal story with you, I think you'll find amusing. Just recently, a world renowned male public official said to me, 'Christina, there isn't a man on earth that would ever take anything you have to say seriously, because you are nothing more than an insignificant little woman with a big mouth.' In response to that statement, I'd like to say, even if it were true sir, it wouldn't matter one bit. Because whether you like it or not women voters out number male voters by nearly two to one. So I invite you sir, to stick those** figures, along with your crude remarks into your calculations, and see just how they compute."

And the crowd went wild! Then I added, "My dear sisters, I know that with the power of the love and compassion found in the hearts of every grandmother, mother, sister, and daughter as a gender, can accomplish what our forefathers have failed to do. That is to truly create a nation which stands under God with liberty equality and justice for all! I also believe in my heart that once we stand together to make the hard changes needed to save our world, then our grandfathers, fathers, husbands, brothers, and sons, will join our cause!"

With that they lost it again! When I finally calmed them down, I said, "Now I know there has been much said over my reasons for accepting the invitation to address this year's convention, so right now I'd like to put an end to all the speculation by saying, after many months of soul searching, my family and I have decided that I should run for office as the Democratic Party's Candidate for President of the United States of America, in the year 2000!"

At that moment, the sound of the cheers of admiration and love which rang-out, had the intensity to reach every ear on earth, and put the fear of God, in the hearts of every politician in Washington, D.C...

Once I knew I had everyone's full attention, I calmed the crowd back down and continued by saying, "I believe it is way past time for our great nation to take a new direction into the future. A direction which will lead not just America, but the entire world toward a rejuvenated earth, and a renewed faith in the relentless ability of the human race to persistently rise, and meet, the challenges of the future every time. Although history has shown us the incredible capabilities of the human spirit, it has also shown us that without strong leadership set on a direct and determined course, we might not have survived to this point. Knowing this has caused me great concern, because with all the possible leaders I see on the horizon, who might one day lead our nation, I truly could not find one, I felt would be capable of leading us over the numerous obstacles, which await us all in the twenty first century. I also know first-hand, due to the corruption and deceit, many of our politicians are found involved in today, America is not what she once was. And the leadership of the current administration fills our lives daily with lies and fake news, just to divide us and destroy our precious democracy. This is why I come before you as a fellow citizen, who knows that there is a great need to bring honesty, and a renewed conviction of integrity, back to our nation's government. This is one reason I have decided to run for President. I ask for your support of my candidacy because I still believe America is the greatest nation on earth! With the strong leadership skills, I will bring to the White House if elected, will help to bring forth the opportunity for all of us, to make our powerful nation once again the most respected

American Goddess

on earth!   I also believe that together we can make the changes necessary, to bring our Educational System to a level which will rival the world!   Together we can have a truly viable and fair Welfare System, which will enable our less fortunate citizens to live a productive and self-rewarding life!   Together we can create a Comprehensive National Health Care Program, which will protect the millions of Americans who are now uninsured and spare the fear our senior citizens feel of losing their life savings, due to an unaffordable Health Care System.   Together we can once again have a cleaner environment, where we will not be drinking polluted waters and breathing toxic air. Together we can eliminate our nation's deficit, and if elected, I guarantee this will be accomplished within my first term!   Together we can wipe out poverty, hunger, malnutrition, and the deadly diseases which are ravaging our world as we speak! Together we can overcome a history of bigotry, prejudice, sexism, racism, discrimination, and the disease of ignorance, which is prevalent within our society today!   I know these things can be accomplished because together, we are not just mere mortals, we are divine beings empowered by God, which is our birth right thanks to His unconditional gift of love.   That is why together we can create the miracle, which will produce a nation known for equality, tolerance, open-mindedness, and fairness for all its citizens!   I know the challenges of the twenty first century can only be met if we have faith in one another and believe in ourselves as a people with a common purpose.   Once we truly decide to work together for the good of all humanity, then I know we will find the way to conquer the overwhelming burdens our nation, and the world face today.   My friends, all my claims will not be merely promises blowing in the wind.   This I can guarantee, if you stand with me by voting for me, and my hand-picked running mates who have decided to run with me on the Democratic Party's ballot, for crucial offices in the House and the Senate.   By asking for your vote for myself, and my hand-picked running mates, I am inviting you to join us in the greatest, peaceful revolution this nation, and world, has ever known.   And I promise, if you will allow me the opportunity to lead our nation into the twenty first century, as the first woman President of the United States of America, then together the dreams of our people will once again have renewed life.   Now I pray that the love, blessings, and power of God, be with us all as we rise together as one, to meet the challenges of the twenty first century!"   Then I raised both fists in the air, and shook them triumphantly as I shouted, "Thank you, America, God bless us all, and Amen!"

With that nearly one million people leaped into the air and began cheering so loudly, that the ground rumbled!   And their cheers evoked a renewed sense of hope, and optimism, for a brighter future.

All at once they began shouting a chant in unison, "Christina for President in 2000!" The sight of this breathtaking display of humanity, showing their love for me, and their faith in my ability to the entire world with enough power to reach the heavens, humbled my heart to the point of tears.   Then almost as if being thrown into a bottomless pit, the realization of the awesome challenges I had just given my word I'd lead our nation through, hit me.   I knew at that moment, if I had to, I would give my life to give my fellow being another chance for a new beginning.

CHAPTER 69

When we held our press conference that evening, the male reporters began firing their so-called sophisticated questions at me like gang busters.

My answers remained calm, cool, and dignified until Tucker Carlson from the Fox news network asked a question which resembled a statement of judgment, "Christina, you don't even hold an associate degree from a Community College, and you expect the American public to believe you can accomplish your noble goals?"

Realizing the questions were becoming more of a challenge similar to an all-out attack of my intellect, rather than an interest in where I stood on the issues, I put my dukes up by deliberately delivering my answers so precise and fast, I had their heads spinning.   "Tucker, if a doctorate degree was what held the solutions to our nation's problems, then we wouldn't have all these problems to solve, now would we?"   I wanted to add smart ass, but I managed to control the urge.

The next question came from Ed Henry, "Christina, you morally proclaim your desire to bring honesty and integrity back to our government, but I have to wonder, how you can make such a virtuous claim, when the way you've obtained your empire, Powers Incorporated, looms under a shroud of deceit and possibly chargeable criminal activities?"

"Ed, your question sounds more like an accusation, that I may have committed a crime, or crimes, to have accomplished the incredible task of rising from the ashes of a crushed life, to be standing where I am this evening.   And frankly sir, that angers me! So to put an end to this kind of nonsense, right now I plainly state, I will not hide my past business tactics from anyone.   And I guarantee, you will not find a skeleton in my closet America isn't already familiar with."   Then I boldly stood in front of a room full of hungry reporters and said, "Gentleman, due to your rude manipulation of this interview by shouting over your female colleagues, I think it's time to say goodnight."

As I turned away Tucker yelled, "Christina, you haven't answered one question on the issues, and you're dodging the press already?"

I turned back to him and calmly answered, "If you recall Tucker, I wasn't asked one question on the issues.   Now I'd like to thank you gentleman for the enthusiasm you've shown over my candidacy."   Then I turned away and headed for the door, but they still refused to stop screaming their questions at me as I walked past them.

The press was still on my heels when I reached my entourage, who were all standing at the exit door of the conference hall, with stunned expressions on their faces. The whole frantic scene caused me to smile almost to the point of laughter as I said, "What's the matter with you guys, seen a ghost?"

With that, Barbara shook her head as if to rattle her brains loose.   Then with frustration in her voice, and in front of all the reporters who were breathing down my neck she said, "What happened to your diplomacy, Christina?   Did you think it would be a wise move to throw it out the window tonight?"

I simply hugged her warmly as I lovingly, yet seriously replied loud enough for all to hear, "Barbara, this isn't Hollywood, and we're not here to win a popularity contest. This is the future of the human race, and we're here to try and save it."   Then I turned as I looked at everyone there and added with a sense of urgency, "This isn't a party! The survival of our future on this planet is at stake, and if I'm going to lead our nation in a last-minute attempt to save it, then I cannot be intimidated by anyone or anything. I refuse to diminish the gravity of the situation one bit.   Everything is going to be placed on the table, so the voters can see for themselves just what we're truly facing.   If the country doesn't like what I believe we need to accomplish together in order to succeed, then the ultimate decision on the direction this nation takes, will be theirs to make.   I honestly believe because of this I will win, but whether I win or lose, at least I will have tried with all my heart to do something about it."

Then Sharon Peach, a reporter for the Seven Hundred Club politely asked, "Christina, one question please?"

I smiled gently as I replied, "Of course."

"You come across as a Christian woman and yet you say it's up to us to save ourselves.   My question is how can you say that, when you know that Christ will return to do that himself?"

I smiled at her spiritual innocence and warmly replied, "I'm not disputing your beliefs, but I also know God is already here within us, and I believe He has been trying to do just that through us for centuries.   What I'm saying, is that I'm sure when He makes his presence known, He'd rather find us working together as one to save the gifts He is given us, then working apart to destroy them."   Still looking at everyone I added, "Now that was the last question, I will take tonight.   Thank you."   When I turned to leave that time, they were all so speechless by my statements, they couldn't have remembered their next questions if they tried.

The following morning October 17th, Taylor, Michael, the entire gang, and I, hit the campaign trail with intensity, as we began the most vigorous campaign schedule ever. The crowds we drew were so large that we stole the headlines from the major political

American Goddess

Party's' candidates for the next two weeks, with headlines like, "**Within three days of her speech, Christina Powers has received over thirty million signatures throughout the country, and her name has now officially been placed on all fifty ballots as the Democratic Party's, nominee for President.**" But when the republicans stole the headlines back, they stole them back big time with headlines that read, "**President Stump joins King Mohammed in Jerusalem to ratify the historic peace accord between Israel and Palestine and to proclaim Jerusalem as the new Capital of Israel.**"

Two weeks later the Independent party stole the headlines with news of their own, "**Ohio Senator Ann Brown has joined the race to be nominated by the Independent Party as the first black female candidate to represent their party for President of the United States.**"

When I stole the headline's back, I wished I hadn't, because they were all similar to this one, "**The Senate has subpoena Christina Powers to appear before a Senate Hearing, called to investigate possible tax evasion and questionable Wall Street business dealings. The Senate has also barred Christina Powers a place on the American ballots until the investigation is completed.**" Beneath the headlines it read, "**We haven't even reached 1999, or the primaries yet, and the race for 2000 is gearing up to be the most dramatic in American history.**"

The morning after my forty fourth birthday, December 11th, 1998, I found myself and my attorney Tom Davies, pushing our way through a mob of reporters, as we walked down the so-called American Halls of Justice, to appear before a Senate Hearing. When we entered the Senate Chambers, the press was kept out by security, and we were promptly informed by a clerk, "The Senate Commission has decided to hold a closed hearing in order to avoid press frenzy."

My reply to her was, "On just whose authority was this decision made?"

A familiar voice from behind answered for her, "As Speaker of the House, I made that decision, Christina." I swiftly turned to see Senator Edward Kenny standing behind me and seated behind him were eleven of the most crooked old goats in Congress.

For a moment I had to fight back my laughter at this menacing sight, then I calmly replied, "Hello, Edward." Of course, I graciously nodded my head at his gang of cut throats as I added, "Good morning gentleman." I smiled sincerely and continued, "I hate to be a bother, but we already have a problem. You see a closed hearing is unacceptable to me, so right now I would like to informally and respectfully, request an open hearing?"

Their smug faces grew sterner as Edward answered for them all, "I'm afraid we've already made our decision Ms. Powers, so your request is denied." I simply said, "You don't really think I'm going to let you gentleman get away with this witch hunt without the public watching, now do you?" I slightly snickered as I added, "I happen to

528

remember my rights, and if you want me to appear here, then I want you to provide me with an open forum."

Edward answered quickly, "Then I'm afraid you're going to have to make your request formally Ms. Powers, and until then I suggest we proceed with the hearing."

With that Tom interjected, "I can give you a formal request right now, sir."

Edward sternly replied, "Mr. Davies, your request will have to be made through the proper channels, and to each one of us individually."

Tom responded with wide eyes, "But that could take weeks sir and you are beginning this investigation today."

Without changing his demeanor once, Edward answered, "I'm not discussing this any further Mr. Davies, now let's begin."

I then turned and began to walk away and when I did, Edward cleared his voice and deeply said, "We have a subpoena Ms. Powers, if you try to leave, I'll hold you in contempt. And I really don't think you want the voters to see me have to do that," sarcastically he emphasized, "now do you?"

I turned back and answered, "I'll answer your subpoena Senator Kenny, as soon as I return from the lady's room." I sarcastically added, "Or does your subpoena exclude that as well?"

When I entered the lady's room, I made one call to Pierre on my cell phone, and then headed straight for the hall where the press was waiting.   When I opened the door, the reporters were caught off guard by seeing me emerge from the hearing so soon, but they regrouped quickly and dashed to my side.   Once I had their attention, I promptly informed them just how the Senate Commission was deliberately attempting to violate my civil rights, by denying my informal request for an open hearing.   Then I added, "Right now I'd like to publicly give the Senate Commission notice that at this very moment, a formal request to immediately hold open hearings is being faxed to everyone on the commission.   It states, '**If my request is not swiftly granted, I will institute a lawsuit against the Commission, as well as the entire United States Senate, for violating my Constitutional Rights as an American citizen.**'   I've taken these strong steps because I'll be damned, before I'll allow this Commission to attempt to falsely crucify me behind closed doors.   Now if you will excuse me, the hostage must return to this illusion of Congressional Justice."

When I reemerged in the Senate Chambers, I watched in total amusement and dismay, at the mentality of these self-appointed judges, as they tried to nonchalantly break from their hasty conference huddle, to somehow reply to the hand delivered faxes' they had received while I was in the lady's room.   When we were all calmly settled, Edward with an amazed look on his face said, "What's the meaning of this, Ms. Powers?"

American Goddess

I simply answered, "Come now gentlemen, it's bad enough you don't know the Bill of Rights, don't tell me none of you can read either."

With that Tom choked so hard he almost spit his coffee all over the Senate Chambers, then I added, "Please Senators, just open the doors to the press and hopefully I won't have to make this farce any rougher on this Commission then I already plan to."

Not two minutes later the press was cordially invited in, and when everyone was settled Senator Kenny said, "Before we begin Ms. Powers, I must insist that you refrain from calling this Commission a farce. The mere fact that Powers Inc. has numerous subdivisions which are not publicly listed as being owned by Powers Inc., suggest that you have something to hide."

I was polite and unpretentious as I replied, "I assure you Senator, the only reason that is true, is because over the years as I've accumulated my corporate holdings, I didn't feel it necessary to broadcast that information to the entire world. I promise you though, when these hearings are concluded and I'm found innocent of all charges, I will personally have my signature placed on every payroll check which is ultimately paid by Powers Inc..."

From that moment on the whole country had an unbelievable bird's-eye view of every tax return and business transaction I ever made. After three months of their intense scrutinizing, all Edward could say for the commission when they finally finished their investigation on March 18, 1999, was, "Ms. Powers, we have undisputable documented evidence that by leaving the country for approximately two years, you evaded criminal prosecution for the tax evasion of your 1972/1973 tax returns."

With that accusation I immediately rose from my seat and swiftly replied, "Senator, this Commission knows quite well that I was never charged of a criminal act, because at the time my then Uncle, 'Frank Salerno' had total 'Power of Attorney' over all financial affairs. We both know if anyone were to have been charged for tax evasion, then Frank was the one legally liable. Since you had the audacity to cast a shadow of doubt over that incident, I remind the Commission that it was I whom two years later paid those taxes along with all the fines that accompanied them, and in full!"

With indignation he replied, "We're not done yet, Ms. Powers. There is also the charge of insider trading in reference to the day you brought Wall Street to its knees, as you so ruthlessly acquired the controlling interest of three major American corporations. Until you can prove to the commission that you had no previous knowledge of that day's events, you will still be barred from your place on the American ballots."

I held myself with dignity as I replied, "With all due respect Senator, I was investigated at that time and cleared of all charges. You know as well as I do, all I did that day was capitalize on the selfish greed of big business.   And please correct me if I'm wrong Senator, but wasn't one of your family's corporations one of those I acquired that day?"

At that moment with heartless frustration, he tossed his gavel down and said, "Case dismissed!"

Even the press cheered for me after that.   They continued cheering for me right through their nightly news broadcasts that evening, with reports similar to the one Tom Bradly gave on NBC, "Christina Powers disgraced the Senate Commission today as she triumphantly wins the right to remain on the American ballot, as the Democratic Party's candidate for President.   When asked how she felt about the decision, she enthusiastically replied, 'Vindicated.   Now hopefully the Senate will allow us to truly concentrate on what's really important, like the issues.' Then to add insult to injury, not two hours later she kept her promise to the Senate Commission, by having her signature stamped on an incredible four hundred and seventy-two thousand payroll checks from all across the country.   As it turns out, now that all the corporations held by Christina Powers are being listed under the one name of Powers Inc., Christina Powers is second to only King Mohammed Fehd of Saudi Arabia, for the title of the wealthiest entrepreneur on the face of the earth.   To top it off, her holdings are the most financially successful and environmentally conscious in the world, with corporate names like Tord Automotive, Easting House Electronics, Kenny Baby foods, Bradford Computers, and the Mitsubisa Corporation of Japan, just to name a few of her credits.   It's now known that it was Powers Inc. which was truly behind last year's two hundred billion-dollar Mitsubisa Corporations takeover of the Model Oil Company of Dallas, Texas.   Then upon close examination of the corporations actually controlled by Christina Powers, we've discovered they lead the world's industries across the board, with salaries, and benefits for their employees, and boast the highest employees' satisfaction rate in the 'country.' After revealing the extraordinary magnitude of her vast holdings to the world, at a press conference this afternoon she was asked, 'What's next, Christina?'   It's said she simply smiled at the reporter and stated, 'Change the world!'"

Thanks to the Commission we had three crucial months to make up.   When we hit the campaign trail the next morning on March 19th, 1999, we hit it with twice the vengeance as the first time.   Thanks to the commission again, the crowds that came to hear what I had to say on the issues, were also twice as large as the first time.   Of course, I hit them right between the eyes with the reality of the most urgent issues of the day, as I gave speech after speech, marveling and shocking the crowds.   Because everywhere I went, I clearly outlined my extremely radical solutions, on how together we could attempt to solve our nation's problems.

American Goddess

As for the press, well they stuck to our twenty-bus caravan like glue, as we bounced across the country from city to city and state to state.   And thanks to the press, excerpts of every speech I gave were broadcast across the nation so much, that by the time I was ready to make my trip abroad on August 1st, I was leading all my opponents in the polls by at least a twenty five percent margin.

The first stop on my trip was Russia, to meet with the newly elected President, Nicolai Puton in Moscow.   After our cordial introductions we sat down to a six-hour meeting, where I politely reminded him of all I had already contributed and accomplished over the years throw Powers Inc., to the democratization of the Russian Republics.   I also informed him of what I would propose to accomplish in the future between our two nations as President.   After that I asked for his international support of my candidacy, and he offered it enthusiastically.   Once I felt within my heart, I could trust and rely on this man as a future ally, I proceeded to fill him in on the details of the conspiracy I had uncovered between the Arab World and the Chinese Government to conquer and rule my nation and his.   Upon seeing the proof for himself, he agreed to bog down his upcoming peace talks with these nations until I was in office.   We could then join the political, economic, and if need be, even the military forces of our nations together, in order to put a kink in Mohammed's dream of world dominance.

Next was Switzerland, where I had a little over four hundred billion dollars in foreign and American currency stashed.   When I met with President Metal, and the six members of the Federal Council, I used that little bit of clout, along with my future plans for specific joint financial ventures between our two nations.   I was seeking their nation's internationally known historic support of any Republican Party's' candidate for President of the United States.   After which I received their overwhelming support for my candidacy.   Once again when I knew I could trust them, I showed them the same documented evidence of Mohammed's scheme, as I showed President Nicolai Puton. After they saw for themselves that Mohammed was planning to undermine their banking industry, they overwhelmingly agreed to help delay the peace talks as well.

From there it was off to meet with the leaders of Germany, France, Italy, Turkey, England, South Korea, Japan, and of course China.   I wanted to explain to each of them individually, what I would propose to accomplish economically, and environmentally, between their Nations and America, if I were President.   I also wanted to feel out the Chinese leaders, and I didn't like what I felt.

Three weeks into my trip, I was informed that my friend King Mohammed had just made a surprise visit to the States; where on the White House lawn he loudly proclaimed, "I have come on behalf of the Leaders of the Arab world, and the Nation of Israel, to through our full support behind President Stump's candidacy for President. We throw our full support behind his campaign, because he has proven to us and the world, that he is a man of his word, when he helped mediate the now historic Peace Accord between Israel and Palestine." I was also informed that after his speech my lead in the polls dropped substantially, but when I returned home on September 3rd with the international support of the leaders of every nation I met with, except China, the polls bounced back quite nicely.

CHAPTER 70

After our trip, we took two days to recuperate at the Powers Headquarters. That day as I was getting ready to go back on the campaign trail Frank and Tom entered my office, and with a look of confusion Tom said, "Christina, we have a problem, the New York State Election Committee has rejected your birth certificate. The Commissioner called me personally and said he was so confused that his staff could not find your records that he decided to research your birth records himself. It appears your birth certificate which was filed with the county clerk's office never had the hospital stamp on it and when checked with the birth hospital there is no record of your birth. On further investigation your birth record was never listed with the State of New York. Since he could not validate your birth certificate, he said he has taken your name off the ballot until this issue is resolved. Do you have any idea why they can't find your birth records?"

I was stunned and it showed on my face as I gasped, "Oh my God." I stood up from my desk so quickly that I had to grab the edge to steady myself because I became lightheaded.

Frank grabbed my arm, "Christina are you alright?"

When the color finally came back to my face I looked at him with a bewildered expression and said, "No Frank I'm not and you're right we do have a problem, a big one that I'm not sure how to handle. Talk about being blind-sided, I never saw this one coming."

Tom shook his head, "I don't get it Christina, what kind of problem could there be with your birth records?"

Just then Michael burst into the office, "Christina I was just asked by a reporter why your birth records cannot be found."

"I know honey; Tom and Frank just informed me."

Michael gave me a confused look as he asked, "What happened? I thought your birth certificate was legal."

"I thought so too, but I guess mobsters don't know how to legalize a fraudulent birth certificate."

American Goddess

Frank, shaking his head said, "What are you guys talking about? Why would you have a fraudulent birth certificate?"

I looked at Tom and Frank who both had dumfounded looks on their faces and I started to laugh just a little as if I had just gone a little crazy and said, "You guys had better sit down for this one. It's like this, I was never born Christina Valona. A few years ago, I discovered that shortly after my birth my mother had Frank Salerno 'doctor' my birth certificate to conceal my true parent's identity in an attempt to keep me safe. With everything going on it never even crossed my mind that the counterfeit birth certificate was not legally registered with the state or I would have never submitted it."

Tom cleared his throat, "Christina two questions, do you have your authentic birth record and were you born in the States?"

"Yes Tom I do and I was."

"Well then as your attorney it's a very simple fix. I'll just submit your original birth certificate and we go on. In this case, it doesn't matter who your parents are as long as your records are legal, besides the whole world knows you as Christina Powers anyway."

Frank interjected, "Tom did you hear her, she said her mother had Frank Salerno 'doctor' her birth certificate to conceal her true parent's identity in an attempt to keep her safe." Then, he gave me an overly concerned look as he continued, "Christina why would the identity of your true parents put you in danger?"

I sighed with a sense of utter defeat and said, "At this point guys if I have to reveal who my true parents are, I don't think this campaign is going to ever get on the road. Tom is there any way you can get the counterfeit birth certificate legally registered?"

He shook his head and chucked, "Christina you're trying to become the first woman President of the United States of America; do you really think we could get away with that?"

"No Tom I don't, I just didn't want to reveal my true identity, but I guess in order to do what I know I have to do to keep my family safe then once again I have no choice. I have to reveal to the world whose 'forbidden child' I am. I only discovered the truth after Frank's murder trial. I learned then that my mother was Norma Jean Montensel and my father was John Fitzgerald Kenny and I was named Christina Kenny."

A look of shock came over them both then Frank said, "Are you telling us that you are Marilyn Monroe and JFK's daughter?"

Just then Pierre buzzed me on the intercom, "Excuse me Christina, but we seem to have a problem, may I come in to speak with you?"

"Sure." I answered with a disgusted tone already anticipating the problem.

Pierre wore a look of total confusion when he entered my office, "Christina we've been getting hundreds of calls from reporters all over the world asking why you submitted a fraudulent birth certificate to election bureaus all over the country.   I don't know what to tell them.   Do you have any idea what they're talking about?"

I shook my head with utter frustration as I said, "I don't have any choice, I have to go public now.   Pierre please call a press conference for 6:00pm this evening in our main conference hall."

Michael interrupted, "Christina are you sure this is the safest thing to do?   You could end up having fanatics coming out of the woodwork after you."

"Michael it's too late already, I have to go public.   If I don't I'll have to drop out of the race, I'll look like I'm guilty of something for hiding my true identity and now that the reporters know it won't be long before one of them finds out on their own.   Either way, the political parties are going to crucify me.   As for the fanatics coming after me, I'm sure Frank and his security team can handle keeping me safe." I turned back to Pierre, gave him a confident wink, "Go ahead Pierre call the press conference, I'll be ready with something to say by then."

As Pierre left the room Frank said, "Christina, I still don't get it, how can you be Marilyn Monroe and JFK's daughter when Marilyn never had a child."

"My mother never had any children she wanted the world to know about Frank. She had very good reasons for concealing my identity."

That's when Tom interjected, "Do you have any idea how you're going to tell the world who you really are and still be considered a viable candidate?"

I shook my head, "Right now I don't have a clue Tom."   I looked toward Michael as I continued, "Baby please tell Jimmy that I'm not going to be able to have lunch with him and Taylor today.   I am going to go meditate for a while and hopefully I'll know what to say by the time I give the press conference."

CHAPTER 71

As soon as I entered the conference room the reporters started shouting questions at me like the one Tom Brokoff asked, "Christina are you going to tell us why

American Goddess

you submitted a fraudulent birth certificate to the election committees all over the country?"

I climbed the podium and immediately had to regain control of the all the reporters shooting questions at me, and the first thing I said was, "This is a press conference people.   Now please take the seats provided each of you and we'll get this press conference started."

The place began to quiet down so I said, "Ladies and gentlemen I have called this press conference to explain to the American Public the incident concerning my missing birth record and why my birth certificate cannot be found.   First, as everyone knows I was raised Christina Valona by Frank Salerno a man I believed at that time was my biological uncle.   Shortly after his death, I discovered that this was not true. I learned from my dear friend Barbara Goldstein that my mother had Frank Salerno 'doctor' my birth certificate to conceal my true parent's identity in an attempt to keep me safe.   That night I discovered Barbara had been a close friend of my mother's and she felt that after Frank's death it would be safe for me to learn who my true parents were.   She gave me an envelope and inside was the original copy of my birth certificate with some pictures of my mother and me along with a letter from my mother to me explaining why she did what she did.   I am at this very moment having copies of my true birth certificate hand submitted to election committees all across this country and shortly to all of you right here in this room.   I feel the only way I can truly explain to my fellow American's why I continued to hide my true identity is to read the letter my biological mother, 'Marilyn Monroe' wrote to me two weeks before her untimely death."

The gasps of shock and disbelief echoed throughout the auditorium.   Knowing that the entire country was doing the same thing, I swallowed my fear hard as I said, "Please, please allow me to continue and then I will answer your questions."   When the room quieted down, I began to read,

"My beautiful Christina, I instructed Barbara, my longtime friend, to give you this letter in the event of my death. You see my darling daughter, I am your real mother and have spent all these many years watching you grow up, but afraid to approach you for fear that your father and his family would endanger your safety in some way. I met your Dad at a dinner party, and we were immediately attracted to one another. In time we began a secret affair because your father was already married. He led me to believe he would leave the marriage for me. Only we discovered that his family and his father's political ambitions for your dad would not permit that to happen.   I had just discovered that I was carrying you, when your father stated that we could never be together and our affair would have to remain a secret, he said, "The world can never know."   At that moment, I became afraid to tell him about you. You see your father was a United States Senator and came from a very rich and powerful family. I knew they were capable of taking any action to protect their son's political aspirations and I had to keep you safe.

American Goddess

I know the world will say that I was just another dumb blonde sex-symbol, but I am far from that my sweet Christina. I didn't tell anyone that you were born because I was afraid for your safety. That is why I asked Frank Salerno to raise you. I turned to Frank who was my friend because he was rich and powerful. I entrusted him with you swearing him to secrecy. I knew that he could protect you and also give you a beautiful home with anything that you wanted until I could come and take you away with me. Then, your dad ran for the office of President of the United States and won. All those years I never stopped loving him and when he became President, I knew I could never tell him about you or how much I still loved him. Even though I married several times, no one replaced him in my heart. When I finally reestablished a relationship with your dad, I thought he was going to walk away from everything for me; only I discovered that was not true. It was then that the FBI began to watch my every move and I became even more paranoid about your safety. When I turned to Frank, he betrayed me and I learned that he was more interested in having me as his trophy wife then being your surrogate father. When he proposed to me, I was horrified and refused him. He became incredibly angry and tried to hurt me. I ran from his house and was more determined than ever to make enough money with my next movie, so you and I could just disappear. Once again, I learned the hard way that the only person I could depend on was myself. All those people in my life who I thought really loved me, did not. They would leave me like my dad or were unable to love me like my mother who was sick, and all the rest just used me.

I want you to know a little about me. All I ever really longed for was to be loved and wanted. I never knew my dad, and my mom was too sick to take care of me. I went from foster home to foster home until one day my mom came back for me. We were happy in our own little house, only not for long, because mom was once again hospitalized. I ended up in an orphanage until a couple came and brought me to live with them. They were extremely strict and mean to me. Many nights I cried myself to sleep because I just wanted my mom back. If you are reading this letter my sweet darling, then you know that something terrible has happened to me. I may not be able to tell you what, but I can tell you why. I am a threat not only to the Kenny family whose son is your father and the United States President, but now to Frank as well, who continues to harbor a great deal of resentment toward me, for refusing his marriage proposal.

Please know my beautiful baby girl, that you have always been the most important thing in my life. I love you with all my heart and soul. I know in my heart, that if you had the opportunity to know me, you would love me just as much as I love you. Not a moment has gone by without my wondering what you are thinking and doing. I have lots of photos of you growing up and I keep them in a secret place. Every night I take them all out and study each one carefully. I know every hair on your head, your laughing eyes, your little adorable nose and those beautiful little pink lips. How I long to hold you, how I long to kiss you, how I long to show you how much I love you. No matter what happens to me, please know that I never stopped loving you and will always be with you.   I pray for you to have a far better life than I had; wherein, people will love, adore and shower you with tons of attention. One more thing my sweet angel, I beseech you not to ever reveal to the world whose daughter you really are. I fear they will come after you as well. Goodbye my sweet darling,

All my love, your Mommy, Marilyn Monroe"

When I finished you could hear a pin drop.   Everyone was stunned for what seemed like minutes until finally Ken Carpenter from the New York Times asked, "Christina everyone knows Marilyn Monroe never had any children and you're expecting the American public to believe you're her daughter?"

"I was asked that same question just this morning Ken and I will give you the same answer; my mother never had any children she wanted the world to know about. The reason she wanted to keep my identity secret was because she feared if anyone knew who my true parents were my life would be endangered.   My mother did what she did because she loved me with all her heart."

Sam Donaldson from NBC news asked, "Christina, you submitted a false birth certificate and lied to the American people and 'the World' about your true identity; why should we believe you now?"

"That is a very fair question Sam and if you will open the envelope my staff is handing out, you will find copies of my birth certificate along with the letter I just read and photos of myself and my mother Marilyn Monroe left for me.   I can assure the American people and 'the World' that my true birth record will be found and once again I did what I did because I was honoring my mother's wishes.   The only reason I have come public now is because I have to in order to run for the Presidency."

Mark Hampton from CNN asked, "Christina do you still plan on running for President and if so can you tell us why should the American people believe anything you may say after this deliberate attempt to deceive the Public?"

I felt a little indignation with that one so I came out fighting as I said, "Mark I believe the American people will understand and forgive me for doing what I did.   And yes, I do still plan on running for the office of President.   As for the American people believing anything I may say after this; well I think my record speaks for itself.   I would have never dishonored my mother's wishes if I did not feel the issues our nation faces are much larger than continuing to honor my mother's wishes."

Cindi   Alton from   ABC   news asked, "Christina it plainly states on your birth certificate that your father was John F. Kenny.   Are you trying to carry on your 'father's legacy'?"

I smiled big for that one as I answered, "Cindi I can assure you my running for President to carry on my 'father's legacy' was the furthest thing from my mind when I made my decision to run.   I am running for the office of President of the United States

American Goddess

of America for one reason; and that is I want to help save this nation for our children's future. I believe if drastic steps are not taken soon to make our America great again, then we will no longer be the beacon of hope citizens all over the world have known us to be."

Cindi quickly came out with a follow up, "Christina one more please. I believe the American public will understand why you kept your identity secret and forgive you, but you still attempted to deceive the public for our Country's highest office. This makes me wonder what else you may be hiding from the public and I have to ask why the American People should believe you now?"

"Fair question Cindi and I will answer as bluntly as possible. First, I give the American People my word that I am not hiding anything else about myself. Second, I attempted to continue to hide my true identity because my father was assassinated, my mother's death was suspicious, my uncle, when he tried to run for office was also assassinated, and my mother was correct that if my identity was known by certain individuals my life would be in danger. Knowing the risk I am taking with my life by revealing my true identity to the world, I still feel strongly the threats that face our nation today required me to take that risk. I love this country and if I saw anyone, I felt had the ability to lead our nation into the 21st century; then, I would not be running. As for anyone believing me, I am the CEO of successful businesses all over the world. I have stepped up to help bring the nation of Ghana from civil war and poverty to peace and prosperity. I have placed my life in harm's way to help free the international hostages in Iraq and have brought international press on nations that continue to treat woman like second class citizens. I have put the spotlight on travesties and injustices every place I saw it. I did all this because I truly care about the welfare of people all over the world. That is who I am. I give my word to the American People that I will give my all to our nation because I see what our nation and the world will face tomorrow. I want to help to make a brighter future not just for our nation's children, but for children all over the world. I know that America can overcome the numerous obstacles we face now and, in the future, if we have strong leadership. If we work together, we will accomplish the task of maintaining our status in the world and continue to give our children the opportunities we now have as American citizens. Now, I think I've said all that needs to be said on this subject and I thank you all and the American People for your time."

Ken Carpenter shouted, "Christina please one more question. How do you plan on carrying out all your noble goals?"

"I will be informing the country on how I plan to do just that as soon as I get back on the campaign trail. Now that will be the last question and once again, I thank you all for coming." Then, I walked out of the room leaving the world stunned.

539

American Goddess

CHAPTER 72

That night the whole world knew my true identity and let me tell you everyone had something to say about it. Even my adversary King Fehd called me on my private line and the first thing he said was, "You are the daughter of a king and you lied to me. I know who you are, and I now know you know who you are and that is why I will give you one more chance to be my bride and bear my son. If you refuse me now, then I will have no choice but to destroy you and everything you represent."

"What kind of moron are you? I've already told you I'm not the woman you think I am and if you threaten me one more time, I'm going to be forced to destroy you and everything you represent asshole! Now, don't call me again unless you come to your senses and are willing to work with me to make this world a better place."

"Christina, I promise you I will make you come to me on my terms or you will die."

Trying to keep my calm I simply replied, "King Fehd I promise **you** that if I see you again that will be your last day on earth. Now, I think we have said enough so good-bye."

As I went to hang up, he screamed, "I will behead you for that you bitch!"

I was steaming when I got off that phone and all I could think about was how to get this crazy bastard before he gets me; because I knew in my heart that he meant what he said.

The controversy over my true identity took the headlines for the next two weeks and when the dust finally settled, I had the support of the entire country. It took another two weeks before I was placed back on the ballots in all fifty states.

Then it was back on the campaign trail. Our first stop was, Prince William Sound, Alaska, where a crowd of over fifty thousand strong braved the chilly weather to hear me address the 'country's' environmental and energy issues. That's when I hit Mohammed, his Arabian Brothers, and the entire oil industry right where it hurts, as I revealed my alternative energy plans for Americas future by saying, "My fellow citizens, my campaign stop here, at the tragic sight of America's worst oil spill in history, the 1989 Exxon Valdez disaster, where ten million plus gallons of oil poured into these once pristine waters, is a symbolic stop. Because if I'm elected President, we will work to see that this type of disaster never occurs again. We would accomplish that by revamping, and then instituting an entirely new energy policy for our nation."

I received an enthusiastic round of applause, after which I continued with, "First, we would mandate that every automobile sold in the United States be electrically powered by the year 2006. This move alone would reduce 60% of our nation's phenomenal oil consumption. I know this can be accomplished, because the scientific crew at Tord Automotive has developed a prototype engine, which takes twelve hours to charge on a normal household current, and it doesn't need to be recharged until after fifty six hours of continuous use. The engine is capable of reaching top speeds of seventy-five miles' p/h, is as quiet as a kitten purring, is powerful enough to pull two busloads filled with passengers up a two mile incline without losing power once, and to top it off, it's rechargeable enough while in motion to give you that fifty six hours of continual use. Although this engine sounds wonderful there are some draw backs. The first drawback is the overall cost, because to mass-produce these vehicles it will take vast capital investments. The second drawback is the price such a vehicle would cost the consumer, because a basic auto with this technology would run about forty-nine thousand dollars. The third drawback is the havoc this technology will place on the American oil industry. Now, these are the three big problems we will face by doing this, but I believe it's possible to overcome these problems by doing three things. We would create an environmental/energy super fund, in which capital would be raised to fund the following: First, to give thirty-year interest free loans to the automotive industry to enable them to take on such a vast overhauling of their companies without cutting into their current profit margins. Second, the fund would also be used to pay half the cost of these vehicles for the public and private industry, for the first ten years. Third, we would give thirty-year interest free loans to the American oil industry, so they could revamp their companies to build and maintain America's new power supply, which will be totally provided by solar and wind power, thus eliminating another 30% of our oil consumption. This would be accomplished by allowing each company the right to line an equal share of the American interstate highway system with high power solar panels and state-of-the-art super wind powered turbine generators. These generators are sensitive enough to produce large amounts of power even when there is no natural wind flow, because they are capable of producing power from air currents created by the flow of traffic. And I would hope the American public would prefer to see this type of technology lining our highways, then the poisonous smog we will be forced to see and breathe if we don't do it. Then, the oil companies who agree to provide this new power source would be given the exclusive rights to sell this clean, efficient, energy to our nation's power plants.

To take on the extraordinary challenge of overhauling our nations' entire energy industry, from a polluting, ozone destroying, acid rain producing, petroleum dependent one, to an Democratic, clean, efficient one, will cost five hundred billion dollars a year for the next ten years, but it can be done. We can raise the funds to do this without overburdening ourselves, simply by putting a one-dollar surcharge on every new and used auto and auto related items sold in America, for every automobile registration renewal, for every annual inspection sticker, as well as on every electrical appliance sold in this nation. By paying an extra one dollar for each of these items I have outlined, we would raise a phenomenal nine hundred billion dollars a year, and by the year 2010, we would be a totally self-sufficient, **non-polluting, energy powered nation**. There would still be an annual reserve of four hundred billion dollars, and then out of that fifty billion will go into our Nation's current national disaster fund, the environmental cleanup super fund, and the remaining three hundred billion will be placed in a holding fund to be used to improve the nation's infrastructure. Just some of the benefits we will reap from this technology will be a cleaner world to live in, and fresher air to breathe. And because we have more than enough of our own oil, to supply the rest of our oil needs, we will have a drop in our nation's trade deficit by nearly six billion dollars a year as well, due to the ceasing of all oil imports.

We would see an increase in our gross domestic product, as we sell our services and new technology abroad, because everyone in the world will want to own the electric vehicles, which only the American automobile industry will be able to provide. Thus, creating a need for a threefold increase in auto workers in our nation, and they will be earning annual salaries of one-hundred thousand and up. And for us all as individual citizens, we will save enough a year on the price of our mass transportation, and automotive fuel bills, to more than offset the one-dollar surcharges. I know what I'm proposing will be an incredible undertaking, but I also know the American People can do it. If you have the courage to join me in this venture, then I promise you, one day we will eliminate any possibility of ever having another disaster like the Exxon Valdez again." This time they cheered their approval.

At the press conference which followed my speech, I released detailed copies of my environmental/energy program, and for the next three weeks it was all anyone heard about. Before the experts could even begin to study and debate its feasibility, my opponents were calling my plan ludicrous. However, when the smoke of the controversy finally cleared, all my opponents were forced by solid documented evidence, to eat their words, and publicly admit that the plan could work.

When they did that, my lead in the polls over my closest opponents rose from a twenty-five to a thirty five percent margin, and that's when my adversary King Mohammed Fehd, struck back with a statement released to the American press which read, **"After close examination of Christina Powers' proposed environmental/energy program, I must admit with the rest of the world that it is absolutely brilliant. Although, at the same time we cannot neglect the fact that it is naively flawed. The reason I make this strong statement is it is foolish to think anyone could throw American industry into such a complete upheaval in only a ten-year span, without causing major damage to the American economy as well as the economies of the rest of the world. I also believe to**

American Goddess

even suggest taking on a challenge of this magnitude in less than thirty years, shows a lack of realistic leadership skills.   To help prevent this possible worldwide economic disaster, I will personally offer thirty-year low interest loans to any automobile manufacturer in the world, who would be willing to mass-produce a new generation of super-efficient automobiles.   If the world's auto industry would take up this offer, then we could feasibly reduce fifty percent of the world's oil consumption, as well as the pollution it causes, in a realistic fifteen years, and without leading the world into an economic nightmare.   I also feel when the time does come for the world to limit its dependency on oil as drastically as Ms. Powers Carr has proposed, then I would hope we would turn to Geothermal Energy Plants instead of defacing our landscape."

When asked by the press to respond to King Mohammed's statements I replied, "His accusations are exactly what any oil rich sheik would want us to believe, but they are unfounded because the creation of the super fund is what will prevent an economic disaster from happening, and he knows it.   Not only that, but his suggestion to build Geothermal Energy Plants all over the world is what truly shows a lack of realistic leadership skill.   If we start drilling thousands of holes into the core heat source of the earth, it will cost the world's economy quadrillions, and it has the potential to be catastrophic for life on this planet."   Even with my rebuttal, I took a seventeen percent nosedive in the polls, and when I discovered this I thought, "Touché Mohammed, but you haven't seen anything yet, because I still have a few tricks up my sleeve that will blow you away."

American Goddess

CHAPTER 73

The following day, October 17th, I pulled out one of those tricks by revealing my plans for America's future education/early childcare program, at a rally of one hundred thousand, where I addressed the 1999 convention of the United League of Teachers at the Meadowlands Arena in New Jersey.

I began my speech by saying, "I am honored to have been invited here today to address this convention, because from the depths of my heart, I believe that the teachers of America have chosen the most important and vital profession in our nation. At the same time my heart is saddened because your calling has been taken for granted, abused, and neglected for nearly four decades now by our nation's leaders. I'm here to say, I think it's time it stops."

With that statement the crowd cheered and when they decided to stop cheering I said, "It boggles my mind to think that our elected leaders are allowing us to head into the twenty first century with an educational system which is in total disarray. What's worse is no one seems to know what to do about it. Well I happen to have come up with a little idea, which I believe will do more than solve the problem, because it is ludicrous to continue struggling with a flawed system when we don't have to. Right now, our nation spends a mere seven hundred million dollars a year to teach fifty million American students, with only three million teachers. Then our Government has the gall to expect our three million teachers to perform miracles on the academic level. Well I don't know about you, but I don't have to be a mathematician to know that the ratio in this equation is atrocious. That ratio is why I've come up with a three-stage proposal which will solve the problem indefinitely. The first thing we must do in stage one, is to obliterate our current education system and replace it with one that works. Step two of stage one; we would eliminate all local school property taxes, thus returning two hundred million dollars back into the pockets of our citizens; eliminate all state contributions to their school system, thus returning two hundred million dollars back into the states treasuries. Next eliminate all current federal contributions to the Nation's schools and channel that three hundred million dollars into our military, to give a twenty five percent across the board salary increase to everyone in our armed services. Step three of stage one; we would create an education/early childcare superfund. And we could create it without crushing the public financially, by simply adding a one-dollar surcharge on every movie ticket, book, record, and video sold or rented in our nation. Get ready for this folk: with this surcharge we would raise a phenomenal seven hundred billion dollars a year. This is nearly six times greater than our current education expenditures. Now for stage two. First, we would triple the classroom space of our schools. Second, we would add an additional three million teaching positions, which will fill half the additional new space we will have and cut our student classroom sizes in half. Third, we will increase their average annual salary from forty-two thousand to sixty thousand. Fourth, we would supply each classroom with the most sophisticated learning tools available today and increase the school day by one hour. Now for stage three. First, we add another three and a half million positions into the system with starting salaries of forty thousand and up. One million more teaching positions, five hundred thousand registered nurses, five hundred thousand licensed practical nurses, another one million will be trained teachers aides and day care aides, and five hundred thousand in support staff. Second, we will place this additional staff into the remaining new space to provide early childcare and preschool training to every child in America, from three months to kindergarten. We would then operate this part of our school system on a twenty-four-hour, seven day a week basis, and we would be capable of providing three nourishing meals a day to our children. Not only that, but there would be no charge for the day care provided, thus relieving our families of at least a four hundred dollar a month childcare expenditure. For those who choose to continue with their current childcare providers, we will pay their monthly childcare expenses for them, up to four hundred dollars per-month. Third, we would pay the tuition for every American who chooses to continue their education, and we will double the tuition paid to our colleges, so they could afford to provide the highest in educational standards and increase their staff as well as their payrolls. My friends, even with all these expenditures we would still have an annual surplus in the superfund of two hundred billion dollars a year, and one hundred billion of that would go into our holding fund to be used on other programs, which I will address at a later date.

Now, to name just some of the benefits we would reap from this program. First, we would have the best school system and the most educated society in the world. Second, we would have a drop in our now 14% unemployment rate to a 6% unemployment rate. Third, we would have an increase in per-capita personal income, an increase in public spending, and a decrease in our public debt. And I'm sure when you examine my entire program; you will agree that the benefits will more than compensate for the one-dollar surcharge. Now I'd like to thank you for listening and say, 'May God Bless us all!'" And with that the crowd roared their approval.

The next day the headlines read, "**Christina Powers astonishes the nation once again, with her proposed education/early childcare program.**" When the experts completed studying my proposal, they all agreed unanimously, it was the most brilliant, and comprehensive, educational agenda they had ever seen. With that acknowledgment made public, my 18% lead in the polls soared to a 42% lead. When that happened, my opponents scrambled to fight back with statements similar to the one President Stump made, "Yes it's true that Christina Powers' radical educational program is unique, but it is not feasible for the United States, because it is more of a socialistic approach to the problem, than a democratic one."

American Goddess

When asked to respond to the accusations of my critics, I answered, "My opponents may place any label they would like on my education proposal, but it won't change the fact that I'm simply using good business sense, and until I see someone come up with a better suggestion, then I'll stick with my own. If they think my education program is radical, wait until they hear me address next months' Governor's Social Welfare Conference in Washington, D.C."

The next morning while Michael, Tom and I were working on my Citizens Care Program speech for the Governor's Social Welfare Conference it hit me like a lightning bolt and I shouted, "Oh my God I am a fucking genius!"

Michael started to laugh as he shook his head and said, "What brilliant scam have you come up with this time and how much more work is it going to cause us?"   I smiled mischievously as I said, "It's not going to cause us any extra work right now." Then I buzzed Pierre on the intercom and continued, "Pierre please call the dynamic trio for me and have them come to my office as soon as possible."

Pierre started to laugh then said, "I assume you want Lucille, Barbara and Gloria."

I started to laugh as I said, "Is there any other?"

"You got it boss I'll send them right in."

As soon as Lucille, Barbara and Gloria entered my office I said, "Thanks for coming so quickly ladies.   I have called you three in because I have a task, I know only you three could pull off for me.   I want you to set up a 2000 New Year's Eve Celebration this year at the Disneyland Theme Park in Orlando, Florida.   Then, extend an invitation to all of America to celebrate the turn of the millennium with me, my family and all of our biggest name performers.   I also want to create the exact replica of the outfit my mother wore when she performed 'Diamonds Are A Girl's Best Friend'. I want to do a tribute to her that night.   Ladies I want this to be the biggest party anyone has ever thrown, and I want it broadcasted all over this country.   Are you ladies up to the task?"

They looked at each other with wide eyes at first then Lucille smiled and said, "Party, that's my middle name. You want a party; we'll give you a party."

I smiled as I said, "I knew I picked the right party girls."

As they left the room Michael said, "You don't miss a beat, do you?"

I kissed his cheek as I said, "Not if I can help it. Now let's get back to work on the Citizens Care Program."

American Goddess

CHAPTER 74

When the States Governor's Social Welfare Conference rolled around on November 29th, I found myself placed first on the list to address the conference, from the three top Presidential Candidates who were invited. After a hardy round of applause, I began by saying, "I am honored to have been invited here today, and I feel privileged to have the opportunity to address such a distinguished group of Civil Servants on an issue as important as our Nation's Social Welfare Program. As we all know, it is a disaster, because we're doing nothing more than spending billions of dollars a year to keep our less fortunate citizens trapped in poverty, as we crush their spirits and devour their dignity. To the shame of us all, not only do we allow our Government Leaders to destroy the hopes and dreams of those of us who are dependent on our so-called Social Welfare Program, but we allow the Government to foster concern to 82% of our citizens who depend on Social Security benefits. Well, I for one can no longer idly stand by and watch this travesty take place without trying to stop the hypocrisy of it all. It disgusts me to think that our nation spends three billion dollars a year on the current Social Welfare Program, which breaks down to ninety million on cash benefits, seventy million on food stamp benefits, and one billion forty million on Medicaid benefits. While at the same time our Social Security Administration spends an additional seven hundred billion dollars a year in benefits, which breaks down to two hundred and fifty billion on retirement benefits, twenty billion on survivor benefits, one hundred and thirty billion on disability benefits, and three hundred billion on Medicare benefits. Then there is another twenty-five billion spent on unemployment benefits, and on top of these figures we have to add six billion contributed from our employees and employers for their disability and unemployment insurance deductions. The grand total spent on all three programs from the federal, state, and the private sector is seven hundred and thirty billion dollars a year. This is why I propose to the nation a three-stage plan, where the first stage would call for the elimination of all three programs as they exist today and place them under a one blanket protection plan which we would entitle, 'The Citizens Care Program.'
In stage two we would first take five hundred billion from these funds and return it to our workers by eliminating the social security taxes. Second, we would return another six billion to the employees and employers, by eliminating their disability and

unemployment insurance deductions. Third, we would return fifteen billion to our states, and relinquish them from the responsibility and expense of managing their Social Welfare Programs. Fourth, we would return the remaining three hundred and twenty billion to the federal Government to be set aside for future use. Now for stage three. First, we would create a Citizens Care super fund. Second, we would give an across-the-board flat rate payment of twenty thousand dollars a year to the twenty-nine million Americans who are retired or disabled, which will total fifty-eight hundred billion dollars a year. Third, we would eliminate all welfare benefits, because with free childcare being provided, we could put the sixteen million now receiving benefits, into either on the job training programs, such as what our school systems and community action programs will offer, at starting salaries of no less then fourteen thousand dollars a year. If they choose to continue in our free education system, we will give them a grant of fourteen thousand dollars a year. And as long as they maintain a B-average, we will continue the payments until they have completed their studies and enter the work force. This will add another two hundred and twenty-four billion to the budget. Fourth, we would eliminate the rest of the unemployment benefits by offering the twenty-two million Americans, who would still be unemployed, the same opportunity as those who were on our welfare system, at a cost of three hundred and eight billion dollars. Fifth, we would eliminate the food stamp program, because there would no longer be a need for it. Sixth, we would eliminate the medical programs, because everyone will come under our new National Health Care Program, which I will reveal at a later date. My proposal will come to a grand total of nine hundred and sixty-seven billion dollars. The revenue for our new Citizens Care superfund will come from placing a one cent surcharge on every one of the two hundred quadrillion BTUs' of electrical energy consumed in our nation each year. This will raise a phenomenal two hundred trillion dollars a year. One hundred and fifty billion will come from the Federal Government's power usages, thus drawing from that reserve I mentioned, two billion from the states, five hundred billion from business, and one trillion ninety-eight billion will come from household use. This breaks down to around a fifty dollar a month increase in a family of fours' average electrical bill. What we will gain from this program would be the eradication of poverty, hunger, unemployment, and illiteracy in our nation and in our lifetime. And we would still have an annual surplus in the fund of one trillion thirty-three billion dollars and one trillion of that will be placed in our holding fund for uses in other programs, and it will still leave us a thirty three billion dollar surplus in the Citizens Care super fund. And I'm sure that the elimination of school taxes, and the cost of health care {which as I've said I will reveal at a later date} from the backs of our nation's businesses, will more than offset their contribution to this program. I'm also sure that the elimination in the

American Goddess

Social Security Tax, along with the Unemployment and Disability deductions, will do the same for our working citizens.

Now I'd like to thank you for lending me your ear as I ask for your support of my candidacy, and I pray that God May Bless all our futures."

With that I received a standing ovation and the look on my opponents faces when I left the podium with the Governors still cheering, told me that neither one of them were prepared to follow that act.

As soon as I exited the conference building, I was mobbed by the press shouting their question.   So I stopped and said, "Please forgive me, I don't have the time to answer your questions right now, but I will be releasing a detailed plan of my proposal to the press way before your deadlines gang, so don't panic.   I'm sure once my Citizens Care proposal has been completely scrutinized; everyone will see it is just as viable as my other proposals.   However, I would like to take this opportunity to mention that I will be hosting the ABC Powers television networks 2000, New Year's Eve Celebration this year, at the Disneyland Theme Park in Orlando, Florida.   I extend an invitation to all of America to celebrate the turn of the millennium with my family and me, along with many of our closest friends.   For those of you who will be able to attend our celebration in person, I promise it will be the most extraordinary blow out New Year's Eve bash this world has ever seen.   Not only that, but the Disney Corporation, Universal Studios, and Sea World will be opening their parks for free that entire day, and Powers Inc. will be supplying all the amenities.   So if it's at all possible, please try to join us."

The next day the headlines read, "**Christina Powers takes a 68% lead in the polls after revealing her Citizens Care Program!   And since her invitation to the nation to join her in ushering in the New Millennium, there has been a record one hundred thousand reservations being made every hour at hotels throughout the State of Florida.**"

Once again, I dominated the headlines as the experts began their debating, but three days before Christmas I was knocked from the front pages again.   Only this time it wasn't by any of my presidential opponents, it was by Mohammed.   With captions like this one, "**King Mohammed stormed out of the peace talks in Moscow today and stated, 'President Puton is a stubborn arrogant man who is impossible to reason with. This concerns me, as it should concern all, that such a man is seated at the helm of the second most powerful nation on earth.'**"

Two days after these headlines I received a call from President Puton who said, "Christina, I have done all I can to stall the peace talks, but he is now threatening to begin an oil embargo if I continue to be so obstinate.   With us heading into the worst winter ever predicted, and our banking system about to go broke I'm forced as you Americans might say, to play hardball, because as you know we are still not capable of supplying all our own oil needs.   To place my nation's people under such a hardship

American Goddess

at this time could ultimately destroy the thin fabrics of our struggling democracy. But I want you to know that I'm still in your corner."

"Please Nicolai, don't give in to him. I will help meet your nation's oil demand by giving you a cut rate from my Model Oil supplies."

"That's not a good idea Christina. If we do that then he will know for sure we are working together. Not only that, but he is promising to advance us three billion dollars to help stabilize our banking system before it collapses. I have no choice but to take the funds from him just to stabilize our fragile economy and try to keep our fledgling democracy on track."

I could hear the stress in his voice, so with a tone of confidence, I answered reassuringly, "I understand completely Nicolai, so please don't feel bad. Besides, I think you may have bought us enough time to beat him to the punch, and I promise, I will be in touch as soon as I'm in office. As for your banking cash flow problem I will transfer three hundred billion to your banking system tomorrow."

After that call Michael, Taylor, Jimmy, Pierre and I headed for Ravena to celebrate Christmas with Tess and the rest of Michael's family. It turned out to be the most heartwarming, loving, family, Christmas, I can remember. Not only were we rejoicing in the enthusiasm of my candidacy, but we were also celebrating the personal triumph of Michael's baby sister, Michelle, who had just received her Doctoral Degree in Psychology, as well as his niece, Mary's, wedding. Their excitement helped to make our Christmas even brighter that year. But like most cherished, peaceful, family gatherings, it ended too soon, and the morning after Christmas we found ourselves psyched to the hilt, as we all headed off to Orlando to prepare for our New Year's Eve celebration.

American Goddess

CHAPTER 75

As soon as we checked into our room that evening, Michael turned on the TV to catch the evening news.   And we were stunned by what we were seeing, and hearing, as Dan Rather said, "Folks, we are witnessing the most phenomenal mass movement of humanity in American history.   As an estimated two million Americans descend on the Orlando area.   Just take a look at this footage, of the traffic jam on Interstate 95, with autos backed up from Florida to Virginia, and it's the same scene on all the major arterioles into the State.   The traffic is so thick that officials at Powers Inc. are already parking vehicles in South Carolina, Georgia, and Alabama, and bussing their passengers into Orlando.   Not only are the roadways backed up, but the airlines and railways are all struggling to meet the demand!   But even with all the frustrations of the massive delays, it's apparent the spirits of those trying to get to Orlando are courteous, patient, friendly, and excited.   This just goes to show us that when Christina Powers throws a party, she does it as she's lived her life, with flare.   Now I'm going to step out of character for the first time in my career, to say I believe the woman is an absolute genius.   And with the new figures giving her an astonishing 78% lead in the polls, it's clear to the world, it would take a miracle for anyone to beat her now."

By the time New Year's Eve morning arrived there was an unprecedented two and a half million people filling the Orlando theme parks.

We started the party 10:00 am on the nose.   That morning was so sunny and breathtakingly beautiful, that the whole nation felt as if God were smiling on us.   To make sure everyone was at the heart of the action Lucille, Barbara and Gloria had one-hundred-foot-tall screens strategically placed throughout the parks and in every major city across the country.   The first thing I did that morning was introduce Barbara, to begin our celebration with the singing of the National Anthem.

Throughout the day I made cameo appearances and when the 9:00pm hour hit, I stayed on the stage and introduced one performance after another, as I enthusiastically built the excitement of the moment right up till forty minutes before midnight.

That's when I said, "Ladies and gentlemen I'm going to leave the stage for a few moments and when I return, I will be doing a number as a tribute to my mother Marilyn Monroe."

The audience cheered as I walked off the stage and when I returned, I had on a blonde wig and was wearing an exact replica of the outfit my mother wore when she performed 'Diamonds Are A Girl's Best Friend'.   I looked so much like my mother that the crowd went wild and when I started to perform the same routine as my mother did

American Goddess

in 'Gentleman Prefer Blondes' the cheers were so loud we had to max out the volume on the sound system just to be heard.

When I finished my performance that night there was no doubt to anyone whose daughter I truly was.   I was so proud of my true parents that I was beaming when I left the stage.

After a moving performance by Michael Wilson of 'My Way', I walked out on the stage and shouted, "Way to go, America!"   With that the audience let out with a roar. While they roared, I shouted again, "We sure know how to party, don't we?"   And we cheered some more.

When we stopped cheering, I said, "My friends, I thank you for coming to celebrate this glorious day in history with us.   Thanks to you, my heart has been filled to capacity with feelings of unconditional love, as we've all experienced the power of humanity united this day.   That power has touched me so profoundly, that I am confident we will survive whatever the future may hold.   Now on a more personal note, I would like to say that after 11:59pm this evening, I will be retiring from the entertainment industry to dedicate my life whether I win or lose this election, to saving the future for our children. That is why, while we're standing together ten minutes to the edge of a millennium; I would like to perform for you one last song which I've written just for this occasion."

With that they cheered and with tears of love and joy filling my eyes, I waved my arms in the air and the orchestra began.   When I joined the orchestra, my voice echoed the lyrics with more power than I'd ever sung before,

"We are united at the dawn of a new millennium, with dreams so free, as we stand together to make history.   For in your eyes I see visions, of what the world will be, when we take each hand and make our stand, to fight against the evils besieging this generation of man.   For united is the only way we can defeat the darkness devouring our land and destroying the future, for our little ones.

If you would only hold my hand, and take that stand, then together we'll see the power of the spirit that burns within every woman, child, and man, as we conquer the darkness raging war all through our land.

So come walk with me, victoriously, into a future filled with endless possibilities. 'Cause I know when we've joined each hand, we'll have reached a power beyond the comprehension of man.   Then together we will save the future, for our little ones. Oh, for our little ones, we must join each hand, for our little ones, we must make that stand, for our little ones, we must save our land.   And we will have done it, all, for our little ones.

Yes, for the little ones, whose spark of life flares in their eyes, with pure love so unconditional. So let's give them all, half the chance, to reach beyond the stars, and grasp their dreams, by fighting back the darkness, which is devouring, our air, land and sea.   And we will have done it all, for our little ones.

American Goddess

For united we'll stand and together every woman, child, and man, will conquer the darkness, devouring our land.   So, take my hand and we'll run carefree, like a child running to a playful sea, toward a future that will be, bright clean, and free.   And we will have done it all, for our little ones.   Oh, for our little ones, we must join each hand, for our little ones, we must make that stand, for our little ones, we must save our land. And we will have done it all, for our little ones.

Oh, for our little ones, we will join each hand, for our little ones, we will make that stand, for our little ones, we will save our land.   And we will have done it all, for our little ones.   And we will have done it, all, for our little ones', forever to be freeeeeee.

When the orchestra stopped the audience cheered so loud, I knew in my heart we were truly going to save our nation.   Then I shouted, "I love you, America!   God bless you all, and happy millennium!"   With that the firecrackers filled the air and our cheers filled with love, pride, and hope, echoed across the country.   Our celebration as one nation under God that night, was so spiritually moving, that we could feel the spirits of the angels rejoicing amongst us.   For there were no Catholics, Protestants, Jews, Evangelicals, Muslims, Buddhist, Hindus, nor Blacks, Hispanics, Gays, Lesbians, Transgenders or Whites, there were only children of God, equal in body and soul.   Nor was there an evil or judgmental remark heard, as we reveled in our oneness.   And we took that feeling of oneness home with us in our hearts and onto the campaign trail when the celebrating ended.

CHAPTER 76

By the time we reached the Republicans Primary on July 27th, I had an 82% lead in the polls, but after they officially re-nominated President Stump and Vice President Larson as their candidates, my lead slipped to 60%.

Then on August 16th, after the Independent party officially nominated Senator Ann Brown and New Jersey Governor Chris Chirsty, for their President and Vice-Presidential Candidates, my lead slipped again, only this time it was to a reachable 48%. When we held the Democratic Party's primary on August 24th, I knew I had to regain a strong lead and fast, because with Mohammed still lurking in the shadows, I didn't want there to be even a slim chance of possibly not winning this race. That is why I took the gamble and had Michael and our beloved eight-year-old son Taylor, stand with me when I addressed the assembly at the opening ceremonies.

I'll never forget that night when Michael and I stood beside our little man backstage, with only two minutes to go before I was to address the entire nation by opening the Democratic Party's 2000, Primary Caucus. Taylor was so beautiful in his little blue tux, and his baby blue eyes just gleamed as he waited full of enthusiasm to help me with my address. I felt so proud of him as I knelt down and ruffled his silky dusty-blonde hair gently through my fingers. I looked at him lovingly, and with a slight hint of nervousness in my voice said, "How are you feeling, honey?"

Michael interrupted with an enthusiastic, "He's going to do just fine, Mom."

With that Taylor smiled and confidently replied, "I'm all right, Mom. Just like Dad said, 'I'm going to do just fine,' so don't worry. Besides Mom, don't you remember the lady in my dream? She told me, Dad and me, were going to help you win, remember?"

I kissed his cheek and softly answered, "I remember, baby."

Just then Jimmy came running up to us and said, "They're ready!" Then looking at Taylor he added, "Are you ready, little buddy?"

He answered with a smile, "I'm ready, Uncle Jimmy." Then he hugged Michael and me as he continued, "I love you guys, don't worry."

"We love you too, son." Michael proudly answered.

I hugged him again and with tears in my eyes said, "I love you with all my heart, honey." At that I grabbed Michael's hand, then looking at them both I added, "I'm so proud of you both, now let's go 'break a leg' guys." And off we went.

I proudly stood with my family at the podium and boisterously said, "Ladies and gentlemen of this delegation, my family and I, on behalf of the Democratic Party's Chief Executives, welcome you to the Democratic Party Year 2000 Primary Caucus." After their cheers, I continued, "I have asked to open this caucus with my family, because we believe the futures of our children rides on the outcome of this Presidential race. And as parents, my husband and I fear that if my proposals are not implemented in this nation and soon, we will not have a future for our children.   We also know in our hearts as we look at our own son that if I'm given the chance, I will take the proper steps toward saving our environment.   We will have a future with plenty of trees left to give us the fresh air we will need to breathe in that future, because we'll be recycling everything.   And we'll have clean water again, without all the acid, and disease-causing bacteria's and viruses, because we will stop our factories from polluting them. Also, someday our streets and parks will be clean and safe for our children again, because our schools will replace the streets and malls for hangouts.   It's as simple as that.   Then not too far in the near future, everyone will truly begin to care for our planet again.   And we'll have done it for our children.   Now we ask you as a family, to join us by giving me your support."   Then I looked at Michael and said, "What do you say, honey?"

He smiled and answered, "You've got my vote."

Then I lifted Taylor up and said, "How about you, little man?"

He smiled confidently as he answered, "On behalf of children all over the world, I cast our vote for my Mom 'Christina Powers' for President of the United States of America!"

Then we all waived as I said, "Thank you, and God Bless!"   With that we received a standing ovation.

The next evening, I won the Party's Nomination for President hands down. Immediately after the announcement, the national anthem began to play, and everyone stood up.   Afterwards the balloons fell as the cheers rang out.   This went on for ten minutes and when things calmed down, I said, "God bless you, America!   And thanks to you, my Vice-President candidate, Senator Eartha Kit, the Democratic Party's first black African American woman to ever be on the ticket as the Vice-Presidential Candidate and I, will be heading for the White House in November."   And as they cheered, I shouted, "But we're not going alone.   Oh no, we're going five hundred and thirty-five strong, and were not coming back until we've taken back Congress and the Senate!"   With that their cheers turned into screams.   Then, I shouted even louder, "Look out Washington, America's cleaning house!" And that's when they really lost it.

After the primaries we regained 9% of our losses, so heading into the debates we held a 57% lead in the polls.   After much dickering with my opponents over the topics, we finally agreed on September 18th, to hold two debates.   The first was to be held on October 12th, at California State University's Berkeley campus in San Francisco.   The topics agreed upon were, Foreign Affairs, Crime, and National Defense.   The second debate was to be held on November 2nd, at New York State University's New Paltz Campus in New Paltz, New York.   The topics there would be Health Care, and The

American Goddess

Nations deficits. Once the debates were finalized, I began studying between each campaign stop, every angle of the topics like a chess player. I had to make sure I knew every step either of my opponents might take and be ready to respond accordingly. So when we reached the first debate on October 12th, I felt more than ready to handle whatever surprises my opponents might present.

When I entered the auditorium at Berkeley the night of the first debate, I was cheered by the filled to capacity crowd. As I climbed the steps to the podium I waved to the press who were set up to beam our images all over the world, for what was built up by them, to be the most dramatic debates in American Political History.

Once I reached the podium, I greeted my opponents with a hardy handshake, and some small talk as we waited the ten minutes until airtime. The debate was being narrated by Dan Rather, Tom Holt, and Barbara Waters. By the luck of the draw, I was to be last of the three candidates to address the issues. This gave me the advantage, because I could then compare my issues to my opponents, while the public had them fresh in their minds.

As we chatted, the loudspeaker came on, and Barbara Waters said, "May we please have everyone take their seats. We'll be beginning in just a moment now." With that I took my seat and thought, "Please God, help me make this good."

"Good evening America," Dan Rather began. "Welcome to Debates 2000! This is the first of two scheduled debates to be held between the three American Presidential Candidates. My colleagues, Barbara Waters, Tom Holt, and I will be narrating this evening. Now to begin the debates we go straight to our audience for the first question from a Mr. Tom Volapié."

With that Tom, who was standing at the mike set up in front of the auditorium said, "My question is on Foreign Affairs. Right now, we are spending billions we can't afford, on maintaining the NATO alliance and the United Nations. And at a time when peace treaties are being signed all over the world, I have to wonder, why we don't take some of that money, and put it toward paying off our deficit instead of adding to it. Thank you."

With that Barbara Waters said, "The question goes to, President Stump."

Donald cleared his voice and replied, "What I propose to do is to slash the four hundred billion we now spend on these programs in half and add two hundred billion a year to paying off our deficit. Thank you."

Then Barbara said, "Senator Brown, the question now goes to you."

The Senator shook her head slightly sarcastically, "We cannot cut these programs as the President has suggested, but we can freeze the expenditures at current levels, and refuse all new applicants' entrance into NATO, as well as the U.N. Thank you."

Barbara spoke up again, "The question now goes to, Ms. Powers."

American Goddess

I smiled warmly and replied, "I respectfully disagree with both my opponents' views.   First if we are to learn anything from history, it should be that whenever people thought we were about to achieve world peace, a world war would break out. So that is why I would propose taking two hundred billion from our one trillion four hundred billion dollar holding fund, and invite the former Russian Block Nations, plus the current Russian Republic, into NATO.   And because they have proven to the world that they believe in liberty and justice, we will grant them all, favored Nation Trading Status.   Then we would strip China of that purchase right, and place 30% tariffs on all imports from China.   We would continue to do this until they ban all the slave labor sweat shops and have proven to the world that there will never be another Tiananmen Square incident.   China must allow freedom to flourish in the streets and in the hearts of their people once again.   And the thirty billion we would earn on China's new tariffs will be channeled into helping the struggling economies of all the former Eastern Bloc Nations.   Thank you."

This time Tom Holt began the narrating by saying, "Thank you Mr. Volapié, for your question.   Our next question comes from, Mrs. Rose Shavone."

Rose wore a shy, warm, smile as she leaned into the mike to say, "Recently our nation's leaders have stated that the downsizing of our military has cut costs and increased productivity.   My question is, if that were true then why do the statistics show there has been a 30% drop in the morale of our armed forces, because they feel they are being forced to work with unsafe and aging equipment thanks to the President and Congress' new budget cuts.   Thank you."

Then Tom said, "Mr. President, the question goes to you again sir."

Donald stood tall as he answered, "I agree there is a morale problem in our military today, and I agree that our military should be compensated appropriately for their loyal service to our nation.   I also feel there is a need to upgrade our aging weapon systems.   But as everyone knows peace treaties are being signed and we are no longer the worlds peacekeepers.   That is why I have insisted that the NATO members pay for their own defense.   I also disagree with Ms. Powers on inviting new members into NATO. NATO is no longer needed!   I also have a great personal relationship with President Puton and there is no longer a need for hostilities between our two nations.   But I do propose adding another one hundred million dollars to our military budget to increase salaries.   And since I won't have a fictitious holding fund to draw it from, I will eliminate the joint military exercises between Japanese, South Korea and American troops.   Thank you"

Tom began again, "Senator Brown, the question goes to you now."

With a tone of disbelief, the Senator said, "Mr. President, I would rather stick my hand into the ladies' fictitious holding fund, and come up with nothing, before I'd cancel

American Goddess

military exercises between Japanese, South Korea and American troops.   Especially since all we need to do is pull one hundred billion from our three hundred billion-dollar NATO budget."

With indignation Stump snapped back, "Being a Senator Ms. Brown on the National Security Commission and knowing there is no longer a threat form the Russians you would think you would prefer to have that one hundred billion for our nation's infrastructure."

That's when Tom tried to say, "The rebuttals come at the end of the program, Mr. President."

At the same time Stump was angrily saying, "How dare you question my strategic abilities!"

That's when Dan jumped in, "Candidates please.   The question now goes to, Ms. Powers."

I smiled almost to the point of laughter then said, "Ladies and gentlemen of America, if my programs are implemented the military will have already received their largest salary increase ever, so morale would already be on its way up.   And to keep bringing up morale, I would pull from our then existing holding fund, two hundred billion dollars and begin to update our weapon systems.   I believe the most important thing for our nation's safety and security is to have a military no one in the world will want to challenge and if elected that will be my first priority.   This is the only way to boost our military's morale and at the same time we will be boosting American Industry. Then we would eliminate the ridiculous, 'Don't ask, Don't tell Policy' of our former and current Administrations, and allow all homosexuals the right to enter the military. Not only that, but we will allow homosexual couples the right to legally marry.   These couples will be recognized and honored in our nation as any heterosexual marriage is today.   We will open up the doors for those couples who want to adopt children and allow them to do so.   I know in my heart these couples will lovingly and eagerly adopt those children which have been abandoned to, and lost in, our current Child Welfare Programs.   This will not only provide loving families for our forgotten children, but it will also save our nation millions of dollars in childcare cost.   Thank you."

With that Dan said, "Thank you Rose, for your question.   Our next question comes from, Mrs. Violet Orland."

Violet wore a strong, proud, expression as she stood at the mike and said, "My question is more of a concern to the American Family personally, because the crime in our cities is so out of control, it's to the point we're afraid to walk the streets in our own neighborhoods.   And I for one want to know what you plan to do to help save our cities form this ever-growing threat of violence?"

Dan began, "The question is once again on you, Mr. President."

American Goddess

Donald smiled confidently as he replied, "First, I will continue to toughen the penalties for all crimes committed across the board, no matter what the crime. Second, I would build a wall between the United States and Mexico to stop all illegal immigrant crossing. Third I would deport all non-documented aliens. Fourth, I would add five billion dollars to our nation's current crackdown on drug smuggling.   Thank you."

Then Dan said, "Senator Brown, the question is now yours."

The Senator's smile was even brighter than Donald's when she said, "This is something we agree upon Mr. President, only your proposals are too weak to do any good.   That's why I will make all drug offenses fall under federal guidelines and enforce the death penalty in all fifty states for anyone caught dealing drugs to our nation's children.   Thank you."

Dan cleared his voice and smiled as he said, "The question goes to you, Ms. Powers."

I smiled appropriately and answered, "Ladies and gentlemen, 80% of our nations crime today is drug related.   So the answer to our problem would be to simply eliminate drug trafficking in our cities.   This is clear to all the experts, and that is what our nation has been trying, and failing, to do for years now.   Only we're finding that the way we're going about it is doing nothing more than merely scratching the surface of our drug trafficking problem, and sending us deeper in debt, as the drug cartels laugh all the way to their Swiss Bank Accounts.   Now that it's clear our strategies are not working; I think it's time to change strategy and beat the drug cartels at their own game.   First, we would legalize all illegal drug use in this country and place it's usage under strict government controls.   Second, we would produce the drug supply ourselves and drop the price right out from under the cartels' feet.   Third, we would pass strict prison sentences on anyone caught with drugs in their possession, if they are not listed with the government as a user, or if the drug found on the person was not sold by the government.   Fourth, we would offer to buy our drug supply from the cartels, thus making them a legitimate tax paying business, only it would be at a much lower price than they are getting now.   And fifth, we would take the fifty billion dollars a year we would earn on the drug sales, and the fifty billion dollars we would save on our drug war with the cartels, and funnel that one hundred billion into our not so fictitious holding fund.   Which by the way; will be holding one trillion one hundred billion dollars.   The other thing we would do to help curb crime is to legalize all forms of prostitution because we are never going to be able to stop this behavior.   We would do his by creating safe houses for prostitution where we would be able to test all the prostitutes and their 'johns'; thus, helping to prevent the spread of STD's.   By doing this we would be offering a safe work environment for those who choose this career and put a stop to the abuse many of those in the field receive from their pimps.   This could potentially save us fifty million dollars a year on court

American Goddess

costs, fifty million a year on related medical expenses and bring another one hundred million dollars into our holding fund. Thank you."

With that the room gasped. Barbara quickly turned to face the audience, as she said, "Please, no outbursts." Then turning back toward the podium, she continued, "The first rebuttal is on you, Mr. President."

Donald looked straight at me and said, "You have some way-out proposals' lady, but tonight's takes the cake. Legalizing drugs, prostitution and homosexual marriages in America is unheard of, and the American people would never stand for it. Thank you."

Barbara's face was nearly white as she said, "The next rebuttal is yours, Senator Brown,"

The Senator's dark cheeks were bright red as she said, "I agree completely with the President, only I think for Ms. Powers to even suggest legalizing drugs, prostitution and homosexual marriages in our nation, shows citizens she may not be such a former drug user after all. Not only that, but I think she should be barred from the next debate because of it. Thank you."

The whole audience looked like ghosts as Barbara, choking on her words said, "And the last rebuttal is yours, Ms. Powers."

I stood tall, calm, and cool as I replied, "I respect my opponents' opinions, but I strongly disagree with them. And I'm sure once America has had the opportunity to examine my drug reform package in detail everyone will see this is the only way we can truly fight and win the war on drugs, and drug related crimes in our nation. Not to mention the millions of lives and dollars, we will be saving from eliminating drug and prostitution related illnesses, like AIDS, STD's and Hepatitis. And as far as my proposal to allow homosexuals to marry, all I can say is, it is way past time we treat all our citizens equally. Thank you, America."

Barbara took a deep breath as she stared dead into the cameras and calmly said, "Well you heard it, America! And I'm sure we'll be hearing a lot more of it in the days to come. Now on behalf of my colleagues and I we thank the candidates, and the American people, for making this debate possible." And the moment she said, "Good night." The room exploded into shouts of controversy.

As we were being ushered backstage by security I thought, "God, please help them see I'm right."

The next day the nation rocked, and the headlines echoed the rumble for the next two weeks, with front pages like this one, "**Christina Powers shocks the world once again as she reveals her controversial Drug Reform, Foreign Affairs and National Defense Polices. At the same time her opponents remind the nation of her family ties to the mob, and her formerly known lifestyle of drug abuse, sexual perversion and** abortion. And as the accusations fly the numbers show Christina Powers is taking a beating because of it, with a whopping 15% nosedive in the polls."

The next day's headlines were even better, "China and the Arab world condemn Christina Powers' Foreign Polices as all of Eastern Europe applauds them, but still Christina slips another 5% in the polls."

After that came the big bang as the headlines read, "All the analysts agree Presidential Candidate 'Powers' Drug Reform Package could feasibly work. But she still loses another 5% of her lead in the polls." And that brought these headlines, "Undercover sources reveal, Drug Cartels have placed Christina Powers on the top of their hit list, to prevent her war on their drug industry. Even with this news Christina's lead still slips another 5%. As the polls slip, we must ask, is Christina Powers really as in touch with the American People as we once thought she was?" Even with all the controversy my programs and past lifestyle seemed to cause, I still managed to hold on to a 27% lead in the polls as we headed into the second debate.

American Goddess

CHAPTER 77

It was 7:46pm, November 2nd, when I entered the auditorium of New York State University's New Paltz Campus, for the start of the second debate. I knew this was my last shot at bringing it home for the entire Democratic Party. This, I had to have because without them America would end up with nothing more than another lame duck administration, and I sure as hell didn't want that. So as usual I was prepared for anything including a little mudslinging, but what transpired that night surprised even me.

It seemed to begin the moment Peter Jensen said, "Good Evening America, and welcome to round two, of debates 2000. Where I, and my colleagues Maria Schreibert, and David Toppal, will be narrating tonight's eagerly awaited debate, between our three Presidential Candidates."

With that the cameras zoomed to Maria who said, "Since Health Care and The Nations Deficits are the only two issues slated for tonight's debates, the format will allow for a rebuttal following each issue. One final note, by the draw of the straw tonight's lineup will be President Donald Stump, Business Entrepreneur Christina Powers, and Senator Ann Brown. Now without further delay, let us go to our audience for the first question from, Ms. Mildred Mancusco."

Mildred wore a meek smile as she leaned into the mike and nervously said, "Good Evening Candidates, I am a member of the Duchess County Association for Senior Citizens, but I speak for the concerns of young and old alike, because the rising cost of Health Care today has us all frightened. And our question is, what will you do if elected, to help control and slow down those costs? Thank you."

This time it was David Topal who narrated, "Thank you, Mildred. Now the question goes to you, Mr. President."

Donald appeared very sure of himself as he began, "I plan to implement a National Health Care lottery, and the proceeds will go into our current State Medicaid Programs. Then we will begin to supply Health Care coverage to the twenty-nine million Americans who have no insurance now. And if we make this move today, we will begin to substantially reduce Health Care costs in the future. Thank you."

Then David said, "Ms. Powers, the question now goes to you."

I smiled confidently as I replied, "Today our Nation spends a total of eight hundred billion dollars a year on Health Care costs, and we boast the best Health Care System in the world. That is for those who have Comprehensive Health Insurance. But for those who are not fully covered or have no insurance at all, it's the worst. This is why we must provide Comprehensive Health Insurance to all our citizens, without crippling or even compromising the quality of our Health Care in the slightest way.   To do that I propose we first take one hundred billion dollars from our one trillion one hundred billion dollar holding fund, and invest it in our current medical research programs.   This must be our first step, because with all the new diseases projected to be heading our way in the next few years, we need to establish a strong front-line defense.   Second, we would assume all Health Care insurance payments being made today, by our nation's employees and employers.   Third, we would mandate all current Health Care Insurance Companies and Home Health Care Providers, to hold open registration for every American citizen. Then the government will pay the increased insurance premiums, so we can provide all Americans with comprehensive health, eye care and dental coverage, without having to overhaul the current system by cutting costs or diminishing the quality our Health Care Providers offer.   Now to free ourselves from the Health Care nightmare we're in and guarantee we will continue to have the best Health Care system in the world, will cost our nation one trillion two hundred billion dollars a year.   To pay for this, we would take the one trillion from our holding fund.   The other two hundred billion will come from placing a 10% land tax, on the two trillion dollars' worth of the tax-exempt real estate held in our nation today, by its religious organizations.   By stripping them of all their current tax exemptions, we will ensure that our holding fund remains solvent indefinitely. Thank you."

The audience gasped as Peter Jensen said, "I must remind the audience members to please refrain from any further outbursts.   Now the question goes to you, Senator Brown."

The Senator turned to me and sarcastically shouted, "What are you, the Anti-Christ lady?"

Peter interrupted, "Senator, the rebuttals come after you've answered the question."   As Ann was still saying, "First you want to legalize drugs and homosexual marriages, now you want to tax the churches?   What are you going to do next, take our children's college funds from them, because you think they won't have to pay for their education anymore?"   Peter tried a second time, "Senator, please!   We must follow the format."

Then the Senator snapped at Peter, "I'm fully aware of the format Jensen, you don't have to remind me."

Peter came back quickly, "Then please abide by it Senator, and answer the question."

The Senator was visibly angered as she said, "Both my opponents have missed the mark completely on solving our Health Care problems.   Especially since all we have to do is put a mandatory freeze on all medical costs until our economic growth matches that of the medical field.   Thank you."

American Goddess

Maria, with wide eyes said, "The first rebuttal is yours, Mr. President."

Donald shook his head dishearteningly and replied, "America, first I have to wonder if the Senator thinks we're all stupid. Her proposal would do nothing but cripple our Health Care system, and she should know that.   As for Ms. Powers, who wants to tax our churches, as she legalizes drugs and condones homosexual marriages; well, all I can say to that is, read the laws of God written by Moses, Paul, and all the apostles in your Bibles and then judge her accordingly.   Thank you, America."

Maria lifted her eyebrows at me as if to say, 'Answer that one smart ass...' as she said, "The rebuttal is now yours, Ms. Powers."

I shook my head and shrugged my shoulders as I simply answered, "America, my proposal is one which will provide the best Health Care in the world, to all of our citizens.   I also believe in my heart that if Christ were here today, he would require his churches to give all they had to the healing of the masses, not just 10%.   And if everyone would just read the words of Christ in their Bibles, and stop reading the words of Moses, Paul, and all the apostles as the President has suggested, then maybe we would all learn the true lessons of unconditional love.   After all, isn't that what Christ said God is, Love?   Thank you."

Maria looked startled, as she continued, "Senator, the rebuttal is yours."

Ann cleared her voice then sternly said, "Bravo Ms. Powers.   That truly was an excellent performance; especially coming from a woman who deliberately seduced one of our nation's most prominent religious leaders just to destroy his ministry.   But if you think, by simply making a profound correlation between Christ's healing ministry and our Nation's health care problems will magically convince the American public to let you get away with taxing our churches, then you're nuttier then I thought.   And just in case you haven't noticed Christina, Christ isn't here, so I suggest we try solving our nation's problems without him.   And as for you Mr. President, well your lottery program for our Nation's health care, isn't any better than what this woman has proposed.   Thank you."

I nearly bit my tongue and I struggled to keep my composure as David Topal said, "Thank you candidates, for those candid views.   Now we go back to our audience for the second question from, Mr. Edward Severino."

Edward wore a proud expression as he leaned into the mike to say, "Thank you Mr. Topal, and my question is how will your Administration combat our Nation's growing deficit?   Thank you."

David smiled as he said, "Thank you Edward, and once again the question first goes to you. Mr. President."

Donald glanced toward me as if to see if I were listening, then said, "As I've said, I will have two hundred billion transferred from our U.N. and NATO expenses, into a fund to pay off our deficit.   I will do this because we must continue to keep America first and

American Goddess

make America great again. Then thanks to our health care lottery, we will be able to transfer another three hundred billion now spent on our Medicare, and Medicaid Programs, into this fund, thus giving us five hundred billion dollars extra a year to pay off our deficit.   Thank you."

This time Peter began the narrating, "The question is now yours, Ms. Powers."

I rubbed my hands together and prayed to myself, 'God, please help me.' as I said, "Ladies and gentlemen, this is the Biggie.   Because if we don't pay off are growing two trillion-dollar deficit and soon, our Nation will eventually be plunged into the darkest depression our people have ever known.   If that happens, I know we won't survive it as a Democratic Nation.   This is why I propose we create a Deficit Buster Superfund, and we will raise the revenue for this fund in four ways.   First, we would take the current five cent soda bottle deposit many states have today and make it national. Second, we would place an additional five cent surcharge on every glass, plastic, and aluminum container sold in our Nation.   Third, we would place a one-dollar surcharge on every hotel room, airline, bus, and train ticket, as well as every restaurant bill totaling over five dollars sold in our Nation.   Fourth, we would place a ten-cent surcharge on every dollar gambled in our Nation.   By adding another one thousand dollars a year to a family's personal expenses for this fund, along with what we earn from our tourist industry, and American corporations, we will raise a phenomenal, nine trillion dollars a year.   I promise you right now, this one step, will enable us to be a-debt-free Nation in only eight years.   And once that is accomplished, we will eliminate all other superfund surcharges, along with all Federal taxes, except those on our churches, and we would still have a nine trillion dollar a year budget.   America, I know the first eight years will be tough, but if you will do this with me, then at the end of those eight years we will have the wealthiest and most powerful Nation this world has ever known.   Then, and only then; will we be able to help the rest of the world join us in saving our planet for our children.   Thank you."

With that, the entire audience began to cheer as Peter said, "Please!   No outbursts! It's not fair to the other Candidates."   Once they calmed down, Peter continued, "Now please control yourselves from any further outbursts, thank you.   The question now goes to you, Senator Brown."

I could see on the Senator's face, she was past angry as she looked at me and said, "People, how can you let yourself be taken in by this woman?   Just take a look at the life she's led, and you will see for yourself, she has no moral right to hold office as the President of our great Nation."

Peter interrupted by saying, "Please Senator, I've told you the rebuttals come after the answers."

American Goddess

The Senator shook her head with frustration as she continued, "I simply propose we institute a National budget buster lottery and pay off our Nations deficit with the earnings.   Thank you."

This time Maria began by saying, "The first rebuttal goes to you, Mr. President."

Donald stood defiant as he said, "America, I agree with the Senator.   This woman is a known Hollywood harlot, and it would be a disgrace to our Nation if she were to become our next President.   That reason alone should be enough for anyone not to vote for her.   She will destroy all the achievements of my last four years and send our economy into a nosedive. Thank you, America."

Maria looked as though she was holding her breath when she said, "Ms. Powers, you have the next rebuttal."

I nodded my head politely, then said, "I wish the problems of Health Care, and our National deficit could be solved as simply as my opponents would like us to believe, but that is not reality.   What is reality is the fact that it will take proposals like mine to get us out of the mess our current policies have created, and everyone here knows it.   To do anything less, would only be providing the patient with a bandage when he needs major surgery.   This is why I ask all of America right now for your vote for my candidacy, and everyone who is running with me on the Democratic Party ballot.   Or all we will end up with is another do nothing administration.   As for the remarks my opponents have made over my morals, you have been asked to read your bibles and if that's the case then I'd like to quote our Lord when He said, 'He who is here without sin, be the first to cast a stone' and the minute I said, "Thank you America, and God bless."   Someone yelled, "Way to go, Christina!" And that's when the entire audience let out with a cheer, which took Maria, Peter, and David, two minutes to quiet down.

Once the room was calm Peter said, "Senator, the rebuttal is now yours."

The Senator looked at me, then to the audience, and with a disgusted tone said, "What kind of rebuttal can I come back with after a statement like that?   So all I'm going to say is please give me your support on November 4th, Election Day 2000.   Thank you, America and May God be with us all."

With that Peter said, "Well America, we've reached the end of debates 2000.   And now that you've heard the candidates address the issues, it's up to you to decide who will be going to the White House only two days from now by casting your votes.   On behalf of myself and my colleagues, I'd like to thank the candidates and you the American people for making this debate possible.   Good night, America."

That's when the audience resumed their cheering, and as they cheered, I went over to shake the hands of both my opponents.   While I mingled with the other candidates, security came out on stage to usher us to our individual interviews with one of the debate narrators.

American Goddess

My interview was with Peter Jensen, and when I entered the press booth, Peter handed me a clip-on mike as he instructed me where to sit. When I was settled, he said, "We'll be ready on three." Then holding his hand in the air, he lifted one finger at a time as he said, "One, two, and three. Good evening once again, America. Thank you for tuning into tonight's after the debates' candid interview with Presidential Candidate, Business Entrepreneur, Christina Powers." Then he turned to me and continued, "Thank you for joining us, Christina."

I smiled graciously as I replied, "Thank you for inviting me, Peter."

After which he continued by saying, "Christina, according to tonight's audience poll, you've won this evenings debate triumphantly. So my first question has got to be, after the intensity of tonight's debate, how does that news make you feel at this moment?"

This time my smile was one of relief as I answered, "I feel greatly encouraged Peter, because without the confidence and support of the American people, none of our dreams for a brighter future will be possible."

Peter smiled as if he were truly pleased for me as he asked his next question, "Christina, economy experts and government leaders all over the world are saying, you seem to have magically devised numerous innovative solutions for all our nations' problems today. It's comments like that, which make American citizens, want to know how you came up with your programs."

I chuckled slightly then said, "It was easy for me Peter, because all I did was analyze our Nation's problems, as if they were problems confronting any business. Then I examined all the possible solutions for each problem and picked the best solution. It was as simple as that."

Peter Shook his head in amazement as he continued, "So what's next, Christina?"

I sighed wearily then said, "Well, for right now, I'd like to just spend tomorrow relaxing at home with my family. Then on Election Day, Michael and I will be placing our votes at our local firehouse, and then heading for our campaign headquarters at Rockefeller Plaza in Manhattan to await the election results with our family and friends."

Then Peter said, "Christina, are there any last words you'd like to say to our audience, before we sign off tonight?"

I was quick with the response to that one, as I said, "Only this, Peter. America, when you place your votes two days from now, please remember if you genuinely want to change our Nation, then I must have your vote all across the Democratic Party ballots. Now I look forward to seeing you all at the polls on Election Day. Thank you and once again I'll say, May God Bless us all."

As soon as the interview ended, I walked out of the press booth to be tackled by Barbara, Eartha, Jimmy, Taylor, and Michael, all screaming, "We did it! We did it!"

American Goddess

CHAPTER 78

After the debate Jimmy and Pierre, took Taylor home to bed, as Michael, Barbara, Eartha, Frank, Tom and I, headed to the Poughkeepsie Radisson, for our end of the campaign trail celebration party.   At the party I gave a quick pep talk, after which I thanked everyone for a job well done.   Then I said, "Now please go have a wonderful time my friends, because the Party is on me!"   After about an hour, Michael and I said our goodbyes, and headed home.

We didn't arrive home until after 2:00am.   After checking on Taylor, who was sleeping soundly, Michael and I cleaned up quickly and headed for bed ourselves. Once in bed together, Michael pulled me lovingly into his arms and gently said, "You did it, Punkie!   And just think, in two days they'll be calling you, Madam President."

I kissed his chest as he spoke those words, then said, "I didn't do it honey, we all did."   I lifted myself onto my elbows, so I could gaze into his eyes as I continued, "And I especially couldn't have done it without you, my love.   You held me up when I was tired, and you encouraged me when I was down.   You have been my strength and you and Taylor have been my inspiration through this whole long ordeal."   I kissed him lovingly, and with tears in my eyes added, "I love you Michael, and I thank you for all of it.   But most of all, I thank you for loving me."   With that he pulled me to him where we touched our oneness, as we melted into the fire of our loving passions.

The next morning November 3rd, Jimmy and Taylor woke us at 8:30am, by throwing a pile of newspapers on the bed.   When we sat up, Jimmy handed us both a cup of coffee, then plopped his ass on the bed beside me and said, "Wake up girlfriend, and take a look at these headlines."

With that I sipped my coffee and as I did, Taylor jumped between Michael and me, causing our coffees to spill as he excitedly said, "Listen to what the New York Post ran, guys, 'The polls give Christina Powers, and the entire Democratic Party, a whopping 56% lead after her triumphant victory in last night's debates!'"

568

American Goddess

When he finished, I kissed his cheek and said, "You've been hanging around your Uncle too much."

He returned my kiss and said, "Did you hear me, Mom?   I said you have a 56% lead in the polls!"

With that I jumped on him and began tickling him as I said, "Yes, I heard you honey, and it's wonderful news!   Now you take Uncle Jimmy and get out of here, so your father and I can get out of bed."

It wasn't fifteen minutes later, we were all downstairs having a peaceful family breakfast, when Carman entered the dining room with the phone in her hand and said, "Excuse me Christina, but its Pierre, he said it's urgent."

I thanked her as I took the phone and asked, "What is it, Pierre?"

His voice was panic stricken as he shouted, "Christina!   The President has granted a request from King Fehd, to withdraw two hundred billion dollars from the American Banking System!   And the bottom of the Stock Market is beginning to drop out as the banks head to Wall Street scrambling to raise the cash."

I was stunned for a moment then I said, "I don't understand.   Why are the banks going to the stock market for the cash?"

Pierre's reply was a bit calmer, "Because that stupid President of ours, had Greenspine put a freeze on the Federal Reserve leaving the banks no option, but to go to the market."

With that news I became infuriated and it echoed in my quick response, "What!   Is he nuts?   Something like this could cripple Wall Street and he knows it."

Pierre's voice became anxious again as he yelled back, "What should I do?"

I thought for a moment then said, "Call President Metal of Switzerland, and tell him what's going on.   Then tell him I need him to wire two hundred billion dollars from my Swiss Account, the number is 6627659826, to our Bank of New York Account.   Just make sure it goes straight to our Manhattan Branch, and not through the Federal Reserve.   Then start calling all our stockholders and tell them not to panic, because I'm on top of it.   You got that?"

He nervously answered, "I got it, Christina."

Then I added, "Just keep your cool Pierre, and I'll be there in two minutes."

When I hung up the phone, Michael yelled, "Two hundred billion dollars!   What the hell's going on?"

I yelled back, "Just come with me to the office, and I'll tell you on the way."

With that the four of us flew out of our chairs, as Michael yelled, "Can't we even get out of our PJ's?"

I hollered back, "There's no time!"

Then Jimmy yelled, "But it's pouring out!"

American Goddess

I turned to him and said, "You won't melt." Then I shouted, "Carman, have James bring us a change of clothing." With that the four of us ran out the door, straight into a cold November downpour.

When we dashed into the command center of Powers Incorporated, Pierre had everyone on the phones to our stockholders, desperately trying to prevent them from panic selling. When I reached Pierre's side, he was on the phone with President Metal. I took the phone from him and swiftly said, "Jeff, its Christina. Do you know what's happening here?"

His voice was noticeably shaken as he answered, "I heard Christina, but I can't authorize that kind of withdrawal all at once."

My voice was sharp and to the point, "Jeff, President Stump has got to be conspiring with Mohammed, to have authorized this withdrawal. And you know damn well, if Mohammed gets away with devastating the American economy, Switzerland will be next."

He grunted painfully then said, "I don't know, Christina. You're asking me to risk Mohammed's financial wrath, and you're not even in position as the President to run that interference you promised."

My voice echoed the urgency as I quickly replied, "Jeff, you know how he's been jockeying into position to devour our economies. He's just jumped the gun because he knows I'll stop him once I'm President. And, Jeff, if we don't jump the gun with him, we're not going to have a chance of stopping him; because he'll have crippled the American economy before I've even been sworn into office."

He grunted again then said, "All right, Christina. I'll start the transfer right now. I just hope you can handle him once he finds out."

With a sigh of relief, I said, "Thank you Jeff, and don't worry about Mohammed. He's not in a good enough position to try and take this any further right now."

With that I hung up the phone and right on the spot, I started to change my clothes as fast and inconspicuously as I could. Then I called Martin Flynn, the President of the American Stock exchange and said, "Marty, its Christina Powers. I want you to inform the floor, I'll be covering the withdrawal in ten minutes, with a two hundred-billion-dollar deposit."

When I was finished with Marty, I turned to Ann Markel my assistant vice-president and said, "Ann, turn on the big screen TV. I want to see what's happening with the stocks exchange."

When the TV was turned on, we caught Dan Rather in mid-sentence excitedly saying, "And as Greenspine, the head of the Federal Reserve continues to deny the banks access to over one hundred billion dollars cash, the Dow Jones has just dropped another 60 points. America this is looking more like a 'Black Friday' than a

American Goddess

pre-election Monday as the American banking system struggles to raise the cash for King Mohammed's two hundred-billion-dollar withdrawal."

Then he put his hand to his ear monitor as he began to shake his head with disbelief, and said, "Hold on, folks!   We have just received word that Christina Powers has transferred two hundred billion dollars cash, from a Swiss Account into the Manhattan branch of the Bank of New York.   And as the news of Christina Powers' incredible bailout of the American banking system hits the floor of the stock exchange, people are beginning to cheer as the stocks began the fastest rebound Wall Street has ever seen.   This is unbelievable!   Christina Powers has just prevented a Wall Street nightmare with one hell of a swift response."   With that announcement everyone in the room including myself began to cheer.   And as we cheered, I noticed that Dan went to correspondent Ken Carpenter in Washington.   I couldn't hear what he was saying, but when the camera came back to Dan, he looked as if he had just seen a ghost, so I yelled out, "Everybody be quiet, something is up."

When we could hear again, Dan was saying, "We are witnessing an unprecedented turn of events America, as the United States Congress grants King Mohammed of Saudi Arabia, an on-the-spot approval to begin a two hundred-billion-dollar takeover attempt of Powers Incorporated."

With that news my blood began to boil as I yelled, "Why those bastards!   They're trying to destroy us."   Then I turned to everyone in the room and started shouting orders, "Ann, get everybody on the lines to our foreign accounts, and start transferring our cash holdings to our American Accounts, now!   And for God sakes, tell them not to let one-penny go through the Federal Reserve.   Pierre, get President Metal back on the line! Michael, get the President on the line!   Jimmy, you get Marty Flynn back on the line!"

Jimmy handed me the phone first, and with an angry tone I said, "Marty, begin a two hundred and twenty-five billion counteroffer for me, and stay on the line.   We're going to fight that bastard until he takes cover in the oil muck he crawled out of!"

With that Pierre reached a phone out to me and said, "It's, President Metal."

I grabbed it quickly and forcefully said, "Jeff, I need that other one hundred billion dollars, and I need it now!"

All I heard was, "Aa!   Aa!"

So I yelled, "Jeff, did you hear me?"

Finally, he nervously replied, "I heard you Christina, but I can't do it."

I snapped back, "What do you mean, you can't do it?   Don't you know what's going on here?"

I could hear the stress in his voice as he snapped back his reply, "Yes, dammit!   I know what's happening, but I can't help you now!   Mohammed just pulled five hundred billion cash out of our reserves!"

American Goddess

That punch nearly took my breath away as I shouted, "And you let him?"

He shouted back, "I had no choice; he was going to cut off our oil supply immediately if I didn't."

I sighed in anguish as I said, "You just slit our throats, Jeff." With disgust in my voice I added, "I have to go." And I hung up.

My heart began to pound so hard I thought my head was going to burst. Then I buried my face into my hands, and when I looked up, all I could see were the frightened faces of those I loved counting on me. So I took a deep breath and shouted, "Damn, him! We're not licked yet, guys. Pierre, get Al Greenspine from the Federal Reserve on the line pronto! Michael, where's the damn President?"

Michael shouted, "I'm on hold!"

I shouted, "Ann, get Tom Davies on the phone. Tell him to publicly declare this takeover attempt illegal, and appeal to Congress to overturn its approval."

And as Ann screamed, "Gotcha!" Jimmy stuck a phone in my face and shouted, "It's Flynn, he needs you, now!"

I grabbed the phone and said, "What's happening, Marty?"

His voice was nearly quivering as he answered, "Mohammed just upped the ante to three hundred billion!"

With force I answered, "Then counter the bastard by twenty-five billion, and keep countering him until he retreats. And Marty, I want you to stay on the phone with Jimmy and keep me informed." Then I handed the phone back to Jimmy as I shouted, "Ann, turn up that volume, I want to hear what Dan is saying."

The moment the volume was up we heard Dan Shouting, "Ladies and gentlemen, Wall Street is rallying once again as Christina Powers makes a two hundred- and twenty-five-billion-dollar counteroffer in an attempt to block King Mohammed's takeover bid of Powers Incorporated. Hold on, America! It appears as though the battle is on as we receive word that in the last ten minutes the offer and counteroffer taking place between these two financial giants for ownership of Powers Inc., has reached four hundred billion dollars and climbing. As this battle wages on Wall Street, sources at Powers Inc. tell us all attempts by Christina Powers to reach the President, to try and convince him to block this foreign takeover attempt of Powers Inc. have been simply placed on hold."

With that Michael grabbed my shoulder as he said, "It's the President."

I took the phone and calmly said, "Donald, I implore you to put a stop to this battle by declaring this takeover attempt illegal, thus null and void."

He arrogantly replied, "I'm not stopping anything, Ms. Powers! America is a free market Nation, and this type of corporate battle is what makes our free market so profitable. Don't you remember?"

American Goddess

I answered with a dignified tone, "I remember quite well Mr. President, but this is a hostile foreign invader, who is trying to take ownership of what amounts to nearly one third of our Nation's largest corporations.   And that adds up to economic treason Mr. President, and you know it!"

He raised his voice angrily as he answered, "Christina, this is a world market we live in today and there's no such thing as national loyalty anymore.   So I'm afraid you're on your own." And as he said, "Now I must go, I don't want to keep my caddy waiting."

I was shouting, "Up yours' you bastard!"   And I slammed the phone down so hard, it broke in half.

That's   when   Jimmy   shouted,   "Christina! We've reached five hundred and twenty-five billion!"

Hearing that I turned quickly toward Ann and asked, "What do we have in foreign currency?"

She nervously snapped back the answer, "Seven hundred billion, Christina."

Then Pierre anxiously shouted, "Christina, its Al Greenspine." as he tossed me a cordless phone.

I snatched it in one hand and demandingly said, "Al, I have nine hundred billion dollars on deposit in American banks, and you're illegally keeping it from me knowing that Powers Inc. is under a congressionally sanctioned hostile foreign corporate takeover attempt.   Now I expect you to abide by the law, and release those funds for me right now, so I can at least have a fighting chance of winning this battle."

With all that he calmly asked, "And if I refuse?"

So I calmly answered, "I'll hang you by your balls for treason, the moment I take office."

He calmly replied, "Consider it done."

So I simply said, "Thank you."   As I hung up the phone, I threw my fist into the air and shouted, "Yes!" And once I did, everyone began cheering again.

When everyone stopped cheering, we became fixed to the TV screen to hear Dan saying, "As soon as the word hit Wall Street, Al Greenspine released the hold on the Federal Reserve allowing Christina Powers access to nine hundred billion dollars Powers Inc. has on deposit, King Mohammed raised his takeover attempt to a phenomenal one trillion dollars, causing the stocks of Powers Inc. to soar to unheard of heights.   As Wall Street waits for a counteroffer from Christina, the panic selling that's taking place on the floor has sent the stock markets across the board plummeting into a spiraling nosedive. Now the question everyone is asking, is, 'Will the American economy survive what's being called, the battle of the giants?'"

I turned to Frank and shouted, "Frank get President Puton on the line for me now!"

American Goddess

As soon as President Puton was on the line I said, "Nicolai, I know you know what's happening here and I need you to transfer the three hundred billion I deposited into your Nation's banks into my account now and I'll get it back to you as soon as this is over."

He calmly replied, "I can't do that Christina."

"What do you mean you can't do that, if I lose Powers Inc., we will all be at his mercy."

He started to laugh at me sadistically then said, "Well now you know how the big boys play you stupid bitch!"

I could almost feel flames shooting out from my eyes as I shouted, "You prick!   No one double crosses me and gets away with it!   I'll be coming after you next you bastard!" Then I threw the phone across the room and it shattered all over the floor.

With that my heart lodged in my throat and as I swallowed it, Jimmy stuck a phone in my face and said, "It's, Flynn!"

I took the phone to hear Marty screaming, "Christina!   It's one trillion dollars, what the fuck do you want me to do?"

My mouth was so dry, I was coughing on my words as I answered, "Counter Marty, and keep countering.   That is until we've reached another six hundred billion.   If that happens, get back on the line with Jimmy, and I'll tell you what to do next."

When I handed the phone back to Jimmy, he grabbed my hand and with a look of desperation said, "That's everything we have, Christina!   All of it!"

I squeezed his hand reassuringly and answered, "I know Jimmy, but we can't let him win."

From out of the blue, Pierre said, "No it's not!"

I turned toward him and said, "What do you mean?"

He smiled as he answered, "There is still six hundred billion in our employee pension accounts."

With that, Ann said, "We can't touch that, it's illegal."

I looked at her and asked, "Who is heading our union negotiation team?"

She answered quickly, "Joe Aiello."

I smiled and said, "Great!   Get him on the line for me."   Then I turned to everyone in the room and shouted, "Get on the phones right now, guys.   I want every employee we have to stop working and start watching Dan's report.   I want them to see for themselves the battle we're in before I ask them to commit their pension to the fight." Turning to Michael I added, "Get a phone link to every business we have, and then have them get ready to patch me in on their intercom systems.   I need to address every employee personally."

Just then I gazed over quickly to see Taylor nervously fidgeting with some papers, as he sat in the swivel captain's chair, three feet from me, at the head of the command center.   When he caught my glance, he smiled warmly, and then motioned his lips to silently say, "I love you, Mom."

American Goddess

I immediately placed my arm around his shoulders, as I knelt at his side to whisper in his ear, "I love you too, Punkie Doodle. Are you doing all right?"

He slanted his head toward me and gazing deep in my eyes said, "I'm scared, Mom."

Squeezing him tightly, I confidently said, "Don't you worry, baby, we're going to get through this just fine."

As I held my baby reassuringly, I heard Ann saying, "Excuse me Christina, but I have Joe on the line."

I kissed Taylor's cheek and said, "Say a little prayer for us, okay." I kissed him again and continued, "I love you, baby, but I have to go back to work now. Just remember Daddy and I, are right here if you need us."

He smiled as he nodded his head and said, "All right, Mom."

When I stood up, I thanked Ann then asked, "Did you brief him on our situation?" She nodded a 'yes', so when I took the phone I simply said, "Joe, I need you to set up a tell-a-link with the heads of all our unions for me, and I need it in ten minutes. Now I'm giving you back to Ann, and I want you guys to keep this line open." Then I added, "Are you going to be able to handle this for me, Joe?"

With a tone of unequivocal confidence, he answered, "I'll be talking with you in ten minutes, Christina."

I replied, "Great, Joe, I'll be waiting."

When I handed the phone back to Ann, Michael's secretary Lucille Karatzas came up to me and nervously said, "Christina, there has got to be a hundred thousand reporters surrounding the building, and they're all screaming for a comment from you."

I patted her shoulder reassuringly and said, "Tell them I'm busy."

Then Michael yelled, "Its ready, Christina. Our employees are watching Dan's report and the intercom system is set up so they can all hear you."

I turned to Ann and said, "Is Joe ready?" All she could do was nervously nod 'no.'

Just then, Taylor yelled out into the chaotic pace of the room, "Mom! They're flashing a red emergency bulletin across the screen."

All eyes and ears hit the TV to hear Dan say, "America, we've just learned that Congress has denied the petition made by attorneys from Powers Inc., to declare King Mohammed's takeover attempt of Powers Inc. illegal and order it null and void." Beginning to shake his head he added, "Hold on, folks! We are getting more. It seems events are catapulting out of control so rapidly in this volatile battle, we can hardly report it fast enough." Then he nodded his head to someone off to his left and said, "I got it!" Turning back to the camera he added; "It appears as the battle reaches the one trillion three hundred-billion-dollar mark, Christina Powers will be addressing the four hundred thousand American employees who work for Powers Inc. via a phone call which will be patched into their intercom systems. When she does, we will be airing it live."

That's when Ann said, "Christina, its Joe."

575

American Goddess

I calmly reached for the phone, cleared my voice and said, "Are you ready for me, Joe?"

He confidently replied, "Go ahead Christina, everyone can hear you."

I took a deep breath, swallowed hard and abruptly said, "Good Morning, this is Christina Powers, President of Powers Incorporated and your employer. By now I'm sure you're all aware we have been battling a hostile foreign corporate takeover attempt of Powers Inc., by King Mohammed Fhed of Saudi Arabia. This battle has only been raging forty-nine minutes, and we've already reached one trillion three hundred billion dollars. That figure can only tell us one thing. Mohammed wants to own nearly one third of America's industries, which breaks down to your jobs, as well as mine, and he wants it bad! But I promise you, as long as I have the ability to fight him, he won't get it. Now I don't know how long this battle will continue, but I do know if we lose it, Powers Inc. as it is known today, will be bankrupt, and Mohammed will have taken control of what will become the wealthiest and most powerful corporation on the face of the earth; because whoever wins takes the whole pot, which adds up to the money and the corporation. The reason I've brought this to your attention, is to ask you to join me in this battle to save our families' livelihoods, and keep ownership of Powers Inc. in American hands, by allowing me to use the six hundred billion dollars, which belongs to you, the employees of Powers Inc., in your pension plans, as a little insurance policy in our battle to block this hostile takeover attempt. I know what I am asking is a lot, but I hope you can see what's really at stake here. Now due to the urgency of the situation, I'm going to ask you all to decide for yourselves whether I may access those funds or not, by holding an on-the-spot vote. I need your answers as soon as possible. Thank you."

We turned back to the TV screen to hear Dan saying, "You heard it, America. This is a high stakes battle and with the stakes rising, Christina turns to her employees, for as she put it, 'a little insurance policy.' As of this minute the battle stands with Christina's counteroffer of one trillion four hundred and twenty-five billion dollars. Now we're going to switch over to Ken Carpenter in Washington where top Church leaders, along with thousands of citizens are gathering outside the White House demanding the President order a stop to this madness."

That's when Ann handed me a phone and said, "It's Joe Aiello."

I took another deep breath as I grabbed the phone and said, "What kind of news do you have for me, Joe?"

He shouted his answer, "You got it, unanimously!"

With tears welling in my eyes, I shouted back, "God bless you, Joe." Then I shouted to everyone in the room, "They're with us," which caused everyone to let out a cheer that sounded a lot like a sigh of relief.

When we stopped cheering, it was back to the TV and Dan, who was excitedly saying, "America, it's been nearly ten minutes and Wall Street has still not received a counteroffer from King Fhed.   And as far as we know, Christina has not had a reply from the employees of Powers Inc. either."   His eyes lit up as he continued, "Hold on a minute folks, we've just learned that Marty Flynn, the President of the American Stock Exchange, is about to make a public announcement.   Right now, we're going live to Wall Street and our correspondent, Dorothy Diguida, 'Dorothy, can you give us a clue as to what Marty will be announcing?'"

The camera went to the stock exchange balcony and Dorothy, who said, "Dan, I'm sure he wants to calm the market as quickly as possible.   I'm also sure he's hoping the fact that fifteen minutes have passed without a counteroffer by King Fhed, will help him do just that."   Then Dan asked, "What's the mood on the floor Dorothy?"

She simply said, "I can only describe it as panic Dan, take a look for yourself." Then she waved her arm for the camera to span the floor, and as it did, the whole world got to see the havoc and fear this battle was creating on the faces of everyone in that room.   As we watched, Dorothy interrupted, "Hold on Dan, Marty's about to address the floor now."

When the camera zoomed to Marty, he straightened his suit jacket and said, "Ladies and gentlemen, I have faxed three formal requests to King Fhed, asking for his counteroffer and each one was declined.   So it appears that at one trillion four hundred and twenty five billion dollars, Christina Powers saves the American economy from a devastating blow, as she wins her battle to keep controlling interest of Powers Inc., and remain President of its Board of Directors."   With that the floor began to cheer.   And when they cheered, we all cheered.

When we finally calmed down enough to hear Dan again, he was saying, "It's not even noon yet America, and this has been the most incredible day in the history of the American Stock Exchange, as the woman the world is now calling, 'America's tiger' saves the day.   As the news spreads across the country, the markets are already showing signs of a possible quick rebound."

That news lifted a ton of weight from my heart, and the moment I sighed with a sense of relief, Dan's voice took on an air of shock and urgency as he shouted, "Oh My, God!   America, we've just learned the United Arab Emirate, China and Russia have joined King Mohammed, in his attempt to takeover Powers Inc., by upping the ante to a whopping two trillion dollars!   And once again it appears the next move is up to Christina Powers.   But with a ball this size being thrown into her court, the question now is, 'Will she be able to counter this one?'"

When I heard that I grabbed for the closest chair, as my legs nearly gave out from under me.   Then I clutched my blouse and with my soul in anguish cried out, "GOD! Help us!   I don't know what else to do!"   And as if being struck by a bolt of lightning, it hit me.   Then I shook my head in an attempt to slow my thoughts as I quickly turned to Michael and said, "Call a press conference on the front lawn immediately."

He looked at me with wondering eyes and replied, "It's still pouring out honey.   I'll call it in the lobby."

I grabbed his hand forcefully and said, "It has to be outside."

He hugged me tenderly, "I'll go set it up right now."   When he left the room, I began to pace the floor in deep thought.

Within five minutes Michael opened the door and said, "They're ready for you, Christina."

I ran my fingers through my hair in an attempt to look like something, and as I did, Taylor ran to my side, grabbed my leg and began to cry.   I snatched him up into my arms, held him tightly and fought back the tears as I gently said, "Oh baby, don't cry.   No matter what happens we'll be all right, I promise you."

Michael flung his arms around us both and confidently said, "Hold on guys.   I know we're going to win this."

I kissed them both, and as I handed Taylor to Michael, I caught sight of the teary-eyed faces on everyone in the room, so I stood tall and defiantly said, "There's no way he's going to beat us."

When I left that room, there was a speck of hope rekindled in every heart. The moment I exited the front door of Powers Inc., the sound of the cameras snapping startled me as it overpowered the pounding of the rain.   I stopped for a split second to see thousands of people gathered in the cold downpour, breathlessly waiting my response and I thought, "God, please guide my words."   Then I swallowed hard and began to walk across the parking lot toward the open field where the microphones for the press were deliberately set up in front of the towering pine forest which ran along the banks of the majestically beautiful Hudson River.   By the time I reached the mikes and took my place in front of the cameras with this awesome display of Mother Nature behind me, I looked like a drowning rat.   Then I pushed back the wet hair from my face, and with all the strength I could muster said, "America, I stand here to tell you this is not just a battle for Powers Incorporated any longer.   It has become a battle for America's financial survival.   The reason it has become that is because it is a calculated conspiracy to commit financial treason against the American people by our own Government Leaders, because they know come tomorrow night, they will all be ousted. They have sold us out for great gain I'm sure, to the oil rich Arab nations who are at this very minute attempting to devastate our economy, and financially enslave us. Mohammed is orchestrating all this because he knows with our current financial might, we will break the chains of oil that bind us, and his ability to one day financially rule the world will have been destroyed."

American Goddess

With that the rain seemed to begin to fall harder, and I found myself flinging my arms out from me, so the drops could be seen bouncing from my flesh. Then I shook my arms forcefully for a moment before continuing, "People, do you see this rain? Can you feel it beating on your skin? Well, I pray you can, because they're the tears of the Spirit of God being poured out for all life on this precious Mother Earth of ours. The spirit is crying because it knows this isn't just a battle between Mohammed and Powers Inc. for the survival of America; no, this is a battle between good and evil, for the survival of the human race. And if we don't stand together right now to defeat this force of evil attacking our Nation, then this will become America's darkest hour, and our dreams for a brighter future will be ashes blowing in a toxic wind. This is why I have fought and will continue to fight this battle. But the reason I stand in the pouring rain right now is to plead with corporate America to join me in this battle to save our Nation, because I know without you it cannot be won. And if you think I may be mistaken concerning Mohammed's intentions, just take a look at your current stock levels, and you will realize once he obtains Powers Inc., he will be in a perfect position to swoop down and completely devour the entire American Stock Exchange, and at rock bottom prices. Now with the blessing of my entire staff, I'm going back inside and I'm going to fight that bastard until I can fight no longer. On my way back, I'm going to pray that you join me. Thank you and May God be with us all."

With that everyone began to cheer, even press members, and as I headed back toward the building, they followed me cheering all the way. When I entered the building, everyone inside began to cheer.

Once I entered the command center, I took the phone from Jimmy and forcefully said, "Marty, counteroffer, and don't stop until it reaches two trillion five hundred billion."

Then I handed the phone back to Jimmy and walked over to where Michael and Taylor were standing. We all just stood transfixed to the screen as Dan said, "What we just heard America, was a heart wrenching plea for the survival of our Nation. Inside sources tell us that Christina Powers has just countered King Mohammed, with an offer of two trillion twenty-five billion dollars. As we wait for the counteroffer, all America sits breathless on the edge of our seats wondering, will 'Corporate America' respond to Christina's plea?" With that his eyes lit up as he grabbed his headset and began shouting, "Hold on! Hold on! You're going too fast." Then he screamed, "America, Wall Street is rocking again as the Disney Corp. commits five hundred billion dollars to the battle. Wait! Universal Studios just matched it. Listen to this folk; Exxon and Texaco have jointly committed eight hundred billion dollars." Then with tears beginning to flow from his eyes he shouted, "Christina, I know you're watching. Listen to this, American citizens by the thousands are offering to put up their life savings and their

American Goddess

homes to join the fight.   Hell, I'll give twenty million myself!" Then he wiped the tears from his cheek with his sleeve, and with a choked voice said, "God Bless You, Christina."

With that, we all began to jump up and down hugging one another as we wildly screamed, "We won!   We won!"   And when we finally calmed down enough to pay attention to Dan again, it was just in time to see him jump out of his seat and shout, "America, we've just learned that King Mohammed, China, Russia and the United Arab Emirate, have just backed down to the financial might of a united industrial America, by declaring they will cease all further attempts to obtain Powers Inc."   And I'm sure you can imagine how we all reacted to that news.

It took us at least twenty minutes just to contain ourselves enough to head home. When I opened the front door to leave the building, I was shocked to see that the rainy morning had given way to a sun filled afternoon and there was the most beautiful double rainbow right over our heads that I had ever seen.   Once the crowd saw me coming, they began to shout in loving unison, "Christina!   Christina!"

I was so moved that I started to cry and as I wiped the tears from my cheeks I thought, "God, thank you for getting us this far."

The next night as I waited alone in my room at Rockefeller Center for the election results, I heard a tap on the door, and the soft loving voice that followed was Michael's. "Christina, may I come in?"

I answered, "Come on in, the door is open, honey."

When he reached my side, I stood up to embrace him, and putting his arms around me he lovingly said, "Are you all right, Punkie?"

I kissed his cheek and replied, "I couldn't be better, Michael."

With that Taylor and Jimmy ran in the room together, and as Taylor excitedly said, "Mom, they're about to announce the winner!"

Jimmy flipped on the TV to once again see Dan Rather, only this time he was saying, "Ladies and gentlemen, it's not even 9:00pm, here in New York yet, and after the largest voter turnout in American history, we can safely say Christina Powers has won her bid for President of the United States of America with an unprecedented 97% of the popular vote, which gives her an across-the-board sweep of the electoral vote.   Not only that, but she's taking the entire Democratic Party to Washington with her."   We could hear the entire city come alive as they shouted victoriously.   Then Dan shouted, "And this news has just brought the house down here at Rockefeller Center, and from the reports we're getting, it's the same scene all over this Nation as our citizens take to the streets.   As the country celebrates, we here at the Powers Campaign Headquarters will be waiting for Christina to come down and give her acceptance speech."

I clicked off the set and the minute I did, my personal phone, which was lying on the desk began to ring.   Michael's eyes opened wide as he looked at me and said, "Do you think?"

American Goddess

As I reached for the phone I replied, "I'm sure it is." So I answered by calmly saying, "I'll bet you two trillion dollars you're not wearing that smirk on your face now, Mohammed."

He screamed with hatred in his voice as he snapped back, "You, bitch! You may have won this one Christina, but I've only begun to fight."

I replied with a condescending tone, "I've told you once Mohammed and I'm going to tell you again. You haven't seen anything yet. Now I really must go collect the spoils of my victory by taking the helm of the most powerful Nation on earth."

I hung up the phone, grabbed Taylor's right hand, Michael's left and said, "Well first family, let's go greet our relatives." With that we headed for the ball room.

When we walked out on the stage the cheers of love, and joy, which rang out, had the power to bring tears of pride to the eyes of every American no matter where in the world they were at that moment. As we reached the podium I thought, "God, this is just the beginning. I know we still have so many more hurdles to leap before we reach our goals." I gazed back at the cheering crowd and thought, "There's still, Mohammed, 'God,' what will we do the next time he rears his evil fangs?" With that I glanced at Taylor and Michael, who were both gleaming with pride and this time I thought, "**Oh well, I'll figure it out tomorrow...**"

To be continued

This novel is dedicated to America with love from your friend, James Aiello